WRAITHBLADE

North Lincolnshire Council
www.northlincs.gov.uk

Library items can be renewed online 24/7, you will need your library card number and PIN.

Avoid library overdue charges by signing up to receive email preoverdue reminders.

To find out more about North Lincolnshire Library and Information Services, visit www.northlincs.gov.uk/libraries

www.northlincs.gov.uk/librarycatalogue

S.M. BOYCE
WRAITHBLADE

THE WRAITHBLADE SAGA
BOOK ONE

Wraithmarked
CREATIVE

WRAITHBLADE: BOOK ONE OF THE WRAITHBLADE SERIES
Copyright © 2021 by S.M. Boyce. All rights reserved.

This book is a work of fiction. Names, characters, places, and incidents are either a product of the author's imagination or used fictionally. Any resemblance to actual events, locals, or persons, living or dead, is entirely coincidental. All rights reserved. No part of this publication can be reproduced in any form or by any means, electronic or mechanical, without expressed permission from the author.

Cover Illustration: Mansik YAM
Cover Design and Interior Layout: STK•Kreations

Trade paperback ISBN: 978-1-955252-01-0
Ebook ISBN: 978-1-955252-01-0

Worldwide Rights
1st Edition

Published by Wraithmarked Creative, LLC
www.wraithmarked.com

This one's for you, Dad.
The anchor in any storm,
the breeze in my sails,
the lighthouse on the rocky coast,
and a guiding light in the darkness.

"Though you plant the seed of thought in another, be patient, for how and when it sprouts is not yours to control."
—*unknown*

CHAPTER ONE
KING HENRY

"Damn them."

Henry sucked in a breath through clenched teeth as the searing pain in his side scorched his withered soul. Hot blood streamed over his fingers from the many stab wounds in his back and stomach. His shirt stuck to his chest, the Montgomery family crest woven into its silk threads stained almost black.

Those traitors.

Those *thieves*.

Come to take his throne.

His throat tightened, and he could no longer quell the violent cough building in his chest. Dark red splatters hit the ancient stone in the labyrinth of corridors beneath his great castle. These passageways were as old as the land around them, as steeped in blood as they were in history.

Henry refused to become a mere footnote in the books the scribes kept.

His knees buckled, and the corridor tilted beneath him. The cold air of the castle depths stung his throat as he pressed his shaky fingers against the cool rock for balance. His vision blurred from the loss of blood, and he paused for a moment to breathe. To regain his composure.

Somewhere behind him, the drip of water hitting stone echoed through the hall, steady as the ticking of a clock.

He would not have long until they found him once again. His escape from the attack had been a fluke, really—a stroke of luck amidst the chaos. If he were to survive this treason, he would need to act quickly.

Each breath tasted of iron and rust. With every beat of his racing heart, a bit more of his life poured into his hand. He couldn't cover all the wounds to stem the bubbling flood, but he did somehow force himself to stagger on. Each step left a thin trail of dark red along the gray rock beneath him, enough for even a novice tracker to spot and follow. He couldn't hide his route. Not anymore.

He had one last hope, now. Only one escape from the walls that should have protected him.

His leather boot caught on a raised stone in the castle floor—*his* castle, damn it all—and he stumbled. The cold, rocky wall caught him, and a jagged corner on one of the blocks dug into his arm as he struggled to catch his balance. He coughed, and more spatters of red flecked the ground before him.

He had to get to the Rift.

It was his only hope.

"Just die, you coward," a voice echoed down the hall. "Come out here and die like a man."

One of the hunters, searching for him.

You are near death, a grim voice said, echoing through his mind like a reaper.

Unprompted, a specter appeared before him—a once-great king's ghost that had granted him so much. His fame. His wealth. His title. This ghoul alone had gotten Henry to where he was, and now it seemed as though the creature would be his undoing.

The Wraith King.

It was the chill down a grown man's spine, present and able to kill even when it couldn't be seen. Henry was immune to its sword and bony fingers, the only man alive to claim as much.

"Move," Henry demanded, blood pooling on his tongue.

It didn't.

Henry pushed himself off the wall, staggering forward through the ghoul. Its skeletal face neared, and as he took a step toward the tattered black scraps of its cloak, its haunting form dissolved into the air.

"Kill them," Henry demanded with a weak nod over his shoulder. "You could decimate them all."

Perhaps, if not for the blades two of them wield, it admitted. *They have prepared for tonight, and you have not. They have something that can kill even me, and you are not worth dying for.*

"Coward," Henry muttered, still stumbling forward.

The creature laughed, the rasp dry and haunting. *I am wise when you would be a fool, old man. I lose very little if you die.*

Henry scoffed, and more blood pooled in his mouth alongside his growing disdain for this... this *thing*. This wretch didn't obey him. It merely tolerated his presence, when once they had conquered entire armies together. To think of the sheer number of men he had killed to control this monster—even his own soldiers, his own friends—and now, he wanted nothing more than to rid himself of it.

It had cursed him.

Henry pushed his dying body toward a great archway at the end of the hall, toward the lone sconce flickering in the shadows of an ancient chamber. His vision blurred again, and the fire's amber light floated farther away with every step.

Lost in his pain, consumed by his singular purpose, Henry's ragged breaths caught in his chest like cold air on a mountain. This far beneath his castle, in tunnels only a handful of souls knew existed, he would make his escape. He would heal, and he would return with a vengeance.

This far gone in the power of the Wraith King, vengeance was all he knew.

The archway finally neared, as did the elaborate circle of glistening green stone in the center of the small room beyond it.

By some miracle, he had made it to the Rift—a pillar of magic that had cost more coin to construct than most kingdoms hoarded in their treasuries over an entire century. Though some said it was old as time itself, Henry knew better. As breathtaking as it was to behold, this enchantment was made by men, and the legends elevated its status beyond what it was in order to keep its power from the common folk.

The commoners were given trinkets—toys to play with, devoid of real magic. True power, like this, was reserved for kings.

For men like Henry.

His knees fell hard on the gem-like stone, and he leaned a bloody hand against the perfectly polished crystal for support. As he stained it red with what little life he had left, the pillar glowed beneath him.

Magic this powerful demanded sacrifice to function. He would oblige it, but not with his own body. To use the Rift, he had to bleed a man dry, and he wouldn't sacrifice himself.

Now, he simply had to wait for one of those fools to find him.

He strained his ear, listening intently now that he had made it. The distant drip of water, slow and rhythmic, filled the void between him and the traitors, until—*there*, yes. There, through the steady pulse of the water, came the dull echo of footsteps, emerging like a beast from the shadows.

It seemed he wouldn't have to wait long.

Raggedly breathing as he knelt on the glowing platform, Henry briefly closed his eyes. He couldn't sleep. With this much blood loss, sleep would mean death. He merely needed a moment, just one, to catch his breath.

"There you are," one of the hunters said, his voice louder now.

"That's right," Henry replied gruffly. "Here I am."

He could feel the weight of the assassin's stare on his neck. With his back to the traitor, he could imagine the smirk of a common man who thought he could kill a king.

But Henry was the Chosen One.

A man of the people, ascended to royalty by the Fates themselves. He had scraped his way through hell to claim the great throne of Saldia. He had united the continent beneath his might. He had forced kings and queens alike to bow before him, only to slice off their heads as punishment for their rebellions against his rule.

He would not lose it all tonight.

Normally, a single man would hardly be a challenge. After the attack, however, every breath ended with the question of whether or not the next would come.

Henry had to conserve every ounce of energy if he were to survive this.

And he would. He had to. With the suffering he had endured up to this point, this would not be his day to die.

After all, there was retribution to be had. There was still much blood to spill before he went to the grave—and more souls to take with him along the way.

CHAPTER TWO
CONNOR

The chilling howl of the blightwolves echoed through the dense trees of the Ancient Woods. In reply, a cold wind kicked through the canopy of the wise old forest. The rushing torrent of air crashed through leaves like waves on a shore, momentarily even louder than the creatures haunting its grove. This wood had seen kingdoms rise and fall in its many centuries, and the mournful cry of the giant wolves held little fear for these timeless oaks.

The howl briefly faded, echoing across the mountains.

An omen of death.

Any breathing thing in its right mind froze in place, waiting for the terrors to pass through the cold spring night.

The hard branch of an old oak pressed against Connor Magnuson's back as he adjusted in his perch, high in the canopy. He had learned early on to sleep in the trees. It was a lesson he had gathered from all the skeletons he had stumbled across in his travels through this forest, their bones gnawed through and licked clean.

Blightwolves showed no mercy—not to man, woman, or child. Legend said they knew only hunger. Death would come for Connor eventually, but he hadn't clawed his way through life thus far to end up as some beast's dinner.

The brisk wind hounded the oaks again. His tree swayed as he tightened his threadbare coat and rubbed his arms to keep warm. Though he sometimes thought of home, of the small manor his father had built back in

Kirkwall, he had long ago stopped wishing for fire and solace in the night. Those were luxuries out in this forest he had chosen to call home—luxuries a drifter like him couldn't afford.

He settled into the rhythm of the breeze through the gnarled oaks around him, a song he had grown accustomed to during his years in this massive stretch of forest: the creak of withered trunks as the wind danced through them; the clatter of leaves, like applause from a long-dead crowd to a performance even time had forgotten; his own quiet breath, added like an afterthought to an orchestra.

And a scream, shrill and short, in the distance.

It snapped Connor from his sleep like a slap to the face. He stiffened, straining to hear it again through the gale. It might've been a dream, nothing but a memory he had so often tried to bury. After all, it had sounded so familiar.

But there, again, in the distance.

A woman.

No—a girl, her thin voice breaking with fear.

From the direction of the scream, a green glow burned through the forest with unnatural intensity, barely one hundred yards away. It blazed like majestic emerald smoke, a beacon of mischief in the night.

In that blistering instant, a puff of his breath froze on the cold air before him, tinged with green.

After only a few seconds, the dazzling glow faded, and the midnight forest consumed the once-brilliant flicker of light.

Magic in the middle of a cursed forest.

A little girl screaming for her life.

In that moment, Connor had a choice. Up in the trees, isolated and a full day's trek from the nearest town, no one knew he was here. It was why he traveled the forests, drifting between villages and brief intervals of work where it could be found.

The freedom of being overlooked, of being forgotten—that was the one power he had left to his name.

But the forests hadn't hardened the last shreds of his heart quite yet.

The blightwolves' fading howls lingered on the air as they chased something to the north. If he was going to make a move, now was his only chance.

After a cursory pause to question his own judgment, Connor jumped into the dead leaves that lingered from autumn and raced through the tightly packed trees of the Ancient Woods toward the shrill scream of a child that shouldn't even be out here.

And he wouldn't be the only one.

The blightwolves sought the weak and vulnerable. The small. They hunted without care for what they killed, so long as it sustained them for a time. Some said the beasts had intelligence, that the bright green spellgust ore rumored to be in the nearby mountains had morphed them into something unholy. Into creatures of insight and wit that sought to cause mankind—their only competition as predators—as much pain as possible.

Connor couldn't say. Like all men with even an ounce of self-preservation, he kept his distance from the beasts.

Still, he couldn't bring himself to let a child die, and there were other dangers in these woods to consider. Bandits. Slavers. Rogue soldiers away from the watchful eye of the king's guard. The Discovered—a different sort of human entirely, with green scales on their bodies and crystals on their faces, said to wield more power than any man could dream of.

Out here, there was little in the way of law, save for the sword a man carried and the courage he had to face his own problems.

As the thick oaks whizzed past him, mere shadows in the darkened night, Connor caught glimpses of the twin moons of Saldia as they slept in the sky. The two crescents cast a shimmer of soft blue light across the forest.

He slowed as he neared a clearing close to where the green light had been, and he paused to take in his surroundings. Only fools rushed into battle with no thought or plan—and Connor was no fool.

The ruins of a great cathedral stood in the middle of the field, the twin crescent moons framed perfectly on either side of the lone surviving spire that stabbed the sky. The crumbling walls betrayed a maze of what were once hallways and rooms inside the ruins. Once-white boulders littered the field, stained with moss and time.

For a moment, nothing moved. No one screamed. Not a sound swept through the cold meadow save for the brief echo of a distant howl.

Until, in the ruins, a shadow flinched.

From the depths of the old building, a man staggered through the tall meadow grasses. They parted before him with every unsteady step, and he dragged something behind him as he stumbled into the field. Whatever he held flailed, its wild limbs scratching at his arm in the darkness as he held tight.

It took only a moment to recognize a braid of yellow hair as the victim fought against her captor.

This man held a girl.

A child.

"You must have one," the man wheezed. "A Rectivane potion. You peasants always have one hidden somewhere. Give it to me. Do it now, you filthy little maggot, or I'll kill you and whatever family you have!"

Muffled screams escaped the little girl as the man's hand tightened around her mouth. As they struggled, she kicked his leg. He fell off balance and set his empty palm against a nearby boulder to steady himself, but his fingers slipped along the rock and stained it with dark red streaks.

From the woods, a silhouette raced toward the pair of them. For a moment, Connor's chest panged with the dread of facing a blightwolf—until the shadow stepped from the darkness on two feet. A woman raced across the field with a dead branch in her fingers, and in a brief flash of moonlight, terror shone in her eyes as the man adjusted his grip on the child.

Her child, most likely.

The girl wrestled with him, his blood smearing across her cheek as his wide hand remained planted over her mouth.

Connor drew one of the twin swords on his back. Whatever this was, it would not end well.

In the whistle of the wind, there wasn't so much as another breath. He scanned the trees for signs of a trap. For arrows straining against a bow. For the flash of steel in the low light of the moons.

He had a few enemies, sure, but none clever enough to plant a trap like this.

With one last cursory look around, Connor noticed something truly odd, and it gave him pause despite the scene unfolding before him.

A house in the trees.

Through one of its foggy windowpanes, a second young girl watched the meadow with wide eyes. Perhaps only a few years older than the one on the ground, she pressed her blonde head to the glass.

A house in the trees. A bloody man crawling through the ruins of an ancient building. A woman and her children, alone in a field at night.

It seemed as though he had stumbled into something quite beyond him.

"Let my baby go!" the woman screamed, her voice shrill with panic as she broke the branch across the dying man's back.

The man winced and fell to the ground, dragging the child with him. The girl scratched her tiny hands against his face, and blood oozed through her golden hair as she tried to wriggle free.

Yet his grip only tightened, his thumb pressing deeper into her cheek.

The little girl's brows tilted upward with panic as she fought him. Her frantic gaze roamed the woods, desperate for help.

Without a word, Connor slipped the thin scarf around his neck up and over his mouth to hide his face.

In moments like this, he'd learned it was best to keep his identity secret. The king's guard had been after him once, years ago. They thought they had killed him back then, and he didn't want them to learn they had failed.

A man's name is all he truly has, his father used to say. *Don't let anyone tarnish yours, Connor.*

A twinge of nostalgia tugged at the memory of his father, but he ignored it and stepped into the clearing.

As he emerged from the shadows, the woman gasped. Her wide eyes darted toward him, and he assumed she couldn't decide if he was friend or foe.

She would find out soon enough.

It took only a few moments to close the distance between him and the tangle of makeshift fighters. The woman lifted the broken half of her branch, but Connor didn't look her way.

He was focused on the man—the only threat in the field.

When he reached the wheezing figure on the ground, Connor lifted his boot and cracked his heel across the man's nose. The snap of bone tore through the chilly night, and the stranger groaned in pain. His grip on the little girl instantly loosened, and she scampered out of his grasp.

"Get inside," Connor ordered without looking at the woman. He stood with his back to her, strategically placing himself between her and the man who had held her daughter captive.

If she were capable of killing anyone, she would've killed the man on the ground. Though she was still a stranger, he could safely turn his back to her—at least for now.

The soft thuds of feet running through the grass joined in with the biting chill of the wind through the trees as the man tilted his head, his face slick with blood. He spit onto the ground, staining it red, and wobbled as he tried to stand. Before the man could so much as get to his feet, Connor kicked him again, nailing his stomach so hard that the man fell onto his back.

A river of blood gurgled from the dozen or so stab wounds along the stranger's torso as he moaned in agony. Most of the fine silk of his purple shirt had been stained black with blood, and the vague hint of a coat of arms lay in gold thread beneath it all.

Connor grabbed the man's collar and lifted him until they were nearly nose-to-broken-nose. Narrowing his eyes, he glared down at the pathetic man who would dare threaten a child.

"Explain yourself," he demanded through the fabric masking his face, his voice gruff and deep.

The stranger paused, his eyelids only half open. His eyes slipped in and out of focus, and with a cursory glance across the grass, Connor quickly realized why. A thick streak of blood led from the ruins of the cathedral, one long stain of everything a man needed to survive.

Whoever this was, he didn't have much time left.

"Otmund sent you, then?" the man asked, his sour breath hissing through his teeth as he winced with pain. The stranger coughed, and Connor leaned back in the nick of time. Red splatters hit his chest, rather than his face, but he didn't care about his clothes. He had seen worse.

Connor waited for the answer that still hadn't come, refusing to move until he got it. "I don't know who Otmund—"

"Worse," the stranger interrupted, weakly waving his hand as if it suddenly all made sense. "You think you'll take the ghoul for yourself, don't you? To be the Wraithblade? Fool."

The man coughed again, but there wasn't much blood in him left to splatter across anything anymore.

"He's a clever bastard, that Otmund," the man continued. "He'll kill you, too, no matter what he promised you'd get from this." The stranger clutched Connor's wrist, his grip impossibly tight for how close to death he had to be. The man's eyes widened, and his other hand grabbed Connor's collar just as tightly. "You deserve what's coming for you, boy. When you get to hell, I'll laugh. You and me—we'll spend eternity in the fires. From the moment I die, you're a dead man walking."

Connor opened his mouth to speak, to ask the man what the hell he was talking about, but a second silhouette passed through his periphery.

He froze, wondering if the wolves had finally come, or if the woman was foolishly back to help. At first, all he could see was the darkness. The night. The vague hint of tree trunks beneath the moonlit canopy.

As he glared into the woods, the shadow moved again, and his blood ran cold.

A hooded wraith hovered at the edge of the forest, its skeletal features hidden partially by shadow as it watched them both with cold impartiality.

As the last of the stranger's life bled from him, the creature floated with no feet among the ancient trees. Only the thin white bone of its hands peeked through a dark cloak that fluttered in a breeze all its own.

A chill shot through Connor's heart like an icy knife through the chest. With the wraith's appearance, the chaotic scene finally made sense.

The demands.

The threats.

The gall to endanger a child.

Connor finally knew who this dying man was.

This was none other than the dreaded King Henry, ruler of Oakenglen and master of the freemen of Saldia. A man, maybe, but clearly more, said to be something *other* entirely. A man to be feared. A man who had conquered a great ghoul. A man who had used Death itself to slaughter his enemies and secure him the throne.

They were monsters, both of them.

With a final sputtering breath, the king went limp in Connor's grasp. His body arched toward the grass as his weight tested Connor's strength. The dead man's eyes remained open, carrying the same expression now as when he'd spoken his final words.

From the moment I die, you're a dead man walking, the king had warned.

And now, the merciless king was dead.

The ghoul at the edge of the woods drew a jet-black sword from the depths of its dark robe. The tattered ends of its cloak billowed in the winds of death, in a gust far stronger than the gentle breeze of the forest.

It watched him, waiting. For what, he had no idea, but he suspected his moments were numbered unless he could find a damn clever way out of this.

The dead king's grip loosened from around Connor's wrist, and the limp hand fell to the grass. Jaw tensed, Connor gently set the dead man on the ground, his eyes focused on the ghoul.

On the bigger threat.

The wind whistled through the trees, tense and angry and *bitterly* cold. The world around them went silent as the forest waited, curious as to what might happen next.

The king's body glowed briefly green in Connor's peripheral vision, so soft and subtle he almost missed the gentle hum of the dead man's body. A warped shadow rose from the corpse and hovered above the man's chest, suspended in time.

In the second it took to breathe a single breath, Connor's gaze drifted from the ghoul at the edge of the woods to the shadow hovering above the king's corpse.

And, in that moment, it became painfully clear the king had been right. Connor was a dead man walking, the target of a supernatural monster.

Nearby, the king's dead fingers spasmed.

Fast as a blur, the wispy shadow above the monarch's corpse darted toward Connor. In the same instant, the specter of death followed suit. It flew through the air like a banshee, the empty eye sockets of its skull trained on its quarry.

On Connor.

The ghoul hit him hard in the chest, knocking him backward. From the moment of impact, the specter melted into nothing, into the air itself.

And yet, its frigid grip tightened around Connor's throat.

Blistering agony tore through his chest, as sharp and raw as if the creature were trying to claw its way into him, tearing at his lungs, trying to tunnel its way clean through his body. He gritted his teeth, his voice catching in his throat, blocked by the ghost's hand on his neck.

Connor bit back a tortured yell as its claws dug into his skin. Into his heart. Into his very *soul*.

He flew through the air with no understanding of where he was or when the pain would end. His body sailed across the grass, scraping across rocks embedded in the dirt. The jagged stones gouged his back and legs, stabbing his spine and ripping open his limbs as the monster drove him backward.

It lifted him, finally, and slammed him against a tree. The invisible hand tightened around his throat. Searing pain burned through his veins as the creature ripped through his body, his boots dangling over the grass.

The agony was unlike anything he had ever experienced in his short life. In twenty-five years, he had assumed he had seen most, if not all, there was for a poor man to see. Yet this—this was true torture. True agony. It burned his soul and turned his blistering blood to ice. Though he still had his skin, he could feel the tiny knives of the creature's nails as it all but flayed him alive.

An unnatural cold seeped into Connor's bones—the sort of chill he figured came in the moments before death.

To *hell* with death.

To hell with a cadaver's curse on his life.

Connor had survived thus far on his sheer stubbornness and wit. He had survived the oceans to the west and made the deadly forests of the south his home. No ghoul would kill him. No king, for that matter.

No monster would eat him tonight.

Through the agony, Connor pried his eyes open, determined to know what was truly happening—but there was nothing around him save the dead man's corpse, a streak of blood across the grass, and three pairs of terrified eyes watching him from a house hidden in the trees.

His mouth parted as he tried to speak, to tell the woman and her two girls to run, but the words came out as a wheezing gasp.

Death is coming for you. A grisly voice rumbled through his head like lingering thunder. *Are you ready, peasant?*

"If I die—" The weight of unseen fingers crushed his throat, cutting off the words as he rasped them, but he pushed through the pain. "If I die, I'll take you with me. No matter what you are, I swear I'll find a way."

I admire your courage, the grim voice admitted. *Very well. You may breathe.*

As quickly as the agony had begun, it ended. The grip on Connor's throat disappeared. He fell to the ground, wheezing and gasping for air, coughing as the edges of his vision went dark. The world around him spun, and he fought with everything he had in him to remain awake. If he fell asleep, it was all over.

He wouldn't let this… this *thing* win.

"What did you do to me?" he choked out, coughing onto the grass as he fought to stay conscious.

You will see, the dark voice answered in his mind, loud and gruff despite the empty night around him. *What's more, I will soon see if you are worthy of it. There are men who can kill us both, Connor Magnuson, and you will face one of them soon. Prevail, and I will make you powerful beyond imagination. Fail, and we will both die. Prepare yourself.*

A flash of brilliant green light cut through the night yet again, glimmering from somewhere in the depths of the ruins. An emerald glow sliced through the dark sky, and the world around Connor hummed as magic crackled to life.

"What is that?" he asked hoarsely, not really expecting an answer as he pressed his fingers against his aching throat.

A Rift, the ghoul replied, as if Connor knew what the hell that was. *They acted faster than I anticipated. Consider this as our brief truce, peasant.*

"What the hell is—"

A portal, the ghost snapped. *A portal bringing death for us both. Stand and face what's coming for you.*

The glimmering green light billowed around them, as bright as an emerald sun, and he lifted an arm to shield his eyes. Its brilliance matched the glow he'd seen when the little girl screamed, and yet it was somehow more than even that.

More than just magic.

It struck a familiar chord in the depths of his memory, and he steeled himself as he tried to place it. He sifted through his thoughts until, through ragged breaths and the agony of a bruised throat, he remembered.

Years and years ago, when he was little, his mother had always ushered him inside when the King of Kirkwall's knights had paraded through town, their bare arms decorated with the glimmering green augmentations that allowed them to use magic without potions or enchanted items. Only the rich could afford to buy the ink or hire the skilled artists who knew how to augment the body.

Only the powerful—or those who served them—wore augmentations.

As a young boy, he had pressed his nose against the glass to watch them from afar, his mind buzzing with the possibilities of what their augmentations allowed them to do. His mother had always shooed him away with a simple warning—those men and women, the augmented, they were not to be trusted. They were the influential people in this world, given access to magic far surpassing what the common folk studied.

They were gods among mortals, and they possessed power far beyond anything a boy could dream of.

As Connor coughed up blood into the grass, the sting of fire in his lungs brought him back to the meadow. His body screamed in protest, furious and aching for rest, but he finally pieced it all together.

The stab wounds in the king's side.

The streak of blood across the meadow.

A powerful man, banished to the woods to die.

And now, a second flash of green. The first had brought the dead king here, and Connor suspected it would soon bring other horrors.

Connor, however, wasn't the sort to lay down quietly and die. If they came for him the way King Henry had warned they would, he would see to it they choked on their own blood before they took even a drop of his.

CHAPTER THREE
CONNOR

As Saldia's twin moons hovered in the star-studded sky, the surreal green glow of the Rift dwarfed the forest. The dazzling light froze the world around it, casting long shadows across the dirt under Connor's feet.

He squinted, shielding his eyes as he struggled to snap out of his daze and move. Though he commanded his body to stand, it wouldn't obey.

His limbs ached. Every labored breath tore through him like lightning through a storm. Every agonizing beat of his heart sent another ripple of anguish down his spine. Whatever the ghoul had done to him had all but broken him.

That had always been his life, though—the test before the lesson, the agony before the reprieve.

This was nothing new, and it would *not* destroy him.

With one hand still planted in the dirt, Connor gritted his teeth and forced himself to stand. He teetered, the edges of his vision blurring as he fell sideways into a tree. The rough bark gouged his shoulder, but he didn't care.

At least he could finally get on his feet.

Whatever had come through this portal, he would face it like a man. If possible, he would take it out completely. Retreat would've been the best option, of course—there was no shame in withdrawing to fight another day. In this state, however, he wouldn't get far, and he didn't want to leave the woman and her children to die at the hands of whatever slunk next from the shadows.

His father wouldn't have left them to fend for themselves, and neither would he.

The ghoul had backed him into a corner, and Connor would need to fight his way out. Though the creature had called for a truce to deal with whatever chaos was coming, Connor knew better.

The peace wouldn't last, and he would face the monster again.

From the glimmering emerald glow dwarfing the ruins, two silhouettes appeared at the entrance to the ancient labyrinth of crumbling passageways. The light behind them glinted off their golden armor as they held their swords at the ready. With their faces obscured by their golden helmets, they stalked past the time-stained boulders of the once-great cathedral.

The air crackled with magic. It pulsed like green lightning through the quiet night as more soldiers emerged from the labyrinth of crumbling stone and stepped into the meadow.

Four.

Seven.

Ten.

Their silhouettes blocked the source of the light as they stepped into the field, their broad shoulders and polished helmets an omen of the inevitable battle to come.

Connor gritted his teeth and rested his back against a tree as he prepared himself for the worst. Still barely conscious, the idea of fighting off a small army in this state daunted even him.

But if that was what it took to survive, then so be it.

As they slowly made their way through the ruins, their boots sinking into the thick line of the king's blood, those who hadn't already done so drew their swords and quickly scanned the turf around them. The silent soldiers drank in the scene, and it wasn't hard to guess what conclusion they would draw.

A trail of blood.

The king's corpse.

Connor, covered in dark red splatters, resting by a tree at the edge of the meadow.

Regardless of the truth, he would become known as the peasant who had killed a king.

A death sentence.

As the ten soldiers paused before him in the field, Connor's training kicked in. His time studying in secret with one of their own, a retired soldier who'd had no idea who Connor truly was, had served him well these last few years—but tonight, his skill would be tested.

Tonight, he would have to see if his mentor Beck Arbor had, in fact, taught him all he needed to know to survive.

Connor studied their armor, their swords, and their movements down to each step. He needed as much information as he could glean from them. Judging by the gilded armor and the Oakenglen crest on their chests, these were the king's own guard.

One by one, their eyes snapped to him. They no doubt saw a peasant in over his head, but he could see more than they realized.

Three had limps—slight, almost imperceptible, but they no doubt had old wounds in their feet or knees he could exploit. Two carried their swords angled lower than the rest, indicating possible weak shoulders or injured elbows. One had a patch over his left eye, which meant he would favor his right side and have inferior aim than the other soldiers.

These subtle hints at his opponents' weaknesses gave him an advantage, one that could mean the difference between life and death.

His life. *His* death.

He eyed his sword in the grass between him and the soldiers, and though he still had one of his twin blades in the crisscrossed sheaths on his back, he fought better with two. They were extensions of him, designed by Beck Arbor himself.

These blades had cost all of his coin to commission, and to survive a night like this, he needed them both.

"Let me through, idiots," a man snapped, his voice tinged with impatience.

The guards stepped aside, none of them taking their eyes off Connor as yet another man pushed through their ranks. Wearing an elaborate green cloak and a black silk shirt beneath it, he paused before them to survey the field. In his hand, he held only a small dagger, its blade glowing as brightly green as the still-open portal behind him.

A furious growl rumbled through Connor's mind—the specter, making itself known yet again.

Caught off guard by the sudden snarl, he tensed and scanned the forest around him. Dark. Void. Despite the noise, nothing stalked between the trunks. Wherever the phantom had gone, it had apparently chosen to watch from afar.

Behind the small army gathered at the edge of the ruins, the Rift's light faded in a rush. The crackling hum of magic dissolved in an instant, swallowed by the cold spring night as it returned to its familiar eerie quiet. Only the soft rustle of wind through the canopy filled the clearing, as the animals had no doubt been scared off by the second rush of magic and the screams that had preceded it.

With the blazing glow suddenly gone, Connor blinked rapidly to clear the imprints of light from his vision. As his eyes adjusted to the darkness, the small army remained still, their swords at the ready.

Connor had to buy himself some time, both to heal and to figure out what the hell was going on.

In the low light of the moons, the fine silk of the man's shirt shimmered. He absently lifted the glowing green blade, his thin beard shifting as he frowned. His cold eyes roved over Connor, the creases in his brow deepening as the cogs in his head turned. As he no doubt pieced it all together.

Those cold, focused eyes snared Connor. It was the gaze of a killer, trapped in the squat body of a scholar.

As the seconds wore on, Connor flexed his fingers with anticipation. He hadn't dealt much with noblemen, but he had seen and heard enough to know they were more deadly than any warrior.

A soldier had a sword, but a nobleman had *authority*. Real power. Justice meant nothing to those who created the laws for their own benefit, and peasants served as easy scapegoats when things went wrong.

Ten soldiers. One nobleman. More guards could come through the Rift at any moment, which meant Connor was clearly outnumbered and way out of his depth.

The only way out of hell is through it, his father used to say.

So be it, then.

Into the flames he would go.

Connor's body hummed with the urge to throw the first punch, and he once again glanced at his sword lying in the grass. It waited for him near the dead king, its cold steel shimmering in the moonlight.

This far away, he stood no chance of grabbing the sword before the soldiers reached him. To get to it, he needed to be careful and clever.

Though he had hoped a moment of respite would ease the agony of the specter's attack, the pain had yet to subside. Each breath still stung, like his lungs were being ripped out of him. Scorches of agony blistered through his chest, as if there were a bony claw reaching in and twisting as it carved him hollow.

He had to focus. To block out the misery. To numb it and concentrate on the more imminent threat.

In the dark and silent forest, the nobleman walked over and studied the king's body. He stood in silence for several seconds, wrinkling his nose with disgust.

If you speak first, you lose, Beck Arbor had always warned him. *You think you're about to fight? You shut your damn mouth, and you wait. You listen. You observe.*

Despite every instinct warning Connor to grab his sword, consequences be damned, he waited.

And he observed.

No matter what he said, they would never believe a peasant. They would never ask for his side of the story.

As the nobleman stared down at Henry's body, his shoulders stiffened.

He raised the glowing dagger above his head, and with a grunt of effort, he drove it hilt-deep into the corpse's gut. With a muttered curse, he spat on the dead king's face.

Oh, joy.

This night just kept getting better.

This was even worse than Connor thought. These weren't the king's soldiers at all—at least not anymore. They belonged to the man—or men—who had killed King Henry.

Now, Connor was a witness to the treason, which meant he would not be allowed to live.

"I wish I could have seen it," the nobleman said with a cursory shake of his head as he wiped the bloody dagger clean on Henry's pant leg. He quickly scanned the field, his eyes once again settling on Connor. "Tell me what happened. Who has it now?"

Connor's jaw tensed, still not sure he understood the depths of what he'd gotten himself into. Instead of answering, he simply waited, his fist tightening as he prepared for war.

The man snapped his fingers impatiently. "The ghoul, boy. Where is it?"

Ah.

The specter.

Connor stiffened, debating what to say, but it seemed wisest not to say anything at all. With each precious second that passed, he tried to piece it all together, to stay ahead of the man who clearly understood what was going on.

Who has it now? the nobleman had asked.

With Henry dead, the ghost must have changed its loyalties. They had been allies, once, but it clearly hadn't tried to keep him alive. It had watched impartially as Henry had died in the bloodstained meadow grass, far from home.

For whatever reason, the ghoul no longer obeyed the king. His only clue for where the phantom had gone was the warped shadow that had risen from Henry's corpse.

A pang of dread shot through Connor's chest as a gruesome thought struck him.

Perhaps the ghoul had never been a specter in the night, floating and killing of its own accord. Perhaps it had lived within the dead king and used him to survive.

If so, its host was dead, and it seemed to have already chosen its next warm body.

Connor.

These men wanted the wraith, and they were here to kill him for it.

Or, rather, they were here to try.

"Can you talk?" The nobleman skeptically lifted one eyebrow.

The scholar walked closer, sizing him up along the way and no doubt piecing things together for himself. Connor stood straighter, itching to draw the sword on his back, but his gaze darted to the soldiers behind the nobleman.

After a moment, the squat man with the dagger paused and studied him with a piteous expression. "You have it, don't you?"

Connor frowned. He wasn't about to admit a damn thing.

The soldiers surrounding the nobleman angled their swords toward Connor as they closed in. Their armor rattled with each step, the metallic rush of the chainmail beneath the golden plates the only sound in the eerie night. Each of them glared at him through the slits in their helmets, ready to run him through.

This was bad.

"Stand down, imbeciles," the nobleman said with a lazy flick of his wrist.

They obeyed, stopping midstride.

"Don't mind them," the man said. "They're just tense. We all are after tonight. There have been so many complications." He rubbed his eyes with his empty hand as he held the glowing dagger loosely in the other. "It didn't go perfectly, but I suppose it went well enough. I'm afraid you're just another snag in a long list of blunders from this evening. It's time to make things right. It's time to fix that man's mistakes," he added with a nod behind him to the corpse.

Connor took the moment to briefly glance not at the king, but at the sword lying beside the body. It wasn't far, and with careful execution, he could reach it.

"How old are you?" the nobleman asked, almost bored. "Twenty-four maybe? Twenty-five? It's a pity. With a build like that, you would've made a decent soldier." He shrugged and straightened the sleeve of his cloak with his free hand.

With that, the scholar examined the canopy. At first, and to Connor's relief, his gaze darted past the house. Safely tucked away in the leaves and shrouded in shadow, perhaps the woman and her daughters would be safe.

The nobleman paused, however, and squinted into the branches hiding the woman's home. He tilted his head in confusion and took a wary step closer, as if he couldn't believe his eyes.

"What do you want?" Connor snapped, trying to steal the man's attention away from the tree.

"It appears our little peasant isn't a mute after all," the scholar said with a wry smirk.

Behind him, the soldiers chuckled.

The nobleman did not, however, look away from the tree, and his eyes lingered on the house in the canopy. "Is your family up there?"

"No." He frowned, irritated that this man was still talking, but he couldn't begrudge the bought time. With every word the nobleman spoke, Connor recovered a little more energy for the inevitable battle.

The soldiers adjusted their grips on their swords, their armor clanking as they shifted their weight. They were all anxious for a fight. He could almost smell their eagerness. Their bloodlust.

It was like iron on the air.

"Look, young man," the nobleman said. "Get on your knees and surrender. This will be over soon, and I'll even do you a kindness. I'll make it painless for you, but only if you make this easy."

"You want me to just hand myself over?" Connor scoffed at the absurd request. "What man would do that?"

"A smart man who knows when to quit," the stranger countered. "You have no idea what's at stake. How many lives are on the line. The fate of our world rests on the choice you make next."

"Does it, now?" Connor asked dubiously, his fingers twitching as he subtly rolled out his shoulders. It took everything in him to block out the pain in his chest as he prepared to grab his other sword from the sheath on his back.

He had been in tighter quarters before, with just as much on the line. He had even squared off with Oakenglen soldiers before and won, but he'd never fought a nobleman. With the ghoul in play, this skirmish transcended anything he'd ever faced.

New day. New challenge. The same stubborn grit as always would see him through it.

"You're not going to win, young man." The nobleman tilted his head, as if speaking to a child. "Let's be honest, shall we? You're common. You were born to pay your taxes, serve your superiors, and then die. You have no higher purpose. You have no blessing from the Fates. You're not the next Chosen One, and there's no way you'll walk out of this clearing alive. It's unfortunate, but if you have the ghoul, you're nothing more than a mistake."

Connor frowned, his eyes narrowing as he glared at the man draped in finery before him. A man who thought himself superior.

"Look at the fate of the last Chosen One." The nobleman gestured to the corpse behind him. "Isn't it safer to simply not matter? You're just a peasant. Don't try to be some foolish hero in a battle you don't understand."

About that, at least, this man was right. Connor had never tried to be a hero. He'd always simply survived, drifting without purpose or direction. Every breath was a victory over those who had tried so hard to kill him, and he'd never asked for more than that.

The nobleman looked again at the house in the trees. "Michaels, Gregory, collect anyone in there. We can't have any witnesses."

His time was up. He could no longer stall. It had come to this—fight a small army by himself, or kneel and let a man slit his throat.

Not much of a choice.

Connor hadn't survived the icy salt of the West Ocean for it to end here. His father hadn't given his life for Connor to just lay down and die.

Blood swirled in his mouth from whatever the specter had done to him. The edges of his vision blurred briefly and went dark again, but he pushed through and shook his head to clear his thoughts.

Two of the soldiers—the one with the eye patch and one with a more pronounced limp than the others—broke away from the troop and strode toward the treehouse as the woman and her children disappeared into the shadows of the home.

"Leave them out of this," Connor demanded.

The nobleman laughed, and the two soldiers ignored the command without so much as a backward glance.

"Dead men don't give orders," the nobleman spat.

"This one does," Connor said dryly.

The scholar's smile faded, and he raised his glimmering dagger in warning. With a brilliant glow like that, the weapon had probably cost more coin than Connor would ever see in his life, and it likely had magic he needed to avoid.

He drew the sword from the sheath on his back and twirled it—an invitation for the battle to begin. A murmur fluttered through the soldiers as they all tensed.

"This is your last chance," the nobleman warned. "Make this easy, or I will skin you alive myself."

In Connor's periphery, the limping soldier reached the tree and set his boot on the first step of the ladder nailed into the trunk below the woman's house.

"You want the ghoul?" Connor glared at the nobleman. "Come and get it."

The scholar shook his head in disappointment. "Very well. Break him, boys, but bring him to me alive so that I can slit his throat myself."

The remaining soldiers approached, quickly closing the gap as they stepped around their master. In seconds, they would be close enough to attack.

Eight on one.

Connor took one last steadying breath. He had little in the way of options, out here in this Fates-forsaken meadow, but he would do what he had always done.

One way or another, he would carve his way out of hell and kill any man foolish enough to attack him.

It was the only way he knew how to live.

CHAPTER FOUR
CONNOR

Though he rarely sought it out, trouble always seemed to find him out here in the forest.

Eight soldiers circled Connor as he stepped slowly backward into the woods, sidestepping the tree that had supported his weight through the nobleman's arrival. Though he didn't know this stretch of the forest very well, he had a brief and fleeting advantage among the trunks. The uneven ground would throw off a soldier used to open fields, and their heavy armor weighed them down.

His advantage wouldn't last long, but he would make it count.

The eight guardsmen fanned out as they circled him, their swords raised and ready to strike the moment they saw an opening. He needed to get to his second blade, and as he tightened his grip on the one in his palm, he waited for the opportunity to strike.

A sword swung at him from his left, and he deflected the blow. The clash of metal echoed through the silent oaks, and a shock snaked up his arm from the force.

A test, no doubt, to gauge his reflexes and skill.

In unison, two more soldiers attacked from behind. He ducked, crouching with one palm pressed to the cold dirt. Their blades sank into a nearby tree with two meaty thunks. The men grimaced, isolated from the group and briefly vulnerable as they tried to pry their weapons from the trunk.

He wouldn't give them the chance.

Connor drove his blade into the nearest man's gut, and the sharp metal sank between the plates of armor meant to protect the soldier. The man screamed with surprise and pain, his eyes wide through gaps in his helmet as Connor's second attacker finally wrangled his sword free.

With his blade still in the first soldier's gut, Connor rolled onto his back and set his foot on the dying man's hip. He groaned with effort and used his momentum to lift the man's body into the air. The soldier flew overhead, and Connor yanked his sword out of the soldier's torso as he cast the corpse into the circle of guards.

His muscles protested the quick and violent motion, his body ripped to shreds from the damage he'd already endured tonight, but he forced himself to push through the pain.

He'd suffered worse.

The dying man collided with three of his brothers in arms. The clang of steel against armor mingled with panicked shouts as they fell beneath his weight. Connor had hoped to take out more of them, but three would suffice.

The goal—divide and conquer. Split up the group and pick them off, one by one.

Easier said than done.

As the soldiers collapsed beneath their comrade, an opening to the meadow appeared. Connor bolted toward it just as two swords sliced through the air behind him. He launched himself over the fallen as they struggled to stand.

He landed in the grass, free of the circle of soldiers.

Success.

More of his strength seeped back into his body with each passing second—another minor victory.

Lying in the grass ahead of him, his sword glinted in a moonbeam. He dove for it, rolling on one shoulder as he grabbed the blade with his left hand and got himself some much-needed distance from the small army trying to kill him.

One soldier, as good as dead.

Nine to go.

At the edge of the forest, the two guards sent to collect the woman still climbed the long ladder to the towering treehouse overhead. The woman and her daughters didn't have much time.

Neither did Connor.

At the edge of the field, the nobleman waited with a scowl on his face, his hand still clasped around that little dagger.

Connor's chest spasmed from the lingering pain of the ghoul's attack, and he swayed slightly as he fought it off. With no other choice, he called on every ounce of energy he had left.

To focus.

To fight.

The seven soldiers still in the field split up. At the edge of the forest, the three he'd knocked to the ground hurled their dying comrade off of them. His body rolled across the dirt as they struggled to stand under the weight of their own armor. The other four raced toward him, their swords glinting in the moonlight, and he had only moments before they got close enough to swing.

His ploy had worked. Forcing them to stagger their attacks meant he had a better chance at surviving the night, provided he could remain in control of the battle—and that was a big *if.*

As Connor adjusted his grip on his swords, he quickly scanned their armor as the four closest soldiers reached him. There weren't many openings in fine suits like these, as they had been designed for close-quarter combat.

Their main weakness was speed. The plates of armor along their arms and chests would drag every movement, no matter how practiced these men were. The weight would slow them down even as it shielded them.

Of course, he did have a few targets. A thin gap at their throat from the opening at the base of their helmets. The vulnerable sections around their underarm and the back of their knees. And, of course, the gap of armor at their gut.

All devastating, if not deadly, blows.

As the closest soldier neared him, Connor's head finally cleared. The pain dripped from his bones, momentarily numbed by the allure of a good fight. He could feel everything—every breath, every beat of his pulse, every rush of the wind through the sky above.

He'd reached a place of tranquility. Of peace, despite the oncoming threat of death.

Though he always felt at one with his swords in the heat of a battle, this moment, this sensation—it struck him as unique.

The night sky. The weight of the hilts in his palms. The cold air swirling through his lungs.

It all seemed so clear.

Every movement became almost painfully slow and obvious, even in the darkness of the starlit forest. Every tilt of the guards' shoulders betrayed their next move as his instinct and training took over.

With an effortless glance, he placed all seven of the soldiers still in the field—their steps, their direction, and their next attack. The nobleman waited on the sidelines, clutching that glowing dagger as if it could protect him simply because he held it.

It was all so *easy*.

He didn't understand this new sense of power that radiated through his veins, but he wasn't going to question it. Not with his life on the line. The specter had done so many horrible things to him already, but it had promised him power beyond all imagination.

Perhaps it had done at least one good thing to him tonight.

As the first soldier neared and swung, Connor easily sidestepped the blade and drove one sword through the thin gap at the man's neck. The blade dug into the man's throat, crunching through the spine as the bloody tip careened out the other side of his body.

Two dead.

Eight left.

Mind clear, wits sharp, Connor kicked the man's golden chest plate to knock the corpse aside. His shoe left a bloodstained boot print on the polished armor as he drew his sword from the man's neck. The guard collapsed to the ground and twitched in the dirt, grasping at his throat as he sputtered for air.

It was hard to have pity for a man who had wanted to run him through with a sword mere seconds before.

Two more soldiers descended without so much as a glance at their fallen comrade. One swung at Connor's neck, while the other aimed for his side.

Connor darted backward, regaining ground as he knelt and swung both of his swords with practiced ease. One blade blocked the attack to his left, and the shriek of clashing metal sang through the night. In the same motion, he drove the other sword into the second guard's exposed underarm. The man yelled with pain, cursing loudly as he fell to his knees and dropped his weapon.

No mercy.

No choice.

Not tonight.

Connor stood and kicked the surviving guard in his rump. The man fell onto his face, momentarily disabled. The injured soldier screamed obscenities and held one hand to his injured armpit. With his target distracted and disarmed, Connor drove one of his blades through a slit in the golden helmet.

The guard went deathly still. Connor set his foot on the soldier's chest and withdrew his bloodstained sword, leaving the man to collapse in a heap on the crushed meadow grass.

Three dead.

"Useless!" the nobleman muttered, his voice almost impossible to hear over the clatter of armor and the hiss of swords slicing through the air.

The surviving guard pushed himself to his feet, though a clump of dirt stuck in his helmet blocked his left eye. He charged, and Connor barely ducked out of the way in time. The soldier's momentum sent him stumbling forward, and his sharp blade sank clean into the grass.

If Connor hadn't ducked out of the way, the sword would've chopped his head clean off.

They weren't heeding orders anymore. It seemed as though the soldiers no longer gave a damn about the order to merely break him.

Now, they wanted him dead.

The soldier struggled to yank his sword from the dirt. With the blade nearly down to the hilt, he bent over and strained with effort. The sword shifted, coming loose, and Connor didn't have much time before the man was armed again.

With a quick twist of his hip, Connor kicked the soldier's wrist just as the guard freed his sword from the dirt. The blade fell to the ground with a heavy thud. The royal guardsman cursed under his breath and shook out his hand. Before he could even reach for his weapon, Connor swept out the soldier's legs and knocked him clear onto his back.

As the remaining soldiers neared, Connor knelt on the guard's chest and crossed his blades at the man's throat. The sharp metal slipped through the gap between the armor and helmet.

The soldier froze, his green eyes wide as he stared into Connor's very soul. He must've known what would come next, and Connor held the man's gaze.

If you're going to take a life, Beck Arbor had always said, *at least look the man in the eye while you do it. Own the gravity of what you've done.*

With his blades crossed and pressed to the man's throat, Connor sank his full weight into the hilts and dug the deadly steel into the man's skin. The guard's head lolled toward the grass, his eyes rolling backward as he choked on his own blood.

Four dead.

Four more remained in the field, and the other two had only just reached the top of the ladder into the canopy.

It wasn't often Connor found himself in a skirmish like this, where he had to take a life or lose his own. Each time he did, he fought to ignore the reality of it all—that these were his fellow men. They were children, once. Many of the soldiers in this field were probably husbands and fathers with families who relied on them. They were breadwinners. Protectors. Heroes, to some. People depended on these men, people who would be lost or even destitute if they died.

More than just the soldiers' blood stained Connor's hands tonight.

He buried the guilt deep down as two of the four remaining soldiers in the field reached him. One ran with his sword held high, but the other couldn't quite lift his weapon all the way—likely a weakened right shoulder Connor could play to his advantage. The last two soldiers trailed behind, both slowed by the slight limp in their gaits.

Tripping over a corpse could cost him his life. He needed a fresh battlefield in which to work.

With golden bodies littering the meadow, Connor took several cautious steps backward. He watched the king's body from the corner of his eye and kept his distance as he maneuvered closer to the ruins.

The fastest guard reached him, and Connor pressed his back against a boulder. The soldier swung, the blade whizzing through the air from the sheer force of his blow, but Connor ducked aside at the last moment. The polished sword hit the rock, and sparks skittered into the air as the harsh screech of metal on stone cut through the night.

Connor had avoided decapitation, but he hadn't moved fast enough.

The guard threw a left hook that hit him sharply in the nose. Connor's head snapped back and smacked against the rock behind him, the stone like a second fist to his skull.

His world spun. The sky blurred into the grass as nausea burned in his throat. For several crucial moments, Connor couldn't so much as tell up from down.

A searing pain tore through his left arm. In a dizzying rush, the world around him steadied as an icy pang shocked his system. The guard stood before him, the hilt of his sword twisting slightly as the man drove his weapon deeper into Connor's bicep.

From the shadows of his helmet, the soldier smiled as he twisted the sword to worsen the wound. His white teeth glowed in the moonlight.

Agony splintered through Connor's brain, and instinct took over. He kneed the man in the gut. His kneecap cracked against the armor. It wouldn't be enough to hurt the soldier, but he didn't care. It was enough to throw the man off balance, and that was all Connor needed.

The guard staggered backward. His grip on the sword loosened, and Connor kicked him hard in the chest. The soldier fell, his heavy armor taking him to the ground as his blade remained in Connor's arm.

Gritting his teeth to ride out the pain, Connor dropped the sword in his right hand and grabbed the hilt of the guardsman's weapon. He quickly yanked the blade from his arm. Searing agony shot through him. He stifled the tormented yell clawing at his throat, refusing to give them the satisfaction of hearing his pain.

He stumbled, his head buzzing as the searing fire in his left arm worsened, but he managed to snatch his second blade from the grass. By some miracle, he held fast to both of his weapons, but he couldn't keep his grip for much longer.

That injury might've just cost him the battle.

If you're going to lose, Beck Arbor had told him once, *then you'd better go down in a blaze of bitter glory. Take those bastards with you.*

Connor's neck strained from the misery thundering through his body. His brow wrinkled from the splintering agony of the massive hole in his bicep, but he refused to back down now.

He struggled to stay on his feet as the downed soldier stood. The other three surviving guards joined the fray, and together, they circled him yet again.

Take those bastards down with you.

Connor lifted his sword, ready to block another blow, but he couldn't keep an eye on all of them. As the soldier in front of him lifted his sword to strike, another of the four kicked Connor hard in the leg. He fell to his knees, only to see a boot seconds before it nailed him in the face.

Blood pooled in his mouth. He landed hard in the grass, and the twin moons blurred above him as the soldiers crowded closer. His arm burned, like hell itself had poisoned the wound. His lungs gasped for air.

It appeared he'd finally lost the advantage, but the fight wasn't over yet.

If he died tonight, it would be as Beck Arbor wanted—in a blaze of bitter glory.

CHAPTER FIVE
CONNOR

Four dead. Four remaining.

Connor would have to be clever as hell to escape this mess, and he refused to leave the woman and her children to die.

Determined to claw his way out of this grueling scrape with death, he inched backward on the grass in an attempt to put distance between him and the guards. Disoriented, his world still blurring while he tried to get his bearings, he braced himself as the soldiers crowded above him.

A blade dove toward his jaw, and he lifted his sword to redirect it. The clang of steel rang through his brain, muted and distant.

As the misery of his wounds numbed his mind, his instinct took over. He lost control, registering each of his own movements a second or two after they happened.

Clang.

A blow toward his head, deflected.

Clang.

A swipe toward his heart, blocked.

Clang.

A stab toward his gut, diverted.

His tired, tortured body didn't have much left to give.

One of the soldiers kicked him sharply in his side, and he bit back an agonized yell as the man's sharp boot broke a rib. Breathing became even more excruciating than before. He groaned, still pushing himself backward, still trying to regain the upper hand he had so briefly enjoyed.

A glint of metal in his periphery caught his attention right before a soldier plunged his sword into Connor's left shoulder.

He could barely stifle the tormented yell as he clenched his jaw shut, not willing to give them the pleasure of knowing how badly that had hurt. His grip on his left blade loosened, weakened from the injuries to his bicep and shoulder. With a thud, the sword hit the grass as he eased himself toward the ruins.

Toward cover.

Toward a second chance to regain the advantage.

The soldiers sneered as they crowded around him, a few of them laughing as they blocked the moonlight. The soldier who had stabbed him knelt and drew a thin dagger from a sheath at his waist.

"What trophy should I take?" the man asked. "A toe? A thumb? Maybe some teeth?"

"Take his nose," one of the other soldiers said. "Let's see the peasant's face before we kill him."

The men laughed.

In the whispered back rooms in local taverns, Connor had heard rumors of this practice—to slice off a souvenir as a trophy from a worthy opponent. A finger, usually, or an ear. It was outlawed and frowned upon by the highest levels of the law, and yet here a royal guardsman wanted to do it while his target was still alive.

The soldier grinned with victory as he neared, those white teeth of his glowing in the shadows of his helmet.

Like a target, begging for a blow.

"What'll it be, urchin?" the guard asked. "Have you nothing to say before I gut you?"

Connor had never been one to waste energy on words.

With what little strength he had left, he drove his remaining sword into the man's helmet, right through the slits that allowed him to see.

The crunch of bone and the squelch of wet meat cut through the snickering laughter of the other soldiers as fresh blood dribbled down Connor's blade. The man went still. His full weight now rested on Connor's sword.

Five dead.

At least they had finally stopped laughing.

The mood shifted, and the remaining soldiers swung at Connor in a moment of sheer chaos. With a strained grunt, he shifted the dead soldier's body into the line of fire. Their swords clattered against the fallen man's armor as Connor used the corpse as a shield.

"Michaels! Gregory!" the nobleman snapped from somewhere nearby, his voice shaking. "Forget the house and get down here!"

With the fallen guard's corpse as his shield, Connor grabbed the dagger out of the dead man's hand and stabbed it into the nearest soldier's boot. The man let loose a string of curses and limped away, giving Connor a brief opening as the other two grabbed their friend's body and threw it aside.

His shield was gone, but Connor finally had an opening.

He yanked his sword from the dead man's face and pushed himself to his feet, swaying as he backed away. His momentary retreat had barely given him any distance from them at all, but it was something, and it would have to do.

His fingertips buzzed with a tingling sensation, and he could barely even ball his left hand into a fist. Blood trickled down his fingers from the wounds in his bicep and shoulder, and he'd lost one of his swords in the fray.

It appeared he was down to one blade again, and he now had significantly less energy.

As the thud of heavy footsteps rumbled from the treehouse, the three remaining soldiers in the meadow circled Connor in a tight formation. He stumbled backward, trying to keep his distance, but they didn't have the injuries he did.

They would reach him, and they wouldn't hold back.

It was time to change tactics. With his world spinning and his entire left arm out of commission, he could only use his blade to attack. Trying to parry every blow would waste energy he didn't have, and for now, he would have to try to avoid getting hit altogether. He just had to make do until he could find a way out of the circle.

This was going to *hurt*.

If he died tonight, he would take every man here with him.

Connor lifted his blade, the sword heavier with each passing moment. He drove it toward the nearest guard's helmet, but the man blocked his blow.

Damn it.

Another soldier swung, driving his blade toward Connor's chest, but he leaned out of the way without a second to spare. The sword thudded against the armor of the soldier behind him, denting the metal.

With a pained groan, Connor drove the hilt of his sword into the nearest soldier's face as the other two lifted their swords to attack. His hilt landed with a satisfying crack, and the man stumbled backward as blood dripped down his chin from a broken nose.

A blade pierced Connor's back, just below his left shoulder. The steel dug into a rib, and the crack of bone tangled with the cold jolt of lightning that crackled up toward his skull. He grimaced, grunting with agony as he pushed through the pain.

As the soldier with the broken nose held a gloved hand to his face, Connor slammed his shoulder into the man's chest, driving him backward. Together, they barreled out of the circle and into the bloody meadow, their momentum taking them both to the ground.

The armored man fell hard as Connor ripped off the soldier's helmet. It clattered to the dirt as Connor lifted his sword, taking only a moment to notice the soldier's matted brown hair as he drove his blade into the man's throat.

Kill or be killed.

He had no pity left for these men.

The guard gurgled, his eyes locked on the moons above as he gasped for breath. Considering all of the wounds in his body, Connor could barely breathe, either.

As the soldier died at his feet, Connor struggled to stand. He swayed, the ground tilting as blood dripped from his fingertips. He limped toward a nearby boulder, his left hand barely strong enough to hold the wound at his side.

He leaned his back against the white stone and surveyed the meadow. Six dead.

The two surviving soldiers from the battle in the meadow stood nearby. Blue ribbons of moonlight glinted over their swords as they studied him. With slow and careful steps, they marched over the twitching bodies of their fellow guards.

The last two soldiers reached the base of the ladder, their swords thankfully clean. If they had stumbled across the woman and her children, at least none of the three had died yet. All alone at the edge of the field, the nobleman clutched his glowing green dagger.

In the distance, the blightwolves' howl lingered on the air, an all-too-familiar omen of death. Since death had already come to the meadow, the only unknown was who else would die tonight.

The surviving pair of soldiers in the field reached him first, and the taller of the pair swung a sword stained with Connor's blood. Connor leaned his head out of the way with barely a second to spare, and the blade scraped against the boulder. The clash of metal on rock dazed him, loud as thunder in his ear as sparks ignited in his periphery, too close for comfort.

Though tempted to retaliate with a blow of his own, he held his last sword at his side. He had to conserve his strength.

Every breath, every movement mattered.

He was on the verge of exhaustion, his body pushed to its limit while his blood tarnished the white stone behind him.

The soldiers hesitated, both no doubt just as depleted as he was—and, perhaps, afraid. He had taken out six of their fellow guardsmen, after all, when any other peasant would be dead.

But Connor was no ordinary peasant.

One of them neared and raised his sword to attack. A slight limp to his left leg caught Connor's attention, though the man's gaze rested squarely on Connor's good shoulder. With Connor's wounded left arm hanging uselessly at his side, it would make sense for an opponent to take out his last chance at survival—his ability to hold a sword.

He couldn't let that happen.

Weakened and dazed, Connor kicked out the man's left leg. Though he'd aimed for the man's inner thigh, his boot nailed the man's knee. The soldier groaned and buckled, falling against the other guard as he sank to the ground.

Fueled by the last reserves of a man on the cusp of death, Connor let out a pained yell as he drove his sword into the thin strip of skin between the soldier's helmet and shoulder plate. The blade dove into the man's exposed neck, slicing through muscle and bone.

Seven dead.

With Connor's sword still in its seventh victim, the other soldier rammed the hilt of his blade against Connor's temple. The blow knocked him to the grass.

Connor hit the ground hard, his ear ringing from the impact. His grip on his sword never lessened. With a meaty squish, the blade slid from the seventh victim's corpse. The guard's body slumped to the dirt beside him.

His chest heaved as he struggled to breathe. Jaw tensed, he forced himself to inch backward across the grass as the remaining soldier stepped over his friend's body.

The lone survivor of the meadow soldiers hoisted his sword into the air and brought it down toward Connor's face. Connor lifted his own blade, and he redirected the strike as yet another clash of steel rang through the night.

The force of the blow reverberated down Connor's arm, nearly shaking the sword from his grasp.

Seven dead. Three to go.

"You must have a death wish," the soldier seethed, his face shrouded in shadow as he blocked out one of the moons overhead.

"Quite the opposite," Connor admitted.

In a world that had tried for so many years to kill him, Connor's fault seemed to be that he was too damn stubborn to die.

A wise man would've quit by now. He would've saved his own skin and escaped. There weren't many people in Saldia who would walk toward wild magic in a forest, and maybe that made Connor a fool.

He didn't care.

A man's years were numbered, no matter how he spent them. Though it was rarely easy, Connor had always striven to do what allowed him to sleep best at night. Here, in this field, that meant fighting.

No pain would stop him. No injury would cripple him. In the end, all a man had was his mind and his sheer, stubborn grit.

The soldier's comment ignited the relentless thread woven into Connor's soul that had always pushed him to overcome.

Tonight wouldn't be his night to go down in a blaze of bitter glory. Tonight, he would send these bastards to the grave without him.

One way or another, he would find a way to *win*.

Exhausted and pushed to his limit, he did his best to hold tight to his last sword as the soldiers swarmed him.

Three of the ten guards had survived. The closest guard stood straighter as the other two finally reached him, fresh and eager to join the fight. They glared at him through the slits in their helmets, their blades glinting in the moonlight.

"Don't kill him, idiots!" the nobleman shouted. "Cut off his legs if you have to, but don't kill him yet!"

As Connor's world spun, one man kicked him hard in the side—he couldn't tell who, not anymore. Pain splintered through him like lightning, and he couldn't even get a moment to breathe. Every exhale became a cough as he sputtered up blood.

The edges of his vision went dark. A boot hit him hard in the face, and for a moment, he couldn't see at all. Between the ragged breaths of the soldiers trying to kill him, crickets chirped in the distance as life inched toward the meadow again.

A rush of wind snaked through the trees, their leaves colliding like the crash of the ocean on a shore. The memory of waves brought him home to

Kirkwall. To the sea. Though he caught brief glimpses of grass and blood, he barely clung to consciousness.

His body ran on instinct. Intuition and muscle memory—that was all he had left. He felt himself roll onto his wounded shoulder and lift his sword, and yet again the clash of steel rang through the night.

The clamor mixed with the soothing crash of the ocean, like blood and nostalgia.

A good man is resilient, Connor, his father had once said.

He could almost hear the man's voice, distant and echoing through the night.

He gets back up when others would stay down. That's my wish for you, son. When life kicks you in the teeth, I want you to always get back up.

Someone nailed him sharply in his side, the boot connecting hard with one of his many stab wounds. The flash of steel overhead caught his eye, and through the blurry blacks and grays of the world around him, he lifted his sword yet again. The familiar chorus of clanging metal shattered the otherwise peaceful night as he blocked yet another blow.

But he didn't move fast enough to block the next attack. A sword pierced his thigh, and he bit back a tortured yell.

Get back up, his father had always said.

Another blow. Another clash of steel.

Get up.

Calling on the last shreds of his strength, Connor stifled an agonized gasp, gritting his teeth as he forced himself to sit up. He swung his sword as a man leaned over him. His steel gouged the glistening gold of the royal guard's armor, leaving a long streak in the perfect metal. The man lifted his own sword to attack, but Connor snuck his blade behind the man's leg and slit the vulnerable, cloth-covered skin on the back of his knee. Blood gushed over the broken stems of grass around them as the man fell backward.

As another boot drove into his side, Connor rolled toward the injured man and drove his blade into the now-wider gap in the armor at the fallen man's gut. It would be a slow death, a painful one, but this soldier wouldn't stand again tonight. This one was no longer a threat.

Eight dead—or close to it.

Get up, Connor.

His father's voice, hazy and distant. Just a memory, but one that fueled him.

He forced himself to his feet, swaying slightly as the two remaining soldiers took wary steps backward, their intense gazes fixed on him as they waited for his next move.

With nothing but instinct and nerve left to his name, Connor raised his sword and glared them down, daring them to come for him.

Daring them to die.

CHAPTER SIX
CONNOR

As the enchanted wind of the Ancient Woods howled through the trees, Connor struggled to breathe. For a moment, only the whisper of wings through the cold night broke the stunned silence.

The two men lucky enough to survive the encounter thus far inched away from him, their swords raised as they retreated. Corpses littered the field, food for the blightwolves if the beasts got peckish later tonight.

Connor studied the nobleman as he stood at the edge of the cathedral ruins. Something seemed wrong—simply off, somehow—and in his dazed state, it took Connor a moment to realize the man had moved.

In the chaos, the nobleman had made his way toward the ruins. Toward the Rift.

Toward the exit.

The scholar's cocky smirk had long since disappeared, and he watched Connor with a chillingly cold gaze. Brows furrowed. Body tense. Dagger raised. The man sized him up not as a peasant anymore, but as a true threat.

It seemed like the nobleman was about to run, and Connor wasn't sure if that was a good thing or the worst possible option. For all he knew, opening the Rift again might've called in an army.

If he allowed the scholar to leave, the man would probably hunt him for the rest of his life. The nobleman had to die here, tonight, along with the soldiers he'd commanded.

Aristocrats were hardly known to be the forgiving sort.

In an effort to steal precious seconds to catch his breath, Connor allowed the two remaining soldiers to withdraw toward the man with the glowing dagger. The two guards stepped backward over the armor-clad bodies on the ground as their brothers in arms choked on their own blood, dying slow deaths all around them.

When Connor had recovered as much as was possible, he limped toward them. He swayed, agony in every step and every breath even as he resolved to finish this once and for all. Warm blood trickled down his calves. His shirt clung to him, hot and wet. Red smears stained his fingers and slicked his grip on his sword, but he was a survivor.

He had been through worse than this and lived. A coward in the field hiding behind braver men wouldn't be the one to kill him now.

A biting wind blew past him, carrying the chill of a winter night despite the spring air. With the gust came the weight of someone's gaze on his neck. He was tempted to look behind him, but he resisted, instead watching the soldiers' reactions to see if they saw anyone.

They did.

The two surviving guardsmen went pale, their eyes darting to the shadows beyond him, somewhere to his left. Even the nobleman's gaze shifted away from him.

Damn it all. Connor was no longer the immediate threat.

He grimaced and braced himself, prepared for the worst.

For the blightwolves.

It had to be them.

He glanced over his battered shoulder, careful to keep his three opponents in the corner of his eye, only to find the ghoul hovering off to one side.

The demon had finally decided to join them.

Though his shoulders ached with tension as a new enemy joined the battle, he couldn't deny the ribbon of relief snaking through his core.

Even the ghoul was a far cry better than a pack of blightwolves.

The phantom hovered at the edge of the woods, utterly immobile save for the fluttering shreds of its tattered cloak. It was hard to tell what the creature was looking at, given the holes where its eyes used to be, but it waited in the lingering silence.

The nobleman lifted his dagger, its blade aimed toward the ghoul. His hand trembled even as he squared his shoulders.

Get that dagger at any cost, the ghoulish voice in his head demanded.

"I don't take orders from you," he snapped. "You want my help? Kill them first."

"Please, no," one of the soldiers begged. His voice shook, and his eyes widened at the sight of the creature.

Connor scowled, confused. These men had come for him, just moments ago. They had been willing to kill a woman and her children on the orders of a coward—only to beg for their lives before the specter.

What gall.

The ghoul drew its black sword, and its tattered cloak flourished with the practiced movement. *Very well. I will take the soldiers if you take the nobleman. Otmund must die.*

Otmund.

In the hazy, blood-soaked corners of Connor's delirious mind, the name rang a bell.

Without waiting for confirmation, the ghoul darted forward and impaled the nearest guard against a boulder. Its long blade dug deep into the rock, cutting through the stone as though it were made of freshly tilled earth. The man screamed, but it ended in a gurgle. Impaled by the supernatural sword, his arms hung limply at his sides. Blood bubbled out of his mouth, and his wide eyes stared into the specter's vacant gaze.

After the jarring attack, the remaining two men scattered.

The nobleman ran into the maze of crumbling corridors, toward the Rift, and the last surviving guard ran with him. They tore through the maze, sliding across the slick grass as they barreled through the night.

Afraid.

As fast as he could, Connor limped after them, all but throwing himself forward as his injured legs struggled to keep up.

"Make this easy, Otmund!" he shouted into the night, echoing the demand the nobleman had given him at the edge of the forest. "Die like a man!"

As he rounded a corner, Connor tripped and slammed into the wall from the sheer force of his momentum. His wounded shoulder ached as a jagged stone dug into the wound. He grimaced, pausing for a second to catch his breath as the two figures raced down the path ahead.

No time to rest.

He pushed forward, scrounging whatever energy he could muster as he sprinted into the darkness. The silhouettes rounded another corner ahead, and as he reached them, he peered around the edge to find a dead end.

At the end of the crumbling hallway, a green circle of stone in the grass glimmered in the soft moonlight, covered in vines and mostly forgotten.

The Rift, no doubt.

Otmund stepped onto the stone, the dagger at his side as the lone guard turned on his heel and raised his sword toward Connor. The man in golden armor stared him down, and through the shadows, Connor saw the outline of an eye patch over the man's left eye.

Thirty yards away.

Without warning, Otmund leaned toward the guard's left side, hiding in the man's blind spot as he reached with his dagger around the soldier's neck and slit his own warrior's throat.

The soldier dropped his sword and reached for his neck as he sputtered and fell to his knees. With a strained grunt, Otmund grabbed the soldier's arm and dragged him the last few feet to the green circle of stone. A waterfall of blood streamed down the man's neck, staining his fingers with a thick sheet of red. Unfazed, the scholar hauled his dying body onto the platform with a strained groan of effort.

At the brazen and brutal act, Connor grimaced. He tripped and slammed into a wall, disgusted that the nobleman could've done that to his own soldier.

Twenty yards away.

He could still end this, but he had to move. Despite the gurgling wheeze of the dying soldier, Connor pushed himself onward. Limping, his body threatening to quit, he gritted his teeth to ride out the pain. The ground tilted underneath him, and he stumbled again into the wall.

And yet, he forced himself onward.

To finish this.

Ten yards away.

"Otmund!" Connor shouted, his voice tinged with hate as he pushed through his injuries.

The stone beneath the nobleman glowed green, humming with life and magic. The ground around them vibrated with life and thunder, accepting the sacrifice of the soldier's blood.

No.

Connor wouldn't let Otmund get away.

When he finally reached the scholar, he lifted his sword to strike the final blow. He leaned into the attack and yelled with the last of his strength as he swung for Otmund's neck, trying to slice the man's head clean off. A soft man like Otmund, with barely any muscle to his name—he didn't stand a chance against Connor.

At the last second, the nobleman ducked. He whimpered as he crouched to the bloodstained stone, and the sword sailed over his head.

In his broken and bloodstained daze, Connor had missed. His blade clanged against the wall. Sparks skittered into the night from the raw force of his blow.

For a brief moment, his right side was exposed.

It was all his enemy needed. Otmund drove the small dagger into Connor's torso and dug the blade in clear to the hilt.

From the moment the glowing green dagger bit into his skin, its magic paralyzed him. It was as though venom had seeped into his blood. It snaked through him, shattering his mind. Muscles tore. Blood boiled. Poison clawed at his heart, his lungs, his head. It boiled him from within, and everything in his body threatened to melt from its mere touch.

Beyond the ruins, the ghoul screamed in agony, as though it had also been stabbed.

As he had suspected all along, this was no ordinary dagger—but he never could've guessed something so small could inflict this much pain.

Splotches of white exploded through his vision as his body surrendered to the agony. Though he tried to fight it, the dagger's magic was winning.

"I only needed you, anyway," Otmund said.

A hand grabbed his collar and gave it a hard yank. The motion dragged him a few inches along the dirt and stirred up a fresh wave of rippling agony. His neck tensed as he fought to clear his head, and he groaned with misery.

He needed to stand. To fight. To push through, as he always had.

Another tug dragged him a few more inches across the grass, and despite the fresh surge of pain, his vision cleared somewhat.

Otmund loomed over him, just a few feet away from the glowing green circle in the ground. It hummed with power as they neared.

Connor gritted his teeth to brace himself, even as the wound's poison ate away at his very soul. He shifted his weight onto his good shoulder and lifted one foot. With all the strength he could muster, he kicked Otmund in the back of the knee. The man grimaced and fell, his hands hitting the ground hard as the dirt stained his beautiful cloak.

A blinding green light shot from the Rift and into the sky, a beacon in the night. Crackling energy tore through the air, splitting its way through the calm stars as the portal opened. This close, the dazzling light seared his eyes, and Connor impulsively raised his arm to block out the glare.

The hand clutched his shirt again. As the fingers twisted around the fabric, Connor grabbed the nobleman's wrist and violently twisted it. The bones shattered beneath his grip. Otmund yelled in agony, and his grip disappeared.

Blinded by pain and the Rift's magic, Connor tightened his hold on his sword and swung recklessly into the light.

His blade hit something.

Someone.

Otmund yelped and muttered obscenities. Something heavy thudded to the ground, but as Connor forced himself to open his eyes and peer through the glaring light, a silhouette grabbed the dagger off the grass.

Connor struggled to stand. To finish this. He staggered to his feet as the backlit silhouette bolted into the brilliant light.

He stumbled, his feet threatening to give out at any moment from the torture he had endured tonight.

From the specter of death trying to burrow into him and doing Fates knew what to his soul.

From the magical dagger even a ghoul seemed to fear.

From the stab wounds, delivered by none other than the king's guard.

He forced himself to look into the blinding green light as the nobleman stepped through. The glare dimmed. Briefly, through a hole no wider than a single man, Connor could finally see what lay beyond the Rift.

The walls of a stone room.

A sconce in the darkness beyond.

Dozens of men in gold armor, standing behind the nobleman.

As the magical gateway inched shut, the army beyond the portal merely waited. Though he stood within arm's reach, no one walked toward him.

The invasion he'd anticipated wasn't going to happen. Though he couldn't be sure, it seemed as though they were merely making sure he didn't follow Otmund through.

With a sharp hiss, the brilliant green light faded. His ears rang in the silence that followed, and the Ancient Woods' familiar moonlit darkness returned. The cold gust of the southern wind raced by, and with it came the distant hoot of an owl.

No screams. No battle cries. No buzz of wild magic.

He didn't trust it, this silence. With his hand pressed against the wound from the dagger, he leaned his bloodstained back against the cold ruin wall.

Otmund and his men could come back at any moment, and if they did, he didn't think he could hold them off again. Not given the army he'd seen on the other side.

Either they'd been waiting on reinforcements, or their fear was the only thing keeping him alive right now.

His world spun, and he could barely think anymore. With the nobleman gone, the last of his energy slipped away like the blood pouring through his fingers.

He needed to get to high ground. Given all the death that had happened here tonight, the blightwolves would inevitably come.

As he limped out of the ruins, time blurred by, and he reached the exit to the labyrinth after what felt like only seconds. He paused by a boulder to take in the carnage left over from the battle. The golden corpses in the meadow grass. The stench of iron and blood on the south wind.

Cover.

He needed cover.

Connor staggered toward the nearest tree, even as it blurred and moved ahead of him. The ground beneath him tilted. He stumbled, unable to even walk in a straight line anymore. He couldn't see the woman or her children, and he had no idea what had happened to them. If they had escaped and left him to die. If the soldiers had killed them after all.

Connor dropped his sword, and though he needed to go back for it—though he wanted to stay armed—he couldn't bring himself to do it now. Every breath was precious, and every step needed to bring him closer to a tree.

Blightwolves wouldn't care about his weapons. He could collect them in the morning—if he survived the night.

With each shaky step, he tried desperately to hold pressure to his wounds, struggling to keep as much of his blood within his body as possible. Each of his labored breaths scraped against his throat like glass.

He didn't even care about the ghoul anymore. Didn't know where it was. With the blightwolves most likely on their way, he had to deal with one death threat at a time.

His world tilted again, this time more violently than before. He didn't even know he was falling until the cold grass collided with his face. He tried to breathe, but the musky taste of dirt stained the air. The world around him blurred, nothing but green and brown streaks.

Get up, his father's voice echoed in his head. Distant. Hollow.

The wolves howled, closer than before.

Soft, gentle hands brushed against his cheek. The warm fingers soothed his sweat-stained skin. A voice swam through his mind, a woman's voice, but he couldn't understand her words. It reminded him of a mother soothing her child to sleep.

Sleep sounded like a good idea.

Sturdy hands lifted his right shoulder and rolled him onto his back. The silhouettes of several people blurred across the shadows above him. Something tugged at the fabric still covering his mouth. As it came free, cold air stung his face.

In the distant sky, Saldia's twin crescent moons floated in a sea of stars. They had seen so many live and so many die, and even when he was gone, they would witness so many more.

With that lingering thought, his world went black. The last thing he heard was his father's voice, almost too quiet to register.

Get up.

CHAPTER SEVEN
OTMUND

"Fates be *damned*!"

In the tunnels below Oakenglen, Otmund kicked the woman's corpse that lay across the magical green stone of the Rift. As his boot railed against the servant girl's side, her hand twitched, and he briefly thought there might've been a spark of life left. Her dead eyes tilted toward the wall as her head lolled to the side, the long slit across her throat coated with flecks of dried blood.

The gash in his leg stung as he stepped over her body, the girl nothing but another useless servant who had found her way into his bed and come to bore him.

Peasants didn't matter, and yet he had been bested by one.

Agonizing pain shot up his arm, and he sucked in a quick breath through his teeth as he rode the wave of pain from his fractured hand. If he didn't get a Rectivane potion soon, his wrist might not heal properly.

Despite the ache, he had more pressing issues to tend to. Namely, the commoner that had stolen a long-dead king's soul.

The Wraith King.

The ghoul.

A pool of blood stained the stone floor beside him, the only remnant of the guard Henry had killed to slip through the Rift the first time. While Otmund had faced off with the madman in the woods, the soldiers had apparently carted the man's body away.

A waste. There had been some blood left in him—enough to use for a potion, certainly.

Four dozen golden-clad king's guard soldiers stood around him, borrowed and bought from under the king's nose. Otmund had only swayed their loyalty temporarily, as they were as tired of the man's cruelty as every other ally Otmund had acquired in recent years. The trained warriors studied him as he paced back and forth, their eyes narrowing with suspicion.

They were no doubt skeptical that he had come back alone when he had gone in with a small army of their brothers.

A Rift only opened for about sixty seconds for each body sacrificed on its stone, depending on how much blood spilled. To them, the great Lord Otmund had chased a dying king through a Rift with as many men as could slip through, and yet he had come back alone.

The peasant had become far more than a complication and far worse than a simple mistake.

As Otmund paced the small room, fuming at his failure, he scanned the soldiers who lined the wall and spilled into the corridor. Seven of the forty-odd men rested their hands on the pommel of their swords, a subtle movement he had seen them make often at court when a potential threat had visited their king.

Now, however, they watched only him.

"You fools had best take your hands off those swords," he snapped, glaring at the nearest of them.

From the shadows of the soldier's helmet, the hardened warrior narrowed his eyes and glared back in silent defiance.

Only the best made it to the king's guard. These soldiers had proven themselves in battle and risen among the ranks of their brothers in arms. Augmented with inhuman strength and unparalleled senses, their innate skill only further complicated the puzzle of the peasant with two swords.

The commoner who had won against ten of the finest warriors in Saldia.

Otmund paused with his back to the soldiers, facing the Rift, staring into the air where the ancient magic had torn open the world to let him through. Without the skirmish at the edge of the gem-like stone altar, he might not have survived.

He had only spilled some of the soldier's blood, just enough to open the portal for about twenty seconds. It had seemed like a lifetime with a madman on his heels.

With a steadying breath, he dismissed the guards with a lazy flick of his undamaged wrist. They didn't deserve to be spoken to, not now.

For a brief and painful moment, however, no one moved.

No clink of retreating armor. No gentle sighs of relief from men who wouldn't die today.

They remained.

Otmund wondered if he had overlooked something—or someone—in his planning. If this was the moment in which *he* was no longer useful. The moment in which someone more powerful had grown bored of *him*.

There were so many players in this sport, and he had coerced so many into dancing for him. Perhaps they had grown weary of his whispers in their ears. Perhaps they had finally seen his plot for what it was—and what he wanted.

Otmund had always been overlooked. The squat puppeteer no one saw. The silent mastermind no one expected.

He didn't speak. He didn't dare to. He held his ground, shoulders tense as he waited for the first fool to act. The cogs in his mind spun, piecing together his next move.

Because, like the stranger in the field, Otmund was a survivor.

After a few stressful moments, the rustle of armor and the soft thud of boots across the stone floor filled the small space as the men filed out. The few men he could see through the corner of his eye studied him through the slits in their golden helmets as they retreated.

He let out a sigh of relief, so quiet he could barely hear it himself.

These men were borrowed, after all. For now, he had to make do with what obedience he could wring from them, however temporary. When he finally sat on the Oakenglen throne, he would see to it they behaved properly by making examples of those who didn't.

Henry's method had been to place heads on spikes, but Otmund had more nuance. He could see further into the future and see the game for what it was. To the people, he would be the savior. The liberator of Saldia. He alone would sit on the throne Henry had so foolishly conquered for him.

The people would rally. Sing. Celebrate. They would say he was chosen by the Fates to free them, and if they started to suspect the truth, he would make his puppets dance again to remind them of his greatness. Wars would be won. Other lands conquered. Whatever it took to keep them fat and quiet, Otmund would pay the price. They would feast in his honor, never knowing the truth of the man for whom they cheered.

From the West to the East and as far south as the Barrens, Henry had conquered it all. Murdered kings in their own courts. Forced prideful men and their wives to bow before him. Married off other men's daughters to strangers in distant lands, just to remind them of his absolute authority.

The known world loathed Henry Montgomery, and Otmund would unite them all through their shared hatred as he took his rightful place in history.

When the last of the clanking metal receded into the dark corridor behind him, Otmund ran his good hand over his balding head.

Everything in him screamed to take the other soldiers through the Rift, to overwhelm the stranger who had so clearly been wounded, but these guards weren't dependable. They had tried to *kill* him, the idiots, instead of listening to orders. Their bloodlust had gotten the better of them, and if one of them had fused with the Wraith King instead—Otmund rubbed his eyes at the mere thought of an insider at the capital suddenly obtaining ultimate power.

No, his next move would require finesse and patience.

There were too many unknowns. This stranger could've been a mastermind, bent on stealing the Wraith King for himself from the beginning. There had been a house in the trees, which suggested a family had made their way outside of the southern towns. Perhaps he truly was a nameless peasant, useless and disposable, in the wrong place at the wrong time.

"But the way he fought..." As his broken wrist ached, Otmund rubbed his jaw with his other hand and paced back and forth across the Rift. The wound in his leg stung with every step, and he vented his rage by kicking aside the girl's corpse.

He bit the inside of his cheek, eyes glossing over as he relived the horror of watching a lone man decimate his army, one by one.

It shouldn't have been possible, not so soon after obtaining that much power. It took time for the soul to merge with the body and for the new Wraithblade to master his powers. More importantly, it took time to earn the loyalty of the Wraith King—or the ghost's disdain.

If Otmund faced the stranger again, he would have to better prepare for the battle. He would have to cheat, or else he would lose.

Cowards cheat, his father used to say. *Noblemen negotiate.*

Otmund scoffed. His father would've been disappointed to see what had become of him, but then again he had never much cared for the old fart's opinion.

His father, the last Lord of Mossvale, had been a damn fool. He'd been a man of the people, by all accounts a fair and just lord in their stunning land, and yet history would forget his name. All of his work and self-sacrifice had been for naught.

If Otmund had followed in his father's footsteps, the Soulblud family name would've faded from memory. No one cared about the late Lord Soulblud, but Otmund had already begun to carve his own name into history.

He had spent too much money rebuilding roads and reforming tax codes, mere trivial nonsense that hadn't added to the coffers. Too much time talking to the peasants. Too much time remembering their names.

It had been a waste of talent and a mistake Otmund wouldn't make.

The rulers of Mossvale were forgotten, all of them, swept aside by the powerful and treated as butlers for the rich. Mossvale had nothing but roaring waterfalls, breathtaking architecture, and exotic women.

Wealth, sure, but Otmund's riches were dwarfed by that of the courtesans in the capital. No resources to barter for political gain save rivers and natural beauty. The land served tourists and nothing more.

Otmund deserved *better*.

The Wraith King was his one chance to be powerful. To have the world bow before him and for him to be served as was his right. He wasn't going to let some peasant take it from him.

A peasant who fought with dual blades.

A peasant who could kill an army.

A peasant who had been in the right place at the right time.

Lost in his thoughts, Otmund paced the edges of the circular room. As he absently rubbed the back of his neck, his sleeve slid up his arm and revealed the forbidden augmentation that enhanced his thinking. The nondescript circle, so simple and plain in its design, hid the power of the stolen spell that gave him a clear and steady mind.

This stranger in the field was nothing more than another puzzle. One he could solve.

It had taken an army to kill King Henry, and he wouldn't have access to those resources again. It had taken years of twisting minds and corrupting souls to get the resources required to catch Henry momentarily off guard, and one of the most important people in that betrayal had disappeared into the night.

He groaned and pressed his good palm flat against the wall as he tried to compose himself. Anger never got him anywhere.

If some stray peasant wielded the power of the Wraith King now, Otmund would have to be clever and lure the man to him. More importantly, he would have to ensure no one killed this stranger before he had a chance to do it.

He couldn't let anyone discover what this man was truly capable of with the Wraith King at his side—especially not the peasant himself.

With a deep and settling breath, Otmund finally cleared his head. He had killed a king, after all. Even if this stranger in the field were more than a peasant, he wouldn't pose much of a threat. The man didn't stand a chance, and he, too, would die.

Painfully.

Otmund would have his day, and when the time came, he would not make the same error again. Henry's death had been five years in the making, but with the peasant, he wouldn't wait. He wouldn't give this stranger in the woods the chance to slip through his fingers, nor would he give the man time to regain his strength.

By his count, he had roughly two seasons before the stranger posed a true threat. Henry had taken two seasons to master his powers, and even then, he had needed another three years to build an army.

Otmund had time, but not much.

He rolled his shoulders as the ache in his broken wrist worsened. After orchestrating Henry's death, he had only a few favors left to cash in, which meant he needed to be cautious with how he spent them.

For now, it was time to use the Lightseers. There were still a few minds he could twist to his favor.

When he caught this commoner, Otmund would personally skin him alive, just as he had promised. And when the time finally came, he would enjoy every moment of the man's pain.

CHAPTER EIGHT
CONNOR

Connor woke with a start.

As he bolted upright, agonizing pain splintered through his body. Every vein burned. Every beat of his heart flooded his limbs with fire, like he was being roasted alive from within.

His leg. His back. His left arm. His shoulder. The injuries from his battle sizzled, screaming at him, and yet the injury in his side seared the most.

He let out a strangled groan of pain as he pressed his palm against the wound Otmund had given him with that infuriating little green dagger. Fates above *and* below—that hurt like hell. He fell backward and clenched his teeth to help him push through the pain.

Damn that rat bastard.

The haunting sensation of claws ripping through his chest followed shortly after, tearing through him just as it had when the ghoul first attacked him in the field. He sucked in a steadying breath, eyes shut as he tried to ride out the second excruciating flood that tore through his body.

With short and shallow breaths, he waited for the biting sting to subside. It gradually receded, and though it didn't fade completely, it finally reached a level he could tolerate.

At first, he simply listened to the world around him with his eyes closed. The heavy silence weighed on his chest like a soggy blanket. Birds sang, their voices muffled. A board creaked in the house. His back lay flat against a lumpy surface that scratched at his skin.

Instead of bolting upright this time, he merely opened his eyes and cast a wary glance at his surroundings. Wooden walls. Light pouring in from behind his head. A chair in the corner. A hand-carved dresser, sitting across from him with one of its drawers open and empty.

"Where the hell am I?" he muttered, running a hand through his hair as he tried to piece together the last fragments of memories from the night before.

The silhouettes overhead.

The hands lifting him off the grass.

The soft murmur of a woman's voice.

He adjusted his weight on the straw mattress beneath him, cursing under his breath with each ripple of pain that shot up his spine. Moving far slower than he would've liked, he finally managed to sit up and peer out the window behind him.

Daylight.

Judging by the soft sunbeams fluttering through the trees, it couldn't have been more than an hour after dawn. He cast aside the rough sheet covering him and swung his legs over the edge of the bed, but his entire body protested every movement with fresh ripples of pain.

As he stared down at his ripped and bloodstained pants, he paused to let the rush fade.

The wound in his side still ached worse than the other injuries, and the muscles in his back spasmed in retaliation to the pain. Whatever magic that glowing green blade held was cursed, and Connor never wanted to see the damn thing again.

If he did, he vowed to smash it with a rock.

With the sheet gone, the cool air brushed across his bare chest, and he looked down to see himself covered in blood-stained bandages. He rolled out his good shoulder, the muscles stiff and aching, and he cracked his neck while he slowly got his bearings.

A blurred shadow in his periphery caught his attention, and it took a moment for him to realize it was his own bicep. He hesitated, squinting at the massive muscle that couldn't possibly have belonged to him.

He poked it to ensure he wasn't hallucinating.

Solid muscle, and unmistakably *his*. Sure, his years in the forest had toned his body, but he'd never had a build like this.

Connor studied his hands, his forearms, his biceps, his chest. All his muscles had grown as he'd slept, now far larger and stronger than they'd been yesterday.

Either that, or he was delirious.

On his sternum, a thick black scar stretched across his skin where the ghoul had ripped into him. He ran his finger over it, and the patch of black glowed briefly green.

Last night came back to him in a rush.

The scream.

The green flash of light through the forest.

The dying man crawling from the ruins.

The royal guardsmen.

The specter, drawing a jet-black sword.

A brush with death, so close he could still taste the blood.

Yet again, he ran his finger along the dark scar. Beneath his touch, the mark glowed as brightly green as fresh spellgust ore.

Magic.

It had to be.

Nothing else in Saldia carried that brilliant light within it.

Magic—and in *his* body.

In a violent rush, his head cleared. His eyes glossed over with shock, and the weight of what this meant sank clear into his bones.

According to the ballads of Henry's twelve-year conquest of Saldia, the wraith had given the man unnatural power, far beyond what any potion master could conjure with a cauldron. His skill, strength, and unrivaled might had surpassed even the augmented soldiers he'd fought on the battlefields.

Entire kingdoms had crumbled beneath Henry's sword, all thanks to the phantom fighting at his side. No one knew what the wraith was or where it had come from—just that it fought like Death itself.

Last night, Connor had met that ghoul for himself and survived. It had clawed its way into his very soul, but it hadn't killed him.

I will make you powerful beyond imagination, it had promised.

Out there, in that field under the Saldian stars, Henry had died. As hard as it was for Connor to fathom, it seemed as though the wraith had already chosen its new master.

It had chosen him, and if that was true, he now had access to magic.

Real magic, not like the watered-down counterfeits sold in the southern towns.

Dark magic. The kind treacherous people usually wanted for themselves.

According to the stories, the wraith had been by Henry's side in every battle, in every interrogation, in every courtroom. Some said the wraith had corrupted Henry; others saw the specter as a blessing from the Fates, given to a worthy man so he could rule the unfit.

Everyone could agree, though, that Henry would've still been a merchant if not for the ghoul. They said it in hushed tones for fear of him somehow hearing, but they said it nonetheless.

If the ghoul had sculpted Henry into a king of kings, Connor now had the power of emperors and the undead at his disposal.

Flooded with the weight of it all, he let out a string of muffled curses.

He didn't even know what the hell to do with power like that. His whole life, he'd scrimped and saved to get an augmentation of his own, but he'd never pooled together enough coin. Like so many others, he'd always craved magic. He'd just never had the chance to wield it.

Until now.

And others would try to take it.

His ear twitched, picking up movement beyond the closed door. Labored breathing. The huff of air from lungs. The murmured voices of two—no, three people. Two men and a woman, from the tone.

"…asleep, yet…"

"…where are we going…"

"…not until I say…"

Snips and pieces of a conversation without any context, sure, but he could still hear words through a solid door. His hearing had never picked up a conversation from this far away. He leaned toward the voices, astonished.

Everything in him had been enhanced overnight. His vision. His hearing. His body.

"What the hell did that ghost do to me?" he muttered, staring again at his hands.

Quick footsteps pattered across the hardwood just outside the door, and seconds later, the entry swung open. A familiar woman walked in, her cheeks flushed as she threw two bags on the dresser and yanked open the remaining drawers. Her dark blonde braids circled her head, pinned to her scalp in elegant loops, and a loose strand fell across her face as she worked. A few tight wrinkles pulled at the edges of her eyes when she frowned. Muttering under her breath, she reached into each of the dresser's drawers and carelessly shoved the rolls of fabric into each bag.

This was clearly the woman from the meadow—and she was very much alive.

"So much to do," she whispered, her eyes glossing over as she worked. "Where did I put those—no, aren't they in here?"

"It's good to see you're not dead," Connor said.

The woman gasped and spun violently around, the bags thudding onto the floor as she pressed her back to the wall. With one hand on her chest and her eyes as wide as plates, her jaw dropped open. "You're awake!"

"Did you do this?" He gestured to the bandages on his abdomen and thigh.

She shook her head. "My boy did. Wesley's a bit younger than you, but I'd wager not by much. He's quite the medic, that one. I'm Kiera. Are you thirsty? You must be. I'll get you something to eat, too. We don't have much, but what's ours is—"

"Don't," Connor said on reflex.

He didn't accept handouts. What he ate, he worked for.

"Hush, you, and lay down." She waved him backward, lips pursed with impatience as she ordered him about. "I'll get you something to eat."

"That's not—"

"How hungry are you?" she interrupted with a cursory glance over his torso. "You look like you could swallow several horses and still have room to eat the barn."

"I—uh—thank you?"

"Hush, now, and lie down. You need to rest." Kiera jabbed her finger into his chest, avoiding any bandages as she coaxed him backward and grabbed the sheet off the ground. With a flourish in the air, she stretched it out above him, and it gently settled over his body once again.

"Look," he said as he tossed the sheet aside again. "You were kind to bandage me and bring me away from the blightwolves, but I'll get out of your hair."

He stood, wavering slightly as he got to his feet. He lost his balance, and he let out an irritated sigh as he had to sit back down.

With each movement, every inch of him roared in protest. Damn that stupid little green blade.

"Mm-hmm," she said dubiously, crossing her arms as she studied him. "Excellent fighter or not, you're in no condition to travel on your own, and I won't allow it. You'll travel with us."

"Us?" Connor asked with a glance toward the open door and the empty hallway beyond.

"If you won't rest, at least get some clean clothes on," she ordered, ignoring him.

He tried again to stand, but the pain in his torso sparked a surge of nausea that burned in the back of his mouth, and he didn't have the strength to argue. Instead, he rubbed his temple and leaned one elbow on his knee while he watched her flit about the room.

Kiera looked over her shoulder at the drawers and rummaged through a few options before selecting something amidst the clutter. With a soft grunt of effort, she yanked out a few pieces of clothing and carefully laid a simple brown tunic and a pair of green pants on the edge of the mattress.

"You're about my husband's size, I think," she added with another cursory glance over Connor's muscles. "Though the fit won't be completely right. You can wear these for now, and I'll sew you something proper once we get to the new place."

"New place?" Connor asked, pinching the bridge of his nose as the world spun around him. "What new—"

"Hush and change," she chided. "I'm going to get you something to eat."

With that, she left the room and shut the door behind her, the forgotten bags and scattered fabric still laying askew across the floor.

For a moment, Connor sat in the stunned silence the woman had left in her wake, barely following her train of thought. If she possessed the ability to listen, she didn't use it much.

He chuckled.

To her credit, she certainly had a fighter's spirit. The hovering, the insistence that a grown man do her bidding—honestly, she reminded him a little of his mother. The way she spoke. The way she carried herself like a matriarch.

His smile fell, and he rubbed his jaw to distract himself from the memories.

A second set of footsteps thudded toward the door, far heavier than Kiera's. Louder. The heavy thumps of a man's boots.

Connor tensed, anticipating conflict. Though Kiera had mentioned a son and a husband in her whirlwind of an introduction, he hadn't seen either yesterday.

The door opened again, and this time, a stocky man with broad shoulders filled the doorframe, blocking the route to the hall with his bulk. He ducked as he entered, his dark hair and a thick black beard framing his weathered face. His eyes instantly landed on Connor, and he scowled.

Connor met the man's gaze, eyes narrowing at the potential threat.

"There we are," Kiera said with a broad smile as she stepped around the fuming man, her arms overflowing with food. A loaf of bread sat tucked beneath one arm. She held a balled-up cloth in one hand and a clay pitcher in the other.

Connor watched her through the corner of his eye as she sat on the edge of the mattress opposite him and placed it all on the rough linen. The corners of the balled-up fabric opened to reveal several strips of dried meat.

The salty aroma of venison snaked into the air, and his stomach gurgled at the idea of food. His throat ached at the promise of a drink, but he refused to indulge himself with a looming threat blocking the doorway.

Her eyes creased as she smiled warmly, and she watched him in the ensuing silence. With her hands on her lap, she waited patiently for him to begin.

But his gaze never strayed from the burly man standing by the door. Even in an ordinary fight, when Connor wasn't recovering from a brush with death, this guy would've been a challenge. His broad shoulders and thickset body implied incredible strength, and Connor had no inkling of the man's fighting ability.

It seemed he had found himself in a fresh pot of trouble.

Kiera peered over her shoulder, her gaze drifting between the two men, and she rolled her eyes. "Ethan, enough. After what he's done for—"

"I think it's time he and I had a chat about last night," the man interrupted, his gruff voice booming through the small room.

"Ethan, *really*," Kiera snapped. "You could show a *little* gratitude for the man who saved your wife and children's lives."

"Kiera, take the girls and leave with Wesley," Ethan ordered without taking his eyes off Connor.

His wife groaned, shaking her head in exasperation. "We don't have time for this, Ethan. There's no telling when an army might come through that damned portal again. And that young man," she added pointing at Connor. "He saved us. We would be dead without him, so I would like you to show a bit of kindness!"

Ethan didn't respond. His expression didn't change an ounce. He simply shifted his attention, turning the intensity of his gaze on her.

Kiera frowned and tilted her head toward Connor, a soft apology in her gaze as she smiled again. "When he's done being an ass, I expect you to come and live with us, at least until you get better."

Ethan groaned. "Kiera—"

"I won't have no for an answer." She quirked one eyebrow, her gaze fixed on Connor. "Now, you eat up. I expect you to eat all of this, you hear?"

A grin tugged at the corner of Connor's mouth, but with Ethan glowering at him, he resisted the impulse to indulge it.

Without another word, Kiera grabbed the packs she had been working on and stuffed them to the brim before slinging them over her shoulder. The sleeve of a yellow blouse hung from the opening in one bag, the hem trailing along the floorboards, but she didn't seem to notice. The woman charged through the door and shut it behind her. Her footsteps receded into the house.

In the silence that followed, Ethan crossed his arms as he stood between Connor and the exit. "Well?"

"You're welcome," Connor said with a nod in Kiera's direction.

Ethan frowned, chin lifting slightly at Connor's cheek. "Fine. We'll do this the hard way."

The burly man grabbed the chair from the corner of the room and dragged it slowly across the floor, letting the legs scrape against the wood. With a quiet groan, he slammed it down in the center of the room and sat on it backwards, leaning his forearms against the backrest as he stared Connor down.

A classic intimidation tactic, but Connor couldn't blame him. This was Ethan's house, his family had just been threatened. He no doubt needed to ensure Connor didn't have other intentions.

"Tell me your name," Ethan demanded, his steely gaze never once wavering.

For a moment, Connor debated not answering. He was hardly in the mood for this. He had done the man a favor and had no intention of spending another moment in the man's house.

Such was the life of a drifter, after all. He had to keep moving.

As Connor adjusted in his seat, his muscles screamed again. Momentarily disoriented from the brutal jolt of pain, he cursed under his breath and held the enchanted wound in his side.

Showing weakness at a time like this could cost him his life, depending on Ethan's morals and motivations—neither of which Connor could guess at quite yet. He had to swallow the pain and bury it deep down until he could find a quiet place to heal.

To mask the true depths of his misery, he leaned his back against the headboard and tried to stem the rising tide of fire through his blood.

It didn't work.

He could barely contain a pained grimace, and the room around him spun. Despite the risk, he briefly closed his eyes to re-center himself.

Hurt. Unarmed. Half-naked. He was clearly at the disadvantage here, with wounds that would take ages to heal. He needed to find his swords, and to do that, he needed a chance to rifle through the bloodstained grasses.

This man held the clear advantage, and Connor would have to play his cards carefully.

As he adjusted on the mattress, the water pitcher sitting on the sheet tipped over. In a lightning-fast movement that seemed impossible for such a massive man, Ethan snatched the handle to keep it from spilling. The motion appeared to be instinctive, like a father reaching for a child about to fall.

Ethan silently offered the pitcher to Connor. His expression didn't change despite the act of kindness, and Connor couldn't deny the ache in his throat any longer.

With a subtle nod of thanks, he grabbed it and drank straight from the jug. A thin stream of water snaked down his jaw, cold and delightful. The fresh water tasted like spring, crisp and light, and he closed his eyes in gratitude as it rushed down his throat.

The simple act ignited a deep hunger within him. His stomach growled, and a primal ache ripped through him, as if it had been waiting for the opportune moment to demand food.

Despite the deer he'd caught two days ago, it suddenly felt as though he hadn't eaten anything in weeks.

He eyed the bread and dried meat, his stomach rumbling, and it took every ounce of his willpower not to lunge across the bed.

"After a fight like that, I'd be parched, too," Ethan admitted.

The comment sparked dozens of questions in the back of Connor's mind, but he couldn't give them the time of day. Not with an insatiable hunger like this.

He set the empty jug on the floor and grabbed the bread, barely hesitating to smell it before he took a hefty bite. Kiera had offered it to him, after all, and he could justify eating their food by accepting it as payment for saving their lives. The warm crust cracked beneath his teeth, fresh from the oven, and he couldn't help but close his eyes to relish the rich and hearty flavor.

"My name's Connor," he said between bites.

"Connor," Ethan echoed, his shoulders relaxing as he finally got a name. "You did right by us, and even if Kiera doesn't think so, I'm grateful. My name's Ethan Finn, and as you've probably guessed, that was my wife. You've already met Isabella and Fiona, our daughters. Wesley is our son, and you'll meet him in a bit."

Connor doubted it.

He was a loner, used to wandering through the woods. As kind as these people were, he had no intention of staying.

"Do you want to tell me what happened out there?" Ethan asked, tilting his head slightly as he waited for an answer.

Connor shook his head as he swallowed the last of the bread. "Instead of that, maybe you can tell me where you were when your wife and daughters were left alone in a cabin in the middle of blightwolf territory?"

It was a fair question. A man's duty was to protect his family, first and foremost. As far as he could tell, Ethan had no right to sit here and interrogate him, least of all judge him.

Ethan's eyes narrowed briefly, as if daring Connor to say it again, but he ultimately sighed in resignation. "You heard the blightwolves, too?"

Connor nodded. "Every soul in the Ancient Woods can hear the blightwolves."

"They've been coming around the house more," Ethan admitted, rubbing the creases by his tired eyes. "I figured they could smell us and were trying to root us out. Trying to hunt us. Now, though, I wonder if they could feel something happening in those damn ruins. Wesley and I were leading them away, trying to throw them off our scent and get the beasts farther from the family."

Connor scoffed as he brushed crumbs off his hands. "How can a man lead blightwolves anywhere? They're bloodthirsty and brilliant."

"A bow, arrows, and a bit of nerve," Ethan countered, squaring his shoulders. "That's how."

Huh.

Impressive.

Ethan rubbed his jaw. Dark bags under his eyes suggested he hadn't slept, probably because there was a strange man in his house.

"I owe you a great debt," he said again, this time more sincerely.

"You don't owe me anything." With the bread devoured, Connor grabbed the strips of meat. "Consider yourself paid in full."

"A light lunch isn't remotely enough to—"

Connor ignored the man's protests as he tried once again to stand. Though pain ripped through him, he braced himself against it. This time, he was able to retain his balance by leaning against the wall.

"Cut the humble horseshit," Ethan demanded as he stood as well. "I give credit where credit is due, and my family's lives are worth more than a few strips of dried venison."

"Of course," Connor said. "That's why I ate the bread, too."

Ethan groaned. "Look—"

"I wasn't trying to be a hero, Ethan. I did what I had to." He grabbed the shirt Kiera had given him and tenderly tugged it over the bandages covering most of his body. Jolts of pain shot through him with every movement, but he did his best to ignore them.

"You could've run, but you fought off the people who would have killed my family." Ethan gestured toward him with a massive palm. "You risked your life and got your ass handed to you in the process. That's what heroes do, right?"

Connor frowned, glaring briefly at the burly man as he bit into another strip of dried meat.

"Kiera told me what happened in the field," the stocky man continued. "I know about the soldiers. The nobleman's order to kill all witnesses. The way the guards circled you. The way you took them out, one by one. Kiera had to cover the girls' eyes for that." Ethan stroked his beard, his brows tilting upward with remorse at the mention of what his daughters might have witnessed last night. "I know what happened, but I don't know *why*. I want to know why you were in these woods."

Ethan absently set the chair against the wall, his back to Connor, but there was weight to the question. Of everything Ethan had asked so far, it seemed this was the only lingering answer he truly needed.

Perhaps Kiera had seen the ghoul. Perhaps they rightly suspected something otherworldly had happened last night, beyond witnessing the Rift open.

Connor hesitated as the delightful tang of the dried meat sat on his tongue. Truth be told, he didn't owe this man anything, and what he said next might save his—or Ethan's—life. Omitting the truth could protect the man's family if any more guards came looking for him.

After all, according to the dead king, Connor was a dead man walking.

He could tell a partial truth by admitting what he was, and that would likely make it easier for him to leave. Usually, when he confessed he was a drifter, people chased him out of town. Merchants were welcome, as they brought goods into the local economies. Travelers and tourists brought coin.

But drifters brought new blood that wasn't guaranteed to stay. Vagrants weren't accountable to the townsfolk, and it made them nervous when a man could disappear into the night and not be tracked.

Transients didn't take the roads. Men like Connor knew better than to leave a trail because nothing good came from those who followed.

"I'm a drifter," he confessed. "On my way to Bradford to find work."

To his surprise, Ethan let out a calm breath. In a sudden rush, all of the man's tension dissipated. His shoulders relaxed, and his scowl disappeared. The deep lines in his forehead eased, and an almost jovial expression washed across his face, as though the scowl had been nothing more than a mask to intimidate a potential threat.

His reaction didn't make a lick of sense.

"What were you expecting?" Connor asked, eyes narrowing with suspicion.

"Nothing." The older man dismissed the question with a wave of his hand. "Can you walk?"

Connor nodded even though he wasn't entirely sure if he could. With a Rift that close, he needed to figure out how to move—and do it quickly.

"Good," Ethan said. "We need to leave. Kiera was right, but don't tell her I said that. The soldiers could be back any minute."

Without another word, Ethan left the room. The door remained open, a silent invitation for Connor to join him.

Once more, Connor was alone as the heavy silence weighed on his shoulders.

He didn't understand these people, but they had saved his life. He would find his blades, thank Ethan, and leave them be.

With a ghoul in the shadows and an army on the horizon, it was the only choice that made sense.

CHAPTER NINE
CONNOR

With Ethan gone, now somewhere in the depths of the house, Connor finally had a moment to think. The man's heavy boots thudded against the wooden floor, receding down the hallway and already out of sight.

He needed to survey the scene in the field and, if possible, find answers as to who Otmund really was and what he ultimately wanted. He also needed to find the ghoul—or, more likely, find a way to avoid it altogether. If it had warped Henry's mind, like the stories claimed, he didn't want to give it the chance to corrupt him, too.

Last night, the monster had driven its black sword through man and boulder alike with astonishing ease. To an enchanted creature like that, perhaps mortals truly were inferior.

And, now, it had marked him. He ran his thumb over the dark scar on his chest, and it glowed briefly green through the fibers of his shirt.

Connor stretched. Though the room briefly spun around him, he kept his balance. His joints popped as he regained his composure, and a flood of relief washed through him.

The clean pants Kiera had offered still lay on the mattress, along with a few remaining crumbs from the bread he had devoured. As he tugged off his bloodstained pants and pulled on the clean pair, he eyed the crumbs and pitcher.

His stomach still growled, and even crumbs looked tempting.

Ignoring the ache for more food, Connor walked down the hall and rounded the corner to find Ethan waiting in an empty kitchen. The unlit stove in the corner was stained black with soot. Half-burned logs sat in a pile of ash, the embers long dead despite the lingering scent of burning wood in the air.

A long, hand-carved table with inlaid designs along the edge took up most of the room. To Connor's relief, his pack and empty sheaths sat on its surface, along with a pile of his daggers. A stool lay on its side in the middle of the walkway, and Connor stepped over it as he snatched his bag off the table.

It only took a few moments for him to buckle his crisscrossed sheaths to his back and rifle through his bag to ensure his meager possessions hadn't disappeared overnight.

His coin pouch. His supply of dried venison. His flask. To his surprise, nothing had disappeared.

For now, he slipped the various daggers into the bag. He could take the time to hide them on his body later, when he didn't have an audience.

"You don't travel light," Ethan said, his gaze locked on the bag of weapons over Connor's shoulder.

"Can't afford to."

"Fair enough. I suppose a drifter can't be too careful. That's a hard life to choose."

"Never said I chose it."

Connor grabbed the last dagger from the table's surface and shoved it into his bag. Beneath the weapon, an elaborate tree had been etched into the corner of the wood. He brushed his thumb along the artwork, momentarily stunned by the intricate craftsmanship.

The artwork continued down the edge of the table, and he ran his finger over the magnificent carvings. Trees. Acorns. Fanged deer. He had seen these ornate pieces of art in a few of the wealthier taverns he had visited, but never in a home.

Only rich men could afford something like this.

"Did you buy this?" he asked.

"No, I carved it." Ethan gave a modest little shrug. "We can't move it with us, but I was a carpenter by trade. I'll make a new one."

With that, the stocky man opened the door and stepped out onto a makeshift porch. As they walked outside, a gust of wind blew through the trees, and the house swayed gently beneath Connor's feet. He frowned, the sensation eerily similar to standing on a boat, and his childhood on the sea kicked in as he intuitively leaned into the shifting porch under his feet.

A large, perfectly square hole in the porch revealed shifting patches of the ground below, and Ethan sat at its edge. Without warning, the massive man slipped through it, disappearing in an instant. Connor peered through to find Ethan carefully climbing down the ladder nailed to the trunk as the house swayed in the gale around them.

In the sky above, a hawk cried before diving through a gap in the trees, and Connor's newly enhanced eyes caught every movement. Though his body still ached with every step, he crossed to the edge and studied what he could see through gaps in the canopy.

The lone spire of the ruins stabbed at the sky, its crumbling white stone covered with ivy. Sunbeams illuminated an idyllic field below, and only the occasional dark brown stain on the white boulders served as grim reminders of what had happened in the night.

Even from up here, everything seemed clearer. He peered across the canopy, his vision sharper than ever before as he scanned the miles of forest beyond.

"You going to stay up there?" Ethan shouted from the ground, a hint of impatience in his tone.

"Not a chance in hell," Connor muttered.

With a few stiff and unstable steps as the strong winds shifted the porch beneath his feet, Connor made it to the hole and tenderly sat at its edge. His muscles screamed, but the more he moved, the less they hurt.

Only the searing wound in his side truly throbbed.

He grimaced as he slipped through the opening and gripped the wooden ladder nailed to the trunk, taking each rung carefully as he eased himself toward the ground.

From the occasional fight with bandits to being ambushed twice in his sleep, Connor was familiar with pain. Whatever Otmund's weapon had done to him, however, was different than anything he had experienced in his life. He wouldn't be able to walk this one off—he had to heal, and that unfortunately meant rest.

Damn it.

On the ground, Ethan leaned against a nearby tree, arms crossed as he studied Connor's every movement. A smirk tugged at the corner of the man's mouth, like he couldn't quite believe this was the hero that had saved his family.

"You try getting stabbed with a cursed dagger, and we'll see how quickly *you* recover." Connor winced again as he reached the last rung of the ladder. His boots hit the dirt, and the wound in his side ripped open. He grimaced with discomfort and pressed his hand against the injury.

"Fair point." Ethan chuckled as he kicked off the tree and strode into the meadow.

As they stepped through the trees and into the decimated field, Connor paused. Patches of dark red grass baked in the sun. Handprints covered the white boulders, smeared and faded from whatever had licked them in the night. A dozen swords littered the ground, along with the occasional golden breastplate or helmet.

But no bodies.

Around him, the gore-soaked grass trembled in a light breeze as he stepped into the overgrown arena where he'd fought for his life. Where a nobleman had come to kill a king. Where a specter had stalked through the shadows.

Where his life had changed, possibly far more than he could fathom.

Connor retraced his steps from the onslaught, surveying the path his battle had taken across the ground. The boot prints in the dirt. The broken stems. The flattened grasses where he had been knocked on his back.

A golden helmet lay in the center of the meadow, streaks of dried blood along the dented nose plate. Beneath it, a small pool of slobber drowned the crushed weeds.

The blightwolves had feasted.

In the sea of glinting metal that littered the field, one weapon caught his eye. The first sword he'd lost in the battle lay on the ground nearby, its simple iron hilt only a shade darker than the blade itself. He braced himself as he reached for it, but the wound in his side stung even more than he'd expected. With a pained grimace, he slid his tailored sword into one of the twin sheaths on his back.

With every step, Connor's muscles screamed a little less. His world steadied a little more. Out here, the scent of grass and honeysuckle floated on the air, more vivid and beautiful than it had been yesterday. More breathtaking than it ever had been before.

It was as though he could smell them all for the first time, as if he finally saw the world as it was supposed to be seen—as a vibrant cacophony of experiences lingering on the air.

Either the vividness was the ghoul's doing, or it was just the effect a near-death experience had on a man's mind.

A long streak of the king's blood led into the ruins, and Connor followed it. As he reached the time-stained boulders along the edge of the cathedral, his second sword gleamed in the sun. He reached for it, his body shouting again as he sheathed his second blade.

Along the nearest wall, a long streak of blood dragged across the crumbling ruins. More of it caked the grass, almost black as it baked in the sun. He paused at a red handprint on the white stone of a nearby wall and held his palm up to it.

It matched perfectly.

Death itself had nearly taken him last night.

Determined to find something—anything—that could explain what had happened, he followed the streak of blood into the ruins, deeper and deeper along the route the nobleman had taken to escape him. Though Ethan and Kiera were worried an army could come through at any moment, he doubted it.

If soldiers were going to rush through, they would've done it by now. A few dozen men had waited on the other side for the portal to close, a warning to him should he try to enter, but they had never so much as inched toward the opening.

Their fear held them at bay, and though Connor hadn't seen the ghoul since he'd woken, he knew it was here. It had to be.

Waiting.

The long streak of blood ended at the large green circle of gemstone embedded in the grass. He knelt, examining it, wondering what this could possibly be. Last night, the nobleman had sliced a man's throat to open it. Though red streaks stained the pebbles beside the green stone, the circle itself showed nothing. Not a drop. Not so much as a smear, as though it had absorbed every bit of the blood spilled on its surface.

As Connor knelt before the pedestal, an elaborate circle in its center caught his eye. Five small divots lined the ring, and a small green stone lay in one of them. He tried to lift the tiny gem, but it wouldn't budge.

A Rift, the ghoul had called it. A portal of immense power that could effortlessly take a man from one place to the next, and yet it lay abandoned in an empty field.

Connor drew one of his swords and dipped the blade along the side of the stone, wondering how deep it went. The blade slid into the grass, screeching as it scraped against the perfect stone, and he buried his blade to the hilt before the screeching stopped.

It went on forever.

He wondered how the hell this thing worked. It was a portal to another part of Saldia, that much he knew, but that was about it. This was ancient magic, far beyond anything he'd ever seen.

Boots crunched the grass, the now-familiar heavy gait trailing behind him. Connor looked over his shoulder as Ethan rounded the corner, wrinkles creasing around the burly man's eyes. "Wesley and I tried to lift that, once."

Connor frowned, sheathing his sword as he stood. "What happened?"

Ethan chuckled. "It zapped me. Hard. Knocked me out for an hour and scared Kiera half to death."

"So, it can't be moved?"

"Doesn't seem like it can, though I'm not sure why we would want to."

"It's a portal to other parts of Saldia," Connor said with a shrug. "That could prove useful if I ever figured out how to use it."

Ethan huffed. "A portal that could bring your enemies to your door."

"Or you to theirs," Connor pointed out, lifting one eyebrow to make his point.

The burly man sighed. "Don't go hunting for them. You don't know what you're up against."

Connor frowned. "Do you?"

"No," the older man said with an irritated glare. "That's the point."

Connor chuckled, cracking his neck again as he studied the portal, still wondering if it could be of any use. Apparently having had his fill, however, Ethan muttered under his breath and retreated into the ruins. Connor debated staying and studying the ground for clues or something he might've missed yesterday, but the blightwolves had eaten his evidence. He could've stayed here all day and not found a damn thing.

With an irritated groan, he stood. The walls around him blurred as he lost his balance, still disoriented from his wounds, but he set one hand on the wall until his world steadied. His vision sharpened once more, more quickly this time, and he followed Ethan out of the once-great cathedral.

"I'm grateful the blightwolves only hunt at night," Ethan confessed as Connor reached him.

"You and me both. Listen, Ethan. You and your family gave me food, kindness, shelter, and clothes. A good deed for a good deed, and I consider any debt you had to be paid. This is where I let you go back to them, and I go on my way."

The man laughed, the slight wrinkles in his forehead more pronounced out here in the brilliant sunlight. "I can't make you do a damn thing. We both know that, but here's what you haven't considered. Hell opened up on you last night. You're in the middle of a war between king's guard and rich men and who knows what else. No one should go through that alone. Sit at my table, eat my damn food, and heal yourself before you go off on some reckless journey to figure out what's coming for you. You hear me?"

Ethan paused, quirking one eyebrow as he dared Connor to disagree. He didn't.

The carpenter prodded Connor's shoulder. "And I have to add that if you *don't* come back with me now, Kiera will hunt you down. You have no idea what that woman is capable of."

With that, Ethan walked off into the forest, chuckling under his breath.

Connor hesitated, his hands on his hips as he watched the man walk away. He shook his head, not entirely sure what he wanted to do.

He'd saved their lives, but they had also saved his. They brought him into the safety of the trees and out of the blightwolves' jaws, so they clearly didn't pose a threat to him.

If they had wanted him dead, they would've left him for the blightwolves to eat.

To follow them, though, to take more of their food—it didn't feel right. He'd lived this long on his own, and it was the only life he knew.

As he rubbed his jaw, lost in thought, the wound in his side bit into him again. A torrent of pain shot through his body, knocking him off balance. His shoulder rammed into a nearby boulder, which shot another tsunami of agony down his spine. He hissed through his teeth. The pain rattled his mind, and he bent over, resting his hands on his knees as he rode out the wave.

Otmund—whoever he was—wanted Connor dead. The nobleman had managed to kill a king, so he didn't seem like the sort to give up easily. Living with the Finns for any amount of time would endanger them.

As another gale whipped through the woodland, the treehouse swayed in the corner of his eye. He studied it, a home buried in the trees, hidden almost perfectly amongst the canopy. Only the occasional window or plank of wood peeked through gaps in the leaves.

These people weren't stupid. They fought with the blightwolves on a regular basis, and they had chosen to live in the freedom of the woods, same as him. They had an inkling of the danger he was in, and for whatever reason, they wanted him along regardless.

With one last look at the blood-stained field, he made his choice. Healing from a battle like that could take ages, and strangers showing him kindness was a nice change of pace.

"Fine," he muttered as he followed Ethan's path into the quiet forest. "You win, you stubborn old coot."

CHAPTER TEN
CONNOR

As Connor trudged through the thick woods with Ethan at his side, neither man spoke.

With every gust through the trees, the forest breathed fresh life into its canopy. The wind swirled around them, carrying leaves and twittering birds through the dancing gale. Leaves clapped together in the rush of spring, and timeless oaks swayed in rhythm as nature took hold of them.

For the last eight years, this expansive wood had been the only home Connor had known.

Each step through the rotting leaves stretched his body a bit more, and he rolled out his shoulders as he tried to loosen his aching muscles. Apart from the sharp pangs from the injury in his side, most of the pain had faded. The spins had lessened. Each time his boots crunched the sparse forest grass, he felt a little more like himself.

He'd fought professional soldiers before, but he'd never been in a battle like that.

In Yarrin, three soldiers had nearly killed him when they mistook him for a wanted criminal. After taking four stab wounds to his legs, he'd hidden in a mountain cave for almost a full season before he could fully walk again. Even that miraculous recovery had been after spending most of his money on a Rectivane potion. Though weak, the brew had helped.

He'd gambled and won. Not all men were so lucky.

Yet now, after nearly a dozen injuries to his back, legs, and sides, he meandered easily through the trees. For some of the wounds, the rough bandages scraping at his skin with every step served as the only reminder they had existed at all.

The pain was almost completely gone.

Several of his joints popped as he stretched his arms above him. The wound in his side stabbed into his soul yet again, but he grimaced and tried to ignore the surge of pain. "What potions did you give me?"

Ethan shook his head. "Once we got you onto that bed, you were out cold. We couldn't force-feed you anything, much to Kiera's horror. We assumed you would die, but we couldn't leave you to the wolves. Not the man who saved my wife and babies." Ethan sighed, his massive shoulders drooping as he looked away. "We vowed to be with you to the end, if that's what it took to give our thanks."

For a moment, Connor didn't respond. Instead, he let the chirping birds fill the silence as he processed what Ethan had said.

He wasn't used to kindness like that. Not out here, where it was eat or be eaten.

"Wait." He grinned as something occurred to him. "All that intimidation in the house was fake, wasn't it? Deep down, you're soft."

Ethan laughed, the sound carrying through the quiet trees as his eyes creased with surprise. "Watch what you say, my friend, or I'll leave you lost in these woods."

As they strode through the forest, Connor sidestepped a patch of dirt to avoid leaving a footprint behind.

A good drifter left no tracks and no trace.

"No potions," he absently muttered, pausing to glance over his shoulder in the vague direction of the meadow. "That can't be right."

"It doesn't make sense to me, either," Ethan confessed. "But you're alive, and that's what matters."

Connor didn't agree.

His enhanced strength, his improved hearing, his sharpened sense of smell, his superior vision, and now the rapid healing—none of it had an explanation, save for one.

The ghoul.

It had promised him immense power if he obtained Otmund's little green dagger. Perhaps the demon had gifted him skills in order to get it, even though they had failed.

Of course, all magic came with a price, and he wasn't sure he wanted to owe a favor to a demon.

"Tell me something, Ethan." He sidestepped a fallen branch, careful not to break any of its limbs as he passed. "Why do you and your family live out here? You've clearly been here for some time, given the ornate detail and woodworking in the house. You're a day's walk from the nearest town, hidden in the canopy. Why?"

The burly man went quiet again, his shoulders tense as he scanned the branches above them. As they stalked through the trees, he didn't answer except to groan when he walked around fallen logs or ducked under branches.

The minutes passed in silence, and Connor allowed the lull to settle into the air. One way or another, he'd get his answer.

"Kiera liked the old ruin," Ethan eventually said. "Thought it was just a decaying church. We had no idea it held magic in it. Sure, we had seen the little green circle and tried to lift it. I thought we might be able to sell it and get some good coin for our trouble. But even before it shocked me, it weighed as much as a damn castle. There's no moving that thing." He shook his head, absently scratching at his elbow as they trudged through the woods. "I don't understand magic. I've only dabbled in it when making a Rectivane potion or two, but I was never any good. Kiera's potions speed up healing by several days. Mine can barely give you an extra minute."

"You didn't answer my question." Connor studied the woods around them as he spoke, the trunks in the distance sharp and clear thanks to his newly improved vision.

He wondered if it would last—or if, like all magic, it would eventually fade.

In a sudden, violent rush, the injury in his side burned. He groaned as the trees around him spun, his feet shifting beneath him. His shoulder hit a trunk, the wood cracking beneath his strength, and he growled with pain as he held the injury from the glowing dagger.

The only one to still hurt.

As waves of agony pummeled him, the rush of the ocean crashed through his brain. Of home. Of the rock that split open his back. Of the shouts of soldiers overhead.

That was all he had left of home, anymore—bad memories.

The pain weakened his resolve, and it took everything in him to shove the visions back where they belonged. He shut his eyes, pinching the bridge of his nose with his free hand, and he took several steady breaths.

"Ride it out," Ethan said. A strong hand gently patted Connor on the back.

"I'm fine."

"Sure you are."

"Where are we going?" he asked to change the subject. "We've been walking for hours."

Once again, Ethan went quiet. Connor squinted at the man as the pain subsided, and the world solidified around him. The stocky carpenter stared at the ground, eyes glossed over in thought as he absently held Connor's shoulder, like he'd forgotten where he was and what they were doing.

There was something Ethan wasn't sharing.

"We're headed for a second house we built a while ago." The burly man rolled up the sleeve of his shirt in the warming spring day as they continued their hike. "We won't stay there long, but it'll do for now."

Ethan cleared his throat a few times and led the way through the underbrush as the canopy swayed overhead. The leaves trembled in the wind, crashing together as the gust had its way with them.

In the distance, the soft grunts of a large animal echoed through the trunks, its heavy footsteps thudding as it meandered away from them. Wood splintered somewhere nearby, and the trill of furious bees hummed through the air.

As Ethan led the way, Connor frowned. The man was clearly holding something back. Drooping shoulders. Cracking voice. Somber shift in mood.

It all signaled grief.

Whatever had happened at this other home, it hadn't ended well for the Finns—and Ethan didn't seem to like the idea of going back.

"Oh, would you look at that." Ethan ducked behind an oak and peeked around the trunk at something out of sight.

Connor stopped midstride and followed the man's gaze to find a brown bear twice the size of a normal man sitting against a weeping willow in the distance. Through a gap in the dangling leaves, the massive beast growled as it dug its snout into a beehive. Its matted fur perfectly matched the shade of the decaying leaves on the ground around it.

Bits of the hive clattered to the forest floor, fracturing against the hard dirt, while bees frantically buzzed around the creature's head. Several dove, no doubt trying to sting it, but they couldn't seem to pierce its hide. It munched happily, snorting as it smacked its sugar-stained mouth. Honey stretched between its teeth as it chewed. Two long fangs protruded from its jaw, curving upward toward its nose with every bite. Only the occasional flick of its ear to bat away a bee gave any indication it knew they were there.

Ethan grinned, lowering his voice as he leaned toward Connor. "These bears are cowards, but they're entertaining to watch. This far south, they don't hibernate like northern bears, but they still eat like they have to."

The fanged bear paused, its head tilting toward them at the sound of Ethan's voice. Its eyes landed on Connor, and the creature stiffened as it registered a possible threat. When he didn't move, however, it grunted and returned to its honey.

Two rabbits raced over the flattened leaves, darting like ghosts through the underbrush. The first reached the bear and hopped effortlessly onto its leg. The second misjudged the hop and fell to the ground, its chubby little legs kicking in the air as it rolled on its back. Without moving, the bear continued to munch—and the first rabbit happily nibbled on whatever fell into the thick fur on the beast's massive stomach.

Ethan laughed. "I could probably join them and steal some honey. I think it's too fat to care."

Connor leaned against a tree, his attention shifting from the bear to the burly man hiding behind a tree trunk only half as wide as he was. He stuck out like a sore thumb as he watched some of the only creatures that could survive in the Ancient Woods.

Nothing out here feared death, not really. Each day could've been the last, and life was lived to the fullest.

To live out here, one had to be a little insane—man and beast alike.

Ethan grinned, his shoulder against the oak as he studied the scene, completely ensnared by the micro-war raging between beast and bug barely twenty yards away. Connor couldn't help but watch the man's face—the way it lit up, the joy he found at nature and discovery—and it stirred something deep within.

Nostalgia.

His father had done this back in Kirkwall. He'd used to take Connor on nature walks when he was little, pointing out all that the island's Firebreath Forest had to offer and warning him of what nature did to protect herself and her creatures. He had always spoken of the woods as if they lived, as if they breathed, as if they watched over all who entered.

As if the trees themselves bled magic.

Ethan chuckled and gestured for Connor to follow him once again, and something deep within Connor shifted. It was painful, this nostalgia, but he couldn't lie.

He had missed it.

Kiera's mothering demands. Ethan's blunt honesty. The undercurrent of compassion. Connor didn't know what to think about this family that didn't want him to leave, since most turned him away.

Even Beck Arbor.

"So, tell me about your family." The stocky man clapped his hands together as they trudged through the woods. "Do you have a wife? You're about old enough for one, I'd wager."

Connor grimaced at the very idea. No woman would've wanted this life, and children deserved better.

For several moments, only the delicate chirp of birds in the canopy filled the silence.

"That's fine." Ethan patted Connor roughly on the back, and it sent small ripples of pain down his spine from the force. "There's no need to share what you don't want to revisit."

"Thank you."

"It's a long walk, though," the carpenter warned. "I hope you don't mind me filling the silence."

Connor shrugged. He preferred the stillness, but he didn't care enough to voice his opinion.

"Poor Fiona," Ethan said with a shake of his head. "That's my youngest. She's the one who, well, in the meadow—"

"I remember."

"The flash of green light woke her. She said she saw a man crawling through the dark and wanted to go help him." Ethan rubbed the back of his head. "She's got a good heart, that one, but she's too trusting."

"Most children are."

"And that man." Ethan's nose wrinkled in disgust. "Grabbing her like that. Getting his blood on her face, in her hair."

That man.

These people hadn't realized who it was.

The Finns didn't know a king had died in their meadow.

Connor let out a slow breath, unsure of what to say. The trembling girl had fought to break free from the dying king without understanding any of what had happened to make him so cruel. Even if he hadn't hurt her physically, a girl that young would be scarred for life.

"And then you," Ethan added calmly. Quietly. "You come out of nowhere, swinging two swords like you were born with them in your hands, and you took on ten men like it was nothing."

"I'm covered in scars, can barely walk without my world spinning, and

I still don't know what the hell that nobleman stabbed me with," Connor corrected. "That wasn't 'nothing' to me."

"How did you learn to fight like that?" Ethan tilted his head as he cast a wary glance toward Connor. "The way Kiera described it made you sound like a specter striking fear into the hearts of his enemies."

Connor's blood ran cold at the mere mention of the word.

Specter.

Perhaps Kiera had seen the ghoul, too. Perhaps she knew what it had done to him, but he doubted it. If they suspected the demon had tied itself to him in any way, they likely wouldn't have been so generous.

As much as Ethan's probing dug into the past Connor didn't want to share, he had to admit these were fair questions. If he were inviting a stranger into his home who could kill him in his sleep, he would've wanted to know a thing or two, as well.

So be it. He would indulge this.

"After I left home, it took a while to figure out how to survive," he admitted. "I worked when I could. Stole what I had to. An old farmer caught me hustling darts in a tavern one night, and he cornered me afterward. I found out he was a retired king's guard, come to live out his last years on the old family homestead. I thought he was going to turn me in."

"Shit," Ethan muttered.

"That's what I said, too," Connor admitted. "I thought I was a dead man, I really did, but the old man struck a bargain with me. Instead of sending me to the gallows, I would work the farm. In exchange, he would feed me, clothe me, and give me two hours a day to train. Sir Beck, I called him, just to annoy the daylight out of him. The farmer didn't have any money, but I didn't need pay. Not with all he did for me."

For a while, they strode through the calm forest, leaves crunching beneath their feet. Birds twittered overhead, and Connor lost himself for a moment in the memory of Sir Beck sitting on a stump as Connor swung the old man's sword. He'd given lecture after lecture on that stump, his speeches filled with everything Connor had done wrong and the few things he'd done well.

"It sounds like he did right by you," Ethan said.

Connor rubbed the back of his neck. "He was a decent man, but it was a business transaction. There wasn't much in the way of affection. Just a teacher and his student."

"That's still a gift in a world like ours."

"I suppose."

Running on instinct and intuition, Connor took a careful step around a bush to avoid snapping any of the twigs. As he stepped around the scrub, however, a tiny imprint in the mud caught his eye, roughly the size of a little girl's boot.

"They need to be more careful," he warned with a nod to the footprint.

Ethan sighed. "Good eye."

He kicked up a nearby rock and slid it across the boot print, obscuring it with a thick streak. "Wesley is getting better with hiding his and the family's tracks, but he still needs a bit of practice." Ethan hesitated. "Maybe you could give him a few pointers?"

Connor nodded as another surge of homesickness hit him. "If that's what it takes to earn my keep."

Ethan clicked his tongue in disappointment. "That's not what I meant. Sure, we could use a hand around the house to help fix it up while you recover, but we don't abide by fair trades. Good men do right by each other. It's how I live."

The words hit Connor sharply in the chest, the motto eerily familiar to something his father used to say.

A man is never taller than when he bends to help someone in need.

The words stung him. His home had been ripped from him once, and there was no point in looking for another one.

He went silent. They walked for several minutes without a word said between them, save for the occasional muttered cursing as Ethan climbed over a fallen log. To distract himself, Connor scanned the world around them. Ever vigilant. Always wondering when the ghoul would appear again.

Yet nothing moved but the birds overhead and the branches in the wind.

As he pressed his palm against a trunk to climb a boulder, a small brown lizard with a green lightning bolt down its spine scampered up the tree. It slithered over his fingers, pausing briefly to watch him before carrying on with its day.

In the somber stillness of the forest, a silhouette darted between the trees. He paused mid-climb, tensing as he studied its movement.

A deer, perhaps—just another fanged buck wandering the forests of Saldia, but he wanted to be sure.

As Connor glared into the trees, the frayed ends of a tattered cloak billowed from behind an aspen roughly fifty yards away. The silhouette slunk past another tree and disappeared behind the towering fir.

And then, nothing. The forest chirped around him, still and serene, as if the ghoul had never been there at all.

The specter was still here, watching and waiting just beyond reach. He simply wasn't sure what—or who—it was waiting for.

When it made itself known, he needed to be ready to face it again. Not just for his sake, either, but for the Finns as well.

CHAPTER ELEVEN
CONNOR

As the sun slowly set over the Ancient Woods, the low rumble of a waterfall seeped through the trunks. Though just a quiet murmur at first, the rush of water quickly became a thunder. As Connor trudged toward it, the air thickened, and his shirt stuck to his skin. The earthy musk of moss and wet grass lingered on the wind, thick and heavy as a mist wafted through the trees.

"We're close," Ethan said, his deep voice breaking their hour-long silence.

The ground beneath them angled upward, and the hill took them closer to the thundering water. A few yards away, a brook wandered downhill through the underbrush and fallen logs, whisking away a few wayward leaves in its current. The gentle gurgle of water over rock whispered through the forest like a lullaby, and as Connor's boots crunched across the leaves, he momentarily closed his eyes to enjoy it.

A drifter's life didn't have many pleasures, and he always took a moment to enjoy the ones that came his way.

At the top of the hill sat a small lake. Cascading ripples in the surface obscured the red and white pebbles only a few feet below the clear water. A river snaked away on the opposite bank, with boulders jutting from the waterway as it curved through the trees. Vibrant green bushes and soft purple flowers crowded the sandy riverbank, each of them shivering in the breeze.

Across the lake, a light brown deer with white spots on its fur lowered its horned head to the water to drink. As it opened its mouth, its thick fangs protruding over its lips, it glanced toward him. The deer paused as they caught each other's eye, but it didn't run.

Beside him, Ethan knelt and dipped his hands below the water. His fingers glowed beneath the surface, a soft golden light that hummed through liquid clearer than glass. The man washed his face, immune to or unaware of the magic. He rubbed his neck and took a deep breath as the water dribbled down his back.

Connor dipped his flask beneath the crystal-clear water and took a long swig as he studied the world around them, scanning the trees for the tell-tale signs of a house.

He figured that was about the only place Ethan's family would live.

Sure enough, a short way off, the planks of a ladder nailed to a trunk caught his eye, each step disguised as a knot in the tree. As Connor drained the last of his flask, he lowered it beneath the water to fill it again and nodded to the ladder. "Are we here?"

Ethan nodded. "Good eye. This way."

He gestured for Connor to follow along the bank. As they walked, the deer flinched and finally bolted off into the forest, its white tail flashing a sign of retreat.

After a few moments of scanning the canopy, Connor finally spotted it—the silhouette of a house nestled in the branches, nothing but a shadow in the approaching dusk.

"He's here!" a little girl shouted gleefully from the treetops. "Papa's here!"

"Fiona, don't—" Kiera said, interrupted by the scamper of boots across a floor.

As the trees swayed in the wind, the corner of a porch jutted through the leaves, and gaps of light shone through holes where several of its planks were missing or splintered. The handrail hung from a single nail, barely clinging to life and drifting slightly as the porch shifted.

A door slammed, the harsh crack of wood on wood cutting through the trees, and a shadowy figure darted past the broken handrail. A board creaked, painfully loud in the quiet evening, and a tiny silhouette climbed down the ladder. As the house groaned, protesting each movement of the trees it relied on, a few more bits of the home came into view. A missing shutter. The cracked glass of a windowpane. A few boards missing from the corner of the house. The hint of mold on the air.

It had been abandoned, clearly, but the grief in Ethan's voice earlier made Connor question why.

The small silhouette reached the dirt, and as she stepped into the light, Connor recognized the golden braids of the tiny girl from the field.

Fiona.

Several boards creaked overhead as Kiera stepped onto the porch and peered over the edge. In the low light, her features came into view. The creases around her eyes were deep and happy as she followed her youngest daughter's trail along the bank. A young man stepped out of the shadows to join her, tall and lanky, with the same blond hair as the rest of the children.

Wesley, no doubt.

Ethan knelt, arms stretched as he waited for Fiona, but the little girl's eyes darted toward Connor. "It's you!"

She raced toward him and wrapped her arms around his waist. Her cheek pressed against the wound in his side, and the pressure sent bolts of agony through his core. He winced, gritting his teeth as he gently pried her off of him.

"Hello," he said dryly.

"Where's my hug, child I created?" Ethan muttered, giving an exasperated shrug as he spread his arms open again.

Fiona giggled and hugged Connor more tightly than before. He winced as a fresh wave of pain shot up his spine.

"*You* created her, did you?" Kiera said with a scoff as she climbed down the ladder and hopped to the ground.

"I was involved." Ethan rested one elbow on his knee.

"Come here, my boy," Kiera said with a grin as she pulled Connor into a tight hug.

"Boy?" Connor asked, smirking at her gall. "I believe you mean 'grown man who saved your ass,' Kiera."

"Fine," she said, laughing. "That, too."

It was strange, this familiarity. It seemed so foreign, something he hadn't had in a long time. He simply stood there, uncomfortable and stiff, but the people around him didn't seem to care about his discomfort.

With a little whimper, a young girl climbed down the ladder and jumped into Ethan's arms—Isabella, most likely.

Her father hugged her tight and kissed her on the forehead, but she just watched Connor. Brow pinched and eyes wide, she studied him with quiet apprehension, like she thought he might eat them all.

Fiona, meanwhile, wrapped her hands around Connor's waist again. He frowned, lifting his arms as he debated what to do with her. Prying her off hadn't worked, and she didn't seem to understand the concept of personal space or how to treat injured men.

"All right, all right." Ethan hoisted the middle child onto his shoulder as he stood and shooed away Fiona. "Give the man space to breathe. Everyone, this is Connor."

The tall, lanky boy slid down the trunk with practiced ease, barely using the ladder at all. "My name is Wesley."

"I figured," Connor admitted.

Giggling erupted through the forest as Fiona grabbed a fistful of lake water and tossed it at Isabella, who still sat on her father's shoulder. The droplets splashed across Ethan's face, and he grimaced with all the irritated patience of a man who'd endured this before.

Isabella finally grinned, and she hopped off her father's shoulder to chase after her sister. They ran along the bank, and the giggling only got louder.

"Girls!" Kiera wagged her finger at them as she followed. "What have I told you about noise?"

"I need a hot meal and a bed," Ethan said with a heavy sigh as he dried his face with his shirt hem. "I suspect you do too, Connor."

"Maybe in a minute."

Ethan nodded. "Whenever you're ready."

Without another word, he climbed up the ladder and disappeared into the house. Meanwhile, Wesley joined his mother in herding his sisters away from the lake.

And just like that, Connor was alone—sort of. Through the chaos and chatter all around him, the racket staining the quiet day, he couldn't quite understand why they trusted him. A stranger. True, he had saved the girls' lives, but he was a stranger, nonetheless.

When the girls switched from splashing water to slinging mud from the lakebed, Wesley and Kiera turned their backs on him to pry the two apart. Connor ran a hand through his hair and slipped into the forest, even though he didn't know where he was going.

As always, he had no direction. He simply kept moving.

He walked until he couldn't hear the chatter anymore, until the thunder of the waterfall faded entirely. Truth be told, he didn't have an idea of what he wanted to find out here. A moment of silence, maybe, or a second to be truly alone. A chance to decide what to do next.

As he paused by an oak, a sharp pain shot through his stomach as it rumbled. Despite the near-constant fistfuls of dried venison Ethan had given him along the walk, his gut had never stopped complaining. No amount of food seemed to be enough. No amount of water, either. With everything the couple had given him already, he didn't exactly want to ask for more.

It didn't seem right.

A jolt of pain hit him hard in the chest, like a dagger through the heart. He groaned and cursed under his breath. The twinge flared again, so he lifted his shirt to examine the scar on his sternum. It glowed green, pulsing with magic he didn't understand yet.

So many questions. So few answers.

And a ghoul lurking somewhere in the forest.

His ear twitched as the soft crunch of footsteps on the ground floated past. A pause between each step suggested an adult with a longer gait trailed after him. He'd been walking with Ethan all day, and the stocky man's stride had more of a weight to it, with a bit of a rumble to each step. Kiera's gait was more of a light patter, with a soft shuffle to the heel.

Wesley, then. Apparently, the boy had followed him out here.

Connor crossed his arms and sat on a nearby log, flattening his back against the nearest tree as he took a moment to breathe in the evening.

He leaned his head against the trunk as a small creature scampered through the decaying leaves. A squirrel hopped onto the other end of the log, its tiny fangs protruding past its lips as its head tilted with curiosity.

Great. One of these damned things.

Connor groaned, resting his temple on one finger as he watched it, waiting to see what it would try to steal from him. These little monsters were always running around, snickering and stealing what they could from anyone in the woods, but they rarely worked alone. If this one wanted his attention, another one likely crept through the woods nearby to swipe something from his pocket.

He tilted his head ever so slightly, watching his periphery for signs of movement. Sure enough, a small creature with matted brown fur inched its way down the trunk behind him.

These little bastards.

He shook his head in annoyance and scoped out the forest as he waited for them to do something stupid. In this stretch of the woods, the diverse trees packed closely together. Oaks, elms, maples, a few birches and a willow here or there gave the stretch of woodland plenty of spaces for small game to hide, as well as plenty of nuts and shrubs for them to scavenge. Where small game lived, predators roamed, and that meant he would have decent hunts here.

As dusk settled into the forest, he scanned the growing shadows for possible warrens or dens. With this much game, the blightwolves likely hunted here, too.

The squirrels inched closer, getting comfortable as he kept tabs on them both. As the one in his periphery neared the flask at his waist, it reached out for the thin rope securing it to his belt loop.

Nope.

Connor grabbed the fanged squirrel by the scruff of its neck and tossed it toward its friend on the other end of the log.

In an instant, they both snarled at him, chittering angrily as they complained and whined at being caught. With a final hiss, they scampered away, kicking up leaves as they ran.

The crunch of footsteps grew louder, and Wesley finally appeared from behind a tree. As he leaned against the trunk, the lanky boy crossed his arms and watched the squirrels dart into the underbrush. "I hate those rotten things."

"Everyone does." Connor closed his eyes and leaned his head against the tree behind him. "I came out here to be alone."

"Yeah, don't we all?" the kid said, laughing.

Yet, he didn't budge.

"You've been around your little sisters too long," Connor said dryly, the corner of his mouth twitching as he suppressed a grin.

"You're probably right," Wesley admitted. "Oddly enough, personal space is a luxury out here."

For a moment, neither of them spoke, and Connor simply enjoyed the quiet forest. He strained his ear, listening for the twitter of birds and any other signs of life around him. Nothing new caught his attention, so he focused instead on his steady breath.

The boy shifted his weight, and a small crack shattered the silence as he stepped on something. Connor peered through his half-closed eyes to see a few pieces of bark fall to the ground at Wesley's feet.

His ear twitched as more bark fell, his hearing sensitive and attuned to the forest. With his newly enhanced senses, he now picked up what would've before gone unnoticed.

These new skills fascinated him, but as much as he enjoyed the power, he hadn't yet been told the cost. Though he had little experience with magic, plenty of folksongs warned of how deals with the dead rarely ended well.

Necromancy was illegal for a reason.

"You're decent at covering your tracks," Connor said, breaking the silence as he rubbed his eyes. "You missed a few of Fiona's prints in the mud, though."

"I knew it," Wesley muttered, shaking his head in disappointment. "I hate missing things."

Connor shrugged. "It happens. You'll get better."

"Maybe." The kid bit the inside of his cheek as he pulled out a coin from his pocket.

The copper metal caught the low light lingering in the forest, flashing briefly as Wesley flipped it absently through his fingers. His eyes glossed over as he played with it, and the flashing pulse of sunlight across the metal sang along his knuckles as the coin slipped in and out of his palm with practiced ease. With a slight twist of his hand, the coin disappeared and seconds later reappeared in his other palm.

"Now, there's a neat trick." Connor leaned one elbow on his knee, watching the show.

"What? This?" Wesley lifted the coin, pressed between his thumb and pointer finger, before he continued flipping it along his knuckles. With a shrug, he sat on the other end of the log. "It's just something to keep my hands occupied."

"You'd make a good thief," Connor said with a wry grin.

Wesley laughed. "Don't give me ideas. Mother would kill me."

The kid slipped the coin into his pocket and stretched, his joints cracking as he leaned into it. His sleeves slid down his arms with the motion, and the green glimmer of something familiar burned along the kid's forearm.

An augmentation.

A jolt of concern shot through Connor. No boy in the middle of the woods could afford an augmentation.

It seemed the Finns had hidden more than he realized. Perhaps they weren't too trusting, after all.

Perhaps *he* had been.

Without a word, he grabbed Wesley's arm and lifted the sleeve as the kid froze beneath his grip. Wesley stared at him with wide eyes, barely breathing, but he wisely didn't fight.

Sure enough, the green outline of an augmentation smoldered on Wesley's pale arm, the design reminiscent of a tangled knot. The lines glimmered, their dazzling light faded to almost nothing.

Its magic was almost gone, but the boy had an augmentation nonetheless.

"What the hell is this?" Connor asked, glaring at the kid as he pointed to the ink. "What magic does it give you? Tell me!"

"It's just for my eyesight." Wesley's voice cracked with fear as he tugged on Connor's tight grip. "I can't see a thing without it. This terrifying woman near Bradford redoes it every three years." His voice trembled as he stared up at Connor, and he didn't break eye contact.

Commoners drank potions. Only the wealthy wore augmentations.

"What did she call it?" Connor pressed, glaring at the kid, jaw tense. "What potion did she use?"

A test.

Connor knew the answer from his time with Beck Arbor, and only because the old man had needed a sip every few hours to maintain his ability to see. If Wesley was lying to him, he'd know in an instant.

"Eye—eyebr—uh, damn it," the kid muttered, trying to tug his arm out of Connor's grip. "Eyebright! That's it, the Eyebright charm."

The boy didn't flinch. He didn't cower, despite the fearful warble in his voice. More importantly, he'd held Connor's gaze and hadn't looked away.

He'd told the truth, then.

Connor released his grip on Wesley's arm and took a step back, his attention drifting again to the augmentation as the sleeve covered it once more. Even a common augmentation like an Eyebright charm could cost major coin, more than a family in the woods should've been able to afford without heavy debt. Yet, Wesley had spoken of it so casually, as if it were normal.

Besides, augmentations needed to be done every two years, not every three. To go an entire year without it meant the family truly stretched their budget.

Connor shook his head, disappointed in himself. He kept looking for ways the Finns might've been scamming him, but it seemed like they were just good people.

A strange thing to find out here in this lawless wood.

"Sorry, kid," he said with a heavy sigh. "I won't do that again."

"Thank the Fates," Wesley muttered. "You're scary as hell."

Connor shrugged and sat again on the log.

Wesley, however, stood out of reach and watched him with wide eyes. Connor set one foot on the dead tree and propped his elbow against his knee as he held Wesley's intense stare.

"Go ahead," Connor eventually said. "Ask."

Wesley shook his head and sat on the log. He leaned forward and rested his elbows on his knees as he absently picked at the skin around his nail. The hoot of an owl cut through the sleeping forest as Connor waited for the inevitable questions.

It seemed like children always had questions.

"All those bodies," Wesley eventually muttered, his voice quiet and distant. "Mother tried to shield me from it, but I need to see these things. I need to know what the world is really like. I'm a grown man."

"*Practically* a grown man," Connor corrected. "You're only what, fifteen?"

"Seventeen." The boy frowned, his eyes narrowing with the scowl.

Connor rubbed the stubble on his jaw, momentarily lost in the memory of bloodstained grass baking in the sun. "You don't need to see that kind of gore yet."

A smile pulled on the edge of Wesley's mouth, and his frown faded away. "You sound like my dad."

"He's not wrong."

"Yeah, well, that doesn't change the fact that something terrible happened yesterday." Wesley stood and paced across the dirt. "Mother said lots of men came through. Twelve of them, and one escaped."

Ten soldiers. One nobleman. One king.

Connor frowned. "Yes, one got away."

The important one. The one who had answers.

"We don't get a lot of visitors out here," Wesley continued, squaring his shoulders as he gestured to the trees around them. "Which makes me wonder where you came from. Why you stopped to help us at all. Why you came with us here, only to disappear into the woods the second you arrived."

Connor didn't respond. He didn't need to.

"Are you going to leave?" Wesley asked.

"If you all don't give me a moment alone, I damn well might."

Wesley frowned. "I'm serious."

"So am I, kid."

The young man crossed his arms, and his boots shuffled through the dead leaves as he paced beside the log.

Connor rubbed his eyes. "Why? Is that what you want? For me to leave?"

"Hell, no. A fighter like you? Of course we want you to stay. But that's why you came out here, right? To dart off and not come back?"

Connor adjusted in his seat, leaning forward as he held Wesley's eye. "What would it matter if I did? I'm just a drifter, kid. I'm a nobody."

"You're not a nobody to us," Wesley said quietly, unable to look Connor in the eye this time.

"Seems like a bit much," he admitted. "You all just met me."

The kid shrugged. "We would also be dead without you."

Huh.

Fair point.

Wesley finally looked Connor in the eye again. "Father and I came back as you were limping into the ruins. If you hadn't been there, the soldiers would've seen us, and we would've died trying to protect the family. You saved our lives, Connor, all of us. There's a gratitude for that sort of thing that doesn't go away." He paused. "A respect that doesn't die."

Connor sat with that for a moment, unfamiliar with the weight that came with this sort of esteem. He wasn't used to people giving a damn about him, and he wasn't sure if he liked it.

Wesley scratched the back of his head. "Look, supper will be ready in a few minutes. You should come eat."

The kid left without another word. His boots crunched along the leaves as he retreated to the house.

As the footsteps faded, blissful silence settled once more into the woods, and the flutter of wings through the canopy stirred up the approaching night. Even with all the death from yesterday, life went on.

The world always went on, no matter who died.

As Connor sat against the tree, still as a stone, a horned boar meandered around the trunks. It snorted as its snout brushed along the ground, kicking aside dirt in its hunt for mushrooms.

It flinched when it saw him and froze in place, waiting to see what he would do.

For a moment, they simply watched each other, two threats sizing each other up in a lonely forest. A boar like this could've impaled a man with horn and tusk alike, but Connor had his swords. If the animal was foolish enough to attack him, it would become dinner.

When he didn't move, it slowly returned to its hunt, pausing now and then to look at him with distrust—tense and ready to bolt.

With a sigh, Connor leaned his head against the trunk. His stomach growled, and something Wesley had said rang again through his mind.

There's a gratitude for that sort of thing that doesn't go away.

He frowned and stretched out his fingers, lost in thought as the final daylight faded.

It's a respect that doesn't die.

CHAPTER TWELVE
CONNOR

The ghoul waited in the ancient forest.
Connor could *feel* it.
In the pitch-black darkness of the cold spring night, he surveyed the local woods not far from Ethan's decrepit cabin in the trees. Long after a hearty meal and an awkward conversation about a past he didn't want to share with them, he crouched in the shadows.

Waiting.

Listening for the old ghost's voice in his head. Preparing for the now-familiar rush of winter air despite the blossoming spring.

It was out here. He *knew* it.

His bones ached, much as they had in the field when the specter attacked him. The hairs on his neck stood on end, the weight of someone's stare heavy on his conscience as he hunted a demon.

He'd come out here, far from the house, to save the Finns from its wrath when he finally found it. Good people like that didn't need the nightmares this thing would've given them.

The night wind barreled through the canopy, and several dried leaves tumbled across his boots. The warm scent of cinnamon and bark caught on the air, the Ancient Woods' fragrance the same no matter how far north or south he had ventured in it—moss, grass, maple sap, and a hint of carrot. Only yesterday, the scents had all mingled together in a nameless cologne, but now he could decipher each unique component.

Yesterday, he had shivered in the cold, clutching a coat to his body to keep himself warm. Tonight as the same wind howled, he knelt by a tree with calm determination, immune to the chilly air.

Magic, no question. Now, he needed to understand its limits and the consequences that lay ahead.

To do that, he had to hunt the ghoul—though he suspected it also hunted him.

With a fresh gale through the leaves, the mood of the forest abruptly shifted. The sensation carried a sense of familiarity with it, of danger, much as it had by the ruins when a greater threat than Otmund had loomed behind Connor.

Heavy.

Somber.

Deadly.

He rolled his weight to the balls of his feet, his attention shifting behind him as a shadow darted between the trees. He strained his eyes in the darkness, his newly heightened vision effortlessly adapting to the low light. The silhouettes of the nearby oaks sharpened as the forest revealed itself to him.

In a flash of black smoke, the ghoul appeared where before there had been only empty air. Framed by two towering trees, the specter hovered before him, and the vacant sockets of its skeletal face stared into his very soul.

Connor went painfully still—not out of fear, but to strategize. It had killed the guard by the ruins with ease. It was not to be trifled with, and though it could've killed him by now, it had chosen not to.

He needed to keep this brief truce of theirs alive.

Its bony teeth glowed in the low light, and its dark hood covered much of its exposed skull. The tattered cloak billowed around the beast as the white bone of its hands reached for the black sword tied to its waist.

Many times before, in the long and lonely nights Connor had spent in this forest, the blightwolves had run beneath his perch in the woods. Each time they passed below, Connor had looked death in the eye and drawn his sword.

This forest ate fearful men alive. It relished in their screams and thrived off their pain. Out here, only the strong saw the dawn.

Connor was many things—hermit, wanderer, a bit of an asshole—but first and foremost, he was a *survivor*.

"Do you talk?" he asked, his voice gruff as he met the creature's glare with his own.

I cannot. Its chilling voice echoed in his mind, though its mouth never once moved. *Only you can hear my thoughts.*

"Aren't I lucky," he muttered. "Obviously, others can see you. Those two soldiers about pissed themselves back at the ruins."

One of them did, the specter confirmed.

A quiet chuckle escaped him despite the grave situation he faced. He wasn't proud of it, but that little fact somehow eased the pain in his side.

Served them right.

He rubbed the back of his neck and studied the specter. Though the ghoul rested its hand on its sword, it had yet to attack. As he hadn't encountered anything like this in his life thus far, he didn't entirely know where to take the conversation from here. He needed to tread carefully.

A creature like this probably thrived on others' fear. It could probably sniff out cowardice, like many of the brawlers he'd often encountered in the pubs as he traveled. The prowling, the shadow through the trees, and now this sudden appearance—they were intimidation tactics, meant to make him feel small.

It didn't work. Not on him.

A man had to lay down his boundaries and hold those who crossed them accountable. This creature—whatever it was—would be no different from any brigand he encountered on the road. He had to be smart, but he wouldn't cower.

A risk, certainly. If holding his own meant going to an early grave, so be it. He doubted many survived their encounters with this thing, and if today was his day to dine in hell, he would go out on his terms.

"Why have you been in hiding?" he finally asked. "I've noticed you lurking in the shadows. What are you waiting for? What do you want?"

Watch your tongue, the phantom demanded, darting closer. *Do not dare speak to me in such—*

"I don't serve you," Connor reminded the ghoul, squaring his shoulders as it threatened him. "Whatever bargain you had with King Henry is over. Even if you could control him, you'll never own me."

As they stared each other down, each waiting for the other to move, Connor took a careful step toward the hovering specter. His training kicked in as he examined it—its stance, its blade, its cloak, its face.

No limps. No vulnerabilities. No weaknesses.

A true threat, unlike anything Beck Arbor had prepared him for.

As far as he knew, a ghoul like this could've done anything. It had killed a man in the blink of an eye, and yet it hadn't so much as made itself known to the Finns.

He needed answers.

You are a curious peasant, it said.

He frowned. Kings and lords spoke like that, but he hadn't expected such contempt from an undead specter.

In the field, you fought with courage, it continued, and its voice echoed like ripples on a dark pond. *Out there in the ruins, you took on more men than you could handle, and it nearly killed you. That's what fools do, and fools do not make demands of me.*

"You're fun," he said dryly. "Fine. How do I make you go away?"

Break our connection, it answered.

"And how do I do that?"

Die at the hand of someone stronger, it said without a trace of emotion.

Connor flexed his fingers to stem his annoyance, and he longed to draw his sword as he stood rooted to the forest floor. He was just a merchant's son in exile, and yet he had somehow stepped into something far beyond him.

Though the ghoul still had its hand on the hilt of its sword, Connor didn't want to draw his own. Not yet. Doing so might've escalated their conversation into something deadly.

"What the hell are you?" he asked.

I am the Wraith King, the ghoul answered, its bony fingers curling into a fist as dark smoke rolled through the trees. *Even a commoner like you must know of me. I was a living legend. A warrior king. A renowned necromancer in my own right, feared for my power over Death. You fools thought I was gone, but Aeron Zacharias was powerful enough to bring me back from the grave.*

A pang of surprise splintered like lightning through Connor's head.

Oh, he had heard of the Wraith King.

Every mother in Saldia told her children of *that* nightmare—the man who had conquered their land centuries ago. A man who had slaughtered their people and used them as slaves to build the massive Slaybourne Citadel. He'd stolen hope. He'd fractured homes. He'd decimated any who challenged his rule.

The master of Slaybourne was no mortal man, but a man of war, blood, and fear. A man of murder, lawlessness, and chaos.

Of pure evil.

This wasn't just some enchanted mutation before him, floating in the winds of death. This was the relic of a real man. A heartless man. A murderer and a conqueror who had set off a Dark Age throughout Saldia five hundred years ago when he had set the entire continent ablaze.

He had killed anyone who got in his way—children and soldiers alike.

In the weeks after Henry's coronation, there had been rumors that he'd obtained a dark ally who was powerful beyond the mortal world, but no commoner could've guessed the reality of it all. If anyone had known it was the Wraith King who had fought beside him, they never would've charged under Henry's banner.

By allying himself with this abomination, Henry had doomed his soul and lied to the people who served him.

"I know about you." Connor drew the twin swords on his back, his grip tightening on the hilts as his eyes narrowed with hatred. "We've all heard the songs. We remember your crimes."

Horrors and lies are easier to rhyme than the truth, the dead man said.

Connor scoffed. "You expect me to believe we all misunderstood your intentions? That you're innocent? Wronged by history?"

The spirit shook his head, the skull drifting back and forth as his exposed teeth glowed in the night. *You are right to fear me.*

"I don't fear you," he corrected. "I'm disgusted by you."

Of course. The ghost chuckled, his voice grim and ghoulish in the night.

For quite a while, Connor stood there and waited for the wraith to move. To speak. To atone. The silent hum of the forest filled the air between them as the blades weighed on his palms, ready to strike—though he doubted mortal weapons would have any effect on a creature like this.

It didn't matter. He would do what he could.

In the tense lull, the soft snore of an animal floated by. An owl's cry pierced the night, and the rustle of wings fluttered through the air. The peaceful life of the forest continued without a care for the ghoul in its midst, and the serene woodlands clashed with the surreal phantom before him.

The master of Slaybourne, draped in a decaying cloak and without his crown, hovered two feet off the ground—a dead man returned to the world he had conquered. A world that had finally healed from the scars he had carved into its memory.

The Wraith King pointed a bony finger at Connor's blades. *Do you think those swords can kill me?*

"Let's find out." He twirled his weapons as his body tensed for battle. The metal flashed in his periphery, sharp and clean.

If he was going to die here, in the woods he called home, his death would be on his terms.

You are brave, the dead king said. *I will grant you that.*

"And yet you sulked around the woods, watching me from afar."

You are injured, the ghoul said with an exasperated sigh. *I made a calculated choice, mortal. You are weakened and unable to fight the large man that protects the family that has fed you. That peasant will likely kill you if any of them discover your connection to me. Though I find you repugnant, you're the closest thing to a warrior I have nearby, and I certainly can't fathom fusing with one of those helpless humans.* He nodded his great skull in the vague direction of the Finns' house. *Regardless, I always observe in the beginning to see what sort of man the new Wraithblade is.*

"Always?"

You are not the first mortal forced upon me, nor will you be the last.

Connor rolled out his shoulders, eager for the fight to begin already. "I intend to do as little dying as possible."

Don't they all? The Wraith King shrugged, his ghoulish body floating back and forth as he paced between the oaks with nothing but empty air where his feet should've been. *It's the way of life, boy. Intentions mean nothing. Death will claim you eventually, and I will pass to whatever man kills you. It has happened to them all, so far. Not one has discovered a way to live for eternity, not even the necromancer who brought me back. He was nearly a god, and even he failed. What makes you think you're any different from the kings and lords before you? You are a mere laborer. Your reign will likely be the shortest.*

The slur didn't faze Connor. Laborer. Peasant. Painfully common. Those words didn't mean anything to him anymore. He saw them for what they were—insults from cowards who needed to crush other men beneath their feet to feel powerful.

"You're right about one thing," he said. "I'm a peasant. A stain on your boot. If you despise me so much, why haven't you killed me? I suspect you'd be able to." He nodded to the black sword at the Wraith King's waist.

A dangerous question, but undoubtedly the most important of them all. If this thing could kill him in his sleep, Connor had to find a way to end this now.

Because of our connection, I cannot harm you, the Wraith King said calmly. *I have tried.*

"How comforting." Connor frowned, not entirely certain he believed the ghost's claim.

Through a gap in the canopy above them, the clouds blocking the moons glowed silver in the sky. They rolled past, exposing Saldia's dual moons amongst an ocean of stars in the pitch-black night.

The Wraith King turned his back to Connor as the heavens shifted. The dead king stared up at the crescent moons while the leaves above him clapped together, reaching a crescendo as the gale blew harder through the forest. As his cloak fluttered around him, he crossed his bony arms, lost as he watched the sky.

A ghost. Stargazing.

Connor's shoulders relaxed, and he begrudgingly sheathed his blades. It seemed no epic skirmish between man and wraith would happen tonight.

Perhaps the dead king had told him the truth. Maybe he couldn't kill Connor after all.

This forest has changed. It is darker, and so very cruel, the ghoul said wistfully. *I like it.*

Connor suppressed a surge of bubbling irritation, and he absently scratched his head to keep himself from saying something he would regret.

The specter gestured to the sky. *When was the last dragon sighting? Henry knew so little of the dragons, much to my disappointment. Since you live out here in the wilds, perhaps you've seen one.*

With a chuckle, he shook his head. "Dragons are extinct. No one's seen one in centuries."

Only a fool would believe dragons could be so easily eradicated. The dead king scoffed. *They are like me, made of old magic and forged in the fires of war. They watch this world, influencing so much more than you can even see. If you haven't seen one, it's because they wish to remain hidden—for now.*

Connor frowned, half-wondering if the old ghost was having a laugh at his expense. Dragons were a relic of the past, nothing but bones in the mountains, and few spoke of them as anything other than a myth. They couldn't be real.

Then again, he hadn't thought he would ever encounter the king's specter in person, and now it had fused to his soul.

He rubbed the stubble along his jaw as he returned his attention to the phantom floating before him. Though the thought of living dragons intrigued him, perhaps it would serve him best to focus on one demonic evil at a time.

"Explain something to me," he said. "Back in the—"

Royalty is not accountable to peasants, the Wraith King interrupted.

Connor's jaw tensed as he ignored the jibe and plowed ahead. "Back in the meadow, you waited to appear until I'd killed most of those guards. I had them in retreat. If you're this great and all-powerful ghoul, why didn't you handle them yourself?"

I wanted you to prove yourself, the wraith answered. *As the nobleman said, you are a mistake. I wasn't about to protect a weakling, though I confess I am pleasantly surprised that you're not completely useless.*

"Oh, good," Connor said, crossing his arms as he leaned against a nearby tree. "I passed a demon's test. How lucky for me."

To his surprise, the Wraith King chuckled, the sound brief and quiet.

As Connor rested the back of his head against the rough bark, he studied the billowing black ribbons of the ghoul's tattered cloak. "What's your name? Your real one, I mean."

What? the specter asked, his voice tinged with confusion. With his back still to Connor, the Wraith King's head pivoted perfectly around on his bony spine to face him, and the black hood twisted with the movement.

Connor cringed, suppressing a shudder at the unnatural movement.

"Your name," he said flatly. "Your family, your lineage—none of it survived in the stories. Maybe the scholars in Lunestone or Oakenglen know, but none of us common folk do. Or have you been the Wraith King for so long that you've forgotten who you really were?"

The floating ghoul drifted slightly away, like he'd taken an unconscious step backward, and he tilted his head in confusion. *No one has ever asked me that before.*

Bewildered, Connor's brows furrowed with doubt. "I find that hard to believe. People get stuck with you, and they don't even want your name?"

Most of them seek me out. You are the only one thus far to be 'stuck' with me. The ghost shrugged. *I see them for who they are, not how they want to be perceived. No Wraithblade can lie to me or to himself, not once we bond. Most men only look at me for what they can get, not who I was. I'm a specter. A soldier. Something they try and fail to control. Nothing more.*

The wraith darted closer, his skull and spine correcting with the motion as he appeared almost instantly in front of Connor. What remained of the dead man stared down from beneath the great black hood, unnerving and silent.

Connor pinched his eyes shut in surprise. Damn it, he couldn't let this relic of a man know these antics got to him.

You're curious, the ghoul said. *Not the usual pompous ass who aims to usurp someone or overthrow some kingdom I couldn't care less about. It's strange. There's a compassion to you I haven't seen before. I think it only fair to warn you, then, that such stupidity will likely get you killed.*

"Thank you. That's helpful," Connor said dryly. "You're not going to tell me your name, then?"

No.

"Fine," he said, waving the question away with a flick of his wrist. "It doesn't matter."

He pushed off the oak and turned his back on the Wraith King, who would have killed him already if that were going to happen. Lost in thought, he set his hands on the back of his head.

Bound to an old ghost the world still feared.

Hunted by a nobleman who controlled the king's guard.

Faced with the lethal unknowns that lay ahead and the looming threat of the gallows.

"The nobleman in the meadow," he said without turning around. "Those guards. Tell me what happened. Who they are."

It entertains me that you continue to make demands. Why do you think a king will answer?

"King of what, exactly?" Connor tilted his body, quirking one eyebrow as he glanced the dead man up and down. "Slaybourne has been lost for centuries. Even if we found it, nothing remains of the kingdom you ruled except a few ruins, and you're certainly not the king of any men. No one obeys you, least of all me. You're just a dead man with a sword, floating in the wind."

The wraith stilled, rising a foot or so in the air as he stiffened. A low growl rumbled in Connor's head like a brewing storm, and an icy wind circled them both.

A ghost's rage, cold and violent.

A silent warning to shut his damn mouth.

"You can't kill me, remember?" he pointed out, setting his hands on his hips as he met the wraith's vacant gaze. "Like you said, I'm just some irritating peasant. We can get along, or I can annoy the living hell out of you until the end of my days. What'll it be?"

The wind howled as it whipped around them in a frenzy, but Connor didn't flinch. He waited, eyes narrowing as he dared the dead king to make his next move. It had been a mistake for the ghoul to admit he couldn't kill the Wraithblade, and Connor figured the ghost already regretted sharing that little bit of honesty.

They would have a truce, or they would have war. Connor wasn't the sort to tremble beneath another man's anger.

With a violent hiss, the cold wind broke. The leaves beneath them scattered, exposing patches of dirt and grass as the ghost raised his chin in defiance.

You are infuriatingly persistent.

"Thank you." Connor gave a mocking little bow. "Now, about Otmund—"

Henry got lazy, the Wraith King snapped. *I recommend you learn from his mistakes.*

"Lazy?"

He started trusting those around him, the ghost answered. *When he should have instilled fear, he permitted what he perceived to be devotion. He was wrong. He let down his guard, he was betrayed, and the same will happen to you if you continue to be such an infuriating twit.*

"Noted," Connor said, rolling his eyes. "And the nobleman?"

Otmund.

"Right, I know the name." He rubbed his face, doing his best to stem the rising exasperation burning in his chest. "Why was he out there? What did he do to you and Henry?"

This. The ghost lifted his left hand to reveal the stubs where his ring finger and pinkie used to be.

Connor's mouth parted in disbelief, and he squinted at the missing digits as he took several cautious steps closer. "That cowardly little man did this?"

The Bloodbane dagger did this, the ghoul corrected, floating backward to put space between them once again. *The same dagger that gave you—and me—that wound.*

The phantom lifted the shreds of his cloak to reveal the right side of his body. A green gash glowed in the depths of his skeletal form, the exact size and shape of the injury in Connor's side.

Connor set his palm against the bandage around his waist, his fingers pressing lightly against the gash that still haunted him even as the rest of him healed.

I have never seen anything like that dagger, the ghost admitted. *Yet, they had two the night they killed Henry.*

"They? Who else did this?"

Two daggers. Three names. Otmund Soulblud. Zander Starling. Celine Montgomery. These are the people you must find, and you must do it before they find you.

"Celine—the queen? Henry's wife?" Connor frowned, unable to believe what he was hearing. "What does she have to do with this?"

Everything, the ghoul answered.

"Slow down." Connor lifted his hands, flashing his palms as he tried to wrap his head around what the ghost wanted. "Was it just these three? Were there more?"

Many more. Three people alone cannot kill a king like Henry, nor can they defeat a man as powerful as me.

Connor ignored the ghoul's arrogance. "Who else was involved? Who do I need to look out for?"

Everyone.

"That narrows it down." He shrugged, exasperated. "Thank you."

Save for a few threats worthy of my attention, most names hold so little meaning, the ghost said, his tone bored. *Furious faces blur together. Men and women betray each other. The same games play out again and again on every throne. Mortals are so tiring.*

The ghoul sighed, and with the sound, several leaves caught on the wind. They spun and twirled through the empty air beneath his cloak.

As the centuries pass, there are so many names to remember, the wraith added. *In the end, it's not worth wasting the energy to recall.*

Connor rubbed his temples. Getting answers from an all-knowing wraith was like milking a fanged bear.

Impossible.

"Who is Otmund?" He rubbed his jaw as he retook control of the conversation.

A lord, the dead king said.

He gestured for the ghoul to continue. "And?"

The Wraith King shrugged. *And that is all I know.*

Connor found that hard to believe. "Fine. Who is Zander Starling?"

A man of power and magic. Surely, you know the name?

"The only time I've heard the name 'Starling' was in reference to the Lightseers."

Exactly. The Starlings own the Lightseers. Red hair. Frost-colored skin. Unmistakable and deadly. Only that family possesses the power and wealth required to create the Bloodbane Daggers. Now, both Otmund and Zander have one. You must acquire these weapons before they're used to carve out your heart.

Connor rubbed the back of his neck as he paced between the trees, trying to piece the puzzle together. He didn't know much about the world of the wealthy, but the Starlings were synonymous with the law.

If a Starling wanted the Wraith King dead, he couldn't trust any

Lightseer he came across. They would all try to kill him—or worse.

Wherever you can, look for Aeron's notes, the wraith added. *Even a great man like Aeron Zacharias couldn't memorize all of his magic. He must have left notes behind. They exist, somewhere, and you must find them.*

Two daggers and a dead man's notes.

He'd hoped the wraith would've had more in the way of answers and less in the way of tasks to complete.

As a commoner far removed from the courts of kings and lords, the Wraith King's cryptic warnings simply weren't enough information for him to use. Otmund had worn silk from head to toe, but that didn't mean much. He could've lived anywhere, owned anyone, and had the means to hunt Connor across the known world, for all he knew.

Yet again, Connor had to figure out how to survive while he found his footing on this new path that had swallowed him whole.

Adapt or die. It was the Saldian way.

Always had been, and always would be.

CHAPTER THIRTEEN
CONNOR

In the depths of the Ancient Woods, smoke wafted past Connor, charred and hot. It stole his focus, and though he needed to pry more information from the Wraith King, smoke on the wind couldn't have been a good sign.

The scorched air spiraled through the canopy, just a shade or two darker than the sky, and the subtle scent of charcoal and wheat drifted through the air. Kiera must've been cooking in the chilly night, but it seemed foolish to advertise their presence to anyone or anything that happened by.

He hesitated. To be fair, he wouldn't have noticed it before his connection to the Wraith King. It would've just been another strange scent on the wind, something he wouldn't have been able to trace.

Perhaps they were safe after all—just not from people like him.

You've noticed the changes, the ghost said with a hint of surprise in his tone.

Connor nodded. "What did you do to me?"

I did nothing. Our connection has an effect on the mortal body. The ghoul tapped the bony hole where his nose used to be. *Healing, hearing, smell, sight, sex—everything is enhanced. It's always curious to see how the Wraithblades experience the change when they first fuse to me. It's the same every time, but some powers go unnoticed in those of weaker minds. I find the feeble ones to be so wasteful, as they are usually unable to discover anything for themselves. They bore me, but you are more aware than even some lords. Yet again, where I expected tedium, I instead find you to be surprisingly interesting.*

"How flattering," Connor said dryly. "Are there more changes? Did I overlook anything?" He crossed his arms, waiting and not entirely sure if a man as legendary as the Wraith King would even answer.

The ghost merely chuckled.

"I'll take that as a yes."

Correct.

Connor gestured for the ghost to continue. "And they are?"

You will have to discover them for yourself. The wraith paused and tapped a bony finger on his jaw in the ensuing silence. *Or, perhaps I will teach you when you earn your keep. When you impress me.*

Doubtful. Connor huffed. It seemed more like a dangling carrot than a true promise. Just something to make him dance.

He didn't indulge the whims of kings and lords. What he did was done on his terms.

As insects buzzed in the peaceful night, Connor paced along the edge of the small clearing where the ghoul had first appeared. Leaves crunched beneath his boots, and he hooked his thumb through a belt loop as he sifted through what he'd learned so far.

Everybody wanted something, even a ghoul like this. He was a man, once, and that greed probably hadn't faded with the centuries.

If anything, it had likely grown stronger.

"You want me to find the Bloodbane daggers," he said, more to himself than anything else. "You want to know the weapon that can hurt you is under control. That no one can use it against us."

Us.

The word had rolled off his tongue, effortless and natural, but he couldn't let himself get too comfortable. Even if the Wraith King couldn't harm him, Connor couldn't forget who this old ghost really was. A living boogeyman. A banshee in the night.

A threat.

Those blades are the only weapons I know of that can kill me, the ghoul confirmed. *As you've seen firsthand, it is especially brutal to mortals as well.*

With power like that, it must cost a fortune to create. There likely aren't more.

Connor frowned as the dull ache in his side twinged, and he rubbed the back of his neck while he debated how accurate that could be. Wealth had eluded him, but he doubted money meant much to those in power.

The wraith tilted his skull as those bony arms crossed over the black cloak. *You are not afraid.*

It wasn't a question.

Connor shook his head. "The only way out of the darkness is to go through it. The trick is to look for lights along the way."

His father used to say that, and the words brought with them an ache for the ocean.

Yet again, the ghoul darted forward, the movement so fast and sudden Connor couldn't even blink before the Wraith King's white skull hovered inches in front of him. With his nose nearly brushing the king's bony face, he stared into the hollow voids of the dead man's eyes, wondering what the ghost could truly see.

You proved yourself in the meadow, the specter said. *Though you failed to obtain the blade, you did send a dangerous enemy into retreat. For that, I will grant you one gift—the knowledge of only one of your new abilities. Not because I am charitable, but because it was earned. You will learn I am a man of my word.*

With that, a bony finger pressed against Connor's forehead. A jolt of pain shot down his spine. He grimaced, his body rooted in place from the violent burst of magic. Smoke billowed around Connor's neck and circled down his arms, curling down his body like fog across a lake. A surge of fire burned through him, and he stifled a tormented yell as the wound in his side erupted with a fresh blaze of agony.

As the specter's bony finger lifted, weight settled into Connor's palms. He tightened his grip on impulse, holding tight to something he couldn't see as the billowing smoke wafted over his hands.

When the ethereal fog dissolved in the breeze, it left behind two jet-black swords in his palms. Fire as dark as the shadows around them crackled along the steel as they rested in his grip, perfectly balanced, as if they had been forged especially for him.

He lifted them, marveling at their beauty as the moons' soft blue light shimmered along the sharp edges.

Money did nothing for Connor. Food held little joy. Except for a rare fling now and then as he passed through towns, he hadn't chased skirts. But weapons—when he saw a beautiful sword or a brilliantly designed axe, he couldn't contain himself.

Beck Arbor had called it weakness. Connor called it a rare indulgence.

"Wow," he whispered, his fingers tightening around the hilts. He swung them to get a feel for their power.

First one, then the other. Both at once. They gleamed and glistened through the air, polished and perfect.

Each slice felt graceful, and the swords remained light in his palm. No resistance. No heft. They floated through the air as if they weighed nothing, easier to wield than any weapon he'd ever held in his life.

As the Wraith King hovered nearby, Connor swung both blades at a nearby tree to test their power. The true test of a sword's might: most blades cut the bark, but a good blade sank deep.

The black steel sliced through the tree like a shovel through soft earth. Effortless.

The oak groaned as the sword sailed clean through it, and its bark shattered as the blades sang. The leaves in its canopy swayed, heavy in the peaceful night. The splintering roar of crashing branches scared a flock of birds into the stars, and the tree toppled with a final crash into the underbrush.

He gaped in shock at the downed tree before examining the weapons once again.

Gorgeous and deadly—his favorite combination.

The Wraith King joined him, hovering at his side as they stared out at the fallen oak. *These superior blades can be summoned or dismissed without the need to sheathe them. A warrior's enemies should never know he's armed until it's too late for them to run.*

Connor grimaced, the delight of his new weapons shattered with the comment. "I suspect I'll have a lot more of those now, thanks to you."

Most likely, the ghost admitted. *Now, put them away. It would be unwise to reveal them to the other peasants in that house.*

Connor looked down at the swords and then at the Wraith King, raising one eyebrow in confusion. "How?"

The Wraith King groaned in disgust. Though the ghoul couldn't form expressions on his face, Connor could practically feel the revulsion rolling off him. *Of course, I had to get a host who knows nothing about magic. Do you know anything of value besides how to be a condescending ass?*

Connor adjusted his grip on the dual blades. "Oh, I'm the condescending ass now, am I?"

With a bony finger the wraith scratched at his exposed skull, right around where the ghoul's forehead used to be. *This frustrates me.*

"You're equally annoying to me," he assured the ghost.

A low growl rumbled through his brain, but he ignored it and examined his new swords instead.

Fine. Since we will be stuck together for a time, I must understand what work lies ahead of me.

Connor narrowed his eyes in suspicion. "Work?"

You. This. The ghoul gestured to all of him. *You will face magic. True magic. I must be able to anticipate if an approaching threat can kill you or not, and to do that, I must know what you understand of magic. Tell me.*

He frowned, and in his periphery, he caught a glimpse of one of his own blades in their sheaths on his back. He'd never been one to give in to others' demands.

Come, now, out with it, the wraith demanded. *Potions, augmentations, enchanted items—which of these is familiar to you? Or are you utterly useless after all?*

As the enchanted swords rested in his palms, the blackfire still rolling across their steel, he sat with the ghost's demand. Pride or curiosity—one would win, and he had to choose.

To get what he wanted, he would indulge the wraith's irritating demand.

"I know how potions work," Connor said, trying his best to hide his annoyance.

Do you, now? the ghost asked skeptically.

"Surprised?"

Doubtful is the word I would use, peasant.

"Fine, we can play this game." He circled the ghost while he spoke. "Potion making is like cooking. If you leave it on the fire too long, it burns and becomes useless or significantly less effective. Too little time on the flame, and it doesn't have the potency you need for it to be truly effective. Every potion is different. Each recipe is nuanced and unique. It's all about perfection."

That's overly simplified, but it will do, the Wraith King shrugged. *You are aware of spellgust, then?*

"Everyone knows about spellgust."

Which types have you used?

"Not many," he admitted, leaning against a nearby tree as the tip of the black swords brushed the dead leaves beneath his feet. "Mostly just the powder they sell in the potion shops."

Disappointing. It's the foundation of all magic, and yet you're aware only of the common mineral. He groaned and floated away, muttering to himself. *I had to get a peasant, damn it all.*

Connor's jaw tensed as he fought the urge to say something he would probably regret. The Wraith King might've been stuck with a peasant, but Connor was stuck with a colossal asshole.

If it weren't for the blades and his newly enhanced senses, he'd have thought he'd gotten the shorter stick of this arrangement. Those alone saved the wraith from Connor finding a way to banish the dead king back to wherever that necromancer had found him.

An idea sparked to life in the back of Connor's brain while the wraith paced the forest, but he wasn't sure if he liked it.

In fact, it could easily get him killed.

Though the limits of magic were set in stone and unwavering, two moralities had sprouted over the centuries to guide men in how to use it. Lightseers preserved the natural order, permitting death so that the world could renew itself.

Necromancers, however, had only one guiding rule: defy death at any cost.

Perhaps he needed to find a necromancer of his own. The magic users who dealt with death might've had the answers the wraith didn't want to give, but finding one would've come with substantial risk.

People whispered breathless rumors about necromancers in the taverns, and the common folk only turned to a necromancer when all other magic had failed. Their potions were forbidden by common law and served as the last-ditch effort for most. Over the centuries, they had been reduced to rumors and folklore, nothing more than the enchantress in the night who would sooner take a man's soul than help him.

But the fortress of Nethervale to the northeast had yet to be conquered, and though rare, necromancers still existed.

I know that look, the Wraith King's voice echoed in his mind.

Connor's gaze darted to the old ghost, though the rest of his body remained immobile. The cloaked skeleton watched him from the shadows of that dark hood, still as death.

"I bet you do."

You're scheming.

"Perhaps."

Hmm. The ghost hovered closer. *And what schemes are burning through that commoner's mind?*

"Keep threatening me, and you'll find out," he answered coldly.

You dare threaten me? The Wraith King straightened his bony back and curled his fingers into fists. In a rush of wind, the light around him dimmed. A cloud passed in front of the moons, and their light faded from the sky, casting the night in even deeper shadow.

Weight settled on Connor's shoulders as he held the wraith's gaze, and the gale only strengthened as he refused to back down. It kicked up the leaves along the dirt, carrying them until a circle of decay swarmed through the air, with only him and the wraith in its center.

The dead king's cloak billowed furiously in the cyclone, and his hood finally fell back to reveal a long crack across the top of his skull. The line traced from the crown of his head to his left temple—a long fracture no one could've survived.

You don't fear me because you are a fool, he warned. *You believe I cannot hurt you, when in fact I can destroy you. I am the voice in your ear, the whisper in your soul, the finger summoning you into the shadows. I can make you doubt yourself. Hate yourself. Ruin yourself. I am not a companion. I am not a guide. I am the darkness, and you will appease me. I am Death's own son, and you will feed my bloodlust. I do not idle well, mortal. Fail me, and I will ensure the world watches with glee as you're strung up on the gallows.*

As the wind screamed past Connor's ear, he didn't move. He didn't recoil. The weight on his shoulders grew heavier, and he had to tense his core to keep from being shoved to his knees. Unwavering, he resisted the intense air and the ghost's magic.

In many respects, the ghoul was right. The Wraith King had immortality, and Connor had but one lifetime. To make matters even more dire, his newfound connection to this ancient king likely meant his days were numbered.

It hit him, then—the price for the magic that had saved his life in the meadow. By stepping in to help a screaming girl in a field, he had sealed his own fate.

The price for his magic had already been paid.

A lifetime with a wraith who demanded sacrifice. Who thrived on war. Who ached for blood on his sword.

Connor wasn't a man of regret. The sands of time never changed, and he saw no need to wish the world were different. With his enhanced senses and new blades, he was stronger and more capable than before. Even if he had no direction in life, he couldn't deny the power that burned through his blood with each heartbeat.

The wraith was a curse for some. For those clever enough to adapt to their new life, however, he was a dark blessing.

More importantly, Connor wasn't a man of fear. The Ancient Woods and the monsters lurking in the trees had carved the terror out of his heart years ago. With no family and nothing to lose, nothing scared him anymore, least of all the threat of damnation.

He had looked death in the eye too often to fear it.

"You want blood," he said, his voice calm and steady despite the howling gale around him.

I do, the wraith confirmed.

"You want war."

Correct.

"You won't get either from me." He tossed the stunning black blades to the soil at his feet. They smacked against the dirt, dissolving into wisps of smoke that faded into the cyclone around him.

The gale dispersed. The howling stopped, and the leaves gently fluttered to the ground like snow on a still day. Connor's ear rang in the sudden silence, but he stood taller and dared the ghost to make the next move.

You refuse to give me what I desire because you know so little about what awaits you. About what's possible.

"Enlighten me, then."

The ghost laughed and circled him, those bony hands behind his back. *You've never seen true power, but you will. It's coming for you. It wants you dead. You said you know of potions? Fool, I can assure you those are but peasants' playthings compared to what lies before us.*

Connor scoffed. "If the legends are true, you used potions more than anyone. You decimated entire armies with your concoctions."

Wrong, the ghost corrected, looming overhead. *I destroyed them with enchantments. With augmentations. Potions are baubles, nothing but a means to an end. It's the enchantments that hold true power. Enchantments like those swords. Enchantments like the one in your chest.*

The ghoul prodded the scar on his sternum with a skeletal finger. A surge of pain shot through him at the ghost's touch. His head thudded with a dull ache as he steeled himself and pushed through the wave, refusing to let the agony show on his face.

You don't have a single augmentation, not even one for hygiene. The dead king lifted his chin, a hint of disdain in his voice. *You stand no chance against an augmented warrior, much less one with an enchanted weapon. Tell me, have you ever watched a soldier wielding an enchanted blade? Have you watched an augmented soldier fight? Do you have any inkling of what lies ahead of you? Of what you could be if only you listened to me?*

Connor simply crossed his arms and let the silence linger. In the dead king's anger, he was starting to reveal truths about magic Connor had never heard before.

Best to let the fool speak and betray what he knew. It would likely come in useful.

When the first real danger crosses your path, you will die, the Wraith King warned. *Spellgust is the breath of life, you infuriating peasant, but you've barely touched it. Augmentations and enchanted items—the powerful ones, anyway— connect to the body. As a soldier trains, each movement, each motion, comes to mean something unique to the magic they wield. Spellgust connects to the blood, and their muscle memory and training grants them complete control over their power. The soldiers you will face were forged in the most refined spellgust known to this world. You merely fell into a puddle.*

It had no doubt been intended as an insult, but the lecture gave Connor an idea.

The ghost said something else, but he tuned out the grim voice so he could focus. If the swords were truly connected to him, as the wraith had said, they couldn't have been destroyed by simply throwing them to the ground.

His heels dug into the dirt, and he tried to recall the weight of the blades in his palm. The way they had balanced so effortlessly in his grip. The exhilarating rush of inhuman strength as he had sliced through a tree in a single blow.

Of the raw *power*.

As he sat with the memory, leaning into it with his full focus, the black swords materialized in his palms with a puff of midnight smoke. Dark flames licked the air as the black steel glinted in the low light of the forest.

With a devious grin, he spun the swords in his palms and aimed the tip of each blade at the skeleton floating before him. His eyes narrowed as he dared the ghoul to continue insulting him. "You were saying?"

Impressive, the Wraith King admitted, not bothering to mask the annoyance in his voice. *You have potential. I've had worse students.*

"I've had better teachers," he countered.

The ghost huffed in anger.

Another rush of agony splintered through Connor's side as the Bloodbane wound spasmed yet again. The ghoul flinched, and the dead king's bony hands pressed against his own cloak as Connor clenched his jaw to ride out the pain.

Both of them shared the same injury, a stark reminder of their connection despite their hatred for each other.

As the rush of agony faded, Connor's stomach growled, evidently unsatisfied with the feast of seared meat and bread he'd eaten barely two hours ago.

He leaned against a tree trunk as nausea burned in the back of his throat. "What the hell is this insatiable hunger? Is this your doing, too? I've been ravenous since I woke up. I can't seem to get enough food."

You don't think all of this power comes without a cost, do you? The Wraith King floated through the trees, darting between the oaks as he spoke. *Your body is taxed from hosting both your soul and mine. It will need more food, more sex, and more water. It will burn hotter. You will never again feel the hot buzz of too much ale because you will never be able to drink enough to obtain it. You're not just a man anymore. You're something greater, and that comes at a price. I have always found it's best to take what you need, as even a king would quickly run out of coin otherwise,* the ghost added, pointing a bony finger in the vague direction of the house in the trees.

At Ethan's family.

On instinct, Connor raised the flaming black steel and stood between the ghost and the Finns. "You will not touch them."

The Wraith King chuckled. The harsh laughter cut through Connor's head, quick and humorless, and the ghoul dissolved into the breeze.

Once again, he stood alone in the silent forest.

Take this time to heal, but do not dally, the phantom's ghoulish voice echoed in Connor's mind, despite the empty woods around him. *You are useless while injured, but I will not be patient for long.*

Connor pivoted on his heel, scanning the depths of the trees, but nothing darted between the old oaks even as the ghost spoke.

I need blood, the wraith continued. *War. Battle. I am not satisfied living as a drifter in the woods. Your life as a vagrant is over.*

"Don't you threaten me," Connor warned, glaring into the night.

The ghoul didn't respond.

A flock of bats fluttered overhead, their leathery wings snapping against the air as they screeched into the night. He waited, his new swords at the ready as the tiny shadows careened through the air, but the ghoul didn't reappear.

The Wraith King was gone, but his bloodlust would lure him back.

It was just a matter of time, and when the wraith's grim voice echoed through his mind again, Connor would be ready.

CHAPTER FOURTEEN
CONNOR

Still tense and on edge as the forest hummed with life around him, Connor examined the flaming black swords in his palms.

He hated to admit it, but the Wraith King was right. If he walked around with blades like these, he would get the sort of attention he didn't want.

Without the Wraith King's help, he had to figure out how to get rid of them.

They had disappeared when he'd dropped them before, but with weapons as beautiful as these, he refused to treat them with such disrespect regardless of where they'd come from.

Adapt or die. One way or another, he would figure this out on his own, wraith be damned.

If the wraith was to be believed, it all came down to muscle memory. In his years with Beck Arbor, Connor had unconsciously picked up the habit of twisting his wrists outward the second or so before he sheathed his blades. It was a quiet habit, one that had snuck up on him from his time shoveling hay. The motions were so similar he barely registered the difference, and to him, it had always meant the duel was done.

He drummed his fingertips lightly against the swords in his hands. Briefly, he rolled out his shoulders as he lifted the blades before him.

"Here goes nothing," he muttered to himself.

With a quick twist of his wrists, he gently loosened his fingers and waited to see what would happen.

The flaming blades shifted in his palms and nearly slid out of his grip, but they didn't fade. He frowned in disappointment.

"Okay," he said as another flock of bats fluttered by. He squared his shoulders and deepened his stance, his heel grinding into the soil as he watched the swords intensely.

Muscle memory.

Practiced ease.

This had to be quick. Intuitive. He had to get out of his own head and let the magic connect to his body instead.

Again, he twisted his wrists outward and loosened his grip in one fluid motion. This time, the enchanted weapons dissolved in a puff of black smoke.

"Ha!" Connor stared at his now-empty palms and grinned with victory. To hell with the ghost. He could figure this out on his own.

He absently curled his fingers as the cloud hiding the moons slipped away, and a gentle blue light returned to the meadow. How surreal to think he could summon blades at will.

An orphaned drifter now had magic even the lords and kings of this world probably wanted. Otmund couldn't possibly have been alone in the hunt, not for power like this. Once they found Connor, he would never have another moment of peace.

To take the advantage, he needed to uncover the truth—of what he was, of what he could do, and of those who hunted him.

And, perhaps, find a necromancer to help him make sense of it all.

As his thoughts raced with risk and possibility, he returned to the house in the trees. The path took nearly an hour as he debated his options, and he only broke from his thoughts when the crash of the waterfall thundered through the forest.

The rumble of water grew louder and louder with each step. Though the falls masked most of the woodland creatures' nightly song, his ear still twitched at the occasional snap of a twig.

Nothing escaped his notice. Not anymore.

Though the wound in his side screamed in protest as he reached for the ladder nailed to the tree trunk, he climbed into the canopy. After only a few minutes, he heaved himself through the gap in the porch. The tired wood creaked beneath his weight, and he doubted this house would last long.

The Finns had abandoned it, and in its retirement, the decaying wood had lost its fight with time. They needed to build a new home and let this one die.

On the other side of the closed front door, a board creaked. A man let out a slow sigh, the sound muffled by the thick wood between them, and Connor paused with his hand on the doorknob.

Apparently, Ethan had waited up for him.

How odd.

He opened the door to find Ethan sitting on one of the stools in the kitchen, elbows resting on his knees as he stared into the stove's red embers. A puff of smoke spiraled out of the open stove while Connor paused at the threshold. The oven cast a warm and soothing glow across the cozy space even as a cold wind snaked through the open entry.

Ethan shivered. "Shut the door."

The latch clicked shut as he indulged Ethan's request. He crossed his arms and leaned against the wall, waiting in the house's warm silence. A man who hadn't slept in close to two days wouldn't have sat awake long into the night unless he'd felt the need.

"That first room is yours," Ethan said with a nod toward the hallway. "It's not much, but you're welcome to it."

Connor's eyebrows furrowed as he peered into the narrow corridor. In the dark hallway, he noticed a sliver of a doorframe, the rest of it just out of sight. "Thanks. I promise I won't stay long."

"Nonsense. The room is yours, Connor. Stay as long as you like and come back whenever you want. We'll make sure there's an extra room in the new house, too, once we finish it."

The man's generosity left him speechless. Each time he thought he understood the Finns, they managed to surprise him yet again.

Ethan nodded toward the porch. "Did you find what you were looking for out there in the woods?"

"I did," he answered, uninterested in discussing it further.

For their own safety, the Finns didn't need to know about the Wraith King.

He walked into the hall, ready to put this day to bed, but Ethan grabbed his forearm as he passed. The grip rooted him in place, strong and sturdy.

Connor had broken men's noses for less, but he allowed it for now. The Finns had been good to him, and he tried to show a bit of patience.

"I know you're caught in the middle of something dangerous, Connor," Ethan said quietly. "Something deadly. All those men? All those bodies? It has to be the sort of thing that'll chase a man across the plains."

Connor didn't answer. He didn't need to.

"Kiera said she saw something out in those woods," Ethan continued. "Something she had never seen before. Something she couldn't name."

Disappointment snaked through Connor as he watched the man piece it all together.

He'd encountered kindness in the past, long before the Finns. Once or twice, he'd been offered room and board with the warning it would eventually end. No matter how hard he worked or what he did to help, their compassion never lasted long. Even Beck Arbor had sent him packing, and he'd learned over the years that no family welcomed a lost orphan into their home for long.

Once a vagrant, always a vagrant. The forest was the only home he had left.

"It's fine," he said in the silence that followed. "I'll leave."

"What? No, Connor, no. That's not what I meant at all." Ethan waved the thought away. "I know you probably won't stay here long, but there's always a room for you with us. No matter what's chasing you. No matter what trouble you find yourself in. Whenever you need to escape whatever is waiting for you out there, I want you to come here. We're grateful to you, and if you want the change of pace, you don't have to be a vagrant wandering the woods anymore."

Truth be told, Connor didn't know what to say. He stood there for a moment in numb surprise, caught off guard by the idea that anyone would've invited him into their home—not temporarily, but always.

No one had offered him *that* before.

When he regained his composure, he simply nodded in gratitude. Ethan released his hold on Connor's arm and stared again into the oven. The burly man's eyes closed, and a small smile pulled at the corner of his mouth as the warm embers cast an amber glow against his face.

Connor stepped into the small room they had offered him and shut the door. At first, he could only stare at the honey-brown walls, still looking for the catch. The lie. The con. As the quiet seconds ticked by, his gaze eventually drifted to the simple wooden bed along the far wall and the hand-carved dresser sitting opposite.

A palace, really, for a drifter like him.

CHAPTER FIFTEEN
OTMUND

Otmund reclined in an ornate mahogany chair as the heel of his palm pressed against the white marble table before him. Through the open windows and the blue silk curtains lining the stone walls of the northern tower, the sun shone brilliantly on Lunestone.

Home of the Lightseers. Home of his favorite—and most treacherous—toys.

He drummed his fingers on the cold table in time to the steady cadence of footsteps by the windows. His nails tapped along the rigid and unyielding stone, the marble not unlike the man who paced along the far wall.

In the silence that stretched between them in the opulent meeting room, Otmund waited. The pacing stopped, and Teagan Starling set his hands behind his back as he gazed out over the lake. The chatter of voices below wafted through the open panes as the curtains floated gently on the early spring air.

Though he wished the Starling patriarch would say something already and get this over with, Otmund stretched his fingers out over the marble to keep himself from breaking the lull in their conversation. He curled his hands into fists several times to keep himself from speaking.

In any negotiation with a Starling, the first to talk always lost.

Teagan's broad shoulders blocked out much of the sun glinting off the water below. His white suit stretched against his muscled bulk, the hardened warrior in better shape at fifty-six than most men were in their entire lives. That trademark Starling hair of his caught the light, the strands still ablaze with the reds, oranges, and gold of a flame despite his age.

Once a soldier, Teagan had retired to rule the most powerful magical religion in Saldia. He controlled their army, their elite assassins, their crusades against the necromancers, and most importantly, their enforcement of magical law amongst the common folk.

The Lightseers.

He governed them all from Lunestone, ordered them to fight the necromancers he told people to fear, and used his position to undermine and execute the enemies who threatened his wealth. All in the name of preserving Saldia.

And thus, why he had proven so useful to Otmund.

The distant crash of Everdale Falls rumbled through the sky, and the occasional creak of a mast or the flapping sails of a delivery ship piercing the otherwise quiet room. The world beyond continued as it always had, peaceful and still despite the clandestine uprising currently underway.

The people hadn't yet learned the king was dead, but it couldn't be hidden for much longer. As soon as the commoners knew, they would need to see his successor. They would need a story to believe, to cling to, to assure them their new ruler was the rightful one.

With no heir to the throne, and given the queen's disappearance, filling King Henry's chair would be no easy task.

A void of power would only incite a bloody revolt to claim the throne, and Otmund wanted this transition to be as smooth as possible. Henry had been a brutal warlord, but the man had been smart enough to keep the people working, fed, and deep in debt.

Their debt had kept him in power.

Otmund let out a slow breath, his jaw tensing as he waited for Teagan to speak. It was a stroke of genius really, what Henry had done. The dead king had built the economy around himself and made himself the source of both magic and coin. In doing so, he had made Saldia dependent.

To lose him would mean they would lose their livelihood as well. It was a policy Otmund planned to expand once he took the throne.

He frowned, doing his best to mask his irritation with the stretching silence, lest Teagan notice. He squeezed his eyes shut and buried his anger deep within, next to his undying hatred for that peasant in the meadow.

To make his deadly puppet dance, Otmund needed to appear calm and impartial. Even a thread of weakness or emotion would've untangled this delicate web he had spent so many years weaving.

A man like Teagan preyed upon insecurity and doubt.

With a long and heavy sigh, Teagan turned on his heel and lifted his chin, raising one thick red eyebrow as he glared at Otmund. "You are wildly incompetent, and your failure to capture the commoner is proof of your ineptitude. I question whether you should remain in the Lightseer Chamber at all after this, much less keep your title. No Master Strategist should've ever let this man escape. You've grown soft."

Teagan had always wielded words like weapons. The slur on Otmund's aptitude, his intelligence, and his ability weighed on his pride, but he resisted the impulse to defend himself.

As with all things Teagan controlled, the insult was merely a trap. A ploy. Something to unsettle Otmund and knock him off balance, in order to reveal any lies beneath the surface Teagan might've needed to see.

It was bait Otmund wouldn't take. Besides, by letting the silence linger, he had won the hardest battle.

Now, to win the war.

He leaned his elbows on the table, forcing himself to relax as he shrugged. "You're one to talk, old man."

"Am I?" Teagan's eye twitched, the movement so subtle that Otmund almost missed it as the Starling slowly closed the gap between them. "When I'm given a mission, I finish it. When I face an enemy, I crush him. You let this peasant escape, Otmund. A *peasant*!"

Teagan slammed his massive fist on the table, and the ancient stone rattled beneath the force of both his anger and his augmented strength. He leaned his palms against the surface, his fingers curling as his nose wrinkled with disgust.

"And it somehow gets worse," he continued in a gravelly voice. "The peasant is irrelevant compared to the Wraith King, and you let that abomination escape! Your one purpose, your one reason for even being there last night, and you failed."

"It's contained," Otmund said as he forced himself to be calm. "The man's injured, close to death, and lost in the Ancient Woods. He should be effortless for one of your elite Lightseers to obtain. Bring him to me, and I will seal the Wraith King away, just as my grandfather did all those years ago in the Blood Bogs."

"Effortless?" Teagan's voice dripped with a chilling disdain that Otmund hadn't heard in quite a while.

The last person the Lightseer Master General had spoken to this way was the now-dead King Henry.

"Effortless," Otmund confirmed, refusing to let his growing terror show through his mask.

"The man who killed ten soldiers by himself, effortless to contain?"

Otmund frowned, the movement only a brief and subtle twinge at the corners of his mouth. His brows furrowed, and he couldn't help but impulsively look away, out at the beautiful sunlit day, out at all the fools and common folk who had no idea what was really happening behind the scenes of their enchanted world.

Usually, he lied with ease. The peasant had killed nine of the king's guard, but Otmund hadn't admitted to killing the tenth.

Best to blame it on a scapegoat. In this case, the commoner.

Teagan squared his shoulders, turning on his heel with militant precision as he once more surveyed the lake below. Hands clasped again behind his back, he inspected his domain with a deep, growly breath. Though Otmund couldn't see his face anymore, he figured the man had closed his eyes to center himself like he always did before he started barking out orders.

So predictable. That was the difference between them.

The Starlings had more coin and magic than any other family in Saldia, even the kings and queens. Teagan owned the Lightseers, controlled their crusades, and operated the magical organization like a religion with him as their god. His ego was too massive, too wild.

Otmund, on the other hand, knew finesse. Control. Stamina. One thing a Starling could never master was having a bit of patience.

"Celine can never know about this," Teagan said calmly.

"Obviously."

Henry's widow didn't need to know the Wraith King's soul was still free.

Otmund resisted the impulse to roll his eyes at the ludicrous comment. Even with Teagan looking away, it sometimes seemed as though the man could see everything, always. As if the fates had granted him omniscience. If anyone could've concocted a potion to do that, it would've been him. Some of the best recipes Otmund had ever stolen were written in Teagan's hand.

Clever, capable, and cunning. The Starling patriarch was the mortal god of the Lightseer religion for a reason.

Teagan rubbed his thick beard, muttering briefly to himself before he shook his head. "On the other hand, she might be helpful in tracking the soul down. Out of all of us, she's the most familiar with it, and if we concoct some lie—"

"No," Otmund interjected, taking a massive risk by interrupting the influential man standing before him. He couldn't let Teagan continue down this path, so he refused to let the idea form completely before he squashed it.

Teagan glared over his shoulder, his brow creasing with irritation at Otmund's audacity, but that was how their relationship worked. They insulted each other, but they also needed each other to get what they wanted.

Every time.

"I mentored her as she came of age," Otmund reminded the Lightseer. "I know her better than anyone, even better than Henry did."

"Then you should know she's not fragile."

"Precisely," Otmund agreed. "That's what concerns me. She's not a desolate widow, drowning in her grief. She left in the night without telling any of us, knowing full well her days were numbered if she stayed. She has a vendetta against the Wraith King, Teagan, same as we do, but she has always been hard to control. If she moves before we—"

"Fair enough." Teagan frowned, his gaze briefly dropping to the table before he returned his attention to the world outside.

Outwardly, Otmund didn't move. He didn't so much as blink or smile. Inwardly, however, he finally relaxed now that this little flame of an idea had died. Celine would only complicate things—ruin things, possibly. With Henry dead, she was no longer useful, and Otmund needed to ensure she was as far from this transition of power as possible. She would eventually discover the truth of how he had played her, but he needed to have the Wraith King by then. If she intervened, warrior queen that she was, she would've just gotten in the way.

Whoever killed the new Wraithblade would obtain the Wraith King's soul, and Otmund was determined not to let anyone else get there first.

Thankfully for him, most people didn't know how the Wraith King worked, or any of the other simmering souls for that matter. If he hadn't secretly copied all of Henry's notes over the last decade, neither would he.

"Does anyone know where she is?" Teagan asked.

"No," Otmund confessed. "Not even me."

He didn't even know if she was still alive. The warrior queen had always said Henry was her one love before the Wraith King had corrupted his soul. Perhaps it had killed her fire. Maybe she would hide in the forests until she died, or perhaps a peasant would find her floating in the river. Though he had mentored her since she had first begun to master advanced magic, he couldn't deny that her death would be the best thing for him—to simply have the meddlesome woman out of the way.

"We need to finish this together." Otmund slid into his prepared remarks as he leaned back into his chair, one of fourteen identical mahogany thrones around the vast marble table. "I need your best assassin to go after this commoner and bring him to me. Kill any witnesses, but capture him alive. Only I know the simmering soul magic enough to—"

"You've said this before," Teagan interrupted. "Only you know how to disable the soul to safely store it away. You bore me when you repeat yourself, Otmund."

"Am I wrong?" he countered, raising one eyebrow.

The Starling patriarch didn't answer. Instead, he tilted his head, snaring Otmund with a glare that could've wilted entire gardens. The man's thick brows furrowed, and the silver scar along his jaw crinkled as those cold gray eyes narrowed.

Many had trembled before this scowl, cowering in their seats as they nervously stared at their hands. Even the man's own children, some of the best warriors the Lightseers had to offer, had recoiled in fear of him in this very room.

Otmund, however, knew better. He hadn't weaseled his way into the Lightseer Chamber by trembling in his chair. Like all men, the Lightseer Master General could be played.

"It's for the good of the people, Teagan." Otmund pressed his fingertips together, the pale tone of his skin a sharp contrast to the black silk in his clothes. "The public needs to see you as a hero, as a man of merit. The man who kills the creatures hunting in the dark. This commoner is nothing more than a new trophy for you to show them. The assassin who killed a king. The mastermind of Henry's death, strung up on the gallows."

Teagan stilled, lifting one eyebrow in surprise as he waited for Otmund to continue.

Yet again, Otmund resisted the impulse to smile as he sewed a new tapestry of lies into one of his favorite puppets. "It's perfect, Teagan. A scapegoat. A head we can put on a spike. We'll have a public execution to shift the blame as power transitions to a new king. To a Starling."

Teagan stood a little taller as he cast a quick glance out the window. Across the massive lake, on the far bank, Oakenglen waited for a new king—but Otmund would see to it no Starling ever sat on the throne.

Oakenglen belonged to him, and he would play the powerful people of this world against each other until his dying breath.

"You must want more than coin." Teagan narrowed his eyes, returning his attention to Otmund. "For you to give me such a tantalizing prize at the end, you must want more than the list you wrote out before. You're waiting until the last moment to bleed me dry, and it won't work."

Ah.

It had perhaps been optimistic to think Teagan would fall for this ploy. Though Otmund had asked for a sizeable transfer of treasuries to fill the vaults back home, his list of demands clearly hadn't been long enough to make them believable. With a prize purse this large, he needed to make a greater demand for Teagan to believe there wasn't treason at the end of the road.

After all, Otmund didn't exactly have a magnanimous reputation. No one would've believed he had done this for the greater good.

At least the Lightseers weren't stupid. In the end, it made them more useful.

"I confess, there is one more thing," he lied, stringing the man along to buy himself a few more precious seconds to strategize. He had to come up with a bigger ask, and he had to do it quickly.

"Get the hell on with it," the Lightseer Master General snapped.

In the back of Otmund's mind, an idea came sharply into focus. He paused, sitting with it as the precious seconds ticked by, but this could very well work.

Worth a try, anyway.

"I want Quinn," he answered.

In the stunned silence that followed his demand, Teagan's brow wrinkled with confusion. The lines around his eyes deepened, but Otmund held the man's stare.

Teagan scoffed. "You want my daughter?"

"I do," Otmund lied.

"You're twice her age," he pointed out, still baffled by the request. "She spent her childhood summers with you. She thinks of you as an uncle, nothing more, and yet you want her as your wife?"

"You understand why I didn't mention this before, I assume," Otmund said, more confident with his lie the longer he sat with it.

Teagan shook his head. "She will fight this and make your life a living hell. Many men have tried to strongarm her into marriage, and half of them are dead, Otmund. If you try to go through with such a ludicrous demand, you should expect a lot of pain."

"That's why you will force her into it," Otmund replied. "She respects you. She listens to you."

The Master General set his hands on his hips. "This is unwise."

"You asked for my price, Teagan." Otmund shrugged. "You want the Oakenglen throne. I want Quinn."

Truth be told, he didn't want her. Maintaining a wife's needs had always seemed like a waste of time, and children irritated him. Teagan's youngest would be married off soon, and the timing simply worked out in his favor.

Headstrong, battle-hardened, beautiful, and talented with magic, Quinn would be useful to him even if he did end up with her. Several of his playthings had mastered potions that could tame wayward minds, and he could always drug her into obedience if the need arose.

Either way, he couldn't lose.

"We will discuss this another time." Teagan grimaced and shook his head as he returned to the windows. "For now, I know who I will send after the peasant. I know the man wore a scarf over his face, but have a sketch drawn by one of the artists in the east wing for whatever parts of his build, clothing, gear, and eyes you can remember. Once you're done, get the hell out of my castle."

Otmund stood without another word, chin held high as he walked into the hallway. A gale ripped through the room as he left, shoving on the door as he held it open—likely Teagan's doing. He barely slipped through before the wind slammed the door behind him, blocking out the steady sunlight streaming in from the windows.

With no witnesses in the empty hallway, Otmund's mask fell.

Safely out of Teagan's sight, he cracked his neck and stretched out the fingers on the now-healed hand the peasant had broken. He didn't trust the Starling patriarch worth a damn, but for the moment, their desires had aligned.

Before this was over—once Teagan figured out what Otmund was really up to and what he really wanted with the wraith—he would have to kill the old man. With the ghoul at his disposal, however, that wouldn't be difficult.

He had orchestrated the king's murder, after all. He had whispered in the right ears and planted the seeds of an uprising. Teagan thought it was his idea, of course, as did many others. Everyone thought they were the mastermind, but Otmund had woven the plan for them all. The players had all done their part, rushing to his side like marionettes beneath his fingers even while they thought he danced for them.

As he jogged down a flight of steps that would lead him to the east tower, he kept an eye on the wall sconces, searching for the one he needed. When a small green jewel inlaid in the gold caught his eye, he paused in the empty stairwell and gently pulled on it. The sconce tilted, rolling on a secret hinge, and the fire in its glass sputtered as a hidden door in the wall popped open. He shoved the door with his shoulder and slipped inside, taking the familiar stairwell as the secret passage sealed behind him.

The Starling children would feud for this mission, for the esteem, and for the pride of catching such important prey.

Let them bicker.

Two of the Starling children had retired already. Only Quinn and Zander remained active, and with those two both trying to out-do each other, Otmund was sure to catch this peasant—all without cashing in even a single favor.

In the meantime, he had a few other strings to tug on before he left Teagan's domain, including the one he very much suspected would be sent on this little mission.

His prized doll.

For now, he would bide his time and allow the Starlings to track the man in the woods for him. He would let them risk their lives while he remained in the shadows—overlooked, underestimated, and safe from it all.

When they brought the peasant to Lunestone in chains, Otmund would be waiting. He had always been the puppet master, pulling string after string while the world bowed to his will.

This peasant didn't stand a chance.

CHAPTER SIXTEEN
ZANDER

In the highest room of Lunestone's northern tower, two balcony doors sat open to invite in the cool spring day. Windows flanked the balcony on both sides, their panes sparkling in the dazzling Saldian sun. Sunbeams stretched over the stone floor, across the ornate golden rug, and toward the red door on the opposite wall.

A room reserved for the elite. For the Starlings.

In its center, a circular table filled most of the viable space. The black marble offered a stark contrast to the golden floor, but Zander Starling had long ago grown accustomed to finery.

He leaned his elbows against the imported stone, engrossed in the parchment lying on the table before him. Standing, with his mahogany chair pushed aside and forgotten, he studied every detail on the paper, right down to the ink blots along the edge from the artist's haste in making the sketch.

Finally, he could see the man in the woods for himself—the one Otmund had allowed to escape.

Zander tapped his finger against the parchment, narrowing his eyes as he memorized every element. The fabric over the man's face, hiding most of his features. The short hair, unkempt and wild.

Those brutal, narrowed eyes, ready for a fight. Familiar with death.

Now *here* was a fun challenge. An opponent worth killing. The hunt, the stakes, the thrill—Zander craved it.

No, he needed it.

More than anything.

Footsteps thundered down the hallway, muffled through the thick red door, and his ears twitched as he recognized his father's gait. He took a settling breath, determined to convince the man to give him this assignment.

The latch clicked, and as the entry swung open, the Starling patriarch stormed into the room. With pinched brows, his scar stretching from his scowl, Teagan slammed the door behind him without so much as a glance in Zander's direction.

"Quinn will join us after we take our wine," his father said. "Watch what you say, lest she hear us through the door."

Zander shook his head, his fiery hair dangling in his periphery as he glared again at the sketch on the table. "I don't understand why you're sending her, Father, instead of me. I cut off that abomination's hand. Let me finish this."

"You took two fingers," Teagan corrected. "Besides, Quinn is the logical choice."

The Lightseer Master General stalked to the windows and stared out over the lake below, his back to Zander. Outside, the water visible around Teagan's broad shoulders glimmered and glistened in the brilliant sun.

He always did this when he gave orders—back turned, chest out, shoulders strong, voice demanding and certain. It worked on the Lightseers, and Zander planned to use the technique when Lunestone finally passed to him.

Instill fear and lead with unwavering confidence. Only then would the masses obey.

Zander ran a hand through his fire-red hair and closed his eyes as he did his best to bite back the scathing comments clawing at his throat. He knew better than to criticize his father, at least out loud.

If he wanted this assignment, he needed to use subtlety.

"Quinn is capable," he forced himself to admit, gritting his teeth as he gave her the only credit he could truthfully utter. "However, short of liberating Saldia from King Henry's rule, this is easily the most significant mission the Lightseers have ever been given. I don't understand why you would allow her the chance to—"

"Fail?" Teagan finished, immobile as he observed the water.

Zander frowned, studying the man by the open balcony as a cool spring breeze rustled the loose strands of his hair. "Yes."

"You want to go." His father tilted his head just enough for Zander to catch the smirk at the edge of the man's mouth.

"Of course I want to go," he confessed with an exasperated gesture toward the sketch. "Besides, of all people, Quinn couldn't possibly—"

"Your little sister knows what she's doing."

But do you, Father?

Zander bit his knuckle, doing everything he could to choke back the words that so desperately wanted to break free. If he spoke his mind, he could find himself on the other end of a pointless and painfully boring quest as punishment.

With a steadying breath, he closed his eyes again and managed to calm himself down. "Why her?"

"Because you have other things to address closer to home."

"More significant than this?" Zander curled his fingers into a tight fist and leaned his knuckles against the cold stone table as he glared down at the sketch.

"Yes," Teagan said, shrugging. "And no."

Ah.

A game had begun, then. There was more at play than Zander realized. Whatever was at stake somehow had more significance than a stranger in the woods who had stolen the Wraith King from under them all.

In the silence that stretched on after his father's comment, he waited. The chime of a church bell rang through the open balcony, and the world outside moved on even as the political situation of their world forever shifted.

Every player in this game who knew the stakes, however, must've been waiting for the moment to strike. To take what they felt was theirs.

"Your youngest sister is twenty-three." Teagan paced in front of the open balcony doors. "Your other sisters retired properly, and yet Quinn refuses to follow their example. She refuses to choose a husband and hang up her sword. She craves more missions, more assignments, and more war. Starling women have a duty, Zander. To be strong, to learn the ways of the world, and to retire so they can train the next generation. Yet, every time I urge her to consider the next stage of her obligations to this family, every time I press her to set the example for the women across Saldia who long to mirror her every move, she simply refuses."

"Then force her."

Teagan chuckled. "That works for the common folk, I suppose, but our family is and always has been unique, Zander. A Starling woman can't be coerced. We can't make our daughters do anything. When your girls get older, you will understand."

Zander frowned, his gaze shifting toward the window as he once again bit back a retort.

"You don't agree," his father observed.

"Is it that obvious?"

Teagan nodded. "It always is. Your anger gets the best of you. You must learn to control it before you take my place."

"I apologize, Father." His jaw tensed as he swallowed the bubbling opinions desperately clawing at his throat. Lecturing the Lightseer Master General had never ended well for him in the past, and he wasn't about to say something stupid to ruin his chances of stealing this mission from Quinn.

Around his father, silence usually served him best.

"Victoria and Gwendolyn were so easy to retire." Teagan let out an irritated groan. "I don't understand why Quinn has been so difficult. Victoria has always wanted to be a queen, and the kingdom of Dewcrest served her ambitions. She never cared for battle, and she retired the moment I allowed her to. Gwendolyn retired late, certainly, but she did it nonetheless."

"Gwen only did it out of pride," Zander pointed out. "So that she wouldn't be an assassin at Henry's beck and call."

"True," Teagan acknowledged. "However, even she seems to be happier without her sword. Quinn simply baffles me. I can't figure out what that girl wants beyond the battle." He shook his head. "There has to be something."

"She has never been told no, Father. Perhaps you coddle her and give her too much freedom."

Teagan snared him in a frigid gaze. Zander held his father's eye, and even as his body tensed with the anticipation of a brutal lashing, he held his ground.

He did, after all, have a point.

"You're mistaking arrogance for confidence," Teagan chided. "Stop imposing your will on others for once and think through the consequences of your actions."

"Am I wrong?"

"Incredibly so," his father answered. "Say we do this your way, Zander. Say I force her. Say I take her sword and hang it beside her sisters' blades. Say I choose a husband for her. Say I ship her off to Wildefaire, or Kirkwall."

"Or South Haven," he muttered. "Or beyond the known world."

His father chuckled, and the man's icy glare dissolved as the lines around his eyes creased. "Fine, say I send her to South Haven. She's miserable in a land she's only seen a handful of times, shunned by the locals who hate us. She aches for her blade, for battle, and for the thrill of a good fight. You think she will stay indoors and be a good wife? You think she will focus her energy into learning a skill to pass on to her children? You think she will simply wither away in obedience because you or I command it?"

Zander didn't answer. He knew where this was going.

"No," Teagan answered for him. "A warrior like her? Don't be daft. She will break the law. Seek out danger. Disappear for days on end, on some nonsense quest only she cares about because we won't give her any crusades that matter. A Starling is the epitome of Saldian power and grace, son, and if she still has any fight left in her when she retires, she will stain our name."

"I see," Zander said, finally piecing his father's plan together. "That's why you want to give her this mission. To break her first." He rested his knuckles on the table, and they cracked as he smiled. "I like it."

Teagan groaned, his irritation seeping through the stony mask of indifference he usually wore. "You two must learn to get along, Zander. Perhaps when she's retired and the two of you are no longer competing for missions, you will see the good in her."

Unlikely.

Zander kept his mouth shut, even as the word vibrated within him.

"I don't want to break her," Teagan corrected. "It's nothing as violent as that. I simply believe it's time we rid her of these dangerous habits and this thirst for battle she somehow developed. When she fails to find this man in the woods, I will send you instead. I will allow her thirty days for this mission, but I suspect she will waste an entire season out of pride."

"That's risky, Father. Given what the Wraith King can do—"

"I know. That's why you must be ready to act the moment I give the word for you to intervene."

Finally.

Zander sneered and turned his head away from his father to hide his glee at the idea of stealing this from her. "Yes, sir."

"Once her time is up, you may chase this man, even if she hasn't returned." Teagan sighed. "Perhaps you succeeding mere days after her deadline will finally kill her fire. Based on Otmund's reports of this peasant's injuries and fighting style, even a full season won't be enough time for this stranger to mount any sort of assault on us. If she fights it or gives you trouble, I will intervene—and, yes, at that point, I will break her."

It still seemed dangerous. The Wraith King's mere existence threatened the very foundation of Lunestone's power. Something this important couldn't have possibly been worth teaching a life lesson to a girl playing war.

Though he kept his mouth shut, he assumed his opinion was plastered across his face—in the scowl pulling at his cheeks, in the tensed jaw, in the bleached knuckles on his fists.

In the end, his opinion didn't matter. It never did, except the rare occasion when his father explicitly asked for his thoughts. In Teagan's decades leading the Lightseers, they had yet to fail.

It was always better to give the man what he wanted.

Zander sat and pulled his chair closer to the table. Lacing his fingers together, he set his chin on his hands and stared again at the drawing before him.

It took everything in him to not reach for the dagger at his side. The enchanted blade lay secured in a sheath beside his own Firesword, *Valor*. Though he would never have to retire *Valor*, the Bloodbane dagger weighed on his hip, familiar and heavy, only recently cleaned of Henry's blood.

In the scuffle and chaos of Henry's assassination, the two Bloodbane blades had swapped hands many times. Perhaps his father didn't know who wielded them now, and if he did, perhaps he wouldn't tell Quinn it existed.

They wanted her to fail, after all.

She needed the weapon to stand a chance against this villain in the forest. Her dying at the hands of a madman in the woods seemed like a suitable solution, to Zander at least, and he had no intention of giving her one of only two weapons that could kill a wraith.

The soft patter of footsteps outside the door caught his attention, and he rubbed his jaw in frustration at the interruption. Knuckles rapped softly on the wood.

Teagan took his seat at the head of the marble table. "Enter."

The door swung open, and a thin serving girl with long brown hair entered. She carried a golden tray of bread, cheese, and two goblets of wine. Per custom, she set the first of the gem-encrusted cups in front of the nearest person, in this case Zander. As the goblet clinked against the stone surface, she kept her gaze averted out of respect. The scent of lilac washed over him as she passed, her ankles and slippered feet visible beneath her white skirt.

Familiar with being served, Zander leaned back in his chair and waited to speak again until she left. They never discussed anything unless everyone in the room needed to be privy to it, as they could never be too careful.

The Lightseers controlled much of Saldian politics through the kings and queens they advised across the known world. The policies they set in this room—as well as the motivations for those plans—were never discussed with anyone else.

As the serving girl rounded the table and set the second goblet before his father, Zander took a sip of his wine. The golden tray glinted in the light as she placed it on the table between them, and a brown curl fell over her shoulder as the tray slid across the marble.

Her job done, she retreated, her gait a little quicker now. Teagan's eyes lingered on her as she left, his gaze hungry, as though he had noticed a new plate of food at a feast.

Perhaps he was sleeping around again, even though he had promised his wife so many times before that he was done. A surge of protective anger burned in Zander's chest, since he hated watching his mother cry when she found out about a new mistress, but he buried it with another sip of wine.

His father commanded the Lightseers, and Zander had no authority to question the man's morals. Besides, it was nothing new.

As the door shut and the servant girl's footsteps receded, Teagan took a sip of his wine. "Last night, several more Discovered were seen in the north, near Hazeltide's northern border. A handful escaped his army when they intervened. It's believed they're hiding in the Frost Forest."

Zander frowned, rubbing the red stubble along his jaw as he sat with the news. "Are the Discovered losing control? Are these things killing people again?"

"It appears so. We still don't know what they are, Zander. They might look like us, but they're not human. The way they react to our spellgust and reagents is dangerous, and we need to study them in detail." Teagan paused, a thin smile on his face as he glanced at Zander over his wine. "That's why the Hazeltide soldiers managed to capture one this time. Alive."

"*Alive?*" Zander leaned forward, gaping in disbelief as his father nodded. "How? Every time we've gotten close, they've lost control of their magic and killed everyone around them, including themselves. How could

Hazeltide, of all the kingdoms, possibly—"

"Luck," Teagan interrupted. "Hazeltide is full of whores, addicts, and conmen, but you can't deny that kingdom has incredible luck."

"Can I see this creature?" Zander asked. "Where is it? Are they bringing it here?"

"I thought you wanted to kill the man in the woods?" Teagan grinned, reaching across the table to tap the sketch with his finger.

"This is a suitable distraction until Quinn fails, I suppose."

His father laughed, shaking his head as he stood and returned to his place by the windows. "Yes, well, as long as I have your permission, boy."

Zander pinched his eyes shut and took a steadying breath to calm the rising surge of annoyance at the subtle slur.

Boy.

Leave the strategizing to the adults.

Go. Listen. Obey.

Never mind his thirty-three years. Never mind his four children. Never mind his hundred and three successful missions through the years. Until his father passed Lunestone to him, Zander would never receive the respect he truly deserved.

When the rush of irritation finally receded, he wove his fingers together and leaned his elbows on the table. "I assume I'll have to travel to Hazeltide to study something this dangerous?"

Teagan nodded and drank again from his goblet.

"Beyond studying the Discovered, what do I need to do while I'm in Hazeltide?"

"Figure out where they're coming from," his father answered. "When you find their entrance, don't block it. Don't close it. Simply sit, wait, and learn. Capture any you can and use the strongest enchantments you can find to contain them. The more of those things we can study, the more useful they might be."

"Why wouldn't we block them from entering Saldia? Each one of these creatures kills a dozen or more people each time—"

"Because they might be useful, Zander." His father lifted his chin as a cloud passed over the sun. "Because they are more powerful than us and more in tune with magic than we are. I want to know why."

Zander tensed his jaw and took another sip of his wine. "Very well, Father."

"You leave in two weeks."

"Why must I wait?"

"There is a power void in the capital. Before you leave to study your new toy, you must ensure the void remains until summer." Teagan looked over his shoulder, catching Zander's eye. "Concoct whatever stories the public will believe, but they must not know Henry is dead. Understood?"

Zander nodded. It seemed he had quite a lot to occupy him until Quinn failed, and it was for the best. He had never much been one to sit idly and wait.

Two loud knocks thumped against the door, and Zander flinched. He hadn't heard any footsteps. No breath or other indication that anyone stood outside the door at all.

He frowned, glaring at the red entry and already well aware of who it must've been.

"Come in, Quinn." Teagan took another swig of his wine.

Zander glared at the door with a fury he no longer bothered to mask. The entry swung open, and his little sister joined them. Thick red and orange hair framed a flawless face, complete with a smattering of freckles across her nose. Her soft hazel eyes darted toward him briefly, passing over him as if he weren't even there, and she returned her attention to their father as she shut the door behind her.

"You wanted to see me, Father?" Quinn leaned against the wall, crossing one ankle over the other as she rested her head against the stone. Arms crossed. Posture relaxed. At ease despite the severity of the situation.

Never sitting. Always standing along the edges. Never really one of them.

Her tailored black coat hid the augmentations covering her arms, each one of them evidence of the pampered indulgence of a spoiled daughter.

Teagan nodded. "What did you hear through the door, my dear?"

"Oh, uh—" She cleared her throat and scratched at her jaw.

Caught.

"Quinn," their father said, a warning in his tone.

"King Henry is dead," she answered. "But I already heard that rumor. It sounds like you're sending Zander to ensure there's not a panic in the Capital."

"Very good." Teagan nodded and smiled at her. "Excellent deductions."

She stood a little taller at the compliment. "It's true? King Henry is really dead?"

"It's true. How many in the castle know?"

"Only a few of the elite. We're keeping it contained. Do you know what happened? How did—"

"I have a mission for you," he interrupted with a nod to the sketch on the table.

Zander could've offered it to her. If it were anyone else, he would've lifted it and saved them the few steps around the table, but he didn't. He simply watched as she snatched the parchment off the marble.

Quinn had been vying for a spot on the Lightseer Chamber for years, and deep down, he had always been concerned their father might indulge her little fantasy and grant it. Even if this was her final mission—her final chance to butt in and take his glory yet again—he simply couldn't wait to be rid of her.

She scanned the drawing. "Who is this?"

"A traitor," Teagan said calmly. "He's the man responsible for the death of King Henry."

A lie.

The dishonesty eased Zander's concern that she might somehow win back their father's favor yet again. His shoulders relaxed, and he sipped his wine to hide the smirk on his face.

She might've been their father's favorite, but at least the man didn't trust her completely. She was his little doll, something he paraded around and showed off, but only Zander had the potential to ever be the man's equal. Only Zander could ever earn their father's true respect.

Now, for the ultimate test—whether or not the Lightseer Master General told Quinn the secrets of the simmering souls. If she were to stand a chance of surviving this mission, she needed to know what she was about to face.

"He overwhelmed and murdered Henry, Quinn," their father said as he handed her an envelope from his pocket. "You must be careful."

"What about Henry's ghoul?" she asked. "Was that thing destroyed?"

"We believe so," their father lied. "Whatever that atrocity was, it shouldn't affect your mission."

Zander's hidden smile stretched into a full grin. He drained the last of his wine as he did his best to hide it.

Teagan tapped the envelope in her hand, and the paper crinkled at his touch. "Everything we know so far is in here. Take the sketch. Take this information and bring him in alive. You have thirty days."

"Alive?" she asked, a twinge of disappointment in her voice.

"Alive," their father confirmed, lifting one stern eyebrow to admonish her before she had the chance to do anything mischievous.

"If this is the man who killed King Henry, shouldn't he be brought to justice? Why should we allow him to live if he—"

"You're not the executioner," Zander snapped. "Father is solely responsible for delivering this man to justice, not you."

Her eyes narrowed. She glared down at him, her nose creasing with disdain at the interruption.

"Zander is right, my dear," Teagan said. "It is not your place to punish him. You may break his bones and cut off his limbs if you like, so long as he's brought in alive."

A small pout tugged at her lips, but she eventually nodded. "I understand. I won't disappoint you, Father."

"I know you won't." Their father curled one finger under her jaw and lifted her chin as he proudly smiled down at her.

With that, she slid the sketch and the envelope in the pocket of her tan riding pants and left the room. As she passed Zander, her eyes darted again to his. With her back to their father, she smirked ever so slightly in victory.

He scowled as the door shut behind her. Sometimes, he wished he could wring her skinny neck, but he took solace in knowing she would be married off within the year. Soon, he would be rid of her, and some poor fool would be stuck with her for life.

If he only had to see her at the winter feast each year, he could live with that. If not—if she didn't break and instead held onto her fire—he wasn't sure how much longer he could stand his father's precious miracle child. The one who almost wasn't. The baby who had crawled back from the grave, too powerful for even Death to claim.

The one Zander had always suspected might not have been legitimate—despite that blazing red hair.

CHAPTER SEVENTEEN
QUINN

As night fell outside Quinn's suite in Lunestone Castle, she furiously packed her bag. Clothes littered the sofas and chairs spread across her suite of rooms in the western tower, but she didn't care about the mess.

After all, she only had thirty days to hunt down the man who had killed their king.

Dozens of weapons lay strewn across the long table in the center of her sitting room. Though the spartan workbench clashed with the blue silk curtains and cotton couches her mother had insisted on adding, Quinn had slowly tailored the suite to her own tastes over the years. After staining too many sheets with blood and grime as she had cleaned her swords on her bed, her father had ordered this table built and a suite in the castle redesigned for her. Living in his manor on the far end of the lake's large island had kept her away from the missions, away from the training, away from her fellow Lightseers.

Even if the other elite kept their distance from her, she preferred to be close by. It was the only way to snatch opportunities like the one she had gotten tonight.

Side by side, her twenty-five gleaming daggers lay in a neat row beside her Firesword *Aurora*. With her bag half-filled, Quinn tenderly ran her fingers over the enchanted blade. The magnificent sword glowed at her touch, connected to her, and a ribbon of emerald-green light snaked through the steel.

Partners, to the end.

With a cursory glance to the two small axes already packed in her bag, she began to slide the sharp and deadly daggers still on the table into the various sheaths and hiding places along her body. Her boots. Her calf. A hidden sheath on her thigh. Sure, she used magic in most fights, but sometimes a sharp blade ended an argument faster.

Per Starling tradition, a woman wielded her blade to defend her home against those who would destroy it. Until she retired, she remained ready to serve the Lightseers and wield her magic in ways few ever dreamed.

Flames flickered in the sconces along the walls, and the ornate furniture cast long shadows across the many rugs that kept the drafty rooms of her suite warm. The tapestries depicted Starling battles from centuries ago, and though she had researched each story exhaustively, they all ended the same—the Starling lopped off someone's head, and then the kingdom they had saved feasted in their honor.

Dull war stories. Nothing real. Nothing worth remembering.

As she stuffed an extra shirt into the bag, the door to her bedroom caught her eye. It sat ajar, the bed swallowed by shadows in the growing night. A moonbeam caught the silk draped over the canopy frame.

It would be a long time before she slept here again.

When she grabbed the final dagger off of the table, she lifted it in her palm. Firelight glinted off its cold steel. With her fingers tight around the hilt, she drove the dagger into the table. Dozens of other marks littered its surface, each of them symbolic.

One mark for every mission. One cross for every failure.

Only seven crosses mingled with the other marks, their gouges deeper than the others. They served as reminders of the mistakes she had made and the lessons that had made her stronger through the years.

She left the dagger upright in the wood, a sign to any who entered that she would return eventually.

Finally, she reached *Aurora* and held it aloft. Amber light from the sconces sang along the blade as the weapon weighed on her palm, friendly and familiar. A green spellgust stone glowed in the hilt, the source of all the blade's magic.

Starlings embodied fire. Her family were the only ones to master the element in ways others could never even dream. And, per the law her ancestors had written, only Starlings wielded Fireswords against those who threatened the land.

An honor. A timeless tradition. A responsibility she didn't take lightly.

Quinn had been born into a life of privilege and blessings, and she thanked her lucky stars every day for it. She had always vowed to earn her keep, one way or another.

She slid the sword into its sheath and strapped it to her waist. The augmentations along her bare arms glowed, and she tugged on her coat to hide them. Beyond Lunestone and the larger cities, augmentations scared the common folk. Her augmentations set her apart and warned the villagers that she had access to magic and money beyond anything they could fathom.

Some worshiped her. Others despised her. Regardless, they all feared her, even if she hated the way they avoided her gaze.

All she had to do was exist, and most people kept their distance.

The tap of boots against the stone floor outside interrupted her thoughts, the sound muffled by the thick door to the hallway. Moments later, a sharp knock rattled the wood, and she groaned with annoyance. Zander had probably come to taunt her. To demoralize her or do anything he could to ease his wounded pride.

Again.

"Come in." She sat on the table with one hand on *Aurora's* pommel. The dagger still sat upright beside her, half its blade embedded in the table as she glared at the entry.

Instead of her ass of a brother, however, a familiar bald head peeked through a gap in the door. Otmund smiled, his eyes crinkling with mischief as their gazes met. "I'm not supposed to be here. You won't tell your father I came to say goodbye, will you?"

She chuckled, her shoulders relaxing as she heaved a sigh of relief. "He kicked you out again?"

Her mentor shrugged. "Doesn't he always?"

"What can I do for you, Uncle?" she asked. "I assume you know about my mission if you're seeing me off."

As much as she admired his cunning and mastery of magic, it unnerved her that he seemed to know everything. About Saldia. About Oakenglen.

About her family.

"I know exactly where you're going, actually." Otmund rubbed his hands together as he looked absently around the room. "It's a mission I asked for."

A small smile tugged at the corner of her mouth. "You asked Father to assign this to me?"

"Let's just say I pulled a few strings." His mischievous smile widened, confirming it for her.

"Thank you," she said sincerely. "This is easily the most important mission I've ever been sent on."

His smile faltered. "And the most dangerous."

She shrugged. "It's part of the job."

"You're right." He tilted his head, his eyes creasing with pride. "I know you won't disappoint us."

"I wouldn't dream of it. When I bring this man back, maybe Father will stop talking about my retirement."

"Perhaps." Otmund's eyes shimmered yet again with mischief.

Her eyes narrowed in playful suspicion. "You know something. What aren't you telling me?"

"You'll see," he said, waving the question away.

"You're no fun." Wringing information from Otmund was like pulling teeth.

She enjoyed his company. Always had. In the magical summers she and her mother had spent in Mossvale when Quinn was little, he had always been kind to her. Like a second father, but one who understood affection. The one who understood her thirst for mischief. The one who had taught her ways to use magic beyond what even her father seemed to know.

Quinn was not, however, an idiot. Not all his mischief was lighthearted, and she wasn't such a fool that she couldn't see through his charm.

He always wanted something, and he had an uncanny way of getting it. Every time.

"Be careful." Otmund set his hands on her shoulders. "I wouldn't want my favorite Starling hurt over something as trivial as a man in the woods."

"A treasonous *assassin* in the woods," she corrected, tilting her head slightly to drive home the point. "Nothing about this mission is trivial, Uncle."

This wouldn't be a pleasant jaunt through the forest, after all.

He sighed and gently squeezed her shoulders. "You're right. Forgive me. I'm just nervous for you, my girl, but I believe in you. I know you can do this."

In a world that expected her to be perfect and punished her failures with pain, Quinn couldn't deny the pang of joy that came from someone simply believing in her. He knew that, however human and flawed she might've been, she could still do great things.

This mission would not end with another cross on her table.

She would not let her father—or Otmund—down. One way or another, this man in the woods would return to Lunestone in shackles. And if he gave her any trouble, her father had already granted her permission to chop off a few limbs.

CHAPTER EIGHTEEN
CONNOR

Another day had passed, and with it went more of Connor's pain. The Bloodbane injury was healing far faster than he had expected, but it wasn't gone.

Not yet.

As the last threads of sunlight faded from the ancient forest around him, Connor closed his eyes to savor the taste of spring on the air. The bite of fresh grass. The oaky musk of fallen bark. The hint of jasmine hiding somewhere amongst the trees.

Without warning, the wound in his side spasmed. He stifled a yell, the agony crackling through him in an unexpected rush, and he pressed his palm against the cloth bandage as he rode out the tsunami of pain. The forest floor tilted underneath him as what remained of the dagger's magic ate away at his body, and he set his free hand on his knee for balance. The pain lessened a little more with each dawn, but not enough for him to strike out on his own.

That damn Otmund. Come hell or high water, Connor vowed to kill him for this.

He forced himself to take slow and steady breaths, counting the seconds in each inhale to calm his racing heart. As his pulse finally slowed, the pain subsided—but it didn't disappear.

As he meandered through the woods not far from Ethan's home, he discovered a meadow. With one hand still on his injury, he leaned against a tree and eased himself onto the soft ground at its roots. Rain-dampened soil stained his pants, seeping through the fabric, but he didn't care.

He stared out at the meadow grasses as they shivered in the wind. In the approaching dusk, their blades hummed with a faint green light. Overhead, stars gathered in the darkening sky, nothing but pinpricks in the eternal black.

The Wraith King had stayed silent today, without so much as a flitting appearance between the trees. Perhaps the ghost had continued to study him, or perhaps the dead man had simply grown bored.

Either way, an ancient warlord wouldn't be content to wait in the woods. Yesterday, the ghoul had demanded blood and movement, and Connor suspected his new undead companion wouldn't stay silent for long.

Their truce meant he could take the time he needed to heal, but it wouldn't last much longer than that. As much as he hated to admit it, they needed each other.

Damn it all.

Out here in this unforgiving forest, Connor had a choice: stay and heal, but put these good people in danger; or leave and brave the woods with an injury that slowed his timing and compromised his chances of survival.

Shit choices all around.

The crunch of heavy boots on dry leaves shattered the forest's peaceful silence. A few twittering birds in the canopy hushed, and the flutter of wings on the air signaled their departure as someone unknowingly scared them off.

Connor's ear twitched as the footsteps approached. Loud thuds. Long strides between each step.

Ethan.

"Where the hell did that man get to?" the carpenter muttered under his breath, a good twenty yards away. "Too good at covering his tracks, that one—"

"Over here, Ethan," Connor said.

A sharp intake of breath followed—a quiet gasp of surprise, no doubt. Several leaves crackled, flattened to dust under the man's heavy boots as he shifted his weight, and Connor waved his left hand out from behind his tree to signal where he was.

"Speak of the devil," Ethan shouted as his footsteps thundered closer, his voice almost painfully loud to Connor's enhanced senses. "What are you doing all the way out here?"

"Surveying the land to make sure there are no immediate threats," he confessed. "Old habits are hard to break, and I needed a walk. From the state of that treehouse, you haven't lived here in years. There's no telling who or what moved in while you were away."

The stocky man rounded the tree, breathing heavily as he leaned against the old pine and stared out at the soft green glow of the meadow. "Well, now that's a pretty sight."

"It is," Connor agreed. "But it's also a bad omen. I don't see grass glow like that in the Ancient Woods. I've only ever seen that happen around spellgust mines, so I assume there must be a natural deposit nearby."

"Then we'd best not stay long."

Connor nodded. "Where there's spellgust, there are soldiers. If they haven't found this mine yet, it's just a matter of time."

Ethan cursed softly under his breath and rubbed his eyes, a hint of the dark bags from yesterday still visible despite a good night's rest. "It feels like the forest gets smaller each year."

"Quite the contrary." Connor stood, grimacing as the wound in his side ripped a bit with the movement. He set a hand on the tree for balance. "The forest to the south is as wild as ever. Fewer mountains means less spellgust, fewer blightwolves, and fewer soldiers."

"Perhaps I took us in the wrong direction, then," Ethan muttered, his shoulders drooping as he glared off into the growing shadows amongst the trees.

"What do you mean?"

"Ah. Well, uh—" The man rubbed his jaw, and his eyes slipped briefly out of focus. "We're originally from Lindow, a few days south of here. Let's just say I took the family north to escape the place and leave it at that."

Connor frowned. Commoners like him and Ethan only needed to escape when they found themselves on the wrong side of the law. If his time in Kirkwall had taught him anything, it was that good men could make mistakes and wind up dead for it.

"You don't have to tell me," Connor said.

Ethan smiled with gratitude. "The south may have more options, but it's best if we stay near Bradford. We know the folks there, and they don't mind our way of life. A new town with new faces might not be as welcoming."

"Fair point."

Silence settled into the air as they watched the glowing meadow grass bend in a soft breeze, the magic in the woodland's roots on full display in the fading light. The trees swayed around them, in perfect harmony with the timeless forest's ballad of wind and birdsong.

With a sharp and brutal pang, the injury in Connor's side spasmed again, and he gritted his teeth to ride out the pain. A twinge of guilt snaked through him as he thought again of Otmund, of the Wraith King, of the storm brewing in this world—with him at its center, and Ethan's family in the line of fire.

"I shouldn't stay, Ethan," he admitted.

The carpenter snorted derisively. "Nonsense. We won't have it any other way. There's plenty of food."

"You don't understand. I'm risking your lives by being here. That man in the field will be looking for me. I, uh…" He leaned his head back against the tree and stared into the darkening sky, wondering how to word this. "I have something he wants. Something that could get you all killed."

Ethan nodded, looking off into the trees as he crossed his thick arms. "I know."

"I highly doubt that."

"We live in the Ancient Woods, Connor." The man scowled, not bothering to mask his irritation. "We're not soft and squishy folk. There's magic out here. Real magic. The dark sort. We've seen it, and we've seen what it does to people. Whatever you stepped in back in those ruins, you're not getting out of it. You're a part of something we don't understand, sure, but we didn't bring you here lightly. We know there's risk, and we did it anyway because it was—and still is, you hear—the right thing to do."

Connor rubbed his eyes as he thought again of the wraith now fused with his soul. "I'm not convinced you want to take this risk."

True, the Wraith King couldn't kill him—but the ghost could, conceivably, kill these people. He couldn't control the ghoul, and he had no idea what horrors waited for him the moment the world learned of what had happened.

A king had died at his feet, and Oakenglen loved a good scapegoat to blame for its troubles.

"Risks. Bah." Ethan squared his shoulders, hands on his waist as he stared Connor down. "Do you think we sit in that tree, laughing over freshly baked bread every night? Do you think this is easy? Every spring, slavers comb through this forest on the way to Dewcrest, snatching travelers to sell on the black markets. You know what they do with those people?"

Connor stiffened, wondering where this conversation was going. The carpenter simply glared at him, those broad shoulders tense as he waited for an answer.

"I don't know," he confessed.

"They sell them to potion makers." Ethan gestured into the woods in the vague direction of the main road. "They take them underground, force them to drink untested potions to discover what those recipes do, and bleed them dry when they're no longer useful because human blood is a reagent. Did you know that, Connor? It's a highly coveted reagent, might I add, to make a potion stronger."

"How do you know all of this?" Connor flexed the fingers on his left hand, frowning as he listened. None of this seemed consistent with a man who couldn't even make a Rectivane.

"Because I've lost good friends," Ethan snapped, and a vein throbbed in his temple as he rubbed his jaw. "Good men, dead and gone because of a potion maker's greed."

Ah.

Connor absently rubbed his neck, wondering how many of the augmented soldiers he'd idolized as a boy had also bled good men dry.

"Dewcrest and Hazeltide have blossoming black markets," Ethan continued as he stared out over the enchanted field. "There's coin to be made, and they're running out of people. So, those bastards come here."

The stocky man kicked off the tree, and pine needles shook loose from the branches as the trunk shook. Ethan stalked into the glowing meadow grass, the blades brushing against his tunic. A shimmering glow blurred after him as he walked, as distorted and faint as starlight.

"Every year, I set traps." Ethan smacked a nearby clump of the tall grasses, and the blow stirred flecks of emerald green light into the air. "I plant fake blightwolf prints. I leave signs of the creatures to deter the slavers from going near the house. Every year, Wesley and I lead them away. If the slavers weren't enough, I have to listen for the blightwolves every night and risk my life to drive them off if they get too close. I don't want them to stake out the house and set a trap for us."

A gust rolled through the meadow. The grasses bent, shivering as the wind shook loose more dots of light. The feral magic curled into the air and sailed over the trees.

Ethan gestured to the forest around them. "Living out here isn't a fairytale, Connor, and no one in that house takes this choice lightly. Even the girls understand the danger. At every moment, my family's lives are in peril, but we know the risks that come with living in this forest just as well as you do. We hide our tracks. We're silent at night. We're careful, always, and if we one day fail—if the slavers or wolves find us, despite our caution—at least we lived good, free lives. No politics of the towns. No robbers in the shadows. No daughters disappearing into an alley when—"

He choked, and he couldn't finish the thought. Connor raised one eyebrow as Ethan turned his back, and a lull settled into the field.

The burly man cleared his throat, the cough harsh and grating in the otherwise whisper-quiet woods. "Look, I don't care if you're a superior fighter to me. I don't care what's chasing you now. Whatever you know about this world and this forest, don't you dare imply I'm some weak-willed fool who doesn't know how to protect his own damn family."

Ethan stared off into the meadow with his thick arms crossed over his chest.

In the silence that followed, a bird sang through the treetops. Connor let its voice fill the night because he didn't know how to respond. No one had spoken to him like that in years, and with one palm still against the tree, he sat with the weight of what he'd just heard.

He couldn't deny the facts. He needed to heal, and the Finns had given him a place to rest. Every day he stayed, they faced death from every direction, but these were hardy folk used to risking their lives. Hell, even getting breakfast ready could've killed them if they weren't careful.

Danger and doing right by each other was all they knew.

"Supper is ready," Ethan said, breaking the quiet. "Let's get back to the house."

The stocky man headed into the forest, gesturing for Connor to follow as he disappeared behind the pine tree. At first, Connor didn't move. He hooked his thumb through his belt loop and stared at the fading dots of glowing dust on the breeze.

With a sigh, he eventually pushed off the trunk and followed Ethan.

The carpenter strode through the trees at a quick pace, his boots crunching over leaves with each step, and Connor trailed behind. His footsteps landed effortlessly on the ground, naturally finding the gaps between the decaying debris of autumn as he passed silently through the forest.

After a few minutes, Ethan looked over his shoulder, his brow pinched with concern. The moment his eyes landed on Connor, he jumped with surprise.

He paused and set a hand on his chest, laughing with shock. "You're eerily silent, my friend."

"Apologies," Connor said with a wry smile.

They walked together through the trees, shoulder to shoulder as they neared the treetop hut. Connor kept his attention on the forest, ear straining for the telltale howl of a blightwolf as the last ribbons of light faded.

Thankfully, the forest remained quiet tonight.

"How's that injury on your side?" Ethan asked.

"Better," he lied.

"How long until you're fully healed?"

He laughed. "Are you trying to get rid of me after all?"

"Trying to put you to work is more like it. I need help building a new house if you'll lend a hand."

Connor had vowed to earn his keep. "Of course. I can't be sure, but I figure I'll be better within a week or two. Before, a blow like that would have laid me low at least a season, if I'd managed to survive it at all."

Ethan frowned. "Before what?"

"Oh. Uh—" Connor tilted his head away to hide a frustrated grimace. He needed to be more careful.

People couldn't know about the Wraith King. Not yet, and maybe not ever.

"Nothing." He flicked his wrist, hoping the conversation would simply die.

"Ah," Ethan said, apparently piecing it together. "Before the ruins. Before you found whatever it is other people want."

"Perhaps."

"It's all right, Connor. You don't have to tell me."

Not that he would, of course. The Finns were better off if they simply didn't know.

The charred haze of campfire smoke coiled through the air, the warm scent soft and subtle at first. It grew stronger and thicker with each step toward the house. The gurgle of the brook whispered through the trees shortly thereafter, soothing in the looming night.

Tall red flowers swayed in the soft evening breeze as Connor and Ethan neared the waterway, and reeds along the bank tilted with the current as the water ambled eastward.

With each step, Connor drank in the forest, knowing his days in this wood were numbered. The thunder of a waterfall rumbled, and a strange sense of nostalgia washed over him as the familiar mist clung to his face and neck.

Ethan set one hand on the ladder into the canopy and hoisted himself up the trunk. "Everyone else is already inside. Let's eat."

Connor waited at the base of the tree to give the man a head start as the towering oak swayed gently back and forth in the wind. When Ethan reached the halfway point, Connor hoisted himself up the ladder as well. Each step pulled on the injury in his side, but he forced himself onward. A ladder made finding evening cover in the trees much easier than climbing a trunk on his own.

It could've been far worse.

His fingers wrapped around one of the rungs halfway up the trunk, and as he tightened his grip to pull himself upward, the wood splintered in his palm.

With his balance gone, he fell.

Connor cursed under his breath as he slipped down the trunk, and with seconds to spare, his other hand tightened on another rung. The movement sent ripples of pain down his side as his injury screamed. He pressed his forehead into the rough bark and gritted his teeth to stifle a yell.

Not one to dally, he reached for the next rung and continued up the makeshift ladder despite the pain—though he hurried this time, eager to get this over with. When he finally pulled himself through the framed wooden opening and onto the rickety porch, he paused to survey the structure. A few missing planks in the porch floor gave him a clear view of the ground thirty feet below, and the unstable railing swung on a single nail as the tree swayed.

Ethan offered him a hand, and he took it. The man pulled him to his feet and headed for the front door, ignoring a small hole at the corner of the house large enough for one of those damned thieving squirrels to pass through.

Connor gestured to the porch. "This place isn't structurally sound, Ethan."

"We won't be here long. Just enough time to build some place better."

Ethan opened the door, and the warm aroma of clove and roasting meat rolled through the entry as they stepped inside. The sweet and crusty fragrance of fresh bread mingled with the spices in the air, and Connor's stomach growled on cue. Every part of his primal soul ached for him to simply grab whatever food he could find, but he straightened his back and forced himself to be calm.

A man was only as strong as his self-restraint, and he wouldn't succumb to the Wraith King's demand that he take what he needed. He would wait and eat what they gave him.

Wesley sat at the table that filled most of the kitchen, his bowl pushed toward the center as he leaned his elbows on the wooden surface. He smiled as Connor entered and tapped his finger along the wood in an inconsistent rhythm.

Hungry, but patient. A good kid.

In the far corner, Kiera leaned over the stove as steam billowed from a pot and snaked through a makeshift vent to the outside. Armed with a wooden spoon, she stirred a stew of some sort and breathed in deeply, her eyes fluttering closed as she smiled.

When Ethan shut the door behind them, her eyes snapped open. "There you two are! Good. We're all famished. Girls! Time to eat!"

An eruption of giggling and the patter of feet raced along the hallway floor as the girls obeyed their mother. Ethan sat at the head of the table with his back to the door and reached his arms toward the ceiling, his joints popping as he leaned into the stretch.

Connor waited, still unfamiliar with suppertime protocol. He usually took his meals under the stars and ate whatever he found that wouldn't poison him. Short of last night and the occasional inn, he hadn't even eaten at a table since his days with Beck Arbor—and that had been in stony silence, alone, usually long after the old man had gone to bed.

Fiona raced around the corner and hopped onto the nearest stool before patting her palms against the table surface. The little girl licked her lips, staring at the pot on the stove as she waited as patiently as a seven-year-old could.

Isabella peeked around the corner leading into the hallway, with barely any of her body visible as she hid behind the wall. Her eyes landed on Connor and instantly widened. With a little gasp, she retreated into the shadows of the corridor.

"It's okay, Isabella." Ethan rested one elbow on his knee and leaned toward her hiding place. "He won't hurt you."

"Sorry, Connor." Kiera let out a weary sigh as she carried the iron pot to the center of the table. "It'll take some time for her to get used to you."

"It's fine." He didn't have much experience with children, anyway. He had been on his own for so long that he didn't even know how to talk to one.

Still standing on the outskirts of the family as they gathered around their table, he rubbed the stubble along his jaw, not entirely sure what to make of these people.

They pulled at a part of him he'd assumed was long dead.

"You're at the other head of the table, down there." Kiera nodded to an empty stool behind her as she returned to the stove. "Across from Ethan."

As Connor sat, Isabella snuck into the kitchen. With her eyes glued on him, she nervously inched her way toward the stool next to her father. Kiera grabbed the loaf of bread out of their makeshift oven and placed it beside the stew as she took her place to Ethan's right.

Last night, the conversation had been stiff and awkward. He'd felt like a visitor, imposing on others. Tonight, however, felt different.

Tonight, he sat at a family dinner, something he hadn't experienced in eight long years.

"We need to scout for a new place," Ethan said as he ripped off a piece of bread from the loaf. "Kiera, did you have any—"

"Hell, no, Ethan." She laughed as she ladled stew into her bowl. "I picked the last place, and we all saw how well that went."

Wesley and Ethan chuckled in unison.

"What about you, Connor?" the man asked as Kiera reached over

Wesley and poured some stew into Connor's bowl. "Do you know any good places to the west of Bradford?"

"I don't."

As Kiera ladled soup into his bowl, he smiled to her in silent thanks and swirled his spoon through the broth. Chunks of meat and potatoes swam through the stew, and his hunger got the best of him. Though he ached to shovel it all into his face, he paused to savor the aroma of something warm and hardy—rather than his usual diet of quickly roasted meat—before he took his first bite.

Heaven.

"I haven't been this far north in probably five or six years," he confessed. "Even then, it was only to run an errand. I didn't scout much of the forest."

"Where were you headed?" Ethan asked. "What was this errand?"

"Don't be nosy." Kiera gently smacked her husband on the shoulder.

The carpenter shrugged. "It's an honest question."

"It's fine," Connor said with a wave of his hand. "I went to Bradford to get a few potions for an old farmer. Nothing impressive. Nothing important."

Ethan nodded. "Ah, that makes sense. The sorceress in the woods is a legend in these parts. She makes the best potions for miles."

"So I've been told," Connor said with a glance at Wesley.

"Watch your language," Kiera chided. "Such slurs, Ethan. Honestly, you're better than that. She's a witch, pure and simple."

"Is sorceress a bad word, Mama?" Fiona asked.

Kiera scowled at her husband. "Perhaps you'd like to answer that?"

Ethan chuckled. "It is, Fiona. It's very rude to call someone that. Calling them a witch is a sign of respect, and it's more polite than using sor—" He cleared his throat as he glanced over at Kiera. "It's more polite than using the other word. Witches and warlocks don't follow the Lightseer or necromancer codes. They practice on their own. Calling someone a sorceress is like calling your mother a nag. They won't like it."

"Ethan!" Kiera smacked him on the shoulder, harder this time.

Laughter bubbled around the table as Kiera shook her head and shoveled more stew into her mouth in an attempt to hide her own widening grin.

Connor took a bite of bread. "This sor—uh, *witch* wasn't there when I visited Bradford. I visited the potion master in his shop on the main road through town. I hadn't heard of the woman in the woods back then."

"Look at him, all brooding and serious," Kiera said with a smirk as she set down her spoon. "Is this really how you are, or is this all an attempt to look dark and threatening to impress us?"

He chuckled as laughter erupted again around him. Instead of answering, he chose to eat another spoonful of stew.

Poking fun. Jokes. Happiness.

He couldn't deny how much he had missed this.

"Don't let her nag you, son." Ethan grinned and cast a sidelong glance at his wife.

Connor stilled, and the word echoed in his mind like a song.

Son.

Wesley said something, and another bubble of laughter echoed through the room, but Connor tuned it out. His ears rang, the words blurring together, and a sense of looming danger washed over him.

The Wraith King waited in the shadows outside. Otmund wouldn't dally, and Connor suspected the world would soon hunt him. The brewing hurricane would hit with rage and thunder, but he couldn't face it until he had healed.

Limping blindly into the darkness would've only gotten him killed, and he had nothing to prove to anyone.

For now, he needed to heal. If he went into the forest with an injury like this, he wouldn't last long.

Besides, he could let himself breathe and enjoy life, if only for a short time. With everything that would soon hunt him, he figured he wouldn't get something like this broken little hut in the trees for a while—or, possibly, ever again.

After all, he was a dead man walking. King Henry had said so himself.

CHAPTER NINETEEN
QUINN

The frigid wind whipped through Quinn's hair as she leaned against her mount's neck, and her fingertips pressed into the soft fur of her winged tiger Blaze.

Together, they flew over the ancient forest in tune to the steady howl of air past her ear and the soft pant of Blaze's breath. The powerful muscles in the vougel's back rose and fell with each wingbeat, but the regal creature would need a break soon. They had flown through the night and rested briefly at an inn to get his strength back, but she didn't have time to waste.

One day of her hunt, gone. Only twenty-nine left.

As dusk fell on the somber forest below her, Quinn had to make a choice: find a tavern in Bradford and wait out the night in safety, or hunt in the darkness with the blightwolves.

Exhaustion tugged at her tired eyes, and she stifled a yawn. Blaze growled softly, the sound almost muted in the howling wind, and he banked to the right as they followed the main road south. Per usual, Blaze kept as close to the clouds as he could to go unnoticed, and by now Quinn had grown accustomed to the thinner air as they soared ever higher.

The common folk didn't like vougels. Centuries of folklore and tavern songs had convinced them these beautiful winged tigers were omens of death and war, instead of the majestic and proud creatures they truly were. She didn't want to cause a panic by taking Blaze too close to the local villages and farms—unless she needed to press them for information, of course, in which case a bit of intimidation and fear would serve her well.

She patted her vougel gently on the neck, and Blaze growled with delight. Their connection opened, as it did every time they touched, but she didn't say anything. She simply savored the rush of his emotions as they came through.

Contentment. Joy. Devotion.

Good. He was happy. Despite a vougel's stamina and ferocity in battle, a grumpy Blaze meant next to nothing would be accomplished once they landed.

As Quinn's eyelids drooped again, she rubbed her temple and swung her pack off her shoulder and into her lap. With the bag's leather safety strap wrapped tightly around her palm, she let her vougel take the lead. Though she had opted long ago to go without reins, he listened intently to her silent and subtle commands. He already knew their route, and he followed the soft brown line of the road that carved through the thick oak trees of this foreboding forest.

She rifled through the pack, past the clothes and stowed weapons until her fingers brushed the glass bottles of her potion collection. What she could take with her was only a trifle compared to the vast stores of magic in her suite back in Lunestone, but these specific concoctions served her best when on the road. A small, custom-sewn cloth protected each of the carefully catalogued potions, and she had labeled each with a secret code only she knew to protect her stores from thieves.

Even these few dozen potions could've fetched a small fortune on the black market, and she wouldn't let even one break. Zander usually destroyed a third of his vials when on a mission, but to him, money meant nothing. Magic meant nothing. *People* meant nothing.

Quinn would never be like him.

In the low light, her Eyebright augmentation kicked in, enhancing her vision so that she could root around the many bottles in the dark.

Five of the bottles had a simple cross drawn on them—her Rectivane potions, reserved for the aftermath of a battle when she needed to quickly heal.

Two had skulls—a harmless combination of jasmine and rose teas thrown into the mix to thwart any thief who might've tried to force poison down her throat.

Two more were marked with a heart—though technically illegal, the Brackenbane potion dissolved objects on contact and came in useful quite often.

Finally, she found a little blue vial with a four-leaf clover drawn on the label—her Dazzledane charm. Just the boost of energy she needed.

With so much at stake, she could rest when she found the assassin. For now, she needed fuel.

The cork left the vial with a soft pop, and Quinn sipped the shimmering silver potion. The liquid crackled on her tongue, vibrant and lively, and her fingers tingled as she swallowed.

Her body hummed with life. With *energy*. With the fire of the sun. Her breathing slowed. Her shoulders relaxed, and she rolled her head on her once-tired neck. Every muscle eased as the exhaustion faded. She shivered with delight as the magic took hold of her body, and though she held it near her mouth, she forced herself to cork the bottle yet again.

One sip, and only once per day—it was all she had ever allowed herself. Men and women alike faded away to nothing from drinking too much of this magical mixture. A quick boost of energy quickly became dependence, until they drank nothing at all but Dazzledane potions. Until their hearts gave out, strained and broken from the magic's effect.

No sleep meant an early death, and addiction wouldn't be Quinn's undoing. If she died young, it would be in battle and at the hands of a superior warrior.

She had toyed once or twice with slipping the brew into Zander's morning coffee each day, of course, to get him addicted. A harmless prank in the Starling household, and nothing worse than the time he'd hidden charmed honeybear steaks in her bag to try to get the dreaded black unicorns of the north to eat her on a mission. But his augmented sense of smell would've sniffed it out, and besides, she had more grace and subtlety than her ass of a brother.

Quinn slipped the potion back into her bag and hoisted the leather sack over her shoulders again. As the thick canopy of the gnarled old forest sped by below them, she leaned against the winged tiger's neck. Blaze tilted his massive wings, banking as a southern wind tore past, and Quinn leaned with her mount to keep the balance even. The two of them moved in perfect sync, connected by more than just their decade together. They had fought in wars and saved each other countless times. Though many used the Bridletame Hex to control their animals' minds, she had done her best to simply earn Blaze's respect.

Otmund had suggested she use the Rift to go directly to the ruins where he had tried to catch the assassin, but animals hated using Rift magic. Even some enchanted animals panicked at the Rift, despite being controlled into almost complete obedience with potions. Quinn knew her steed well enough to not push him into using magic he couldn't handle.

Deep down, Quinn couldn't deny her gratitude for avoiding the Rifts. The haunting screams of the men they slaughtered each time always lingered with her for weeks afterward. The way they all begged for mercy, for a few more seconds of life. It didn't matter that the Rift's victims had killed others or earned a death sentence for their own actions. Delivering justice didn't soften their shrieks of panic when they haunted her at night.

Killing an armed man came easily to her, but slitting a defenseless man's throat, regardless of what he'd done, seemed wrong.

Blaze descended, and his wing caught a rough gust of wind. The violent burst of air shook them, and Quinn kept low to his neck to avoid resistance. As she peered over his shoulder at the forest below, she scanned the trees and road for signs of life.

Her ear twitched, attuned to the angry gusts billowing past them, and she listened for the blightwolves' howl. Those beasts were known to travel a hundred miles in a single night, and she didn't want to come across even one of them. Though a dozen towns and hundreds of hamlets sprawled through the expansive forest, she had never been able to understand why anyone would've chosen to live out here.

Maybe that was why the assassin had escaped to these woods—to disappear. Many people vanished out here, though rarely by choice.

As the final threads of light faded behind the mountains, her augmented vision fully adjusted to the encroaching darkness. In the distance, a large break in the trees appeared, and a lone spire rose above the surrounding canopy.

The ruins.

"Faster, Blaze," she said, her voice barely louder than the wind.

Blaze dove, the powerful vougel's wings cutting through the air as he easily maneuvered the turbulent southern winds. This forest had a life of its own, right down to its air, and it had knocked many a warrior from the sky.

Quinn, however, trusted Blaze with her life.

When they reached the clearing, the winged tiger circled, and the two of them studied the land below to check for any surprises that might've been waiting for them.

Quinn drew *Aurora*, and the moment her fingers brushed the magnificent silver hilt, the connection between her and her enchanted weapon erupted to life. With a practiced flick of her wrist, she summoned forth its fire. Brilliant orange flames erupted over the metal blade, the spellgust stone in its hilt glowing with magic as she prepared for the worst.

The meadow didn't move.

The tall ruins lay dormant, silent and sleepy. The golden glint of metal below caught her eye, but only briefly. Only in passing, now and then, when the low light of the forest caught whatever remnants of the battle lay scattered across the field below.

Nothing so much as breathed among the trampled meadow grass, and dark shadows stretched into the clearing from the crumbling walls as the spire clawed at the sky.

"Take us down," she ordered.

Blaze descended, and his claws dug into the grass as he growled. The low rumble built in his throat as he surveyed the empty meadow.

Both of them tensed. Quinn lifted *Aurora*, and the blazing fire of her blade cast a warm glow across the clearing. A golden helmet glinted in the firelight, barely two yards away.

A large scratch scarred the back of the helmet, the mark thicker and wider even than Blaze's claws.

Quinn waited to dismount until she had a better view of the field. She sat up in her saddle, leaning her free hand against the vougel's neck as she listened to the unnerving silence.

Aside from the gentle crash of leaves trembling in the wind, she heard nothing.

She waited for a full minute, never one to trust the quiet. When no arrows flew through the air, and when no one yelled or charged from the woods, she finally dismounted. Sword drawn, she took several careful steps into the field, waiting to see what would happen.

Nothing.

Quinn frowned, twisting her wrist to disable the fire in her blade before she sheathed it at her waist. Blaze snarled, his nose wrinkling as he stalked behind her, the soft pads of his feet snapping what few meadow grasses hadn't already been trampled by whatever the hell had happened here.

Nine golden helmets and an assortment of chest plates littered the field, the bodies they had belonged to long gone. Judging by the massive claw mark on the helmet, however, she had a theory as to where the corpses had gone.

Quinn set her hand on her vougel's neck, her fingertips opening their connection. The enchanted golden band around the tiger's forehead glowed briefly, and the green stone in its center ignited with Quinn's touch—an enchantment using a variation of the Bridletame Hex, meant merely to enhance Blaze's intelligence and awareness.

When the Lunestone Beastmaster had first made the enchanted helm, he'd added the traditional spikes to the other side of the spellgust stone to ensure the enchanted item worked at peak efficiency. Since she had explicitly ordered him not to do that, she had broken his nose for trying to jam metal spikes into Blaze's forehead. Frankly, the man was lucky to still be alive. She had killed men for less.

Other Lightseers needed enchantments to control their mounts. She didn't, and anytime someone had been foolish enough to endanger Blaze, she had destroyed them for it.

"Perimeter check," she ordered.

The winged tiger nodded and darted off into the forest.

As he disappeared into the shadows, Quinn inspected the edges of the meadow. Black crust stained several patches of the grass, the bloody stalks evidence of the death this place had seen. She scanned the white stone ruins, only to discover several bloody handprints, also black with time. A long tongue mark smeared the one nearest to her, and she grimaced with disgust. She set her palm against the stone beside it, the bloody fingers dwarfing hers, and she wondered who the hand belonged to.

The assassin, perhaps—or one of his victims.

She knelt beside a breastplate and lifted it, sniffing gently, trying to figure out what had been here as her Scentscathe augmentation kicked in. The sting of dander and the rot of decay hit her hard, and she retched at the stench.

The breastplate thudded to the ground, and she resumed her hunt. In a dried patch of mud beside a boulder, a massive paw print lay embedded in the dirt. She set her foot in it, and the pad alone dwarfed her entire boot. The creature's toes radiated from her shoe, the entire print easily larger than her head.

Quinn frowned as she surveyed the battle scene again. The wolves couldn't have been far. She and Blaze had to be careful.

In the lone patch of mostly unbroken meadow grass, a small path of bent stalks led toward the trees, just wide enough for a man's body. A long smear of caked blood trailed along the route, as though someone had been dragged. She knelt at the start of the path to run her fingers across the matted grass, and more black blood flaked off the stalks.

The trail led to the edge of the woods and ended at a tree. Much to her surprise, she found a ladder nailed to the great oak's trunk.

As another gust rocked the forest, the old oak before her groaned as it swayed in the wind. Through a gap in the canopy, she caught sight of a window.

A *house*.

In the trees.

How odd.

A flash of white fur and golden stripes in her periphery snared her attention as Blaze returned. He trotted toward her and growled softly. Since no man had screamed during the vougel's patrol, she could safely assume Blaze hadn't found anyone hiding.

Many dangerous things could've been waiting for her up there.

Lost in thought, she absently stretched her fingers wide. Her palm tilted toward the sky, and flames erupted in her palm.

The fire snapped her out of her daze, and she cursed under her breath. This was an old habit, one she had tried and failed to break for years. When deep in thought, fire burned within her, too hot to contain.

Her Burnbane augmentation crackled across her fingers as flames licked at the air, but she didn't need it right now. She shook her hand to extinguish the magic.

Without taking her eyes off the house, she climbed into the saddle on Blaze's back. With two taps on his side, she gave the silent command to take off.

He obeyed.

The vougel leapt into the air. His wings snapped against the wind as he took her into the canopy, and when they reached a small porch, he hovered just beyond the railing.

Effortlessly, Quinn swung one leg over his back and jumped onto the porch. She crouched against the wood and listened to the silence. The house groaned beneath her, swaying again in the wind, but no one moved.

No heartbeats inside. No breath but hers. No whispered voices, lying in wait.

Just silence.

The leaves rustled around her, a soft applause on the wind in the otherwise silent night. Ear strained, shoulders tense, she waited for the fight to come. For a man to race from the shadows beyond the open door.

She stood, squaring her shoulders. "Stand guard, Blaze."

Her vougel snarled and dove toward the ground, his paws thudding against the grass as he obeyed.

Quinn stalked toward the open door, and a loose board creaked beneath her boots. As instantly as she heard it, she lifted her foot. Though anyone keeping guard would've seen Blaze, she still needed to be careful.

She drew *Aurora*, ready to torch the house if she had to.

With her shoulder, she nudged open the entry, only to find an abandoned kitchen. A hand-carved table. Six stools, one of them resting on its side. A makeshift hearth in the corner with a vent above it to let out smoke. A dark stain on the table. Breadcrumbs in the corner. The charred but faded scent of woodsmoke.

Evidence that people had lived here recently.

With her sword raised, Quinn took slow and steady steps into the dark hallway. Carefully, she pushed open the door to the first room to find an old straw mattress stained with blood. A bloody sheet lay crumpled on the floor. An empty pitcher sat on the floor by the bed, surrounded by breadcrumbs. The empty room held a dresser and a chair. Nothing else but the window and the view of the leaves outside.

She walked through each of the rooms in the house, and though she prepared for a fight each time, no battle came. Bed, dresser, chair, window—identical, all of them, and empty.

When she reached the last room in the deceptively large treehouse, a small silhouette under the bed caught her eye, the shadow barely the size of her hand. She knelt and tugged out a small toy rabbit made of old tattered cloth and stuffed with sand. A blue button served as its one remaining eye, though broken black threads marked the spot where the other one should've been. She examined it, chewing her lip as she began to piece it all together.

Children had lived here, but no bodies remained in the house. If the assassin had come to this meadow, these people could have been his family—or, perhaps, they were simply in the wrong place at the wrong time, and he had thrown their bodies to the wolves.

It struck her as odd to think of an assassin with a family, so she suspected these people had likely not survived their encounter with him.

If so, this assassin had killed children. She rubbed her face and gripped the little toy tightly, and though she had always tried so hard not to make assumptions, she couldn't help but imagine him looming over a terrified little girl with his sword raised. Ready to strike. Ready to kill.

"Focus," she chided herself.

Now, to figure out where he had gone.

Quinn eyed the toy rabbit in her hand. Long ago, when she was little, her father had taken her on one of his routine trips to meet the sheriffs along the southern road. To her delight, he'd taken her to Lindow, a town famous for its toy shops. An entire street in the city, devoted only to toys.

Heaven, for a ten-year-old.

Out on the main street, while her father and the sheriff had droned on about topics a ten-year-old like her couldn't pretend to care about, a little girl had walked by with one of the town's famous stuffed bunnies.

One strikingly similar to this, if her memory served her.

But Starling children didn't beg for treats or pull on their father's sleeve to ask for playthings. However much she had wanted one for herself, she had remained silent.

A dutiful daughter. A good girl.

Quinn didn't love this clue, but so far, she had nothing else to go on. The assassin had covered his tracks too well. If he had come here, going south to recover from a bloody battle with a brutal king would've made more sense than heading north toward the very city he had just escaped. East or west would've taken him deeper into the Ancient Woods, and she doubted he had a death wish after going through so much effort to escape Oakenglen alive.

King Henry had possessed ancient magic, the sort that only the members of the Lightseer Chamber truly understood. Perhaps this assassin had obtained some of Henry's darkness for himself—the dead man's infamous recipes, perhaps, or some of his fabled enchanted weapons. Maybe the assassin had set out to recruit an army of his own.

Still kneeling in the treehouse with the toy bunny in one hand, Quinn's jaw tensed as she recalled watching Henry lead forces against Hazeltide to conquer the neighboring kingdom. She had only been thirteen, but her sister Gwendolyn had wanted her to see this nightmare for herself, to know what awaited them if Henry was allowed to conquer the continent. The newly crowned king of Oakenglen, clad in golden armor on his black unicorn, had ridden into battle beside a ghoulish specter with no name.

Hopefully, that abomination had died with its king.

With nothing else to go on, Quinn held the toy in both hands and studied its tattered face. Aside from a loose sheet and a toppled stool, there was no sign of struggle in the house. No spatters of blood. No stench of death. If the assassin did have a family, perhaps he'd taken them to safety.

Perhaps he'd taken them home to Lindow.

She groaned with irritation, infuriated with all the unknowns.

Quinn gently set the toy on the bed and returned to the porch. As she sheathed her sword once again, she leaned over the edge to better judge the distance to the ground. Blaze stood guard below, and he craned his neck to stare up at her.

Not far. Thirty feet, at most.

She hopped over the railing with a quick grunt and braced herself for the landing. Her Strongman augmentation kicked in as her boots hit the dirt, and her enhanced strength protected her body from the jarring blow.

Easy.

Blaze shoved his head against her shoulder in a rough welcome. Desperate to find a better clue, she absently patted his neck as she once again scanned the field. A stuffed animal and a loose connection to a southern city didn't give her much to go on.

Her vougel growled impatiently, and she laughed as she ran her fingers through his fur. The green gem in the circlet on his brow glowed again with their connection. "Fine. Go hunt. If you detect the blightwolves, get back here quickly."

Blaze growled with pleasure and darted off into the forest. Though the night wore on, Quinn rubbed her face in frustration and returned her attention to the meadow. Even as she scanned the edges of the clearing, nothing important caught her eye save for a long gouge in a nearby tree, likely from a blightwolf's claw.

No trail. No tracks. Nothing to go on but a whisper.

After a more thorough check around the perimeter, she would head south and listen in the taverns for gossip. If she didn't hear any word of him within four days, she would return and try the road to the north.

With only twenty-nine days left in the most important mission of her life, she didn't have the luxury of wasted time.

Nothing stopped Quinn Starling, especially when she had something to prove.

CHAPTER TWENTY
CONNOR

Dappled morning sunlight danced along patches of grass on the forest floor as Connor swung the twin shadow blades around his head. Blackfire billowed over the enchanted steel as he trained, their flames scorching the air.

His eyes narrowed, focusing on a log as his grip tightened on the hilt of his right sword. The injury in his side had weakened his right hand, and he needed this practice to retrain his muscle memory.

The weapons cut through the air with each swing, lopping off loose branches and anything else that got too close. A gust rocked the canopy, and the leaves above him shivered in the warming spring air. The sun meandered its way across the sky, taking its time.

Though he wore his silver blades in the sheaths strapped to his back, he hadn't drawn them since he'd met the wraith. Old habits were hard to break, however, and he liked their familiar weight on his shoulders.

His boot dug into the soil as he pivoted on the ball of his foot, kicking up leaves. Dirt rained across the base of a tree trunk from the movement. With each step between the trees, he ran through another phase of an old sword form Beck Arbor had taught him all those years ago.

The blades clashed above his head as he crossed them to block an imaginary sword from lodging in his skull. As he paused to catch his breath, the weapons glinted in the brilliant sunlight streaming through the emerald green leaves above.

His chest heaving, and happily exhausted from a morning of training, Connor studied the majestic blades as he held them aloft. With a well-practiced twist, he dismissed the blackfire scorching the blades, and it dissolved with a hiss. A dark sheen glistened across the weapons, which shimmered like two black jewels in his palms.

Magnificent.

Lethal.

His.

He spun on his heel, and the weapons flashed in the sun. They hissed through the air, vicious and brutal, ready to kill on command.

Each day over the last week, he had made his way to a different part of the woods to practice, always careful to listen for Wesley's now-familiar gait trailing behind him. To master these weapons, he needed to be alone—for the Finns' safety and his own sanity.

He didn't need Fiona darting underfoot to chase a fanged rabbit or throw mud at Isabella while he swung a sword that had felled a tree.

At first, he had struggled to summon the blades. Several times, the wraith's impatient sigh had echoed through his head as he'd stared at his empty palms, and that had only driven him to try harder.

Just to prove the dead king wrong.

With time, the weapons appeared in his hands with ease. Thus far, he had kept them a secret from his surrogate family in the woods, and he intended to keep it that way.

The Finns didn't need to know the truth of what he was—not now, and maybe not ever.

As he somersaulted across the dirt, he completed the form by driving one sword deep into the ground. A light hum sang from the blade as it obeyed him, and his left knee sank into the cold soil. His chest heaved as he caught his breath. With his right hand still on the sword stabbed into the dirt, he wiped the back of his left hand over his brow to wipe away sweat.

Though the wound in his side throbbed, dull and steady, at least he could move again. Each day, the gash shrank, and more of the pain receded. It hadn't stung for three days. It hadn't ripped open in five.

In less than a week, he probably wouldn't even feel the dull throb anymore.

Finally, a gruesome voice echoed in his head. *You are nearly well again.*

On instinct, Connor snatched the shadow blade from the dirt and lifted it, spinning on his heel to face a now-familiar specter hovering between two nearby oaks. The sword rested against one of the specter's ribs as Connor squared his shoulders, never one to enjoy being caught off guard.

Ghosts didn't have footsteps, and he'd almost never been able to tell when this one would appear.

"I see you're still here," he said, lowering the blade. "I was beginning to think you had slunk off to the shadows to sulk."

We leave in the morning, the wraith said, ignoring his jibe.

"You aren't the captain of this ship," Connor snapped. With a twist of his hands, he dismissed the stunning black blades into a cloud of smoke. The foggy haze settled like dust on the air.

What ship? The ghost gestured to the woods around them. *We are in a forest. There is no boat.*

Connor hesitated, lifting one eyebrow in surprise as he frowned at the dead king floating before him. "No, not a real—it's just an expression. It means you don't decide what I do next."

And you think you're wise enough to decide what we do from here? The ghost circled him, the ribbons of that tattered old cloak billowing with the movement. *Every day spent in this forest is a day lost for the hunt. Zander and Otmund may have already given their blades to other warriors, for all we know. I allowed you to heal, and you are well enough to travel again. Therefore, we leave at dawn.*

Connor laughed, and he stretched as he paced among the trees. "You 'allowed' me to heal, did you? I take it you and I see the world differently."

You cannot waste any more time. Find the Bloodbane daggers. Kill the people who wield them. Find any of Aeron's notes that remain. Take whatever throne you wish along the way, but you must get me those weapons.

Connor cracked his neck, and a surge of relief shot down his spine as the movement eased the tension in his joints. "Who said I want a throne?"

All of you want a throne, the old ghost snapped with an irritated wave of his bony hand. *It's inevitable. One way or another, you want this queen or that city or those resources. It's the same, every time.*

"Except this time, you're stuck with a peasant."

Yes, the ghost said, his voice dripping with annoyance. *Does that mean you have no ambition? Am I doomed to rot in these woods until someone finally kills you?*

Connor chuckled and shook his head. "So impatient."

The ghoul crossed his skeletal arms. *And right.*

He turned his back on the ghost and set his hands on his head as he stared off into the forest.

As much as he hated to admit it, the Wraith King had a point. The longer he spent in these woods, the less of a chance he had to truly understand who—or what—was after him.

He still needed to choose how to wield the simmering power in his blood, but he just wasn't the conquering sort. Since he'd left home, he hadn't wanted anything except to see another dawn.

One threat at a time.

Whatever it takes, survive.

The Ancient Woods never stayed quiet for long, and the chaos would come. It was inevitable, and he needed to prepare.

Though he didn't need a throne, he did quite enjoy being alive, and that meant he *did* need power. Resources. A fortress of his own, perhaps, a fortified defensive position that allowed him some sort of protection from whatever hurricane tried to rip him apart.

More importantly, however, he needed to understand the ghoul and learn how to control this dead man fused with his soul. If these Bloodbane daggers had the power to kill a wraith, he also had to do everything in his power to find those weapons and either contain or destroy them.

His smile fell, and he set his hands on his waist as he surveyed the Ancient Woods. The forest had been his home for the last eight years, and he couldn't quite fathom what waited beyond them. Oakenglen, a city two hundred times larger than any town he had visited. Entire kingdoms and forests far more dangerous than even these woods.

Death waited for him beyond the rickety walls of the Finns' treetop home. Whether his or someone else's, a lot of blood would spill before this ended. Even if he didn't want to overthrow anyone, every legend and story he'd heard in his life started the same way and ended with the same moral.

Those who rule this world crave power, and they will obtain it at any cost.

People he didn't even know were going to come for the wraith, and he had to be ready.

"Why are you being so helpful?" Connor spun on his heel and sized up the wraith hovering by a nearby tree. "A week of silence, and suddenly you give me practical advice? Something I can actually use?" He frowned. "It's highly suspect."

Because I need blood, you irritating peasant. The Wraith King curled his bony fingers into fists as he stared down at what remained of his hands. *I am a creature of war. I need movement. Direction. Purpose. Your idle life in this forest bores me. If I have to watch another one of those damned squirrels for my entertainment, I will start killing things.*

"Ah," Connor said, nodding. "Now you sound more like yourself."

I've waited as long as I could. You needed to heal, and thus I permitted the reprieve, but now you're growing lazy and fat.

"Fat?" Connor flexed his bicep and pointed to the thick muscle straining against his shirt. "I'm in the best shape of my life, you old twat."

The heavy thud of Ethan's footsteps carried through the woods, distant and faint but growing closer. Judging by the slight shift in his gait and the occasional labored breath, he'd been walking for a while.

The Wraith King's skeletal head tilted in the direction of the carpenter's footsteps, and the ghost went eerily still as he listened. *You have until morning to leave.*

"Or what?" He curled his hand into a fist as he dared the ghost to threaten him.

The wraith's skull pivoted on his spine, the empty eye sockets snaring Connor as he dissolved into the wind without an answer.

"Damn that old ghost," he muttered.

Tense and on edge after the unspoken threat, his shoulders ached as he scanned the now-empty woods for any sign of that bastard ghoul's billowing cloak. He tapped his thumb on his leg and sat with the wraith's threat, wondering what he intended to do if Connor refused to oblige his whims.

Now more than ever, he needed to learn everything he could about the Wraith King. The ghost had begun to toy with him, testing how to control him, and Connor refused to become a pawn for some dead thing floating on the breeze.

A race had begun between them, and only one of them would win.

"There you are!" Ethan huffed as he leaned against a tree, and an axe rested on his shoulder as he caught his breath. "I need firewood, and several oaks toppled out here recently. Come help me chop some logs for the fire."

Connor nodded, gesturing for the man to lead the way, but he more so wanted to put distance between them and the Wraith King—if such a thing were even possible.

If the ghoul was connected to him, it must've gone wherever he did.

"Were you talking to someone?" Ethan shifted the weight of the axe to his other shoulder. "I thought I heard you mumbling."

"Just talking to myself," Connor lied.

"I do that, too."

The carpenter led the way through the woods, each clump of trees nearly identical to the last, until they reached a trio of fallen oaks. The trunks stretched across the dead leaves, their splintery corpses fractured by whatever had toppled them.

Ethan kicked the nearest fallen oak with his boot and handed the axe to Connor. "Here's a good log. Let's start with this one."

Connor took it and hoisted the blade over his shoulder with practiced ease while Ethan leaned against a nearby pine and crossed his arms to watch. The axe thudded against the base of the wood, the blade digging deep into the bark, and Connor easily pried it loose for another swing.

This would've gone so much faster with his shadow blades, but Ethan didn't need to know about those.

"Amazing." Ethan gestured toward Connor's injury. "I still don't know how you're healing so fast, but I'm grateful not to chop."

The axe dug into the log again. "You'll get your turn."

Ethan laughed. "Since you're healthy now, you should help me scout for a new place. I could use your survival skills in picking out a new location. I figure we head to the stretch of forest west of Bradford, toward the Westhelm Mountains. I've heard tales of hundreds of waterfalls and plenty of caves to live in. It'll be a better stretch of land than these wilds while we build a new home."

Connor buried the axe again in the oak and twisted it to break the wood apart at the half-hewn seam. It groaned beneath his might, the wood splintering as he forced it to obey, and the first section of the trunk broke off.

Easy.

He paused, taking a moment to catch his breath as he examined the shattered log beneath him. Despite getting stuck with an irritating ghoul, he couldn't deny how much he enjoyed the perks that came with being the Wraithblade. The enhanced strength and senses served him well, even if he did eat more than an army to fuel his new power.

He looked Ethan in the eye. "I can't stay much longer."

The burly carpenter sighed, studying the splintered log, and eventually nodded. When he didn't say anything else, Connor picked up the axe and continued his work. The steady thud of the blade through shattering wood mixed with the occasional rustle of a small animal skittering through the nearby underbrush, but the conversation died.

With each swing of the axe, Connor could practically feel the unanswered question lingering in the air between them.

What are you?

Truthfully, he didn't know how to answer.

Ethan scratched at his beard as his gaze drifted across the forest floor.

"Look, son. I—"

A chilling scream echoed through the trees, and Connor's blood ran cold at the gruesome wail. He and Ethan stared at each other, frozen in place, their brows pinched with concern as the screech faded.

"This way." Connor handed off the axe to Ethan and instead drew the twin swords he always kept sheathed to his back. The shadow blades would've probably served him better, but he didn't want to risk Ethan asking too many questions—or worse, piecing things together for himself.

Body tense and every muscle in him primed for battle, Connor led the way through the trees.

The forest had stilled. Nothing sang. Nothing moved. Every living thing in the woods waited for the danger to pass, even as Connor and Ethan ran toward it.

As they neared their best guess of where the cry had come from, the steady drip of water punctuated the eerie silence. It reminded him of rain sliding off a leaf, but it hadn't rained today. With the nearest stream almost a hundred yards away, the sound didn't make sense.

Whatever it was, it couldn't have been water.

A nauseating stench rolled over him. The sour bite of blood coated the air and crawled into his lungs. Through the thick branches around them, a red mist hovered in a small clearing not far away. Something dark stained the grass, and as they neared, the stench of death grew stronger.

Connor raised his swords ahead of him as he prepared for the worst—a rabid blightwolf, perhaps, out in the middle of the day. It had happened once before, long ago, before he'd known what nightmares waited for him in the shadows. Back then, he'd barely escaped with his life.

As they neared the crimson mist, sunlight flashed through the red droplets on the air, and the drip of water grew louder.

With his silver blade, Connor pushed aside a low-hanging branch. A deer leg hung from a nearby tree, and blood dripped steadily from its hoof into a small puddle on the ground.

Drip.

He'd been right. It wasn't water at all.

Drip.

Footsteps crunched the leaves behind him, and Connor raised his arm to keep Ethan from seeing this. His blade cut through a clump of low-hanging leaves as he pressed his elbow into the carpenter's chest.

Ethan paused midstride, his way blocked, and Connor looked over his shoulder to catch the man's eye. Wordlessly, he shook his head in warning to keep the carpenter from saying anything.

Their lives probably depended on their silence.

Drip.

With a cautious step, Connor walked to the edge of the field by himself. The rusty sting of blood on the air overwhelmed his newly enhanced sense of smell, and he creased his nose in disgust as he tried to block out the stench.

In a rush, the steady drip became a cascade. Red rivers poured from the branches above him, drenching his shirt and hair. He grimaced with revulsion and stepped out of the bloody rain as the torrent soaked the field like a two-second monsoon.

When the storm ended, the red mist settled again on the air. Only the steady drip of blood punctuated the silence that followed.

He walked into the field again, this time keeping his attention on the branches that stretched above most of the clearing.

Limbs protruded from every tree. Hooves. Legs. A tail. Bloody tendons stretched between the oaks like gruesome garlands, the forest's leaves stained red in the aftermath of the poor creature's grisly death.

In the center of the field, a stag's head hung from the thickest branch in the canopy. The dead deer's spine coiled around the wood, and the blood-soaked bones anchored the corpse as it swayed. The beast's tongue lolled out of its mouth, its eyes milky as it stared blankly down at him.

Under his breath, Connor let out a string of curses as he surveyed the gruesome scene.

Beneath the decapitated head, someone—or something—had carved a single word into the soil, the grooves now filled to the brim with blood.

DAWN.

"Bless the Fates," Ethan muttered from the edge of the clearing. He dropped the axe and spun around, bracing his hands on his knees as he heaved his breakfast into a nearby bush.

Connor pinched his eyes shut, and though his cheeks flushed with nausea at the disgusting scene, he managed to keep it at bay. He sheathed the swords, since they wouldn't have any effect against a wraith.

Sure enough, while Ethan heaved what was left of his morning bread into a nearby bush, a shadow floated between the trees across from Connor. The ghoul's skeletal face haunted him, those empty eye sockets staring into his soul moments before it disappeared behind a gnarled oak.

"I'll leave in the morning." His shirt and hair drenched with blood, Connor turned his back on the grisly scene behind him. "It's no longer safe for me to stay."

"No, son." Ethan wiped his mouth on his sleeve and forced himself to stand, his back to the morbid spectacle. "I won't let you walk into the unknown if you're being hunted by something that can do this. I won't—"

"That's not what I mean, Ethan." Connor set his bloodstained hand on the man's shoulder. "If I stay, it will no longer be safe for *you.*"

CHAPTER TWENTY-ONE
CONNOR

As Connor slept, the darkness tormented him. It sang through a thick fog, calling to him like a siren on the sea, stealing the wind from his sails as it beckoned him closer.

Wind. Water. The spray of a wave as it crashed upon his boat as it sank. The sting of salt on the air, coating his lungs.

A woman's hand on his chest as she pulled him under the waves, whisking him away to freedom and death.

He woke with a start and the sense that someone watched from the shadows. The muscles in his back flexed as he lay in bed, his body coiled for a fight.

As his eyes snapped open, a face hovered above him—skeletal and serene. Empty eye sockets swallowed what little light remained in the room. The specter hovered mere inches away from his face. The tattered black cloak blocked his view of the room beyond.

Instinct took over.

Connor grunted with surprise and summoned the shadow blades on impulse. The jet-black swords appeared instantly in his hand, and smoke wafted through the room as it blended with the tattered shrouds of the ghoul's cloak. He drove both blades into the specter's heart—at least, where it would have been, if he'd had one.

The creature didn't flinch.

Ow. The Wraith King's mocking tone rang through Connor's mind.

As the surge of surprise began to fade, Connor cursed under his breath and relaxed into the mattress. "You're an ass."

The ghost chuckled.

Connor rolled out of the bed and shook out his shoulders as he glared at the specter floating above where he'd been sleeping moments before. "What the hell are you doing in here? It's not dawn yet, and I told you to stay away from them."

You did, didn't you? The dead man tilted his head and watched Connor, as if waiting for a reaction.

A dull ache thudded against Connor's skull, and he rubbed his temples to soothe it. With an irritated groan, he glared out the window and tried to gauge the time of day. Darkness and thick leaves blocked most of his view, though thin slivers of golden light crept across the top of the canopy visible from his room.

Hints of the first breaths of dawn.

He wouldn't leave, not yet. Until the sun rose, the blightwolves owned the forest.

In the stretch of silence that followed, a low and haunting howl twisted through the air. Moments later, several other wolves joined the cry. Connor froze on impulse, accustomed to his time in the trees and not the safety of a house. It took a moment for his shoulders to relax as the cry faded away.

"Get the hell out of here before they see you," he demanded, glaring at the ghost.

Even if you can't see me, I am near, the ghost warned. *Do not dally.*

With that, the wispy black threads of his cloak dissolved into the air. His face faded last, until nothing remained but the gnawing sensation of someone watching from afar.

Connor rubbed his tired eyes. He had another hour at least before he could leave. Sleep would've done him good, but the idea of laying back in that bed didn't exactly appeal to him anymore.

His stomach growled. Always hungry. Never satisfied. His body burned with the heat of this new magic, demanding more.

Always needing more.

Sleep wasn't going to happen, so he made his way toward the kitchen in the hopes Kiera had left something out for him. The wound in his side ached briefly, but the pain passed almost as instantly as it had come.

As he rounded the corner into the kitchen, a small silhouette by the door to the porch shifted its weight. He hesitated, eyes narrowing as he examined the shadow. It took a moment to recognize Isabella's long blonde hair as she sat with her back against the wall. With her knees tucked to her chest, she sobbed quietly into her arms.

At first, he merely stood there. Comforting others had never been his forte. In the dark and quiet house, with her soft sobs cutting through the silence, he didn't know what to do.

A long howl pierced the night, closer than Connor would have liked, and he glared out the window. Through a gap in the trees, a shadow darted among the oaks—too quickly for even his eye to follow.

Isabella gasped, and her head snapped up as she listened to the haunting cry on the wind. Her eyes darted to Connor a second later. She yelped again in surprise and scooted back along the floor, pressing herself into a corner as she stared up at him with a wide and fearful gaze.

It gutted him to have a little girl look at him with so much fear, like she thought he was going to break her arm at any moment, just to hear it snap.

He sighed and rubbed the back of his neck as he pulled out a stool, careful to keep a respectful distance from the terrified child. The wooden legs scraped across the hardwood floor and creaked as he took his seat. He rested his elbows on his knees and leaned away from her out of respect. With his hands clasped together, he frowned as he tried to figure out what to say.

"I'm not going to hurt you, Isabella," he promised. "I won't let any of those blightwolves hurt you, either."

She curled up again, her back pressed against the corner of the kitchen as she pulled her knees once more to her chest. Without so much as a whimper in answer, she watched him, waiting for him to make a move.

His little sister had been a fearful girl, too. As the silence stretched on, he let his mind go where he usually never permitted it to travel—to the past. To a time before Beck Arbor had taught him to fight. To a time before he'd drifted from town to town, looking for work.

To home.

"I used to live in Kirkwall, you know," he said softly, his eyes glazing over as he studied his hands. "Have you been there? To the island?"

In his periphery, Isabella shook her head.

"It's beautiful." He absently rubbed his thumb against his palm as he spoke. "White buildings along every inch of the coast. Forests growing between the homes. When you sail up to the island, all you see is that ocean of green and white, towering over the waves."

"That sounds pretty," Isabella said in a tiny voice.

"It is." He nodded, lost in the memory. "Ships in every harbor. Big white sails, filled with salty air. You need to see the ocean, someday. You'll fall in love."

"Why did you leave?"

He turned away to hide his pained grimace from the little girl who didn't know better than to ask a question like that. "It's complicated."

"Papa says that a lot." Isabella leaned her chin on her knees as she stared at the floor. "When he thinks I'm too young to understand."

"Fathers are smart. Especially yours. You should trust him."

"I do," she admitted with a soft sigh.

A deafening howl cut through the air, closer than ever, and Isabella froze in place. Her eyes widened again as she craned her ear to listen. Connor stood, carefully circling the table so he could peer out the window.

Through a gap in the trees, the waterfall crashed into the small lake beside the treehouse. The thunder of its waves blocked out any chance of hearing the wolves' footsteps across the grass. He waited in the lingering silence, aching to spot the blightwolves' shadows, but nothing moved.

"I wish they would go away," Isabella whispered.

Connor shook his head. "That's not how the forest works, Isabella. We're in their world. They don't abide by our rules."

"But they scare me."

"They should," he admitted.

When she didn't say anything, he shifted his attention back to her. The little girl stared at him with even wider eyes than before, and her lips parted with breathless fear.

Oh.

Apparently, that had been the wrong thing to say.

He cleared his throat, searching for the right words to salvage this. He didn't want Ethan to give him an earful because he'd broken the little girl's spirit. "You know, I had a little sister back in Kirkwall. She was scared all the time, too. You're not the only one."

"Really?" Isabella asked, her voice tinged with hope.

Connor nodded. "She used to be afraid of thunder. Of lightning. She said it was too wild. Too chaotic." He grinned. "Imagine being scared of something as natural as the weather."

Isabella chuckled. "Did she get braver?"

"She did. Over time, she realized she would be fine as long as she stayed indoors during those storms. In the house, she was safe."

His smile fell. In the end, the house had been her undoing, but he pushed the thought away.

Isabella sat a little straighter. "So, if I stay up here—"

"Then you're safe," he finished for her. "Up here, nothing can touch you. No one can get you."

The girl's shoulders relaxed, and she smiled. "And if more of the bad men come? Are you going to save us again?"

For a moment, he didn't answer. He couldn't. He hadn't had anyone to protect in a long time, and back then, he had failed.

"Of course," he promised.

The sharp thud of boots in the hallway caught his attention, and he leaned against the stove as Ethan appeared in the doorway. At first, the carpenter scowled as he glanced between the two of them, no doubt trying to figure out what had happened and if he needed to be concerned.

Isabella closed her eyes, a smile lingering on her face while she laid her cheek on her knees, and his shoulders relaxed at the sight.

"Isabella, go to bed," he ordered.

"Yes, Papa." Yawning, she stood and rubbed her eyes on her way to the hallway. When she reached her father, she wrapped her arms around his waist and hugged him tightly before disappearing into the shadows of the corridor beyond.

Ethan rubbed his hands together briefly to warm them as he took the chair Connor had sat in moments before.

"I guess nobody's sleeping tonight." Connor took the seat across from the burly man and leaned his elbows on the table.

"You scared me there. I just heard you two talking and…" Ethan rubbed his face, as if the words alone were too difficult to say.

As if he had somehow expected the worst.

"Thanks," Connor said dryly, frowning as he stared out the window at the brightening leaves outside.

"No, son, it's not you." Ethan shook his head as he tapped his knuckle at the table. "It's a father's fear. It's…"

He trailed off again, his eyes glazing over with yet another thought.

In the back of Connor's mind, a few stray bits of information he had previously ignored suddenly wove themselves together. "You mentioned something once about daughters disappearing, Ethan. What happened? Why did you have an extra room in this house? I doubt you have much company. There's no need to put all that effort into building an extra room for guests."

The burly man across from him let out a weary groan. "Even as our children grow and learn about the world, fathers never stop worrying. If anything, we worry more. Wesley isn't our first child, Connor. Your room used to belong to our eldest girl. Before—before she—" Something caught in the man's throat, and he cleared it roughly as he looked down at his hands.

Connor rubbed his jaw, his heart twisting with the confession. "Ethan, I'm sorry."

"I failed her," the carpenter admitted. "I couldn't protect her. A powerful man in Lindow took a liking to her. He was easily twenty years her senior, and obviously, she wasn't interested. He came to me, trying to arrange a marriage she didn't want, but that's not the man I am. I told him to piss off. Not even a full season later, she was found dead in an alley behind a tavern she had never visited." The life in the burly man's eyes faded, devoid of the humor and joy he usually carried with him. "She was only sixteen."

"Ethan…" Connor didn't even know what to say.

"I couldn't prove it was that tyrannical asshole, and in the end, the sheriff blamed wandering bandits that he claimed had gotten away. No justice. No accountability. Her killer still lives in the same house, a free man. Ever since then, we've been out here. Safe."

In the silence that followed, the blightwolves howled again.

"Safe from people, anyway," Connor said.

"I've always wondered which is more dangerous." Ethan shook his head. "But I worry about what this does to my children. I sometimes think I made the wrong choice."

Connor leaned forward and set his elbows on the table. He couldn't offer anything in the way of advice. He wasn't going to pretend he had answers, especially not about kids. He'd chosen the woods as his home, too.

Only the Fates could know if he and Ethan had chosen correctly.

"At least out here, you have each other," Connor said.

"And you," Ethan added, finally looking him in the eye.

Connor watched the burly man, his jaw tense. He didn't know what to say. He wasn't used to people needing him, much less wanting him around.

A twinge of pain shot through his chest, and Connor impulsively rubbed the scar left over from where the Wraith King had fused with his body. He drummed his fingers on the table with his other hand as he pushed through the pain.

Ethan ran a hand through his hair. "I know you said you can't stay. I get it. Do you at least understand why these people want what you have? Whatever it was you found in the ruins?"

"I don't," Connor confessed.

"Can you tell me what you found, son?"

"I shouldn't."

"Then let me guess." Ethan sat straighter, and the wrinkles around his eyes creased as he stared Connor down. "Advanced healing. Hunger that rivals mine—don't think I haven't noticed the way you stare at the leftover food when the rest of us are done. You resist out of courtesy, but you shouldn't."

Connor chuckled. "Guilty."

"Eat what you need. What we have is yours."

He scratched the back of his head, not loving the idea of taking their food, but Ethan had offered. Even at the mere thought of another meal, his insatiable stomach growled.

"Look," Ethan continued. "Whatever you have either caused the scene with the deer, or there are more vile things than men chasing you. Whatever you found, it isn't child's play. This isn't light, charm-based magic or the sort of enchantments common folk like us understand. This is one of the darkest parts of Saldia, the dangerous magic mothers warn their children about. Am I right?"

Connor stretched out his neck as he debated what to share. Ultimately, Ethan had done right by him. The man deserved a bit of the truth.

"Yes," he admitted.

Ethan nodded and stood, crossing his arms as he paced back and forth along the far wall. "Whatever this is, it's old and dangerous magic. The sort of thing you hear about in legends. If those old stories are right, you need to master it, Connor, before whatever this is masters *you*. That's the way the old stories go—the magic takes root and corrupts good men's souls. You have to be clever."

"I know."

"Listen, son, I know you have a conscience in there, but you need to know something about the people in the southern towns." Ethan tapped his finger on the table to make his point. "If you go around saving others and showing off what you can do, you're putting yourself in danger. The people out there, they're not like us. They won't be grateful just because you saved their lives. You're different, and you're more powerful than any of them. They'll fear that. They'll fear *you*."

"Maybe."

"Definitely," Ethan corrected. "When you leave, where are you headed? What's your next move?"

"Information. I need to find a necromancer."

"A necromancer?" Ethan balked. "What you have is real magic, son. A necromancer will try to steal it."

"I know," Connor admitted. "I don't have many options, and that's the only lead I have so far."

"Hmm." Ethan tapped his finger on his jaw, briefly lost in thought as he considered the request. "You should head to Bradford, then. Look for the sorceress in the woods. The one who made Wesley's augmentation. No matter what Kiera says to be polite, that woman is no witch. She's not neutral. She's dangerous."

Connor frowned. "She makes potions and augmentations, right? I need someone who has connections to real necromancy. How can she help me?"

Ethan shuddered. "That woman is dreadful, but she knows things about magic no one should know. Being in her house is like walking into the land of the dead—it's just not natural. Not right. The way she stares into her cauldron, I figure she's capable of anything. That woman didn't study with the Lightseers, I can tell you that much. Word in town is there's no potion she won't make and no recipe she doesn't have. Even the illegal ones."

"Probably not a Lightseer, then," Connor agreed.

"She's a necromancer. No question. She skirts the law, and the sheriff has tried more than once to arrest her. If you need someone who has navigated the shadows before and come out alive, she's the only one I know of."

It was a long shot. He didn't know for sure if she would be able to help him, but at a minimum, she would be able to point him in the right direction.

For a price.

"How do I find her?" Connor asked.

"Her hut is on the outskirts of the north end of town, but it's never in the same place twice. If you try to wander there yourself, word is you'll end up deep in blightwolf territory and entirely lost. The people of Bradford only talk about her in whispers, like they're afraid she has ears in every wall."

Connor laughed. "There's probably a potion for that. I don't know enough about magic to say for sure."

"Don't you go to her hut alone, son," Ethan warned, ignoring the joke. "Not even you. Hire a sellsword, hire an army, do what you must—but don't go alone. Whenever we need Wesley's augmentation redone, we hire a mercenary from a local tavern to make sure she behaves. There are a few familiar with her if you ask the right people at the pubs."

"I can't imagine a woman like this is cheap."

"Hardly." Ethan huffed with irritation. "Quite a bit of coin, that one. I can't afford her, but we bring her reagents that only grow out here in the wilds. It's enough to offset the cost. I have some devil's ivy you can bring her. I overheard her adding it to a fire potion, once, and she always knocks off a bit of the price when I bring her some. I can also give you some reishi mushrooms. Try as she might to hide it, the sorceress's eyes always go wide when we bring her those, so I think they're her favorite. Both reagents are rare enough to be worth something to her."

"I can't take—"

"Shut *up*, son," Ethan said with a laugh. "You'll take them. It's not like we create potions, anyway. All any of us knows how to make is the Rectivane potion, and that doesn't need either of these reagents, you hear me?"

Connor smiled in gratitude. "I suppose so."

"Be sure not to mention her to the townsfolk, of course," Ethan added. "It's illegal to deal with necromancers."

"That never stopped you."

"Neither you nor I are very fond of laws, now are we?"

Connor laughed, and he tapped his fingers on the table as he sorted through what the day ahead might bring. "How do I find her if her hut moves?"

"It's probably all smoke and mirrors, but there's a process," Ethan said with an annoyed grumble. "There's a withered tree to the north of town. Right off the main road. You can't miss it. Leave a coin in the hollow of the trunk, and wisps of light will lead you to her. Or, if she doesn't want your company, rumor is she will lead you to the blightwolves instead."

"She sounds charming," Connor muttered.

"Prepare yourself," Ethan warned with a grumble.

In the silence that followed, the two men lost themselves in thought. It was strange for Connor to simply sit with someone, to enjoy the quiet and not have to fill it with noise.

To no longer be alone.

With a heavy sigh, Ethan leaned forward and studied Connor's face. Bags pulled at the burly man's eyes, and any trace of a smile had long disappeared. "If you ever need a place to hide, we're here for you. If we leave this house before you make it back, we will leave symbols in the trunks to guide you to us. You're a good man, and you give me hope that there's still compassion in this world that has been cruel to us."

"Thank you," Connor said. "Be careful, Ethan."

"I'll try."

After a soft pat on Connor's shoulder, Ethan retired into the hallway. The thuds of his boots on the wood faded slowly, and seconds later, a door clicked shut in the quiet night.

Connor looked out the window, enjoying the last few moments before sunrise. Truth be told, he'd expected to see the wraith hovering in the trees, urging him to leave.

Instead, the silhouettes of a dozen massive wolves darted past the waterfall and into the fading night.

CHAPTER TWENTY-TWO
ZANDER

In the labyrinth of hallways beneath Oakenglen, Zander leaned against a cold stone wall. Arms crossed, he waited in the shadows of a little-used corridor.

Urgent and panicked conversations bubbled out of a nearby room, the door still cracked because the fools hadn't properly closed it. The royal advisors had panicked, and their failure to contain the crisis disappointed him.

When a Starling finally sat on the throne, he would behead them all and simply begin anew.

The door opened a second later, and two men in plain black tunics carried a gurney between them. A white sheet covered the body they held, and as they stole through the damp tunnels, they cast wary glances over their shoulders. The worry lines in their brows betrayed their fear, and they had every right to be concerned.

They likely wanted to keep the corpse's identity a secret, but Zander already knew who it was.

He watched as King Henry's long-lost nephew—the only family relation to survive exile—was carted off to the morgue beneath the castle. It would be a quick trip, and no one would even know the fifteen-year-old had been alive. He'd been only a few years old when Henry had taken over. Celine had managed to whisk her sister's child away to the far corner of Saldia after Henry had started getting a little too liberal with the executioner's axe.

As he waited for the fools to round a corner down the hallway, Zander tapped his finger on his chin and tried to recall exactly how many people

Henry had killed. At least twenty of his own family had lost their heads, most of them nephews and nieces who might have eventually vied for the throne.

The old king had been a fool really, but perhaps his time with the wraith had fueled his arrogance. Too afraid of losing even a thread of power, Henry had failed to secure the kingdom in the eventuality of his death. No natural-born heir. No named successor. No preparation at all.

Perhaps Henry had thought he would never die. It wouldn't have been a surprise, of course, given his connections to the Wraith King. If a man spent too long with a necromancer's abomination, he would've inevitably started to think he was immortal, too.

The buffoon.

As the two men in black carted the young would-be king away, the boy's arm fell out from under the sheet. His fingertips hovered above the floor, limp and lifeless. The young man hadn't even had an inauguration before his assassination.

The public would never even learn he'd been alive.

The heir should have escaped into the Lost Peaks the moment he found out he was supposed to be king. Coming to Oakenglen had been the greatest mistake of his short life.

Zander couldn't possibly have been the only one in this castle pulling strings. Powerful families from all over the known world—and possibly beyond—had converged on the capital. Each wanted their own puppet on the throne, but Zander and his father had the advantage.

They owned or influenced most of Saldia already. Capturing Oakenglen would simply be the final jewel in their crown.

Zander had always believed the Starlings were fit for both royalty and war, and he intended to see this broken land mended once and for all. The question, really, wasn't which family would own the throne next—but, rather, which Starling child would be the first to wear the crown.

If their father dared nominate Quinn, Zander would have to ensure she met the same fate as the would-be king he had poisoned. And, like tonight, not even the great Teagan Starling would discover the truth.

CHAPTER TWENTY-THREE
CONNOR

Connor had never been one for goodbyes.

He stood at the kitchen table with his full pack in his hands, eyeing the breads and dried meats lying beside the bag and his blades on the table. His silver swords glinted in the morning light through the window, but for now, he ignored them.

It didn't serve him to stall, so he focused on the task ahead and stuffed his pack with whatever food could fit.

The first golden threads of dawn glowed against the leaves outside, the honey-yellow light waking up the forest as the shadows retreated. His eyes stung with exhaustion, but he simply rubbed them and pressed onward. It wasn't like he would've gotten a lot of sleep around the impatient Wraith King, regardless.

Part of him hated the brutal old ghost for what he had done to the deer—or, more importantly, for the threat he had made against the Finns. The ghoul didn't have to say it aloud for Connor to get the message loud and clear.

Ignore me, and they're next.

Though he'd begun to let down his guard, and though he enjoyed their company, the drifter in him ached for movement. He hadn't spent this long in one place since his time with Beck Arbor, and his bones ached for the unknown.

The drifter's fate—to discover himself as he lost his way.

He needed to leave and put as much distance between the Finns and the Wraith King as he could muster. It would take much of the day to reach Bradford, and he couldn't waste a moment more.

A few light footsteps in the hallway caught his attention—gentle, slow, delicate.

Kiera.

"You're up early," he said without turning around as he buckled the pack.

She chuckled, and the floor creaked slightly as she shifted her weight. "You hear everything, don't you?"

"Pretty much." Connor set the bag aside and leaned against the table as he faced her.

She rested against the wall, her arms crossed as she watched him. A frizzy curl fell from her tight bun, a hint of gray amongst the gold as the wrinkles around her eyes deepened with her smile. "A big fellow like you is going to need more food than that."

He shook his head. "Ethan insisted I pack this much, and it's more than enough. I survived on my own in the forest for years, Kiera. I don't want to take any more of your food."

"You act like I'm giving you a choice." Kiera lifted her chin in defiance as she knelt beside the stove and rifled through their stores. Moments later, she pulled out a cloth filled with more dried meat and offered it to him without a word.

As he reluctantly snatched it from her, he grinned. With a few well practiced tugs, he unbuckled the pack to shove the meat inside, grateful for her stubborn generosity.

His gaze lingered on the twin swords lying side by side on the wood, their custom dual sheaths beside them. With the shadow blades he now wielded, these no longer served much purpose despite their years of service. It would've benefited him to have backup weapons, but he wanted to make sure the Finns could defend themselves.

"How many weapons do you have?" he asked.

"Enough." She quirked one eyebrow, as if daring him to offer her the blades.

"Kiera," he said, a warning in his tone. "Be reasonable."

"I never much enjoyed being reasonable," she admitted with a lazy little shrug. "Besides, we have swords and a few daggers, not to mention the axe. We're fine."

"Suit yourself." He tugged on the harness, and the sheaths pressed tightly against his back as he sheathed both weapons.

The heavy clomp of boots in the hallway broke the silence. Moments later, Ethan entered the kitchen with three glowing potion bottles in one hand and a small coin purse in the other.

"Absolutely not," Connor snapped, turning his back to the stocky man as he finished tightening the last of the buckles on his pack.

"Don't fight it." Ethan set the bottles and coin purse on the table beside Connor with a resounding thud. "Nothing surpasses a Finn for sheer stubborn pride. You'll just lose in the end and waste time in the process."

Connor scoffed. "I'm not taking your food, your money, *and* your potions. That's not happening."

"Consider it payment." Ethan tapped his finger on the table to emphasize his point. "Payment for saving our lives."

"You're the ones isolated in the forest a day away from anyone's help." Connor gestured to the two of them as morning sunlight streamed through the kitchen window. "I'm headed *into* town. *Toward* resources."

"We have plenty," Kiera said. "We didn't come out here unprepared."

Connor rubbed his eyes in frustration. "Don't you start in on this, too."

"Look," Ethan said quietly, leaning his fists against the table as he watched Connor. "Do this for me. Take it. Just in case."

As he stood there in the kitchen, Connor simply watched the older man for a moment. With his blades on his back and the bag in his hand, he could have simply left—but his damn conscience got the better of him.

He grabbed the potion bottles with an exasperated sigh, and he kept Ethan's eye as he intentionally left the coin purse on the table. With a few quick tugs, he stowed the potions in one of the side pockets.

"Fine," Ethan said as he stood up straight. "Do you know what those are?"

Connor shrugged. "Rectivane potions, I assume. In case I get hurt."

"Exactly. Kiera brewed them herself. Every smart man has a couple on him, and we noticed you didn't have any," he added, raising a skeptical eyebrow.

"You went through my things?" Connor flexed his fingers to ease the impulsive ribbon of irritation that snaked through him at the thought.

Ethan smirked. "What was left of them, anyway, after the soldiers got to you."

"You were a strange man in the middle of the woods who appeared out of nowhere." Kiera set her hands on her hips. "Of *course* we looked through your things."

Connor frowned.

Fair point.

The soft patter of footsteps echoed down the hallway, but from the gait, he couldn't tell which of the little girls raced toward him this time.

Moments later, Fiona scampered into the kitchen with a broad smile on her face. When her eyes drifted toward the bag sitting on the table by Connor, however, she skidded to an abrupt stop. "You're leaving?"

"I have to, kid," he said.

She lifted her tiny hands to her chest and took a few steps backward, as if she didn't know quite what to say. Her lip quivered, and she rubbed the back of her hand across her nose to hide a sniffle. Without another word, she ran up to him and hugged him tight, and her tiny little fingers dug into the back of his shirt.

At first, Connor simply stood there with his hands in the air, not quite sure what to do while this tiny human clung to him. When she didn't release him, he patted her head in an attempt to soothe her.

She sniffled louder this time, so it apparently hadn't worked.

"Try not to die, please," she said in a sweet little voice.

"Yeah," he said. "That's the plan."

With that, she ran back into the hallway and disappeared to the thump of Wesley's footsteps in the hall.

"Isabella's not coming," the boy said as he rounded the corner into the kitchen. "No offense, Connor."

"None taken."

"She's terrible at goodbyes," Kiera said softly. Her gaze darted toward the wall in what he assumed was the direction of Isabella's room.

Wesley stood at the opening into the hallway and settled into a wide stance. "I don't suppose you'll let me come with you?"

"No," Connor and Kiera said in unison.

Wesley shrugged, grinning, and his eyes swept over the adults in the room. "I had to ask."

"Take care of them," Connor ordered as he offered his hand to the young man.

Wesley shook it. "I'll do my best."

With that, Connor slung the pack over one shoulder. It always made for a bulky experience with the swords also on his back, but he made it work. Carrying the bag by hand got old quickly.

As he headed for the door, Wesley patted the bag. "Be careful out there."

Connor reached the ladder and climbed down. As he descended, he glanced up at the three heads peering through the hole in the porch above him. He wasn't used to kindness in this world, and he oddly enough found himself hoping this wouldn't be the last time he saw them.

If there was as much chaos after him as King Henry had promised, however, he refused to bring it to their door—no matter what Ethan had offered in terms of a safe harbor.

CHAPTER TWENTY-FOUR
QUINN

Eight days in Quinn's hunt, gone. Only twenty-two remained.

She lounged against a tree in the Ancient Woods just outside of Rutherglen and roughly a two days' walk from the Rift in the crumbling cathedral. The trunk's bark scraped against her back as she shifted her weight, and the roots protruding from the grass pressed into her thigh as she took a bite from a shiny green apple. The tangy juices nipped at her tongue, and she shivered with delight.

The greatest joys in life came from the smallest things. Sunlight through the canopy, casting dappled shadows on the grass. A flower along a riverbank, bending in the wind. Fruit fresh off the vine, so crisp that it snapped with every bite.

The apple tree above her swayed as a wind blew through its leaves, its apples ripe a full two seasons early. Someone around Rutherglen must've cared for this tree with a Rootrock hex for it to bloom out of season, but with no official title marker nailed to its trunk, the fruit was legally fair game.

It probably didn't have a title marker because its owner didn't have a hexes permit, which eased the last ribbons of her guilt at eating someone else's food. She took another bite and rested one ankle on her knee as the tart juices coated her lips.

Two sparrows dove through the canopy above her, twittering in the forest's gentle breeze as she took her mid-morning break to let Blaze hunt. With a whole week lost to a dead lead, she didn't have time to waste.

Her vougel, however, needed a good meal.

The crunch of bones snapping between his powerful jaws shattered the peaceful morning air, and she peered around the trunk as Blaze ripped off another chunk of muscle from the deer he'd caught. He munched happily as he lay on the ground beside the carcass, purring even as the beast's blood soaked the normally pristine white fur across his chest. He studied the birds as they danced overhead, his tail twitching playfully.

Quinn ran a hand through her thick hair, the fiery locks longer than she usually liked to keep them. Pretty hair got in the way of a good fight, but it was the one bit of vanity she allowed herself.

After all, she wasn't the only Starling to indulge a bit of pride.

Her trip south hadn't yielded a single clue, and though she had been right about the toy being sold in Lindow, there was no sign of the assassin. Not even a rumor, much less a sighting or a lead. Even though it made no sense for him to have taken any direction but south, it seemed as though her initial clue had taken her down a dead end and wasted valuable time she wasn't ever going to get back.

Damn it all.

As she bit again into the apple, she closed her eyes and leaned the back of her head against the apple tree's rough bark. Sunlight broke through a gap in the leaves above, and she listened to the forest around her as the light warmed her face. Cicadas chirping. The rustle of something running through the underbrush. The soft growl of a beast, far enough away to pose no threat. A sob.

Quinn sat upright, her eyes snapping open as she strained her ears to listen.

In the silence that followed, Blaze tore into the deer yet again. Meat ripped from bone. Tendons snapped. His joyful munching masked any chance of detecting the subtle sobbing she had heard.

To make him stop, she whistled, the chirp quick and quiet. A wordless command.

Be silent and observe.

He paused mid-bite, watching her as half a deer leg hung from his mouth. A drop of blood fell from the hoof onto his paw, but he remained perfectly still.

Through the twittering song of the birds overhead, a woman whimpered. The distant sound meandered through the trees, far enough away that Quinn couldn't quite place the direction it had even come from.

She stood and set her half-eaten apple at the base of the tree. Some lucky rabbit or boar was going to stumble across a free lunch today.

With a wave of her hand, she quietly ordered Blaze to follow. Her boots fell softly onto the grass, too quiet for even an augmented person to hear as she jogged into the forest. With her ear craned, she drew her sword and listened for any hint of the sobbing's source.

Hopefully, a young woman was simply upset and trying to find a bit of peace and quiet in the ancient forest. Quinn, however, wasn't one to take any chances. If someone needed help, she wasn't going to abandon them to the whims of the Ancient Woods.

Blaze groaned and stood over his half-eaten meal, his brow furrowing as he glanced from the carcass to her and back.

"You can eat later." She paused mid-stride and nodded into the forest. "We have work to do."

He growled, his eyes lingering on the deer before he obeyed. When he neared, Quinn listened to the forest's song, waiting to hear the whimpering again so that she could orient herself amongst the trees.

While they waited, she set a hand on his bloodstained neck to check on his mood. His soft fur brushed against her fingertips, and their connection opened almost instantly.

A surge of annoyance bubbled through, followed shortly thereafter by trust. She smiled and patted his neck, grateful for his dedication and faith in her.

Her ear twitched. There, again—to the north. A woman's voice, muffled by the thick forest.

Quinn darted off into the woods, and Blaze easily kept her pace. They shot through the forest with practiced ease as the sobbing grew louder. Neither of them made a sound, their muscles coiled as they prepared for the unknown that waited for them amongst the gnarled oaks. Her training and a good, old-fashioned Prowlport charm ensured her boots fell silently on the soil as she made her way through the forest.

Any Lightseer worth their merit went undetected at all times—until, of course, they wanted to be seen.

"Shut yer mouth, ya whore," a man snapped from somewhere nearby.

The woman's sobs floated through the trees like a mist, from everywhere and nowhere all at once.

Fire crackled in the midday forest as Quinn reached a tangle of bushes and knelt behind them. Blaze sank to the ground and pressed his blood-stained belly to the dirt as he kept his head low and his eye on Quinn, waiting for the order to attack.

In a verdant forest rife with greenery, the white and gold tiger couldn't possibly have hidden himself for long. In situations like these, they had to lie low and use their stealth to avoid detection.

As Quinn peeked around the bramble, she scanned the forest for signs of life. A wagon sat parked in the middle of a small meadow, its horses gone and their unbuckled harnesses lying on the grass. The wagon jostled to the tune of heavy boots thumping around inside. A glass shattered. Men laughed, their voices muffled by the wood.

Barely ten yards away, a man lay on the grass by a still-burning fire in a makeshift pit lined with mismatched rocks. Blood dripped from the fresh gouge in his throat as he stared vacantly into the forest, and a milky white sheen covered his once-brown eyes. His dirt-stained cheek rested in a dark red pool that seeped into the grass around him.

The sobbing continued, and the hard smack of skin on skin only made the woman cry harder.

Bandits, it had to be. And, from the sound of the woman's sobbing, potential rapists.

A jolt of rage scorched through Quinn, and her furious heart skipped several beats. She scowled, and flames crackled to life between her fingers as she barely managed to contain her fury. The unconscious fire in her palms licked the hilt of her sword as her grip tightened.

Everything in her ached to bolt into the meadow and kill everything that moved. The bloodlust came in a rush, and she barely silenced the urge in time. To regain her composure, she squeezed her eyes and gritted her teeth.

A Lightseer wielded power and authority far above the men and women they protected. To act with emotion would've dishonored not only her, but her family and her cause.

She went still, forcing the depths of her rage back into her soul. The seconds that passed felt like a lifetime when all she wanted to do was help, but she wouldn't have been useful to anyone if she had given in to bloodlust and made stupid, emotionally driven mistakes.

Though her heart finally settled, her hatred still burned like embers in a fire, deep within her chest. The fire in her hands flickered and died, though the magic in her blood ached to be freed.

It wasn't true calm, but it would have to do. These lawless forests needed more of the king's army patrolling it to keep the peace, and she would see to it she had a talk with her father when she returned with the assassin.

For now, Quinn and her sword would suffice.

She gestured for Blaze to wait behind the bush for now, and she strode into the field. From a quick scan of the trampled grass in the small meadow, she noticed five unique prints. One woman. One dead man. Therefore, she had at least three bandits to contend with.

Hardly a challenge, since men like this rarely wielded magic. Bandits along the main roads usually preferred to find weak targets and relied on sheer brawn and carnage to win.

They didn't stand a chance against her.

Quinn's grip tightened around *Aurora's* hilt, the heavy blade a deadly extension of her arm after their seven years of training together.

Sunlight glinted off the deadly steel as she quickly crossed the gap between her and the wagon. It creaked, the floorboards protesting as someone dragged something heavy toward the door at the other end.

Her ear twitched—two sets of footsteps. Two men inside, one heavier than the other and with a limp in his gait. They spoke in low tones, their curses muffled by the wagon's thick walls as another glass shattered inside.

"Please," the woman begged from the other side of the wagon. "Please, don't—"

"Shut yer gob, damn you," a man snapped. "This would be over faster if you stopped fightin' me."

The rage in Quinn's soul burned hotter, the fires lighting again even as she tried to remain calm. To focus. For all she knew, this could've very well been a trap. She doubted it, of course, but a Lightseer had to be vigilant.

She strained her ear to listen, her enhanced hearing picking up on the swish of skirts and the ragged breath of a man. The woman sobbed again, quieter this time, and the wagon creaked as they jostled.

Two men inside. One man and one victim outside. As she scanned the empty forest again for other signs of life, it seemed clear she only had a few bandits to kill today.

A pity. To vent all this rage, she would have preferred more.

She rounded the corner of the caravan, not bothering with stealth anymore. The woman's cheek pressed against the side of the wagon as a man held the back of her neck, rooting her in place. With her eyes squeezed shut, she faced Quinn. Loose curls stuck to her tear-stained freckles as she stifled her sobs. Her fingers curled against the side of the wagon. Long scratches carved through the soft blue paint, evidence of where her fingernails had dug into the wood.

At first, the man didn't even notice Quinn. He fussed with the woman's skirts as she squirmed beneath his grip, still trying to get away. His dark hair fell into his eyes as he tried to keep her still, his full attention on her even though he had yet to unbuckle his pants.

The woman was a fighter. She hadn't let him have his way. Quinn admired that, but the flames of her hatred for this man burned even hotter.

Men like this—they had chosen this life. They *chose* to shatter families and kill decent people who were just trying to make a living.

He deserved what she was about to do to him.

"Let her go at once," Quinn ordered.

The bandit flinched and cursed under his breath. He staggered backward, his eyes wide as he finally looked at her, and he shoved the woman aside. His victim fell to the ground beside the wagon, hidden in the shadows of her wheeled home.

"Look away, madam," Quinn said to the woman, though she never once took her eyes off the bandit.

Through the corner of her eye she watched as the woman curled into a ball and buried her face in her hands.

The man tensed, his shoulders practically to his ears as he took several wary steps backward. She kept pace with him, taking a step forward for each he took backward. As he inched into the meadow, the sunlight illuminated a dark red splatter along his beige shirt.

More evidence of his crimes.

He drew the sword at his waist as he sized her up. "You're one of them Starlings, ain't you?"

"I am. How many of you are there?"

"Plenty." His tongue darted over his cracked lips as his gaze drifted to her chest.

Sizing her up, no doubt—*a threat, or prey?*

She had seen that look too many times before, from too many men who assumed she had only gotten into the Lightseer elite because of her fire-red hair.

Those fools didn't last long.

"They're slavers!" the woman shouted from underneath the wagon. "Please kill them, m'lady! I beg of you!"

Quinn glanced over her shoulder, careful to keep the man in her periphery, and found the woman watching them through gaps in her fingers.

Not bandits, then, but something far worse. The evidence of theft, attempted rape, and outright murder only sealed their fate.

A death sentence—one Quinn, delightfully, had the authority to deliver.

"They killed my husband! My—" The woman wailed again, squeezing her eyes shut as she sobbed into the dirt. "They killed my Morris!"

The slaver's nose wrinkled with loathing as his gaze darted toward the woman on the ground. "Shut yer mouth, whore!"

"Don't speak to her like that," Quinn ordered.

Unfazed, the man licked his cracked lips yet again. "You best keep walkin', Starling. This don't concern you."

"On the contrary," she countered, her tone even and calm. "This very much concerns me now."

With a subtle turn of her wrist, her magnificent blade erupted with fire. The man flinched, and his eyes widened with fear. As flames licked the enchanted steel, the green gem in its hilt glowed with unbridled power.

His hands trembled. He aimed the tip of his sword at her, but Quinn had heard enough.

"For your crimes, I sentence you to death," she said, walking through the obligatory Lightseer Code even as she raised her Firesword. "Per my duty to the people, I will deliver your sentence myself, and you will die on *Aurora*'s blade."

It seemed to click for him, then, that she was most certainly not prey.

Mouth gaping with terror, he bolted. His sword thudded to the dirt. He ran across the meadow, surprisingly nimble on his feet, but Quinn easily kept his pace. She reached him within seconds and swung.

Her great blade sliced the back of his neck.

He crumpled instantly to the ground, his fingers twitching as his head dove into the dirt. The stark white of bone glistened briefly through the wine-red blood streaming from the gash. The skin around the wound sizzled, black and charred from *Aurora*'s enchanted flames. The stench of burning flesh snaked through the air like an aroma from a sick and twisted bazaar, but Quinn had long ago grown used to the revolting odor of burning men.

As he convulsed on the ground, Quinn drove her sword through his back. The great blade instantly severed his spine. Its flames consumed his body like wildfire, torching his entire form in a single, brutal moment. The stench of burning meat intensified, and she wrinkled her enhanced nose in disgust that men like this existed.

The would-be rapist let out a guttural scream as *Aurora's* magic consumed him, but it didn't last long. In seconds, the fires dissolved, and only his blackened corpse remained.

Dead—perhaps too soon. Maybe she had been too kind, but she couldn't waste time with two more targets to eliminate.

Still impaled by her blade, his shriveled carcass shuddered as his last scorching breath left him. Quinn rested her boot against his backside and used it as leverage to yank her beautiful sword free of the coward's corpse. Black soot drifted into the air as bits of him dissolved into ash.

"Mitch, ya damned fool!" a man shouted from the wagon. "What's all that noise?"

The thud of heavy boots on wood caught her ear, and she returned her attention to the wagon as two men emerged carrying a large, hand-carved chest between them. They trundled down the stairs, both of them peering around the wagon as they tried to get their bearings. One man wore an ornate purple and gold shirt that didn't match the stark browns his companion wore—more stolen goods, most likely.

Both men froze the instant they laid eyes on Quinn. Their eyes drifted in unison to the blackened cadaver beside her.

"Fuck," muttered the man in the ornate shirt.

Quinn rolled out her shoulders, ready for the next battle. "Yep."

The two men dropped the stolen chest and bolted into the forest. The trunk's lid popped open as it hit the dirt, and shimmering silks spilled out onto the grass as Quinn dismissed the fires along the sword with a subtle twist of her arm. She sheathed *Aurora* and whistled into the air—the cue for Blaze to join the hunt.

The bloodstained vougel roared as Quinn sprinted after the surviving slavers. His battle cry shattering the serene woodland. The white tiger bolted through the trees, a snowy blur amongst the browns and greens of the forest.

A hunter as honed and ruthless as Blaze didn't need camouflage.

The two slavers darted through the oaks, their ragged breath like a beacon in a fog even as their brown clothes blended with the trees. Every now and then, one of them glanced over his shoulder, his eyes wide with fear.

As Quinn and Blaze quickly closed the gap between them and the men, the two slavers split apart. One ran to the south, the other to the north. Quinn whistled and gestured toward the man who had veered off to the left, and Blaze roared as he headed off after the unfortunate slaver.

It wasn't a matter of if, but when he would die under the vougel's claws.

Though Quinn always enjoyed a good run, she'd had enough of these men. They had wasted yet more precious time. She sprinted after the northern-bound slaver, her eyes narrowing as she studied his movements. He had the slightest limp to his left leg, and she could use that to her advantage.

Quinn lifted her left arm, her fingers stretched as she manipulated the air around her with her Airdrift augmentation. A breeze that obeyed only her swirled through the trees and danced through her fiery curls.

Unlike fire, however, air resisted control. It had taken years to master, and even now, it always tested for weaknesses in its master's aim. As the air resisted her, Quinn groaned with effort and hurled the gust of wind at the back of her quarry's knees.

The air broke against his legs, and he shot forward from the force of the blow. His head bounced twice against the hard dirt as he fell, and he slid to a stop along the dead leaves of last autumn.

Quinn dropped to her knees as she reached him and slid across the dried leaves until she came to a stop. She snatched his collar and lifted him by his beautiful silken shirt, her lip curled into a snarl as she prepared to rid the world of another criminal.

"Please!" He grabbed her delicate wrist, and the calluses on his palms scratched against her smooth skin as his terrified brown eyes glistened with tears. "Please, I beg of you, let me live. Take me to prison if you must, but don't kill me!"

"You're a slaver. The Fates have no pity for a man like you, and neither do I."

"Please! I'll—I'll tell you where the others are." He raised his arms to protect his face, trembling in her grip as she held him aloft. "I'll lead you to them and the women we've stolen so far. I swear!"

Quinn paused, tempted by his offer. A chance to kill an entire roving band of slavers and rescue those they had captured thus far had quite the allure.

A piercing scream tore through the air, and the slaver in her hands flinched as he stared off into the trees. A low growl rumbled through the woods, followed by yet another agonizing scream. The cry cut short, and the sickening crunch of snapping bones followed.

"Please," the last surviving slaver begged.

Quinn stared at him with cold ambivalence. People like this man—people who preyed on the weak—deserved no pity. As her right hand held his collar, she dropped her other hand to her side. Flames crackled along her left palm while she debated his fate, the fires of her Burnbane augmentation as natural to her as breathing.

She didn't have the luxury of time. With a king's assassin on the loose, she didn't have weeks to devote to a slaver hunt, even with a lead as amazing as this.

The sheriff in Rutherglen, however, did.

"If you try anything, you will die," Quinn warned. "If you try to escape, I will let my vougel hunt you. If you attack me, I will kill you myself, and I will ensure it is as painful as possible. Do you understand?"

"Yes. Yes! Oh, bless you. Bless you." As she held his collar, he kissed her wrist, her arm, her hand—anything his putrid lips could reach.

She grimaced with disgust and dropped him. As he groveled at her feet, she wiped off the slime leftover from his sloppy gratitude. With a twitch of her fingers, she dismissed the fire in her left palm and grabbed his collar from behind this time, hauling him to his feet with ease.

Her dozens of augmentations gave her an advantage over nearly everyone she encountered, and she thanked her lucky stars every day for the blessing.

Quinn fetched a pair of thin iron cuffs from a pouch at her waist and twisted his arms behind his back. He whimpered at the jarring movements but stood in place, wisely remaining immobile. His compliance almost disappointed her. Part of her wished he would've tried to escape. Part of her wanted to drive her sword through him, or better yet, channel lightning straight through his heart.

But the Lightseers protected the people, and she had a duty to ensure the other slavers were found. Sparing his life would save countless others. She would take him to the sheriff in Rutherglen, and even though it would cost her several precious hours in her hunt for King Henry's assassin, she would never betray the people who trusted her to keep the peace.

She shoved the shackled bandit hard in the back, and he stumbled back toward the field. With her hand firmly grasping the sleeve of his shirt, she guided him through the trees.

As they returned to the meadow, a white blur bounded through the oaks toward them. The man panicked and bolted, babbling terrified nonsense as he tripped over himself and ran into a tree.

Technically, he'd tried to run, but Quinn forgave it as a moment of stupefied terror. She kept hold of his shirt and rooted him in place even as he tried to break free, his panic getting the better of him.

Blaze reached them, he stretched out his wings with victory. His tail darted happily back and forth as a severed arm hung from his mouth. He purred, waiting for permission to eat as blood dripped from the dead slaver's fingertips.

"Drop it," Quinn warned. "We don't eat people, Blaze."

His ears drooped, and he growled.

She quirked one eyebrow, daring him to disobey her. "Now."

The vougel spit out the severed arm and grumbled, stalking off into the meadow as he folded his wings against his side. His tail swished violently back and forth, a clear sign of his annoyance as he pouted.

In the meadow, the woman from earlier sat by the smoldering embers of the fire and held the dead man's corpse in her arms. She sobbed into his face and clutched him, their wagon and the overturned chest of silks ignored. Quinn paused at the edge of the field, not wanting to interrupt, and her heart twisted as she witnessed the woman's grief.

Deep down, she hated herself for not reaching the field in time to save them both.

Delivering the woman safely into town and giving the slaver over to the sheriff was going to be a massive delay, one no other Lightseer she knew of would indulge. To Quinn, however, it was a delay worth making.

A Lightseer was only as good as the people they protected, and this was the only life Quinn knew. She would never dream of failing her father, but she couldn't fail herself, either.

CHAPTER TWENTY-FIVE
CONNOR

As the afternoon sun crept through the sky, Connor knelt by a stream. A few pebbles in the bank pressed against his knee, and the damp soil seeped through the fabric of his pants. The gurgle of the brook sang through the air as the trees swayed above him, the forest's lullaby as soothing as ever in the surreal silence.

After so long with the Finns, the deafening quiet loomed like a fog. He had once craved this over the chatter and nonstop giggling, but now the air seemed almost empty.

He scooped a handful of water and splashed it on his neck, and a delightful shiver snaked down his spine as it soothed his hot skin. With one arm resting on his knee, he washed his face and relished the chill in the otherwise hot day.

In the ceaseless southern wind, leaves trembled above him. The shivering canopy cast dappled light across the brook as the gust took hold. He peered through the leaves, catching a brief glimpse of the sky as a cloud rolled past.

Out here in the wilds, survival was a dice game, and a man's wit was about the only thing he could count on to keep him alive. Creatures waited in this grove, hungry and aching for a good meal. Once the sun set, this forest became theirs, and any living thing became prey. Between roving bandits and rogue soldiers from the city, the daylight hours didn't exactly offer safe haven, either.

To reach Bradford before nightfall, he had to find the main road soon.

Traveling through the trees protected him from the outlaws and lawmen patrolling the main road, but it slowed him down.

Though he had never been overly fond of people, the road was faster. He would simply have to take the risk and stare down anyone who sized him up for a fight. If he did encounter a roadblock or a troop of bandits, perhaps the Wraith King would finally prove himself useful instead of a nuisance.

The phantom wanted blood, after all.

The empty flask at his waist bumped against his thigh, and he unhooked it from his belt to refill it. As his hand dipped below the clear surface, several green goldfish swam up to his fingers. They nibbled gently at his knuckles, and as they hovered near him, they glowed—softly at first, but brighter the longer they stayed.

As Connor knelt by the creek, a herd of deer wandered to the water downstream. He paused, careful not to move as they lowered their heads to drink, their fangs dipping into the stream as their black tongues lapped at the current. His stomach rumbled, and he debated hunting for some fresh game to preserve his food stores.

Above them, a branch creaked, and a horned owl with a body as large as his torso settled on one of the lower limbs of a nearby tree. The deer ignored the rustling leaves, their focus on the creek, and Connor figured this herd of prey was spoken for. He wouldn't get a meal out of them—not if that owl had already staked its claim.

No sense staying quiet, then.

He stood, and the deer bolted into the forest. Their white tails flashed in the low light as they retreated, the bushes and underbrush shaking with their escape. The owl's head pivoted toward them, and it paused briefly to track their movements before it flew off after the herd.

Instead of fresh venison, Connor settled for dried meat. He rifled through his pack and grabbed a few strips as he trudged through the forest. Though it didn't stifle the surging hunger, he suppressed the urge to eat the rest.

As he swung the pack over his shoulder again, the rattle of coins somewhere in the bag caught his attention. Still chewing, he frowned and dug again through the pack, since his coin purse had never left his belt. One of the smaller pockets on the outside of the bag jingled, and as he unbuckled it, he found the small coin purse Ethan had tried to give him.

He groaned with disappointment.

On the way out of the house, Wesley had patted his back—which meant that sneaky little bastard had hidden the money. Connor shook his head, admittedly impressed Wesley had gotten the better of him.

You frustrate me, a grim voice echoed in his mind.

The Wraith King.

The great specter appeared between two nearby oaks, floating through the air as if he were pacing back and forth even though his feet never touched the ground.

You are affiliated with me, the Wraith King said. *You represent me now. You should be living like a king, not a peasant, even if you are painfully common.*

"No one knows you exist," Connor pointed out. "Even Henry didn't tell the people who you really are. He would have never admitted it because no one would have respected his authority. Except for the people who want to kill you—and me, thanks for that—everyone thinks you're dead."

It doesn't matter, the ghost insisted. *Power like mine is wasted in the woods.*

"That's why we're going to a village," he said with a wry smirk. "Mud covered roads. Drunk peasants brawling in the taverns. You'll love it."

The wraith groaned with irritation. *Go to Slaybourne.*

"Pass."

Rebuild my great citadel, the Wraith King continued, as if he hadn't spoken. *Bend men to your will, remind them of my greatness, and build your army. Take this land back. Pillage a town for the hell of it if you want. I don't care anymore. At this point, I'll settle for petty theft along the southern road. Do something—anything other than walking aimlessly through a forest, for the Fates' sake.*

Connor rolled his eyes and swung the pack over one shoulder. Without a word, he continued through the trees as if the Wraith King weren't there at all.

Well? the ghost prodded, floating beside Connor as he hiked. *Say something.*

He shrugged. "Why bother? You're only going to ignore or insult me."

You learn quickly, the ghoul admitted. *But the conversation gives me mild entertainment, so I will settle for listening to your misguided nonsense.*

"Right, nonsense. Of course." Connor gestured toward the forest around them. "Why can't you simply enjoy the day? Why all this talk about war? Why must you conquer everything you see?"

You truly don't understand?

"Never have," he admitted. "When Henry conquered Saldia, it seemed like such a waste of life. All those people dead, and for what? To make a rich man richer?"

Of all the lords and kings in Saldia, I had to fuse with a laborer, the Wraith King mumbled. *I suppose I shouldn't fault you. Perhaps you simply can't understand what it means to have ambition. You're just a directionless drifter with no purpose and no meaning to his life. Why should I expect more from you?*

Connor stopped in his tracks and glared at the dead asshole hovering beside him. "Killing men doesn't give anyone meaning. It just passes the time until you die—or until someone kills you. Maybe I'm tired of the bullshit you powerful folk call ambition. Maybe I want something *more.*"

To his credit, the Wraith King finally stopped talking. Instead, the dead man's skull of a face angled toward Connor, and those empty eye sockets studied him in the silence.

With an irritated huff, Connor adjusted the bag on his shoulder and resumed his hike, not much caring if the Wraith King followed. In his periphery, the ghoul dissolved on the wind. The black wisps of his cloak faded into smoke, and he was gone.

Perhaps the specter was right. Maybe Connor didn't have ambition. In the end, it didn't matter. That stupid old ghost was just as lost and devoid of purpose as him.

CONNOR

True to Ethan's word, Connor reached the outskirts of Bradford around dusk, just before it got dark enough to wonder if the blightwolves would howl. Wide enough for five horses to ride side by side, the cobblestone road beneath his boots curved its way through the forest as he headed north.

To his surprise, there hadn't been a single bandit on the road. He doubted that luck would hold, but he appreciated the reprieve.

At least something had gone right today.

The woods around him ended in a large stretch of grassy fields surrounding the walled town, and the winding road led to an open gate. A soldier in a dark uniform stood above the gates, his hand wrapped around a spear as he watched something inside the wall.

Connor slipped into the woods to form a plan. For all he knew, Otmund had warned the sheriffs along the road that he might've been coming. He didn't want to fight off dozens of guards again—and definitely not with an audience of townsfolk this time.

He had walked unnoticed through a town before. As long as he kept his head down and didn't draw attention to himself, he would be fine.

Two massive flames burned on either side of the gate, their green fire crackling with furious intensity. A blended perfume of honeysuckle and lavender radiated from the fires, along with the stinging bite of pine. Large pots filled with the emerald flame burned every ten feet along the towering stone wall.

He often saw these potions burning around towns and houses to keep the blightwolves at bay. He rarely saw this many ablaze at one time, though, and Bradford apparently had enough money to care about its citizens' safety.

A luxury in this day and age.

Still crouched in the forest, Connor tugged his hood over his head.

Wearing a cloth over his face would only raise suspicion, and he needed to blend in as best he could.

Disgraceful. The Wraith King's ghoulish form appeared beside Connor as they stared at the walled town through gaps in the oak trees. *You should be conquering this village, not sneaking into it.*

"Mm-hmm," Connor said dryly, not really listening anymore. "You need to disappear. I can't have any of them seeing you and telling Otmund where I am."

The Wraith King studied him, and for several moments, the ghost didn't move. Connor got the feeling the specter couldn't decide if he would listen—perhaps he wanted a bit of fun, and a battle would be an easy way for him to get the blood he wanted.

But this wasn't a negotiation.

Connor's brow furrowed, and he stood to face the ghoul beside him. He got as close to the skull as he could and glared into the holes where the man's eyes used to be.

"Listen to me closely." His voice dropped an octave, to the gravelly tone he usually reserved for bandits when they drew their swords on him. "You can't kill me directly, but I know you well enough by now to guess what you'll do."

You think so?

He scoffed. "I know so. You love causing trouble. You thrive on pain. You're bored, but you haven't thought any of this through. With the enemies I'm facing, you'll get your blood. You'll get your war, and I doubt you'll have to wait long. But if you make a scene at any point while I'm in public—whether it's today in Bradford or tomorrow in some other village—there are ways for me to destroy you. The old legends tell us that much."

Oh? the ghost challenged, a hint of laughter in his tone.

The ghoul thought of this as a joke. Connor, however, did not.

"Don't try me," he warned. "Every legend ends the same way. It doesn't matter how dark the magic is or how corrupted it has become. There's always a way to shatter it. So, if you don't listen when I tell you to do something,

I will do everything in my power to find out how to kill you for good. No coming back. Dead, once and for all, with no one else to torment and no way to sate your bloodlust. Even if it means I lose my swords—"

My swords, the ghoul corrected.

"My swords," Connor repeated, more firmly this time. "If I lose my new weapons and my senses, so be it. I won't be your puppet, no matter what you think you can dangle in front of me." He paused, his eyes narrowing as he dared the wraith to challenge him. "Are we clear?"

The ghost waved his bony hand dismissively. *You wouldn't give up this power. You can claim you don't care about those blades, but even you are smarter than that.*

"I survived just fine without them."

He ignored the twinge of disappointment that snaked through him at the thought, but he hadn't lied. In the end, they were nothing more than objects he didn't truly need.

Connor curled his hand into a fist and pressed his thumb into his chest. "You've seen every type of king and lord, but you've never met a man more stubborn than me, I can guarantee you that. If there's a way to get rid of you, there's nothing like a crafty peasant to figure it out. We don't abide by your rules, and we're used to clawing our way through hell every day, just to see the next sunrise. We're not weak, like you rich folk think. We're clever."

For a long while, the Wraith King didn't answer. He simply hovered in the silence, his skeletal face vacant and impossible to read. Connor tensed his jaw, daring the dead fool to test him.

You intrigue me, the Wraith King admitted. With a dry laugh, he dissolved into the wind.

"Son of a—" Connor groaned with annoyance.

If the dead king didn't stay hidden, the old ghost was going to learn the hard way that Connor was a man of his word. No matter what powers the wraith gave him, he wouldn't become some dead man's puppet.

He wasn't the sort of man who could be bought.

With his hood covering much of his face, he stepped onto the main road. The uneven cobblestones pressed against the thinning soles of his boots, and though he likely needed to find a new pair soon, he wouldn't waste the money tonight.

The clop of hooves cut through the air from behind him, approaching quickly. He peered over his shoulder as a young man flew down the path, his eyes on the town as he thundered by. Sweat coated the horse's neck, and foam gathered on the bit in its mouth as it stormed past. Connor stepped aside as the horse neared, and its rider didn't so much as look at him as they nearly ran him over.

You're going to suffer that insult? the Wraith King asked with a hint of disgust. Though he didn't appear, his voice echoed through Connor's mind.

"It's just an idiot on a horse." Connor made his way down the road, keeping an eye on the guard at the gate as the soldier waved to the rider. "If you let every little insult rile you, you'd be dead within a week. Letting your pride get the best of you just makes you easier to manipulate."

Hunt him down and kill him, the Wraith King demanded, ignoring everything Connor had just said.

With those words, Connor's blood ran cold. A sudden and powerful rush of energy burned within him, like a torch lit in the night. A thirst for blood and vengeance bubbled beneath his skin, hot and fierce.

Foreign and overwhelming, the sensation scorched his soul, commanding him to act.

To conquer.

To kill.

You have the power, the Wraith King pointed out. *No man should disrespect you again. If he belittles you, then he belittles me. You and I are one in the same, and I do not tolerate contempt from any living soul.*

Connor gritted his teeth and swallowed hard, briefly shutting his eyes to block out the sensation and the sound of the Wraith King's voice. "If you killed every idiot in the world, there wouldn't be anyone left to rule. We're all stupid at one point or another."

I do not understand you, the Wraith King said with an infuriated growl as Connor neared the gate. *Why wouldn't you kill those who insult and annoy you?*

"For the same reason I'm still alive and you're dead," he muttered, careful to ignore the guard's lingering gaze.

To his credit, the Wraith King laughed. *Touché, peasant.*

Connor grinned. Perhaps the irritating ghost had a sense of humor after all.

As he stepped through the gates and into the marketplace, the bustle of shouting voices overlapping each other drowned out all sense of order in the chaos. He had a good two inches of height over most of the people around him, and he took the chance to look for a tavern among the shops.

Hundreds of people crowded in the dense streets, bustling between the vendors who had set up their stalls outside the local storefronts along the main road through town. The crowds parted as the rider from before led his horse through the crowd and wandered off down a side road, slower now that he had reached the safety of the town walls. The wide cobblestone road stretched between the long rows of white houses, their brown trim a stark contrast to delicate storefronts.

Signs hung over each door along the main road, each etched with a symbol to let the illiterate know what they could buy inside. A frothy mug hung over a nearby door—the first tavern to welcome folks into town.

The door to the pub opened, and a man with no shirt drunkenly staggered into the doorframe. He tripped down the stairs and landed on his palms. His head lolled, and he heaved his dinner onto the front steps as laughter rolled from the candlelit room behind him.

Though Ethan had recommended he find a sellsword in one of the taverns, Connor opted to start his hunt elsewhere.

He scanned the rest of the storefronts, still looking for something useful. A farmer, perhaps, or a butcher—anyone who could get him more food at a good price. A toy maker's shop stood nearby, a thin little building with a small window display facing the street.

In the window, two charmed dolls danced and spun on a table by the windowsill. Their skirts swished every which way as they twirled their arms and went through their choreographed routine. The red lips painted on their faces didn't move, and their eyes never once blinked as they twirled. Their honey-brown skin glistened in the setting sun as their blue silk dresses swished and spun.

To his surprise, Connor thought immediately of Fiona and Isabella. Perhaps they would've enjoyed something like that. If he ever saw them again, maybe he would bring them each a gift.

A produce stall sat just beside the entrance to the toy shop, and as the man tending the stall leaned over to talk to a woman holding a long carrot, his produce shivered. A large leafy plant wriggled in its basket, its vines tangled around the front post as its bright red blossoms shivered in the breeze. Buckets along the front of the stall overflowed with a bountiful harvest, from pumpkins to radishes to strawberries—food from every season.

Spellgust had endless possibilities if one knew how to use it. It was something Connor had always admired about magic, even if he hadn't always understood it. Beck Arbor had used potions to grow crops out of season, much to the delight of the local merchants. It had cost more to make, of course, but produce out of season often fetched triple the normal price.

His stomach gurgled so loudly that a little girl in the crowd gasped in surprise. Her mother scowled at him before hurrying her child on.

Steal, the Wraith King said in his mind. *You need to eat, and you have precious little coin.*

"No," he muttered under his breath. He rubbed his jaw to hide the fact that his lips were moving when he wasn't talking to anyone the townsfolk could see.

In the distance along the edge of the road, the familiar symbol of a potion bottle etched into a hanging sign caught his eye. The wooden plaque swung on iron hooks outside the largest shop so far. Four windows advertised the potion master's wares, the displays lined with open books and glowing potion bottles.

Though he briefly debated ducking in to find a few extra potions that might've helped him on his travels, he resisted the impulse. His money would be better spent on a sellsword and hiring a necromancer. He scanned the other signs instead, looking for another frothing beer mug, until he spotted four men in dark cloaks weaving through the crowd.

Toward the potion shop.

Interesting.

He stepped to the side of the bustling road and leaned his shoulder against the toy shop wall as he hid behind the produce vendor's stall to watch. The men trotted up the stairs to the potion shop and glanced over their shoulders at the crowd before ducking inside. As the last man entered, he drew a thin dagger from the belt at his waist.

Damn it.

Patrons wouldn't have glanced over their shoulders, as if wary of witnesses. Legitimate businessmen didn't draw a dagger before entering.

Thieves, probably. Sneaking into a shop at dusk, no less, while guards watched the walls for signs of the blightwolves. Usually, a town's sparse militia didn't focus much attention on patrolling the roads until nightfall, since most thieves would never have been so brazen as to break in with so many people walking the streets.

Clever bastards.

He groaned, torn between staying focused on his mission and doing what his father would have done.

Do right by people, and you'll never go wrong, his father had always said.

As a Kirkwall merchant, his father had sometimes thrown debt ledgers in the garbage and sent starving single mothers on their way with enough food to last the week. Whenever they had tried to pay him back, he conveniently had no records of the debt they owed.

Connor rubbed his eyes, his damned conscience winning yet again.

You've finally noticed something useful. The Wraith King's dark voice boomed in Connor's mind. *I'm impressed, peasant. If those bandits are any good, perhaps you could recruit them.*

"You should know me better than that by now," he muttered.

You—curse the Fates, you fool, are you going to try to stop them?

As Connor scanned the road, quietly hoping a guard had noticed the thieves, he didn't reply. No one else so much as looked at the potion shop.

It seemed as though the potion master wasn't going to get any help from the town's lawmen tonight.

The wraith groaned in disgust. *You would save a stranger? You refuse to take what you need, and yet this is the way you sate my bloodlust? What has this potion master done for you?*

"I do right by people." He tilted his head toward the buildings beside him to hide the fact that he spoke to what others perceived to be empty air.

The ghost scoffed. *Doing right by the Finns didn't work out well for you. Now, I'm stuck chaperoning you through a dull old town.*

Connor shrugged. "Can't win them all."

He slipped back into the crowd and darted through the chaotic street. Merchants shouted around him, and women huddled together, chatting arm-in-arm as they walked through the bustling market. A black curtain behind one of the shop's window displays dropped, most likely to hide whatever happened next from any passersby.

As he reached the steps, he paused to collect his thoughts. If this fight tumbled into the streets, the sheriff might get involved, and all hell could break loose.

His father's words swam through his mind yet again.

What good is a man who sees evil and does nothing?

Connor took a deep breath, squared his shoulders, and reached for the doorknob.

Damn his bleeding heart.

CHAPTER TWENTY-SIX
CONNOR

A s Connor twisted the doorknob to the potion maker's shop, it refused to turn.

Locked, despite the bustling street and a near-monopoly on the potions business of Bradford.

Part of him warned against interfering. After all, he didn't know the potion master personally. For all he knew, the man could've been making a black-market deal for spellgust or human slaves.

The idea seemed far-fetched. An illicit deal wouldn't have happened during business hours, when anyone could have knocked on the shop window or peeked around back to check in on things. It simply didn't make sense.

With his back to the street, he covered his mouth and nose with the black scarf around his neck. Whatever lay beyond this door, he was more certain than ever that it wouldn't end well.

Careful not to draw attention to himself, he leaned into the door. His grip on the knob tightened, and the muscles in his arm tensed until the lock gave way beneath his newly enhanced strength. The handle shuddered beneath his hand, limp and broken, as the door creaked open.

A little bell above the entry chimed, destroying whatever element of surprise he might've had.

An odd cologne rushed from the dark shop, a blend of too many ingredients for even Connor to name—cardamom, bergamot, oak resin, jasmine petals, willow bark, and so many more. The herbal concoction barraged him, and he nearly gagged. His eyes briefly watered as the overwhelming scent crashed into him.

A line of thick pillar candles burned on a shelf across from him as he entered, their flames flickering in the draft that followed him inside.

A trembling voice piped up from the depths of the shop. "P-please, don't—"

"Shut your mouth, old man," a hoarse voice snapped.

"Do you want coin? Potions?" The man whimpered, and something clattered to the floor. "I'll give you what you want, just let me live and—"

The sickening crack of metal on bone shattered the still air, and a body thudded to the floor.

Connor closed the door behind him, and the bell chimed again. His fingers curled into a fist as he scanned the shelves around him and prepared for the worst.

A walkway lined with stacked books and loose papers led through the dozens of shelves, their surfaces littered with jars of dried mushrooms and flowers suspended in oil. The path led around a corner, and though Connor couldn't see beyond the dozens of ivy plants blocking his view, he strained his ear to listen.

No wise man went into this sort of situation blind, but the conversation stopped.

He listened to the ragged breathing just beyond the tangled green vines draped over the dark brown shelf. It sounded like perhaps four or five people waited around the corner. Though he walked with silent purpose, the wooden floor creaked beneath someone else's boot. A man quietly cleared his throat. The creak of skin tightening around the hilt of a weapon punctuated the air.

Wary of summoning the black blades in front of strangers, Connor drew one of the twin swords from his back. His shoulders ached from the tension. The threat of a brewing fight hummed through the shop.

The Wraith King was about to get the blood he so badly wanted.

A row of long branches covered in dried blue leaves hung from the ceiling, and he ducked around them on his way to the shelf of ivy. As he reached the bookshelf, a floorboard creaked just beyond it. He knelt, angling his sword upward, ready for the battle to begin.

A man in a black hood rounded the corner, driving his sword into the empty air where Connor had stood moments before. Before the stranger could so much as look down, Connor drove his blade into the man's gut and twisted the sword as it drove through his stomach. Still crouched, he shifted his weight to one foot and drove the heel of his other shoe into the man's thigh, knocking him backward.

The whole exchange had taken only a few seconds, and Connor yanked his blood-soaked blade from the man's body as the fool stumbled backward.

The thief's sword clattered to the floor. He stared down at the open wound in his gut as his back slammed into a shelf. The jars behind him rattled, and a few rolled onto their side as he held his hands over his stomach. Several fell, shattering like rain at his feet, and their oil slicked the wooden floor.

Connor stood, pressing his back to the shelf of ivy as he lifted his sword, ready to deal the next blow.

Vines poked into his spine as he strained his ear and listened again for any sign of a pending attack. The walkway angled around his bookcase and led deeper into the shop—toward the four remaining bodies that waited for him to make his next move.

"Show yourself," the hoarse man ordered.

The first thief gurgled and slid to the floor, no longer a threat as he choked on his own blood. He gasped for air as his head fell backward, and his eyes rolled into the back of his head. The man slouched against the wood, and his hands plopped to the floor. Breathing, but unconscious as blood rushed from the injury in his abdomen. With a stab wound like that, he had minutes at most before he bled out entirely.

Through it all, none of the other thieves moved. They hadn't so much as gasped when he took a blade to the gut, and that told Connor everything he needed to know about these men.

No honor. No loyalty. No chance they would defend each other when he began to rip them apart.

They were weak.

Beyond his ivy-covered bookshelf, a man whimpered again as the clatter of a pot rolling across the floor broke the silence.

The shopkeeper hadn't died, then, and only three thieves remained.

"Bless you, whoever you are!" the old man shouted. "Kill them, and I'll pay you like a king!"

Finally, the Wraith King said.

"Stay out of this," Connor ordered under his breath. "You can't let the shopkeeper see you."

The ghoul sighed, long and impatient, but he didn't reply.

Connor ignored the specter as he focused on the chaos before him. The clomp of boots shook the floorboards as someone retreated further into the shop, likely toward the potion master. The scuffle of someone scurrying across the floor and the ragged breath of the other two thieves gave Connor a loose idea of where the surviving men stood.

Two men remained between him and the old man. The third stalked toward the potion master, likely to kill him once and for all.

What little information he had to go on would simply have to do.

He grabbed a dagger off his belt with his free hand and dropped to the floor. Shoulders tight and back arched for the throw, it looked like he had to make the next move.

Connor hated making the first move in a fight, as it gave away his position and usually cost him the advantage. With the potion master's life on the line, however, he didn't have much time to waste on patience.

While keeping low to the floor, he rounded the corner and threw the small blade in one fluid motion. It meant he couldn't aim, but it would do its job nonetheless. Better to throw them off their game, even if he missed his target.

They had a similar idea.

As he rounded the corner, a dagger sailed through the air toward him and sliced through the space above his head, landing with a dull thud in the shop wall. His blade missed the nearest thief by barely an inch before it shattered a tall glass jar filled with a black flower the size of his head. Liquid cascaded over the shelf like a waterfall, the blade of his dagger embedded deep in the shelf as the hilt of his blade quivered from the force of his throw.

"Not my reagents!" The old man peeked his balding head out from behind one of the glass displays farther down the line. "Do you know how much that flower *costs*?"

He ignored the old man as the surviving thieves took cover. In the momentary lull, he had a chance to survey his opponents.

Three men, each dressed in grays and blacks. Two with dark hair and thick beards. The third crouched by a row of glass displays along the far wall as he took cover from the dagger that had nearly embedded in his skull. A long scar across the third man's mouth twisted as he frowned, and he glared at Connor briefly before he ducked behind the displays filled with knives and jewel-encrusted combs.

The two closest thieves drew their swords and jumped to their feet, racing toward him as their eyes narrowed. His grip on his own blade tightened as he prepared for the attack in the tightly confined row between the candlelit bookshelves.

When he had to fight, Connor preferred large fields. The wide spaces gave him room to recover, react, pause, and plan a new line of attack if necessary. These close-quarter fights usually ended with far more injuries.

The first to reach him swung, the thief's long brown hair flying with the brute force of the blow. Connor lifted his own blade to block it, and the clash of steel nearly deafened him in the small space.

The second thief jabbed his blade over his comrade's shoulder, perfectly aimed for Connor's neck. Connor kicked the first man in the gut, knocking him backward just in time to block the second blow to the shattering clang of steel.

He threw a left hook into the second thief's jaw. Pain splintered across his knuckles as the man's bone shattered beneath his fist. The thief cursed and held his face as he stumbled backward.

The first thief swung his sword again. Connor leaned back, and the steel missed his nose by an inch. The blade sank into a nearby shelf, and the candles behind him trembled from the force.

No reprieve. Not a second to breathe.

Connor drove his fist into the first thief's stomach. As the man gasped for air, the man with the scar strode behind the glass displays toward the shopkeeper trapped at the end of the row. He grabbed the balding man by his collar and lifted him off his feet until they were eye-to-eye.

It didn't seem as though the potion master had long to live.

The two thieves jabbed at him in unison, and Connor blocked their swords to the clash of metal. Though the third bandit's mouth moved, he spoke in a tone too hushed for Connor to hear over the clang of steel.

If the potion master died, all of this risk and blood would be in vain. He had to end this.

Now.

Heat raced through his veins as he kicked the nearest thief hard in the stomach. The man staggered backward, and Connor swung at the second thief's head. The man ducked the blow, and Connor's sword dug deep into a shelf.

The thief smirked and drove his sword at Connor's gut, but Connor twisted out of the way with a fraction of an inch to spare.

In a moment of pure impulse, he did the first thing he could think of.

Since his normal blade had sunk deep into the shelf, he left it. He would get it later. Instead of wasting precious seconds to pry it free, he summoned one of his enchanted black blades into his hand and drove it into the thief's exposed neck.

A risk, but one worth taking. One that gave him back the element of surprise.

The man's eyes widened as he reached for the blade in his neck, but Connor ripped it loose and kicked the man hard in his chest. The thief stumbled backward and collapsed onto the floor. Even as he held his throat, his blood bubbled through his fingers. He stared at Connor, eyes wide with shock, and gasped like a fish vying for its final breaths.

The criminal's blood burned in the blackfire of the enchanted blade, and as the wine-red goop sizzled, a chill snaked through the room.

In an instant, the tide had shifted—this time, in Connor's favor, and he lost himself in the fight.

With that effortless kill, a surge of power burned through his very soul. He succumbed to the skirmish, the sword in his hand as natural as if he had been forged for this, as if he had been born for combat and bred in the blood of those who dared to stand against him.

Ah, the Wraith King said, his voice echoing through Connor's mind. *There it is.*

Connor didn't care. He had two men left to kill.

Though one silver blade still sat in the sheaths on his back, he left his second silver blade stuck in the bookshelf. With only one of his black swords held aloft, his focus shifted to the nearest of the two remaining thieves.

The bandit gasped, his eyes wide as he stared at the dying man on the floor, and he took several wary steps backward. Connor didn't give the thief a moment to debate retreat. Instead, he stalked closer, taking back whatever gap the criminal tried to put between them.

Based on what Connor had heard when he'd entered the shop, every thief here had made the same choice tonight. They had come to rob and kill a defenseless old man, and now they had seen too much for him to show any mercy.

The man squared his shoulders, lifting his blade as a final warning for Connor to keep his distance. "What the hell are you?"

Connor didn't answer.

He didn't need to.

The shadow sword crackled with midnight fire as he swung, and though the man lifted his blade to deflect the attack, the undead black steel sliced effortlessly through the weapon. Half of the long steel sword clattered to the floorboards as Connor's blade cut through the man's neck, severing it from his spine with the treacherously intense magic of a dead king.

Magic Connor now controlled.

The thief's head plopped to the floor with a nauseating thud, like meat on a wooden slab at a butcher's shop. His corpse sank to its knees and keeled over against a shelf, rattling the old wooden structure and the bottles perched precariously on its surfaces. What remained of the thief's sword clattered to the floor.

At the back of the shop, the last surviving thief paused. Though he still held the trembling shopkeeper aloft, his gaze swept over the corpses littering the store before it settled on Connor.

Lost in a moment of astonishment and suspicion.

The lull lasted only a few seconds, and he released his grip on the old man. The shopkeeper collapsed in a heap behind the display, hidden by the rows of jewel-encrusted daggers protected behind the glass.

He kicked the glass display between them, sending it crashing to the floor. It shattered, and the knives displayed inside slid across the wood beneath their feet.

The man drew his sword. "You don't know when to quit."

"And you should've been paying attention." Connor raised the black blade in his hand as dark flame rolled across its surface. The dead men's blood boiled along the cursed steel.

Apparently undeterred by the enchanted weapon, the bandit swung. Connor easily ducked out of the way. The thief's sword dug into the wall, and Connor kicked him hard in the side. Though a bone cracked under Connor's boot, the thief didn't crumple to the floor.

The man staggered backward and cursed under his breath. With a furious yell, he managed to pry his weapon out of the wood. He swung wildly, the blade glinting in the shop's low light as he tried to hit something. Connor simply leaned back, the movement almost too easy as he avoided swing after swing.

You're toying with him, the Wraith King said. *If I didn't know you to be a humorless ass, I would say you're enjoying this.*

Connor groaned with annoyance and swung, ready to finish this once and for all if only to stop the old ghost's commentary.

His shadow blade cut through the bandit's sword, and the man froze in momentary panic. He dropped the hilt of his broken weapon, and both halves of the sword clattered on the ground as he gaped at Connor.

Done with the fight and keen to finish, Connor kicked the survivor in the knee. Bones snapped. The man fell with a pained yell and thudded to the floor. He whimpered, his leg bent at an unnatural angle as he scuffled backward toward the display he had destroyed moments before. He scooted through the broken glass, terror in his eyes as he retreated along the hardwood floor, and Connor lifted his dark blade to deal the final blow.

The thief grasped at the floor around him, his fingers stretching as he tried to find something, anything, to defend himself. He snatched one of the daggers from the debris around him and lifted it as Connor swung.

Their blades collided—and the dagger didn't fracture beneath the black blade's magic. It held, saving the thief's life by a few inches and a bit of luck.

Connor paused, shocked into stillness as he stared at the unbroken dagger in the thief's hand. The man's chest heaved, and in the lingering moment of silence, they both gaped at the locked blades in awe.

It didn't last.

The thief kicked Connor in the thigh. Pain splintered through his leg, but he powered through it. He twisted his blade and sliced the man's wrist clean off. The criminal screamed as his hand plopped to the floor. His severed fingers loosened, and the dagger clattered to the ground.

Connor lifted his blade, his eye locked on the thief's torso as he prepared to end this.

"There's more of us." The criminal cradled the stump of his hand to his chest as he glared up at Connor. "They'll come for you. You're a—"

"Dead man," Connor finished as he drove the blade into the thief's chest. "I know."

The thief gasped, his body stiffening as the sword tore through his heart. His gaze lingered on Connor for only a moment more before his blue eyes rolled into the back of his head. His body went limp, and his weight shifted onto the sword as he fell forward. Connor dismissed the blade with a twist of his arm, and the thief's body collapsed to the floor with nothing to hold it upright.

In the silence that followed, Connor stood in the rubble of what had once been the potion maker's shop. Glass littered the floor between the corpses, and rivers of blood ran along the divots in the floorboards. Daggers and jewel-encrusted hair pins covered the wood, their polished gems stained with crimson.

You enjoyed that, the wraith said in his ear.

Connor frowned, refusing to admit the ghost was right.

The power. The ease. The carnage. None of it should've brought him pleasure, and yet he'd lost himself to the fight.

As he learned more about what the wraith had done to him, he had to be careful. There were more abilities to discover, and any one of them could either be Connor's salvation or his undoing.

A trembling bald head peeked over one of the three remaining glass displays, his wiry eyebrows raised as he surveyed the chaos. The potion master pushed himself to his feet, and he leaned on the display for support. The color drained from his face as he surveyed his bloodstained shop.

"Are you all right?" Connor asked.

"All right?" The man tilted his head, watching Connor as though he'd gone insane as he gestured to the bodies in his shop. "By the Fates, man, *no*! No, I'm not all right!"

Connor scanned the shopkeeper's arms, looking for any sign of an obvious injury. Dried blood stained the collar of his shirt, but he had managed to stand just fine.

He would live.

The old man knelt, and the clank of glass bottles mingled with his ragged breathing as he grabbed a glowing green potion out of one of the displays. He popped the cork and threw back his head, downing the entire thing in one gulp.

"You saved my life," he said as he brushed the back of his hand over his mouth to wipe away the potion from his lips.

"I did."

"Your coin!" The man smacked his palm against his forehead, and he turned on his heel. Still trembling, he sidestepped the corpse leaning against one of his displays and rummaged through one of the wooden cupboards against the wall as the clink of coins sang through the air.

"It's fine—"

"I promised payment," the man interrupted.

"If you insist." As long as the man wasn't acting out of fear, Connor wasn't going to refuse coin.

"Here, my friend. Take it." The old man lifted a sagging leather bag, its seams nearly bursting as its contents strained against the laces holding it together.

Connor quirked one eyebrow, impressed by the payout as he took the heavy bag from the old man's quivering hand. "That'll do just fine."

"What else?" Teak rubbed his hands together eagerly, his eyes scanning the shattered remnants of his store.

"This is enough. Show me an exit out the back, and I'll be on my way."

"On your way?" The potion maker clicked his tongue in disappointment. "No, my friend, you're a hero. You need a proper reward. Let me get you some potions, at least. What survived?"

The shopkeeper hopped over the nearest corpse, and Connor couldn't help but wonder if he was profoundly grateful or just stalling. For him to be so generous with a masked stranger made no sense, not even in the aftermath of a near-death experience.

Connor had done his father proud, and he didn't need random potions as a reward.

With the man's back turned to him, Connor tugged his steel sword from the nearby shelf and yanked his dagger out of the back wall as he searched the cluttered shop for an exit.

The black flower sat on the shelf, the pollen stems in its center twirling and wriggling with a life of their own. The center of the flower glowed pink, and blue light radiated from the base of each petal as it all but hummed with life.

A sweet perfume coiled in the air above the petals—a beautiful blend of honey and the salty tang of a summer ocean, rolled into one. He took a deep breath, his curiosity piqued as he studied it.

He'd never seen a flower like that before. The potion master had been mortified when the glass shattered, and if it was a prize possession in a potion shop, it probably held secrets and power unlike anything he could imagine.

A mystery for another day, perhaps. He had too much riding on finding the sorceress in the woods to sit around asking questions about reagents.

As he stepped over the last thief he killed, he paused and studied the dozens of jewel-encrusted daggers strewn across the floor. Blood leaked from the dead man's severed hand and pooled around the elaborate blade that had blocked his shadow swords.

Unlike the flower, the dagger was a mystery worth pursuing.

As the old man rummaged through the depths of the shop, Connor snatched it, and he balanced the blade on his finger. It leaned toward the handle, its hilt too heavy to be properly balanced, and he grimaced with annoyance.

Sloppily made. And yet, nothing else to date had blocked his swords. Instead of whatever random potions the shop keeper wanted to give him, he opted to take this.

Behind the shattered glass cases, an open door led to a stockroom in the back of the building. The fading daylight outside streamed around stacks of crates, hinting at an exit. There must've been a window, at least.

He ducked into the storeroom, careful not to make a sound as the shopkeeper disappeared around the shelf of ivy. Sure enough, a lone window on the far wall served as the only exit, and he sidestepped a stack of crates to reach it.

Through the panes, a ginger cat tip-toed along a nearby garden railing, its tail raised as it walked its metallic tightrope through towering green bushes. Across the narrow alley separating this shop from the others, another path between two rows of buildings gave him a clear sightline to the next road over. The bustling crowds rushed past, and the good people of Bradford unknowingly offered him a chance to simply disappear.

As the shopkeeper droned on, his voice muffled by the stockroom's clutter, Connor sheathed his silver blade and stored the dagger in his pack. The window slid easily open, and he ducked through. Though his shoulder got stuck as he tried to slip his muscled torso through the window, he wasted only a few moments before he dropped effortlessly to the small garden below and crouched.

The hum of conversation and the clatter of wheels on cobblestone blurred together in the air, and he scanned the alley for signs of life in the growing dusk. The ginger cat shot him a lazy glance over its shoulder before it hopped off the railing and trotted off down the empty lane.

Alone—just the way he liked it.

CHAPTER TWENTY-SEVEN
CONNOR

On the outskirts of Bradford, Connor sat at the bar of a tavern as far from the potion shop as he could manage. At most, he had perhaps a day before word of the dead thieves spread through the town, if even that long. That meant he had until dawn to find this sorceress and get the hell out of town.

After putting some distance between him and the potion shop, he'd stuffed the bag of coins deep into his larger pack to protect it from pickpockets. The bag still jingled with every movement, and he needed to figure out a way to quiet the clinking.

Killing a pickpocket would've just added to his already growing body count.

Now and then, a group of men at one of the tavern's five long tables lifted their heads to watch him. They stared for a moment before returning to their huddle to whisper. Three other clusters of men at the tables by the door did the same, and though they spoke in hushed tones, Connor's enhanced hearing picked up snippets of their conversations.

"…think he's one of the bandits from up north…"

"…that caravan of amber merchants never showed up…"

"…what could he want, do you figure?"

Connor groaned and tapped his knuckle again on the bar as his stomach roared for food. After the payday he'd gotten, he'd chosen to treat himself to a hot meal.

Unlabeled bottles filled the shelves in front of him, each half full of brown liquid. One intricately etched brown bottle balanced on a half-destroyed section of the lower shelf, and a large nick in the wood rendered half of the shelf unusable.

Apparently, this bar saw its fair share of armed fights. Given the amount of whispering around him, he understood why.

Just what he needed—gossip and drunk men itching for a fight.

At the far end of the bar, the tavern keeper frowned at a fat man with a thick beard. They argued in hushed tones, each occasionally poking the other's chest with his pointer finger as the conversation escalated and the scowls deepened. The salty stench of sweat mingled with the warm and mouthwatering promise of chicken as the tavern's blended cologne wafted through the air.

They'd been arguing for ages, and that alone had delayed Connor's dinner. If the other taverns weren't so close to the potion maker's shop, he would've left by now.

A serving girl with long brown curls and an arm loaded with empty plates leaned her shoulder against the lone door in the back wall. The door swung open, its hinges creaking, and the honey-drenched scent of roasted meat poured out into the tavern as she disappeared into the kitchens.

It took every ounce of Connor's self-restraint to not kick down the door and grab a chicken off the fire for himself, plates and payment be damned.

He needed *food*.

Down at the end of the bar, the barkeep finally threw his hands in the air in defeat and walked away from the other man, who only kept talking. The fat man gestured after the tavern owner, and Connor only caught the last word of the confrontation.

"...unreasonable!" the customer shouted.

The barkeep shook his head as he stalked toward Connor, deep lines etched along his mouth from his scowl. As he neared, he grabbed a polishing cloth stained with patches of brown and threw it over his shoulder as he glared at Connor from under thick brows. The grizzled man's salt-and-pepper beard covered his neck, frizzed and dry with age, and his broad shoulders blocked out most of the bar behind him.

"What do you want?" the man asked, leaning against the wooden surface.

"Food and beer," Connor answered. "Before I starve."

The man let out a slow breath of relief, as if he had expected Connor to say something else, and he pulled a mug out from underneath the bar. The cup thudded against the dried wood as he reached under the counter yet again, this time for a pitcher. Yellow liquid frothed and bubbled as he poured.

With the mug full, the man leaned one elbow on the bar and set his palm over the cup. "Five coin."

Connor scoffed. "Tell me you're joking."

The tavern keeper shook his head, his frizzy beard almost glowing in the dancing firelight of the wall sconces behind him. "Five coppers for the food and beer, another three if you want a room for the night."

"At those prices, I'd rather sleep in a tree."

He shrugged. "Suit yourself. You want the food or not?"

Connor's eyes narrowed as he debated punching the charlatan trying to shake him down. He could easily break the man's arm, but he didn't want to make a scene and summon the sheriff. Connor chose not to rise to the bait, even if this inn keeper was little more than a crooked thief.

This city had plenty of taverns he could've visited, but he didn't have the luxury of time. Ultimately, he'd chosen to come here, and that fault was his alone.

He gritted his teeth and reached into the coin purse on his belt for five crown coins. With an irritated huff, he smacked them on the wooden surface. "Give me my damn beer."

"Good man." The tavern keeper grabbed the coins with his free hand and slowly pushed the mug toward Connor. "I don't allow for no nonsense in my tavern, you hear?"

Connor met the man's glare with his own and snatched the cup. "Then don't give me any more of it."

The barkeep pushed off the bar as a young woman with long brown hair set a plate of chicken and potatoes before the fat man several seats away. He ignored the food, focused instead on her low-cut blouse and the line of cleavage visible on her porcelain skin. She wrinkled her delicate nose in disgust and scurried away.

The barkeep whistled, catching her attention before she could duck back into the kitchens, and the two of them spoke in hushed tones on the other side of the tavern. Hopefully, that meant Connor would get his own plate soon. If not, he might well kick down the kitchen door after all.

He drained the beer in one gulp and shuddered as the sour drink burned the back of his throat. Kirkwall had better pints than any inn along the southern road, but he'd grown accustomed to the fermented water they called beer. He cleared his throat and set the mug down as the booze warmed his stomach. It left a satisfying fizz along his throat even as the bitter flavor coated his tongue.

More.

He needed *more*.

Connor signaled to the barkeep again and pushed the mug forward as he approached. While the owner slowly refilled the mug, Connor bit back the urge to simply snatch the pitcher and drink from the source. Hell, he'd certainly paid enough to cover it—and then some.

However, he also needed information, and he couldn't let his irritation or hunger get in the way.

He leaned forward as the beer frothed in his mug and cast a quick glance around to ensure no one listened in. "What do you know about the sorceress in the woods?"

"What sorceress?" the man asked without so much as a glance upward while he poured.

Connor groaned, annoyed that he had to waste precious coin on bribing a con artist, but he reached into the pouch on his belt and tugged out two more crown coins. Firelight from the nearby sconces glimmered along the stamped copper as he set them on the counter. With his eyes locked on the barkeep, he pressed his fingertips against the metal and pushed them toward the grizzled old man.

"I think you know the sorceress I'm talking about."

The barkeep raised one eyebrow as the coins scraped against the wood. Even though he still poured, the mug nearly full, the money had stolen his full attention.

For a moment, he didn't speak. His brows knitted with thought as he debated what to do.

"Oh, *that* sorceress." The man cleared his throat and slipped both coins into his pocket. "Never met her, but there's a girl on this street who goes to that sorceress for remedies."

"What sort of remedies?"

The barkeep wrinkled his nose with disgust and set the pitcher down as he leaned his elbow on the bar. "Unwanted babies, beauty fixes, love potions, what have you. She always pays heaps of coin. Or rather, her father does."

Connor sipped on his mug to hide the smirk tugging at his lips. He figured this girl must have been the man's daughter, as the furrowed brow and deep scowl reminded him of Beck Arbor any time he talked about his children's expensive habits.

"Is the sorceress any good?"

"Best we Bradford folk ever seen," the barkeep admitted with a hint of disdain. "She does magic even the potion master can't match, which is the only reason we let her stay."

"Stay?" Connor asked, chuckling. "She lives in the woods."

"No sane man wants to live near power like that," the tavern owner countered. "The potion master is too good a man to run her out, even though she steals his business. Some go to her because she does magic even he won't fiddle with. Give her gold, and she'll give you what you want." The barkeep paused, and his gaze swept briefly over Connor. "*Anything* you want."

Connor frowned and drained the last of his beer.

The man has a point. The Wraith King's voice echoed through his mind.

You have yet to fulfill the urges every man has, and you won't be able to focus unless—

"Shut *up*," Connor muttered, his mouth hidden behind the empty mug.

"Food's nearly ready." The barkeep grabbed the polishing cloth off his shoulder and shoved the pitcher of beer toward Connor. "Rest is yours. You paid for it."

"How charitable."

The tavern keeper chuckled and grabbed a half-filled mug from an empty seat nearby as he walked away.

Connor stared into his tankard, and his eyes glossed over as he debated what to do next. This wasn't some prostitute in the woods who knew her way around a cauldron. Anyone who knew how to make even a simple augmentation had power—*real* power.

Frankly, Connor didn't know if he had enough coin to buy the information he needed from someone like that.

The door slammed against the wall as someone threw it open, and a gust of cold wind tore through the air as a man stumbled inside. He caught himself at the last moment and kicked the door shut, grinning as he lowered his gray hood. His messy brown hair reached his shoulders, and he rubbed his thick beard as his eyes roamed the room. A thin scar beneath his eye crinkled with his smile, and a hilt peeked through the shadows around his waist. Behind him, the tip of the long sword lifted the edge of his cloak.

Throughout the room, most of the men glanced up at the newcomer. Many shook their heads and returned their attention to their plates, while others leaned to their neighbors and muttered in hushed tones. One man leaned against the wall in the back of the tavern, his arms crossed as he studied the stranger's movements. His eyes widened briefly in recognition, and he disappeared into the shadows of a nearby corridor that led deeper into the inn.

Connor poured himself more of the terrible beer to quell the violent vibrations through his gut as his hunger reached its peak. At this point, even a raw deer sounded appetizing.

Despite the dozens of open chairs and stools around them, the newcomer sat beside Connor and let out an exaggerated sigh while he drummed his knuckles on the wooden surface. His grin only widened as he leaned his elbows on the table and glanced at Connor.

"What a day, huh?" the stranger muttered.

Instead of answering, Connor took a long swig of his awful beer and watched the stranger from the corner of his eye. He'd seen grifters like this before. A man this sociable usually wanted an easy mark to swindle or a chance to steal some coin.

Either way, he wanted something. The friendly ones always did.

The soft sizzle of roasting meat snaked through the air, and Connor sat upright on impulse. The door to the kitchens opened, the hinges creaking as the brunette from earlier pushed her way into the tavern. She held a large plate of chicken and potatoes, and this time her gaze settled on him.

As she reached him, she smiled broadly and made a show of leaning over to set the plate before him. The low-cut blouse betrayed her cleavage, and her gaze wandered his body as the loose sleeve of her dress slipped down her shoulder.

Her eyes lingered on him even as she retreated again toward the kitchen, and despite the food in front of him, he found himself watching her. He didn't know her name—didn't care for that matter.

In that instant, a primal craving took hold of him. It urged him to pin her down and take her there on a tavern table, witnesses be damned. To make her scream with pleasure and beg for more.

Though the hunger gnawed away at his self-control, he grimaced and fought off the temptation with every shred of self-restraint he had left. He'd never had thoughts like these before, nor had he ever needed to fight off such a primal compulsion.

Just give in, the ghoul in his head ordered. *For both of us.*

The thought of the wraith watching the next time Connor bedded a woman sent a wave of disgust through his body.

Instead of answering, he ripped off a chicken leg and bit into it—hating how hungry he was, how ravenous he felt, how overwhelming his senses had become. He had yet to actually eat his fill, and he was starting to doubt it would ever happen.

The stranger beside him leaned in, his voice a whisper. "That's the barkeep's daughter, mate. Don't start trouble unless you can get away with it."

"What the hell are you talking about? I'm just sitting here."

The ruffian flashed him a wry grin. "Pretty bloke like you? That's all it takes."

The tavern owner approached with a newly filled pitcher of beer, and though he set a second mug on the bar for the newcomer, he didn't so much as look at the stranger. As he poured, he glared at Connor in a silent warning.

The stranger grinned and set a coin on the bar. "You're a gentleman and a scholar, my good sir."

"Don't cause no trouble," the barkeep warned, his gaze briefly shifting to the ruffian before he grabbed the coin and walked off with an irritated huff.

"He charged me five," Connor muttered, glaring at the grizzled old man.

"Yes, well, he's an asshole." The ruffian shrugged. "I'm Murdoc."

Connor nodded, not interested in giving his own name to a stranger at a bar.

"Ah, you're one of those talkers, then." Murdoc nodded as though the world suddenly made sense. "I like talkers. Can't ever get you lot to shut up, but in the end, you always have good stories."

"Or, we're just unafraid of silence," Connor quipped as he took another bite of chicken.

"And a smartass, too," Murdoc said with an approving nod. "I like you already."

Connor chuckled. He couldn't help it. This guy seemed genuine enough, if a bit too friendly in a day and age where chummy people usually ended up conning someone or dying an early death.

Or both.

As he ate, Connor debated his next move. Ethan had warned him against heading into the woods alone, and that man didn't waste money. If he had hired a mercenary each time he went to visit the sorceress, Connor would do well to heed the warning.

He grabbed a baked potato with his bare hands and bit into it, too hungry to even taste the food as steam coiled into the air. Truth be told, he loathed the idea of a sellsword, mainly because most of them only helped their client until a better opportunity presented itself.

No loyalty. No trust beyond the coin. No accountability.

A smart man didn't rely on someone who could be bought because one day he would inevitably lose to a higher bidder.

The door smacked against the wall yet again, and another gust of cold air blew through the pub as someone else entered. The sconces flickered, their light casting distorted shadows across the faces of the men gathered around the tavern's long tables.

This time, however, whomever had entered didn't bother to hurry inside and close the door.

As the conversation in the tavern died, the figure's silhouette paused at the edge of Connor's periphery. A tall man dressed in a red shirt and a fine black cloak stood at the open entry. His gaze swept across the room, and his neatly combed hair barely masked his receding hairline. A hooked nose protruded from his face like a bird, and his eyes creased with the early wrinkles of an aging man.

In the somber lull, everyone stared at the newcomer as two massive men entered the tavern behind him. Apart from their hair, they looked strikingly similar—squat noses, broad shoulders, dark eyes. Brothers, perhaps, one with dark hair and the other bald. They towered over the well-dressed man as he scoped the room, their thick bodies covered in muscle that strained against their black shirts. The last to enter slammed the door shut behind him, and the walls shook.

A man dressed that fine could've easily been the sheriff, damn it all.

It seemed Connor's time had come far sooner than he'd thought it would. He hadn't even gotten to finish his food.

It looks like our evening just became quite interesting. The wraith's hollow voice rang in his mind. *I shall enjoy watching you fight your way out of a filled tavern on your own.*

Connor groaned and took another bite of his chicken. If he had to fight off a horde of drunken men, he would at least do it on a full stomach.

CHAPTER TWENTY-EIGHT
CONNOR

As the well-dressed newcomer and his two bodyguards stood by the door, blocking the primary exit, Connor flexed the fingers on his free hand. His chewing slowed while he surveyed the three of them, and his training kicked in as he scanned them for weaknesses. The prissy figure in the silk shirt would've been easy enough to take out, if not for the two towering monsters behind him. At nearly seven feet tall, they shattered his idea of how tall a man could get. He'd never seen a human that big, much less two of them.

Given his luck, they were probably here for him.

A hush rolled over the pub, until only the odd clink from the kitchen pierced the silence. Beside him, Murdoc drummed his fingers on the bar and swallowed hard as he watched the new arrivals with an unwavering gaze. A man seated on a bench behind them even unsheathed a dagger and held it in the shadows beneath the table.

Everyone could taste the brewing fight—that unforgettable tang of steel and bloody knuckles, soon to be wafting through the air.

Though Connor bit into a potato and kept up a facade of indifference, he scanned the back of the tavern for another way out. A dark hallway led to the unknown, offering him a possible escape. There had to be a window back there, at the least.

If the sheriff had come after him already, he needed to leave town. The law would've wanted to ask questions he didn't want to give the answers to. Hell, he might've been charged for murder, despite only killing those bandits to save the potion master's life.

He and his damned bleeding heart couldn't leave well enough alone.

A heavy stillness weighed on the air—the sort that came before broken noses and shattered bones. No one spoke. No one returned to their dinners. No one so much as whispered to their neighbor. The tavern held its breath, waiting for the man to make the next move.

He had full control and everyone's attention. A man of power. A man of prestige.

A man they clearly feared.

The newcomer straightened his silk shirt and lifted his chin as he scanned the faces around him. "I'm looking for someone. A criminal. And, to my horror, I was told he's here, having a *drink*, instead of swinging from the gallows."

With a dramatic flourish, the newcomer swept his hands across the crowds. He took slow and deliberate steps into the tavern and stalked the aisle between the tables as he scanned face after face. The men sitting at the benches leaned away as he passed them, as though he would reach out and wring their necks if they let him get too close.

"You will help me find him," he informed the crowd. "I will see to it myself that whoever tries to hide or help him will face the axe. Either point me to him or stay out of my way. If you do what you're told, no one else has to die tonight."

"Shit," Connor and Murdoc muttered in unison.

They paused, each looking at the other with one eyebrow raised. It seemed the ruffian knew his way around the law as well, which gave Connor a thin glimmer of hope that he wouldn't have to fight his way out of this place after all.

The grizzled barkeep threw down the cloth on the bar and rested his palms against the wooden surface. "Abner, I don't need no trouble—"

"Shut your mouth, old man," Abner interrupted. "I have a score to settle, and you won't interfere."

The tavern keeper's jaw tensed, and he briefly pinched the bridge of his nose as he bit his tongue. "Sir, I beg you to leave."

The newcomer pointed to the bottles behind Connor. "If you want another whiskey shipment at any point in your life, you won't say another damned thing. There are other tavern owners who could do with what I sell, so if you want your customers to stay, you'll shut your mouth."

Ah.

This man wasn't a sheriff at all, but a merchant—and a powerful one at that. Connor let out a slow breath of relief, grateful the law hadn't caught wind of him just yet.

The merchant's eyes shifted to Connor, and he held the man's gaze. Beside him, Murdoc sipped on his mug, his head down and body mostly hidden behind Connor's muscled frame.

Abner's gaze shifted again, and this time it landed on Murdoc. His eyes narrowed, and he lifted his chin as he meandered closer. "There you are."

"Me?" Murdoc set his hand on his chest, and his brows shot up his face with convincing surprise. "I'm afraid you're mistaken, good sir. I'm just a traveler passing through town. Who might you be?"

"Horse shit." Abner grabbed the mug out of Murdoc's hand and slammed it on the counter. It splashed across his hand as he leaned in, his voice dropping an octave. "My servant recognized you the moment you stepped foot in this place. You should've left town, you fool. I won't be made a cuckold. You slept with the wrong man's wife."

The two goons that had followed Abner into the tavern cracked their knuckles and took their place behind their boss. As all three men glared at the ruffian, they ignored Connor completely.

Truth be told, it was a nice change of pace.

Since he didn't want his dinner flattened or knocked off the bar, he grabbed his mug, pitcher, and plate and shifted a couple seats down to get out of the line of fire. As far as he was concerned, this had nothing to do with him.

Abner poked Murdoc sharply in the chest. "I make examples of the men who try to humiliate me."

The ruffian laughed. "Happens a lot, does it?"

"What—" Anber stuttered, and his cheeks flushed red at the insult.

Murdoc downed the last of his beer. "You're only humiliated because I can make her scream like a whore, and you can't even get her to spread her legs for you."

As he polished off the last of his chicken, Connor chuckled.

Abner's face flushed red, and he shoved Murdoc hard in the chest. The ruffian slid easily off the stool and landed on his feet, wisely using the opportunity to put some space between them. He backed toward the door, never once taking his eyes off the three men before him.

Cheers erupted through the tavern as the grizzled owner grumbled under his breath, elbows locked and arms straight as he leaned his palms against the bar.

Another day, another bar fight.

Coins changed hands as men placed bets on the brewing skirmish, and beer sloshed onto tables as drunk men lifted their mugs to cheer their choice of champion.

Abner nodded toward Murdoc, his steely eyes never wavering. "Kill him, boys."

The jeers of the crowd nearly deafened Connor's enhanced ears, and he winced at the sheer volume of their voices in the relatively tight space.

You peasants, the Wraith King muttered. *Always so predictably primitive.*

Connor ignored the old ghost's voice as the two goons stormed toward Murdoc. The dark-haired thug cocked his arm and threw a punch at Murdoc's face. As the meaty fist sailed through the air, Connor expected to hear a resounding crack and mumbled cursing. Men this large usually got their way, and this would probably end with broken bones and lots of blood.

Murdoc, however, ducked the blow as easily as if it were a choreographed dance. The goon lost his balance and fell onto a nearby table. The table slid, and the force of his fall knocked over several mugs. Angry men shoved him onto the floor, and the jeering crowd only yelled louder.

"Huh," Connor muttered as he polished off the last of his beer.

The bald goon threw the next punch, and Murdoc grabbed an empty stool in time to block the blow. The wood splintered beneath the massive man's fist, and Murdoc tore off a jagged piece of one leg as a makeshift spear. He stabbed it into the bald man's forearm until it hit bone, and the goon yelled in agony. He stared at his arm, fingers splayed wide as the jagged piece of wood stuck out of his body.

Ruffian or not, Murdoc put on one hell of a show. The crowd cheered, and Abner's face flushed even more red than before.

The dark-haired goon recovered and pushed himself to his feet. With a grunt of effort, he grabbed a bottle from the nearby table and shattered the base of it as he held it aloft. Whiskey slid down his arm and onto the floor as he wasted half a bottle.

Men at the table shouted obscenities, their whiskey gone, but the massive man didn't even look their way. He quickly closed the gap between him and Murdoc and swung the jagged ends at the ruffian's throat. Murdoc ducked the blow and kicked the man's legs out from under him. The dark-haired goon crashed onto the floor, and the tavern shook. The broken bottle rolled beneath one of the tables, far out of reach.

"Kill him, you idiots!" Abner gestured toward the still-standing Murdoc as both goons struggled to stand. "What do I even pay you for?"

The two men forced themselves to their feet as Murdoc laughed and inched his way toward the door. The dark-haired man dove and grabbed the ruffian's arm. Murdoc landed a hard kick in the man's thigh in an effort to break free, and a loud crack snapped through the air.

The goon winced and doubled over, loosening his grip, and Murdoc kneed him in the face to the tune of more jeers from the crowd. Bone splintered with the blow, barely audible over the chorus of shouts from their audience, and the goon flew backward. He landed hard on a table as blood streaked down his face. Chicken bones stuck to his bare arms as he tried in vain to sit upright.

Murdoc lifted his arms in victory, smiling broadly as the crowd cheered for him.

Connor smirked. This Murdoc fellow had skill, and he seemed to relish the thrill of a good fight.

With Murdoc momentarily distracted, the bald goon darted behind him and wrapped his good arm around Murdoc's neck. Blood poured down his other arm, the wooden spear gone even as he left a red trail along the floorboards.

The bald man's thick bicep flexed as he tightened his grip, and Murdoc clawed at the arm across his windpipe as he gasped for air. He drove his elbow into the man's side, but from this angle, he couldn't get enough momentum to strike a serious blow.

Just like that, the tides had shifted. A moment of distraction was all it had taken for Murdoc to lose the advantage.

The cheers died as the dark-haired goon got to his feet once again. Though his nose sat at an odd angle and blood poured over his mouth, he drove his fist into Murdoc's stomach. Murdoc doubled over from the blow, though he couldn't move far with the bald man holding him firmly in place. His face flushed as he gasped for air.

The skirmish had ended.

Abner smirked, casting aside his cloak with a dramatic flair as he drew a dagger from the sheath at his waist.

The dark-haired man grabbed a fistful of Murdoc's hair and yanked his head backward, exposing his neck as Abner's heavy boots thudded across the floorboards. A hush settled over the patrons as the fight neared its end.

Several men leaned forward in their seats, their eyes on Murdoc as they no doubt wondered how he would cleverly escape certain doom.

Connor popped the last bite of potato into his mouth, absorbed in the scene. Only bones remained on his plate and the pitcher sat empty, but he surprisingly didn't care. Though he wasn't full, his hunger no longer clawed at him. Like everyone else, he waited to see what would happen next.

At this point, Murdoc couldn't escape. He had no chance in hell of surviving this.

Murdoc, to his credit, watched Abner with a strange sense of calm.

Though he struggled to break free of the two men restraining him, his eyes never shifted from the merchant's.

No trembling. No begging. No fear.

Just a soldier, patiently waiting for the end.

Connor had seen that expression before. Beck Arbor had mistaken it once for pride, but he knew better.

Like so many lost souls in Saldia, this man had a death wish.

Abner lifted the dagger to Murdoc's throat. "First, I'll hang you from the eaves of the bedroom to remind my wife of her place. When she has learned her lesson, I'll throw your body to the pigs."

Murdoc grinned. "At least I won't go to waste, then."

Brave—and a bit stupid. Connor had seen worse men go free for far greater crimes. To stand by and do nothing when he could've saved this man's life wasn't right.

He groaned. His damned conscience would be the death of him.

Connor stood and closed the gap between him and Abner in seconds. As the merchant's blade pressed against Murdoc's throat, Connor grabbed the man's hand and, with a flick of his wrist, bent it backward.

Abner yelped in pain, and his grip loosened. The dagger clattered to the floor.

"Oi!" a nearby man shouted at his intrusion. "We got good money riding on this fight! You stay out of this!"

Connor shifted his glare to the stranger in the crowd, who froze instantly beneath his stare. As an eerie chill settled on the room, Connor silently dared the man to speak again. The heckler's eyes instead drifted to the floor, and he wisely shut his damn mouth.

Abner winced beneath Connor's grip. "Let go of me this instant, you son of a—"

With his free hand, Connor punched the merchant hard in the face. The merchant launched backward and landed with a heavy thud on the table behind him.

In the deathly silence that followed, only Abner's wheezing gasps mingled with the wind howling outside.

The merchant sat upright, his once-tidy hair now askew. He held his broken nose as he gaped at Connor. "Have you lost your mind?"

"Maybe. If you're smart, you'll stay down."

The man scowled at him but didn't move.

"Let him go." Connor shifted his attention to the two goons pinning Murdoc in place. "Now."

"Suck my cock." The dark-haired man spat on Connor's boots, and his thick brows furrowed as he dared him to do something about it.

Murdoc's grin widened. "You shouldn't have done that."

In a move too quick for the goon to even register, Connor punched him hard in the jaw. A tooth flew into the air as he crashed into a clump of men along the wall, knocking them all to the floor with his weight. He crumpled to the ground, his head lolling backward as fresh blood gushed from his nose.

Connor glared at the bald goon, who gaped at him with wide eyes. "Do you have something to say?"

"No, sir." The man released Murdoc and raised his bloodstained hands in surrender as he took several cautious steps backward.

"That's more like it." Murdoc brushed dust off his shoulder. "Show us some damn respect."

"Don't speak," Connor ordered.

"Yep." Murdoc scratched the back of his head, doing his best to look anywhere but at Connor. "Closing my mouth."

Connor debated leaving a few coins to cover the damage he'd caused to the tavern, but the barkeep had already gouged him for the meal. As far as he was concerned, they were even.

"Come with me." He gestured for Murdoc to follow as he pushed past the men lingering by the door and stormed outside. The thud of Murdoc's boots on the floor trailed after him, and Connor kept his gaze ahead to avoid the stares of those in the tavern.

So much for going unnoticed.

A gust of cold wind sailed past them as they stepped into the chilly spring night. The tavern door slammed shut behind them, and the muffled murmur of conversation sparked to life shortly after.

The people of this town would start talking, and he needed to leave before the sheriff caught wind of this little incident and started piecing things together.

Murdoc cleared his throat and scratched his ear as he glanced across the street. "You did me a kindness back there."

"No, I did you a *favor*." Connor crossed his arms and glared down at the ruffian as he quickly pieced together an idea. "Now you're going to return it."

"Okay, but be gentle," Murdoc said, lifting his hands. "It's my first time with a man."

Connor grinned and shook his head, unable to suppress the laughter. "You're an absolute idiot."

"I mean, a pretty bloke like you?" Murdoc shrugged. "Men aren't my preference, but I could give it a go."

"Just stop talking." Connor gestured for the ruffian to follow him again as he put some distance between them and the tavern. "There's a sorceress in the woods to the north of town, and I need information from her. We're going to talk to her and—you know what, no. I'm going to talk to her, and you're not going to say anything," he added with a sidelong glare. "You're coming along to make sure she doesn't try anything. After I get my information, you're done. Favor fulfilled."

"I prefer being paid in coin." Murdoc gestured to the pouch on Connor's belt as they slipped into a dimly lit alley.

Connor nodded in the vague direction of the tavern. "If you don't like my offer, you can always try your luck with those three."

"Actually, I've made up my mind." Murdoc rubbed his hands together and blew into his fists to warm them. "After giving it significant thought, I've decided to take you up on your generous offer of unpaid work. Shall we hurry this along?"

"Smart man. We're leaving. Do you have your pack?"

"Don't need one. Everything I need is in my sheath or in here." Murdoc patted the oversized pockets on his pants, and the jingle of a chain broke the silent night.

That seemed like a terrible idea, but Connor kept his mouth shut. "Suit yourself."

As they walked in silence through the alley and slipped onto another street, Connor kept an eye on the occasional groups of men wandering through the once-bustling road. Streetlights cast a soft orange glow along the cobblestones, and a fragrant hint of the potion burning along the town's walls wafted through the air.

At least they wouldn't have to deal with the blightwolves tonight—just a necromancer who may or may not try to kill him.

"Question." Murdoc lifted one finger, his other hand resting on the hilt of his sword as they walked.

"What?"

"Why did you save my ass in there?"

"You're a decent fighter," Connor admitted with a shrug. "I figured I could strong arm you into a favor."

A bit of a lie, but he didn't need the stranger to think he had a bleeding heart.

"Fair enough," Murdoc said. "Do I get your name at any point on this venture?"

"Connor," he said, careful to keep his voice low in case anyone nearby tried to listen in.

"Charmed."

"I have a question for you, Murdoc."

The man lifted one curious eyebrow. "Yeah?"

"Do you have a death wish?"

Murdoc smirked as they walked through the streets, past dark houses with only the occasional light in a window here or there. "Maybe."

CHAPTER TWENTY-NINE
QUINN

Nine days of Quinn's deadline, wasted. She had only twenty-one days left to find the assassin.

Saldia's twin moons hung in the sky, their soft light casting a cool glow on Quinn's dark coat as a gale tore through her hair. The unnatural tempests of this southern forest rustled the trees below, the leaves rippling like waves on an emerald ocean as she kept her eyes trained on the ground. Blaze pumped his wings in a soothing rhythm, carrying her through the night as she leaned against his neck.

They would reach Bradford at any moment, and she needed a lucky break. A clue. A hint. Hell, at this point, she would even follow a rumor if she came across one.

The people south of the Rift hadn't heard of any mysterious assassin or seen anyone resembling the sketch her father had given her. For all intents and purposes, it seemed as though this man had simply disappeared into the Ancient Woods.

"Impossible," she muttered, her voice almost instantly lost in the howling wind.

Quinn frowned and ran her fingers through the soft fur on her vougel's neck as she lost herself in thought. Maybe Otmund had made an error in the sketch, or perhaps she had overlooked something in the meadow by the ruins of the old cathedral.

Or maybe one of those accursed blightwolves had eaten a crucial clue.

The chilling howl of the unholy wolves rolled through the air, hollow and distant as they raced through their forest. As much as a return to the cathedral tempted her, going there after dark risked a run-in with those damned beasts. There had been urgency when she had visited before—a chance to stumble across the assassin himself if she acted quickly enough—but now, the risk outweighed any potential benefit.

Lindow had been an utter waste of time.

With the Rift nestled halfway between Bradford and Wimborne, she'd had an equal shot of finding the assassin by visiting either town. Wimborne hadn't had a single clue for her to chase, so hopefully the people north of the Rift had a lead for her to follow.

On the horizon, the green fires of Bradford burned along the town's great walls. She sat up straighter as the soothing perfume of the blightwolf fires curled through the air, keeping the beasts at a distance.

For now.

Quinn stretched to ease the ache in her back from sitting too long, and while part of her longed for a good meal and a soft bed, she knew better than to think she could have either until this mess with the assassin ended.

Besides, every time she entered a town like this without a glamour to hide her fire-red hair, the people greeted her with celebration—or, at a minimum, fearful awe. All towns treated Lightseers with respect, but the Starlings received so much more than mere admiration.

Zander relished it, of course. Smiled. Waved. Shook hands. Laughed and pretended he cared about the townspeople's plight, whatever it happened to be that visit. He loved the celebrity of it all. The fame.

Quinn had always believed the pomp and celebrations got in the way of her work.

As she surveyed the road that meandered through the forest and across a stretch of open field to the closed gates, however, she got an idea.

Perhaps it was time to make some noise. Glamouring herself and listening to gossip in the taverns hadn't gotten her very far on this particular hunt, so maybe it was time to use the pomp and nonsense in her favor to finally get some much-needed information.

With two light taps of her heels on Blaze's side, she gave the silent order to descend. Instantly, he angled toward the open stretch of road inside the closed gates. As they neared, streetlamps cast a warm glow along the cobblestone. Shielded by their glass enclosures, the fires within each lamp flickered softly despite the fierce enchanted wind tearing through the sky.

The guard standing over the closed gates craned his head to gape at her as she flew past, his grip on the spear in his hand weakening as the whites of his eyes practically glowed in the low light.

Blaze landed easily on the cobblestone street, the dark road empty save for three hooded men standing by a nearby door. Tavern songs rolled through the open entrance beside them, the clink of glasses timed perfectly with the beat of boots against the floorboards. The three of them huddled close in the cold night, their hands tucked under their armpits for warmth as they watched her. Their hoods cast their faces in shadow as they reflexively stiffened.

Familiar with protocol and a little too eager to show off, her vougel fluffed his wings as they strode through the center of town. Quinn suppressed an embarrassed sigh at his vanity, but she opted not to chide him.

"Citizens of Bradford!" she shouted into the quiet night, doing her best to keep the boredom out of her tone as she recited the familiar words her father had so often shouted on his visits to the smaller towns. "I come to your aid!"

Curtains along the main road parted. Doors creaked open. Men and women wandered out onto the cobblestones while children peeked through curtains on the upper floors. A soft murmur bubbled through the street as a crowd gathered.

In a matter of minutes, roughly four dozen people stepped out of their homes and congregated around her and Blaze. Heads bobbed in the crowd, their eyes locked on her as they gaped with wonder at the spectacle.

At the vougel.

At the Starling with hair the color of fire and flame.

At a warrior from Oakenglen—what some considered to be a blessing, and what most thought to be an omen of brewing danger. Lightseers traveled where they were needed and snuffed out the deadly things that ate grown men in the night. Many assembled before her must've wondered what horrors had brought her to their town.

Quinn had long ago grown used to the way she and Blaze drew stares. Used to how often people asked for favors and aid. Used to people knowing exactly who she was. *What* she was.

A Starling.

In this world, the name alone was legend, but all this fanfare only proved how truly separate she was from everyone else.

How alone.

She tensed her jaw and raised her chin, eager for this to be over.

"A Starling!" someone shouted.

"What's wrong?" another man asked. "The blightwolves be howlin' again, is that it? The fires be failin', I always figured it would happen sooner or—"

"Are we safe?" a woman in the crowd shouted as she reached her hand toward Quinn, her green eyes wide with fear.

"Good citizens of Bradford," Quinn said, her voice carrying through the dark street as she tapped Blaze's neck to make him stop his strutting.

The vougel paused midstride and kept his chin raised, his eyes straight ahead and ears alert despite the growing crowd. The perfect mount, eager to practice the ceremony she so rarely allowed him to indulge.

"There is danger in these woods, yes," she admitted, mostly to stoke the fires of gossip so she could finally get a clue. "I'm here on a mission from Lunestone, and I need to find a criminal who is reported to have escaped to your fair town."

A shot in the dark, of course—but if the people thought there was a criminal in their midst, they would've been more inclined to monitor newcomers more closely. It worked in her favor, and at this point, she was desperate for a lead.

"A criminal, eh?" A woman in the crowd huffed, and the shawl wrapped around her head slid back to reveal her gray hair. "Check the bars, m'lady! There be plenty o' criminals in there. Take my husband, too, will ya?"

A ripple of laughter bubbled through those gathered, and it took everything in Quinn to not roll her eyes with exasperation.

She hunted for an assassin, and yet they wanted to make jokes.

"Have any of you seen this man?" She tugged the sketch from her pocket and held it for them to see. In the low firelight from the streetlamps, creases and tears in the well-worn parchment became even more pronounced. "Have any of you heard of strange happenings in recent days or witnessed illegal necromancy?"

The laughter faded. In the frigid silence that followed, Quinn scanned each face in the crowd. Most of the men and women cast their gazes to the ground, and more than one along the fringes slipped off into the shadows between buildings.

Ah.

It seemed these good people were perhaps not as good as they had led the crown to believe.

"I seen him," someone said from the gathered throng.

A few gasps filtered through the crowd as every head turned toward a man leaning against a nearby building. He chewed a piece of straw between his molars, and his hazel eyes narrowed. His dark cloak hid most of his body, and tangled blond hair framed his face like soiled hay. He spit the straw in his mouth onto the ground and watched her, but he didn't elaborate.

"Where did you see him?" Quinn asked.

"My mind ain't what it used to be, I'm afraid," the thug muttered, the corner of his mouth twisting into a smirk. "Mayhaps the pretty Starling could spark my memory with a bit o' coin?"

Quinn pursed her lips as a surge of impatience bubbled through her, but she had dealt with idiots like this before. "I won't pay for what you should freely tell me."

He propped one leg against the wall behind him and gave her a quick glance over. "What can you offer, then?"

The fool.

She drew *Aurora* from the sheath at her waist and, with a flick of her wrist, summoned brilliant flame across the enchanted sword. The man flinched as the warm glow of the Firesword illuminated his face.

"I can offer you my eternal gratitude," she said dryly.

The crowd around her gasped. As she held the flaming sword over their heads, dozens of the citizens backed quickly away. The crowds parted, and a clear path between her and the man appeared as everyone else wisely gave her space. The stranger gulped, his shoulders hunching as his gaze darted from her to the sword and back.

"You were saying?" Quinn prompted him.

He licked his lips and pointed up the street, toward the north. "The potion shop. I seen a man like that walk in around dusk, and word is there been a robbery. Last I heard, the sheriff is in there talkin' to the old man who runs the place."

Despite her best judgment, Quinn's heart skipped a beat with hope. After a week with no news of the assassin, she knew better than to believe she had truly found him.

She would, however, follow the lead—just in case.

"Thank you for providing such useful information." With another flick of her wrist, she dismissed *Aurora's* flames. The fires hissed as they dissolved into the night, and she tapped her heels on Blaze's side in a silent order for him to continue their hunt.

To her relief, the crowd didn't trail after her. These people had dark secrets, and she suspected it had to do with necromancy.

Or, perhaps, with the assassin himself.

CHAPTER THIRTY

QUINN

With her augmented vision, Quinn scanned the dark signs hanging above each door along the main road until she noticed the familiar drawing of a bottle. Closed curtains along the four main windows hid anyone inside. If the sheriff truly had entered already, her target could potentially be in cuffs.

She doubted it. A sheriff hardly posed a threat to the man who had killed a king, but a girl could dream.

Quinn dismounted. Her boots hit the cobblestone without a sound, and she drew her sword again as she neared the door to the shop. The broken knob hung from the wooden hole it should've been mounted to, and the door sat slightly ajar.

A soft growl rumbled in Blaze's throat as the hair along his neck stood on end. The skin around his nose creased with a snarl as he glared at the shop's front door.

He could sense a fight.

"Stand guard," she ordered.

Her vougel nodded and faced the road, his ears pinned to his head as he surveyed the shadows. With him at the entrance, no one would get in or out without her knowing.

Quinn opened the door to the soft jingle of a bell, and she scanned the shelves out of habit. The rush of spices and herbs assaulted her the moment the door cracked open, and she sifted through the scents to find useful information.

Dried meats and the stench of furs, both useless in potions. Dried flowers, weaker than their fresh counterparts. A bit of rosemary and lavender, neither of which were even reagents. Commonplace scents out here in the nothing, where fresh ingredients and powerful reagents were few and far between.

The rusty stench of blood rolled past next, and she wrinkled her nose as it hit her. The metallic odor overwhelmed most of the scents in the air, and she scanned the candlelit shop to find its source. A dark red puddle at the base of a nearby bookshelf caught her eye, though no corpse lay beside it.

Something had certainly happened here, but she still couldn't bring herself to hope she had finally found her target.

As she walked deeper into the shop, another perfume snaked through the cloud of blood and useless reagents. The breathtaking fragrance reminded her of summer and sunshine, with a hint of heaven and heather.

The telltale aroma of a bloody beauty.

Her heart skipped a beat at the mere idea that a potion master along the southern road could have something so rare. In her suspicion, her grip tightened on the hilt of her sword.

"What the hell?" someone snapped from the back of the store. His boots thundered along the floorboards as he neared. "This shop is *closed*, and you shouldn't be—"

A man rounded the corner. The moment his gaze landed on Quinn, his dark brows darted up his face. He froze with his hand on the hilt of his sword, blinking with shock as a lock of his dark hair fell in his eye. A golden badge on his chest glistened in the shop's low light, the five points of a lawman's star giving away his identity.

"Sheriff." Quinn nodded in welcome and sheathed her sword out of respect.

"My lady." He bowed, blinking away his daze as he snapped to his senses. "Sheriff Newborn, at your service. To what does our fair town owe the pleasure?"

"I'm hunting a criminal from the Capital." She fished the sketch from her pocket yet again and handed it to the lawman. "I was told he entered this shop at dusk today."

"You Starlings have uncanny timing." The sheriff scratched at his jaw as he studied the sketch. "I didn't see this man among the bodies, but the potion master witnessed a lot of horror here today. Perhaps he can identify this man for you."

"Take me to him," she ordered.

"Yes, of course." The sheriff gestured for her to come with him and rounded the corner.

Quinn followed and passed a bookshelf laden with ivy as she scanned the shelves for clues. Several notches in the wood hinted at a swordfight. More blood pooled along the floorboards, and small red rivers streamed across the divots in the floor. Shards of glass littered nearly every surface, glinting in the firelight, and the shattered remnants of a display lay in a heap at the back of the shop.

An old man stared down at the broken display, his back to the door, and he rubbed his bald head as he examined the mess. "Who was that at the door, Roger?"

"I'll introduce you." The sheriff gestured to Quinn as she joined them. "Teak Williams, meet Lady Starling."

The bald man froze. His gaze darted toward Quinn, and his mouth parted with shock. "Fates be damned, it really is a Starling."

Quinn's jaw tensed with irritation as she resisted the impulse to say something that would've earned her a verbal reprimand if her father ever found out. "If we could focus, gentlemen, this matter is urgent."

"Yes, of course." The old man cleared his throat. His gaze lingered on her hair before he finally gestured to the floor. "I was nearly robbed, my lady. They wanted gold and spellgust, mainly, and I nearly lost my bloody beauty bloom in the chaos."

As tempting as the mention of the rare reagent was, Quinn forced herself to remain focused. She pointed to the sketch in the sheriff's hands. "Did you see this man?"

"Huh?" Teak's gaze darted from Quinn to the parchment. "Oh, yes, I saw him, my lady."

Quinn's body stiffened. She set her hand on the hilt of her sword on impulse and took another step toward the potion master, almost unwilling to believe him. "This man tried to rob you, did he? That means he isn't operating alone. Who was with him? What did they try to steal?"

"I—uh." The old man stuttered and wrung his hands as he took a wary step backward. "I believe you misunderstood, my lady. He didn't rob me. He saved me. The Shade, we've been calling him. A man of magic, I think, based on what he did to those men's swords. Nothing like I've ever seen—"

"Wait." Quinn crossed her arms, convinced she hadn't heard him correctly. "You're saying he saved you from the bandits?"

The potion master nodded and pointed to the sketch. "I'd be dead now, if not for that man."

"Why are you hunting him, Lady Starling?" the sheriff asked. "If he would do such a good deed, I find it confusing that Lunestone wants him detained. What has this man done?"

Quinn didn't answer. She couldn't—not until this all made sense.

As her mind raced, she turned her back to the men and surveyed the rubble of the potion master's shop. Smears of blood coated the floor. Two halves of a broken sword lay on the floorboards, the clean line through its steel blade evidence of the magic that had given the Shade an advantage in the duel.

For him to save this man made no sense. He was an assassin. A murderer who had left a king's corpse in a meadow to rot.

"Sheriff, we must find this man immediately." Quinn tapped her finger on her chin without bothering to look at him as she gave her orders. "Go. Gather your men and get me a lead. Come to me with any word at all as to where he might've gone or what he might want."

For a moment, neither man spoke. Sheriffs rarely took orders from anyone, much less from a woman, but he knew better than to disobey.

When a Starling walked into a town, they became the law.

"Yes, my lady," the sheriff eventually said. He thundered past her, the floorboards trembling with his heavy steps.

Quinn whistled twice, the chirps short and sharp—the sign for Blaze to not kill the lawman as he left.

Moments later, the bell chimed as the sheriff walked into the street. A muffled yell of surprise snaked through the door before it closed behind him.

Good. Now she had a moment alone with the potion master—and a chance to get the truth.

"A bloody beauty is quite rare," she said with her back still to him. "You must be an important man to get your hands on a live bloom."

"It is certainly an honor," Teak said, and she could practically hear the wistful smile on his face as he spoke.

Quinn peered over her shoulder to find him staring off through an open doorframe into a back room with a sheepish grin on his face. He must've stored it back there, out of harm's way. He watched the reagent like an adoring father watching a babe sleep.

"Even those with the money to buy one can't always find one," she continued, her trap slowly closing around the potion master's throat. "How did you manage?"

"When you've been in the trade as long as I have, my dear, you make friends." He grinned as his eyes drifted to her. After a moment, however, he seemed to remember to whom he spoke, and his smile fell. "That is, my *lady*. Not—uh—I mean—"

"It must be nice to have such well-connected friends," she interrupted, her trap closing.

He cleared his throat and scratched at his neck, looking everywhere but at her. "Yes, well, I'm sure you have quite a few friends of your own who—"

"It seems odd, though," she admitted. Her boots fell silently on the floorboards, her augmentations masking each step as she closed in on her prey. "To sell such a thing out here in the Ancient Woods seems like quite the risk. If it's stolen, you could go bankrupt, but who would you even sell it to? Who could afford such a powerful reagent this far south of the major cities?"

He gulped, his eyes wide as he watched her, waiting for the axe to fall.

Quinn closed the gap between them, and her eyes narrowed as her nose came within inches of his. "Let me save us both some time, Mr. Williams. You and I both know you don't have a legal buyer for that bloom, and it was foolish of you to parade it in broad daylight. Let me guess, you thought it would give you clout in the town. Am I right?"

He stuttered, unable to form a coherent sentence, and his gaze drifted to the floor.

Guilty.

"It didn't just give you clout, though," she continued, piecing together the events that had led to the brazen robbery. "Your greed and pride got the best of you, and displaying the bloom made you a target. Now, tell me who your buyer is."

Truth be told, she didn't care. She needed the truth, and to get that, she first needed leverage.

"My lady, I beg of you." He pressed his palms together and looked up at her. "Please. *Please* don't do this."

"Why do you think begging a Starling will do you any good, Mr. Williams?"

He gaped at her, his eyes wide with fear. "Certainly, there's something you need? Anything at all?"

Normally when someone tried to bribe her, she punched them in the gut. Today, however, she needed this man to comply, and she finally had her leverage.

"There is one way—and *only* one way—I will overlook finding out who your buyer is." Quinn set her hands behind her back, as she had so often seen her father do during interrogations. "Tell me absolutely everything there is to know about the gentleman who supposedly saved you. No matter what threats he made against you, you are to tell me the unfiltered truth. Do you understand?"

Eyes wide and body stiff with fear, he simply nodded.

"Good," she said. "Tell me what you gave him before he left. Do you know him personally? Did you hire him as protection?"

"No! No, my lady, I swear to the Fates themselves." The potion master lifted his palms, his breath quickening as he stared up at her. "He entered the shop just after the bandits, after they locked me in here and tried to force me to give them the bloom and my gold. I paid him when they were dead, but only as a token of gratitude. I never meant to—"

"How much?" Quinn interrupted.

"Fifty gold, I think." The old man rubbed his hands together, and his eyes glossed over with thought. "Perhaps seventy? I was still panicked, that close to death—"

"He forced you to pay him, did he?"

"No, my lady, no." Teak shook his head. "I offered him pay after he walked in and killed the first bandit. I was desperate, you see? I swear to you, I had no idea he was a criminal."

Quinn frowned, still not following. An assassin had walked into the shop without knowing he would be paid. Either he had intended to steal the goods for himself, or he had truly done a good deed.

Of course, if he'd wanted to steal the bloom, he had the power to do it. Judging by the vibrant fragrance, the bloom hadn't left this building.

Strange.

"How many bloody beauties did you have when he entered?" she asked, trying to catch the man in a lie.

"How many?" Despite the dire situation he faced, the potion maker chuckled in surprise. "Getting the one was difficult enough, Lady Starling. I can't fathom how I could have found more."

"What did you give him, then, besides the coin?"

"I tried to give him potions." The old man gestured to his destroyed shop. "Whatever I could find that wasn't broken. When I turned around, he was gone."

"Gone?" She crossed her arms and paced through the rubble. "Did you hear him leave?"

"Not a sound. He must have escaped through the back window, or perhaps he vanished into the air."

She resisted the impulse to roll her eyes at the man's melodrama. "Where is he now?"

"He disappeared, my lady, I swear to you!" He took a wary step backward and ran into the shelf behind him, jostling the potion bottles perched on the display. "I went to the front of the shop to find him some decent potions as a sign of my gratitude, and when I came back, he was gone. The bell didn't ring, and I never saw him leave. He simply vanished."

Quinn pinched the bridge of her nose and scanned the room for exits. As capable as the assassin was, not even he could simply disappear.

He had to be somewhere.

She paused, her back to the potion master as she took a deep and settling breath. "If you're lying to me—"

"Never, my lady," the potion master interrupted, his voice trembling.

Quinn glared over her shoulder to find the old man watching her with wide eyes. Still and breathless, he wisely shut his mouth. This time, he kept quiet and waited for her to finish her thought.

"The Shade, as you called him, is not a hero." She took careful steps toward the potion master as he gulped beneath her glare. "He's a criminal, and I need you to tell me where he went after you two spoke."

"I wish I could, my lady." With a nervous sigh, the potion master ran his hand along his bald head.

In the silence that followed, Quinn simply waited. A liar would've shifted uneasily in the looming quiet. A liar would've looked anywhere but at her.

The potion master, however, simply watched and waited, as though terrified of what she might do next.

She rubbed her neck to ease the tension in her body, the exhaustion of her hunt slowly eating at her the longer this wore on. "Very well."

He let out a slow breath of relief, but Quinn ignored him. Her target had been in this very shop mere hours ago. The blood, the destruction, the broken swords—she was close to finding him.

So very close.

"Thank you for your information," she said with her back to the old man as she surveyed his shop. "You've been very—"

Outside, Blaze roared. The snarl tore through the air, a warning that someone was trying to enter.

The sheriff, most likely.

Quinn whistled twice, the signal to allow their visitor inside. Boots stomped along the stairs, their thumps muffled by the closed door, and the little bell chimed. Footsteps thundered over the floorboards, and the slam of wood on wood shattered the stillness. The sheriff rounded the ivy-covered bookshelf again, his chest heaving as he struggled to breathe.

Quinn glanced him over. "What is it, Sheriff?"

"He's been spotted to the north," the sheriff wheezed.

Her heart leapt with hope. Barely able to stand still, she cracked her knuckles while she impatiently waited for the man to catch his breath.

The sheriff swallowed hard and pointed toward the door. "A local drunk saw him and a sellsword headed down the main road. It looks like they're headed into the forests north of town."

She frowned. "That's suicide. What's out there that he would risk going into the woods at night?"

"A necromancer." The sheriff's nose wrinkled with disgust at the word. "She moved here a few years ago. I've tried to run her out of town several times, my lady. She vanishes, that woman, any time you get close."

A necromancer.

Here, in Bradford.

Quinn rubbed her temple as it all made sense. The sheepish, guilty glances of the townsfolk when she had mentioned necromancy. A rare magical bloom in the middle of nowhere.

She glared over her shoulder at the potion master, suddenly quite clear on who his unknown buyer must've been. His lip twitched, and instead of meeting her eye, his gaze drifted to the floor. To buy from or sell to a necromancer meant certain jail time, and the sorceress hadn't camped north of Bradford without a clientele to fund her illegal magic.

Between the sheriff's ragged breathing and her own racing heart, she simply gave herself a moment to debate her next move.

The sheriff backed toward the door with his hand on the pommel of his sword. "I'll gather our soldiers. We don't have many men in our ranks, but—"

"No," Quinn interrupted. "I will go alone."

The sheriff leaned against a shelf, still catching his breath. "But my lady, I can't possibly allow you to risk your life alone in those woods. Your father—"

"My father sent me to finish this." Quinn snared him with a withering glare, daring him to interrupt.

"My lady, I can't in good conscience allow you to go alone."

Quinn almost laughed. "Have you ever fought a necromancer, Sheriff Newborn?"

"N-no," he admitted. "I've hunted her several times, though, and always come close."

"Because she wanted to dangle the potential arrest just out of reach," Quinn pointed out. "The closer you think you are to catching her, the less likely you are to call in the Lightseers to handle it—which you should have done, Sheriff, the moment she arrived."

He cleared his throat and stared at the floor, his brows knit with anger at his failure.

All Saldian lawmen had augmentations to help them keep the peace, and while they differed from region to region, she doubted he had enough to take on a necromancer. He should've known that, and his pride had put the people he'd sworn to protect in danger.

"I won't risk your men's lives against a necromancer." Quinn adjusted the sheath around her waist. "The magic that woman has likely surpasses yours, and there's no need for your men to die tonight."

She extended her hand toward the sheriff and nodded to the parchment in his fist. He sighed in resignation and, though he couldn't have known its true value, returned the only sketch of King Henry's assassin.

When King Henry was alive, rumors whispered in the back rooms at Lunestone hinted at the dark power he possessed. That wraith of his must've come from necromancy, and Lunestone had not succumbed willingly to his authority. Many good Lightseers had died fighting him off, and their augmented army had still lost to that reanimated pile of dead men's bones.

His demon.

With this assassin now chasing down a necromancer, she suspected history was about to repeat itself. Perhaps the assassin had killed Henry in order to learn the secret to the man's power. Or, perhaps, he simply wanted a wraith of his own.

Whatever his motivations, Saldia wouldn't survive another war.

If he'd learned how to create a wraith, she had to stop him before he found this necromancer and acquired the ingredients for his spell. She had time, but not much.

Quinn had to apprehend this man before this spiraled out of control. Before more people died. Before a new king rose from the shadows of this vile forest and spread his darkness to the rest of the known world.

If she acted quickly, she could end this once and for all.

Tonight.

CHAPTER THIRTY-ONE
CONNOR

The cold night whistled by as a lonesome howl lingered on the wind.

Connor paused midstride on the road, and the scuff of gravel under his boot scratched through the quiet night like a nail on a wooden board. His ear twitched as he strained to identify the sound, but the shrill cry cut short. Too quiet for the massive lungs of a blightwolf. Too brief, and ever so slightly timid. A lone gray wolf, perhaps, hunting for a mate.

So far, no blightwolves prowled this stretch of the forest tonight.

Thank the Fates.

Connor gestured for Murdoc to follow him as the city gates lumbered open. Murmurs above them floated down to the street, too quiet and far away to hear as he and the ruffian stepped out of the town's gates. Connor craned his neck to find two guards leaning on the edge of the wall. Their eyes narrowed as they watched him, their razor-sharp spear tips glinting in the green glow from the fire pots on either side of the gates.

Before the gates even opened fully, they began to close once more. Connor twisted sideways and slipped through a gap barely wide enough for him and Murdoc both, and the sellsword cursed under his breath as he darted through after him.

"Rude, that," the ruffian muttered with a quick glare over his shoulder at the guards.

Rude or not, at least the guards had indulged the request. Connor let out a slow breath of relief and turned his back on the soldiers, grateful word hadn't yet spread about the brawl in the tavern.

It wouldn't be long before the sheriff pieced together who had been responsible for both the shopkeeper's rescue and the tavern brawl. As soon as he did, Connor needed to be long gone.

As the gates thudded closed, the guards' gazes weighed on his neck. The murmurs began again, and this time, he caught part of the exchange.

"…headed to the sorceress?" the first one asked.

The other soldier muttered something Connor couldn't hear, except for the last line. "…crazy bastards."

He didn't bother to look behind him again because, insult or no, the soldier had a point.

To anyone else, he must've looked like a madman. He'd led Murdoc into the northern part of the forest around Bradford, out of the safety of the gates and into the world the blightwolves owned. Even when the blightwolves departed for a time, off to haunt some other stretch of the woodland, the forest's other carnivores wandered into the night to feed on the enchanted wolves' scraps.

Hell, maybe he *was* insane.

Roughly the width of five men standing side to side, the road out of town snaked up a hill and into the forest beyond the safety of Bradford's walls. Their boots crunched along the gravel, and though Connor sidestepped most of the rocks to avoid making noise, Murdoc's footsteps boomed and crackled in the otherwise whisper-silent evening.

When they finally reached the trees, a cloud blocked the light from one of the moons. The puffy white edges glowed silver even as the sky darkened.

"I'm having second thoughts," Murdoc admitted.

"Quiet," Connor chided.

Besides, it was too late for second thoughts—for either of them.

Murdoc seemed like the sort to camp out in taverns and the beds of other men's wives, so he likely didn't realize the danger they faced. Creatures filled these woods at night, their bellies empty and their ears attuned to the slightest sound.

The ruffian's crackling footsteps were bad enough. Connor didn't need the man talking, too.

A twig crunched beneath Murdoc's boot, and Connor glared at the ruffian over his shoulder. The man grinned in a sheepish apology and shrugged, as if that would do any good against the dozens of things in these woods that wanted to eat them alive.

Jaw tense and shoulders tight, Connor briefly pinched his eyes shut to force himself to have a bit of patience.

Hopefully, this idea of his wouldn't bite him in the ass.

It was wise to bring a sacrifice, the Wraith King said in Connor's ear. *I assume that's why you brought along such an oaf, anyway?*

Though the Wraith King had yet to appear, Connor groaned. After walking through a town and encountering other people, life had almost made sense again. Food and supplies had been purchased. Conversation had been made. There had been a sense of normalcy, however fleeting, and he'd let himself almost forget the ghost fused with his soul.

Almost.

He is a decent fighter, the Wraith King continued, apparently unaware of Connor's reaction. *However, even you must be able to tell he will not last long in a battle against true warriors who have magic. He is therefore useless as a servant and a worthy trophy for the necromancer. This sorceress you've found will find his blood useful in many potions.*

"You all right there, Captain?" Murdoc asked a little too loudly.

Connor nodded and held his finger to his mouth in the vain hope this sellsword would finally shut the hell up.

He had no intention of sacrificing the man to the sorceress, regardless of what the ghoul said. Whether necromancers wanted blood for their potions or simply craved human suffering, he wouldn't indulge this one's bloodlust.

If Murdoc didn't close his damn mouth, however, Connor absolutely *was* willing to beat some sense into him with a rock.

You can smell it on him, can't you? the ghoul continued, as calm and grim as ever. *He reeks of ineptitude. I haven't smelled one of these in a while, and I'd honestly thought they were all killed off in my time. A man who's allergic to spellgust is standing right before me, and you won't even indulge me in a little murder. He's nothing but a scoundrel. A waste of breath.*

Connor balled his hand into a fist at the slur. He'd broken men's teeth for saying less, and it took everything in him not to respond. For a brief moment, he wondered if his connection to the ghoul meant he actually could break the ghost's teeth with a well-timed punch, but he shoved the thought away.

He had bigger problems than a bigoted old ghost.

As he led Murdoc into the forest, the branches bending over the wide road blocked out the light. Their thick canopies plunged the path into even deeper shadows, and Connor's eyes adjusted instantly.

Murdoc, however, stumbled. Quick as lightning, Connor grabbed the man's collar to keep him from falling.

"Thanks," Murdoc whispered. "I can't see anything."

Roughly one hundred yards ahead, a scaly blue snout poked from the underbrush along the side of the path. A tongue darted out over the gravel, yellow as the sun. A head broke through the bush, the creature's skull easily as large as the pack on his shoulder.

Connor stopped dead in his tracks, his grip tight on Murdoc's collar to root the man in place as the beast slithered onto the road. Its long body snaked back and forth in a hypnotic rhythm as hundreds of clawed feet clicked along the ground. Its tongue snapped again at the air, smelling its way through the night before it disappeared into a bush on the opposite side of the road.

"It's probably for the best that you can't see," Connor admitted as he drew one of the twin swords on his back.

With one hand gripping Murdoc's tunic in order to guide the man through the darkness, Connor continued down the road. Ethan had said there would be a fork in the path, and now they simply had to walk until they found it.

"You can climb, right?" Connor asked in the barest whisper.

"Yeah, why?"

He didn't answer. Wasted words and broken silence wouldn't serve them now. If the blightwolves came, the two of them would be fine as long as they both climbed a tree to find safety. He didn't fancy the idea of hauling a grown man up an oak, but he'd do it if he had to.

The trill of cicadas buzzed through the forest as the night's orchestra played for those who made the time to listen. The canopy rustled. Somewhere in the depths of the woods, a twig snapped.

With one hand still on Murdoc's collar and the other wrapped around his sword, Connor listened to the night. A branch splintered in the distance, breaking under the weight of something heavy, and he impulsively tightened his grip on his weapon.

Ready to strike.

A gap appeared in the trees ahead, and as they neared, a footpath broke away from the main road. Barely wide enough for two people, it seemed more like a deer trail than a true walkway.

Thin lines etched into a tree along the path caught his eye. Barely a shade lighter than the bark, the carving reminded him of a scar. Someone had chiseled a rough sketch of a potion bottle into the trunk.

It seemed as though they'd finally found their fork in the road.

Connor led the way, still guiding Murdoc along the darkened route as they trudged deeper into the forest. The trail cut through the trees, winding around trunk after trunk.

The trees blurred together. With no distinct landmarks, every oak looked identical to the last. As the minutes ticked by, Connor frowned with concern. Since he had no light from the moon, he quickly lost track of time.

And yet, the path never changed. Just an endless trail winding through the trees.

Perhaps this was one of the necromancer's tricks. A path that went on forever—it seemed like something a necromancer might've been able to pull off. Connor didn't know enough about them or magic itself to tell for certain.

As the path continued, the forest slowly brightened. Though subtle at first, soft blue moonlight cast a cool glow through the trees as the woods thinned. Murdoc's weight shifted as the light returned, and he gently tugged on Connor's grip to break free.

Focused on the forest and whatever they might find within it, Connor released him without another thought.

Through a gap in two trunks, the landscape finally changed, and he caught sight of a withered old tree. The trail curved, cutting between two thick oaks, and it led them to a meadow. The withered tree stood in the center of the waist-high grasses, a beacon that they had finally arrived.

The dead tree stretched its black branches into the night like a scorch mark on a field. No leaves. No sprouts. No hint of life. Its thick trunk coiled and snaked around itself like a tornado frozen in time. At about chest height, a hand-carved hollow served as a makeshift shelf in what had once been the tree's heart.

He paused at the edge of the woods, alert for a possible trap. The night hummed with life, unbothered by his suspicion. Nothing moved but the grasses in the wind. Only the cicadas spoke, their voices carried on the same breeze that danced with the meadow.

Quiet.

Time to see if this sorceress knew anything of value.

Connor left the forest and trudged through the field. The grass around him swayed in time with the midnight melody and bent beneath his boots with each step. Small green pinpricks of light floated off the blades of grass and swirled away into the enchanted night as he fished a coin from the bag at his waist and set it in the tree's hollow.

"This is fun." Murdoc rubbed his hands together for warmth. "We're not about to summon demons, are we?"

"We might," Connor admitted as he scanned the woodlands around them for signs of the necromancer. "Get ready."

At any second, the sorceress would decide if she wanted to speak with them or try to kill them.

Any minute now, a wisp of light would appear and guide them to her hut or to their doom.

Any breath could've been their last.

"Where is she, then?" Murdoc asked.

"Be quiet." Connor strained his ears as branches creaked in the woods, their limbs bending beneath the weight of something heavier than the breeze.

The ruffian crossed his arms as he scanned the meadow. "Is she dancing naked in the woods, maybe?"

"Stop talking."

"A man can dream." His eyes lingered on Connor's sword, and he drew his own in response. "What exactly do you want from this sorceress?"

Connor didn't answer. He didn't need to. The hair on the back of his neck stood on end, and his intuition spiked with warning.

They wouldn't have to wait long for her to appear.

A gust tore through the meadow, fierce and violent. In the tree's hollow, Connor's copper coin glinted in the moonlight.

"Come to kill me, have you?" a woman asked.

Her voice echoed through the field, and though Connor scanned the branches above them, he couldn't place her.

"I've come for information," he corrected. Though his body tensed with the looming threat of a fight, he did his best to keep his voice even. "I want to make a deal."

"Who sent you?" she asked.

A silhouette darted through the forest behind the withered tree and melted instantly into the shadows.

Either she moved faster than any human he'd ever known, or she had ways to divert his attention and toy with his mind.

Regardless, she was good, and he had to tread carefully.

"Ethan Finn," Connor answered. "He said you might know—"

"That's clever," she interrupted. "Finding one of my clients, who I haven't seen in years, and claiming he sent you. Did you torture him for details about me?"

"What?" Connor frowned. "No. Why would—"

"You come here with your swords drawn, reeking of death," she snapped. "Yet you have the gall to lie to me? Do you think I've survived this long in these woods because I'm just lucky?"

"What does she mean, 'reeking of death'?" Murdoc asked. "It's not me, Captain, I swear. I bathed already this week."

"It's not you." Connor gripped his sword tighter and debated summoning his blackfire blades, regardless of the witnesses.

She can sense me, the wraith said. *I am impressed. Perhaps she is a worthier Wraithblade than you, peasant.*

Connor frowned. He wouldn't be replaced that easily.

"I don't recognize you," she continued. "Given your age, I'd know your face if you'd come from Nethervale, so they found someone else. A loner."

She paused, and the forest's song died. No hum of insects. No twitter of birds. Only the unrelenting wind as it wove through the canopy.

"It's a clever ruse, I'll grant you that," she admitted. "Approaching as a possible client. Coming at night when no one from town could see you. You didn't come alone because you knew I would be suspicious if you'd traveled the forest by yourself, so you brought only one other soldier to ensure I would underestimate you."

"You're mistaken," Connor said, more firmly this time. "I want to make a deal. I've brought devil's ivy and reishi mushrooms to barter for—"

"A man like you shouldn't barter with a commoner's reagents," she interrupted. "You have real power, and that means you have to offer something more substantial."

"Captain," Murdoc said quietly as he scanned the empty forest. "I'm getting a bad feeling about this."

"Same," Connor admitted. He slipped his bag off his shoulder and set it beside the withered tree in the likely chance this situation devolved into a battle.

He'd never fought a necromancer before. If the Wraith King's power was any inclination of what lay ahead, this would test everything he had ever learned about the sword and about himself—but he hadn't come this far to die next to a withered old tree.

MURDOC

The southern wind moaned, low and mournful, through the trees. The ancient oaks bent in the gust, and as their branches danced across the moonlit clouds, their trunks groaned with the weight of the gale.

Murdoc's skin creaked across the hilt of his sword as he held it tighter. His ear strained against the wind, but he heard nothing else. No crickets. No chirp of a midnight sparrow. No creatures through the brush, shuffling on to their next meal.

The beasts of the forest had abandoned this field, and no mere witch could've scared them away.

In all his life, a sorceress had never toyed with him this way. The stranger had lied, and whoever waited for them in this forest wouldn't have a few potions to sell or a half-baked augmentation to ink onto anyone's arm.

No deal would be struck tonight. Blood, however, would spill. He could taste it on the wind, like sour skin flaking off a carcass.

He'd cut down the moonlit horrors many times before, and this reminded him of a necromancer playing with her food. The monsters from Nethervale took no prisoners.

Whatever his new Captain had in store for them, it would sting.

It seemed the Fates had sent this man as an answer to his death wish, and he found it odd that they would've shown him such a kindness.

They never had before.

A whistle pierced the night, sharp and sudden. His eyes darted toward the sound. A silhouette shot through the forest shadows, too fast to see.

Murdoc cast a sidelong glance at the man who had brought him here.

Tall. Broad shoulders. Thick chest. Squared jaw. Not just a warrior's build, but a king's. He looked like someone who could've taken down a dragon back in the old days, when the Curse-Strykers summoned thunderclouds from the ocean tides and rained hellfire on the people.

This Connor fellow studied the woods with narrowed eyes. Focused. Clear. Seeing what no mortal could. Compared to the stiff and silent fellow he'd met in the bar, this man seemed far more at home in the woods than with people.

How odd.

From the moment they'd left Bradford, it had been clear this man had a darkness to him. It rolled from him like a fog, so much thicker out here under the moon and away from the town's lamps and lights.

The somber shift in the air around Connor transcended the effects from any augmentation Murdoc had ever seen. This went beyond mortal magic and touched something else.

Something darker.

Something like Death.

Perhaps he had only been brought out here as a sacrifice to this necromancer. He'd heard of it before. He'd been cautioned not to take a job from anyone who headed out into the forests at night. Every year, countless sellswords went missing in the gaps between trees.

He'd chosen not to heed the warnings. If tonight was his final night in Saldia, he would at least let himself enjoy one last good fight and indulge in a bit of banter. The somber fights and scowling faces had never much entertained him, anyway.

Murdoc had to die with his sword in his hand, swinging until his dying breath. That was the rule. His only way to redeem himself.

His last chance to recover a bit of honor before he met the Fates.

CHAPTER THIRTY-TWO
CONNOR

"You've piqued my curiosity," the woman admitted from the depths of the pitch-black forest around Connor. Her voice carried on the southern wind from every direction, swirling through the tall grasses as he tried and failed to place her.

A threat hidden in the woods, with power likely far beyond anything he'd ever seen. If he didn't diffuse the tension in the air, this was going to unravel. She was the closest thing he had to a lead, and he wouldn't let this chance to get answers slip through his fingers.

"Let's talk, then." His eyes narrowed as he resisted the urge to summon his shadow blades. If he drew an enchanted weapon, she would probably attack.

"How tempting," she teased. "I really am curious, but you can't fool me. Whatever game Nethervale is playing, it ends tonight. I don't know how you found me, but I'll send you back to them in pieces."

Before Connor could even reply, a crackle of energy cut through the chilly air. He felt it long before he saw it, like a tide shifting beneath the surface of the ocean. His body moved on its own, before he even consciously understood what had happened.

He grabbed Murdoc and threw the ruffian on the ground seconds before a blistering blast of ice cut through the field. The shard of ice hit a tree with enough force to crack the bark. The oak froze instantly as ice crept across its surface, spreading like frost on glass. The splintering thunder of snapping wood tore through the night as the tree fell, and its roots ripped from the soil. Clumps of dirt soared into the air.

When the tree finally fell to the ground, its trunk coated in a thick sheet of blue ice, it shattered into hundreds of pieces.

Dead in a flash—and the same would happen to them if her ice touched their skin.

"I was right, Captain," Murdoc said as he gaped at the tree. "You're going to be fun."

"Focus!" Connor ordered. "Don't let the ice touch you!"

Another blast snaked through the night, and he rolled out of the way with seconds to spare. The burst of magic landed against the dirt, coating the ground in a thick sheet of ice.

Murdoc scrambled to his feet and stood, his sword raised as he studied the woods where the attack had come from.

Connor followed suit and jumped to his feet. As he found his footing and inched away from the sheet of ice slowly spreading across the meadow, a silhouette appeared from within the shadows of the trees—a woman's hourglass figure, just a shade darker than the forest around her.

Connor hadn't even known a potion existed with that sort of ability, but spellgust had a way of constantly surprising him with its power.

The glowing green ore that bewitched Saldia could never be underestimated—nor could he underestimate the people crafty and clever enough to master its enchantments.

With spellgust, a person could craft any future they wanted. Almost any power they desired. Their augmentations and potions could give them almost any life they craved, if only they had the money to pay for it and the creativity to dream. If they studied the dozens of reagents growing all over Saldia, the only limitations to what they could create were their own imagination and wit.

Less than two weeks ago, Connor had fought ten of the best soldiers Oakenglen had to offer and chased off a lord who had wielded a dagger that could've killed an undead ghoul. Despite all that, he suspected this woman was likely the greatest threat he had faced thus far in his life.

A battle with her wouldn't end the way he wanted, so he needed a different approach. It was time to use man's greatest weapon.

Reason.

"I won't fight you," he shouted. "I don't want to. I need information, and I'll pay you well for it."

"I already know you're clever," she answered. "You can't tempt my greed. I won't let you get close enough to kill me."

"She has *issues*," Murdoc whispered.

"I'm setting my sword down," Connor said, ignoring Murdoc.

It was a risk, but a measured one. If she tried anything, he had his other silver sword and both of his magical blackfire blades as backups.

Logic and a calm tone could still save them from a bloody battle, though she clearly didn't believe anything he said. For whatever reason, she wanted to believe he was here to kill her.

If the necromancers in Nethervale were truly after her, perhaps her paranoia made sense.

A wicked little laugh rang through the meadow. "You're setting down your sword as a token of good faith, I take it?"

"Yes." He stood, his hands wide as he watched the silhouette in the trees.

"That was foolish," she replied.

Another crackle of energy cut through the night, and Connor dove out of the way. Abandoned on the grass, his sword glimmered in the moonlight as ice sailed over it. The blast shattered a nearby tree, and the ice consumed the oak as it toppled.

In a blur, the silhouette at the edge of the forest darted toward him. Arms pumping at her sides, she bolted into the moonlit field. Despite her speed, he caught a fleeting glance of her pale face glowing in the light. Her dark red lips curled into a smirk as her black hair and dark dress billowed behind her.

The woman moved with unnatural speed, and he barely stood in time to face her. She reached him in seconds, and a dagger glinted in her palm as she swiped at his neck.

Fine. If she wanted a fight, he'd give her one.

He leaned back, and the blade glinted as it passed by. She twirled and swung again, but this time, he grabbed her wrist. His strength surpassed hers, and he blocked her mid-swing. The dagger paused mere inches from his head.

Quick as lightning, he twisted her hand. She grimaced, and her smile fell as her closed fist popped open. The blade dropped to the ground and disappeared into the thick grass at their feet.

She didn't even pause to catch her breath.

Her heel dug into the dirt, and she tugged hard on his grip. It threw him briefly off balance, and she used the moment to launch a left jab at his neck. The blow hit, and his throat burned as she momentarily cut off his air. His grasp on her wrist loosened, and she wrenched her hand free.

Two could play that game.

Connor dropped to the ground and kicked her legs out from under her in a fluid motion. She toppled and fell hard on her hands with a grunt of pain. He reached for her arm, trying to pin her in place so that he could finally talk some sense into her, but she rolled out of the way one second too soon.

She knelt in the grass before him and raised one hand. With a subtle twitch of her fingers, the blade on the ground shivered, responding to her magical pull. It slid across the dirt and flew through the air before landing flat in her palm.

Her magic. Her connections to Nethervale. Her enchanted dagger. She had real power, and she could help him.

Now, if only he could convince her to stop trying to kill him.

With an elegant twirl, she swung her arm. The attack looked more like a dance as her skirts twisted, but it ended with the deadly dagger launching at his face. He ducked, and the tiny blade hissed through the air over his head.

She called it back to her and swiped again, this time aiming for his throat. He leaned back in time to avoid it. With his hands near his face to protect his head and neck, he ducked and wove, unwilling to let her strike him. He dodged it once—twice—three more times as she drove him backward across the field.

"Feel free to help," he shouted at Murdoc. Somewhere in his periphery, the ruffian stumbled across the edge of the meadow, but Connor's full focus remained on the deadly necromancer in front of him.

Try as she might, she couldn't hit him. Her ruby-red scowl deepened with each missed blow.

Murdoc ran up behind her, apparently recovered from his narrow escape from an icy death. He raised his sword to strike a blow, but she didn't seem to notice. She didn't even look away from Connor.

Shit.

If Murdoc killed her, all of this would've been for nothing.

The ruffian swung, his hips and shoulders perfectly aligned as he leaned into the attack. As he swung, however, he twisted his blade, and the flat width of his sword sailed toward her head.

If it hit, the blow would knock her out. Even though she had tried to kill them both, Murdoc hadn't forgotten why they were there.

Good.

As Connor ducked another of the woman's attacks, he smirked with gratitude. Murdoc was a better wingman than the ghoul had given him credit for.

With the blade inches from her head, the woman's eyebrow twitched. At the last second, she dropped to the ground. The sword passed harmlessly overhead.

Murdoc frowned with disappointment, but Connor didn't care. If nothing else, the ruffian had given him a suitable diversion.

While the kneeling sorceress regained her balance, he kicked her sharply in the side. Normally, he never would've done something like that, but most women he met didn't try to kill him.

She seemed like an exception to his general rules of chivalry.

He didn't want to hurt her, damn it all. He just wanted to *talk*. He needed to get her on her stomach so he could pin her in one spot long enough to have a conversation, and that was proving far more difficult than he had expected.

She grimaced as she took the blow. Her enchanted dagger dropped to the ground. Instead of reaching for it, however, she grabbed his leg and twisted. Her nails dug into his skin, and the movement took him to the ground.

The sorceress climbed on top of him and threw a punch at his nose. Instead of ducking this one, he grabbed her fist and stopped the blow an inch from his face. With his hand locked around her fingers, she tried punching him with her other hand, only for it to meet the same fate. She grimaced, leaning into his hands, and a chill seeped through her fingertips into his palms.

With a grunt of effort, she rolled to the side, and he rolled with her. He now had her pinned to the ground.

The brief upper hand didn't last.

She rolled them again, and he ended up on his back, looking up at her as her dark hair cascaded over her shoulders. Fists locked, they wrestled across the meadow grass as she tried to break free.

Connor was quickly losing his patience.

He rolled them again and pinned her hands over her head. "Will you sit still long enough to listen?"

Without so much as acknowledging that he'd spoken, she shifted her hips and rolled him onto his back once again. She straddled him, and with her weight on his chest, she wrenched one hand free of his grip. This time, she landed a punch to his throat.

As he choked, she snatched his second sword from the sheath on his back and threw it at a nearby tree. The blade landed hard in the wood, the hilt quivering from the force of her throw.

With a jarringly fast movement, the necromancer stood and slammed the heel of her boot in Connor's gut. He grunted with pain as she rolled out of range and stood, her chest heaving from their fight. He pushed himself to his feet as the burn in his throat slowly faded, and he studied her with barely contained fury.

Murdoc charged at the woman from the other side of the field, his sword raised even as he gaped in awe at her. With a smitten little smirk, he swung. His blade cut through the air, but she stumbled backward to avoid the blow.

"I must say, you're absolutely beautiful," the ruffian admitted as he swung again.

His sword barreled toward her, broad and heavy, but she ducked out of the way at the last second. Her fingertips twitched, and something in the air behind Connor sent a jolt of warning down his spine.

His enhanced senses hadn't led him astray yet, so he listened to the hit of intuition.

Murdoc raised his sword to attack again, but Connor shoved the man aside. He and Murdoc rolled across the ground. Seconds later, the woman's dagger flew through the air where the ruffian had stood moments before. It landed square in her palm, glinting briefly in the moonlight as she wrapped her fingers around its hilt. With a graceful twirl, she launched it at Murdoc's face.

The ruffian twisted out of the way, and the dagger grazed his cheek instead of landing in his skull. Blood dripped into his beard as he scooted backward across the flattened grass, but his grip on his sword never loosened.

A fighter to the end.

"I mean, yes, you're absolutely insane," he admitted with a shrug. "But incredibly beautiful."

A second dagger slid from the depths of her sleeve and into her palm, so quickly it seemed as if she had summoned it from thin air. If Connor hadn't been so close, he wouldn't have even noticed where it had come from.

Her gaze darted between the two of them, sizing them up, and this clearly wouldn't end well if Connor let her have her way any longer. Though he only wanted to disarm her, she seemed hell-bent on digging those daggers of hers into both their skulls.

The woman threw the second dagger at Murdoc as he tried to stand. He fell backward and barely ducked out of the way as it sliced his temple. Blood rolled down his face, the cut deep enough to draw a thin and constant stream.

"We're not trying to kill you," Connor shouted. "But if you keep attacking us, we'll have to."

"Oh, good!" Murdoc leaned up on his elbows, grinning like an idiot. "Since he doesn't want you dead, I don't suppose you're free later?"

"You're either lying, or you're an idiot." She glared at Connor, ignoring Murdoc entirely.

Her delicate fingers nearly glowed in the moonlight as she stretched them apart. Her blades whizzed through the air again, and Connor rolled out of the way as they flew overhead. One of them grazed his neck, cutting deep, and the sting of steel across skin burned through his skull.

For all he knew, these could've been poisoned.

He had no patience left for this woman.

None.

"Enough!" Connor twisted his wrists, and billowing black smoke snaked into his palms as he summoned the blackfire swords. The enchanted blades settled into his hands, and he tightened his fingers around the hilts as he stared her down.

The forest stilled as the bewitched fire crackled across the black steel. Murdoc gaped at the weapons as he lay in the grass, his sword forgotten at his side. The sorceress froze in place, and her fingers curled around the daggers in each palm as her dark eyes narrowed in suspicion.

"With swords like those, you don't want my potions," she said calmly. "Nothing I can do will surprise you. I'm not sure why you're here, but I refuse to believe a thing you say. You want a necromancer as a slave? You want me to lead you to Nethervale? A man like you doesn't want something simple, and I'm fine with the life I live. Whatever you want, you won't get it from me."

She launched both of the daggers, the cursed metal aimed right for his heart. Connor swung his blades on instinct. Muscle memory from years of training guided his hands.

The black flame along his swords crackled as he knocked the blades from the air. They fell to the ground, dented from his blows.

A small victory, certainly, but not a win.

Not yet.

The woman gritted her teeth and curled her hands into fists. With the motion, the ground beneath them rumbled. A vine broke from the dirt at her feet, followed by a dozen more. Clumps of soil shot into the air as she summoned the earth to do her bidding.

Ice. Earth. Enchanted blades.

She would stop at nothing.

Coin hadn't worked. Reason hadn't worked. Even his blackfire blades hadn't stopped her for more than a few seconds.

"Captain, I hope you have a plan!" Murdoc shouted as he scooted backward. A vine launched into the air from the ground where he'd laid moments before, and he snatched his sword off the flattened grass seconds before a vine could coil around it.

Connor grimaced. For her to insist on killing him meant one of two things. Either she had spent entirely too long alone in the woods, or she had the sort of enemies that could put even the Wraith King to shame. It seemed as though this woman had even more secrets than he'd suspected, and this confrontation would not end with her putting away her magic so they could talk.

She charged again, the vines coiling behind her like a tangled spider web, but Connor had no patience left for this woman's paranoia.

At this point, he had only one other option short of running her through with his blade.

"Stop her, wraith," he ordered with a twinge of disappointment. "I want her alive."

Finally, the Wraith King said, barely able to contain his excitement.

The ghoul materialized out of thin air before Connor, looking down at the woman as she charged. She gasped and slid to a stop, and the vines around her wilted like dead leaves in the sun.

The ghost grabbed her throat with his bony fingers and lifted her off her feet as her vines slid back into the earth. Only piles of dirt and uprooted grass remained where the roots had retreated. Her dangling boots kicked at the hems of her dress, the only part of her visible underneath the Wraith King's cloak as he hovered in the air.

Connor stepped around the ghost to find her clawing at those bony hands, her eyes wide as she wheezed for breath. Her hair caught on the wind, and her nails scratched uselessly against the ghoul's skeletal fingers.

The horror on her face reminded Connor of Isabella, oddly enough. It reminded him of the way the girl had pressed herself into the corner of the kitchen, her little arms wrapped around her knees as she had waited to see if he, like so many things in this world, wanted to hurt her.

"Put her down," he ordered. "I think she's ready to talk."

The Wraith King growled with frustration. He held her aloft, testing their shaky truce. Connor waited, his steely gaze on the ghoul, daring him to disobey.

Daring the old fart to test him.

Eventually, the ghost's bony fingers released her neck. She collapsed onto the grass, wheezing as she held her throat. Her dark hair cascaded over her shoulders, obscuring her face as she coughed into the dirt and tried to catch her breath.

The ghoul remained in the field, his cloak billowing in its own breeze as he watched them all with those empty eye sockets. Though Connor hadn't wanted anyone else to see the Wraith King, there was no need for the ghoul to disappear now.

Like it or not, he had his first witnesses.

With his eyes locked on the Wraith King, Murdoc reached around blindly for his sword. A reflex, most likely. Nothing more than a need to feel like he could protect himself, even if a mortal weapon wouldn't do a damn thing against a ghost like that.

Silence stretched through the night as even the cicadas waited with bated breath. Both Murdoc and the necromancer watched the ghoul, frozen in place.

As the minutes passed, however, their gazes slowly drifted instead to Connor.

Good. At least he had their attention.

"I have questions." He stretched out his shoulders as he dismissed the blackfire blades. Smoke billowed from his palms as they disappeared.

He let his words linger on the field as he made a show of retrieving his other weapons. A power play, but one worth making against a necromancer as powerful as this one. She needed to know where she sat on the food chain.

Most of all, the sorceress needed to assume he wouldn't show her mercy if she tried to kill him again—because he wouldn't.

He grabbed his first sword off the ground and sheathed it before crossing the meadow to fetch the other one. He grabbed the hilt, its blade still embedded in a nearby tree, and yanked it from the trunk.

With his weapons sheathed and a heavy silence weighing on the field, he crossed his arms and faced the sorceress who had overcomplicated this from the start.

She held her throat, and her fingers barely hid the red marks where the ghoul had held her in the air. "You may have questions, stranger, but so do I. If you're not here to kill me, then what do you want?"

"I want information. Once you give me that, you can leave." Connor paused, his gaze shifting toward Murdoc. "Both of you."

Don't be foolish, the wraith chided. *You cannot have witnesses, and it would do well to have servants. The man is a waste, but the necromancer will be useful.*

Connor ignored the ghoul and waited for a response, but the sorceress didn't answer. She simply studied the Wraith King with wide eyes. After a while, her shoulders relaxed, and a small smile tugged at the corner of her mouth.

That wasn't fear. That was recognition.

He didn't trust this woman, but she recognized the Wraith King. Somehow, she knew what the ghoul was—perhaps even who he was—and Connor was going to get his answers one way or another. Too much relied on him figuring out his abilities, and soon.

She had skill. She had resources. She had a vast understanding of magic, and he suspected she had use for the wraith's power. Of all his potential enemies, she seemed like the most capable of killing him.

If she tried to take the Wraith King for herself, Connor would sacrifice her knowledge and usefulness. He didn't like the idea, but he'd seen that expression on too many crooks to ignore it.

Greed.

He'd stumbled into a pit of vipers, and damn it all, he would do whatever it took to find his way out.

CHAPTER THIRTY-THREE
CONNOR

A gust rattled the trees surrounding the meadow. Leaves clattered together in a ripple of applause as branches trembled beneath the bewitched southern wind. Clouds crept across the sky, and as their hazy forms obscured the moon, their edges glowed silver in the quiet night.

The Wraith King hovered beside the withered old tree in the center of the field. Around him, the once-tall meadow grasses lay flattened after the skirmish.

Connor's fingers twitched as he waited in the silence, his palms achingly empty as he resisted the urge to summon his swords again.

The sorceress stood and brushed clumps of dirt off her dress. A loose curl caught on the breeze and floated across her face as she studied the specter. With a quick twist of her wrists, her enchanted blades soared toward her.

Connor tensed, ready for another battle, but the daggers landed flat against her palms and disappeared into her sleeves.

"I enjoyed that." Murdoc pushed himself to his feet and brushed a dead vine off his tunic. "What's your name, love? Or do you prefer I call you something derogatory like 'sorceress'? That seems like a kink you might have."

"Stop talking," Connor ordered.

"Yep." Murdoc snatched his sword off the ground and sheathed it.

"Is he your servant?" She nodded toward the ruffian. "He talks too much. You do realize I could hear him long before you entered the meadow, right?"

"I'm aware," Connor said flatly.

Murdoc frowned and leaned against a tree, arms crossed. He pointed a lazy finger and gestured between them both. "Rude."

The sorceress pursed her lips in disappointment and studied the ruffian. "If you insist on keeping him, we need to give him a Prowlport augmentation to make him manageable."

"None for me, thanks," he said with a wave of his hand, as if he were passing on a beer. "I've had my fill of magic."

That settled it, then. For Murdoc to pass on a free augmentation confirmed he had a spellgust allergy. Either that, or he was an idiot.

Maybe both.

"Tell me your name," Connor ordered.

The woman huffed impatiently and set her hands on her hips. Her gaze shifted again to the ghoul, however, and she begrudgingly crossed her arms across her chest. "Sophia Auclair."

"I'm Connor, and this is Murdoc."

"I'm also unmarried," the ruffian added with a wink.

For Murdoc to flirt with a woman like this, he truly must've had a death wish after all.

The Wraith King shifted abruptly. His blurred form darted toward Murdoc, and he smacked the ruffian on the back of the head with his bony hand. Murdoc cursed under his breath and staggered away from the ghoul, his hand nursing the back of his skull as he retreated.

"Thank you," Connor muttered to the ghost.

My pleasure, the wraith replied.

Connor returned his attention to the sorceress. "Sophia, I'm here because I want to offer you a deal."

"You can't afford me." She paused before nodding toward Murdoc. "And no amount of money can be worth bedding him."

Murdoc smirked. "The more you fight this attraction between us, the more I like you."

She opened her mouth to speak, but Connor wasn't in the mood for games or banter.

"If I wanted a whore, I'd have found one in Bradford," he snapped. "Shut your mouth and listen."

Her eyes narrowed, but her red lips pressed together into a thin line.

"Here's my offer—you answer all of my questions truthfully, and I will give you both coin and reagents. I brought devil's ivy and reishi mushrooms, which Ethan said you—"

"That's what the common folk bring me," she interrupted with a dismissive wave of her hand. "It helps cover the cost of their potions or augmentations and saves me a trip to the potion master's shop. You, however, have to pay in full."

"And why's that?" He set his hands on his waist as he challenged her. "Are you just upset that I beat you?"

Her frown deepened. "I wouldn't call that a victory for you, so don't get cocky."

He smirked. In his book, winning always meant victory. She clearly didn't like to lose. "Come on, now. Be a good sport."

"You are clearly something else entirely," she continued, ignoring the jibe. "Someone with real power. That means you can get me things I actually want."

He crossed his thick arms over his chest and widened his stance ever so slightly. The subtle shift in his demeanor mirrored a tactic he'd seen Beck Arbor use plenty of times over their years together, whenever people challenged his authority or tried to overcharge him in the shops.

Be a mountain, Connor, Sir Beck had always warned. *Be a mountain and make them walk around you.*

"And what exactly do you want?" he asked, daring her to scam him.

Money, magic, or power—it was all anyone ever asked for in a negotiation. If she asked for something else, or if she asked for too little, he would catch her in the lie. Given how she watched the wraith, he could already guess what she truly wanted.

If she wished to take his power from him, he wouldn't allow her enough time to even form a plan.

The corner of her lips curled into a wicked little smile. "We'll get to that. First, let me guess what *you* want."

Though he likely wouldn't benefit from giving her temporary control of the conversation, Connor waited for her to continue. He wanted to see where this would lead and how much she could guess on her own.

"You want me to tell you about that." She pointed to the wraith without ever breaking eye contact. "You want me to tell you about what you are, and you want me to take you to the Deathdread."

"Maybe," Connor bluffed.

He had no idea what the hell the Deathdread even was. If she was going to be foolish enough to give him useful information without him even paying for it, he wouldn't stop her.

"Is there more?" she asked.

Of course there was more. He needed to know why his blackfire blades hadn't broken the dagger in the potion shop. He needed to master the powers he had acquired from the wraith thus far. He needed to learn how to control the ghost and keep it from killing everyone around him.

He bit back a sarcastic quip and simply nodded.

"You have questions," she said with a wide grin, echoing his earlier statement. "Lucky for you, I have answers."

He shrugged, remaining aloof as their negotiation began. "And how good are those answers of yours? How do you know any of this? How can I be certain the information I get is worth what I pay?"

"Fair point," she admitted. "I guess you don't."

"That's adorable." He tilted his head and narrowed his eyes, refusing to give her an inch. "If you want to negotiate any kind of reasonable fee, then you'd better give me a real answer."

That wiped the smile off her face. "That's not how this works, handsome. I name my price, and you accept. Given what you're asking for, you don't have the upper hand in this little negotiation of ours."

"Pretty sure I do." Connor nodded to the wraith floating by the tree to remind her of who had the stronger magic. "Besides, you're in hiding. You admitted it yourself. Nethervale is after you, and it would be a shame for them to pick up your trail."

Her eyes widened, and her body went still. "You wouldn't. If you turned me in, you'd never learn what—"

"I won't," he promised, interrupting her before she could spiral into a panic. "I won't tell them anything about you unless you give me a reason to take you out. If you try to con me or kill me, you're fair game."

She swallowed hard, her body tensing as she watched him in disbelief. In fear.

Whoever hunted her, she feared them. Whatever they wanted to do to her, it seemed evident she would've done anything to avoid their wrath.

That, as a matter of fact, *absolutely* gave him the upper hand.

"I bet Sophia's not even your real name." He paced the field with his hands behind his back. He already had the hook in her, and now all he had to do was reel in his line to snare her once and for all.

To remind her which of them truly had the advantage.

"We can't trust anything you say," he continued, his trap closing. "You're trying to con me, for the Fates' sake, and I haven't even told you what I want. After everything I've been through to get here, I'm starting to think I wasted my time. What use are you?"

"What use am I?" She squared her shoulders, and her long fingers curled into tight fists at her side. "How dare you—"

"You don't think I came here unprepared, do you?" He paused midstride and studied her, all trace of a smile long gone.

No games. Not anymore.

The trap had closed.

"Here's what will happen." Connor pointed to the ghoul hovering by the tree. "I've learned quite a bit about the wraith, so here's what I'm going to do. I'll ask you questions I already know the answer to, and I'm going to sprinkle them between those I don't. I'm going to pretend I don't know something when I do. I'm going to pretend to know something when I don't. If I catch you in a lie, sorceress, even *one*, you won't get your payment. One lie, one omission of truth, and you get nothing. You're done, and there's no second chances with me. Understood?"

Beside the withered old tree, the Wraith King crossed his bony arms and chuckled. *I bet you cheat when you play cards, Magnuson.*

Magnuson.

Instead of his usual insults, the ghoul had used Connor's last name. It seemed off, somehow. Odd. Unnatural.

Important.

"Well?" he asked, ignoring the ghoul. "What'll it be, Sophia?"

She hesitated, and as she once again looked at the Wraith King, the fire in her eyes faded. "Fine."

"Excellent. First, tell me how you know anything about the ghoul at all."

With a slow sigh, she rubbed her eyes and shook her head in disbelief. Like she couldn't believe what she was about to do. "I trained at Nethervale with the elite."

"Ah," he and Murdoc said in unison.

I knew I liked her for a reason, the ghoul said.

Connor raised one eyebrow and turned his attention to the specter, silently asking the question he didn't want her to hear.

Curious about Nethervale? the phantom asked.

He nodded.

You should be. They will be useful to you if you can convince them not to kill you. The wraith chuckled. *In my time, Nethervale produced the best assassins in the world. Half their students died, and those who survived feared nothing. Not even me. If the forest is any indication of how the world has changed in my absence, I suspect Nethervale is far superior now than they were in my day.*

"Hmm." He rubbed his jaw as he debated this curious turn of events.

Nethervale. If she had access to the inner workings of the necromancer temple, he stood a chance of gathering intelligence that could turn the tides in his favor. Either that, or it was going to get him killed.

It annoyed him how frequently those two extremes seemed to be his only options, lately.

With a careful glance over his shoulder, he spotted Murdoc leaning against a tree, examining his nails.

Once he knew the sorceress actually had the sort of information he needed, he'd send the ruffian back to Bradford. Any sooner than that, and they would've risked the sheriff catching his scent.

Until then, he had to keep his questions about Aeron Zacharias to himself. Any hint of what the wraith truly was would've sparked a manhunt, and right now, he needed to lay low.

"What did they teach you about the ghoul in Nethervale?" Connor asked, choosing each word carefully. "About the sort of magic that can make a wraith?"

Sophia scoffed and rested her weight on one hip as she glanced him over. "I don't give away information for free. Our next subject is the price."

"You're not giving anything away for free," he corrected. "I'm deciding what this information is worth, and that means you need to clarify a few things for me before we discuss the cost." He frowned and crossed his arms over his chest. "Now, answer me."

The necromancer shook her head and mumbled obscenities under her breath. "I know enough about it to get by. The old masters in the temple guard books and scrolls unavailable anywhere else in the world. I had access to recipes most people didn't even know about. The greatest necromancers trained there, same as me. They all left an imprint on the place, and when you pay me, I'll tell you about it."

"Hmm." Connor nodded to his bag at the base of the withered old tree. "If the reagents I brought aren't good enough, what exactly do you want?"

Her gaze drifted briefly over his body before snapping back to his eyes. "I want a favor."

"I volunteer." Murdoc grinned and raised one hand in the air.

"A real favor," she snapped. "A useful one, from someone with actual power. Just one favor that I can cash in at any time, for anything, for any reason."

In other words, she wanted control. Namely, she wanted to control Connor.

"Absolutely not," he replied.

She balked. "You need me. You need what I know. A favor is hardly—"

"A favor is too broad." Step by threatening step, he slowly closed the distance between them as he spoke. Shoulders back, jaw squared, he stared her down in a silent challenge. "A favor is your way to turn the tides against me if you ever get the opportunity, and I'm no fool. If you want something, you'll tell me now exactly what that is."

"But—"

"Now," he repeated. "Or we're done."

Angering a sorceress with rash and brazen demands, the Wraith King said. *Bold choice. I look forward to dancing on your grave.*

Connor ignored the ghost. When he reached Sophia, he glared down at her with barely a foot between them. Her jawline tensed, the muscle in her cheek spasming as she scowled, but she didn't move.

For several minutes, no one spoke. Only the clattering leaves fluttering on the wind broke the silence as they both waited for the other to break first.

He'd played this game before. It wasn't going to be him.

With an indignant little huff, she lifted her chin in defiance. "Very well. My price is fifty bloody beauties, full to the stem, and not a petal less."

The wraith laughed, his voice muffled as it echoed through his head. *I like her spirit. The royal treasury in Oakenglen may have enough coin to cover forty, but only if the tax hauls have been impressive.*

"Are you trying to set me up for an impossible bargain?" Connor demanded, his voice dangerously low. "Trying to ensure I can't pay?"

"Not at all," she replied, her tone just as chilly as his. "I'm simply making sure I'm properly paid for the risk I take on by helping you."

"What risk is that, exactly?" He gestured to the empty field.

"I know what you are," she whispered, leaning in. A subtle perfume rolled off of her neck, like a summer breeze through a field of jasmine. "I know the sort of people who hunt the Wraithblade, Connor, and I know what they're capable of. If I help you in any way, do you think they'll hesitate to come after me?"

Though he kept his expression even, his heart skipped a beat in surprise. Perhaps she knew even more than he'd suspected.

"Now that you've come here, I can't stay," she whispered, her voice still too quiet for Murdoc to hear. "I built a nice little life here. I had coin and clients. I had what I needed. You uprooted my life when you walked into this field, and you must compensate me for what you've done."

"Until I get my information, I owe you nothing," he reminded her.

"Very well." She cleared her throat and turned her back on him.

With a few silent steps through the broken grass, she put ample space between them. He could practically see the gears turning in her head as she ran her fingers through her thick hair and stared up at the moon.

Crafty and clever, she would pose a true danger to him, even if he got his information and left her behind. Like any mercenary, she would only be on his side until the moment when it would benefit her most to betray him, and he needed to be careful.

"I have a counteroffer." The sorceress spun on her heel to face him again. "You want the Deathdread, and you want information. I want my bloody beauties. All of that happens to be in the same place—the Mountains of the Unwanted. If you guide me there and get me my flowers, then I will answer all of your questions along the way. I'll even make sure you get your book."

So, the Deathdread was a book. From what little context he had, he figured it was likely one with notes and details on the Wraith King, perhaps even written by Aeron Zacharias himself.

That, of course, or she was conning him.

Connor rubbed his jaw, debating the ways she could've possibly set him up to fail with this little plan of hers, but nothing substantial came to mind. Thus far, it made sense.

If he kept her close, he could keep an eye on her. A woman who knew what he was could either be useful or deadly, and he figured having her nearby would give him more opportunities to learn about being the Wraithblade.

Provided he could keep her from lying, of course.

"I also need to find two items that belong to me," he explained, dancing around the details. "Items two very powerful people happen to have. If you help me get those, give me information, and take me to the Deathdread, then yes. We have a deal." He offered her his hand.

"What items?"

With his hand outstretched, he simply held her gaze and smirked. She wouldn't get information out of him that easily.

She sighed and grabbed his hand. Her soft fingers pressed against his palm, almost impossibly delicate for someone so powerful, and they shook on it.

This will be most entertaining, the ghoul said. *Which will survive? The sorceress, or the peasant?*

Connor glared at the wraith, who chuckled at his exasperation. The dead king dissolved into the wind, and the black threads of his cloak burst into ribbons of black smoke that drifted away in the breeze.

Irritating, but not wrong. Whatever came Connor's way, he needed to tread carefully. Every step could be his last, and every breath could end in a heartbeat.

At least his life wasn't boring.

CHAPTER THIRTY-FOUR

CONNOR

As the great ghoul disappeared into the night, Sophia froze in place. With her hand still in Connor's, their handshake apparently forgotten, she stared after the ghost even as he left nothing behind. Her fingers went limp in Connor's grasp.

Awe. Reverence. Maybe a twinge of disbelief. Whatever she felt when she looked at the wraith, he couldn't quite tell.

"You know exactly what the ghoul is." He dropped her hand and leaned against the withered tree. "Which means you must also know who that once was."

She stiffened. "I do. Have you told your servant?"

"Who, me?" Murdoc surveyed the empty field, as if she could've been referring to absolutely anyone else.

Connor shook his head in a silent demand for her to keep it to herself.

"Told me what?" The ruffian chewed the inside of his cheek and glanced between them. "I feel like I missed something."

"It's not important," Connor lied.

The people of Saldia didn't need to know about the Wraith King's identity. If Murdoc found out, Connor figured it wouldn't remain secret for long.

Like so many others, the sellsword would've probably turned on Connor the second he discovered the truth.

"Hmm." She gently rubbed her jawline, as if considering whether or not to honor his silent warning.

Connor frowned, daring her to test him.

The necromancer rolled her eyes and uttered an impatient little scoff. "Fine, yes. As for what it is, it's a wraith. That's not easy magic."

"Have you done it?" Murdoc sat in the grass nearby, his elbows resting on his knees as he stared up at her like a child waiting to hear a story.

She glared at him over her shoulder, her nose wrinkled with disdain, and she shook her head. "Only one man has ever done it, and he did it four times."

"Four times?" Murdoc whistled in surprise.

Connor drummed his fingers on his thigh, not entirely sure he wanted Murdoc to hear this. It towed the line and gave him clues he didn't need to have. Though Connor didn't like the idea of traveling alone with the sorceress, perhaps it was time for the sellsword to leave after all.

First, he needed to know if his secret was safe.

"Do you recognize the ghoul?" He shifted his attention to the ruffian, though he watched Sophia through the corner of his eye. She didn't seem like someone he should ever turn his back on.

Murdoc laughed. "I'm not sure what circles you run in, mate, but I've never seen something like that in my entire life."

"Do you know where the wraith came from?"

The edges of the ruffian's mouth creased as he frowned, and his eyes briefly searched Connor's face. "Where are you going with this, Captain?"

He shrugged. "All I want is the truth."

Will you kill him? the wraith asked. *How will you guard this secret you so desperately want to keep?*

Connor ignored the ghost, his intense glare focused instead on Murdoc.

The man's gaze darted toward the withered tree, and he shrugged. "That has to be necromancy, is my best guess. I don't know much about this dark magic you lot seem to enjoy using on the rest of us." The ruffian gestured between Connor and Sophia. "I only know the basics. The only wraith I've ever heard of is Henry's, and even with that, I've only heard rumors. Never met the man or his beastie, myself. I take it you found yourself one like his? My future wife over there just mentioned there are more, right?"

She leaned her weight on one hip and set her hand on her waist. "No amount of Bridlecharge curse could numb my mind enough to marry you."

Murdoc grinned. "You fight it because you know it's inevitable."

He doesn't know who or what I am, the ghost observed. *How disappointing. I suppose there's no need to kill him, then, unless you would like to simply indulge in a bit of fun?*

"Stop talking," Connor murmured to the stupid ghost, too quietly for even Sophia to hear.

Honestly, this dead man tried his patience.

"Murdoc, your job is done." He nodded to the path that led back to the main road. "You can go back to Bradford. If you keep your sword at the ready and stick to the path, you'll be fine."

"And have my ass handed to me by that Abner fellow? No thank you."

Sophia grinned. "Good at making enemies, I take it?"

"The best." The ruffian winked.

"Murdoc," Connor interjected. "I know I said I wouldn't give you coin, but you've earned it. This is where you leave. You can't come with us, and for your own safety, you don't need to hear any of this."

"On the contrary, Captain." The sellsword leaned back on his palms, calm and relaxed despite the several brushes with death he'd had so far tonight. "You have something far more valuable to me than coin."

Ah.

Here it was—yet another greedy man, after the Wraith King.

Connor frowned, disappointed in Murdoc despite his own better judgment. With the man's jokes and jovial nature, he'd hoped this one would be different.

"And that is?" he asked, his tone dangerously low.

"A suitable solution to my death wish," Murdoc answered.

Connor paused, thrown off guard by the man's comment. "What?"

"A death wish, huh?" Sophia chuckled. "That explains a lot."

"Back in Bradford, you asked if I have a death wish." Murdoc shrugged.

"I do. There's dignity in a good death. In a final breath earned at the hand of someone better than me. I can't give up, and I can't kill myself. The only way out is in a battle. That's the Blackguard way, and I can't leave this world through any other means."

"You're a Blackguard?" Connor asked, his voice almost too quiet to hear.

"No wonder you're so annoying," the necromancer beside him muttered.

Back in Kirkwall, he'd heard tales of the magicless heroes who saved the common folk from those who used magic to take what wasn't theirs. Towns liberated. Farms saved. Villains dispatched in the night.

All by the brave men and women who wore the mark of the Blackguard—a sword beside a shield, its blade aimed toward the sky.

Murdoc leaned his elbows on his knees. His chin drooped to his chest, and he shook his head. "I *was* a Blackguard."

What a well-practiced lie, the wraith said.

Connor gritted his teeth at the ghoul's intrusion, but the dead man had a point. "Prove it."

At first, the sellsword didn't move. He sat there, immobile, and stared at the grass. With a quiet groan, he unhooked the top few buttons on his shirt and pulled aside the fabric to reveal a tattoo on his chest—a sword resting against an upright shield, its blade pointed to the sky.

And, through the black ink, a large cross.

Disgraced.

Disowned by his brothers and cast aside in shame.

"Well, I've seen a lot, but I've never seen that," Sophia admitted.

"It's illegal to have that mark, even with a cross through it." Connor pointed to the unenchanted ink as he examined Murdoc's face for tells of a lie. "You'd be sent to the gallows the moment a sheriff saw it. So, you're either a Blackguard, or you're a very convincing con artist willing to do anything to sustain the lie."

Murdoc laughed. "Think hard about those options, Captain. Which do you think is the truth?"

"Fair point." He rubbed his jaw as he thought over what he knew of the man thus far. "That's why you keep calling me 'Captain,' I suppose. Because the Blackguard soldiers respect rank."

"Old habits are hard to break." The disgraced Blackguard looked up at Connor through the strands of hair hanging across his face. "Take me with you. Let me find my good death. You saw what I could do back in that tavern. Out here, against her, I didn't run when most men would have. Whatever comes, I'll fight to the end."

Either way, the options didn't truly work in Connor's favor. He didn't love the idea of having company he didn't trust, but the fight in the field against Otmund would've gone very differently if he'd had help. In a close-quarters combat situation like that, an extra soldier on his side—even one with an honor-bound death wish—could mean the difference between life and death.

An interesting prospect, if nothing else.

He hated the idea of relying on anyone, much less a disgraced Blackguard or a sorceress, but times had changed. With the Wraith King now fused to him, Connor had to make different choices than he would've made drifting through the woods.

The day he'd left Kirkwall, he'd learned not to trust others. He'd learned to keep the world at arm's length and do what it took to survive.

Trust got good men killed.

Now, however, he had stumbled upon two fellow pariahs in a world that had discarded them all. For them to survive the Ancient Woods, they would have to act as a unit. A team.

If they betrayed him, at least he had the option to abandon them in the brutal forest.

"Fine," he conceded. "You can stay."

Murdoc let out a sigh of relief. "You won't regret this."

"I'd better not."

"Back to business." Murdoc rubbed his hands together in the chilly night. "Sophia, you said there are three other ghosties wandering around Saldia?"

In unison, Connor and Sophia both let out an irritated sigh.

"Fates give me patience," the sorceress muttered.

"He has a point," Connor said.

If the Wraith King wasn't the only soul that had been brought back, it meant Connor had real competition beyond whoever wielded those two green daggers.

Given his luck, no one else with a wraith would want to be allies. Salida was a land of conquering armies, not peaceful nations content with their borders and trade agreements.

War was all the people of this world knew.

"That's death magic for you," Sophia said with a shrug. "Nigh impossible to do in the first place and dangerous to replicate. Most people who try it die in the process."

"So, who was the man to do it?" Connor asked, staring her down. "Whisper his name to me."

"Ah," Murdoc said. "This is the thing I can't know about."

Connor glared at the former Blackguard, but the man simply laughed and laid back in the grass. He propped an ankle on one knee and tapped his foot to an aimless rhythm as he stared up at the stars.

"You two chat." Murdoc waved a hand lazily through the air. "I'll entertain myself."

With his thumb against one temple, Connor returned his attention to Sophia. "Well?"

He knew the answer, of course. The Wraith King had betrayed this little nugget of information the first time they'd spoken. She had already implied she knew something of Zacharias's work, though she hadn't admitted the details.

This was simply the first of many tests.

Sophia hesitated and pursed her lips as she caught his eye. He could practically see her debating with herself, sifting through what to tell him and what to omit.

He didn't betray his knowledge. He didn't betray the flutter of curiosity that snaked through his chest. He simply waited, stony and silent, for her to make her move.

Their entire makeshift truce depended on what she said next.

She leaned in and dropped her voice to the barest whisper. "The only person to ever successfully bring back souls without a body was Aeron Zacharias, the Great Necromancer."

The truth caught Connor off guard. He had expected her to lie.

"That's how death magic works," she continued, louder now. "A body can only operate with a soul, and vice versa. It's a requirement of living on this plane. That's what makes the wraith unique. It's a soul with no body that flits between worlds. It can kill, yet it can't be killed."

Not true. He studied her face, looking for signs of a tell—a slight twitch in the lip, or the quirk of an eyebrow—but she simply shrugged.

She truly didn't know about the Bloodbane daggers.

Interesting.

"You were testing me." Sophia tilted her head as she bit the inside of her cheek.

"Perhaps."

She frowned. "The Lightseers try to silence information on Aeron, but we all remember. Some revere him, but the smart ones just want to learn what he did. He was a man after all, same as any of us."

He was a liar, the Wraith King interjected. *Brilliant, of course, but a colossal ass. Much like you, Magnuson.*

Connor chuckled. Apparently, the old ghost wasn't a fan.

She walked to the edge of the woods and lifted a leather bag from behind a tree. Bottles jingled together as she tightened the strap and swung it over her shoulder.

"Are you headed somewhere?" Connor raised a skeptical eyebrow.

He wasn't finished with her yet.

"I packed when I heard you coming," she admitted, no longer bothering to whisper. "I figured if Nethervale had come for me, I needed to move quickly."

"Why does Nethervale want you?" Murdoc asked. "Besides the obvious, I mean," he added with a glance toward her chest.

"Murdoc," Connor said.

"Yes, Captain?"

"She's not interested. Take the hint and stop talking."

"Yep."

Connor returned his attention to Sophia and crossed his arms. "You do have to answer his question, though."

She huffed. "None of the Nethervale elite can leave the temple."

"And?" he pressed.

"I left." She stood taller, her chin lifted in defiance.

Ah.

"And how about you?" She walked back to him and leaned in, that jasmine perfume rolling off her hair as she again lowered her voice to a whisper. "Last I heard, King Henry had the wraith. How did you stumble across it, exactly?"

He rubbed his tongue over his back molar as he studied her. He didn't trust her for a minute, and some things didn't need to be shared. "You don't need to know that."

She shrugged. "Maybe, but I—"

"I'm asking the questions," he reminded her.

The necromancer frowned, and her jaw tensed as her mouth snapped shut.

"What skills do I have, thanks to the ghoul?" Connor asked.

Another test.

"I don't know all of them," she whispered. "Just what I saw from watching King Henry fight."

He cast another glance over his shoulder at Murdoc, but the man hummed quietly to himself as his foot tapped in the air.

Connor grabbed the sorceress's arm and led her farther away, where they could speak in private. "You knew Henry?"

"I knew of him," she corrected. "Did you ever see him on the battlefield?"

Connor didn't answer.

"He was a beast," she said in a wistful tone, her eyes glossing over as she remembered. "A warrior unlike anything Saldia has ever seen. To see him fight was to watch a master, but that's the thing about masters—they never show all their cards. No one knew his limits, maybe not even him."

"You fought beside him, then?"

She laughed. "If the necromancers had fought with him, we would be the ruling class of Saldia, not the Lightseers. We would have conquered Lunestone and turned it into a brothel by now. No, he tried to win over Nyx Osana, but she refused to bow to him. Nethervale bows to no one."

Connor had never heard of Nyx, but he had more pressing matters on his plate than who ruled Nethervale.

Sophia shrugged. "I studied his battles whenever I could sneak away from the temple for a week or two. I trailed his armies and watched from afar, studying his movements, trying to understand his connection to the ghoul who fought beside him. If I could understand the wraith, I could understand death. Overcome it, maybe." Her smile fell, and she looked away. "I never got very far."

Her greed is palpable, the wraith said. *How disappointing. It would be so simple to control her. Too easy, perhaps. I suspect with time she would come to bore me.*

"Tell me what you observed," Connor ordered, ignoring the ghost.

"Not much," the sorceress confessed with a slight shrug. "His appetite was legendary. He could never eat enough. Do you experience that?"

Connor didn't answer.

"Fine," she muttered. "We never had much to go on in Nethervale, since Aeron never shared any of his notes with us. But as I watched, I noticed Henry needed more of everything. More food. More water. More wine. More women," she added with a smirk.

Impressive, the ghoul admitted.

He wasn't going to admit it, but Connor agreed. She had figured all of this out on her own, merely by studying what notes Nethervale had and by watching from afar.

"Go on," he said.

"Enhanced senses and reflexes. He could sense an arrow flying through the air toward him and act fast enough to catch it." Sophia flashed her little dagger, and the dent in its surface served as proof Connor could do the same. "And, of course, those blackfire blades."

"What else?"

Her smile faded. "That was all I was able to tell from afar. To get any more detail, I would've had to be up close."

Connor growled in frustration and paced the meadow. Thus far, she had proven she knew what she was talking about, but he still hadn't learned anything new.

"I take it that's not what you wanted to hear," she observed.

With another glance to check on the still-humming Murdoc, he returned to the far corner of the meadow where she waited. "It doesn't matter."

"Of course it does. That's why you need the Deathdread, and that's why you need me to take you there. According to the scrolls in Nethervale, the Deathdread is the only thing that can tell you everything about the simmering souls."

He stiffened at the mention of the souls—at the other wraiths like his.

"No one knows why he brought them back," Sophia confessed. "We don't even know what he wanted to do with them. We only know that whoever fuses with one of them becomes something other than human." She bit her lip as her eyes swept across his body. "Something powerful. Something dark. I can only assume you want to learn about the others, too."

He frowned. "You think I'm going to hunt down the other wraiths?"

"Of course I do. Any necromancer would."

"I'm not a necromancer," he pointed out.

"You might as well be." She gestured to his torso. "The magic in you isn't blessed by the precious Lightseer Chamber. You're the enemy, and they'll hunt you. You might as well make yourself powerful enough to protect what you've got."

He tilted his head. "And let me guess. You can protect me?"

"You're not stupid enough to fall for that line," Sophia admitted. "You don't need protection. You need an entire army. You need to lead a charge against the people who are coming for you. We need to stop them now before they gain traction and public support like—"

"Whoa." Connor lifted his hand. "Slow down. I'm not trying to overtake anything or usurp anyone."

"Then you're an idiot." Her cold eyes snared him. "All that power, wasted on someone who doesn't even want to use it! You could conquer entire kingdoms! Lay waste to the Barrens and discover what's across the deserts! There's so much to do, Connor. What's your plan, exactly?"

Ah, yes, the Wraith King said, his voice dripping with disappointment. *There it is. The greed. How unfortunate to see she's as pliable as the others. I suppose I'm stuck with you for a while longer.*

"I'm as happy about that as you are." Connor glared into the dark forest around him in an effort to silence the ghost's constant interruptions.

"You can talk to it?" Sophia's eyes darted around the empty field, her tone light with curiosity. "It can talk to you, but we can't hear what it's saying. We can't even see it. Where is it?"

Connor rubbed the back of his neck, not entirely sure how much she should know. She seemed aware of every moment, of every *movement.* Always curious. Always watching.

A defining feature in both a great ally and a deadly enemy.

"Where in the Mountains of the Unwanted is the Deathdread?" he asked, changing the subject. "Are there any other books about the simmering souls?"

He needed to know once and for all if the Deathdread was real. As he pressed her for information, he would have to look for signs of a tell. After even one twitch of the lip or eye, or one nervous glance into the shadows, he would end this.

"No other books that I know of," she confessed with a lazy little shrug. "The Lightseers control Aeron's Tomb and the artifacts stored there."

Artifacts. Plural.

Not a lie, then, based on her calm demeanor.

He scratched at the back of his head. "Why didn't they destroy these artifacts? They're Lightseers. That's what they do—destroy the evil things in the world."

Things like him, apparently.

Sophia snorted in disgust. "That's what they want you to think. They haven't destroyed them because they want to use them for themselves at some point. Everything they don't control is condemned, of course," she added, rolling her eyes. "That's the righteous Lightseer way. There's not—"

Her head snapped to the right, as if she had heard something he hadn't been able to detect.

He frowned. Until now, he hadn't seen anyone with more heightened senses than him, and he hadn't heard a damn thing.

She has an alert system in the woods, the Wraith King said, almost bored. *Someone has tripped one of her alarms, and she's attuned to the artifact while you aren't. She's talented, Magnuson. Try to learn something from her.*

Sophia scowled, her eyes snapping into focus as she glared at him. "Were you followed?"

He scoffed. "Everyone knows where you are. How could I have been followed?"

"Fair point." She knelt and rifled through the bottles in her bag as she whistled for Murdoc's attention. "Blackguard, get up. We might have another fight on our hands."

Murdoc sat upright and brushed grass off his shirt. "Why do you always assume the worst in people, my love? Maybe it's simply a friend of yours."

She glared at him. "Do I look like I have friends?"

Connor scanned the empty forest around them. He studied the trees, and for a moment, he just listened.

Silence.

Utter and complete silence.

In the eerie quiet, not even a bird chirped. There was nothing, and it set his nerves on edge.

"Something's wrong," he said, his intuition flaring.

"That's no client." Sophia tugged out a potion bottle and slipped her arms through the pack's straps. "I've been suspecting this for a while. They must have called the Lightseers here to chase me out once and for all. Connor, I can take you to the mountains. I can take you right to the Deathdread. I've read or stolen every book, scroll, and scratch of paper on this subject, and they all reference that tome. I know exactly where to go and who to talk to if we want to get in, but you have to kill whoever comes after me. As long as we travel together, you have to protect me from whatever Nethervale or Lunestone throws my way."

His eyes narrowed in suspicion. "That wasn't part of the bargain."

"That's the reality of asking for a banished necromancer's help." She shook the bottle in her hand, and a ribbon of green light snaked through the metallic silver potion inside. "I'm no good to you if I'm dead."

"Fine." He scanned the field around them as he sifted through a few ideas of how to get out of this alive. "Stay behind me and find something that can create a lot of smoke. I might have a way out of this."

"Smoke?" she asked dubiously.

"Do you want my help or not?"

The necromancer tilted her head at the absurd question and raised one irritated eyebrow.

He took her silence as an answer. "Good, then we're on the same page. Get me smoke and wait for my signal."

The cool air rushed over his skin as he crossed to the center of the field. He craned his ear, surprised that he still hadn't been able to hear a thing.

"Go see if you can spot our company," he added to the Wraith King. "Stay out of sight until I give the order."

This had better be a real fight, the ghost said dryly. *You promised me blood and war.*

"I promised you no such thing. I merely said it was inevitable."

He felt the weight of Sophia's stare on the back of his neck, but he chose to ignore her. He kept her in his periphery, and as long as she didn't move or threaten him, he would keep her alive.

Truthfully, he didn't know how long this little truce of theirs would last.

SOPHIA

Sophia fished through her enchanted bag and slipped the Brackenbane potion back in its place. Whoever came for her tonight wasn't going to be boiled alive, but it just meant she could save the potion for another day.

The bottles clinked together as she fished out a familiar gray one. The silver liquid inside floated and churned, ready for her to unleash it. Smoke, just as the Wraithblade requested. Perhaps he understood how to make a good diversion, or perhaps he thought of her as a sorceress with an unlimited supply of magic to appease his every whim.

They would soon find out.

Out of the corner of her eye, she watched the strange man who had uprooted her life. He was right about one thing—Sophia wasn't the name she had been born with, but it was a name she had grown accustomed to over the last five years. It would serve her until she got her bloody beauties. Once this Connor fellow paid her, she could finally disappear again.

This time, perhaps for good.

He fascinated her, and she longed to dissect him. She hadn't been around this much raw power since her days with Nyx. Magic like this—real, dark magic—it didn't just reek of death. It simmered with possibility.

Despite his frayed pant hems and the dirt on his travel-worn tunic, she suspected he had quite a few juicy secrets bottled up inside that delightfully muscular body of his. For starters, he had a knack for ordering people around, and that didn't seem like a peasant's trait.

As she had mentioned already, he had most definitely piqued her curiosity. Perhaps she could make use of his incredible power.

Or, even better, maybe she could take it for herself.

CHAPTER THIRTY-FIVE
CONNOR

An owl screeched in the quiet night. The shrill scream sliced through the air like a banshee's call, and a single tree in the clustered canopy shivered as something scampered to safety.

In the silence that followed, the enchanted southern wind sighed into the trees. The ancient branches creaked beneath its might, and the weight of something watching from the shadows settled on Connor's chest. The empty path into the woods loomed before him like an open gate leading into a fortress, and the threat of a fight seeped from it like a fog rolling over the grass.

He lifted his scarf over his mouth and nose as he waited. Whoever hunted the sorceress didn't need to know his identity, too.

His ear twitched as he listened, his hearing attuned to the forest he had called home for so long. Any moment now, a twig would snap. A bird would startle, and the flutter of wings would warn of the encroaching danger. A boot would fall too heavily into the dirt, and his opponent would reveal themselves—intentionally or not.

Yet nothing came.

Nothing but the excruciating silence.

A boot shuffling through the grass beside him interrupted his surveillance. Murdoc joined him, sword drawn. Though Sophia leaned against the withered tree, her body stiff as she studied the woods, Murdoc stared at the grass. The former Blackguard leaned his ear toward the forest, no doubt listening when his sight couldn't penetrate the shadows between the trees.

Connor resisted the impulse to critique Murdoc's stance. He'd already seen the man fight. Instead, he nudged Murdoc and wordlessly pointed to the cloth he'd secured over his mouth and nose. The former Blackguard nodded and tugged a thin bit of fabric from the pocket on his shirt before tying it around his own mouth as well.

In the blink of an eye, the energy around them shifted.

The air thickened. His body tensed with warning. The hair on his neck stood on end, but the Wraith King's arrival had become more and more familiar as the days passed.

"Well?" Connor asked without so much as a backward glance. "What's your report?"

For a peasant, you're quite demanding, the Wraith King said dryly. *Where did you learn such an audacious way of speaking to a king?*

"I guess I'm a natural."

A woman approaches, the Wraith King said. *With red hair and a vougel.*

"Red hair? Describe it."

Red and gold, like a fire. I've seen her before in Henry's court.

Connor shook his head in disappointment. "This is a Starling, isn't it?"

She is, the Wraith King confirmed. *Even though most mortals bore me, the red hair is hard to forget.*

"Damn it."

"A Starling?" Sophia's red lips parted with shock as she took several wary steps away from the tree. "Are you sure?"

Connor nodded. "I've never met one, but from what I hear, they're hard to miss."

"Why would they send such a high-ranking Lightseer after me?" Sophia tugged on the ends of her hair and paced the field. "Which one? The woman, or one of the men?"

"A woman," Connor answered. "Maybe they found out about your time in Nethervale. Maybe they know who you are."

"If that's true, I'm as good as dead," she whispered. "Damn the Fates, this night couldn't get worse."

"Well, now don't jinx us, woman." Murdoc rolled out his shoulders as he prepared for the fight. "The Fates love a good challenge."

The barest whisper of a footstep in the distance caught Connor's attention—the brush of a shoe against grass, barely loud enough to register.

"Quiet," he ordered.

The meadow stilled, and both of his companions froze in place. Even the wraith waited, hovering beside him as the moons lit the meadow with a soft blue glow.

"You should leave," he said to the ghoul.

I will not hide, the ghoul warned. *Not forever. Not from those who matter.*

"Now," he demanded.

You don't understand the Lightseers as I do. You must do as I say.

"I know I'm a dead man if one of them sees you," he countered.

A dead man, perhaps, the ghost mused. *Or a serious threat worthy of their respect. You will eventually become one of the two, Magnuson. Which will it be?*

With that, the ghost dissolved into a gust of wind. Though the Wraith King's warning echoed in his brain, he didn't have time for riddles or predictions. He needed to focus on the danger right in front of him.

The drifter's way—handle one threat at a time.

At the break in the trees where the path led into the forest, a silhouette appeared. At first nothing more than a figure, she kept an even pace as she neared. Her fiery red hair glowed like embers in a hearth as she reached the edge of the wood, and the rest of her followed shortly thereafter. Soft skin. Hazel eyes. A smattering of freckles across her nose. A black jacket and dark pants.

Augmentations probably covered most of her skin, and Connor had to be wary. The hilt of a massive sword strapped to her side glimmered in the low light—likely her Firesword. A staple of the Starling fighting style, according to law and legend.

Under different circumstances, Connor would've thought she was beautiful in a brush-with-death sort of way. Tonight, however, he saw only a woman who wanted to murder him, and it killed his interest.

Besides, that seemed more like Murdoc's kink.

As she stepped into the field, a massive tiger appeared from the shadows behind her. Its eyes glowed gold in the low light, and gilded stripes covered its white fur. Its massive wings laid tucked against its side. Its nose creased with a snarl as the Starling woman paused at the opposite edge of the meadow.

Connor curled his fingers into a fist, the magic of his blackfire blades a breath away if he needed it.

"The sorceress is under my protection," he warned, not bothering with pretense or courtesy.

"Rude," Sophia muttered.

He ignored her.

"That's too bad for her." The Starling warrior set one hand on her slender waist. "I'm here for you."

Connor stiffened. His mind went blank, and those simple words momentarily numbed him.

This night had very suddenly gotten far worse than he'd ever thought possible.

"That's a twist I wasn't expecting," Murdoc admitted, his voice muffled through the scarf across his face.

The redhead shrugged off her jacket. As the black leather slid off her shoulders, the intricate green ink along her arms glowed with augmentations that wove seamlessly together, like an intricate puzzle as old as time itself. A chain hugged her neck, too tight to slip over her head. A diamond glittered at the space between her collar bones. A second chain hung from the gemstone and ended in a dazzling purple ornament shaped like a shield, with a gilded phoenix in its center.

Judging by her hair, that had to be the Starling family crest.

As her skin practically glowed in the moonlight, she tucked the necklace into her cleavage. From the way she smirked, he figured she had often used her body to distract her prey.

It wouldn't work on him. Not with his life on the line.

Murdoc chuckled. "So, this is how I die. My wish was granted faster than I thought it'd be."

"Don't decide to lose just yet," Connor muttered.

"Right." The ruffian let out a shaky breath. "Good point."

"My name is Quinn Starling." The woman cracked her knuckles, and a glittering flash of magic rippled across the green augmentations on her arms. "We have two options here. Option one—all three of you resist, I beat you senseless, and then I get to arrest you. You'll be taken to Oakenglen, where you'll be subjected to investigation, interrogation, and imprisonment in our Capital's filthiest prison." She shifted her gaze to Connor and narrowed her eyes. "Or, option two, you alone can come with me and make this easy for your companions. I'll let the sorceress go if you come willingly."

"There's three of us, and one of you," Murdoc pointed out. "Well, one and a half if you count the tiger-bird. What makes you think you can win that easily?"

The vougel snarled, and its claws sank into the dirt beneath its paws.

"Don't taunt them, idiot," Sophia whispered.

"Well?" Quinn ignored Murdoc, and her eyes remained locked on Connor.

"Sorry, princess." He shook his head. "Easy isn't how I do things."

The Starling warrior chuckled, but it was half-hearted. Short. Humorless.

"You're not going to win this," he continued. "No matter how good you are, you're outnumbered, and I'm not going with you tonight. You'll lose, and it will hurt. If you step aside, we'll go on our merry way, and you can say you couldn't find us. Don't make this more painful than it needs to be."

"You don't want to fight me," she warned. "I've won before with worse odds."

"No, missy," Murdoc corrected. "You don't want to fight us. We have a secret weapon that you—"

Connor elbowed Murdoc hard in the shoulder, and the former Blackguard muttered the rest of his speech incoherently under his breath.

First thing when this was over, he would have to teach the man how to keep a damn secret. This woman might not have known about the wraith, and he intended to keep it that way for as long as possible.

"This is your last chance." Quinn drew the sword at her waist, and with a subtle twist of her hand, flame ignited along the blade. It crackled and sputtered, as blazingly red as her hair.

"Let's do this then." Murdoc squared his shoulders and settled into a fighting stance.

It seemed as though everyone around him wanted blood except for him, and Connor just groaned with disappointment. Footsteps in the grass behind him caught his attention, and he glanced over his shoulder as Sophia inched behind him with her gaze firmly fixed on the Starling warrior. She held a bottle in her hand and stiffened as she watched the Lightseer on the other side of the field.

"Throw it," Connor ordered.

"Throw what?" Quinn asked with a grin. "Is this your secret weapon?"

But Sophia understood.

Something sailed overhead, and the crack of a bottle shattering on the ground broke the silence. Smoke billowed into the air, thick as a fog on the open ocean, and it instantly obscured the forest with white mist.

The cloth across Connor's face doubled as a filter for the smoke.

A few years ago, he'd taken some coin to kill a rabid bear outside of a southern village. The thing had begun to hunt people, and though he didn't enjoy taking life, it had to be done. He'd lured it into a mist rolling off the sea, and that had disoriented the beast enough for him to drive his sword through its neck.

Against a Starling, this plan of his stood a hefty chance of failure. If she figured out what he was up to, he would just have to think on his feet and pivot, like he'd always done.

Deep in the smoke, the vougel roared, its deep and resonant growl piercing the night like a shiver. The smoke would throw off its sense of smell, and that would work in their favor until the mist cleared.

The crackle of fire through the air joined the tiger's snarls. Connor waited and listened. As the crackling fire grew louder, he tracked her movement. Even though he didn't hear a breath or even a footstep, the blazing sword in her hand gave her away. The tiger's growl rumbled through the mist, growing distant as it stalked off in another direction.

Connor summoned the black swords into his hands. A plume of dark smoke sank onto the grass, and he took a steadying breath to prepare himself for the chaos that would erupt any moment.

For now, he kept the blackfire at bay, and his enchanted swords seemed almost empty without their ethereal flame. The fire would've probably given away his position, and he didn't want to take the risk of being unarmed when a Starling swung at him.

As the fiery red sword cast an orange glow through the mist, he inched toward her. No sound. No breath. Not even a shuffle of his boot over the grass. Not a single noise to give himself away as he circled through the smoke to catch her from behind.

He needed to disarm her. With an opponent as influential as a Starling, he stood a chance of getting some information out of her if he played his cards right. She had to know why the Lightseers were after him, and she might've even known what they had learned about the ghoul.

Besides, killing her would've angered the most powerful family in Saldia. He didn't want to give the Starlings any more reason to hate him. Giving them a thirst for revenge by killing one of their own would've sealed his fate. If he killed her, even accidentally, he would never go anywhere unnoticed again.

He lifted his blades to attack. Tonight, he needed to injure her just enough to slow her down and keep her from following them out of the field.

As he raised his swords, a gust of wind tore through the meadow. The smoke dissipated in a sudden rush.

When it cleared, she stood before him. The blade of her Firesword crackled with flame, already aimed at his head.

Their eyes met, and she smirked.

Damn it.

With her Firesword in her right hand, she curled her left hand into a fist. The gust that had cleared the smoke disappeared on command.

"Not bad." He grinned, impressed despite the gravity of the situation. Even in the smoke, even with his stealth, she had detected him.

She had talent.

Quinn twisted her blade, jabbing it toward his face. He swung, and the steel of his left blade knocked hers aside. The fires billowed as the enchanted swords hit.

With his right blade, he swung at her face to test her reflexes. She effortlessly ducked backward, and his sword passed overhead. Her blade twisted, and his slid along the steel. With a grunt of effort, she swung her blade over her head and aimed it for his.

He crossed both of his blades and blocked her Firesword with his enchanted steel. Lingering trails of smoke wafted between them as they glared each other down, their swords locked.

With a passing glance over the field, Connor took stock of his surroundings. Sophia had vanished, but Murdoc hadn't moved at all. Over by the withered old tree, the vougel crouched close to the ground, and its tail twitched as the Blackguard finally noticed it. He spun on his heel, his sword raised in challenge.

The tiger roared. To the best of his ability, Murdoc roared back.

Quinn kicked at Connor, their blades still locked, and he twisted his body to avoid the blow. He leaned into the movement, his swords closing on her fiery blade, but she twisted her weapon at the last second and wrenched it free.

With a grunt of effort, she swung at his neck. Crackling fire blurred through the air. He summoned the blackfire along his enchanted weapons and blocked the blow.

Dark flames roared across the jet-black steel, and his swords sizzled as they hit hers. The fire between their blades surged, the red and black mixing together with the blow.

He twisted his blades, sliding them along the length of her steel. The violent movement threw her off balance, but only briefly. The fingers in her free hand stretched wide, and fire ignited instantly in her open palm.

With a strained grunt, she threw the fireball at his face. He ducked, and the heat of her magic rolled across his forehead as he narrowly missed having his eyebrows burned off.

His momentum took him to the ground, and he rolled over the grass to put some distance between them. She charged, sword raised, and he jumped to his feet to meet her. With an effortless twist of his blade, he sliced at her neck. She leaned backward at the last second, and his sword instead lopped off a lock of her red hair. The ends of her loose red curls smoked as she quickly patted out the embers to keep the rest of her head from catching fire.

Her scowl deepened, and even though he'd only cut off a bit of her hair, she looked ready to kill him.

Apparently, the Starlings took more pride in their looks than most people realized.

Her sword spun in her hand as she adjusted her grip. Brows furrowed, she circled him. Connor settled into his stance, ready for whatever came his way.

She's playing you, the wraith warned.

He gritted his teeth, trying to ignore the ghost. He had to focus.

Fast as a bolt of lightning, Quinn charged. He swung, figuring she would do the same.

She didn't.

The Starling warrior crouched and kicked out his leg, knocking him onto his ass. He fell hard, and his black blades dissolved as he lost his grip on them both. She drove her sword into the grass near his head, but he rolled out of the way with seconds to spare.

Recovered and ready for the next blow, he crouched with one knee pressed into the cold dirt.

Barely six feet apart, the two of them knelt on the ground. Chests heaving from the fight so far, they studied each other. With a flick of his wrist, he summoned the shadow blades back into his palms.

Quinn raised one eyebrow. "Impressive."

"As are you," he admitted. "Friendly truce?"

She chuckled. "I'm afraid not."

Behind Quinn, the vougel roared again. It beat its wings across the field, sending ripples of air over the matted grasses as Murdoc swung at its face. His blade sliced the tiger's muzzle, and it snarled with pain. The gust from its wings knocked him off his feet, and he rolled as the tiger snapped at the space where his head had been moments before.

A vine shot from the depths of the forest and wrapped around the beast's leg. It growled, wriggling to get free. As it moved, Sophia stepped out of the forest, only for the tiger's wing to nail her hard in the stomach. She flew backward and landed against a tree. Her head snapped back against the bark, and her body went limp as she slid down the length of the trunk.

"Bad two-ton monster!" Murdoc chided. "Don't you know it's rude to hit a woman?!"

"You can still save them," Quinn said, her eyes never leaving Connor's.

He shook his head. "They're not the ones who need saving."

She chuckled. "You're a good fighter, but don't get cocky."

In the span of a single breath, she summoned a blast of fire into her hands and hurled it at him. He lifted the swords in time to block it, and the black steel cut through the magic even as the blistering heat rolled across his face. His shadow blades ate the enchantment, and her fire dissolved entirely as his blackfire burned hotter.

He spun the blades in his hands, their flames larger than ever before thanks to her accidental donation.

Quinn grimaced, and her nose wrinkled with disdain as she charged. Fresh flame roared to life along the blade of her Firesword. The sizzling crackle of fire collided with the clang of steel as their blades met again.

She raised her sword to slice his neck, but Connor crossed the dual blades and twisted. The movement pinned her sword between both of his, and he leaned all of his newly enhanced strength into the hilts. She fought him, the muscles in her arms flexing as they tested each other's strength.

With her distracted, he kicked her knee with the edge of his boot. She buckled beneath the blow, her leg giving out, and her grip loosened on the sword. It fell to the ground at Connor's feet as she fell onto her back.

Quinn stared up at him as the fire on her blade dissolved into the cool night air. He set one boot on her sword, daring her to come for it.

"I don't need that to kill you," she warned him.

As he debated how to reply, he knew he needed to tread carefully. A woman this powerful likely had plenty of surprises in store for him if he got too arrogant. If he was smart about this, he could play her against herself, like so many of the egotistical brawlers he'd encountered in the taverns.

Get them a little angry. Make them feel like they have something to prove. Then, they're far more likely to make a mistake—one that could turn the tides of a fight.

"Prove it," he dared her.

When he'd used to goad the smug bastards in the taverns into doing something against their best interest, a line like that had always made them scowl. Knuckles were cracked. Weapons drawn.

Quinn, however, simply laughed.

Dueling a true warrior isn't quite as easy as your peasant brawls, is it? the wraith asked.

The Starling warrior jumped to her feet, no doubt eager to grab her blade again, but he wasn't about to let that happen.

Connor swung. Both of his blades cut through the air, one after the other, and he drove her backward across the grass. The blackfire sputtered as she ducked and wove around it, never once letting it touch her.

Despite her skill, he controlled her direction with each blow. The shadow blades cut through the air between her and the Firesword whenever she tried to maneuver her way back to it.

With each failed attempt, a little more of her smile fell.

As he drove her toward the tree line, she faced a choice—let him pin her to a trunk, or charge into the blades in an attempt to overpower him.

As far as Connor was concerned, the battle was done. Neither option worked in her favor.

Time to end this.

"Give up," he demanded as they neared an old oak.

He swung at her chest, driving her backward once again. Only four feet left until they reached the tree, and this would be over.

She ducked. His second blade whistled through the air, aimed at her neck in an attempt to force her to take another step away from him. Instead of ducking, however, she leaned into it this time.

Into the line of fire—a risk no sane person would've taken.

In the seconds before his sword sliced off her head, a bolt of surprise shot through him. Killing a Starling would've unleashed the sort of hell storm few could've survived.

Maybe she knew that. Maybe it had been part of her calculation in taking the risk.

Damn it all.

He had only a split second to adjust his aim. As she raced toward the blackfire, he twisted the sword so that the flat of the blade would rail against her chest. It wasn't going to kill her, but it would still hurt like hell. It even stood a chance of taking her down and ending the fight once and for all.

Barely a breath before the swords hit her in the chest, she lifted both her palms. Light splintered across the air between her body and the sword, and the thin rays crisscrossed each other until they created a makeshift shield of glowing green light.

His swords collided with the shield, and the light shattered like glass.

Quinn's head snapped back, and she collapsed to the ground with a pained groan.

For a moment, she didn't move. Locks of her long red hair obscured her face. With a grunt of agony, she leaned onto her hands, and her forearms trembled as she tried to sit up. She fell again to the dirt and glared up at him, her chest heaving.

"Stay down," he ordered.

She didn't answer. With her hair scattered in her face, she merely studied him. Lips parted. Eyes narrowed in suspicion. Her words lost in the breathless bafflement as she no doubt tried to process what had just happened.

"You're no Lightseer," she said between shaky breaths. "But I've never met a necromancer who fights like you, either. What *are* you? Who are you fighting for?"

With a scowl, he raised one crackling blackfire blade in warning. "Myself."

CHAPTER THIRTY-SIX
CONNOR

In the flattened meadow grass surrounding the withered tree, Connor held his blade to Quinn Starling's throat. A distant roar tore through the night from behind him, followed by the splintering crack of ice.

The battle raged on, and Quinn hadn't surrendered just yet.

"That was a Shieldspar charm." Her arms wobbled slightly as she tried and failed to push herself to her feet. "How did that sword of yours fracture my light shield? That's impossible. There isn't an enchanted weapon in the world that can break a Starling Shieldspar."

"You lost this fight," he pointed out. "You don't get to ask me questions."

"Are you sure?" She grinned, and her chest instantly stilled. "I was just catching my breath."

Quick as a whip, she swept her legs under his and took out his left ankle. He fell backward, and his blades dissolved in a puff of black smoke that rolled along the dirt as she launched to her feet.

She aimed her boot at his face, but he grabbed her ankle and twisted. She fell again to the ground, and he wrapped his arm around her neck. With her back to his chest and her throat pinned against the inside of his elbow, he leaned his knee against her leg to keep her rooted in place.

"Yeah," he muttered. "I'm sure."

Instead of replying, she summoned fire into her palms. In a fluid motion, she leaned her neck into his forearm and shoved both hands over her head—right at his face.

He impulsively ducked backward, and his grip around her throat loosened ever so slightly.

It was all she needed.

She grabbed his arm and rolled forward, hurling him over her head with strength that didn't match her slender figure. He landed hard on the grass and rolled from the force of the throw.

Without so much as pausing to savor her victory, she bolted for her sword in the grass. Connor got to his feet and ran after her, summoning his own black blades as he ran.

He didn't make it.

Quinn snatched the blade and lifted it as he neared. Red fire crackled to life across the enchanted steel at her touch. Ready to go again, she snared him with her deadly gaze as her vougel roared through the forest.

"I think it's time we end this," she said.

I agree, said the wraith.

Dread shot clear to Connor's toes, rooting him in place even as she charged him.

No. Fates above and below, the last thing he needed was for the wraith to appear *now*.

When Quinn swung, the air in the meadow shifted, and a familiar weight settled onto Connor's shoulders. Though her blade cut through the air, her gaze darted behind him, and her eyes widened briefly in surprise.

That damned wraith. If he weren't already dead, Connor would've killed him.

In a swift and practiced movement, he knocked her sword aside with one of his blades and drove his other into her gut. The black steel cut effortlessly through her shirt and tore through her body as if she were made of sand.

If you ever want to take someone out and not kill them, you're a damned fool, Beck Arbor had always said. *But if you have to do it anyway, aim here. It'll cause them enough pain to end the fight, but it'll also give them enough time to get a potion to heal.*

Connor had only ever used this attack four times. The men he'd used it on had always screamed in agony as his sword drove into them, and he braced himself for the same from her.

Despite the devastating blow, she merely sucked in a sharp breath. Her sword fell to the grass, and her fingers went limp.

Sparks ripped across her arms. Seconds later, a blast of lightning snaked from her fingertips.

The flash of light froze the meadow, each of the players in this fight briefly suspended in time.

Thunder shook the field, rolling from her as if she were a goddess of the sky. The ground trembled. The roar of her magic blistered through his brain as it overloaded his enhanced ears. Vibrations rocked him to his core, but he held his ground. With his shoulders squared and his heels dug into the dirt, he turned his head away from the blinding flash of light.

The lightning struck a tree at the edge of the clearing, and the oak's charred branches crashed into the underbrush. The ends of the wood glowed orange, and coils of smoke spiraled into the air from her magic.

Wild. Unruly. Untamed.

She'd had the power of lightning all along and simply hadn't used it. That meant she either couldn't control it, or she had been waiting for the opportune moment to fry him.

Her fingers wrapped around his forearm, but he dropped his shadow blades and peeled her hand off just as quickly. He wouldn't let her roast him with another bolt.

His swords fractured into plumes of dark smoke as they hit the ground, but the damage had been done. Her eyes darted to his, still wide with shock. He held her gaze, owning the severity of what he'd done.

She staggered, about to fall, but he grabbed her shoulders to keep her upright. Gently, he eased her toward the grass at the base of the gnarled old tree. As she leaned her back against the bark, he knelt beside her.

Blood bubbled from the wound, and she pressed both hands against it to stem the red surge. Shoulders tense, she glared at him. The proud warrior in front of him braced herself, like she was waiting for him to deal the final blow.

He wouldn't.

He'd won, but only by a technicality. It didn't feel like a fair fight, and he almost hated himself for taking advantage of her momentary distraction.

"I don't know what recipe Henry used to make his wraith," she admitted, her voice barely loud enough to hear. She winced, and a bit of blood stained her teeth. "But I don't think you've had enough time to make one of your own. You found a way to steal the king's wraith, didn't you? You—" She pinched her eyes shut and arched her back, the tendons in her neck tightening as she rode out a wave of pain.

"Damn it," he muttered.

Quinn lifted her left hand and summoned fire into her palm.

"Don't." He summoned one of his shadow blades and held it inches from her neck. With a glare, he silently dared her to do something stupid as the blackfire cast a soft gray glow on her face.

Her jaw tensed. The muscle by her eye twitched, but the fire went out with a hiss.

The tiger roared, closer this time, and Connor looked over his shoulder as the beast turned its sights on him. With its magnificent wings spread wide, the creature charged. Its claws kicked up dirt and clumps of grass as it ran, and he braced himself for another battle.

"Blaze, leave!" Quinn shouted.

The vougel slid to a stop, its claws kicking up clumps of dirt into the air. It beat its wings against the air, its tail twitching in frustration, and it roared again—this time at her.

"Go, you stupid bird!" she snapped. "Now!"

It growled in anger, and at first, it didn't move. Its gaze darted from her to Connor as its body coiled, ready to spring.

Connor's grip on his sword tightened, and he prepared for the worst.

"Go," Quinn whispered.

The vougel moaned, the sound sad and soft. Its body relaxed, and the beast launched into the air. A gust cut through the meadow from its powerful wings. It flew overhead, and in seconds, the tiger disappeared over the trees.

Connor waited, shoulders tense as he tried to figure out the trap. The trick. This close to death, she had chosen to save her mount instead of herself. After his run-in with Otmund, he assumed this had to be a ploy of some kind.

And yet, the beast didn't return.

As the final smoke cleared from the small meadow, he took stock of the chaos. Sophia held her shoulder, blood pooling over her fingers as she leaned against Murdoc. A massive gouge across the former Blackguard's chest stained his shirt red, and his sword had disappeared at some point in the battle.

The Wraith King hovered beside the withered tree, and Quinn glared up at the dead man's ghost. Her face twisted with pain, and she slipped her hand into her pocket. The dull clink of a bottle caught his attention.

Crafty.

As she slowly tugged a small vial from her pocket, Connor snatched it from her hand. "No potions for you."

She scowled and glared up at him with hatred as she waited in the lingering silence.

"You sacrificed yourself to save your vougel." He stood, his blade loose in his palm as he circled her. "Why? I've seen people sacrifice their mounts for less."

"As if you care." The color drained from her cheeks as more and more blood seeped over her fingers from the wound. Her voice never wavered, and though she arched her back again from the pain, she hadn't once pleaded for her life.

Connor set his free hand on his hip and shook his head in frustration, wondering how he wanted to play this.

Sophia limped over. "What are you waiting for? Kill her."

The sorceress is right, the wraith said.

"Both of you, shut your damn mouths," Connor ordered. He shifted his attention to the specter. "Especially you."

He had ordered the ghoul to remain hidden, but the dead man had disobeyed. If Quinn hadn't known the extent of what Connor was before, she sure as hell did now. The ghoul had mentioned several times he wouldn't be controlled, but they'd had a truce. Showing himself during the battle had taken this whole mess a step too far.

The wraith *wanted* to be seen.

The wraith *wanted* the Lightseers after Connor. He'd confessed as much during their time with the Finns.

I need war, the wraith had said. *I am not satisfied living as a drifter in the woods. Your life as a vagrant is over.*

"Sophia, get me something to block her magic," he ordered. "What do you have? A potion?"

She opened her mouth to protest, but he narrowed his eyes in warning. Her lips closed, and she let out an irritated groan. Instead of fighting it, she rifled through her bag and tugged out an iron circlet with a single hinge on one end and a lock on the other. "I wouldn't trust a potion in this situation. As long as she's wearing this, her magic is useless."

"Don't you dare," Quinn warned, her eyes darting toward the sorceress.

Sophia tossed the circlet to Connor, but she groaned with pain the moment the band left her palm. Her hand fell again to her side, and she stumbled. Murdoc held her in place, his hand around her shoulders the only thing keeping her on her feet.

Connor snatched the circlet out of the air and wove it around Quinn's neck. He didn't waste time trying to sort through her hair, and his fingers brushed her blazing hot skin as the enchanted item locked with a sharp click.

Her hazel eyes narrowed. "I'm going to kill you for this."

"You'll have to get in line," Connor replied. "There are plenty ahead of you."

The wraith darted into view, blocking out much of the forest around them as he leaned in. *You must kill her, you fool.*

"You complicated this," he reminded the ghoul. "This is your fault.

You can't control me."

The phantom growled with frustration. *You are new to this life, so I will grant you a merciful lesson to save you from your own stupid sense of nobility. Both when I was alive and now as an undead ghoul, I am a specter of death. Those who see me must understand they have but two options—bow to you or die. To allow for anything else is to proudly announce your own weakness to the world!*

Connor leaned in and stared into the empty sockets of the wraith's eyes. "I'm not like the other fools you strong-armed into obedience. You can't trick me into doing what's against my best interest."

A heartless warrior would've sacrificed her mount to save her own life. Whatever orders Quinn had to bring him in, she didn't deserve to die alone in a meadow. Saldia had a shortage of decent people, and she seemed like one of the few. He wouldn't be the one to take her down.

Not tonight, anyway. If that came back to haunt him, so be it.

The wraith shook his bony head in disdain. *If you refuse to kill her, you must at least detain her. In war, it is critical to acquire your most powerful enemies and wring every shred of information out of them.*

"Right, that wouldn't backfire," he muttered. "It's not like we have a prison."

"You can't contain me," Quinn warned as Murdoc and Sophia reached them. "Even if you had a cell, there's nothing you can do to me that will make me talk."

"I have ways," Sophia said with a wry grin.

"Enough, both of you." Connor dismissed his sword and dangled the vial he'd taken from Quinn in front of the Starling's face. "Is this a healing potion?"

The woman went still, her face a stony and unreadable mask.

"I'm going to take that as a yes." He pointed at her Firesword. "Murdoc, take that to the edge of the field. Keep it somewhere we can see it."

Murdoc nodded and lowered Sophia to the ground. As he raced off, the necromancer used the opportunity to rifle through her satchel.

With the two of them occupied, Connor grabbed his own pack from the other side of the tree and yanked out one of the Rectivane potions the Finns had given him. It didn't feel right, wounding a warrior and leaving her to die in a clearing.

He had to make it hard enough for her to heal that she couldn't follow, but he didn't want her to bleed out. A difficult balance to achieve.

Though they could have used one of Sophia's vines as a makeshift rope, he'd made this difficult enough as it was. Without magic or her sword, she had to find a way to get the Bluntmar collar off before she could heal *and* get to the potions in time for the magic to work.

"Listen to me closely." His voice dropped an octave as he set both bottles in the tree's hollow above her head. "I left one of my Rectivanes in case yours isn't enough. You can have both once we're gone. A wound like that gives you a few hours before you bleed to death, especially if you apply pressure. You have until dawn. I figure a warrior like you has been through worse. We're going to leave, and you're not going to follow us. If you do, I won't spare your life next time."

"Nor will I spare yours, assassin," she warned.

He raised one eyebrow in confusion. "Assassin?"

"Don't play coy." Her gaze shifted to the ghoul. "Feigning stupidity doesn't suit you."

"Whatever Otmund told you, I didn't assassinate anyone."

"Is that the lie you told them?" Her voice dropped to the barest whisper as she gestured to Sophia and Murdoc with a bloodstained hand.

He frowned and stood, more tempted than ever to see if he could wring information out of her. Apparently, someone had been weaving lies about him already.

Fantastic.

"Let's go." He nodded to the others. "You two have sixty seconds to find anything you lost in the fight."

If he was lucky, he wouldn't see this woman again. Deep down, however, he knew better than to expect her to leave him be.

As the weeks wore on, his luck seemed to be running out.

CHAPTER THIRTY-SEVEN
QUINN

As the pink and yellow glow of a springtime dawn swept across the forest, Quinn struggled to breathe. Golden light inched across the matted meadow grasses, but her vision blurred. The daylight became nothing but streaks of color.

More blood seeped into her palm with each moment. Her shirt clung to her skin from the constant flow. Pain crashed through her body like waves on a shore, and each surge distorted the minutes that ticked by.

The tip of the sun peeked over the trees, and she frowned with confusion. If dawn had already come, she had been bleeding far longer than she had thought.

Her palm pressed against the wound in her side, and another ripple of agony tore up her spine as she applied more pressure. The back of her head smacked against the bark as she tried to distract herself from the pain.

A futile attempt. This hurt like the fires of hell.

The injury itself shouldn't have caused her this much pain. She had been stabbed dozens of times before and had always managed to push through the anguish, but the assassin's blade had gone deep. Worse, the blackfire seemed to have scorched—or even cursed—her from within.

Every breath sent jolts of agony clear to her toes. Every beat of her heart shocked her system. Every blink of her eyes disoriented her, and her world spun so violently she feared passing out.

Staying awake had been her greatest challenge in the hours since the assassin had left. With no access to her magic, her body protested every movement. Everything took more effort than it should have.

With the Bluntmar collar around her neck, it felt as though her very essence had been cut off from her.

As she ran her hands along its metal surface yet again, still searching for its weak point, her fingertips dipped across the deep scratches in the metal.

Scars from her previous attempts to pry it off.

Yet again, Quinn tried to stand. With one hand still pressed flat against the wound to stem the blood, her other hand clawed at the tree for balance. Her nails ripped off the bark, and flakes of wood fluttered into her hair. Hunched over and unbalanced, she managed to finally get on her feet.

Nausea burned her cheeks. Her head swam. The ground tilted, and her legs gave out. Her knee hit the dirt, and that alone kept her from diving headfirst into the grass.

Every movement mattered.

Every breath could've been her last.

Loose hair stuck to the sweat on her brow, and she wiped her face against her arm to clear her vision. This didn't make sense. None of it. The Bluntmar didn't do anything but block her magic, and yet she could barely stand. Once, she had walked for days with gashes clear through her leg, and yet now reaching a stupid vial tested every ounce of her willpower.

If she ever caught up with that assassin, she'd find a way to run him through with his own sword as payback.

Tenderly, she inched her knees across the dirt and hobbled toward the hollow. He said he'd put her Rectivane potion up there, along with a second one he claimed to have taken from his own stores.

She huffed at the boldfaced lie.

Unable to stand, she reached into the hollow. With her entire body straining from the effort it took to simply remain upright, her fingertips swept across the interior. Something scampered over her hand, and she grimaced with disgust.

If it was one of those squirrels, she'd roast it alive.

Her fingers brushed across a vial, and she snatched it. The familiar glass settled into her palm, and she sank to the ground with a sigh of relief.

Finally.

Laying on her back with her hair splayed across the grass, she allowed herself a moment to catch her breath. Though she wanted to down it right then and there, it wouldn't have had any effect until she removed the Bluntmar collar.

But she needed a moment to rest.

With the bottle clutched to her abdomen, she stared up at the encroaching dawn. Exhaustion tugged at her body. She longed to sleep.

Her shallow breaths rasped in the quiet meadow as the Bluntmar collar weighed on her throat. The heavy circlet served as an insulting reminder of her loss against the assassin who had shown her mercy.

"I shouldn't be alive," she told the sky.

The clouds above her blurred together as she tried to make sense of their movements.

"He won," she slurred. "I lost. Why did he let me live?"

The sky didn't answer.

"Sleep sounds… sleep…" Her eyes fluttered closed, but she forced them open just as quickly.

No.

Sleep would mean death.

She had to get to her sword. No potion could work if a person wore a Bluntmar collar, but enchanted items worked regardless of one's access to their magic. If she could use her sword to get the collar off before she bled out completely, the potion still had enough time to kick in and save her life.

Probably.

The rustle of feathers in the treetops broke through her hazy thoughts. Something big, judging by the heavy wingbeats. The canopy rustled. Branches creaked. A blurry silhouette darted overhead, brief and blinding, so fast she barely tracked its movement.

She would be damned before she became something's breakfast.

Groaning with the weight of the mind-numbing pain, she forced herself to sit up. Agony ricocheted through her body with every little movement.

She had to get to her sword. Her life now depended on it in more ways than one.

Behind her, just out of view, the soft thud of heavy feet against the grass broke the early morning stillness. Leaves crunched beneath paws as whatever it was neared. It growled, but the snarl quickly became a soft purr.

A sound she recognized.

Blaze rounded the withered tree, and Quinn's shoulders relaxed the moment she saw him. The massive tiger tucked his wings at his side and pressed his face against hers. His purring vibrated through her teeth, soothing and gentle.

His soft cheek wiped away the sweat on her brow, and she leaned into him with a grateful smile. She sank her fingertips into the fur on his neck, tainting it with her bloodstained touch.

"You big softy," she teased.

He nudged her cheek with his cold nose, and she impulsively shivered.

They didn't have time for reunions.

"Get my sword." Her words slurred together, but she pointed at the blade stuck in the ground at the edge of the meadow. "Get *Aurora*."

Blaze trotted over to the weapon and grabbed it in his teeth, his head tilted sideways to avoid cutting himself on the sharp edge. With a quick tug, he yanked it free from the ground and trotted back. The steel glistened in the spring sun as he reached her, and the sword thudded against the dirt at Quinn's feet.

She snatched it, though her vision blurred again. The sword shifted in her bloodstained grip. With a muffled curse, she dropped the blade and wiped her hand on the grass. Long red streaks clotted along the blades.

Delicately, she eased the tip of the blade toward the lock and pressed the very end into the keyhole. The shrill scrape of steel on metal cut through the air, and the sword slid in her exhausted grip. The razor-sharp tip slipped off the circlet and pressed against her throat.

Blaze's eyes widened, but she caught the sword in time. Together, they let out a sigh of relief when it didn't draw blood.

Not that she had much left to give.

It took a bit of maneuvering, but she finally managed to set the tip of the blade against the lock. With a practiced twist of her hand, flames erupted along the sword. Heat rolled over her face, and she held her breath as she continued to twist the blade against the lock.

Blaze growled, but she just closed her eyes to focus.

Finally, a loud snap cut through the air. The mechanism broke beneath her blade, and the cursed thing fell to the ground.

Quinn let out a strangled little gasp as her magic swarmed her. The fire of her Burnbane charm flickered to life in her chest. The lightning of her Voltaic hex shot through her veins. The soothing rush of breath in her lungs thundered with the power of her Airdrift charm.

Blaze jumped to his feet, his tail swaying happily, but she set her sword aside. The fires extinguished the moment her skin left its hilt.

The last grains of sand in the hourglass of her life were slipping through her fingers, and that meant she had no time to waste on celebrating their minor victory.

She uncorked the vial the assassin had stolen from her and drank the whole damn thing. A few swigs would have likely sufficed, but a brush with death tended to make mortals like her a little greedy.

Not that the assassin could've understood.

The vial's extra-strength Rectivane potion took control of her body. Her vision went dark, and she fell to her hands and knees as it took root. The magic swam through her, healing everything it touched. Air caught in her chest, rough and heavy as the potion instantly hit her heart.

The wound in her gut rippled with simultaneous pleasure and pain as it stitched itself together. She winced and did her best to brace herself as the potion repaired her from the inside out.

It took ages. She lost count of her breaths and the minutes that passed. Blaze growled softly, but a sharp ringing in her ears dwarfed the sound.

When the pain finally faded, it left in a rush. The ringing in her ears remained, but her arms and legs slowly regained their strength. She let out a long sigh of relief and pressed her forehead against the dirt.

Despite the cold soil pressing against her face, Quinn smiled with gratitude. Through the long gouges in her clothes from the fight, cold air rushed over her skin where the lethal injury had been moments before.

Rectivane potions like this were only made in the Capital, and only by her family. A closely guarded secret of the Starling fortune, these potions were reserved for moments of chaos.

Moments like this.

Though her head still spun, she rolled onto her back to let the potion finish its work. A blurry twig in her hair loomed in her peripheral vision as she stared up at the waking sky, but she didn't care.

With a low growl, Blaze followed suit. He rolled onto his back and laid his massive head beside hers. With nothing else to do, he pawed absently at the air. His giant claws slid from the pads of his feet, glinting like steel in the light.

Quinn chuckled. "You're just a big kitten."

Blaze rolled his golden eyes.

She set her hands on her stomach and relished every breath as if it were new. That had been such a close call.

Too close.

Without a doubt, she had faced off with the man in the sketch. Those eyes. The disheveled hair. The cloth across his face. Every feature and every detail had been perfectly captured in the drawing Otmund had given her.

Her father had said this man killed King Henry. That he was an assassin, but assassins never showed mercy.

She frowned. "And yet…"

Blaze lifted his head and looked at her, curious and confused, but she didn't have the words to explain.

To complicate matters, the man had Henry's wraith. Though she didn't know much about the nuances of forbidden death magic, she had to assume each wraith would've looked at least slightly different. Such was the way of spellgust. Advanced use of its power accounted for the intricacies of how it reacted to each reagent and person.

Advanced spellgust use boggled even the brightest minds, but Quinn had studied her mother's work with glamours enough to understand the basics. A glamour changed specific things, of course—a nose, or an eye—but two people who drank the same glamour would look different. Using the glamour to dye two women's hair brown still resulted in different shades of brunette between the two of them.

Somehow, the assassin's ghoul wasn't just a copy. It had to be the same wraith.

The billowing cloak. The skeletal face. The sword. That wraith looked identical to the one she had seen floating through the pillars in King Henry's court.

The specter that had secured a throne. An enchantment with eerily human features. With no mind of its own, it had obeyed Henry's every whim. According to Henry, it was an undead atrocity stitched together from what remained in the graves of powerful necromancers.

Henry had used necromancy to create an undead ghoul, steal the Capital, and conquer the continent. For as long as she'd had *Aurora*, she had been warned about the wraith's power.

When the wraith had appeared during her duel with the assassin, she had foolishly dropped her guard. For one moment, she had been vulnerable. Her years of training and a lifetime of magical experience had failed her for that one second, but a brief moment was all it ever took to lose. In fact, that was how she had killed some of her most talented targets—by waiting for a window of opportunity to show itself.

Everyone had an eventual moment of weakness, no matter how much magic or training they had at their disposal.

This man would eventually have one, too.

Any other hitman would have taken the opportunity to gut a Starling and enjoyed it. This assassin was already a wanted, hunted man. The Lightseers knew about him, and killing her would have taken out a dangerous threat.

Yet, he hadn't done it. He'd shown her the sort of mercy she would've never shown him.

It didn't make sense. Though it might've been a ploy, she didn't see the benefit for him in leaving her alive. She simply didn't have enough information to know what he wanted. This man possessed unknown resources, and she had no idea of his allies.

For all she knew, he already had an army.

Her mission had just become far more urgent and dire. Though she ached to hunt him down and break his arms for the pain he had caused her, she needed to be rational and calm. Every fiber of her being warned not to let pride get the best of her.

Duty above all else.

The Lightseer code.

Though she still had weeks to capture the assassin before her deadline, her father needed to hear the news.

Perhaps she needed to speak with her sister Victoria as well, since the eldest Starling sister had a broad knowledge of rare reagents. If a recipe could be crafted to take down a wraith, Victoria must've had it in one of her books.

First, however, Quinn would have to bring more information to the negotiation. She needed something useful and significant enough to prove she could handle leading the charge. Zander no doubt wanted to get involved, and he would look for any sign of weakness in her report to seize control of the mission.

Her mission.

There were too many mysteries to unravel about this assassin in the woods for her to give up control just yet.

Most other Lightseers would've simply continued pursuing him to the ends of time. No thought. No strategy. Just brute force and a banner flying overhead to announce who they were.

Quinn was smarter.

As of this moment, she needed to change her tactics. He'd obviously spent time in Bradford, so she would go back in disguise this time. With a suitable glamour, she could blend into the woodwork and listen to any rumors floating by.

A man like that wasn't going to go unnoticed for long, and it was just a matter of time before the whispers started. When they did, he wouldn't escape again.

CHAPTER THIRTY-EIGHT
CONNOR

Throwing Quinn off his trail had cost Connor precious time, and that meant he and his new team would have to spend a night in the trees. A night in the canopy and away from the blight-wolves didn't faze him, of course, but he had yet to discover how Sophia or Murdoc would react.

Time would tell.

With a grunt of effort, he adjusted the deer around his shoulders as he trudged through the woods. Its tongue lolled out of its open mouth, and its horns jostled with each of his steps. Light as a fistful of cloud, it barely weighed on his shoulders at all. Before the wraith, he never would've dreamed of lifting a buck this big, much less draping its bulk across his shoulders.

Times had certainly changed.

At the first signs of sunset, he'd ordered the team to camp and build a fire out of sight of the main road. They wouldn't reach Murkwell until tomorrow afternoon, and since the Lightseers knew about him, walking into yet another town came with risk. It seemed best to bypass the town entirely.

Sophia had repaired their battle-torn clothing with one of her potions, much to Connor's amazement. Having a necromancer on hand had proven even more useful than he'd thought.

Provided, of course, she didn't get him killed—or try to kill him herself.

He marched through the forest alone as the sun cast a red and orange glow through the trees. They had spent the day away from the main road, and he'd paraded his newfound team through creek after creek to dampen their scent while the two of them bickered.

After years alone in the silent wood, Sophia and Murdoc had tested his patience today. Hunting alone had been a momentary peace in the storm of their incessant banter.

The southern wind had died down, though it would likely pick up again tonight. Above him, oaks and pines carved into the sky, and sunlight danced along the ground through gaps in the canopy. The lingering char of smoke wafted through the air, along with the distant crackle of a fire.

Any second now, he would hear their voices as they finished setting up camp. Provided, of course, nothing had eaten them in his absence.

Through a gap between two trees to his left, the wraith appeared in a rush of black fog. The dead man's cloak billowed into existence with a midnight flourish that, weeks ago, had sent a jolt of surprise clear to his toes.

Now, the ghost's tendency to appear from thin air just annoyed him. Nothing but a parlor trick meant to intimidate mortals.

It was foolish to leave the Starling woman. The wraith floated in front of him and poked a skeletal finger into his chest. The sensation of the dead man's bone against his shirt sent a ripple of frost across his skin, but he ignored it.

Without so much as a glance toward the ghoul, he adjusted the deer's weight on his shoulders and stepped around the floating specter. His hands tightened around the beast's legs to keep it rooted in place.

He didn't respond. He couldn't. He was still too angry.

Back in the field, the specter had disobeyed a direct order and revealed himself. The dead man had tested Connor's boundaries, and now he had to hold the wraith accountable.

The more he thought about it, the more the ghoul's actions made sense. The ghost had kept quiet in the town to avoid a swarm of soldiers attacking them, but Quinn had been a prime target—someone with connections, alone in a field.

By appearing before her, the Wraith King had given Connor an ultimatum. The choice between letting her live or slitting her throat had no doubt seemed obvious to a brutal dictator, so he had tried to force Connor to kill an influential figure.

Her death would have created a snowball of war and chaos. Battles. Blood. Mayhem. Allies and armies, fighting for vengeance without the full context of what had happened.

Murdering a Starling would've given the wraith everything he'd wanted and more. Connor refused to play into his hands.

However, he had found one silver lining in the frustrating turn of events. If the wraith so desperately craved recognition, it meant Connor had discovered a simple yet effective punishment—pretending the dead man didn't exist at all.

I see, said the ghost. *You refuse to speak to me.*

Connor didn't react. He climbed up a small hill and sidestepped the mossy pebbles in the soil to avoid slipping. All the while, his gaze remained focused on his path through the trees as he followed his nose toward the smoke.

The wraith shrugged. *It doesn't matter to me if you reply.*

A lie.

Besides, the ghoul continued. *I could've killed her myself. You would have still taken the blame had I run her through with my sword.*

With an irritated sigh, Connor shook his head and opted to break his silence. Apparently, his attempt at punishing the wraith hadn't worked as well as he'd hoped.

Damn it.

"Killing her would've crossed the line," he pointed out. "If you'd gone that far, you know I would've done everything in my power to end you because your mere existence would've threatened mine. I told you I'd find a way to kill you if you crossed me, and I meant it. Revealing yourself to her without killing her outright was your way of testing my boundaries. You wanted to see if you could control me."

That, or it was my way of seeing what you would do to defy me, even if doing so was against your own best interest.

Connor scoffed. "You're not that clever."

The ghost chuckled.

A bird chirped in the canopy. A dozen loose leaves caught on a gentle breeze and spiraled into the branches as a ray of sun cut through the oaks around them. The sunbeam cast a golden spotlight on a dead tree at the base of the hill, and the gnarled old oak twisted around itself in a way eerily similar to the dead oak in Sophia's meadow.

A necromancer. A Starling. A vougel. A disgraced Blackguard. This new life of his tested his understanding of the world.

"Back in the field…" He frowned as words failed him. Try as he might, he hadn't yet pieced together something that had been itching at the back of his mind since he'd first fused with the ghoul.

Yes? A tinge of curiosity floated on the wraith's voice.

"Even though my father was a merchant, he made sure I knew how to protect myself," Connor explained as he resumed his walk up the hill. "I've held a sword for most of my life. After I left Kirkwall, I trained with an elite soldier from Oakenglen. I'm good, but back in the meadow, I fought better than ever before. I didn't notice it as much when I fought the king's guard, since it was all so new to me. But against Sophia and Quinn, my reflexes were better. Every punch landed harder. Every blow had more heft."

Very observant, the ghoul admitted. *Can you guess why?*

"Stop playing with your food and tell me, already. After your stint in the meadow, you're not exactly in my good graces."

The ghoul laughed. *Was I ever?*

Connor did his best to suppress the smirk tugging at the corner of his mouth.

Touché.

I don't apologize, Magnuson. The wraith let out an irritated groan. *You did, however, fight well, so I will tell you this—when you fused with me, you obtained my lifetime of skill. Both my mastery of the sword and my abilities with hand to hand combat. You were decent before, judging by the fight in the ruins, but you're a master now. Listen to your body. Let it guide you. You've inherited my muscle memory, and it knows better than your inferior, mortal brain.*

Connor suppressed the urge to scoff at the shameless boasting. Even though the wraith had an ego larger than a barn, he had to admit that a bit of the bragging was earned. Thanks to the wraith's influence, he'd fought better beneath that withered old tree than at any other point in his entire life.

If he truly had no choice but to fight off a swarm of assassins and Lightseers, at least he'd be able to kick ass more efficiently.

As he neared the fire, the stench of roasting slime and pan-fried mold hit him like a left hook to the face. He gagged on impulse.

Beside him, the wraith tilted his skeletal head and stared off into the lengthening shadows. A breeze blew by, and the ghoul dissolved into the wind without another word.

Either he'd seen something out there in the encroaching dusk, or whatever abomination Murdoc had thrown on the fire repulsed even the undead.

"…but rats are all there is to eat out here," Murdoc's voice carried through the forest as Connor neared the campfire.

"There's far more than rats in this forest." Sophia's voice dripped with disdain.

The warm glow of the campfire flickered in the fading light. Its flames cast distorted shadows across several trunks as Connor approached the small camp they'd set up far enough away from the main road to go unseen and unheard. Though he didn't try to mask his footsteps, no one greeted him. Neither of his new companions so much as moved.

A long stick sat on a makeshift spit over the fire. Red globs of blood bubbled on one end of it, leading to two rats that had been speared through from head to tail on the wooden spike. Murdoc rotated them, his contraption of twigs and fallen branches barely enough to hold their weight as their tails dangled lifelessly over the flame.

The former Blackguard leaned over the meat and wafted their scent toward his face. His eyes watered, and he barely stifled his grimace at their disgusting odor. He choked and swallowed hard. "See? They'll taste great. Unless you plan on wandering out there to catch us a boar, you'd better eat."

Without a word, Connor shrugged the deer off his shoulders. It landed with a meaty thud on the ground beside Murdoc, and its horns speared the dirt by the fire pit.

Murdoc jumped to his feet and drew his sword. Sitting on a rock beside him, Sophia gasped and pressed her hand against her chest in surprise.

"You can't eat these." Connor grabbed the rat-covered stick off the fire and tossed it into the underbrush.

"Hey!" Murdoc stared after his attempt at dinner as the charred rodents disappeared into the depths of a bush.

"Those were slime rats." Connor sat on a rock beside the fire. "They'll give you the shits for a week."

"Delightful." Sophia wrinkled her nose with disgust.

"It's unpleasant," he agreed.

She rolled her eyes. "I meant your description."

Murdoc sat beside him, and the Blackguard raised his eyebrows in wonder as he stared at the buck. "I haven't seen a deer that big in years."

"It should feed us for a while if we cook it right." Connor gestured to Sophia's bag. "I assume you have a way to preserve meat for travel?"

The necromancer groaned. "I'm not a spellgust dispensary. You don't get every wish granted the second you ask for something, just because 'magic.'" Her eyes widened as she mocked him, and her fingers danced in the firelight as she pretended to shoot spellgust from her fingertips.

"Am I wrong?" He stared her down, knowing full well he wasn't.

She scowled, and her gaze swept over the massive animal. "Fine, yes. I might have something. I need to check my stores."

"I guess I'll earn my keep and clean this thing." Murdoc lifted the buck by its horns and pulled it away from the fire. "So, Captain, what's the plan?"

"We can't sleep here." Connor scanned the forest as he spoke. "The deer's blood will attract scavengers, and it might even bring the blight-wolves. We'll need to move toward the road and find a place to spend the night in the trees."

"Sounds cozy," the necromancer mused.

He smirked. "It's not a hut in the woods, but you'll manage."

Sophia swept her dark hair over one shoulder as she adjusted in her seat. "Whatever happens, I'm sure you big, brave men will protect me."

His smile fell, and he studied her face as she pretended to watch the flames. Her eyes glossed over, and more than once in the silence that followed, he caught her glance briefly his way.

Quinn Starling had interrupted their conversation about the Wraith King, and it was time they finished it. He had faced the dark forest for answers, and it was time Sophia fulfilled her end of the bargain.

CHAPTER THIRTY-NINE
CONNOR

As the Ancient Woods darkened around Connor's makeshift camp, the fire between him and Sophia sparked. The blistered logs within the circle of stones popped and fizzled while the flames roasted them. Heat rolled off the campfire, warming his shins as he drummed his fingers on his knee and debated where to even begin.

So many questions. So few answers. So few opportunities to test her for the truth.

His ear twitched as the coarse grate of steel sawing through bone filled the camp, and he cast a glance over his shoulder at Murdoc—the only one of his new team who didn't know about the Wraith King.

He had to tread carefully. There was no telling what sort of contacts a former Blackguard might've had. His kind hunted the darkness and slaughtered the sorts of monsters that left most common folk standing in a puddle of their own urine.

Even with his death wish and general irreverence for danger, Murdoc couldn't be underestimated. For now, the Wraith King's identity was a secret Connor refused to share.

He returned his attention to their resident necromancer as she grabbed a stick and poked the fire between them. "Tell me more about death magic. I want to know why he chose to fuse with me."

Sophia tilted her head, and a coy smirk tugged at the edge of her ruby-red lips. "The wraith is a 'he,' huh? Not an 'it?'"

"You are annoyingly observant." Connor rubbed his temple to mask his irritation with himself at letting a detail like that slip by. "But yes, *he*."

"Interesting." A wistful curiosity fluttered through the word, like a butterfly darting through the air.

He waited, elbows on his knees as he silently demanded an answer.

"I can't tell you for certain," she admitted as she stoked the fire. "There's not much about his kind in Nethervale. What I do know is that the wraith transfers to a new host after the death of the previous one. We assume it—sorry, *he*—seeks out the nearest living human. You were probably chosen because you were closest when his previous host died."

Connor rubbed his jaw, careful not to let any emotion show on his face as she cast another curious glance his way. She had just guessed at Henry's death, and while she could safely assume the king was gone, he wasn't about to confirm it for her.

With another careful glance over his shoulder, he found Murdoc sawing away at the deer's underbelly. The rusty tang of blood snaked through the air as something gushed onto the grass, but the man's expression never changed. Eyes focused, his ear didn't so much as twitch.

If the former Blackguard listened in on their conversation, he didn't seem to have registered anything about how Connor had obtained the wraith.

Still, they needed to tread carefully.

He stared again into the fire. "Who's after me, then?"

"Everyone." Her stick lifted above the campfire as she shrugged, and the branch's tip left an orange streak through the air as the bark burned.

With an irritated groan, he shook his head. "Give me names. I want detail. I'm sick of hearing that 'everyone' answer."

Sophia pursed her lips, and dimples formed in her cheeks. "Fine. Nyx, and therefore all of Nethervale, will likely leave you alone unless you seem weak enough for her to conquer. A few rogue necromancers may be brave enough to come after you, but most will simply watch from afar. The entire elite army won't pursue you unless Nyx gives the order. Lucky for you, she's not interested in the wraith. She says magic like his is a fool's errand and a waste of time, but I think she's just gotten cocky."

He stared into the fire as he listened between the words for signs of a lie, but Nyx's apparent apathy for the simmering souls surprised him. Given her control over Nethervale, he would've figured she of all people wanted the wraith for herself.

Perhaps Sophia had done an expert job of lying, or maybe Nyx had grown bitter that Aeron Zacharias had achieved something no one else in the temple had ever managed.

"The Lightseers will be after you, obviously." Sophia gestured over her shoulder in the vague direction of the meadow. "The Starlings control the Lightseers, so really you're up against that megalomaniac Teagan and his entitled family. They'll have connections in every major city, so I suspect all of the capitals will have your wanted posters in their town squares soon. The towns will as well, in time."

"Delightful," he muttered. "What do the Lightseers want with me?"

The necromancer shrugged. "Who knows? They might want to dissect you. They might want the wraith for themselves. They might want to bottle it up and store it away, which of course would kill you in the process."

"Of course," he said dryly.

"As for the others after you, I can't tell for certain. Wildefaire, Dewcrest, Hazeltide, Mossvale, Freymoor, South Haven, and Kirkwall were mostly subdued in Henry's expansion."

Connor's jaw clenched on impulse at the mention of his home, but he kept his steely gaze trained on the campfire.

"After years of war with Henry, there's probably some resentment for wraith magic in every major kingdom," she continued. "As for Westhelm, no one has heard from them in years. They hate magic users and have a vendetta against Henry for pushing them off their land, since he banished them from Oakenglen. I can only assume they'll be after you, given all that power at your fingertips."

"What about Otmund Soulblud and Zander Starling?" Connor rubbed his temple to ease the throbbing pang of a looming headache. "Where are they?"

Her lips curled into a knowing smile. "These are the two powerful men who have something that belongs to you?"

He simply nodded.

"Odd." Her smile fell. "Zander, I understand. He meddles in everything. But what does the Lord of Mossvale have to do with any of this?"

"That is an excellent question," Connor admitted.

A hint. A clue. She didn't realize it, but she had given him vital information—Otmund ruled Mossvale, a small realm Connor knew next to nothing about. He'd learned about it in his schooling back in Kirkwall, but aside from brief mentions on the maps, it meant very little to Saldia as a whole.

From what little he remembered, a Mossvale lord didn't have the connections, military, or treasury a king would've had. That meant Otmund didn't have the resources to mount a crusade against him.

Or so he assumed.

"Why do you know his name?" she pressed. "What do Soulblud and the Starling heir have that you need to get back?"

He chuckled at her persistence. A necromancer didn't need to know about a weapon that could kill a wraith. With her skill, he figured she would've been able to get both daggers on her own, but he didn't trust her to surrender them to him afterward.

"They each have something that belongs to me," he repeated, dancing around the truth. "My primary aim is to get my property back, and for now, that's all you need to know."

Her frown deepened, and she crossed her arms with an indignant little huff. "Fine, be cryptic."

"You were saying?"

The fire glowed against her face as she quietly fumed. "I don't know anything about Soulblud except that he exists. As for Zander Starling, I've never met him in my life, thank the Fates."

Damn.

"How do we get to Starling?"

She leaned backward and cast him a sidelong glare, as though she weren't quite sure where he was taking this. "We don't. No one does, and no one wants to."

"Indulge me, then."

Her forehead creased as she stared into the fire. "I suppose if I absolutely had to track him, I would wait."

"Wait?"

She nodded. "Wait and listen. To win against a Starling, you need to be patient. You need to look for the opportune moment to attack, which are few and far between with that family. The next time I got word that he went on a mission alone, I would follow and intercept when he least expected an attack. I'd find an isolated area, far from help. If he had even one solider with him as backup, I would abandon the mission and try again another day. In the rare chance this mission actually succeeded, I'd also have a foolproof escape plan because no Starling takes a loss well."

Even though the Bloodbane daggers posed the deadliest threat to his very existence, he had to wait.

Short of her not having an answer for him at all, being told to wait was the one thing he hadn't wanted to hear.

He groaned in frustration and rubbed his face. At least he had plenty of questions to fill the time.

"While we wait, riddle me this." He fished through the mushrooms and dried meat in his bag to find the dagger the bandit had used on him in the potion shop. As he lifted it, its jewels glittered in the firelight. "Do you know what this is?"

"Let me see." She reached for it, her palm turned toward the canopy as she waited for him to hand it over.

With a stern glare of warning not to try anything, he indulged her.

The necromancer twisted it every which way, examining the dagger's jewel-encrusted hilt in excruciating detail before she finally drew it from its sheath. Firelight danced along the steel, though nothing particularly unique stood out to him despite the gemstones in its handle.

"It looks familiar, but I'm not sure why. How is this special? Why do you have it?" Her dark gaze shifted to him.

He tilted his head impatiently, silently urging her to get the hell on with it. He had no intentions of giving anything away before she told him what he wanted to know. He didn't trust her, and if he caught her in even one lie, his threat to abandon her out here in the forest was still very much real.

She shook her head in irritation and slid the dagger back into its sheath. "It's an enchanted item. Look here." Her finger tapped against an oval gem in its hilt, and the stone glowed briefly green beneath her touch. "That's a Firebreath spellgust gem, all the way from Lunestone. The Lightseers have a monopoly." She grimaced, and her nose wrinkled with disdain as she continued to study the dagger. "I take it you don't have much experience with enchanted items?"

He held her gaze, and he merely narrowed his eyes in annoyance. For some reason, she kept thinking he would actually answer her incessant questions.

"Oh, this is just another test." Sophia rolled her dark eyes and tossed her hair over one shoulder. "Fine, I'll indulge you. A stone like that is required for any enchanted item to work. It's where they draw their power, though it fades over the years. Each stone has about two years in it, with moderate use, though items with heavy use need to be re-enchanted sooner. That's all I can tell for certain without knowing how it was made. Where did you get it?"

"The potion master's shop in Bradford."

No harm in admitting that, at least.

"Ah! I knew I recognized it." She examined the hilt again, her shoulders relaxing as the puzzle solved itself. "This was in one of his display shelves in the back, right?"

Connor nodded.

"It's probably a Firestarter, then."

She yanked the dagger out of the case once again and swung it toward the dirt at her feet. A flame erupted at the hilt and barreled down the length of the blade. The tiny fireball sailed off the tip and hit the dirt with a hiss before the flame fizzled out into a thin ribbon of smoke.

"Mystery solved." The necromancer sheathed the blade and returned it to him. As he took it from her, she sighed with disappointment. "I confess, I had hoped it would be something interesting."

"Where I'm from, it is," he admitted. "We don't have these in the West, and I never saw one used on any of my trips down the southern road. I always thought the only Fireswords in existence could belong to the Starlings."

"Legally, that's not a Firesword." The necromancer pointed to the little dagger. "It's only a fraction as potent, and in dagger form, the most it can do is start a campfire. The old man just added some gemstones he imported from Wildefaire, probably so he could charge ten times what it's worth."

Connor frowned. The apparently ordinary dagger had stopped his shadow blades, and so had Quinn's Firesword. Back in the potion shop, however, the thieves' unenchanted weapons hadn't stood a chance.

Either fire-charmed blades could block his weapons, or—more likely—enchanted items possessed the sort of magic to give him a real challenge in a fight. He needed to watch, wait, and assume the worst until he found out for certain.

The Deathdread had more detail. If an answer existed anywhere, it had to be in that book. Since he had to wait for an opportune moment to tighten the noose around Zander Starling's neck, he might as well chase this lead to Aeron's Tomb.

"Tell me more about the Deathdread." He changed the subject before she could ask him anything else about the dagger. "How do you know it's in the mountains?"

"Oh." The necromancer cleared her throat and pressed her knees together. Her fingers danced absently on her kneecaps as she glanced away from the fire.

"Sophia." His voice carried a warning in it.

Don't lie.

She frowned. "Judging by your act of mercy to that Starling woman, you're not going to like my answer."

"Try me."

The sorceress grumbled, and she absently rubbed the back of her neck. "Roughly two years before I left Nethervale, Nyx caught a Lightseer Viceroy."

"What's a Lightseer Viceroy?"

"One of the highest-ranking officers in the Lightseer Chamber," she answered with a slight frown, like she had expected him to know that. "Was that *another* test?"

It wasn't, but he smirked anyway to keep her guessing.

"You irritating—" With a frustrated groan, she rubbed her eyes and wisely shut her mouth before she could finish her insult.

He gestured for her to continue, playing along with the idea that he was testing her on this. "Go on. Indulge me."

"Fine, be infuriating." She huffed. "A Lightseer stupid enough to walk into the Nethervale swamp never sees daylight again. That's the law. The moment a Lightseer wanders into our territory, they're considered dead to the world. There's a reason the Starlings haven't been able to topple Nethervale, and that's because a war between the temples on our soil would cost thousands of elite soldiers' lives. Maybe even hundreds of thousands. But this woman we caught was a Viceroy, and we weren't sure what would happen. We didn't even know if they realized she had come. We had to choose—interrogate her, or negotiate a trade?"

Connor stifled an impatient sigh. "Are you going to answer my question at any point during this story?"

"I'm getting there." Sophia scowled, and her back arched with indignation. "The point is this woman had connections and information. She wasn't the typical captive. Viceroys are valuable. If Lunestone found out we had her, the war between temples might've happened anyway. We had to move fast. I warned Nyx to negotiate a trade, since there was plenty we wanted from the Lightseers, but she ignored me. We chained the Viceroy in the dungeons, and the interrogation began. The Viceroy knew she was as good as dead, but she still wouldn't talk." The necromancer shook her head as she stared at the fire. "It didn't matter. Nyx had any number of magical reagents that could've made her give us the answers we wanted. I could've brewed a potion to force her to tell us whatever we asked, but—"

"That's a thing?" Murdoc interjected.

Connor peered over his shoulder to find the man with the deer's head in one hand and a bloody knife in the other. Red goop dripped over his fingertips as he gaped at Sophia in awe.

"Yes." She didn't bother masking her annoyance at yet another interruption. "It's a thing."

Wordlessly, Connor gestured for her to continue.

She absently brushed her fingers through the ends of her hair. "Instead of telling me to brew a Hackamore potion, Nyx chose to skin the woman alive, finger by finger, inch by inch. Even by my standards, it was brutal—but it worked. She *sang*. At the end, she talked until her heart gave out, and she told us everything we wanted to know." Her dark eyes darted toward Connor. "That's who you're dealing with, by the way, if you have to go against Nethervale. Keep that in mind."

He grimaced with disgust. Pain for the sake of pain. Torture for the brief thrill of feeling powerful over someone in chains.

People like that didn't deserve the air they breathed.

"This mentor of yours sounds charming," Murdoc said dryly as he sawed away at the deer carcass. "I can't imagine why you left."

Sophia scowled into the darkness behind Connor. At her withering glare, the former Blackguard stopped talking.

"We discovered quite a lot from her," the necromancer continued. "With the secrets locked away in that woman's brain, we had access to archives and information we never even dreamed of."

She scanned the forest's growing shadows and gestured for him to come closer.

Apparently, this was the part Murdoc couldn't hear.

Instead of huddling together and whispering, he stood and motioned for her to follow him into the forest. They had a bit of sunlight left before the hunters and beasts of the evening came out of their dens, and they had to use it wisely.

It didn't matter if this was one of the most important conversations of his life. The monsters of the Ancient Woods didn't know patience or compassion.

They obeyed nothing but their hunger.

CHAPTER FORTY
CONNOR

The crackle of the fire faded as they put some distance between themselves and Murdoc. When the orange glow of the flames faded into the soft purple haze that came with dusk in the woodlands, Connor leaned against the rough bark of an oak and crossed his arms.

"You were saying?"

"The Viceroy we—"

"—tortured," he finished for her.

"*Interrogated*," she corrected with an irritated glare. "That woman told us things. Most importantly, we learned the Lightseers did *not* destroy the simmering souls all those centuries ago. They lied to the public to ease their panic after Aeron's rise to power and his violent assassination, but he was smarter than them. He knew they would steal his work and try to destroy it, so he hid the souls across the continent."

"Wait." Connor pinched the bridge of his nose. "If Aeron had four souls, why didn't he fuse with them? Why would he have merely hidden them?"

Sophia's lips curled into a wry grin. "They were untested. He had succeeded, yes, but it was still theory. He didn't know if the fusion would work, nor did he know what would happen when he fused to all four. He needed more time."

Connor frowned. "I fused with untested magic?"

Sophia nodded. "But you're not dead, so it can't be that bad."

He simply rubbed his face and gestured for her to continue.

"That's most of it," she admitted. "The Lightseers have waged an unyielding covert crusade against the souls ever since, and almost nobody knows about it. Even within Lunestone."

In the heavy silence that followed, she studied him intently. Her eyes swept his face, no doubt waiting for him to react, but he merely held her gaze.

"Wait, where did they go?" The trees muffled Murdoc's voice. "I didn't even hear them leave. If they left me to get eaten by a…" His voice faded into a muffled string of curses.

Connor scratched the back of his head while he sat with what she had told him. "You said even some of the Lightseers in Lunestone don't know about the simmering souls?"

Sophia shook her head. "It's a secret guarded at the highest levels. Not even the elite Lightseers know the souls weren't truly destroyed, though a few of their top soldiers do have access to Aeron's Tomb. Only the Viceroys in the Lightseer Chamber know the truth, and it's a closely guarded secret. That's why they didn't denounce Henry when he took power."

Ah.

It made sense, now. The Lightseers could've turned the world on Henry had they explained who his wraith truly was—not just as the Wraith King brought back to life, but as one of Aeron's simmering souls. No one would have followed Henry. No one would've obeyed him. His empire would've crumbled the moment the people learned the truth, and his soldiers would've rebelled.

However, exposing Henry would've also exposed the Lightseers' great lie. As the protectors of the people, they depended on public trust as the foundation of their power. All those years ago, declaring to the world that the simmering souls had been destroyed had only cursed them to fighting their war against Aeron's creations in secret.

To make matters worse, it explained why they wanted Connor. He had a simmering soul, and that meant he was a loose thread for them to cut. The very foundations of their power depended on keeping him quiet.

"It gets better," Sophia added with a smirk. "The Viceroy confessed she had come to Nethervale in search of one of the simmering souls, and she was convinced we had one."

"Did you?"

"Nope." The necromancer pursed her lips in disappointment. "However, I took a bit of glee in the wicked irony of us learning the truth about the simmering souls from someone who'd come to hunt one we didn't have."

His eyes narrowed in disappointment at her bloodlust. "What else did you learn from this woman you tortured?"

"Nyx tortured her," Sophia corrected with a stern glare. "I had no choice but to follow orders. In the temple, you'll die if you disobey."

"Fine," he conceded, still unconvinced. "Is there more?"

"Quite a bit more. The Deathdread, much to our surprise, wasn't a legend at all." She toyed with the hem of her sleeve as she racked her brain. "It's real. They keep it locked away in Aeron's Tomb, deep in the Mountains of the Unwanted. Since Lightseers burn the bodies of anyone they kill, we assume it's just a vault of sorts with a foreboding name, true to Lightseer melodrama. They scoured the world for any of his notes and studied whatever they could find. Most of what they stole is hidden in a second vault deep beneath Lunestone, but not the Deathdread. The Lightseers can't open it, so they assume it's cursed and unsafe to keep close by."

"Interesting." Connor rubbed his jaw, admittedly surprised the wraith had kept silent for this long. Usually, he would've interjected with a snide comment by now. "What are the other simmering souls?"

"The only other simmering soul anyone has ever found is the Feral King. Most who see him don't live long enough to tell anyone about the experience. The few who survived reported a beast in the darkness with glowing eyes, and the man who fused with it went insane. No one has seen him in decades."

"And the other souls?" he prompted.

Her eyes creased with mirth, and she laughed. Her voice carried on the wind, surprisingly loud.

He tilted his head, a bit confused by her reaction. "What, exactly, is so funny?"

"It's nothing." Still smiling, she pinched the bridge of her nose and shook her head. "It's just—I tell you about an undead beast in the shadows that tries to kill everyone it sees, and you aren't even fazed. This thing drove a man mad, and you didn't even acknowledge the horror of it all. Yet, you claim you're no necromancer? This is normal for people like me, Connor. Is it normal for you, too?"

He sat with that for a moment. "I haven't had 'normal' in a long time."

A derisive little snort escaped her. "Apparently not."

"You were saying?" he prompted. The shadows grew longer with every second that passed, and a chill snaked through the trunks as the southern wind sighed.

They didn't have long until nightfall.

"Yes, yes, fine." She waved away his impatience with a flick of her slender wrist. "The other two simmering souls are a mystery. No one has found them, and any clue as to what they are or where Aeron hid them is locked away in the Deathdread. For you to find the others, you'll need that book."

He squinted at her, wondering where she had gotten that idea. "We're not hunting them down, Sophia."

"Right, of course." She rolled her eyes. "Whatever you say, Connor. Now, the only way to get the Deathdread is if we go to Aeron's Tomb, and the only way we can get there is to find a map through the Mountains of the Unwanted. That means to get what we want, we need to coerce a Lightseer Viceroy into helping us."

"And what do *we* want?" he asked, emphasizing the word she had chosen.

We, as if they were a true team.

As if he trusted her.

As if she cared about his survival at all.

"Yes, *we*." Her eyes narrowed, silently daring him to challenge her on this.

With his broad shoulders squared, he trained his stern glare on her face and took an intimidating step closer. "And what do you want besides the bloody beauties? Tell me why you're so interested in the simmering souls."

She frowned. Given her level of skill, it had probably been years since anyone had ordered her to do anything. The necromancer hesitated, and for a moment, it seemed as though she wouldn't answer.

He studied her intently, waiting for her to back out of their bargain. If she wanted her blood-drenched flowers, she would give him the information he needed.

That was the deal, pure and simple.

A pause before answering. A twitch in the muscle by her eye. A quick breath that caught in her throat, like she couldn't get enough air.

All tells of brewing deceit. In the pubs and taverns on his travels, he'd learned the hard way to weed out the cheats from the decent men.

He rubbed the stubble on his jaw as he silently dared her to lie.

Sophia groaned with irritation, surrendering. "Yes, all right. Listen, every necromancer knows about Aeron Zacharias. Every necromancer dreams of finding one of the simmering souls. They crave the power. They crave the legend that surrounds them. I'm no different."

"And what legend is that, exactly?"

They had long since delved into the waters of that which he didn't understand, but she couldn't be allowed to figure that out. To ensure he got the truth from her, she could never figure out what he did and didn't know.

"Those who have a simmering soul are said to be immortal." She bit her lip as she studied him, those dark eyes of hers narrowing with envy. "It's said they'll be gifted with power beyond human comprehension—if they can survive it, of course. If the soul doesn't drive them insane."

A small frown broke through his otherwise stony composure.

"Like many necromancers, I've been hunting the simmering souls for years," she confessed. "I was close, too. As part of the Nethervale elite, I had access to archives other necromancers can only dream of." A wistful smile pulled at her lips as she looked off into the woods. "Even with the horror I witnessed and suffered behind those walls, I had so much."

"Why'd you leave?"

She grimaced, and her body instantly froze. Her eyes glossed over, and her smile quickly became an unsettling scowl. The creases in her brow deepened in the long shadows of the coming night.

He had seen that expression before—namely, on the widows and orphans wandering the streets along the southern road. People who had been tossed aside glared at the world like that, perfectly justified in their bitterness.

He knew that life all too well.

"It's fine." He waved his hand to dismiss the question. It didn't really matter, and he didn't need her to delve into the depths of her soul to speak on a topic that clearly caused her pain.

Another chill swept through the canopy, and Sophia wrapped her arms around her torso for warmth. "We need to find Richard Beaumont. Once we capture and interrogate him, he'll give us the answers we need."

"Beaumont?" Connor chuckled in disbelief. "As in a member of the Beaumont crime family?"

"You heard me correctly." The necromancer glared into the woods as the shadows between the trees darkened. "Beaumont, as in the most dangerous crime family in Saldia."

He groaned with frustration, certain this had to be a joke. "Isn't their motto simply, 'Vengeance'? Why in the blazes would we kidnap one of them?"

"My sources say Richard weaseled his way into the Lightseer Chamber not long ago." Sophia picked at a loose piece of bark on the oak beside her. "He's the youngest to ever get access to the restricted rooms in Lunestone. If anyone has information about Aeron and the simmering souls, it's him, and he will be the easiest of the Viceroys to break. The others have strong security and a lifetime of experience in guarding secrets, but he's still new and painfully self-absorbed. He thinks he's untouchable. He believes no one would dare come after him because he's a Beaumont. It's made him cocky, and that gives us a window of opportunity."

"How do you know so much about this man? Is he one of your contacts?"

"Not quite." She frowned, pursing her lips together as she stared again into the trees.

Connor shifted his weight as he studied her. "From the way you're talking about him, I'd say he was something more to you. Someone significant."

Her eyes flashed with anger, and she stiffened.

"Lover?" he guessed.

"Hell no," she spat.

"You hate him," Connor observed. "Why?"

"I don't have to explain myself to you."

"You're suggesting we kidnap someone I've never even met and, in doing so, we would risk angering an entire crime family. Therefore, Sophia, you very much *do* need to explain yourself to me."

A vein throbbed in her temple, and she paced the patches of grass between the trees like a wild beast in a cage.

"He did something to you," Connor guessed as he studied the deep and bitter lines in her forehead. "Is that it? You hate him this much because he did something horrible to you, and you want to make him pay for it."

"And?" she snapped. "Don't pretend you've never wanted revenge."

Her comment stirred memories buried deep in his soul, and he quickly shoved them back in their place.

"This isn't about revenge," he replied. "This is about gathering information. You can have all the revenge you want after this is over. Right now, you have to focus."

She shook her head. "Fine, you caught me, but revenge will just be a bonus. Based on the letters I read before I left Nethervale, he is guaranteed to have the information we need. That solves our problem, just as I promised, but we can't let him live after the interrogation. If we do, he will tell everyone where we're going, and there will be an army waiting to stop us."

Connor shook his head, astonished at her bloodlust. "There's almost always another way. We can ask decoy questions to throw him off. We can hide our faces. Don't assume I'm going to murder everyone we interrogate. I don't kill unless it's deserved."

"Oh, it's deserved." Her nose crinkled with hate. "I've known for years how to get him to talk, but what's stopped me is finding a way to speak to him in private. I never had the resources before, or the manpower." Her gaze wandered over Connor's body before she returned her attention to the woods around them. "I can brew a Hackamore potion, and we can force it down his throat. He won't have a choice but to tell us everything we want to know."

"You actually have the reagents for a truth potion?" he asked, piecing together her plan.

"No," she confessed. "But the shops in Oakenglen do."

"Let me see if I understand." He rubbed his face and laughed at the absurdity of her plan. "You want us to walk into the Capital—right into the homeland of a king the Lightseers probably think I killed—and interrogate one of their Viceroys beneath their noses?"

"Yes, that's exactly what I'm saying."

"That's reckless." He groaned in frustration. "How do you know he's even there?"

"I know the exact brothel he goes to every other night. He has a favorite whore and often—" Sophia squeezed her eyes shut and took a steadying breath. "Never mind. The point is, I know where to find him. Besides, what else can we do? We need a map to Aeron's Tomb and a way into the mountains. Where else can we get that information?"

As Connor thought it over, the distant campfire popped and crackled in the growing night. Like it or not, he didn't have a better plan. As Sophia had pointed out, chaos had quickly become his new normal, anyway.

"He rarely leaves the Capital." Sophia's voice shattered the quiet lull. "There's no way for us to intercept him outside of the city because he never travels by road."

"What about on his way to Lunestone? That's not in the Capital, if I remember my maps correctly."

"It's not, but from what I've heard, Richard uses the Rifts to travel to and from the Lightseer stronghold."

"Damn it," he muttered.

Her eyebrows shot up her head, and her lips parted in shock. "Truthfully, I wasn't expecting you to know about the Rifts."

His eyes darted toward hers, and he let the silence be his answer. The more she debated what he did and didn't know, the more truth he could wring from her.

Whatever her connection to Richard Beaumont, she clearly had old wounds that would cloud her judgment in an interrogation. The Beaumonts influenced or controlled much of the Hazeltide economy, and they maintained their power through fear.

Given the rumors that had traveled south about that family over the years, any Beaumont had likely done enough to earn a swift death. Still, it wasn't his place to pass judgement, especially without knowing more about Richard's alleged crimes.

They had time to think of a better plan to throw the Lightseers off their scent, so he could figure that part out later. For now, he didn't have an alternative to get to Aeron's Tomb, so interrogating Richard Beaumont would have to do.

"Captain?" Murdoc shouted.

Connor peered around an oak to get a view of the fire. The flames' orange glow flickered against the former Blackguard's face. He set one foot on a log and wiped his blood-drenched hands on a rag.

"Anything else about the souls I should know?" Connor asked Sophia under his breath.

As the chilly spring night took root and the shadows turned black, she shivered and shook her head.

He gestured for her to follow, and they returned to the camp. The last threads of sunlight snaked through the canopy above, giving them one last chance to find cover before night took the forest.

The rusty bite of blood wafted through the air, stronger with every step closer to the campfire—a beacon to every hungry thing waiting in its den. In the shadows just beyond the firelight, a rib bone glowed briefly white. Roughly hewn steaks lay beside the deer's silhouette, stacked atop each other and ready for Sophia's magic.

"We're going to Oakenglen," Connor announced.

Murdoc flinched and took a step back in surprise. His eyes pinched shut when he saw them, and he shook his head. "Stop doing that."

Sophia's red lips twisted into a smile. "Nervous?"

He pointed a blood-stained finger at them. "You two are eerily quiet."

"Are you done?" Connor asked with a nod to the buck.

"Almost." The former Blackguard knelt beside the beast.

"Do you need help, or—"

"I've got to earn my keep, remember?" Murdoc gestured for him to sit. "Now, what's this about Oakenglen?"

"There's something we need to get, and we have to find a way in." Connor sat again on his rock as he waited for Murdoc to finish. "The question is how. I heard the Capital requires papers to enter, and I haven't had mine in years."

Burned up in the blaze, back in Kirkwall.

Sophia nodded. "All the Capitals require papers, and we can't get glamours out here in the towns. Not good ones, anyway. We would have to walk by soldiers that might know our faces. Murkwell has a secret tavern where we can buy papers or possibly find a guide to get us in through a hidden entrance, if we're willing to spend some money."

"I don't trust a stranger who's been paid before we get what we want." Connor scratched the back of his head, debating his options. "Can we hide in a caravan? Maybe sneak our way into a traveling troupe of some sort?"

The necromancer crossed her arms and raised a skeptical eyebrow at the idea. "You want us to hide in a circus?"

Connor shrugged. "Whatever works."

"It's too much of a risk. The guards check every nook and cranny, and they'll look at everyone's papers. That's why there's always a long line at the gates."

"I might have a way in," Murdoc announced as he tossed aside a deer leg.

"You might?" Connor frowned. "Or you do?"

The former Blackguard wiped the back of his hand across his brow, and it left a thin streak of blood on his forehead. "I do, fine, yes. It's a back way into the city through a drainage tunnel. If I show you the way in, though, neither of you can judge me. Do you swear?"

Connor studied the man in silence, not altogether sure he liked where this was going.

Murdoc tilted his head, waiting. "Come now, both of you. Swear."

"I swear," he answered hesitantly.

"I promise nothing," Sophia said.

The former Blackguard set his bloodstained hand on his heart, and his brows furrowed with mock pain. "My dear, don't test our love like this!"

"Murdoc, we need a way in," Connor interjected. "Are you absolutely certain this will work? Is this route of yours secure?"

"It's an old access tunnel that almost no one knows about. It'll work."

"We'll at least take a look, then." Connor rubbed his eyes as he stifled a yawn. "Let's get some sleep. We're going to skip Murkwell and keep to the woods. Staying in the trees will slow us down, but it means we won't run into that Starling woman again."

"Works for me," Murdoc admitted.

"Good." Connor stretched, and a joint popped in his shoulder. "With the delay, we still have a few days before we reach the Capital. Murdoc, wrap up with the deer. We can't keep a fire going into the night, or we'll attract the blightwolves." He paused "Or worse."

The ruffian chuckled. "What's worse than the blightwolves?"

He looked over his shoulder to find Murdoc crouching beside the deer's carcass. "Remember when we left Bradford and you couldn't see the path?"

"Yeah."

"Remember what I said?"

Murdoc frowned in confusion. "You said it was for the best."

"Exactly." Connor stood and grabbed his pack off the ground. "The same is true for the Ancient Woods at any point along the road. Stay in the trees at night, put out your fire, and try not to look down at whatever passes by."

He hoisted the bag over his shoulder and scanned the shadows around them. The dead deer would draw all sorts of things from the hidden crags and hollows. The three of them needed to be as far from the animal as possible before that happened, same as any sane mortal without a death wish.

Danger lurked in every shadow, and something out in the night inevitably wanted to eat them all. It was the way of the world, and he'd never known anything else.

CHAPTER FORTY-ONE
CONNOR

A growl rumbled through the night, like thunder on the horizon. Connor snapped awake. With his arms still crossed over his chest as he sat in the canopy, he listened. The trunk's bark scratched at his back through his clothes, and he stifled the urge to shift his weight.

The leaves around him fluttered in the endless gale of the southern forest, but the woods had otherwise gone silent. At some point in the night, the cicadas had stopped singing. Nothing scampered along the ground. Even the enormous horned owls had gone silent, spooked by something even bigger.

He knew this kind of quiet all too well. It always rolled through the woodland ahead of approaching danger.

Murdoc snored softly in the tree next to his. A vine around the man's waist anchored him to the oak high above the forest floor. In the next tree over, Sophia slept like a corpse. The vines around her waist kept her in place, but it hardly seemed necessary. While Murdoc twisted in his seat, his head rolling along the bark as he tried to get comfortable, Sophia never once moved. She didn't adjust. She didn't twitch. She didn't even sigh with the wind as it tussled her dark hair. Only the subtle flutter of her eyes as she dreamed served as a hint that she hadn't died in her sleep.

How odd.

The charred hint of smoke spiraled through the air, and Connor tensed on impulse. This far from the towns, smoke could only come from one of four places—a wildfire sparked by a lightning storm, a farmhouse's hearth, a campfire, or bandits on a raid.

It hadn't rained in days, and their last lightning storm had been weeks ago. It couldn't have been a wildfire. Given their proximity to the road, the nearest hamlet would've been miles away. This couldn't have been some harmless farmhouse fire, either.

Someone had foolishly left their campfire lit. That, or bandits had thrown torches into caravans to burn evidence of their robbery.

Regardless, the blightwolves would notice.

A muted conversation rolled past, barely audible over the roar of the wind. From the pitch and tone, he isolated a man's voice and a woman's.

Campfire, then. Thieves wandered the road in packs and kept silent. Tonight, some poor fools who didn't know better had built a fire for warmth or to protect themselves from the monsters in these woods.

Little did they know fire acted like a beacon in the pitch-black forest. It simply drew the monsters closer.

If they didn't put out the campfire and get into the trees, something would eat them.

Connor ran a hand through his hair, debating his options. The last time he'd rushed to someone's rescue, he'd fused with a wraith and unleashed hell on himself. Every ounce of self-preservation in his bones warned him to stay in place and let the fools learn their lesson the hard way.

As he closed his eyes and tried to go back to sleep, however, his mind buzzed. The bones leftover from his hunt would attract all sorts of beasts in the night. Though he had buried them far from the road, nothing deterred a southern predator for long. If these strangers died, he would be at least partially responsible.

Damn it all.

He grabbed the branch beneath him and slid off the limb. With practiced ease from years of sleeping in the canopy, he eased his way to the ground and knelt with his knee in the dirt.

In the silent forest, he took a precious moment to listen for danger.

His ear twitched, but he heard nothing. No more growls. No fluttering of wings. Only the rush of leaves shivering in the wind.

The muffled conversation floated again through the air, and he darted toward it. As he wove through the trees, he debated what to tell these idiots. It seemed ludicrous to think anyone could've been so foolhardy, and no reprimand he could think of felt severe enough.

The air around him shifted, and the Wraith King materialized beside him as he ran. The ghoul easily kept pace and darted around a tree to avoid hitting it. *You wish to save them?*

"I suppose so," Connor said under his breath as he cleared a log.

And what is there to gain?

Connor shook his head, his arms pumping as he ran. "It's not always about what you gain."

The ghost grunted, an odd sound of blended confusion and surprise.

"Stay hidden. I don't want them to see you."

Fine, the ghost said. *Try not to be too stupid, Magnuson.*

"Thanks," he muttered. "Good advice."

An orange glow illuminated a small clearing just off the main road, and the shadows of two heads danced across the trunks in the flickering light.

Earlier, he and his team had passed through this clearing on the way to their trees. From what he could recall, the deer bones were only about thirty yards away.

These two didn't have long.

As he neared, more details came into view between gaps in the trees. A young man with blond hair sat beside a young woman with long brown curls. They both gazed into the fire, and she sighed as she rested her cheek on his shoulder.

Kids. Barely eighteen, if that.

Without pausing to even put his scarf over his face, Connor jumped over a bush and landed in the clearing. In unison, their eyes darted toward him.

The girl gasped and fell backward. The boy's arm tightened around her shoulder, and the subtle gesture kept her from falling into the dirt. The two of them gaped at him in silent shock.

Connor pointed to the campfire. "What the hell are you doing? Put that out immediately and get into the trees!"

"The trees?" The girl's brow furrowed, as though he were the only ludicrous fool in the meadow. "Why in the Fates' name would we sleep in the trees?"

The young man stood and drew a dagger in the scabbard on his waist. "Whatever game you're playing, you can't trick us."

"We don't have time for this." Connor nodded to a nearby tree with branches low enough for the girl to climb, even with her thick skirts. "Get into the canopy. There are things in this wood you don't want to—"

The low growl that had woken Connor rumbled again through the woods, closer than before. It floated through the air from every direction, a deadly thunder that carried teeth and hunger on its tailwind.

"What was that?" the young woman asked, her voice barely a whisper.

Paralyzed by their fear, neither of the kids moved. They gaped into the shadows, frozen in place.

With an irritated groan, Connor stalked over to the boy and smacked the dagger out of his hand. It hit the ground with a thud. The kid flinched at the lightning-fast movement and gaped down at his blade.

"If I wanted to kill or rob you, I'd have done it already." Connor glared down at the kid and pointed again to the tree. "Now, get the hell into that canopy!"

The young man gulped. "Yes, sir."

He and the young woman ran over to the old oak, their pack and blankets abandoned beside the fire. Connor stood guard at the base of the oak and surveyed the forest while the two of them climbed at a painfully slow rate.

Though the fire cast strange shadows that kept him from seeing into the darkness beyond the clearing, putting it out now would only slow their climb. Besides, judging by the growls, whatever hunted them had already found them.

"Faster," he ordered, his eyes still locked on the forest.

The young woman's skirt caught on one of the branches, and her boot slipped as she tried to balance. She screamed as her grip loosened, but the young man grabbed her hand at the last moment.

Together, they sighed with relief. Though her hand shook, she reached again for the next branch as they continued their climb.

Connor glanced up into the tree as the two of them paused roughly twelve feet in the air. "Higher. Blightwolves are big."

"Blightwolves?" The young woman paused her climb and peered down at him. "Are you—"

"Will you climb the damn tree so I can leave?" Connor snapped.

She gulped and returned her attention to the branches above her.

This couldn't have been worse. On the ground, Connor was a sitting duck. He didn't want to spend the rest of the night in the same tree as these two, nor did he want his team to think he'd left them.

Even now, given their painfully slow climb, he probably wouldn't have time to get back to his own camp before he became something's dinner.

He had already lost the window of opportunity to return to his tree. Apparently, he had to keep these kids company tonight.

Damn it.

Connor grabbed the nearest limb and hoisted himself up after the children. A tree like this gave him plenty of foot and handholds, so he caught up to them in mere moments. The firelight cast a flickering glow across his boots. Their blanket and pack still rested against the log by the fire, and for now, nothing stumbled into the clearing.

He doubted it would remain empty for long.

"Move like your life depends on it," he told the young man. "Because it does."

The boy nodded and reached for the girl, who took his hand. He hoisted her onto the branch beside him, and together, they stared higher into the tree's canopy.

"You wanted an adventure," he whispered to her. "Does this suffice?"

"Oh, hush, you," she muttered.

Connor glanced down at the ground. The firelight danced across his boots as he entered the thicker section of branches, but they still needed to climb another ten feet or so before he would consider them safe.

As the girl reached for the next branch, an ear-splitting howl ripped through the air.

Roughly three feet above Connor, both of the kids flinched. The girl gasped and wrapped her hands around the nearest branch, but in his shock, the boy's foot slipped along the bark. He cursed under his breath, and he teetered on his heels. His hands flailed through the air as he tried to find something to grab. Connor reached out to catch him, but the young woman clutched the boy's sleeve before he could fall. She stifled a scream as she struggled to pull him upright. When the boy finally latched onto a branch again, he let out a shaky breath of relief.

Growls rumbled through the trees from all around them. The thunder of paws racing across the dirt stirred up the night. Silhouettes darted through the oaks just beyond the firelight.

The blightwolves.

"I changed my mind," Connor muttered to the wraith. "You can reveal yourself and help now."

You want me to kill these beautiful creatures? Still unseen, the Wraith King scoffed at the very idea. *Never. However, if you need a diversion, I'd be willing to knock the children to the ground to give you a chance to escape.*

Connor grimaced. "Never mind."

"Never mind what?" the young man asked.

"You have another five feet to go." He pointed to the canopy. "Stop talking and get to it."

A silver blur darted into the clearing and ran toward their tree. Even larger than a horse, the silver mound of fur and teeth cast a long shadow on the grass as it sped closer.

"Go!" Connor shouted, his eyes locked on the creature even as he gestured for the kids to hurry. "Faster!"

The creature hit their oak, and the wood beneath them groaned from the force of the blightwolf's blow. The tree bent under the beast's weight. The crack of snapping timber reverberated through the night, and the creature stood on its hind legs as it leaned against the trunk.

The girl screamed and clutched the nearest branch as their tree threatened to topple. The young man said something, but Connor tuned him out. A low growl rolled through the branches as the beast paused, going eerily still as it stared up at him with icy blue eyes.

A blightwolf.

Teeth the length of a dagger's blade. Ears pinned against its head. Massive paws, each the size of his face.

Its thick claws, black as the shadows around them, peeled back chunks of fresh wood as it growled. In the firelight, its thick silver fur glimmered like miniature spikes of metal sticking from its hide. With a face as large as Connor's chest, this beast could've eaten horses whole. Wrinkles along its snout creased as it snarled up at him.

He'd never seen one this close—never wanted to, for that matter.

"What the hell is that?" The young man's voice broke with fear.

The blightwolf's gaze shifted to the boy, and the beast jumped. Its claws dug massive gouges into the wood inches below Connor's feet, and its enormous jaws snapped at the air. It bit a branch, and the wood broke instantly in its teeth.

"Higher!" Connor shouted.

The two kids scrambled up the tree as the blightwolf snarled beneath them. On her way into the canopy, the girl's skirt caught on a broken limb. She whimpered and tugged at the fabric with one hand while she desperately clutched a branch with the other. As the beast leaned harder against the tree, the old oak shivered.

The girl slipped, and she screamed as she fell.

"Ellie!" The young man reached for her, but her fingertips brushed his as she failed to grab his hand.

As she passed him, Connor reached for her. His balance shifted, and though he grabbed her wrist, he slipped off his branch as well.

With a strained yell, he threw her upward as the lower branches cracked beneath his back. She landed hard against the trunk, and her nails ripped into the bark as she frantically clawed for something to grab. Her hand finally wrapped around a branch, and she let out a panicked little gasp as she clung to it.

Connor, however, fell.

Several branches broke under his weight, and one smacked the blightwolf in the face as the beast snapped at him. It growled with rage and dug its teeth into the bark as Connor sailed past.

His shoulder hit the ground first, and he instinctively tucked his head toward his chest as he rolled. Pain splintered down his spine, and he bit back an agonized yell as rocks in the soil scraped against his arms and chest. His boots kicked up dirt as he slowed his momentum, and large clumps rained into the fire. The flame sputtered, but it ultimately held.

No time to recover.

He had to move.

The silver blightwolf by the tree growled as it shook the broken branch in its teeth. It cast the limb aside, and the log shattered against a nearby trunk. The great beast shifted its ice blue eyes toward Connor as he knelt and waited to see what it would do next.

If he ran, it would chase him. Somehow, he had to buy himself enough time to get up another tree before it ripped out his throat.

It lowered its head and snarled as it stalked across the meadow. Howls sang through the air around the clearing. Silhouettes darted through the shadows beyond the firelight.

"I could use some help," Connor said again to the wraith. "Do you really want to fuse with one of those kids?"

The wraith let out an exasperated groan.

When the old ghost didn't appear, Connor summoned his dark blades into his palms. The blackfire rolled along the steel, and as he spun them in his hands, the blightwolf paused. Its cold eyes darted toward the swords, studying them with a hint of curiosity. Its ears relaxed. Instead of closing the gap between them, the wolf circled the edge of the field.

"We finally found you." Its words rumbled from the depths of its throat, barely indistinguishable from a growl. They hummed in the air like whispers on the wind, and at first, he thought he'd imagined them.

He stiffened with surprise. "You can talk?"

The blightwolf laughed, the sound rough and hoarse as it nodded. "We do a great many things."

Without even the slightest hint of warning, the creature charged him. The silver blur raced toward him, too fast to see. Muscle memory took over, and he trusted his body's aim as he swung the blades. His steel sliced through the wolf's jaw, and the blackfire scorched its metallic fur.

The blightwolf yelped and retreated to the edge of the field. It growled as the fur around the bloody gash on its face burned, and it narrowed its eyes in anger. Howls from the trees around them pierced the night, stirring the forest into a frenzy.

This silver wolf had to be their alpha. Since the other blightwolves hadn't yet charged, they must've been waiting for the signal to attack.

"Good reflexes," the silver wolf snarled. "Quick to act. Curious scent, like death. Like us. To eat you or not? What a dilemma."

Connor spun the blades in his hands, ready for the next attack. "I vote against you eating me."

It laughed again, the rough noise like a man's dying breath.

The pack's cry faded, and the rumbling thunder of dozens of growling beasts replaced it. The silhouettes darting through the shadows slowed and, one by one, faced him. Teeth glowed in the shadows along the edge of the clearing as they approached.

Blades at the ready and with his blackfire roaring, Connor surveyed the chaos. The blightwolves inched their way into the light from every direction. Claws dug into the dirt with every step. Wolves of every color inched their way closer. Black fur, like obsidian spikes. White fur, like icy daggers. Brown fur, like spears of splintered wood. Teeth bared. Haunches raised. Eyes, glowing in the night.

The perfect carnivores.

The silver blightwolf stepped on the fire, and the flames extinguished with a hiss beneath its mighty paw. As the light faded, Connor's vision adjusted instantly to the darkness.

From the shadows in every direction around him, dozens of eyes glowed green as the beasts sealed off any chance of escape.

The silver blightwolf bolted again toward Connor, its body nothing but a silhouette in the pitch black. He swung, but it ducked out of the way this time. It bit his shoulder, and he stifled a yell as hot blood rolled down his arm. He drove his blade into the base of its neck, and the wolf howled in agony. Teeth impaled his arm, and the beast threw him across the field.

He slid to a stop. Before he could even get to his feet, the wolf pressed its paw into his chest. It weighed on him like a boulder and pinned him to the ground. With a pained yell, he swung at its leg. Though the blade cut through its fur and drew blood, the beast merely growled. Its claw dug into his chest in a wordless warning to be still.

As the claw plowed into his sternum, mind-numbing agony shot through him like a bolt of lightning. His feet went numb. His grip on his sword loosened, but he forced himself to keep hold.

Never one to surrender, he pushed through the pain and swung again.

The wolf snapped at his blade. The blackfire crackled across its jaw. The beast snarled and yanked the weapon from his hand. His sword dissolved into a puff of black smoke, and the wolf shook its head to put out the burning embers on its face.

Get up, his father had always said.

Survive.

Unbearable pain rocked through him. A groggy haze blistered through his head. He grimaced in agony, determined to fight to the end, and he raised his remaining sword. The blightwolf bared its teeth at him. Jaw tensed, he pressed the tip of his blade to the base of its neck.

Nose to nose, they glared at each other.

Stuck at an impasse, each daring the other to act first.

The rumble of the wolves' growling churned the night, as raw and violent as thunder over the ocean—but, bit by bit, the snarling faded.

In the lull that followed, the mood of the forest shifted.

The air thickened, like a fog had rolled over them. The silver wolf paused, and its claw lifted from his chest. He sucked in a greedy breath as its gaze darted behind him, toward something he couldn't see.

He arched his back enough to steal a glance at whatever had caught the wolf's attention. From this angle, his world had turned upside down, but he could still make sense of it. Through his blood-stained hair, he spotted the specter hovering at the edge of the clearing. Black mist radiated from the silhouette, and the blightwolves around it stepped back to give it space.

The wraith.

Connor studied the silver wolf's face, but the alpha didn't so much as glance down. Each of the beasts watched the dead man with the same curiosity as a dog waiting for a command from its master.

I will tell you what to say, the wraith explained. *Do as I say, and you will survive.*

He gritted his teeth at the idea of obeying the brutal warlord, but the silver wolf's claw tapped against his chest. He swallowed his pride and simply nodded.

Tell them we are not unlike them.

"We're not unlike you," he echoed, staring up at the silver wolf.

Its gaze darted to him, and it brushed its cold nose against his as it stared him down.

Listening.

Aware.

We're creatures of death as well.

A muscle twitched in his neck as the blightwolf's claw dug deeper into his chest. "We're creatures of death as well."

Of murder.

He grimaced, unwilling to agree. Hating the idea of surrendering to the hate that fueled the wraith.

But he wasn't wrong.

After fusing with the ghost, more death had followed him in a few weeks than in the last few years combined. The thought stung him like a hornet to the soul, and his shoulders relaxed despite the massive paw on his chest.

"Of murder," he admitted.

You have our respect, and as long as you give us the same, you will have our loyalty in this lawless world. It is a gift we rarely give.

Connor met the blightwolf's glowing eyes. It studied him, a soft rumble in its throat as it waited.

"You have my respect," he conceded. "As long as you give me the same, you have an ally in a world that wants you all dead. It's a gift I don't often give."

"Interesting." As the blightwolf spoke, the stench of rotting meat rolled off its tongue. Connor suppressed the urge to gag and forced himself to hold the beast's gaze.

Around him, the blightwolves growled. A few snarled as they inched closer, apparently too hungry to wait for their alpha to make the kill. A white wolf approached at a slow trot, and its tongue darted over its teeth as it eyed Connor's leg.

The silver wolf snapped at the intruder, and the white wolf slunk back to the edge of the forest with the others.

"The wind tells us everything that happens in our forest." The silver blightwolf returned its attention to Connor. "We will wait to see what it says about you."

With its mouth still in front of Connor's face, the beast howled into the night. He winced as the shriek ripped through his enhanced ears, but he forced himself to stay still.

The others joined in, their powerful cry painfully loud. The wind stilled. The trees held their breath. The ground rumbled, as if the very land trembled at the sound.

A deafening rumble of paws across the dirt mingled with the howling. To his surprise, the pack dispersed. The wolves along the edge of the clearing darted off into the forest, leaving him alone with their alpha.

The weight of the silver wolf's paw on his chest lifted, and it darted off into the shadows with its pack.

At first, Connor could only lay there and listen to the rumble of the blightwolves as they charged off into the night. He stared at a hole in the canopy, at the smattering of stars against the black blanket of the sky, and he drank in breath after surreal breath.

It took a while before he could feel his feet again, but when he did, he sat upright. His grip on the remaining blade loosened, and it disappeared in a rush of churning black fog.

That had been close.

Far too close.

He looked over his shoulder, but the wraith had disappeared.

To his astonishment, the ghoul had saved his life. Whether it had been to prevent himself from fusing with one of the children or whether the old ghost had truly meant to do it, the fact remained—the wraith had done a good deed.

"Are you alive?" the young man asked from the tree.

The young woman sobbed. "Bless the Fates, I hope they didn't eat him."

"I'm fine." Still unclear on what had just happened, Connor rubbed his face to get some feeling back into his body after the bizarre turn of events.

"Oh, thank goodness." The girl let out a sigh of relief. "We're coming down to help you."

"Don't you dare move," he ordered. "You stay right where you are."

He pushed himself to his feet and staggered as he caught his balance. His body hummed with the energy that usually helped him in a fight, but now it had nowhere to go. After such a close brush with death, the unreal flood of shock and awe still pumped through every vein.

"Why did they come?" the young man asked.

Connor kicked the dirt. "Your damn fire, that's why. If you absolutely must travel the road at night, you need to snuff out the campfire. Leaving it going only attracts the things that want to eat you or the people who want to rob you. Sleep in the trees to avoid the blightwolves and other predators on the ground. Next time, travel in a larger group or hire a sellsword to protect you. Or, better yet, get to a city before dark and find an inn."

They were all lessons he had learned the hard way. He might as well save them a bit of pain and stolen coin.

"Stay in the tree until dawn." He staggered out of the field, ready to be done with these two and finally get some sleep.

"You're the Shade, aren't you?" the boy asked.

"The what?" He paused midstride and stared up at the tree.

The young man sat on a branch high in the canopy, but Connor could still make out the boy's silhouette in the darkness. "The hero who protects people."

Connor laughed and rubbed his eyes. "I haven't heard of that folk story, kid, but trust me. I'm no folk hero."

"You are to us. Thank you for what you did. Let us make it up to you. In the pack by the fire, there's coin. Not just coppers or silver, but gold. It's yours. All of it." The young man pointed toward the fire pit, where the silhouette of a bag lay beside the rock they'd been sitting on.

A generous offer, but it was money two young people like them probably couldn't afford to give.

He turned his back on them. "Keep it."

"Wait!" the young man shouted. "Wait, we need to do something for you! You must need *something*."

Connor waved away the comment with an exhausted flick of his hand. "Don't be too loud. The blightwolves might come back."

He stumbled into the shadows between the trees, his ears twitching at every snapped twig or breath of wind through the leaves above him. As the surge of disbelief finally faded, his stumbles became a light jog. He darted through the woods, keen to get back to the relative safety of his tree.

The blightwolves had let him go once tonight, but that didn't mean they'd do it a second time.

Magnuson.

The ghost's voice swam through his heady daze, and at first, he simply ignored it.

Listen, damn you.

A swirl of jet-black fog sank through the trees in front of him, and the wraith's skull emerged from the gloom.

Connor skidded to a stop, his boots kicking up dirt as he stopped inches from the ghost's bony teeth.

"What?" he hissed. "The wolves are out, and I for one would like to be in a tree."

The ghost chuckled. *Yes, you will need a Rectivane as soon as you return to camp. I will wake the sorceress.*

"That—huh." His shoulders relaxed at the unexpected gesture of kindness. "Thank you, actually."

I told you once that I am not a man of charity, but that I give rewards when they are earned.

"I remember." He rolled out his wrist, the magic of the blackfire blades still hot in his hands after their encounter with the blightwolves.

Tonight, you earned another reward.

The ghoul set the tip of his bony finger against the bloody gash in Connor's chest.

Searing pain shot clear to his toes, and he suppressed a strangled yell of agony as his jaw clenched shut on impulse. His breath caught in his throat. His ears rang. His mind splintered, and he couldn't even think.

His fingertips dug into his palms as he fought through the cloud of misery threatening to knock him unconscious. It took everything in him to simply remain on his feet, but he somehow managed.

Deep within his chest, something tore at his lungs. Tiny claws dug into his very bones as the wraith's magic fractured him, unrelenting and cruel.

As fast as it came, the torment faded. It disappeared in a rush, like light pouring into a dark room.

He couldn't see. He couldn't feel his legs. His world went stark white as his body reeled from what it had endured.

With a thud, he fell to his knees. Something heavy slammed into the dirt beside him. Warm metal weighed against his left forearm, like a pot recently set on a fire.

Pleasant. Soothing, even.

He blinked the murky daze from his vision. Bit by bit, color returned. The dark green shadows of the forest mingled with the soft blue glow of the moons. "Curse the Fates, you old fool. Can't you warn me before you do things like that?"

The ghost chuckled.

In his periphery, a hazy silhouette became a tree. The brown blur beneath him became dirt with a smattering of leaves skittering by. The ringing in his ear became the rush of the wind as it whispered through the canopy above.

As the world finally snapped into focus, Connor curled his fingers around a leather strap in his palm. A large, perfectly round shield sat on his forearm, and the air above it sizzled. As black as the night sky, the shield's face swam with thin ribbons of white and green light.

Not even Henry earned this reward, the ghoul cautioned.

Despite the twinge of pain in his chest and the hot blood rolling down his arm from the gash in his shoulder, Connor smiled. Not once in his life had he held something this finely made.

Moonlight glinted off the impossibly smooth metal as it hummed with a life of its own. He ran his fingers over the surface, and though the sizzling metal warmed his skin, it didn't burn.

This transcended even the blackfire blades.

"It's incredible," he admitted.

It is. It was my final creation.

"This was yours?"

The ghoul nodded. *Part of me lives in that shield, same as in the blades. In life and in death, it and I are one.*

"Wait." Connor shook his head, laughing. "Why do you show me these things *after* they'd be useful in a fight?"

The dead man turned his back and disappeared into the depths of the forest, though his grim voice echoed in Connor's mind. *Because a king shouldn't need magic to win. His natural grit carries him through. You have my blades and my shield because you earned them, Magnuson. Use them wisely.*

With that, the ghoul was gone.

Connor's smile fell, and his grip on the shield tightened. Despite the danger lurking in the woods, he gave himself a moment to simply stare after the ghoul and process the offhand comment.

Tonight, something had changed. What or why, he couldn't say, but the Saldian tides had shifted in more ways than one.

A jolt of pain stabbed him in the chest, and his face paled as he set his empty hand over the gash. After he got a Rectivane from Sophia, he could muse and debate the wraith's intentions all he wanted. For now, he needed to heal.

CONNOR

Once again perched in his oak at their makeshift campsite, Connor drank the last of the Rectivane potion Sophia had left for him in the crook of branches where he'd slept. Relief swam through him as the magic set to work. His joints popped. Twinges of pain splintered through his chest, but he let out a slow breath as he pushed through each ripple of agony.

He'd taken a few Rectivane draughts in his time, but none of them had worked this fast or this well. Whatever recipe she used far exceeded anything available to common folk like him.

The wraith's comment about the shield buzzed again through his brain. His brow creased with uncertainty as he studied the ground below.

A king shouldn't need magic to win.

Just as he'd practiced on his way back to camp, he clenched his fist. The shield snapped into existence amidst a swirling cloud of black smoke, its leather straps already tightened around his forearm and palm. The now-familiar sizzle of its warm metal crackled in the quiet night while the first of the crickets began to chirp again. He stretched his fingers wide, and on command, the shield dissolved into nothing.

Two blackfire blades and a shield, all humming with the magic of the undead.

Blightwolves with the power to speak.

A southern wind, carrying his scent to those who watched him closely.

"What a night," he muttered.

If not for the phantom fused to his soul, he might not have survived his run-in with the blightwolves. Perhaps the dead man didn't embody brutality as much as he wanted the world to believe.

CHAPTER FORTY-TWO
MURDOC

The night wore on, and the song of insects Murdoc didn't have names for trilled through the forest around him. His perch in the tree shifted with the southern wind, and his stomach churned as the branch he'd tied himself to creaked in the gust.

He'd come to the Ancient Woods to find his good death, but damn it all, he didn't want it to come from a steep plunge to the dirt below.

With a few measured breaths to stem the tide of nausea, he pretended to sleep and peered through one eye at the man in the tree next to his. While he watched, Connor summoned a shield from thin air. Black smoke swirled around the large circle of flawless metal like a fog from the afterlife, and ribbons of light snaked through its surface.

A jolt of surprise shot through Murdoc at the sight of this new enchantment, and it took immense effort to remain still. Though he kept his breathing even, he couldn't tell if he'd gotten away with appearing asleep.

Any sane man would've paled, aghast at the dark magic in his hands, but Connor—this man was something else.

Murdoc's new captain ran his fingertips along the curved shield as though it were a lover. He twisted his arm this way and that, examining every facet as the bewitched metal hummed with life. As quick as it had come, it vanished in another churning cloud of smoke. Connor leaned back against his tree and closed his eyes with a happy sigh.

Either he had kept this shield from Murdoc and Sophia, or he had discovered a new power out there in the woods tonight. True to form, the man had incredible abilities that evolved the longer Murdoc was around him—the sort of magic that had a dark tint to it.

The sort Murdoc would've hunted in his days as a Blackguard.

During his years in the brotherhood, Murdoc had developed an intuition for these things. Necromancy, death magic, the darkness in a man's heart—they never escaped him, even now that he'd been without a mission for almost a full year.

His chest panged with longing for the good old days, and he gave up pretending to spy on the mysterious man in the next tree over.

With Connor asleep, Murdoc tugged out the secret flask hidden beneath his shirt, one he'd been draining whenever the other two looked away. He would need to refill the moment they reached a market, as he'd been drinking a lot more since joining this ragtag little band of misfits.

His hand shook as he pressed the cold metal to his lips. The flask stung like the bite of frost in the already chilly night. The whiskey followed shortly after, burning his throat and warming his body.

He shifted his weight in the awkward crook in the tree. The branch pressed hard against his tailbone, and a knob on the limb hit his spine. He winced and let out a string of muffled curses as a jolt of pain shot down his back.

Barbaric, honestly. Sleeping in a damned *tree*.

As he adjusted his weight on the rock-hard branch beneath him, the hilt of the sword still strapped to his hip pressed into his side. Instinctively, he grabbed the pommel, his fingers wrapping around his last memento of his time with the Blackguard.

They would've killed him if they ever discovered he'd stolen it back, but he didn't care. It had been forged for him, and it was the one fine thing he still had to his name.

Murdoc stowed the flask in its hiding place under his shirt and tilted the sheathed weapon toward him so that he could examine the black stone embedded at the base of the hilt. A bit of the soot had been rubbed off in his fight with the vougel, and a dull green gem peeked through the black smears masking its enchanted nature.

With a wary glance at Connor, Murdoc pulled out a small pouch from the pocket on his pants. His fingers tugged apart the strings as he pressed against the black stains along the edges of the well-worn cloth to open it. Inside, his meager supply of soot pooled at the bottom.

He pinched a bit between his fingertips and rubbed it on the spellgust gem to properly hide its nature. The magic in this one had faded to almost nothing, but it still had a little power left.

Just enough.

At least scoundrels like him were able to use enchanted items other people made for them. Without the enchantments on this blade, he would've failed over half his missions. The Blackguard brotherhood had always used magic to fight magic, even if they'd never told the public.

Out of habit, he patted the enchanted Bluntmar chain hidden in one of the larger pockets in his pants. The metal jingled, and it had a bit more magic left than his sword.

A scoundrel, prepared to battle the magic of mortal gods if the need arose—and he suspected it soon would.

Connor and Sophia didn't think he could sense the secret war between them, but he'd always preferred to go unnoticed. The world had underestimated him from the day he was born, and he'd found ways to use that to his advantage.

Both of his teammates had power enough to tempt the Fates. The moment the wraith had first appeared in that field, Murdoc had known he would be in it for the long haul no matter what Connor truly was—because the man wasn't human.

Not anymore.

His new captain had saved his life, and since he had never much valued the air he breathed, he owed a debt to Connor. The wraith made this man a target, and Murdoc would give his life if that was what it took to even the score.

He reached again for his flask and took a greedy sip.

A former Blackguard, defending the darkness he used to hunt. He never would've seen this coming, but the Fates had sent this man to him, and it was a challenge he would face like a soldier.

The booze seared the back of his throat, and he suppressed a wheezing cough. People did all sorts of gruesome things to obtain magic like Connor's, and part of him wondered what his new boss had done to get it. Men didn't usually come into raw power like that by honest means, but Murdoc wasn't a Blackguard anymore.

There was no need to stalk the things in the shadows now. Besides, no one wanted his help. No one had appreciated his sacrifice but his brothers in arms, and he'd grown resentful of the civilians who had slept soundly in their beds while he kept the grime of humanity from invading their homes and stealing their daughters.

A Blackguard's life was a thankless one.

He snuck another glance at Connor to find the man with his arms crossed and his chin tucked against his chest. His shoulders rose with each quiet breath, and he didn't so much as fidget even as the tree beneath him bent in the wind.

That man had saved Murdoc's life back there in the bar. Even if he'd claimed it was to coerce a favor, he'd also offered to pay. Just now, he had saved those two people by the campfire, and he had probably saved countless others, too. The Fates made certain there were plenty of opportunities for rescue out here in this lawless wood.

Underneath all that brooding darkness, Connor somehow had a good heart.

The tree beneath Murdoc rocked, and he shut his eyes to suppress another surge of nausea as the venison he'd eaten for dinner threatened to come back up. He'd heard those kids, too. He'd smelled the smoke, and he'd done nothing.

While Connor had done something about it, Murdoc had stayed safe in his tree. After all, he wanted to die on a blade, not as something's dinner.

Everything in him warned against trusting his new Captain to do the right thing. He didn't witness many good men, and those who had good souls usually couldn't even hold a sword correctly.

Magic polluted people. Perhaps it would pollute Connor, too.

No matter what's done to him, a man can't be corrupted, his grandfather used to say. *He can only relinquish his principles. Your values can never be taken from you—they're something you have to give up willingly.*

The old man had given him plenty of wisdom over the years, but that was one lesson Murdoc had never agreed with. He'd seen too many decent people go rancid. Every man had his price, and he couldn't help but wonder what Connor's price could've been.

Deep down, this burgeoning respect and camaraderie he felt for a man he didn't even know was like a whore's love—fake, and it came at a cost. They would travel until Murdoc was no longer useful, and then Connor would either try to kill him or send him on his way.

It had happened plenty of times before, and he knew better than to believe this would be any different.

He ached for the sort of fraternity forged on the battlefield, where men faced death together and spat in its face to the clash of steel and the roar of a battle cry.

A broad grin broke across his features as he let himself remember the good times. The villains defeated. The scars earned through sweat and grit. He leaned his head back against the trunk as the leaves above him shivered in the wind. Those were the days.

No.

With a rough cough, he sat upright. Jaw tensed, he forced the memories back down. Best not to pine for what was no longer here.

He took another swig of his near-empty flask, and he held it to his mouth longer than he should have if he'd wanted to conserve it. At Connor's side, any day could've been his last, so there was never a need to think ahead.

That was the point. He had no need to conserve anything anymore.

Just as he had in the year since the Blackguards had cast him out, he would numb himself with life's pleasures. He would drink and chase skirts until death came for him, resentful of all the times he'd slipped through its fingers.

Those little moments of indulgence were all he had left.

CHAPTER FORTY-THREE
QUINN

In a tavern on the outskirts of Bradford, Quinn leaned one elbow on a table in the back. With one foot propped on the wooden seat beneath her and the other dangling off the edge of the bench, she pressed her back against the wall and lifted a watery ale to her lips.

Almost two weeks, already gone. Only eighteen days remained until her time ran out.

Eventually, this mess would make sense. Until then, she simply had to listen and wait for the opportune moment to strike.

With an exhausted sigh, she swept her hair over her left shoulder. The brunette strands fell flat against her neck, and she impulsively frowned. The glamour her mother had given her worked brilliantly, of course. Every inch of her face had changed. Her nose had narrowed. Her eyes had turned blue. Even the color of her skin had darkened, and it almost hid her freckles.

People traveled across Saldia for her mother's glamours, but the gentle and loving glamourist always saved her best recipes for Quinn.

The potion would last for another two hours. By then, she had to be in the woods on her way back to her makeshift camp, where she had left Blaze in hiding.

A door slammed, and she snapped back into the moment. Footsteps thudded along the wooden floor. A burly man with broad shoulders and a dark mop of hair sat at the bar and rubbed his tired eyes.

The bartender grinned and shook the man's hand. "Ethan! Good to see you."

"And you, Frederick." The burly fellow scratched his thick beard. "What do you have? More of that terrible ale?"

The bartender snatched a pitcher off the counter and stowed it beneath the bar with a hearty laugh. "No shitty ale for you, my friend. Nothing but the best."

Quinn frowned and stared at the pale liquid in her cup.

Ass.

"I haven't seen you in nearly a season." The bartender uncorked a bottle from behind him and poured the man some whiskey. "Long walk through the woods, I take it?"

The newcomer took the mug. "Isn't it always?"

Quinn's ear twitched as she eavesdropped, eager for someone to mention the assassin. Shadow blades. Abnormal power. Cloth across his face to mask his features.

She needed something—anything—to go on. Whatever it took, she had to find out what this man in the woods wanted.

After all, everyone wanted something.

So far, Bradford had proven mostly useless. For three days, she had forced herself to stifle yawn after yawn while neighbors complained about their landlords and whispered about secret affairs between the town's wealthy merchant families. A few bar fights had broken out, but mostly over stupid nonsense or hustlers in the darts corner. A few rumors had confirmed the sorceress was gone, and thus far everyone agreed that she had been taken in the night.

That was the trouble with rumors. Behind the wild guesses, there was always a grain of truth. The difficulty lay in sifting out fact from fiction.

She took another sip of the shitty ale and stifled an irritated groan. There had to be a lead somewhere in this blasted town. The assassin's trail had ended in a stream, and try as they might, neither she nor Blaze could track him.

He was *good.*

If he kept near the road, he could've gone in only one of two directions.

Heading south would take him through a dozen or so villages, and then to South Haven and the Barrens. Aside from an endless desert, nothing waited for him in the south.

Going north would take him to Oakenglen, a place he had just escaped.

Rumor had it the warriors of Westhelm inhabited the Ancient Woods, but no one had found them. Perhaps he had formed a pact with them. Maybe the assassin had struck up some sort of agreement that would grant them their rights back.

There were too many unknowns.

"Any news, Ethan?" the barkeep asked.

With the cup nearly to his mouth, the newcomer impulsively stiffened at the question. He cleared his throat and forced himself to finish his drink as he glanced away. "Nothing much."

An obvious lie.

Quinn frowned. She wanted so desperately to believe he knew something, but she couldn't let her impatience get the best of her. He could've been hiding information on an affair, or perhaps he'd stolen something recently and felt remorse for his actions.

Again, too many unknowns.

She grumbled with frustration and pressed her cup to her lips to drain the last of the ale.

The door burst open with a dramatic flair, and it slammed against the wall as a cold gust rolled in. A young couple entered, each of them barely eighteen, and they paused at the door with vacant expressions.

The young man glanced around the tavern and swept a loose lock of blond hair out of his face, as if he had only just come to and realized where he was. The brunette beside him shivered in the cold. He kicked the door shut and rubbed her shoulders as he led her toward the bar. She walked with her hands clutched to her chest, staring at the ground as if she had witnessed the horrors of hell.

Neither spoke as they reached the bar. Though the tavern had only a handful of people at this time of the morning, those reclined in the corners watched the newcomers in dumbfounded silence.

What an entrance.

They sat. The young woman held her face in her hands and stared at the splintered wood beneath her elbows. Beside her, the young man plopped onto a stool and stared at the wall, his hand over his mouth.

The burly man named Ethan sat down his mug. "Are you kids all right?"

"Not at all," the girl said softly.

The barkeep leaned his palms against the counter as he studied them. "What the hell happened to you? You look like you've seen a ghost."

Quinn's ear twitched, but she quickly shoved aside the impulsive rush of hope. It was a common phrase, and it didn't mean they'd seen the wraith. If she got impatient and started making assumptions, her own rash excitement could blow her cover.

Right now, she couldn't afford to make a mistake.

"Ale first." The young man plopped a gold coin on the counter as he rubbed his forehead. "Whatever you have is fine."

With a small shake of her head, Quinn stifled the urge to say something. The boy had just grossly overpaid, which meant he had little knowledge of money. He hadn't even asked for a price or tried to haggle. That wouldn't serve him well, not down here in the southern towns.

"That'll do." The bartender set two cups in front of them. His gaze darted between the kids as he lifted the pitcher from beneath the counter and poured them some of his shitty ale.

Quinn looked at her own empty cup and grimaced. It seemed like those poor children had already endured enough. They didn't deserve to be subjected to this garbage, too.

"It's a wonder we're even alive." The young woman shook her head, and strands of her brown hair caught on her cloak with the movement.

"The blightwolves have been howling." The barkeeper wiped down the bar to their left. "Did you hear them? Were you traveling?"

The two of them didn't respond at first. After a few painfully silent moments, the young man slowly nodded.

Still reclined in the corner and largely ignored, Quinn sat upright at the boy's confession. Though the blightwolves didn't involve her quarry, they had always fascinated her. The legend. The lore. The endless debates over where they had come from and what had made them.

She ached to know more.

The girl tugged on the ends of her hair. "We didn't just hear them. We saw them."

Ethan leaned toward the kids, and his wooden stool creaked beneath his weight. "You saw the blightwolves? Where?"

"To the north." The boy pointed over his shoulder to the south, but Quinn figured he simply didn't have a knack for direction.

The burly man let out a sigh of relief as the bartender poured him a second drink.

"One of them tried to eat me." The girl shuddered, and her eyes pinched shut with fear. "A great big silver monster."

A fine brown mist flew into the air as Ethan spit out his whiskey in surprise. He slammed his half-filled glass against the counter with a dull thud and stared vacantly at her. Though the whiskey sloshed onto his hand, he didn't seem to notice. "You weren't in the trees?"

"We didn't know." The girl shrugged, her eyes wide. "We're from Hazeltide. We didn't realize you couldn't make a fire on the southern road. We—"

"Ellie." The young man set his hand on her wrist, his tone firm and quiet as his grip tightened.

"Sorry," she whispered.

Ah.

If the couple had come from Hazeltide, that explained their ignorance. The north had only the black unicorns of the Frost Forest to contend with, and few ventured out into the woods alone. They had no idea of what waited for them in the south.

Two young lovers in hiding. It had to be. They were likely searching for a new life down here in the southern towns. Judging by his gross overpayment of the ale, they had probably escaped gilded cages to be together.

Romantic, perhaps, if also a bit foolish. They probably wouldn't last long before they trudged back home, broke and hungry.

Quinn set her cup down and leaned her elbows on the table. Per the law, her duty was to return missing children to their parents. If she hadn't glamoured herself, she would have had no choice but to turn them over to the sheriff for the long trip to the north.

She rubbed her eyes, debating her options, but she didn't want to force them back into their old lives. As naïve as the two of them were, it wasn't her place to decide their fate. Besides, she couldn't afford the distraction.

Ethan tapped one finger on the bar. "You two are lucky to be alive."

The young man took a sip of ale. "We wouldn't be if the Shade hadn't saved us."

"The Shade?" Ethan frowned with confusion. "What the hell is that?"

Quinn's ear twitched, and her entire body stiffened at the familiar term. The potion master had coined it back when the assassin had saved him from the bandits.

The Shade.

I'd be dead now, the potion master had said. *Dead, if not for that man.*

She rubbed her temples. Assassins didn't save shop owners from bandits, nor did they rescue children from the dangers lurking in the Ancient Woods.

None of this made any damn *sense*.

The bartender cast a wary glance around the bar, and his gaze lingered briefly on Quinn as he lowered his voice. "You saw the Shade? Are you certain?"

"I didn't think he was real," the young man confessed. "He even tried to deny it, but there's no one else it could've been. Before our run-in with the blightwolves, I thought the Shade was just a stupid legend we heard about in Murkwell. The merchants told us about him. They said someone was doing good deeds around Bradford. A mysterious man of magic with dual swords who always wears a cloth over his face. He—"

Ethan coughed into his cup. The two kids and the bartender watched him in stony silence at the interruption, but he lifted his hand and waved away their concern. "I'm fine," he said hoarsely. "Fool that I am, I must've tried to breathe my drink."

"We saw him," the young man continued. "He saved our lives. We wouldn't be here without him. He drove off the blightwolves and taught us what to do to survive the forest at night."

Ethan coughed again, harder this time, and his face turned red. "He drove off the *blightwolves? By himself?*"

"It's hard to believe, I know," the young woman admitted with a shrug. "But it happened. I saw it with my own eyes. I fell, and he caught me. If he hadn't… if he didn't…"

She set down her cup and stifled a sob.

"It's okay, dear." The young man kissed her gently on the head. "You're safe. We both are, thanks to him."

Quinn rubbed her eyes in frustration. To the people, the assassin was some kind of folk hero. A man of magic and honor.

If they only knew the truth, they wouldn't revere him.

With a few absent taps of her fingertips on the table, her mind went blank at the impulsive thought. After everything she had heard about this man, she truly had no right to judge him. The people didn't know who this man was, but honestly, neither did she.

He had spared her life when anyone else would have killed her.

For the first time since her father had given her the mission to hunt down a traitor and bring him in alive, she questioned what she had been told.

Maybe the Lightseers didn't have all of the facts about this so-called assassin. It seemed like a betrayal to her family name to even consider the possibility.

She impulsively pressed her palm flat against the table and leaned back in her seat. As her nails dug into the wood, her breath quickened at the absurd idea. It felt like high treason to even have these thoughts, but there were holes in what she had been told.

Duty above all else.

The Lightseer way.

To do right by the people she had sworn to protect, she needed more information. She needed to find out the truth.

Quinn swallowed hard and stared at the wooden table before her. Perhaps her father and Otmund had been conned. If so, the time had come to ask them herself. She had resolved to discover the truth, whatever it took, but she had never dreamed it would've come to this.

After all, it didn't seem possible for the great Teagan Starling to be *wrong.*

CHAPTER FORTY-FOUR
CONNOR

As another sun began to set on the Ancient Woods, Connor rubbed his eyes to wipe away the exhaustion. With the Starling woman on their heels, he'd lost precious time ensuring their trail remained hidden.

Extra effort well worth the price, in his opinion, but Sophia had more than a few choice words to share about "trekking through the muck like peasants."

"Fates, grant me patience," he muttered under his breath.

Wandering through the trees far from the road came with a greater risk of encountering the blightwolves again, and he doubted they would be merciful the next time he faced them. Several days had passed since his run-in with their alpha. Every time the shadows lengthened, the scars on his shoulder stung with the reminder of the beast's teeth. Sophia's Rectivane potion had healed most of it, but not all.

The silver blightwolf had left its mark.

Though he braced himself for their howl each night, it never came. In fact, the wolves had been more silent in the last few days than they had been in years.

It unnerved him. Sometime over the last few weeks, they had picked up his scent. They knew him, and they were watching.

His jaw tensed at the thought.

Behind him, Sophia tripped over a root and stumbled into a nearby oak. "I'm done! Connor, I am *done* with these damned woods! If I have to spend another night in these cursed trees, I swear to the Fates I will kill one of you!"

"I vote him." Murdoc pointed at Connor.

Connor chuckled. "Thanks."

"I can't sleep in those damned branches!" Sophia ignored them both as she ran her fingers through her frizzed and matted hair. "My neck hurts like hell from sleeping upright, and my beautiful hair looks like a bird's nest. How do you do this? Do you really sleep in the trees? Or is this some sick and twisted—"

"Truthfully, Captain, I think you can take her." The Blackguard soldier shrugged as he continued along their route. "It'll be fun to see you go against her when she's this sleep deprived. Think she'll be able to aim, or will she set the forest on fire?"

"I'll set *you* on fire," she snapped.

Connor grinned, his eyes still on Murdoc. "She probably has a potion for that."

"I bet you're right." The former Blackguard shuddered. "I don't want to find out for certain."

"How much farther?" The necromancer wiped the back of her hand across her brow to wipe away the sweat. "It's only a day between Murkwell and Oakenglen by road with a decent horse, but we've been walking for days."

"The road is crawling with soldiers." Connor paused and leaned against a nearby tree with his arms crossed as he waited for Sophia and Murdoc to catch up to him. "Walking through the woods slowed us down, but it means no more interactions with anyone from the Capital."

"Especially that Starling woman," Murdoc added.

"I need a minute." Sophia plopped onto a nearby rock and lifted her flask to her mouth. A ribbon of crystal-clear water snaked from her lips, and her eyes fluttered closed with the bliss of a cool drink.

The mere sight of water parched Connor's throat, and he shook his head in annoyance as he reached for his own canteen. He'd already had to fill it ten times today.

Always hungry. Always thirsty. Always horny. Nothing was ever enough for his body, anymore.

The air shifted, heavy as a storm rolling in off the sea, and a shadow darted from behind Connor. The Wraith King materialized from nothing, his back to them as he clasped his bony hands behind his cloak.

This had become routine for Connor, but Murdoc and Sophia flinched in surprise. The sorceress muttered obscenities under her breath and let out a sigh of relief as she recognized their company.

Look at you, still traveling like a commoner. The Wraith King gestured to the empty forest around them. *Walking on foot. Hiding. Have you learned nothing from our time together? Is a dead man's book truly worth this little endeavor of yours?*

"I get why Sophia's complaining." Connor gestured to the necromancer, who flashed her middle finger at him as she lifted her flask again to her lips. "But why are you? You don't even have feet. Besides, you told me to look for the book. I'm looking. This should make you happy."

"Wait, is that possible?" Murdoc pointed to the ghoul. "Can he actually feel happiness?"

Connor shrugged. "Probably."

The Wraith King huffed. *The book is important, Magnuson, but not urgent. You must prioritize, and there are other matters to tend to first. Besides, it's not the effort wasted. It's the time. You peasants forget money doesn't matter as much as your time.*

"Why do you care? You're immortal. Time can't possibly mean anything to you anymore."

I still get bored. The dead king shrugged in frustration. *You keep forgetting that you represent me, and a warlord never wastes his time. I may be immortal, but I am tethered to this world by our connection, and your heart has a limited number of beats. Only the Fates know when it will stop. More money can be earned or stolen if it's lost, but your days can never be replenished.*

Connor rubbed his jaw, surprised by the rare nugget of wisdom. He hadn't expected a life lesson from a dead man to be useful in any way, but the old king had a point.

The ghost waved his hand vaguely toward Murdoc and Sophia. *This hunt of yours, these companions you've chosen, the way you travel—it's all nonsense. It's all a waste of precious minutes and days you'll never get back.*

Murdoc pointed to the ghost. "I wish I could hear what he's saying because I feel like he just insulted us."

Connor chuckled.

"I'm right, aren't I?" The Blackguard huffed. "Rude."

"What would you have me do instead?" Connor asked the ghost.

Before we find the Deathdread, we must go to Slaybourne, the Wraith King explained. *Bring it back to its full glory. Don't trudge through the mud of other kingdoms. Force them to come to you. Don't steal the book from under their noses. Demand that they bring it to you.*

He shrugged. "After all these centuries, it's just a ruin. What could I possibly gain by spending whole seasons of my life hunting for some piles of rubble?"

There's magic there. There's power that could help you.

"Or you."

The dead king laughed. *What could possibly help me? You think there's some trap lying in wait? You think there's some forbidden potion locked away in the ruins that can allow me to, I don't know.* The ghost shrugged. *Possess you, perhaps? Overpower you in some way?*

He shrugged. "Is there?"

I wish, the ghost confessed. *I've dreamed of taking over one of the Wraithblades, of truly living again and not just as a shadow, but it's not possible. If the magic exists, any knowledge of how to use it died with Aeron Zacharias. You have nothing to fear from Slaybourne and everything to gain.*

"What exactly is there to gain?"

"Is this strange to you as well?" Murdoc whispered to Sophia. "It's like he's talking to a tree."

The necromancer ignored him as she took another sip from her flask.

All the while, her gaze remained on Connor.

You'll find weapons. The ghost paced between the oaks. *Spellgust ore. Enchantments in the soil. My soldiers swore an oath beyond even death. There is magic in Slaybourne, deep to its roots, and there's a reason it's feared. Horrors wait for your enemies.*

Connor rubbed his jaw, not entirely certain he liked the sound of that. If the dead warlord's soldiers somehow remained in the citadel, their loyalty belonged to the Wraith King—not to him. "And what do you have to gain if we go back?"

For a moment, the Wraith King didn't answer. He simply floated between the trees, the empty eye sockets in his skull trained on the forest around them.

I've lost track of the centuries since Aeron brought me back, the Wraith King admitted with a hint of wistful longing in his voice. *The years blur together. I sometimes forget about the seasons. I often forget why I should care about this frail little world, but the one thing I have never forgotten is Slaybourne. My citadel. My fortress. My home.*

Connor rubbed his tongue along his back molar as he studied the dead man floating in the breeze. The ghoul had centuries to hone his skill with manipulation, but the resounding loss in his voice seemed all too real.

Almost human.

As he studied the wraith, he leaned the back of his head against the old oak behind him. After their run-in with the blightwolves, the phantom had made it at least partway into his good graces. He could indulge the ghoul in a bit of reminiscing.

"Maybe we'll go there someday when there isn't impending doom on the horizon."

There will always be impending doom, the Wraith King said. *At least for you.*

With that ominous warning, the ghost disappeared. A bird twittered overhead, singing as the forest brightened again. Dappled sunlight danced along the ground as the emerald canopy trembled in the wind.

Murdoc pointed to the empty air where the ghost had been. "As fun as it is to only get half of the conversation, I would very much like to know what the hell all that was about."

"Nothing." Connor hooked his flask onto his pack and led the way through the forest. "Let's get going."

We are close.

Connor's head snapped up as the ghoul's voice rang through his mind. He paused midstride and scanned the forest for any hint of what the ghost had meant, but nothing looked any different than before.

Endless trees and a relentless wind. Same as always.

"Captain, are you all right?" Murdoc stepped around Connor on their way up the hill.

"I'm fine. I just—"

The world around him shifted. With an abrupt and violent blur of colors, he was in the sky above the forest. His head rotated, as if someone else controlled his movements, and he scanned the valley below.

Saldia's golden sun set along the western horizon, casting an amber glow across the patchwork fields in the distance. The emerald ocean of leaves below him ended at a cobblestone road littered with caravans and bobbing heads. Beyond the gathering travelers, the walls of Oakenglen cut across the grassy fields in both directions.

They had arrived.

The city towered ahead of him, easily twenty times the size of Kirkwall. Hundreds of thousands of buildings crowded together, casting shadows on the streets, and a massive lake ate away at the city's northern border. In the setting sunlight, the hazy mirage of an island danced on the horizon.

The vision abruptly ended.

He fell back into his body with all the force of a thousand-foot fall. Stumbling and disoriented, his shoulder rammed into a tree as he fought to regain his balance. Leaves shook loose, and several landed in his hair as they rained down on him. He pressed his palm against the nearest trunk, and the sharp bite of bark stabbing into his skin helped center him in the moment.

Murdoc raised one eyebrow and set a hand on Connor's shoulder. "Are you sure you're all right?"

He pinched the bridge of his nose as Sophia's familiar gait shuffled across the dead leaves behind him. A surge of nausea burned in the back of his throat, and he shook his head to stifle it. "What the hell was that?"

I shared my vision with you, the wraith explained. *Seeing as I have a superior line of sight and no need to tether myself to the ground, it seemed the most logical and useful option. You're welcome.*

Connor's world finally stopped spinning, and he rubbed his eyes as the wraith explained yet another power. One that had its uses, certainly, but only reaffirmed his need to read the Deathdread. The time had long since come for him to fully understand the wraith's abilities.

There's a cliff up ahead, the ghoul continued. *It's a suitable vantage point. Had I known about it, I would have warned Henry to post a guard tower here. When you retake Oakenglen, you must build one.*

"Except for those daggers, I'm not retaking anything," he muttered.

Suit yourself.

"Murdoc, Sophia, follow me." He tried to mask his irritation as he continued their hike up the hill.

He led them through the woodland, and the ground angled upward as their walk became a climb. Loose rock and clumps of soil gave beneath his boots as he leaned against the trees for balance, but he pushed onward.

"If I have to climb another tree," Sophia muttered under her breath. "Fates help whoever's nearby."

Connor chuckled.

The ground leveled out as the trees thinned. A few old oaks leaned over a ledge, their low branches blocking the view, and he flashed his palm as a silent order to stop.

It looked like they'd reached the cliff.

He knelt to get a better view from beneath the thick branches, and a gust ripped past him as he scanned the massive city below. The southern gates sat open, easily as tall as ten men. Twenty soldiers lined a wide footbridge over the outermost moat, and their spears glistened each time they stopped someone trying to enter. Caravans stretched down the road and into the trees, each of them probably trying to pass through the city gates before nightfall.

Beyond the walls, buildings stabbed at the sky. Densely packed streets bustled with bodies, so far away that even with Connor's enhanced vision, he couldn't make out details. Several rows of walls separated each ring of the Capital as the city stretched toward the lake. In the distance, the hazy silhouette of a castle towered over the city.

"The drainage tunnel I told you about isn't far." Murdoc leaned against a nearby tree and whistled softly to himself. "Now that's a pretty view."

"It is." Sophia grabbed a nearby tree as she leaned over to peer beneath the branches.

While the two of them studied the city, Connor looked over his shoulder at the woodland behind them. A sunbeam broke through a gap in the leaves, and its soft light hit a small white mushroom growing at the base of a tree.

To think, he hadn't left this forest in eight years. When he'd first walked down the southern road toward Murkwell, he had always assumed he would never come back out.

That had been the plan, back then—escape into the most dangerous woodlands in Saldia and pray to the Fates that the world would forget he existed.

It hadn't worked.

CHAPTER FORTY-FIVE
CONNOR

With Murdoc leading the way, darkness had fallen as they trudged through the woods around Oakenglen. Somewhere far beyond the road and walls, the Blackguard hunted for a drainage tunnel Connor was beginning to doubt existed.

The moons shined through the thin forest, casting a blue glow over the dark green underbrush. Frogs croaked in the cool evening air, and crickets chirped somewhere in the distance.

"Murdoc," Connor warned. "If you don't find this damned tunnel soon—"

"It's here," the Blackguard insisted. "I swear. Listen for a river. It's around—"

"I hear it," Sophia interrupted.

She paused midstride, her head tilted as she listened to the woodland song. Connor followed suit, and sure enough, the gurgle of a brook rippled through the trees.

The necromancer stepped in front of Murdoc, and her boots sank into the mud with each step. She grimaced in disgust but plowed ahead and gestured for them to follow.

Within minutes, the gurgle became a chorus of bubbling water over rock as a small river flowed through the woods. A steep bank led into the shallow water, and smooth pebbles at the bottom of the river glistened in the moonlight.

To reach the shallow river, Murdoc slid down a steep bank easily as tall as he was. His boots kicked up dirt as he landed in the knee-high water with a splash. "Which way's north?"

"That way," Connor and Sophia said in unison, as they both pointed upriver.

"Let's go." The Blackguard grabbed a fistful of water and splashed it on the back of his neck. He sighed with relief as he trudged through the river ahead of them.

Sophia grimaced, but Connor slid down the bank without another word. His boots slid quietly into the water, and the cold river seeped through to his toes. His pants clung to his body as the river soaked him through. He frowned with discomfort, but he'd endured worse than wet clothes.

His feet dragged against the current as he trudged after Murdoc. Sophia gently eased herself down the bank, cursing to herself all the way, and she landed with a splash. He paused and glanced over his shoulder to find her on her ass, the water flowing over her chest as her wet hair clung to her face.

"Not a *word*," she warned.

Connor turned his back to her to hide his broad grin. "Do you want help getting—"

"I'm fine."

He shrugged. "Suit yourself."

Ahead, a weeping willow blocked their view of the rest of the river. It leaned over the water, and its long branches dipped into the current as it flowed past.

The slosh of a wet dress through the water approached from behind, and Connor kept his gaze trained ahead of him as the drenched necromancer passed by.

"Eager to get into the city?" He grinned.

She cursed under her breath and ignored him as she sloshed past.

Murdoc reached the willow first, and he pulled the branches aside to reveal a tunnel roughly seven feet tall. A thin trail of brown water seeped from its shadowy depths, draining into the clear river as the waterway rumbled past.

The stench of rotting cabbage and fermenting meat funneled from the dark passage like a haze. Sophia gagged, and Connor narrowed his eyes as he turned his full glare on Murdoc.

The Blackguard waved away his concern with a flick of his wrist. "You get used to the smell after about fifteen minutes."

Connor groaned. "Let's get this over with."

"Wait." Murdoc raised his hands and glanced between the two of them. "Before we go in, remember that you swore not to judge me for this."

"I didn't agree to anything," Sophia pointed out.

"As long as you get us into the Capital unscathed, I don't care what happens." With another glance at the pitch-black tunnel, Connor scanned the riverbank and grabbed a stick roughly the length of his forearm.

In a stretch of tunnel that dark, even he and Sophia would need light.

He offered the would-be torch to the necromancer. She held the dead branch with the tips of her fingers, as though it would infect her if she got too close. "What am I supposed to do with this?"

Instead of answering, he rifled through his pack and fished out the Firestarter dagger.

"Ah." She grabbed it and held the blade against the edge of the stick. With a twist of her hand, flame ignited along the dagger.

In seconds, a torch flickered to life in her hands. Connor lifted it from her grip and led the way into the tunnel. "Let's go. Hold onto the Firestarter for now."

"If you insist."

They trudged into the tunnel's ankle-high water, and the stench worsened with each step. As the blue moonlight faded, the orange glow of the torch illuminated only a few feet of the tunnel at a time.

Something floated by in the putrid water, nothing but a shadow in the low light, and Connor forced himself to keep his eyes ahead. He probably didn't want to know what festered in the slop beneath his feet.

As the tunnel entrance became a pinprick of blue light in the distance, the tunnel never once curved. They walked in silence with nothing to fill the void but the slosh of their feet through the slime. To keep from inhaling too much of the stench at a time, Connor took shallow breaths even as his head spun from the smell.

"Sorry, Murdoc," he said. "I'm judging you."

"Already?" The former Blackguard winced. "Because the smell isn't the worst part."

"Fantastic," Sophia muttered.

An iron gate appeared at the edge of the torchlight in front of them. Murdoc cursed under his breath and ran to it, water splashing beneath his boots. He grabbed the metal bars and shook them with a frustrated groan.

"Fates be damned!" His voice echoed down the tunnel. "They fixed it!"

"Quiet." Connor held a finger to his mouth in warning.

The former Blackguard nodded and ran his hand through his hair in irritation. "Damn the Fates, this is bad. The ladder is on the other side. What do we do?"

"Hold this." Connor handed the torch to Murdoc, and he wrapped his fingers around the metal bars.

Time to test his newly enhanced strength.

"Don't be ridiculous," Sophia chided. "There's no way you could—"

He yanked the bars toward him, and the iron groaned in protest as the bars twisted beneath his grip. His hands screamed as the metal tore into his palm, but he gritted his teeth and willed himself to pull harder.

"Whoa," Sophia whispered.

The muscles in his neck tightened as he strained against the iron. It gave another inch, and Connor squeezed his eyes shut as he pulled again. The thick outline of the veins in his arms pressed against his skin as the iron fought him, but the bars bent inch by inch beneath his grip.

Finally—mercifully—it gave. He stifled a yell as the iron finally snapped, but the scream of metal ripping apart echoed down the tunnel in both directions. He tossed the bars aside, and they clattered against the wall. He examined his chaffed hands as he caught his breath. Though raw and red, they didn't bleed, and that was all that mattered. His arms ached from the effort, and his palms stung with all the fire of a million wasps.

He set his hands on his knees to catch his breath. The putrid air snaked into his lungs, and the musky rot of moldy carrots coated his tongue. He spat into the water and shook his head as he wiped his brow with the hem of his shirt.

"Now you're just showing off." Murdoc pointed to the broken metal bars. Water crashed over the iron like a rock in a river.

Connor laughed and pointed to the new hole in the grate. "Just go."

The ruffian led the way with their torch, and the three of them stepped through the fresh hole in the gate. This time, Connor took up the rear as the orange light stretched ahead of them.

As the minutes passed, the tunnel finally curved. They had probably reached the city, and that meant they were close. The pinprick of moonlight faded behind them as they rounded the bend, and the tunnel narrowed by roughly a foot.

"We're almost there," Murdoc promised.

Sophia lifted her soaked skirts and gagged. "You owe me new clothes."

Murdoc looked over his shoulder and smirked. "Does that mean I get to help you take those off?"

"Focus," Connor chided. "Both of you."

"There!" Murdoc pointed toward the wall of the tunnel. "There, do you see it?"

Along the right edge of the passage, the curved wall flattened. An iron ladder nailed to the wall stretched above them and into a narrow tunnel barely wide enough for a man to climb through. As Murdoc neared, the torchlight revealed a few more rungs of the ladder, but the thick shadows obscured the rest of it.

Sophia shuffled through the putrid water. "Good. Let's get the hell out of this sewer."

"Wait, wait." Murdoc stopped them again. "No judging."

Connor gestured to the ladder. "We already know you're an adulterous Blackguard who's allergic to spellgust. If we accept those parts of you, what the hell are we going to find up there that you're worried we'll judge you for?"

"I—well—huh." Murdoc shrugged. "I guess that's a good argument."

"I'll go first." Connor lifted the torch from Murdoc's hands to get a better look, but the shadows stretched far beyond the torchlight. With the torch pressed flat between the iron rung and his calloused palm, he carefully maneuvered his way up the ladder. Murdoc and Sophia clambered after him, and the iron shivered beneath his grip with every footfall on the rungs.

His elbows scraped against the narrow tunnel with every rung he climbed. The fire ate away at the stick, inching toward his hand as the minutes passed. Even as it approached the end of what he could hold without getting burned, they still hadn't reached the top.

Connor paused and stared down at the Blackguard climbing after him. "How long is this thing?"

"It can't be much farther," Murdoc said in a hushed tone. "We should be quiet from this point on, in case they hear us."

"Who is 'they,' exactly?" Sophia asked.

"You'll see."

"If this gets us caught, Murdoc, I swear to the Fates—"

"We won't," the former Blackguard promised. "I swear on my life."

Connor scoffed. "The life you're trying to end in an 'honorable death' as quickly as possible?"

"Oh, right." The ruffian chuckled. "On Connor's life, then."

As they resumed their climb, a woman moaned in pleasure. The rock muffled her voice, but the unmistakable euphoria of a woman in ecstasy floated past.

Connor frowned and glared down once again at Murdoc.

"What?" The firelight cast shadows on the former Blackguard's face.

"You didn't hear that?"

"I sure did," Sophia answered. "Where exactly does this ladder let out, Murdoc?"

The woman moaned again, her voice still distant and muted by the stone. Her voice grew louder with each passing second as she climaxed somewhere above them.

"Yes!" she screamed. "By the Fates, yes! Harder!"

"Oh!" Murdoc chuckled. "Yes, I can hear it now."

"I'm fairly certain they can hear her in the castle," Sophia quipped. "You're leading us into a whorehouse, aren't you?"

"You said you wouldn't judge me for it." The man whistled impatiently and gestured for them to continue. "Now, shall we?"

Connor laughed and resumed his climb. Of all the ways into Oakenglen, Murdoc only knew a route that involved a woman on her back.

Of course.

The ladder ended in a wooden cover, and Connor handed Murdoc the torch as he set his palms flat against it. He gave it a light push to test its strength, but the damn thing didn't budge.

"Wraith, what's up there?" He shoved again on the lid, but it still didn't move. "What can you see?"

The old ghost sighed with irritation. *I am not your errand boy.*

"If you would rather we rot down in this putrid puddle of—"

Fine.

Connor's vision shifted, and he suddenly stood in a cellar. The edges of the dark room blurred as he got his bearings. Shelves lined almost every wall, and across from him, stairs led to a door. Light shined from beneath it, and a shadow passed across the floorboards as someone stomped by. Another woman moaned with pleasure, her voice deeper than the first, and something heavy thudded against the ceiling above him.

As quickly as the vision had come, it faded. He fell back into his own body and wove his arm through one of the ladder's rungs to keep from falling.

"Thank you." He muttered a string of curses under his breath and held his head as he waited for his world to stop spinning.

Since the cover refused to budge, he figured one of the shelves likely blocked their way. With the tunnel locked by the iron gate, the brothel madam had probably abandoned this ladder or simply forgotten it was here.

"Time to break things," he said.

"What?" Murdoc asked. "What do you mean—"

Connor shoved his shoulder against the cover as hard as he could. The wood creaked beneath his force, and this time, the lid budged. Above him, bottles clinked together, and glass shattered.

"Hurry," Sophia urged. "Before someone hears."

He shoved his shoulder against the lid again, and this time, the weight above him toppled. It eased off the lid, slowly at first, but finally fell onto the stone floor with a heavy and resounding thud that shook the ground. Glass shattered, and a rush of black liquid dribbled into the tunnel.

Connor tossed aside the cover and peered over the edge. Sure enough, they had ended up in the cellar the wraith had shown him moments before. One of the shelves lay across the floor, pools of liquid intermixed with shards of broken glass as the fractured potions drained toward the ladder.

"Let's go." He pulled himself out of the tunnel and grabbed the torch from Murdoc. Though he listened intently for the thump of footsteps, none came.

With the torch in one hand, he reached for Murdoc with the other. The ruffian grabbed his forearm, and Connor hoisted the man out of the tunnel.

"There's an exit over here." Murdoc stumbled as he found his footing on the stone floor, and he darted into the corner on the same wall as the stairwell.

"Get it open." Connor watched the closed door, expecting company at any moment.

The clink of shivering metal echoed up the tunnel. Moments later, Sophia's face appeared from the shadows, and he reached for her hand.

In the hallway at the top of the stairs, footsteps thudded toward them. Sophia's eyes widened, and he cursed under his breath. He grabbed her forearm and hoisted her out of the passage.

With her through, Connor tossed the torch back into the tunnel and set the cover across the hole in the floor to hide it.

As Sophia scrambled to her feet, he scanned the other shelves. Dozens of bottles filled with clear liquid. Empty baskets. Towels. Glittering boxes filled with the unknown.

Whoever investigated the noise would know in a heartbeat that someone had come through the tunnel, since only the shelf above the ladder had broken.

With a disappointed sigh, he begrudgingly grabbed a shelf piled high with towels and pulled. It toppled, and the rolls of cloth fell to the stone. They muffled the crash of the wooden shelf on the floor, but not by much. He followed with a third shelf on the opposite side of the wall, mostly empty save for a few baskets. The shelf shattered on the ground, and the empty baskets rolled clear to the stairs.

The footsteps thundered closer, faster than before. As they neared, the low rumble of stone grinding against stone hummed through the air.

"This way," Murdoc whispered.

Connor brushed the splinters off his hands as he scanned the darkness. In the corner, the Blackguard's face twisted with effort as he pushed open a secret panel in the wall. It resisted, and Sophia leaned her shoulder against the edge of the panel to help.

The footsteps paused. At the top of the stairs, a shadow crossed in front of the crease of light beneath the door.

Time to leave.

Connor joined them and pushed. With his added muscle, the secret door slid open, and he ushered his team into the dark passage beyond. Hinges creaked at the top of the stairs, just out of sight, and the muted hum of conversation floated down the steps.

Murdoc and Sophia darted into the secret room, and Connor slipped in after them. He closed the door behind him as a shadow passed across the fallen shelves.

"What the hell?" a woman asked from within the cellar, her voice muffled by the stone.

Connor pressed his back against the secret door and listened. A boot brushed aside some of the broken glass, and the woman cursed under her breath.

"Useless imported junk." The clatter of wood splintering cracked through the air as she investigated. "What a waste of money. And that sewer! The stench." She gagged. "I might seal this whole damned room if I don't find a way to…" Her voice trailed off to the thud of her feet on the stairs, and the door slammed above them.

"This passage leads to the street," Murdoc whispered from the shadows. "Not that I ever needed to use it, but the brothel is designed for discrete escapes, should the need arise—or should a wife find out where her husband has been."

Connor rubbed the stubble on his jaw as his heart rate settled. "I don't suppose this is the brothel we need?"

Sophia shook her head. "Richard frequents one in the second interior, closer to the castle."

"Ritzy." Murdoc whistled softly. "I hear you can't call the ladies 'whores' up there. You have to use the term 'companion.' They even sing, dance, debate—"

"Focus." Connor pointed down the darkened passage. "Murdoc, can you see enough to lead the way?"

"I can try." The Blackguard reached out ahead of him, and his fingers brushed the stone wall as he blindly wandered into the darkness. "It's a straight line, so it can't be that hard."

Sophia followed after Murdoc. "We have to make a few stops before we reach the brothel. For starters, you both look like vagrants, and you won't last two seconds in the second interior. The soldiers are trained to sniff out people who don't belong. You need clothes and a lecture in manners."

Connor groaned. Propriety. Expectations. Nosy neighbors. He had gone ignored in the woods for so long that he'd forgotten what a cage civilization could be. He hadn't stepped foot in a city since he'd left Kirkwall, and honestly, he didn't know what to expect anymore.

For the last eight years, he'd been overlooked by nearly everyone. Now, he stood out like a wildfire in a field—and with the magic he'd inherited from the wraith, he was more deadly than any blaze.

CHAPTER FORTY-SIX

CONNOR

As flames flickered in the lamps along the road, a dog barked in the distance. Mumbled conversation flowed from a window somewhere along the street to the east, and a dish shattered in the somber air. The constant rumble of wheels over the well-worn cobblestone hummed across the intersecting roads as carriages wandered through the streets at all hours of the night.

Evidently, the Capital never truly slept.

A baby cried from the third story above him. Its wail split through the dark alley where he waited. He craned his neck to find the window above him open.

Delightful.

After a few moments of shrill screams, a woman muttered sweet nothings into the darkness. The infant's cry slowly faded, and a slender hand reached through the open window to shut it.

All of the windows along the alley had now been closed. A blessing, really, since it meant no one could eavesdrop.

The shadows of the alley covered his features, as intended. Across the cobblestone street, a black unicorn flicked its tail in irritation, and the silver harness latched to its chest jostled. The beast snorted, its eyes milky white as a gemstone in the silver band around its brow glowed green.

A creature of the northern forests, tamed by spellgust.

The beast towered over the cobblestones, its shoulder easily as tall as Connor's, and he silently hoped to never see one of these things in the wild. Legend said these beasts ate men whole, with teeth as sharp as the swords travelers used to defend themselves.

The carriage jostled, and the unicorn's ears pinned against its head as the harness shifted. A driver climbed into the seat behind the enchanted creature and snapped the reins against its rump. The unicorn snorted and trotted away, the foot-long strands of fur around its feet shivering with each stomp of its hooves, like ribbons in the wind.

As the carriage rumbled away, the brothel's front steps came into view. Connor had waited in the shadows for hours as the bordello's madam greeted each of her many customers with the same warm smile and elegant nod of her head. Colored glass in the ornate sconces along the front porch cast a honey glow across all who entered, but none of them had been their target.

You should investigate, the wraith said, still mercifully hidden from sight.

He shook his head. "You're shameless. We both know he's not in there. You only want me to walk in so we can make a detour to 'blend in' and have a tumble."

The ghost groaned. *Fine. You've sorted out my intentions. You're so terribly clever. Come now, Magnuson. It's been weeks, and I can't take much more of this forced celibacy. For my own sanity and yours, get the hell in that brothel.*

He laughed. "Show a bit of restraint, will you?"

I have never been one for restraint. The wraith huffed with impatience. *A warlord gets what he wants when he wants it. Go bed a woman, or I might lose my damn mind.*

Still grinning, Connor leaned against the wall, his eyes trained on the upstairs windows as he waited for Richard Beaumont to arrive. Sophia had warned him Richard would arrive in a carriage with the Lightseer crest, and to look for a man with pale skin and hair as black as night.

Apparently, he was the sort of man that didn't go unnoticed.

A curvy silhouette passed through a light on the second floor. As she walked by, the building's red brick glowed almost purple in the moonlight.

In every direction, wrought-iron lamps dotted the cobblestone road.

With each of them placed exactly ten feet apart, their light strangled the moons above. Instead of the brilliant blue he had grown accustomed to in the Ancient Woods, an orange hue covered every city surface like a layer of grit that wouldn't wash off.

It seemed somehow wrong. Perverse, even. A crime against the twin moons floating above.

A flash of royal blue in the corner of his eye caught him off guard, and his head snapped toward it—only for him to recognize the sleeve of his new shirt, courtesy of Sophia.

Well, he'd paid for it. She had simply told Murdoc where to go and what to buy.

New clothes. New boots. The hem's golden thread glimmered in the low light, but he would have to pack this away once they entered the forest again. Such ornate silks might've allowed him to blend in here, but out in the woods—his home—they would be a beacon for any passing creature with an empty belly.

Everything about the city struck him as surreal and somehow even more dreamlike than his encounter with the blightwolves. The buildings packed together along the streets, and though the main road could handle three carriages side by side, the alleys between each home could barely fit a single man.

Along the main road, the lingering chatter faded into silence. Windows shut, one by one. Candles shivered and died as people snuffed them out. Rooms went dark. The people of Oakenglen went to sleep, concerned with their structured lives and the excitement of whatever would come tomorrow. None of them thought about what would happen in the woods tonight or what might eat them as they slept.

He'd forgotten what city life was like. It had been too long.

"How far can you see?" he asked the wraith, careful to keep his voice low to avoid detection.

Since you refuse to do the sensible thing and walk across the street, I've distracted myself with surveillance, the ghoul answered. *I have roughly a half mile of movement in any given direction, and thus far, there are no patrols anywhere near us.*

"Huh." A half mile seemed like a surprising limitation, given the wraith's unbridled power and magic.

It would have to work.

"Check the brothel again—"

He's not in there, the wraith insisted. *I've checked twice.*

He smirked. "I figure you picked out one of the girls, though, while you were passing through."

There's a brunette on the second floor who's knitting, for the Fates' sake, he snapped. *Attractive, endowed, and with nothing else to do. Just go in there!*

"I could understand if I were having this conversation with Murdoc, but I can't believe I have to tell *you* to focus on the mission at hand."

The ghoul grumbled.

Another carriage clambered down the street, but he didn't move. He'd stiffened hundreds of times over the last few hours, expecting each carriage to be Richard, and it never was. In the rare instance when the carriage didn't thunder past, men in fancy robes and clean-cut suits walked up toward the bordello door. Even a few women in elegant evening gowns had entered the brothel, but never Richard Beaumont.

Sure enough, the approaching carriage rumbled past without stopping at the brothel. He groaned in frustration and leaned the back of his head against the rough brick behind him. Past the shingled roofs and dark windows overhead, only a small spattering of stars twinkled in the black.

With the city's endless parade of lights and blazing torches, most of the night sky he knew so well had completely disappeared.

The muted thump of boots on a table and the muffled chorus of a tavern song piped through the door to a tavern on the other side of the alley. A few feet away from the rear entrance to the pub, Sophia shifted her weight as she tried to sleep on a barrel. Her eyes fluttered, and she adjusted on the drum as her head reclined against the wall.

A brief flash of light glinted across the glass of a darkened lamp on the wall beside the necromancer. They had extinguished it to remain unseen. On the other end of the alley, another torch burned beside the back entrance to an adjacent inn. At two hours past midnight, he doubted anyone would stumble into the alley and notice them, but he didn't let down his guard.

No assumptions. Not with this much on the line.

Sophia adjusted again in her seat, and her red hood slipped off her head. Her new crimson gown flowed over the barrel around her, and she looked for all the world like a drunk princess sleeping off a rough night. Her body stilled, but he'd camped with her long enough to know her sleeping patterns. If she moved at all, it meant she couldn't sleep. The woman slumbered like a corpse.

"At least it's not a branch," he said.

"You're such an ass," she muttered.

He chuckled.

The door beside her opened, and a chorus of song rolled into the alley. Murdoc stumbled into the narrow lane with a tray of turkey legs in one hand and three mugs precariously balanced in the other. His fresh green and black tunic fit him a little loosely around the chest, but as he grinned stupidly over his shoulder, he didn't seem to care.

A barmaid with long brown hair and a low-cut blouse blew him a kiss as the men in the tavern raised their cups to the air. Beer sloshed onto the floor, and Murdoc winked at the girl as the door swung shut behind him. The drinking song and hum of slurred conversation faded, though the muffled stomp of boots never ceased.

"Took you long enough," Connor said.

"I was detained." Murdoc lifted his chin with pride and offered him the fistful of steins.

Connor finagled one of the mugs out of the man's grip and took a drink to hide the smirk on his face. "You found a barmaid, didn't you?"

"Three." Murdoc grinned like a child who'd gotten into mischief and was damn proud of it. "But don't tell my future wife."

"I will never marry you," Sophia said.

Murdoc flinched with surprise as he looked over his shoulder at her. Her eyes popped open, and she snatched one of the two remaining mugs out of his hand.

As the lukewarm ale fizzed down Connor's throat, it wasn't enough. His mouth dried almost as quickly as the booze rolled over his tongue, and he wished he could've stolen a whole keg. Maybe that would've finally quenched his thirst, if only for a time.

"Did you get us a room?" he asked.

Murdoc shook his head. "No space. Besides, with the price they quoted me, I'd rather sleep on a roof."

"Don't you get any ideas." Sophia tossed back her head and downed the ale in one go.

"Then find us a room." Connor gestured down the alley, toward the inn.

She shook her head and let out a raspy breath as the ale burned her throat. "Not here in the second interior. We can't afford it, and places in the interior require your papers to get a room. We'll have to go to the outskirts."

"Fine. I don't personally care. As long as we don't lose Richard, I could sleep on a roof, too."

Sophia let out a frustrated groan. "Men."

The heavenly aroma of roasted meat wafted from the plate of turkey legs in Murdoc's other hand. Though he'd probably meant for them to share the mound of food, Connor figured all seven turkey legs would've been enough to satiate his hunger for just a few hours. His stomach growled, and he reluctantly took just two.

"No, Captain, I got you three." Murdoc offered up the plate again. "Sophia and I only need two each."

"Speak for yourself," she muttered.

"You're a good man, Murdoc." Connor set the empty mug on the ground and held the turkey legs in both hands. As he bit into the first one, the warm meat split beneath his teeth. The angelic tang of honey and spices sat on his tongue, and he shut his eyes in momentary bliss.

After the first few bites, however, his hunger got the best of him. He no longer tasted the food. In seconds, the meat vanished, and his stomach rumbled with dissatisfaction. Every fiber in his being warned him to eat, and to eat *more*. He stared at the bone and contemplated eating that, too.

Nothing was ever enough.

"We can't stay here much longer," he said with a glance toward the moons inching toward the horizon. "Dawn will break in about four hours."

"Let's hope our man is an early riser." Murdoc took a bite out of his first turkey leg.

Sophia bit into her turkey and hummed with pleasure. "He's usually home before dawn. If he doesn't show tonight, it just means we came a day too early. He's a horrible excuse for a human being, but at least he's punctual."

Murdoc leaned away from her and wiped his mouth with the back of his sleeve. "It is *eerie* how much you know about this man."

She shrugged.

The whinny of horses cut through the air, and the clatter of their hooves on the cobblestone reached the alley shortly thereafter. Another carriage thundered by, its wheels rumbling over the stone street. Two white horses pulled it as they raced up the road toward the first interior.

The carriage hadn't even slowed as it neared the brothel.

Not their man.

Connor groaned and tore into his second turkey leg. He tried to force himself to savor each bite, but the more he ate, the more he wanted.

It would have to suffice. What he'd eaten so far would keep him going, and only that mattered.

As the hours passed and their shared plate of food became nothing but well-picked bones, Connor debated climbing onto the tavern roof just to give himself something to do. He wasn't used to sitting still for this long except to sleep.

This waiting nonsense set his blood on fire with anticipation.

"Burn off some of your energy and get some rest." Murdoc nodded toward the brothel as he polished off his last bit of turkey. "I'll keep watch."

Connor shook his head. "Our coin needs to be used wisely, and I'm still not convinced these clothes were a good purchase." He gestured to his royal blue shirt and cast a sidelong glare at Sophia.

She raised an eyebrow. "Did we get stopped on our way into the second interior?"

Instead of answering, he turned his back on her and paced the narrow alley.

"Exactly." She huffed. "That means it was money well spent, and you're welcome."

Murdoc cleared his throat. "Look, Captain, not to incite your wrath or anything, but…"

Connor sighed and set his hands on his hips. "Just say it."

"You look like you need to, uh, *release some tension*, if you know what I mean."

Yes. Listen to the wise and all-knowing scoundrel, the wraith echoed.

"Shut up, both of you." Connor rubbed his jaw as he suppressed a primal urge to give in. "I'm not one to pay for my company. Besides, if he visits while I'm up there, I might miss him."

"Suit yourself." The Blackguard leaned against the tavern wall as he scanned the brick building on the other side of the road. "I would be happy to do some reconnaissance. For the good of the mission, of course."

"You're both unbelievable," Connor muttered.

"Why did it have to be a Beaumont?" Murdoc absently scratched at his neck while he studied the bordello. "I mean, as far as crime families go, they're the most terrifying. Why couldn't we stalk a Redgrave? Or a Lockmore? No, it had to be a *Beaumont* for the Fates' sake."

Sophia gestured to the bordello. "It's not like we had options to choose from."

"I mean, what *don't* the Beaumonts steal?" He rambled on as if she hadn't said anything. "People, spellgust, enchanted items. I've heard they smuggled a Discovered into the eastern cities, once, for a buyer. The Blackguard soldiers had all sorts of stories about them."

"Like what?" Connor asked.

With nothing else to do, stories seemed like a harmless enough way to pass the time.

Murdoc drummed his fingertips along his chin. "Some say they own the necromancers. You know, in the same way the Starlings own the Lightseers? A soldier told me once that they control Nethervale's every movement."

Connor looked over his shoulder at their resident necromancer. "Sophia?"

"That's a story for another day." She bit into her last chunk of turkey.

He frowned.

"I'd rather face off with a Redgrave," Murdoc confessed. "Those backstabbing traitors would turn on each other in a heartbeat. We wouldn't even have to brew a potion. Just offer them some coin, and they'll sell each other out. It's a wonder they're still around with that sort of attitude."

Sophia tossed her turkey bone onto the pile. "They deal in secrets. They're still around because they know everything about everyone, including each other."

"You know a lot about the crime families," Connor observed.

She shrugged. "I know a lot about many things."

Murdoc scratched his jaw. "Do you know about the Lockmores?"

"Of course." She examined her nails and picked at the cuticle on her pinkie. "Smugglers. Mischievous assholes, the lot of them."

"Exactly. They sound fun," the ruffian admitted. "I've always wanted to meet a Lockmore. Did you know their family motto is *Mischief is a Noble Art?* If I was ever going to be a criminal, I'd join them. Not the life for me, though. I'm no good at taking orders."

A horse nickered in the quiet night, and Connor's ear twitched impulsively as it approached.

"Murdoc, be quiet," he ordered.

"Yep." The Blackguard cleared his throat. "Closing my mouth."

The clop of hooves against the cobblestone cut through the air, and Connor reclined against the wall to brace himself for yet another carriage to rumble past. Though he hadn't had much opportunity to familiarize himself with the city's layout, the clopping hooves came from the side of the road that led to the first interior, nearest to the castle.

Sophia pushed off her barrel and leaned toward Connor, her voice a whisper. "Have you thought about what I said? We can't let him live, Connor. He'll alert the other Lightseers, and we'll have a reckoning waiting for us."

"Don't start this now," he warned. "I don't kill for information. If someone's going to die, it's because the world is better off without him."

The clomp of approaching hooves grew louder.

Her gaze darted toward the ground, and she toyed with the hem of her sleeve. "I can assure you the world would be better off without him."

Connor frowned, and his curiosity got the better of him. "What did he do to you, Sophia? Why won't you tell me?"

"It's—" Her eyes glossed over, and her shoulders drooped. "It's not—"

The clattering hooves slowed. Led by two stunning black horses, the carriage eased to a stop in front of the brothel. The animals' dark coats shone like silk, a stark contrast to the carriage's flawless white paint and gilded wheels. A coat of arms painted on the door facing the alley featured a blue horse in the center of a white shield.

"That's the Lightseer crest." Sophia stiffened. "Whoever's in that carriage is a member of the Lightseer Chamber. That, or they're one of the elite. Either way, they have connections to Richard."

Murdoc rubbed his face. "I can't believe we're really going to do this."

Across the street, the driver hooked his reins beneath his seat and jumped to the ground. He disappeared around the far side of the carriage. Moments later, hinges creaked as a door opened somewhere out of view. The stagecoach jostled as someone stepped out.

"How good of you to join us this evening, my Lord," the madam said, her soft voice almost indistinguishable over the crackle of the fire in the porch sconces.

The driver climbed back into his seat at the helm and cracked his reins against the horses' rumps. They darted off, and as they towed the carriage behind them, a man climbed the stairs to the brothel door. Not even one wrinkle marred his perfectly fitted suit. A simple black ribbon tied his long dark hair behind his head, without so much as a single hair out of place.

The bordello's madam stood at the open door with her hands clasped in front of her, and she angled her arms subtly inward to enhance her cleavage as she smiled at him. Strands of gray accented her otherwise black hair in the elaborately braided bun at the back of her head. Her purple gown flowed across the floor as she stepped aside to let the man enter.

As the man walked in, he nodded to her in welcome. The subtle movement betrayed a hint of his profile.

Sharp jaw. Narrow nose. Dark brows.

"That's him." Sophia never once looked away from his face. As the door closed behind him, she froze in place, still staring after him. Her brows furrowed, and she trembled with barely contained hatred.

"Listen closely." Connor stepped between her and the brothel, and his voice dropped to a dangerously low tone as he closed the distance between them.

Her eyes snapped to his as she took a wary step back.

"Whatever bad blood you have with this man is between the two of you." He didn't bother to mask the unspoken warning in his tone. "Don't let your hatred get in the way. If your desire for revenge costs us our information, you and I are going to have problems."

At her side, one of her fingers tapped lightly against her thigh. "I'm not an idiot."

"I know." He held her gaze. "But don't think you can play me, either. It won't work, and you'll just burn us both."

She scoffed, but her gaze dropped to the ground in a subtle surrender. Whether or not she listened to his warning, however, only time would tell.

He crossed his arms and studied the brothel across the street. Though Richard Beaumont didn't know it yet, he wouldn't get another moment alone. They would wait until he left and follow him home, even if that meant running across the roofs to go unseen.

By morning, they would know where the man lived, and that meant they could form their plan. Over the next few days, he would learn exactly where to find Aeron's Tomb—and how to get into a place only a handful of Lightseers could enter.

CHAPTER FORTY-SEVEN

QUINN

To hide the slight tremble in her hands, Quinn adjusted the ends of her sleeves as she strode through the halls of Lunestone. Each step toward her father's suite in the northern tower spiked her pulse.

When she approached the corner that would take her to the carpeted stairwell to his office, her shoulders stiffened with dread.

With seventeen days left until her deadline, it seemed unnatural to walk these halls. She hadn't failed, and yet she had dared to return empty handed.

It felt wrong.

Every shallow breath carried her closer to the conversation she didn't want to have. The tendons in her neck tightened, and she swallowed hard to brace herself as she rounded the corner. At the end of the corridor, familiar lilac carpet blanketed the steps up to her father's office suite, and she squared her shoulders as she forced herself onward.

In moments, she would sit before her father and somehow find the words to suggest aloud what any other Lightseer wouldn't even allow themselves to think.

You may be wrong.

About her target. About this so-called assassin.

Her lungs burned, and she forced herself to breathe as the plush carpet flattened beneath her boots. She wiped her sweaty palms on her travel-worn riding blouse and took the stairs one at a time.

One foot in front of the other.

She could do this.

No, she *had* to. For the good of the country. If her hunch had any truth to it—if there was more to this manhunt than even her father thought—it meant King Henry's real killer still walked free. She refused to send an innocent man to the gallows for someone else's crime.

A Lightseer protected the people. A Lightseer honored their duty above even their family and put their life on the line every day for the greater good.

Such had always been the Lightseer way.

As she neared the top of the stairs, golden vines glinted in the rich purple tapestries hung along the walls. A chandelier dangled from the ceiling, its crystals casting a rainbow of light across the gold thread woven into each drapery.

A mahogany desk with intricate carvings across its legs sat against the far wall, facing the stairs. Perfectly centered to the stairwell, it hadn't been moved in decades.

In the chair behind the thick mahogany, a young woman with long blonde hair leaned one elbow on the surface and mumbled to herself. Her lavender quill shivered as she scratched its tip across a parchment on the desk in front of her. When she paused to dip her pen in the inkwell by her elbow, the quill's feather brushed against her soft pink lips.

Black sofas flanked the walls on either side of the stairwell as Quinn stepped into the reception area. Life-sized portraits of her father wearing elaborate robes hung on the wall above the seats.

Each painting captured a distinct moment during his coronation as the Master General of the Lightseers. In the first, he held his Firesword *Sovereign* aloft. Its flames roared, captured in oil paint, as he recited the timeless oaths of his position. In the second portrait, he knelt before her late grandfather as the man placed a golden circlet on his head. Though not a crown and not for daily wear, it represented the weight and responsibility that rested on his shoulders with his new title.

His office hadn't changed in years. In fact, everything around her remained just as it had when she had left weeks ago, except that yet another stranger sat behind the desk.

Though Quinn hated to admit it, she had stopped bothering to learn his secretaries' names after her first year in Lunestone. They never seemed to last more than two seasons, but she couldn't fault her father's high standards. It took a clever mind to keep up with his constantly shifting demands.

As she approached, the woman didn't so much as glance her way. Engrossed in her task, the young woman bit her lip and paused with the pen to the parchment. A blot formed on the paper, and she cursed softly under her breath as she dabbed at the ink puddle with her sleeve.

Nothing new, of course. No one in Lunestone ever heard Quinn coming, and she liked it that way. It kept the castle on its toes, and she often used her stealth to learn how people truly felt about her and her family.

Sometimes, the truth stung, but she could take it.

She waited until the woman finished scratching out her sentence. She chose to remain silent until his new secretary reached for the inkwell, so as not to ruin her letter when Quinn inevitably startled her.

With her arms crossed as she waited, she stretched out her aching neck to pass the time. When the young woman finally sighed and reached again for the ink, Quinn stifled an impatient sigh.

"Is my father in?" she asked.

The young woman gasped and dropped the pen on the edge of the table. A splatter of ink landed on the mahogany, but the parchment remained perfectly clean. Her brown eyes widened as she gaped up at Quinn, and it took a few moments of stunned silence for her to process the question.

She stuttered as she fought to find her words. "Lady Starling! Oh, my, uh—that is, good morning!"

"My apologies for frightening you."

"Not at all." The young lady let out a shaky breath. "Your father is currently in a meeting with the Lieutenant General. Should I announce you?"

Quinn's heart skipped a beat at the mention of Zander's rank among the Lightseers. She had always envied his status as Lieutenant General and his role in the Chamber.

"No," she quickly answered.

Too quickly.

Her father's secretary frowned, and her brows pinched with confusion.

For such a delicate conversation as the one Quinn needed to have with her father, she wanted to do it alone. If Zander caught even a whiff of it before decisions were made and plans were drawn, he would twist her arguments against her and steal this assignment out from under her nose.

The dagger still sat upright in her bedroom, embedded in the thick table, and she would be damned if she got another cross on her record.

To cover her tracks and ease the girl's suspicion, Quinn forced a charming smile. Her mother had taught her how to properly fake charisma during the frivolous dances her parents had forced her to attend over the last ten years.

At least something useful had come from all that dull curtsying and small talk.

Eyes creased. Head tilted to the right, but only just so. Lips curled gently upward to ensure they didn't twitch from the strain of the lie.

As she smiled, the young woman behind the desk relaxed.

"I try not to interrupt them," Quinn lied. "When is my father's next appointment?"

"Roughly one hour, my Lady."

"Secure that spot for me, will you?" She turned on her heel and retreated down the steps without waiting for a confirmation.

"Yes, of course," the woman mumbled, a hint of bewilderment in her tone.

With an hour to spare, Quinn had options. An hour could've gone far in the libraries, and hunting for information about the wraith seemed worth the effort. The fluttery anxiety in her chest would've distracted her from remembering anything she read, though, and she ultimately opted against it.

If the conversation went well with her father, she would ask for access to the restricted vaults far below the fortress. Only the Lightseer Chamber had clearance to visit those ancient tomes, but perhaps he would grant an exception to help her solve this mystery. If an answer about how to destroy King Henry's wraith existed anywhere on this continent, it had to be down there.

A better use of time would've probably been to reach out to her contacts in Oakenglen to see what gossip had spread from the corners of the world. If she sent a note over to the Capital now, her contacts could prepare and brief her after her meeting with her father. Perhaps they had a hint for her as to where the assassin had gone.

She frowned, still unsure if she could call him that.

Assassin.

Despite her brush with death, the term just didn't fit.

A third option tugged on her mind, but she tried to resist it. Per tradition, her father and Zander always spoke in the Starling Room. The space had been reserved for their family only, and many considered it to be the most secured room on the continent.

Quinn, however, knew a way to listen in.

Her childhood years had been spent exploring the fortress her ancestors had built, and no one alive knew this castle better than she did. It had hundreds of forgotten corridors, and one of its many secret passages led right by a vent in their supposedly fortified room.

For the family to continue to hold meetings in an unsecured office suggested she alone knew of the passage's existence, so she had kept her accidental discovery to herself. Judging by the footsteps in the dust, no one else had ever entered.

It was one of those secrets that had always eaten away at her. A dutiful daughter would've revealed the weakness in her family's defenses, but it was her only way to learn about Zander's missions. Without access to the passage, she would've lost one of her precious advantages over a highly skilled sibling who often tried to sabotage her assignments.

♦

In fact, without the secret tunnel, she would've had twelve more crosses in her table. For whatever reason, Zander got off on watching her fail. Luckily, she got an equal high from succeeding despite his interference.

She couldn't afford to lose access to the hidden corridor, and thus, it had remained her secret.

When she reached the bottom of the stairs, she paused and eyed the sconce that opened the hidden door.

Perhaps she would listen in for just a few minutes. Once she got her fill, she would reach out to her contacts in Oakenglen.

As she reached for the golden lamp, a doorknob jostled down the hall. She froze in place and scanned the empty castle around her. Hinges creaked, and sunlight stretched across the windowless hallway. A maid with a scarf over her gray hair stepped onto the carpeted floor and balanced an empty basket against her waist as she shut the door behind her.

To avert any chance of suspicion, Quinn set her hands behind her back and slowly strode toward a nearby portrait. She paused at the canvas and studied the familiar image of her father as he held his Firesword *Sovereign* aloft and stared down with a commanding scowl at those who passed.

"Good morning, Lady Starling." The maid smiled warmly and nodded in welcome as she walked by.

Quinn nodded politely and forced another charming smile in return. "Good morning."

The maid opened the nearby door into the servant's stairwell and headed down a circular flight of steps. As the tap of her slippered feet on the stone receded, Quinn's fake smile fell. She scanned both ends of the empty hallway one last time before she pulled on the sconce.

Time to see what Zander has been up to since I left.

Its flame shivered as the lamp rolled back on a secret hinge, and the scrape of stone on stone rumbled through the hall. A sliver of the pitch-black passage appeared in the otherwise seamless stone wall, and Quinn gritted her teeth with dread as she waited for the noise to end.

She always hated this part. With her enhanced hearing, it seemed like these secret doors practically screamed every time they opened.

Highly adept warriors with heightened senses patrolled these corridors all the time, and opening a secret door always came with the risk of being discovered.

The moment it opened wide enough for her to slip through, she darted into the darkness. On the other side of the wall, she tugged on a dangling chain connected to the sconce outside. It popped back into place, and the door rumbled closed once again.

When the low rumble finally stopped, she let out a calming breath and summoned fire into her palm. The flame hovered above her skin as her Burnbane augmentation ignited her blood with magic. A gentle crackle filled the air as the makeshift torch cast an orange glow across a flight of stone steps that ran parallel to the carpeted stairwell in the hallway.

She took them two at a time, eager to spend her hour wisely.

The dull echo of a conversation wandered through the empty corridor, and she lifted the fire in her hand to get a better view of the passage ahead. As the tunnel twisted through the castle, an abandoned cobweb hanging from the ceiling caught in her flame. The long-dead carcasses trapped in the web burned instantly to ash.

With a grimace, she lowered her flame and continued into the darkness.

The passage forked, and she took the familiar route to the left. The muffled conversation grew louder, and though she still couldn't make out words, she recognized both voices.

Zander and their father.

As their voices grew ever clearer, she dismissed the fire. The pitch-black passage plunged again into darkness, but this time a small beacon of light in the distance called to her like a siren at sea.

A sunbeam cut through a small vent at the base of the wall and cast a perfect rectangle across the floor.

"...more dangerous than we realized," her father said as she neared.

Zander sighed wearily. "I knew it was just a matter of time."

She sat beside the vent and rested her back against the wall, careful not to let her boot slip into the sunlight. Any indication of her presence would've risked losing access to the passage.

More importantly, discovering her in the tunnel would've destroyed her father's trust in her.

Her heart panged with guilt, but she squared her shoulders and forced herself to remain still. This wasn't about eavesdropping on him, after all. She merely wanted to spy on Zander.

But the guilt didn't go away.

Every time she sat here, she risked detection. Every time she listened in, she put her father's faith in her to the test.

Deep down, part of her knew this would eventually backfire. One of these days, her father would discover her, and everything she had done to earn his trust would collapse beneath her.

It was only a matter of time—and yet, she came back again and again. Addicted to the secrets, like a drunk stumbling into a tavern. Bewitched. Ensnared.

Always hungry for more.

CHAPTER FORTY-EIGHT

QUINN

To ease the remorse snaking through her bones at listening in on her father's private conversation, Quinn curled and stretched her fingers until the tension in her bones slowly faded. With her back pressed into the dusty stone wall behind her, her jaw tensed with dread at the thought of discovery.

Thus was her ritual. Riddled with self-loathing and regret, she still wouldn't leave.

"They're ready for a fight," her father said. "The Discovered who come into Saldia are armed, now. They attack any time they see us. A few survivors must've escaped back into the mountains, and they're coming back prepared. They're getting smarter."

Quinn frowned and tried to piece together their conversation from what she had heard so far, but she had precious little to go on. The Discovered had never been captured before. Due to their uncontrollable magic surges, they always left behind nothing but a hole in the ground and a pile of charred bodies.

Human bodies.

She gritted her teeth and stifled a bitter growl. These things killed every time they came near a human settlement, but she only ever got there in time to witness the aftermath. The blackened corpses. The destroyed homes. The horses and oxen, torn in half from the blast.

So much death. It followed after the Discovered like a plague.

The humanoid creatures mostly gathered in the mountains near Hazeltide, but some of her contacts had claimed they'd begun traveling south.

It seemed ludicrous to even consider—Discovered in the south. She scoffed under her breath at the very idea. With the sheer number of towns littered across the continent, they'd be dead before they even reached the Enchanted Forest.

"There's nothing else I need you to do in Oakenglen," their father said. "You're cleared to leave. King Edward has been notified and will have everything ready for you."

"Excellent."

Ah.

The Discovered had been spotted near Hazeltide, then. Edward Hallowglenn had ruled for the last two decades.

Quinn tapped her finger on her knee, wondering what exactly Zander needed to see for himself in a place like Hazeltide.

"Update me on the refineries." Teagan cleared his throat as curtains snapped in the morning wind off the lake. Quinn could imagine them billowing around him as he stared out over the water.

"Is that really urgent, Father? I should leave as soon as—"

"Before you leave for your investigation, we must ensure everything is running smoothly here at home."

"Of course, sir." A finger tapped on the marble table, and someone shifted their weight in their chair. "Our spellgust production is running at one hundred and twenty-three percent compared to this time last year. I believe we may have reached our cap. Any more than this, and we'll strain our personnel. That'll mean mistakes and therefore higher costs, so this is the fastest sustainable rate we can currently manage."

"Good. You've improved it dramatically since you took over. I'm impressed, Zander."

"Thank you, sir."

A twinge of jealousy snaked through Quinn, and she pulled a dagger out of the sheath hidden on her calf to distract herself. The spellgust refinery financed fifty percent of the Starling family fortune, but it still didn't interest her in the slightest.

Not anymore.

Her father had never allowed her to visit the facility nestled on a smaller island off Lunestone's western shore. Because some of the most potent spellgust in the world came from there, she had always wanted to watch the alchemists roast the spellgust in the time-honored traditions. Only a true master of Burnbane magic could take residence as a Firebreather in the Starling refinery, and she had always longed to study their movements to learn from their craft.

To make herself better.

However, the refinery's secrets belonged to the Starling patriarch and his heir. No one else. Her father had made that painfully clear during her many attempts to infiltrate its walls.

Somehow, he caught her every time she tried to sneak in. As the punishment for each attempt grew more severe, she had eventually stopped trying.

While the two of them droned on about production timelines and quotas, she balanced the hilt of her dagger on one finger and spun the blade. The metallic blur hummed on her fingertip, and she did her best to keep it spinning with tiny bursts of air from her Airdrift augmentation.

It was a mindless game she had invented to give her hands something to do when the people around her droned on and on.

"The Isletide sector is finally done," Zander said.

Her ear twitched.

As the second most potent refining method for spellgust ore, the recipe for how to make Isletide Solution belonged to the Wildefaire kingdom. No one else had the rights or knowledge to produce it.

"Fantastic!" Her father clapped his hands together with excitement he rarely betrayed to her, and never in public. "Is anyone aware of what we're doing? Does Wildefaire know?"

"So far, no. Everything has been kept quiet, and only a handful of the architects know of the long-term plan. They're cooperating."

"Why did you tell them?" A frown weighed on their father's voice, and she could practically taste his disappointment snaking through the air.

"They had to know in order to build the appropriate facilities, Father. It was an unfortunate limitation, but none of the workmen suspect anything."

"If the architects talk—"

"I'll take care of them," Zander promised. "No one outside of the island will know."

"Good."

As the dagger spun on her finger, Quinn frowned. If she didn't know her father better, she would've thought he'd just ordered Zander to kill the men who had built their spellgust facilities.

The comment sank into her bones, rough and raw, and she unleashed another tiny blast of air against the spinning blade as she tried to rationalize what he'd said. Perhaps she had missed a part of their conversation, or maybe she had simply misunderstood.

It wasn't the sort of man she knew her father to be. The man who had raised her to live with honor and nobility never would've given the order to kill someone just to keep a secret.

Her father's boots thumped gently against the floor as he paced by the windows. "How soon until production begins?"

"Two seasons, unfortunately. We have to find ways to discretely bring in the materials."

"That is disappointing."

"I still don't see how this can work, Father," Zander confessed. "Our solution will likely look similar to Wildefaire's exports. I doubt we can sell—"

"Not by the time we're done with it," the Lightseer Master General interrupted. "Victoria has already experimented with several techniques, and the product is pristine. That sister of yours is brilliant. Don't forget that when it's your turn to rule Lunestone, son. She's a resource. Honor what she knows."

"Yes, sir," Zander begrudgingly conceded.

"I've seen what she's made out there in Dewcrest. Her recipe barely resembles Wildefaire's Isletide Solution at all. This is where you come in, Zander."

"Of course, Father. What do you need me to do?"

"Craft a story to sell to the public. Make it seem like we rediscovered an ancient secret in the Lunestone vaults. The mystery will make it more appealing, and we can sell it at a higher price. With full control over two refining methods, Whitney Stormglass will never threaten our stake in the spellgust markets again."

A chair scraped against the floor, and a shadow fell across the vent. As the light faded, Quinn stiffened.

After a few tense moments, the shadow passed, and she let out a quiet sigh of relief.

"What was that woman thinking?" Zander asked. "Whatever possessed her to market her Isletide Solution as superior to our Firebreath is beyond me."

"She will learn," their father said ominously. "One way or another."

Quinn's brows pinched with confusion as the dagger spun on her finger. None of this made sense.

None of this seemed *right*.

Queen Whitney of Wildefaire had Starling blood in her veins, albeit diluted over the generations. In the war against Henry, her father's armies had sacrificed thousands of lives and millions of gold pieces to fight alongside the Lightseers. The Ice King, as he'd been known, hadn't surrendered until Henry had kicked down his door, and he'd paid for it with his life.

For the Starling patriarch to threaten the pillar of the Stormglass family's wealth over a marketing slogan seemed trivial. Petty.

It was an act far beneath the man she knew her father to be.

"What else?" the Master General asked from over by the windows. "Any other news from the refinery?"

"Just one, sir." Zander adjusted in his seat, and the wood creaked beneath him. "There haven't been any deaths in the Firebreath fields in a full season."

"That must be some sort of record."

"It is."

"How did you accomplish that?"

"Muzzling the beasts, mostly. We finally figured out how to craft Bridletame circlets large enough for them."

"I'm impressed."

Quinn frowned. As far as she knew, no beasts or creatures had ever been imported to the island refinery. While the dagger spun on her finger, she bit her lip and wondered if another attempt to infiltrate the island's secrets would be worth the risk, after all.

Zander cleared his throat. "If there's nothing else you want to discuss about the refinery, my contacts in the Capital have interesting news."

Her blade spun, still perfectly balanced on her fingertip as she listened. Her eyes glossed over with boredom, and her hearing instantly sharpened. With little else to do, she shifted her full attention to the conversation pouring through the vent in the floor beside her.

"And what news could that be?" Her father huffed impatiently, as if he already knew what Zander would say next.

"There's word the Shade is headed up the southern road, toward Oakenglen. It would seem the Wraithblade is headed to the Capital. He might even be on his way to Lunestone."

Her eyes snapped into focus as the blade's rotation slowed on her finger.

"That's suicide," their father said. "He might be a commoner, but even he must realize we're hunting him."

"Perhaps he's an idiot."

"This man has the power of the Wraith King at his disposal, Zander." Heavy hands smacked against the table, and her father's voice dropped an octave in somber warning. "Never—and I mean never—underestimate someone fused to a simmering soul. It could cost you your life."

Quinn's eyes went wide at the staggering comment. Her blade tilted off balance as her mind went blank.

The dagger fell, and her fingers wrapped around the blisteringly sharp steel out of impulse. Something warm and wet pooled in her palm as the blade split her skin, but she barely registered the pain.

Her world had shattered so suddenly, so *violently*, that she couldn't even think.

The Wraith King, an immortal warlord, had been brought back from the dead by the Great Necromancer. Worse even than that, at least one of the simmering souls had, in fact, never been destroyed.

How easily the truth had rolled off her father's tongue when he thought no one else could hear him.

The air in her lungs stung as she struggled to breathe through her shock.

Of course.

The wraith she had seen floating through the pillars in King Henry's throne room had never been named. According to Henry, it was merely an enchantment with eerily human features. An undead menace with no mind of its own.

Lies. All lies.

To create something so vile, one had to use necromancy. She had always assumed the wraith's ties to forbidden death magic had forced the Lightseers to wage such a brutal war against Henry's campaign. It was a bastardization of the natural order they had all sworn an oath to defend with their lives.

Necromancers sought to defy death. Lightseers sought to honor life and live in balance with nature. They had been at war from the beginning, their moralities split by the endless possibilities of what a clever mind could do with spellgust.

But now, she realized the war against Henry had been about so much more.

The ghoul wasn't just an undead atrocity King Henry had cobbled together from dead men's parts. It wasn't just a shadow on the battlefield with a bloodstained sword. The legend and lore King Henry had woven in his time on the throne had masked the wraith's true nature.

Intentionally or not, the Lightseer Chamber—to whom she had pledged her life and sword—had helped him spread the deception.

The phantom in the field by that gnarled old tree where Quinn had almost lost her life was none other than the Wraith King, brought back to life as Aeron Zacharias's abomination.

And the so-called assassin she had been tasked to capture was none other than the newest Wraithblade—the ghost's tether to the living world.

If this simmering soul still existed, perhaps the others had never been destroyed, either. Her ancestors had lied, and her father had *known*.

Teagan had even tasked her to capture the Wraithblade without warning her about the specter who fought at the man's side.

"We believe the ghoul was destroyed," he had said. *"Whatever that atrocity was, it shouldn't affect your mission."*

In reality, he'd known exactly what the ghoul was, and he had outright lied to her about it.

The thought froze her in place, and she gaped vacantly at the little window of sunlight by her boot as she fought to regain her composure.

"...or what they know," Zander said.

As her shock simmered, the conversation in the next room grew louder than the ringing in her ears. She blinked herself out of her daze and tried desperately to listen.

"Don't underestimate your sister," her father warned. "Quinn is better than you give her credit for, son. You say the Shade is on his way here, and I say your information is wrong. If her hunt had taken her back to the Capital, she would've checked in with us to orchestrate a manhunt. She's an excellent soldier. The moment he steps into the city's walls, he's dead."

An impulsive smile tugged on her lips at her father's faith in her, but the horror of the wraith's identity killed the brief flutter of pride. All she had ever wanted was to make him proud, and yet he'd omitted vital news from her mission.

If she didn't know better, she would've thought her father had set her up to fail.

A flicker of rage ignited in her chest, and as the blistering fire grew, it rooted her in place. She couldn't move. If she did, she would scream with fury and punch through the wall behind her.

Zander groaned in disgust. "Father, is this working? Is your experiment with Quinn really worth the time we've already lost? If the public finds out what that wraith really is, it threatens everything we've built. We need to bottle that abomination and store it in a vault, but we can't do that if she's out pretending to be a warrior."

Pretending?

Quinn's teeth ground together in her barely contained fury, and her grip on the blade in her hand tightened. A ribbon of blood snaked out of her closed palm. The red droplets plopped one after another onto the floor, but her fingertips merely tingled as the shock sank into her bones.

Her father let out an impatient groan. "This again?"

"No one has seen her in days. The sheriff in Bradford even gave us word that she followed a lead into the woods and disappeared." Zander blazed through the arguments so quickly that it became obvious he'd rehearsed. "Think about it, Father. What if she's dead? What if the blightwolves ate her and that blasted vougel of hers?"

"Would you mourn her?" the Master General asked, his tone even. Almost... *bored*.

Quinn swallowed hard at the careless question from her own father.

A moment of silence passed before her brother answered. "Of course."

She could practically taste the lie. It lingered in the air, as putrid and suffocating as a stench that wouldn't fade.

"I know you have a plan," Zander continued. "I know you do everything with intention, Father, but I ask you to reconsider whether or not this is worth the risk. The wraith is more important than my trip to the north. Let me pursue this man. Yes, I want to dissect that creature King Edward captured, but the Wraithblade becomes more of a threat with each passing day. Call Quinn home. Let me end this. We're trying to break her, not destroy the country by letting this madman be out there longer than he should."

As she forced herself to sit still, it took everything in her not to growl like a caged beast. Her body coiled, ready to strike at the first thing she saw, and she fought the urge to tear through the wall to ring Zander's neck. A furious scream built in her throat, and she pressed the back of her head against the stone wall to stifle it.

Tears welled in her eyes, but she forced them back. Her father had warned her throughout her childhood that Starlings didn't cry. They punched things until they felt better.

Specifically, she wanted to punch Zander.

"I believe it was you who wanted to 'break her,'" their father corrected. "She's my miracle child. A gift from the Fates. I adore her, and I want her to be happy. Her duty as a Starling woman has evolved beyond missions and battles, that's all. It's merely time for her to hang up her sword."

"But if she doesn't—"

"I maintain the oath I made when we started this. If this failed hunt of hers doesn't break her spirit, then yes. I will break it for her."

Her heart shattered. The rage in her chest sputtered and died at his confession, like a soldier snuffed out in an instant by an unseen arrow from afar.

Teagan sighed, the sound exhausted and heavy. "Be patient, son. Henry took years to build his armies, and even then, no one learned the truth of what he was. In the scheme of things, seventeen more days won't make a difference. Your chance to face this man is coming. When she fails to capture him, you will have your chance at glory."

When.

Not if, but when.

The ringing in Quinn's ear grew to a deafening scream as she stared at the floor beneath her boots. Her lungs couldn't get enough air. Her head thudded with the searing throb of a migraine, and the ache only further muddied her attempts to process what she was hearing.

"I defer to you, Father," Zander said, his tone dripping with revulsion.

Curse the Fates. She had heard him use that tone before, but only ever in the weeks leading up to disobedience. A handful of times in his career, he'd gone rogue and pursued the missions he believed to be worthy of his time, even if they differed from the ones he'd been given.

Her brother didn't want to wait. He wanted to *act*, and he wouldn't be patient for long.

"Have you chosen a suitor for her, yet?" Zander asked, probably to change the subject. "Somewhere far off, perhaps? South Haven would suit her, don't you think?"

To her horror, her father laughed.

He *laughed*.

"I wish you two would get along," he said. "Why you hate each other with such fervor is beyond me."

Quinn stifled a disgusted scoff. She had only ever wanted to make her father proud. For years, she had tried to help Zander on his missions, like a good soldier, only for him to sabotage her efforts. Every time she tried to help him, he'd made her look like a fool.

In her earliest memory, Zander had pushed her off a balcony. At thirteen, he had easily overpowered her. If not for her newly formed friendship with the young vougel who had saved her, she would've died on the rocks.

Her brother had always hated her, and she had never understood why. For all she knew, it stemmed from some misguided contest for their father's love.

Only one child could be Teagan's favorite.

"Several noblemen in Wildefaire are interested," her father admitted. "Perhaps after we humiliate them with our superior Isletide Solution, we can strongarm them into a takeover and gain control of their refineries with her at the center of the deal."

"That could work. It's far enough away that she wouldn't interfere here at home."

"Zander," her father said, a warning in his tone.

"Apologies."

After a moment of silence, her father groaned. "Perhaps you're right. Perhaps it's best to keep her far from Lunestone. Otmund has made his request, of course, but I doubt I'll honor it."

"It seems odd, doesn't it? For him to want her?"

"I've seen stranger pairs, but she deserves better."

Quinn grimaced with disgust.

As if this couldn't get any worse. The Fates were testing her, and she didn't know how much more of this she could take.

Otmund, the man she saw as family, who had practically raised her during her summers in Mossvale, had asked for her hand.

He had claimed to have sent her on this mission, but he must've been complicit in all of this. Like them, he wanted to break her. He wanted to watch her fail.

Even Otmund had lied to her.

"Perhaps we can arrange a coup across the lake," her father continued. "With the right man at her side, she could sit on the Oakenglen throne. It would be the ultimate prize to have a Starling control that city once and for all. Think of it, Zander." The Master General sighed wistfully. "After that, we'll own everything. Saldia will belong to us, and us alone."

"We already had a Starling on the throne," Zander pointed out. "Celine—"

"Celine doesn't count," their father interrupted. "She's only a quarter Starling, and I never did find a way to control that woman. She's too headstrong. Quinn, however, will do what she's told."

The last flicker of Quinn's rage shattered, and she sank against the stone wall as her body surrendered to the overwhelming shock of all she had heard today. It felt as though her chest had been cracked open and left to drain onto the floor.

Her head swam with her father's words. With his betrayal.

Zander grumbled. "Queen Quinn. Can you imagine even saying that? It's ridiculous to put those words together."

"We would change her name. It's common before a coronation."

She grimaced at the very idea. Not even her *name* belonged to her anymore.

"I should take that throne, Father," Zander insisted. "Not her."

"Watch that greed of yours," the Master General warned. "A man can't keep two thrones. One, yes, but two? Your selfishness will undo you, and you'll lose both."

"But Quinn is too impulsive," her brother argued. "Let me take her place in Oakenglen. Given what I've learned from you, I would be a good king."

"You would be a *great* king, son, but you will be a far better Master General of the Lightseers."

"Thank you, Father." A barely restrained smile brightened her brother's voice.

"This castle? This dynasty I've built for you?" Their father paused, and she could imagine him gesturing to the room around him. "This is your destiny, Zander. Even if you don't sit on the Oakenglen throne, you will control the Capital from a distance. Manage it through your sister's new husband. We'll choose a man who fears us. As Queen of Oakenglen, Quinn will find the purpose she has always craved, and that will be enough to ensure she behaves. It's the smartest move."

"Yes, sir," her brother reluctantly conceded.

"Good. I'll figure out the details of the Oakenglen coup. For now, prepare to leave. I'll have more for us to discuss when you return. You're dismissed."

A chair scraped across the floor, and almost imperceptible footsteps trailed toward the exit. A hinge creaked, and a door slammed moments later. The muffled murmur of a conversation filtered through the closed door, and just like that, they were gone.

Somewhere in the depths of Quinn's hazy mind, a warning for her to move urged her to get up. To stand.

To avoid being discovered as she left the secret passage, she had to hurry. She tried to get to her feet, but her body wouldn't budge.

Every fiber of her being ached to blame this betrayal on Zander. Perhaps he had warped their father's mind, somehow. Perhaps this was nothing more than his final act of sabotage, where he'd spun half-truths or outright lies to convince their father to agree to this plan.

There had to be an explanation that didn't shatter her world.

As she sat there in her breathless shock, a painful sting cut through her hand. She winced and opened her palm to find blood still pooling on the dagger's blade.

In a rush, the blistering pain cleared her head.

The fiery rage crashed back into her chest. As her nose creased with a grimace of utter loathing, she scowled into the empty shadows of her secret tunnel.

Her hand tightened around the blade in her palm, intentionally this time. Jolts of agony shot clear up to her shoulder, but she only tightened her fist. More blood dripped onto the floor.

The pain gave her life. It woke her up.

Under her augmented strength, the steel in her palm trembled. Her arm shook as she held the dagger even tighter. Thick ribbons of pain shot through her wrist, but she didn't care.

She didn't stop.

The blade shattered in her palm. The broken hilt fell, and her free hand snatched it from the air. Fragmented shards of the blade rained like glass onto the floor, barely audible.

Even in the most dire of moments, a good Lightseer made no sound, and she had always striven to be one of the best. Her rage, however, only burned hotter.

Today, her father and brother had spoken with excruciating candor. With her supposedly out of the castle, perhaps they had assumed they could speak more freely.

In the end, it didn't matter. She had unearthed the truth. What she did next would speak volumes of who she truly was. Her eyes squeezed shut, and a single furious tear rolled down her cheek.

It was time to face the facts.

Fact. Her father had never believed she could handle this mission to hunt the so-called assassin. He had sent her after the Wraithblade unprepared, with the intent to break her. Now more than ever, she doubted her target had truly killed King Henry. The stranger in the woods had probably been nothing more than a useful tool in Teagan's plan to break her resolve.

Fact. To her father, the end justified the means. He would do anything to her if it meant she hung up her Firesword *Aurora* beside Gwendolyn's *Honor* and Victoria's *Divinity*. He wanted to retire her, once and for all. The mission she had thought would earn her admiration and respect had been nothing more than a ploy to waste her time and kill her fire.

Something warm dripped onto her thigh. Her eyes snapped open as blood dribbled out of the red pool in her palm. She stretched her fingers wide, and more pain splintered through her body. Ribbons of numbness danced along her fingertips as fiery jolts of pain shot up her arm, and the agony brought her back into the moment. Her vision sharpened as she stared at the dark clots forming along the edge of the deep slice in her skin.

Fact. Quinn Starling didn't surrender. The swing of a sword in the heat of a battle felt like life to her. The thrill of a brush with death made her feel at one with the world.

No one would take that from her, not even the legendary Master General of the Lightseers.

Her father. Otmund. Traitors, both of them.

She grimaced with unbridled disgust. Aside from Blaze, Quinn had only ever trusted four people. Today, two of those four had betrayed her.

Perhaps even Gwendolyn and her mother didn't deserve her trust.

She didn't know what to believe anymore, but she did know one thing for certain: there was more at stake than even she knew. Her eyes narrowed as the bonfire in her chest surged with a fresh wave of rage.

Resolute and more determined than ever, she finally pushed herself to her feet and left the shattered remnants of her blade on the floor. Solving the mystery of the so-called assassin in the woods—the Wraithblade—was no longer about impressing her father.

No honor waited on the other side. No glory. No triumph. Her father wouldn't put his hand on her shoulder and say he was proud of her. Nothing she did would be enough for that man. As she accepted that ice-cold reality, the last of her terror died.

As of this moment, the only approval she craved was her own. Once she left Lunestone, she would use every ounce of her tenacity and willpower to unravel the lies her family had woven.

Even if it killed her.

CHAPTER FORTY-NINE
OTMUND

As he sat alone in a meeting room in the eastern tower of Lunestone, Otmund waited for Zander Starling to join him. He drummed his fingers on the wooden table before him in the silence, with only the breeze off the lake to keep him company. Waves crashed against the rocks below the open window, and a gull cried on the lonely air.

White and blue paint, flecked by years of use, coated the table before him in what had once been the Lightseer crest. With nothing on the walls, not even draperies over the window, the décor in this part of the castle paled in comparison to what he was used to as a Lightseer Viceroy.

The marble tables and plush thrones of the northern tower would've been more comfortable, but he didn't want Teagan to learn of this meeting. Otmund's entire plan hinged on keeping the man from interfering.

Something bright flashed in his periphery, and Otmund glared out the window. Beyond the castle, the sun's rays glinted off the frothing waves, but he hadn't come here to enjoy Lunestone's natural beauty.

He'd taken the Rift from Mossvale to ensure the Wraithblade didn't have a chance to intercept him. As the days turned into weeks, he'd had to be careful not to give the peasant an opportunity to strike.

Quinn still hadn't returned, and her delay frankly didn't make sense. Usually, she was faster than this. Though he had grown accustomed to seeing several moves ahead in this game he played against the Fates, he wasn't sure how much longer he could lie low and rely on his little puppets.

For the new Wraithblade to evade the Lightseers for this long meant they were either underestimating him, or he had impressive skills beyond even what Otmund had witnessed in the field.

Both options deeply concerned the Lord of Mossvale and future King of Saldia.

As he leaned back into his chair, his shoulders tense from night after restless night of wondering where this man could be, he sifted through what he would say to Zander. This new plan of his was desperate, and he knew it—but if it failed, his days were numbered.

The handle rustled, and the door smacked against the wall with a dramatic crash as Zander stormed into the room. The Lieutenant General glared at Otmund from under his thick red brows as he slammed the door shut behind him.

"This had better be worth my time, Soulblud."

"It always is." Otmund leaned back in his chair and donned his mask of cool indifference—the only one that worked on the men of the Starling bloodline.

"Get to it, then." Zander's boots barely made a sound as he passed by the chair Otmund had pulled aside for him. Instead, he stood by the window and peered out over the lake—checking for anyone foolish enough to listen in, no doubt.

The time had come for Otmund to weave a fresh web of lies.

"Quinn has taken too long," he began. "I trust you have a backup plan in place for when she fails?"

"Of course."

"How will you ensure you retrieve the Bloodbane dagger from her? If she refuses to—"

Zander scoffed and crossed his arms over his chest as he glared out the window.

At the Lightseer's brazen lack of restraint, a twisted grin pulled at the corners of Otmund's mouth. He rubbed his jaw to cover the smile and to ensure the Lieutenant General drank in his lies while he played dumb.

"You sent her after this man without the only weapon that could protect her from a simmering soul?"

"Quiet, you buffoon." Zander's gaze shifted to the door. "These rooms aren't as secured as those in the northern tower."

A half-truth, if not a blatant lie. Otmund had scoured the area around this room to ensure it was safe to speak freely, and he knew Zander would've done the same before agreeing to meet here.

"My apologies." He set a hand on his heart as he feigned embarrassment at the gaff he'd intentionally made. "Just in case, perhaps we should ask Victoria to make another?"

"I assume you'll pay for it, then?" Zander scowled, the creases in his forehead deepening as his nose creased with disdain. "The sheer cost to make one of these baffles even me, Otmund. Besides, we haven't been able to catch a blightwolf for nearly two seasons. They're smart and don't fall for the same trap twice."

"A fair—"

"As if I would ever give something so precious to her, of all people," Zander muttered, not even listening. "Besides, don't act coy. I doubt Celine kept hers in exile. Word is she gave it to you. You claim you want Quinn as your wife, but you didn't give her your blade, now did you? You're just as responsible as we are for sending her out there unprepared."

Otmund balked, feigning outrage at the insult despite the fact that Celine's blade rested in a scabbard hidden on his leg. "What an atrocious lie."

"Is it?" Zander pushed off the wall by the window and stalked closer, his unwavering gaze narrowing as he neared. "Those blades swapped hands many times in the chaos, but I saw Celine pull you aside before she left. After Henry escaped, the two of you had no reason to pause and have a conversation. Time was of the essence, and he was getting away. What did she tell you, Otmund? What did you promise her in exchange for the dagger?"

"I mentored her." Otmund pushed to his feet, and his chair scraped against the floor as it nearly fell over. Though Zander towered over him, he craned his neck to keep the man's eye. Anger blistered through him as the future leader of Lunestone inched toward the truth, and a shred of his genuine rage slipped through his mask of indifference. "She was saying goodbye, just as any student would to—"

"You were supposed to kill our *target* out in that field." Zander jabbed his finger hard into Otmund's chest, and a ripple of pain snaked from the point of impact. His voice dropped to a harsh whisper as he got dangerously close. "You were supposed to bottle the ghoul, just as you promised you would when we began this coup. If you hadn't acted so quickly at the Rift, rest assured I would have gone with you to guarantee you followed through on your promises."

Zander allowed the silence to linger, and Otmund resisted the urge to shove the Starling backward to get some space.

"Hmm," the Lieutenant General said, reading something in Otmund's furious gaze. "And yet, how convenient it was for you that your men stumbled across him. As the rest of us searched the tunnels, you somehow found the guard whom Henry had killed to open the Rift. You charged through with only a handful of soldiers, ever the hero. How curious that, by the time the rest of us learned where you'd slunk off to, you had already returned—alone. How *strange*, Otmund."

He held the Lieutenant General's treasonous glare and narrowed his eyes in warning. "What are you implying, Zander?"

"I imply nothing." His voice dropped an octave as he leaned in closer. "I'm *warning* you, Otmund. I'm warning you that I'm aware of what you did, and I believe the list of demands you gave us are a decoy. You truly want gold, spellgust, and my sister?"

"Of course I—"

He snorted derisively. "You think I believe you? You think my father believes you? I suspect you have other goals you're not divulging to the rest of us, no matter how feeble and weak you pretend to be. If I find evidence of such treason, you won't have to worry about keeping your Bloodbane dagger on you because it won't be the peasant who slits your throat in your sleep."

Zander let the silence hang suspended above them and looked him right in the eye, daring him to speak.

Daring him to lie.

Otmund barely breathed. His heart skipped beats with painful irregularity as it raced in his chest, and he figured the Lieutenant General could probably hear it. Sweat licked his palms, and he resisted the impulse to wipe them on his tunic. He held Zander's gaze, refusing to let even the barest hint of his fear through his mask.

The Starling heir turned his back as the lull stretched on and returned to his place by the window. While Zander studied the spring day outside, Otmund's gaze drifted to the floor as he sifted through how this affected his plans. If he needed to change course, he had to do it quickly. Perhaps he needed to word his suggestions differently, or—

No.

Regardless of Zander's threat, this was still going to work. Even better, it would solve two problems for Otmund. It would end Zander's suspicions and get him the wraith, all at once.

He cleared his throat. "I have a solution, if you'd stop being a brute for two minutes."

Zander didn't answer. With his hands clasped behind his back, he didn't so much as acknowledge that Otmund had spoken.

"I spent a few evenings in the vaults—"

"Against my father's orders to leave Lunestone, apparently," the Lieutenant General interrupted. "I will ensure your access is more heavily monitored going forward."

"I am a member of the Chamber!" Otmund slammed his fist on the table, perfectly justified in his rage as the wooden planks shook beneath his fury. "I'm the Master Strategist to your father, for the Fates' sake. I will always have access to Lunestone, and when you stop interrupting me, you'll understand why that is to your advantage!"

"Make your point, then."

"My point," Otmund muttered as he adjusted his shirt with an irritated huff. "Very well. My point is that while in the vaults, I discovered the location of Slaybourne Citadel."

Zander glanced over his shoulder and raised one skeptical eyebrow. "And why is that interesting? It's a ruin by now. After all these centuries, looters must've picked it clean. There can't be anything left."

"The Wraith King earned his title by being a specter of death, Zander," Otmund chided. "He used fear and raw power to crush anyone he faced. You truly believe a man like that wouldn't have measures in place to prevent looters in the event of his death?"

The Starling heir's gaze drifted to the floor, and his brows furrowed with thought.

Good. Evidently, Otmund still had a chance to snare the man in his web. He simply needed to weave it carefully and play the warrior's weaknesses against him.

Pride. Greed. Ambition. Despite Zander's innate talent and clever mind, he shared the same flaws as the most easily manipulated men.

Otmund tapped his finger absently against the table before him to settle his racing pulse. "The legends and accounts we have of the Wraith King claim he was a powerful necromancer. We have a scroll hidden in the vault that alleges he laid traps in his home that would outlive him, merely as revenge on anyone who dared usurp him."

"Rumors." Zander dismissed the claim with a lazy flick of his wrist. "Unprovable nonsense, and I hardly see how it matters."

"I figured you of all people would understand where I was going with this."

Pride—the easiest weakness to exploit.

Zander glared at him over his shoulder, but Otmund didn't so much as flinch.

"Why are you wasting my time with this?" the Lieutenant General demanded.

"Because the wraith has a new master, and that new master has no castle." Otmund pressed his palm flat against the table. Splinters poked into his hand, but he used the blips of pain to distract himself from his fluttery breath as he planted the seeds of a new idea. "If this new master truly is a peasant, it means he has nothing. No stronghold. No base of operations. No fortune like Henry used to buy loyalty as he mounted his crusade. Why wouldn't the wraith go home? The ghoul knows how to reach Slaybourne, even though it's been lost to the world for centuries. We do, too. It's the perfect fortress, and we can't allow him to reach it on his own."

"And why is that?"

"You should truly read the scrolls down there," Otmund chided, scratching yet again at the man's pride. "I'm surprised you haven't."

"There are tens of thousands of scrolls and books in the vault," Zander snapped. "Unlike you, I have important matters to attend to on a daily basis."

"Then let me enlighten you," Otmund offered with a flourish of his hand. "After the Wraith King died, Death's Door locked. Given how secured his city was, nestled in those mountains, no one was able to get in or out once the enchanted gate closed. Only a few survivors from that night managed to escape, and it was their accounts I read down there in the vault. Those who didn't make it out screamed with terror as it closed, as if something were chasing them, and those screams lasted into the night. One by one, each scream cut short, until there was only silence."

He paused for effect and lowered his gaze in an effort to appear traumatized by the true story. After so many years of lying and deceit, it felt strange to report something exactly as he'd heard it.

Zander leaned his palms against the windowsill and looked out over the water as he listened. "You have yet to get to your point, Otmund."

"I'm about to."

"And that is?"

"You and I can help each other. I can give you glory, and you can give me what I truly want."

Zander shook his head, as though he were playing along to a game he loathed. "And what, pray tell, do you truly want?"

"Your sister," Otmund lied. "If I give you the location of the fortress, you'll be able to save her from a gruesome fate of dying at the wraith's hands. Once you kill the Wraithblade, all you have to do is tell your father I was the one who told you where to go. The Wraithblade will be dead, we will have the wraith in our control, and I will finally be in Teagan's good graces. In his gratitude, your father will give your sister to me. We all win."

"That's a simmering soul, you dolt." The Lieutenant General leaned briefly toward Otmund as he lowered his voice. "If I kill the Wraithblade, that abomination will fuse with me."

"Exactly."

"What in the Fates' name are you—"

"It's the only way to bring the wraith back to Lunestone," Otmund explained. "It's the only way to keep it from killing you as you bring it here. You see, Zander, I discovered something else important while down in the vault. I unearthed a way to extract it from you without killing you. It's complicated, but there's substantial evidence it has been done before. I swear on my life and fortune, Zander. This will work."

A brazen lie, but the man didn't need to know that. Otmund had already crafted a story to feed Teagan about how the wraith had corrupted his son, just as it had warped Henry.

It wasn't ideal to lose a puppet, of course, but they were running out of time.

The Lieutenant General leaned one shoulder against the wall by the window, and he lifted his chin as his eyes narrowed with suspicion. Even from here, Otmund could see the cogs of doubt and skepticism churning in the Starling warrior's mind.

Luckily, he'd come prepared with a final argument that couldn't fail. Everyone in Lunestone knew Zander hated his sister, and their feud gave Otmund ample fuel for his fire.

"Think of what it would do to Quinn," he added. "You come in, just as her thirty days are nearly gone, and you save the day. You will succeed where she failed. Just imagine what it would do to her. She would be forced to accept that you're her superior, and perhaps she will finally hang up her sword. I suspect it would break this warrior's will of hers, don't you?"

Zander's body went eerily still, and he raised one eyebrow as his gaze darted toward the ceiling.

Hooked.

Now, to tempt his greed.

"Teagan will be even more proud of you than he already is," Otmund continued. "He will see you as the heir you truly are. And who knows? With Quinn finally married off and out of the picture, perhaps you can even take Oakenglen. Think of it—the man with two thrones. You would be a living legend, with a legacy greater even than your father's."

A lie, of course. Once Otmund killed Zander and obtained the wraith, Oakenglen and Saldia would be his. He would be remembered while Zander became a footnote in history, and the Soulblud name would finally mean something in this Fates-forsaken world.

"It sounds like you want me to set an empty trap." The Lieutenant General paced in front of the window. "We have no guarantee the wraith will even go to Slaybourne. We need proper bait to draw him out of the shadows."

"Where else could he go? He has nothing, Zander. However, if you must take bait with you, take the only weapon that can kill the wraith. I suspect the ghoul wants the Bloodbane daggers, wherever they are." Otmund feigned indifference despite the knife strapped to his leg.

"You may be right," Zander admitted absently as he stared over the water. "It would be wisest to set a trap for him nearby. Why go to the fortress? Traveling to an isolated ruin would be risky."

"Perhaps," Otmund conceded. "But what does he want more? The daggers, or a fortress? If you set a trap anywhere but Slaybourne, would he take the bait?"

Zander didn't answer. The man continued his pacing and rubbed his jaw, lost in thought.

"We don't know enough about this man to know what he'll do." Otmund wove his fingers together and leaned his elbows on the table before him. "We must get to the peasant before he reaches Slaybourne. If he's not already there, I doubt he will wait long. Setting a trap anywhere else risks letting him take back the citadel."

"I can't allow that," the Starling warrior said under his breath. "If he already reached it, we'd be forced to mount a crusade against him. We cannot let this get out of control." He paused, and his hand curled into a fist. "Not again."

The Lieutenant General stared out over the massive lake while Otmund let the silence settle between them. As Zander neared his time as the Master General of Lunestone, it would become much more difficult for his father to control him.

Teagan's era was almost over, and Zander's ambition would be the end of him.

"You have a deal," the Starling warrior said, his voice even and calm.

A jolt of relief shot through Otmund's chest, but he resisted the impulse to smile in victory. "Smart man."

"I'll leave in the morning, but I have things to attend to first. In the meantime, get me a map."

"I come prepared, Lieutenant General." Otmund tugged an envelope out of the pocket in his shirt.

He set the parchment on the table, the folded papers inside too heavy for the wind to take with it. He'd provided more than enough detail on how to not only reach Slaybourne, but advice on how to kill the Wraithblade.

After all, he desperately needed this to work.

"Slaybourne is in the Decay," he explained. "There's a reason that part of our world has always been dead. The Wraith King's magic is still active somehow, all these centuries later. Be cautious."

Zander didn't answer.

As the Starling heir stared out over the lake, Otmund took his leave. He stepped into the hall, careful to silently close the door behind him so as not to break the man's focus. He needed the seeds of this plan to take root deep in Zander's greedy heart.

If this ploy failed, Otmund would need to protect himself, and that meant doing something drastic he truly didn't want to do.

For now, he would go to Mossvale and set his trap for Zander—and for the ghoul. The Wraith King had tarnished many men's souls over the decades, but now Otmund would see if he could be the one to corrupt the dead.

ZANDER

As a spring breeze rolled off the lake, Zander closed his eyes and savored the sweet aroma of honeysuckle swirling in the wind. His mind buzzed with the possibilities Otmund had presented him.

Somewhere in Otmund's plan, there had to be a thread of deceit he hadn't yet noticed. The more he worked with the Lord of Mossvale, the more he doubted the man's facade as a weak but otherwise useful tool. He once thought of Otmund as a pawn, but now he suspected the man was a player.

The plan seemed so simple—take on the mantle of the Wraithblade just long enough to bring the wraith to justice. Even if he had to sacrifice his pride to host such a vile atrocity of nature, at least the thing would die in the end.

But that all depended on whether or not Otmund had truly conceived of a way to extract the wraith without killing Zander.

Never trust another man with your life, his father had often warned.

It was advice he had always heeded.

If he ultimately bore the burden of the wraith for the rest of his life, so be it. His mind was sharper than Henry's had ever been, and he could steel himself against whatever temptations the ghoul dangled before him.

In the end, he already had almost everything he desired. There wasn't much the wraith could use to tempt him.

As word of his upcoming mission to the north spread through the ranks, the entire castle expected him to go to Hazeltide. It gave him the perfect cover to head to the Decay, as no one would suspect he'd changed course. He finally had the chance to do what he truly wanted to do—kill this wraith before it destroyed Lunestone.

The last time someone new had discovered the wraith, hundreds of thousands of people had died. Henry had conquered Saldia like a black tide of smoke and slaughter.

Teagan had bowed before the last Wraithblade, claiming that he'd chosen to play the long game for the sake of Lunestone's future. Zander, however, would not bow to this new conqueror.

He had always revered his father, but the more he dwelt on the man's errors, the more he wondered if Teagan had gone soft. He'd let a simmering soul run free to teach a girl a lesson about playing war, when Lunestone's future depended on the public believing the souls were gone. He'd submitted to a warlord and corrupted the Lightseer name by honoring Henry's demands. He hadn't sent a crusade for a simmering soul in over a decade, and the one Viceroy who had defied orders and gone on her own had never emerged from the swamps of Nethervale.

Though the simmering souls still existed, Teagan had clearly given up on his attempts to destroy them.

He'd given up on his *duty*.

One day, Lunestone would pass to Zander. Perhaps it was time for him to show his father exactly the sort of Master General he would be.

He rolled out his shoulders and, as he debated the risks of his plan, he paced the decrepit meeting room usually reserved for the newly enlisted. His feet tapped against the floorboards, light and nearly undetectable from his modified Prowlport augmentation.

The greatest risk, of course, came from facing the wraith.

In his career thus far, there had been twelve attempts on his life. Each time a necromancer had come for him, they'd waited until he'd traveled alone into an isolated area. Only then had they attacked. They had all lost, of course, and he'd gleaned quite a few useful tidbits about Nethervale as he'd tortured them. It had taken him several assassination attempts before he finally saw the pattern, but now he always went into isolated stretches of the world prepared.

This time, he would be the one to set the trap.

He would walk into the Decay alone to give the Wraithblade incentive to follow, but he wouldn't underestimate the wraith's abilities. He would bring enough enchanted weapons to take down an army.

Zander would ambush the Wraithblade right in front of Death's Door. Never the patient type, he would need to ensure his prey learned only enough of his plan to ensure the man came to him.

The more vocal gossips in the castle would help him achieve that.

Of course, spreading whispers of his plan meant others might wander into the Decay, but only those who knew Slaybourne's location would survive. Though his father would eventually learn about his disobedience, all would be forgiven once he secured the wraith.

He frowned with disappointment as a thought occurred—Quinn would hear about his plan, too. If she interfered, he would have to put her and the Wraithblade in their place at the same time.

As his plan fell into place, he rubbed his freshly shaven jaw and grinned.

He would be the man who finally rid the world of the simmering souls. His name would go down in history as the Great Lightseer, the man who defeated the last shreds of the Great Necromancer. The man who overcame the darkness. The master of light.

He would become more of a legend than even his father.

Zander stared out over the water, more certain than ever that this would work. It was time he gave his father—and all of Lunestone—a taste of what the future held.

CHAPTER FIFTY

QUINN

As the morning sun crept across the sky, Quinn sat on a balcony railing in Lunestone's southern tower and stared out over the lake. Her legs dangled high above the waves as the water smashed against the castle's walls. Wooden boards in the empty pier groaned as the lake churned, and white foam crashed across the planks that would be teeming with life in mere hours as the supply shipments came in.

A gust of wind tore through her hair, and the red curls blocked half of her view. The gale shoved at her back like a child trying to send her over the railing, but she tensed her abdomen and kept her precarious seat.

To the west, massive torches burned atop towering posts along the shores of the island refinery. Day and night, rain or shine, the fires burned. As long as the facility produced Firebreath spellgust for the world to use, those flames would rage.

The heavy winds had cleared any trace of the clouds from the sky. As a consequence, she could see clear to the other side of the lake. Usually, she had to imagine Oakenglen in the distance, but today the city shimmered like a mirage on the horizon.

Her appointment with her father had come and gone. In all her years, she had never once missed a meeting with him. Today, however, she just hadn't been able to face him.

Not yet.

Questions surged through her like a frothing rapid. Deep in her chest, the bitter fire still burned with the sort of rage and resentment she never imagined she could feel.

She replayed the conversation in her mind over and over to numb herself to what she had learned, but it only made her more furious.

Anger like this would only distract her. Distractions led to mistakes, but try as she might, nothing she did could dampen her ire. She couldn't waste time sitting on a balcony, lost in thought, but for the first time in years she simply didn't know what to do.

The game had changed, and her plan had to change with it.

Though she had enough money to go into self-imposed exile, money wasn't everything. From the moment she had first seen her father's sword *Sovereign*, her purpose had been to fight beside the Lightseers she had admired since she was little.

Now, though, she knew the truth. Neither her father nor Lunestone deserved her admiration.

But if she wasn't a Lightseer, she didn't know what she was. It was all she had ever been.

Her father wanted to break her. As long as he thought she was chasing her tail and wasting her time, she had seventeen days left to fly free. The moment he realized she knew the truth, he would try to chain her.

He'd confessed as much already. If she didn't break on her own, he would break her himself.

A ribbon of terror snaked through her at the thought of facing off against her father. Despite her augmentations and strength—despite everything she had done to hone her skills and perfect her art—his wrath horrified her.

Teagan Starling had brought some of the best warriors in Saldia to their knees. They had groveled before him, begging for mercy he hadn't shown. Watching him fight had always struck raw fear into her heart. The lightning. The destruction. The intense and unbridled power. He possessed magic and a keen mind few could ever dream of wielding, and fighting at his side had once inspired her to be better.

But to think of his fury turned on her—she shuddered.

"And for what?" she muttered, unable to quell her rising disdain.

Motherhood—an honorable role for those who wanted it, but that life had never appealed to her. According to tradition, a Starling woman had only a handful of duties and a wealth of freedom, but her duties came first.

Hang up her sword.

Master an arcane skill.

Create the next Starling generation and teach them to honor the patriarch.

To obey *Zander*.

She shuddered with revulsion at the idea of raising a child to obey the man who hated her.

Quinn had always assumed she would be exempt. She excelled on the field in ways Victoria and even Gwendolyn had never mastered, and a sliver of a dream in her soul had convinced her that it would be enough to avoid a life of backdoor deals and arranged marriages.

How foolish.

The young men she had tried and failed to love in her youth had bored her. Liars and braggarts, all of them. In the end, every single one of them had only shown interest because they'd wanted something from her. Recognition. The respect of her father. A glamour from her mother. A favor from her brother.

None of them had wanted *her*.

As the glittering sun turned the waves into diamonds, she grabbed the edge of the railing. Her fingers bit into the stone. The pain of her nails against rock splintered through her, sharp and clear, waking her up. Clearing her mind.

To hell with Zander.

To hell with her *father*.

She would not roll over and let her soul die to appease either of them.

Whisper-quiet footsteps scuffed up the stairs behind her. As lost in her thoughts as she was, she almost missed them, but her ear twitched as she listened.

Heavy. Measured. Confident. Each step was taken with precision and intention.

Her father's gait.

She stiffened, still not ready to speak to him or even look him in the eye. Her grip on the railing tightened on impulse, and the stone cracked under her enhanced strength.

Play it smart, she warned herself. *Don't do something stupid just because you're angry.*

Fire erupted in her palms, even as she held tight to the stone railing. She briefly shut her eyes to stuff away her rage. The flames rolled across her fingers, and it took several seconds of carefully focused breathing for them to recede. As she sat up straighter, the flames mercifully dissolved into the gale rolling across the lake.

Without so much as a glance over her shoulder, she braced herself for the worst as he reached the top step. "Good morning, Father."

"No one alive can sneak up on the great Quinn Starling." He laughed. "Not even me."

Even just yesterday, she would have chuckled and thanked him for the compliment. Today, she couldn't even bring herself to turn around. She kept her gaze trained on the water to keep her temper in check.

"My secretary said you scheduled an appointment but never arrived."

"My apologies, sir." Even though she wanted nothing more than to shove his lies in his face, she forced herself to keep protocol. Anything less than the utmost respect and obedience would've raised suspicion. "I've been racking my brain about the assassin. I must have lost track of time."

A blatant lie to anyone who truly knew her.

His steps neared, a little louder now. "I forgive you. It happens to the best of us."

When he reached her, he set his hand on her shoulder and gently squeezed. In the past, she had always taken it as a sign of affection. Now, she questioned everything he did. Perhaps he saw it as a subtle reminder of his control and authority.

One little push, after all, and he could shove her onto the rocks below.

She resisted the urge to shrug him off. To have him touch her felt like a violation. Her body tensed with the desire to put space between them, but she forced herself to remain still.

"How goes your hunt?" he asked, his voice clear despite the crash of the waves below. "I was surprised to see you back so soon. Have you caught him already?"

She swallowed hard to quell the rising indignation. He knew damn well she hadn't caught him, and he was finding subtle ways to rub that in her face.

"No, sir." Quinn needed a lie to explain why she had come home, and she spun one as quickly as she could think of it. "I followed a dead lead into Oakenglen and checked in to report, as you taught me."

"That's unfortunate." Dissatisfaction hung in the air between them, thick and palpable. "You don't usually need this long to complete your assignments. You so rarely disappoint me, Quinn, that I must confess I'm surprised at your delay."

At his unspoken threat, her body stiffened with dread. The movement had been so unconscious, so habitual, that it made her sick to her stomach. He'd controlled her for so long, and she never noticed.

From his perspective, the first seeds of his plan had probably begun to bloom. He stood at her side, planting doubt in the back of her mind as he prepared her to accept failure.

Teagan gently patted her back. "Perhaps it's time to let Zander take over. Your assignment is of the utmost importance, and we can't afford any more delays. If you have any doubts in your ability—"

"I don't," she interrupted.

His hand left her back, and he stepped into her periphery. A vein in his temple briefly throbbed at the interruption, but he swallowed whatever he had been about to say.

Playing the long game, no doubt.

"Don't let your pride get the better of you, my dear," he warned as they stared out over the water. "Don't let a petty sibling feud get in the way of your mission or our country's safety."

"Never, sir. I only paused to watch the water while Blaze eats. The moment he's ready, I'll leave."

"Leave for where?"

"I have a solid lead," she lied. "On my way into town, I went undercover and picked up reliable information that he's headed west. I'm close."

Outwardly, she remained calm and cool. Her Lightseer training had prepared her for interrogation, and she did her best to channel the unshakeable calm her professors had taught her.

Inwardly, however, she raged with the wrath of a volcano.

"Excellent." He set his hand on her shoulder once again, and she suppressed the urge to shy away from his revolting touch. "I know you will always make me proud, Quinn, in ways Zander can't even fathom."

They were words she had craved her whole life, and yet she felt nothing.

How often have you told Zander the same thing about me? she wanted to say. *How often have you patted his back and made him believe you loved him most?*

"Thank you, sir." Though she tried to force a bit of genuine emotion into the words, she failed.

The shuffle of slippered feet across the stone steps behind them echoed up the corridor, and Quinn frowned as she tried to place the gait. It took a moment of listening to recognize the newcomer, and it wasn't until she heard a familiar sigh that she realized who had joined them.

"Good morning, Mother." She craned her neck to look over her shoulder as her father mercifully let go. "You're up early."

An elegant woman in a dark blue dress reached the top of the steps and leaned one palm against the open doors to the stairwell. As she caught her breath, she smiled warmly at Quinn. Her eyes creased with joy as strands of her blonde hair lifted in the wind.

"Has my darling girl already slayed the monster?" Her eyes darted toward the Master General. "Teagan, darling, I didn't expect to find you up here. What a pleasant surprise."

"Good morning, Madeline." He smiled broadly as he embraced his wife with a kiss on the cheek.

Quinn pinched her eyes shut, finally free of his shadow, and she forced a slow breath to calm herself. After she had stowed away most of the hate in the depths of her core, she swung her legs back over the railing and stood on the balcony with her parents.

"Best of luck," her father said with a nod to her.

"Thank you, sir." She bowed her head as he jogged down the steps. His fiery red hair disappeared into the shadows, and he was finally gone.

Though she still had company, Quinn let out a quiet breath of relief.

"I didn't think you'd finish with your mission so soon." The glamourist tucked a loose strand of Quinn's hair behind her ear and fussed with her jacket. She tugged on the leather and straightened the collar with all the practiced ease of a mother tidying up a young child.

"Mother, please." Quinn playfully smacked away the hands around her collar. "For the Fates' sake, I'm a grown woman."

"You'll always be my miracle baby." Undeterred, she resumed her fussing and tugged out the necklace hidden beneath Quinn's shirt.

The pendant's golden paint glistened in the sunlight, and she flinched at it with mild surprise. She had worn the necklace for so many years that she sometimes forgot it still hung around her neck. Like a lock of hair or a fingernail, it had become a part of her she rarely thought about.

Every Starling wore one from the day they were born, and they wore it until the day they died.

Beneath the phoenix, the family motto had been carved into the heavy pendant, ruthless and elegant all at once.

The wicked die at our feet.

The Starling crest weighed against the chain as Madeline polished it with her sleeve. "What's bothering you, dear?"

"Nothing," Quinn lied.

Her mother scoffed and scrubbed harder at a smudge on the phoenix in the middle of the crest's purple shield. "You might be able to fool your father, but you can't deceive me."

Quinn's smile fell. A thousand questions stormed through her mind, but she didn't dare voice even one of them. "It's nothing. Truly."

"Hmm." Her mother pursed her lips, unconvinced. "Do you know where we are?"

She frowned with confusion. "The south tower."

The master glamourist nodded. "And this balcony? Do you recognize it?"

"Mother, where are you going with this?"

The woman sighed impatiently. "In all your years spent in this fortress, you've only come up to this balcony seven times." Her mother raised one knowing eyebrow and nodded toward the water. "You come up here when you fail, my dear. You come up here when you put a cross in that blasted table of yours."

Quinn groaned and ran a hand through her hair. As the wind tossed several red curls into her face, she turned away and leaned her forearms against the railing. "Am I that obvious?"

"Only to me."

"What do I do, then?" she asked quietly. "If I fail?"

Madeline clicked her tongue in disappointment. "Quinn, my baby, the Starlings don't fail."

"Mother, this is different—"

"You are a Starling, dear, and we *never* give up." The glamourist tugged on Quinn's shoulders and gently turned her around. With her brows knit in determination, she lifted the Starling crest around Quinn's neck into the air to drive her point home. "Even when we fail, even when we flounder, we persevere. That was the first lesson your father taught me all those years ago, when I kept telling him no and he never stopped asking for my hand."

Her mother chuckled, but Quinn leaned again on the railing at the mention of her father. Their courtship had always seemed so romantic, but now she doubted everything he'd ever done.

Perhaps Madeline had been nothing but another victory—nothing more than a powerful woman to conquer.

"Listen to me, my darling." Her mother set her palm flat against Quinn's back, her voice soft and serene as she spoke. "Both success and failure teach us about ourselves. Sometimes, we can learn far more from a loss than we ever could from a victory. No matter what happens after this mission of yours—whether you succeed or fail—you will come out of this a better woman. A *stronger* woman."

Quinn sat with that advice as a powerful gust rolled off the lake. The breath of wind crashed against them, carrying with it the sweet perfume of honeysuckle from somewhere nearby.

Her losses had always been marks of shame, carved into her bedroom table to remind her to be better. They had always fueled her drive for perfection. Perhaps, though, each failure had grains of wisdom in it, if only she looked again at what she had once tried to forget.

"Besides, you're never alone." Madeline lifted the crest around Quinn's neck yet again. "As long as you wear this, you carry the fire of the Starling bloodline with you. Hold it tight and remember—you are one of us. Trust yourself, my love. You always know what to do, even when there's no hope left. I've always admired that about you."

A gentle smile tugged on Quinn's lips. She took her mother's hand in hers as they listened to the waves. "Thank you."

"Now, go out there and finish whatever errand that father of yours sent you on." Madeline toyed with the loose strands of red hair around Quinn's face. "And for the love of the Fates, don't tell me a single thing about it. You scare me senseless every time you come back with another tale of how you nearly died in a battle with some beast or criminal or what have you."

"Yes, ma'am." Quinn reluctantly cleared her throat, and an awkward lull settled into the air between them.

Madeline rubbed her eyes. "You've already had a near-death—"

"You told me not to tell you these things, remember?"

The glamourist huffed. "Soon, you're going to give me gray hair my glamours can't hide. You just wait, Quinn. The day is coming."

Her mother planted a kiss on her cheek, and the woman's satin skirts swished across the stone balcony as she returned to the stairs. When her blonde head disappeared from sight, Quinn draped her arms over the railing and stared out at the water.

Now, she knew exactly what she had to do.

A risky plan began to form, inspired by something the Wraithblade himself had said back in the field by that withered old tree. He'd threatened to kill her the next time they met, and though he seemed like the sort of man who kept his word, this time would be different.

When she next faced the Wraithblade, she would let him think he had won. Quinn Starling, an elite Lightseer who had only failed seven times in her storied career, would surrender to him.

A potentially lethal plan, of course, and surrendering would end one of three ways.

Outcome number one—if he was the sort of man to take prisoners, she would see for herself what this supposed assassin truly valued. She would use her time as his captive to figure out what he wanted, who his allies were, and if he was truly as evil as everyone claimed.

Outcome number two—if he tried to murder her when she surrendered, her orders and the mission she had been given wouldn't matter. Regardless of the consequences, she would kill him herself.

Outcome number three—if he tried to torture or interrogate her after he had taken her prisoner, she needed a backup plan and a means to escape. He would undoubtedly use another Bluntmar collar on her. As much as she hated the idea of wearing that insulting choker, it was an inevitability she had to account for. Her augmentations and potions wouldn't work, at that point, but enchanted items would. That meant she needed to find one he wouldn't steal, even after he took her sword. Something small. Something easily overlooked, but deceptively powerful.

Quinn always went into battle prepared. The deadly feud raging between Lunestone and the simmering souls would change the Saldian tides, and she would not sit idly by as the world burned. Neither the Wraithblade nor her father knew it yet, but this was her war, now.

She merely had yet to pick a side.

After all, she had nothing left to lose. Her respect for the Lightseers and the Chamber had crumbled to dust, and she didn't care about her father's plans for her. Whatever happened, she would face it the only way she knew how—with her sword raised, ready for war.

The Lightseer motto had never rung truer.

Duty above all else.

Even family.

Years ago, Gwendolyn had warned her to keep her own clandestine reserves of coin, spellgust, and enchanted items. It had always seemed like a foolish precaution, since Quinn had the authority to raid the Lunestone armory and treasury at will, but now she was grateful she had heeded her sister's warning. She had millions of coin hidden in every city across the continent, along with vaults full of spellgust, potions, reagents, and weapons.

All secret. All secured.

Someday, she would have to thank Gwendolyn for giving her the single greatest piece of advice she had ever received.

If her father cut her off financially in an effort to bend her to his will, it wouldn't matter. If he banished her from Lunestone and his estate, the only thing she would miss was her mother. Financially, she had enough to get by for the rest of her life.

Teagan Starling couldn't control her anymore.

There were just a few more things to secure. She would raid the treasury and armory one more time, since this was probably her last chance to do so. Victoria and Gwendolyn, despite their blazing red hair and the respect the world held for their family, were forbidden from many areas within Lunestone now that they had retired. That was probably Quinn's fate as well.

She had to make this last raid of the coffers count.

As she pushed off the railing and headed for the stairs, she thought again of the dagger embedded in the table in her room. Maybe she had already failed, since her father's idea of success was to break her.

For now, she chose to leave it upright in the wood until she learned the Wraithblade's intentions and identity for herself.

As of this moment, her father's desires meant nothing. Success was now hers to define.

CHAPTER FIFTY-ONE
CONNOR

In the sky above the burnt-orange bricks of Oakenglen's first exterior, a soft blue glow crept across the navy night. The last of the stars disappeared into the rolling clouds as the sun tossed and turned on the horizon.

Along each of the main streets, amber lamplight dimmed as the approaching day dwarfed their meager flames, and several completely died as their oil emptied.

Connor only had about an hour before the city woke with the dawn.

Oakenglen's middle class dominated this ring of the city. Though he and Sophia had already passed through several streets of white fenced gardens and identical houses in the residential burrows, what they needed lay in one of the first exterior's dozens of shopping districts.

His heavy pack weighed on his shoulder as they paused in an alleyway between a quiet tavern and a playhouse. A row of identical posters along the theatre's brick wall showcased a man cracking a whip at a grotesque wolf. Its fangs protruded from its mouth, easily as long as the man's forearm, and patches of skin across its rabid fur bled onto the stage. Beneath the drawing, elaborate lettering took up the second half of the poster.

Masters Rightfurl and Meagerson present: The Blightwolf.

Connor rolled his eyes. Above him, a candle flickered in a window on the theatre's third floor as someone burned the midnight oil.

He doubted anyone in that playhouse had seen a blightwolf for themselves—or most of the people in the city, for that matter. That had probably given the writers a bit of poetic license to make up nonsense about the horrors lying in wait in the Ancient Woods.

If it kept people out of the forest, so be it. Few truly understood the creatures waiting for them in the blue glow of a woodland night, and even fewer went into the trees prepared enough to handle it.

Their alley opened onto a darkened stretch of the main road where two of the streetlamps had gone out. The cobblestone street led directly to the shops' front doors, and every window along the sleepy boulevard had something for sale behind the glass. A display of furs draped over a trunk. A pile of stuffed bears and horses placed in a rocking chair. A sword as long as Connor's leg resting against an anvil, with a silver plaque displayed on a pedestal beside it.

Above every shop, an identical wooden sign swung on iron hinges over the door. Just as in the towns beyond Oakenglen, a symbol on the wood explained what the shop sold, though hand-carved words also appeared beneath each etched drawing.

Evidently, most people in the city could read.

"We're almost there." Ahead of him, Sophia peered around the corner to check for witnesses before they continued.

The distant clomp of boots on the stone road floated through the air, growing louder by the second.

"Let's go," she whispered.

"Wait." He grabbed her arm and rooted her in place as she tried to dart into the lane. Though she yanked against him with impressive strength—likely due to an augmentation hidden somewhere on her body—he didn't budge.

Her head whipped backward, and she fell into his chest. Her eyebrows knit with anger, and she cursed under her breath as she pushed away from him. "What the hell are you—"

The rumble of boots on stone grew louder, and Sophia's head tilted with the interruption. Her furrowed brows relaxed, and her dark eyes drifted to him as her lips parted with surprise.

Together, they crouched beside the wall, keeping out of sight as six soldiers stepped into the lamplight of a side street barely visible from their vantage point. The guardsmen scanned the dark windows of each tall building as the unit stepped onto the road leading past their hiding place.

Much to Connor's annoyance, the soldiers took their sweet time. They marched in two rows of three, more focused on monitoring the windows than watching where they walked. When they passed through the dark patches of unlit road, their black leather uniforms disappeared from sight. Only the glint of their spears and the stomp of their footsteps gave away their position.

While they waited for the guards to pass, Connor rubbed his tired eyes. Murdoc had only just taken over his twelve-hour watch, but at least Richard wouldn't leave his home without them knowing. After hunting their target through the midnight shadows on their first night in town, they'd nearly lost him when they ran out of dark alleys to hide in. The well-lit roads of the second interior provided precious little cover.

But roofs were much like trees—harder to climb than a trunk, of course, but they offered incredible sightlines over the city. After finding a route onto a neighbor's house, he'd found a way to study the Viceroy without anyone ever knowing.

The six guards stomped up the road, and it took another few minutes for them to round the next corner on their route. As he waited in the dark, forced to crouch and crane his ear in the silence, those few minutes felt like a lifetime.

When the soldiers finally left, Sophia leaned in close. "I envy your senses."

Still unsettled over this little mission of theirs, he ignored the compliment. "I'm not a fan of stealing what we need to brew the Hackamore potion."

"You and I are both wanted by the Lightseers," she whispered back. "We don't know how many people know your face, and as for me—well, let's just assume they do. We can't exactly walk into a shop and buy what we need."

He frowned as she darted into the road ahead of him. She was right, of course, but he wouldn't admit it out loud. With an annoyed sigh, he followed after her.

At first, he'd ordered Murdoc to go shopping on their behalf, just as the man had done to get them their clothes. It had worked out well, since no one in Oakenglen or the king's guard recognized the former Blackguard.

Sophia had refused to even give the ruffian a list, though, because apparently the reagents needed for this potion required painfully specific quality, quantity, and care. One dried petal instead of a fresh one, or one nut roasted with salt, and they risked an ineffective potion. To ensure they got the truth out of Richard, everything had to be brewed perfectly.

Everything in him wanted to believe she was being annoyingly picky, but he didn't know for sure.

When they crossed the road, he and the necromancer crouched in yet another shadowy alley. Their pre-dawn shopping trip gave them the most amount of darkness and cover. During their four days in the city, they'd learned the hour before dawn had the most extinguished streetlamps.

However, it also meant they had almost no time at all to get what they needed and get back to the lowest ring of the city without being discovered.

No pressure.

He set his muscled shoulder against the brick building beside them and scanned the walls above. Silence rolled over the city like a fog, thick and heavy.

When no footsteps or hushed murmurs drifted through the air, Sophia darted through another dark patch of road. Barely ten feet away from them as they ran, lamps cast an orange glow across large circles of the lonely street.

"How much farther?" he whispered into the shadows.

"We're nearly there."

Instead of darting out into the amber lamplight at the end of their shadowy path, Sophia set her back against the corner of the building and peered into an unlit maintenance alley dividing two rows of shops. Doors lined the service road, though none of the buildings had even a single window on the ground floor.

The necromancer stepped into the backstreet and scanned the tall brick structures around them. Her fingers drummed against the air as she bit her lip and studied the darkened windows above them.

Without signs or windows, Connor couldn't tell what any of these shops even sold. "Is this it?"

She nodded. "I've been hunting for a good reagents supply store since we got here, and I found this one yesterday. From what I saw people carry out, he should have what we need. He won't have the same level of protection as they have in the second interior's Spell Market, but he's bound to have something guarding his shop."

"Soldiers?"

"Enchantments. Live guards would be too expensive, even for him."

"What—"

"Wait." She pointed at a small flight of steps two doors down, which led to a nondescript brick building identical to the rest of them. "Here. Stand guard."

He smirked and raised one skeptical eyebrow at the command while she knelt by the stairs. "Since when do you give the orders?"

She groaned and set her leather bag on the steps. "*Please.*"

"All right, then." He grinned, knowing full well it would get under her skin. "Since you asked nicely."

As she rifled through her pack, he scanned the alley. Bottles clinked in her satchel, the jingling painfully loud to his enhanced ears, but the windows on the upper floors remained dark.

With nothing to light the alley but the pale orange glow rolling over the roofs, no one would've seen them even if someone did manage to hear something.

He crossed his arms as he waited and peered over his shoulder at her open bag. Dozens of impossibly small vials sat in militant rows in the satchel, and he squinted as he tried to make sense of their size. Perhaps it was a trick of the low light, but it seemed like he was looking at them from twenty feet above, rather than standing a foot or so away. He'd watched her use her potions before, and none of them were that small.

"There you are," she mumbled to herself.

She reached in, and again, the light must've played a trick on him. Her hand shrank to half its normal size, but it and the bottle in her palm returned to normal as they left the pack.

He rubbed his eyes, not entirely certain of what he'd just seen.

"Be ready." With the potion in her hand, she stood and slung the bag over her shoulder. A flash of amber lamplight glinted across the bottle's metal stopper. Green light snaked through the metallic silver potion in the vial, and the dark liquid left a thin gray film behind as it sloshed against the glass.

He nodded to the potion. "What does that do?"

She gave it a happy little shake and smiled. "It dissolves anything it touches. Only metal and glass are immune, so I can't use it on the knob. He probably enchanted the door to resist a Strongman augmentation, but after watching you rip apart that iron in the tunnel, I don't think there's much that can withstand you. Try out the knob, but don't open the door until I take over."

With a cautious glance at the potion in her hands that could apparently dissolve human flesh, he walked up the stairs and wrapped his hand around the handle.

"Check inside," he whispered to the wraith as he leaned against the door. "Anything we should worry about?"

Hmm, the wraith's voice echoed through his mind. *A nice little trap waits for you. I think her Brackenbane curse will suffice.*

"You want to give me a little more detail than that? What kind of trap?"

That would ruin the fun, Magnuson.

Connor shook his head at the useless ghost and tightened his grip on the knob. As he twisted, however, the handle didn't budge. Just like the iron bars in the tunnel, it remained immobile beneath his hand.

His palm burned from the strain, but he refused to so much as breathe as he fought against it. A door wouldn't best him, no matter what the potion master had done to enchant it.

He gritted his teeth and tightened his fingers around the knob. His biceps flexed from the strain. The handle trembled in his hand, and though it still wouldn't turn, a ribbon of hope snaked through his chest.

Almost there.

The metal burned against his palm, rubbing away layers of his skin as he leaned his full weight into it.

These potion masters and their paranoia. The things these magic users could think of and create simultaneously amazed and exasperated him.

He grunted as the knob resisted, irritated that something as stupidly simple as a door could keep him out despite all the enhanced strength and magic that had made him a wanted man.

The handle finally cracked under his weight, and the little metal knob went limp in his hand. He let out a groan of relief as his arms burned. The door pulled on his grip, but he held it in place thanks to Sophia's warning.

"We have to be careful." She walked up the stairs behind him. When she reached her arm across his to take hold of the door, her soft fingertips brushed his hand.

You know, she would suffice as a companion if you refuse to bed a paid woman, the ghoul said. *She would likely be willing.*

Connor grimaced as he tried to ignore the ghoul. The last thing he needed was to get in bed with someone who might want to kill him and take the Wraith King for herself.

"There's a trap of some sort," he warned.

"Right." She let out a shaky breath. "I heard you ask the wraith."

"It's all yours, then."

His palms stung like hell, so he jogged down the steps to give her space and shook out his hands to ease the fire. They screamed at him, like he'd dragged them across a mile of brick and then poured whiskey on the open cuts. He cursed under his breath as the burn slowly faded.

In his peripheral vision, Sophia eased the door open. Though her shoulders hunched with anticipation, she peered into the darkness. The soothing aroma of lavender washed down the stairs, and she swallowed hard as her grip on the bottle tightened.

Her head snapped to the left. Seconds later, a shrill scream tore through the air, eerily similar to the death rattles he often heard at night in the Ancient Woods.

Connor stiffened and scanned the alley for signs of soldiers. With his back to the door, the scream cut short barely a second after it had started.

When he turned around again, Sophia had disappeared. The door sat open at the top of the short flight of stairs, inviting him into the shadows. The inky black darkness beckoned him closer, like a void that led to nothing.

Like a hole leading to death itself.

He took a wary step closer, listening for any sign of her as the magic in his blood simmered in his aching palms. The blackfire blades hummed, only a breath away, ready to appear at a moment's notice.

Ready for a *fight*.

CHAPTER FIFTY-TWO

CONNOR

Connor waited for hell to pour from the darkness.

The shop's rear door sat open, and lavender-scented shadows waited beyond. Despite the soothing aroma swirling through the air, the chilling screech he'd heard suggested something lay in wait.

The only question was what.

His fingers coiled into fists, and his bicep flexed as he prepared to break someone's face. To grab a creature by its neck, perhaps, and wrestle it to the ground. Or—

"Hurry," Sophia whispered from the darkness.

That one word fractured the tension in his chest.

He let out a relieved sigh as he trotted up the stairs. Death stalked the Ancient Woods every night, but at least he'd been able to prepare for it when the sun set each day. In the city, a death sentence could've lurked behind any corner.

He simply couldn't be too careful. Not in Henry's kingdom.

When he stepped inside, stacks of uniform crates lined every wall of a tiny storeroom, and a narrow hallway ahead led deeper into the building. Sprigs of lavender hanging from the ceiling smacked against his forehead as he entered, and he squinted up at them in annoyance.

A simple wooden stool sat in the sparse floorspace between the boxes, and the air sizzled with the charred odor of burnt steak. Atop the seat, smoke coiled into the air from a melted blob of wood and straw—and, possibly, other things he couldn't decipher in the midst of all the smoke and muck. A pool of brown liquid gathered beneath the stool as the gloopy mess dripped onto the floorboards.

With a satisfied little grin, Sophia popped the metal cork back into the bottle and slipped it into her bag.

"Brutal, but effective." He shut the door behind him and reached for a crate to keep the broken door from swinging open. "Don't you dare ever use that on me."

"How about on Murdoc?"

As the crate slid into place and rooted the door shut, he glared at her.

"Fine, I'll restrain myself." An exasperated little huff escaped her as she scanned the darkness. "It looks like that's the only alarm, so he was probably relying on the noise to attract soldiers if anyone broke in. We still have to be quiet, though. Shopkeepers usually live above their stores. If he heard that, you'll need to knock him out."

"Look at that." Connor grinned and gave her a quick once-over. "Your first impulse wasn't to kill him. That shows some marked improvement on your part. I'm proud of you, Sophia."

She rolled her eyes and gestured for him to follow her into the narrow hallway. "Let's make this quick."

"Remember, only take what we absolutely need. I'm not trying to bankrupt this man."

In reply, she simply groaned.

The dried flowers hanging from the ceiling continued in an endless stream of lavender as they walked deeper into the darkened shop. A soft orange glow appeared at the end of the corridor, and as Sophia rounded the corner, her shadow stretched across the floor.

The hallway ended in a single large room. Dozens of half-filled bottles sat on rows of shelves at the front and back of the store, and a handwritten label affixed to the front of each identified its contents. Two large wooden cabinets took up most of the available wall space on the left and right sides of the shop, though with their doors closed, he could only guess at what they held.

Narrow tables stretched across the center of the room, their surfaces covered in everything from baskets of flowers and vases of fresh blooms to bowls of dried mushrooms and boxes of roasted nuts.

A buffet of magic, ripe for the taking.

Not once in his life—not even in the potion shops along the southern road—had he seen so many reagents in one place. Due to issues with storage and supply, most towns only had dried ingredients. Getting any sort of fresh blooms stirred the townsfolk into a frenzy as they bid up the prices.

He didn't even know the names for most of these flowers, nor could he identify the mushrooms in two of the wicker baskets nearest to him. His gaze wandered over bowls of ground powder and boxes of bark, wondering what these reagents could do with a bit of spellgust thrown into the mix.

The possibilities hummed through him, stirring his imagination. Perhaps a potion in this room could control the weather or light his way through the darkness of the Ancient Woods. Perhaps—

Something flickered in his periphery, and that snapped him from his spellbound daze.

Two large window displays on either side of the door to the main street gave him a clear sightline to the road. The torch across the street roared with a still-thriving flame, and its light cast an orange line across the first few feet of the shop.

On impulse, he pressed his back flat against the wall. Though he shifted into high alert, Sophia wandered aimlessly through the tables and muttered to herself as she walked by each basket of goods.

"Be careful," he chided.

Without looking up from her work, she waved away his worry. "I can't hide and shop at the same time."

"That's reckless." He would need to keep a look out to keep her from getting them both discovered.

With another cursory glance across the store, he searched for the best vantage point. He would need to see out the window and keep an eye on the hallway, all without stepping into the light at the front of the room.

In the back corner, a single glass display featured four small combs encrusted with dazzling jewels, each resting on a satin pillow fit for a princess. A waist-high stool stood behind the display, turning the glass counter into a makeshift desk. A notepad lay on the glass beside an elaborate peacock-feather quill in its inkwell, both waiting for the next day's receipts.

Despite the risk of discovery and the general lack of cover, his chest panged with nostalgia.

The quill dragged him back to Kirkwall. Back to his father's spice store. He imagined his father sitting there at the makeshift desk, scratching out the day's tally with his favorite pen.

We can talk when I'm done, my boy, he'd always said as he wrapped up his day. *I have to finish these notes for the bookkeeper. Two more minutes, and then I'm all yours.*

Connor squeezed his eyes shut to silence the memory. With a gruff cough, he cleared his throat and forced himself back into the moment.

Soldiers could pass by at any time. Distractions like that were a luxury he couldn't afford.

"What did you learn about Richard during your watch?" Sophia whispered as she passed by.

Her enticing perfume rolled over him, a blend of jasmine and honey, but it clashed with the fragrances coiling into the air from the dozens of baskets and bowls around them. His enhanced nose creased as the overwhelming blend burned his lungs.

"Limited staff, from what I could see." He covered his nose with the cloth around his neck to filter out some of the aroma. Though he'd been tempted to wear it while they stole through the city, they'd kept to the shadows, and it wouldn't have made much of a difference either way.

She nodded as she rifled through a pile of white mushrooms. "Good. Staff?"

"A butler who doubles as his driver. Four soldiers on eight-hour shifts. A maid who doesn't stay overnight."

"All good news. From what you've mentioned so far, it seems like he's not well protected." After grabbing a handful of the white mushrooms in one hand, Sophia thumbed through a vase of fresh peace lily flowers. "Since he's in the second interior, it means the Lightseers don't really care about his safety. That works in our favor."

"Is it because he's a Beaumont?"

Without looking away from her reagents, she nodded. "It must be. I can't imagine he charmed his way into the Chamber through honest means, and Gibor probably strong-armed them into it. The Lightseers probably resent both men."

Connor frowned. "Who the hell is Gibor?"

"The Beaumont crime lord," she said with a bored shrug. "That's his name."

He rubbed his temple as he debated how to reply. With her, each of her answers only prompted more questions. More doubt. Any response of hers could've easily led down an endless rabbit hole with dozens more secrets hidden in its depths. She knew so much more than she let on, and he didn't have much patience left for her to keep her secrets.

A floorboard creaked, and Connor's ear twitched as he waited for the thud of footsteps to follow. The rustle of Sophia's dress against the table mingled with the crackle of dried flower petals as she dug through a basket. Nothing else shifted in the oppressive silence, and if the shopkeeper had moved, he had merely adjusted in his sleep.

Good.

"What about the yards around his home?" Sophia reached across a table for a bowl piled high with bark. "Gardens? Open grass? Are there proper places to hide? Is it a secured fortress, or just a house?"

"Just a house," he whispered back. "The guards mostly stand post at the four corners. One of them fell asleep against his spear last night."

As she lifted a white mushroom to study it in the light, her ruby red lips twisted into a wicked little smile. "Excellent."

Connor studied her as she set the mushroom on the table beside her and sifted through the rest of the mushroom caps. "We're not killing him, Sophia."

Her smile fell, and she cast him a sidelong glare. He held her gaze, and a dimple formed in her cheek as her dark eyes narrowed.

He gestured to the reagents at her fingertips. "Come up with something clever to keep the man from talking. I won't slit his throat just to make you happy."

"You don't understand, Connor. He—"

"Find another way."

She shook her head. "There isn't another way. If he tells the Lightseer Chamber about what we discussed, then—"

Ugh. More of this.

As she spoke, he tuned her out as he tried to come up with a plan. Though she had a point about the risks of Richard giving away their destination to the Lightseers, it seemed more like a cheap excuse to justify murder than a genuine concern. If they asked their questions carefully and played their cards right, they were clever enough to come up with a way to avoid killing a man he'd never even met.

She had history with Richard Beaumont. For whatever reason, she wanted him dead. From what little he knew about Nethervale, a necromancer did whatever it took to get what they wanted.

Time for a good, old-fashioned bluff.

"No, that's fine." He shrugged and leaned against the wall. "You're right. We'll have to drag him along with us. I'm sure we can buy enough rope to subdue a Lightseer Viceroy."

"You wouldn't dare," she seethed.

A chill snaked through the room like a breath of winter. Frost crept across her hands. Splintering ice coated her wrists in a slow and steady trail as it crawled up her forearms. Her slender fingers balled into fists, and a muscle in her eye twitched with her mounting fury.

"You said there wasn't another way." He raised one eyebrow, cool and steady despite the shift in the air. "I solved it for you. Is there a problem?"

"A *problem?*" Her voice hummed, thick with a dark and deadly threat.

Don't push me, it warned.

With his shoulders relaxed as he leaned against the wall, he didn't even flinch. He nodded toward the reagents sprawled across the tables. "If you don't like my idea, I'm sure you're smart enough to find another way that doesn't involve murder."

That broke the spell, and she shook her head as her nose wrinkled in disgust. Though her lips parted, she just watched him in baffled silence.

"Fine," she eventually conceded as she returned to the mushrooms. With her back to him, she muttered incoherently to herself as she angrily stuffed the white caps back in their basket.

A victory, though he didn't enjoy riling her up like that. He'd never led anyone before, much less someone as powerful as a Nethervale graduate, but he'd begun to get the hang of it.

"Damn it," she muttered.

"What?"

She glared at him over one shoulder and gestured to the open table in front of her, as if he was supposed to understand what was missing. "This man doesn't have any Chaste tree reagents. Not one. Without Chaste tree, I can't make a glamour."

He shrugged. "Don't worry about it. The Hackamore is what matters. Does he have what you need for that?"

"Most of it. I usually prefer to add maypop flower fruits, and he doesn't have any."

The necromancer scratched the back of her head as her eyes darted across the tables. Her shoulders relaxed as she distracted herself with her work, and that was probably for the best.

Though he didn't like relying on their shaky truce, he wanted to keep it alive.

She pointed to a jar of nuts. "He also has maidenhair tree nuts roasted in salt, when the idiot should've known all you need is olive oil. That's going to affect the final potion, but not enough to sour it. The fool."

With her hands on her hips, she scoffed and glanced his way. A lull followed as she watched him, as though she expected him to add something to the conversation.

"Yeah," he said dryly, though he had no idea what the hell she was talking about. "What an idiot."

"Astonishing, really," she complained. From a row of cauldrons stacked against the back wall, she tapped her fingernail against a massive pot and grunted as she lifted its weight into her arms. "This sounds like iron."

"Does it have to be?"

"Ideally, yes. It makes the potion stronger." Sophia set the large cauldron on a nearby table and darted through the rows of reagents.

The necromancer turned her back to him and mumbled incoherently to herself as she scanned the baskets, bowls, and bottles. One by one, she grabbed small trays stacked at the end of each table and collected the mushrooms, dried nuts, fresh flowers, and long strips of bark she had set aside earlier.

No reagent touched another as she sorted her ingredients and stowed them in the cauldron. Everything had a place. Everything had a purpose, and she walked with the confidence of someone who had spent years mastering her art.

"And now, for the moment of truth." Sophia squared her shoulders as she strode toward the nearest floor-to-ceiling cabinet. She threw open its doors with a flourish, and a soft green glow filled the air.

Connor instantly tensed at the flood of light and walked to the window. With his hands across his chest, he scanned the empty street outside.

A brilliant glow in a closed shop would've been a beacon of trouble to anyone who passed.

"Hurry," he demanded.

Glass clinked behind him as he glared into the street. When she didn't reply, he peered over his shoulder as she pulled three bottles of the glowing green dust out of the cabinet.

Spellgust. It had to be. Nothing else in Saldia glowed like that.

With the spellgust powder tucked under one arm, she crouched to study the bottom row of dark red bottles. Her skirts billowed around her like a crimson fog of fabric, and she tapped her finger against her lips as she browsed.

From his place by the window, he couldn't make out the handwriting on the labels. It didn't matter, though, since he recognized the wine-red liquid. He'd spilled it plenty of times before.

"That's blood," he said.

"It is." She grabbed two bottles. With her arms full of blood and spellgust, she carried her discoveries to the cauldron.

Though it already felt like years had passed since his time with the Finns, the vial of blood reminded him of something Ethan had said.

Human blood is a reagent, used to make a potion stronger.

He ran his tongue over his back molar, wondering how much information he could wring out of the necromancer. "Why do you need blood?"

Sophia's eyebrows pinched with confusion, and a humorless laugh escaped her as she stared at him. "You're joking, right? Or is this another one of your stupid tests?"

"Test," he lied. "Indulge me."

"You realize these are a waste of my precious time, don't you?"

"Just do it."

"If you insist." She didn't bother masking her boredom as she stowed the bottles in the cauldron. "Blood acts as an amplifier for your potion. It enhances the effects of your spell. Shall I continue?"

He nodded, doing his best to look bored.

She pursed her lips. "You annoy me."

Connor smirked and scanned the street again.

Still empty, thank the Fates.

"Blood is one of the most basic foundations of magic." She sighed impatiently, and the clink of glass filled the air as she adjusted the bottles in the cauldron. "Some potions don't need blood, but most do. All enchanted items require at least some. It's also why augmentations are so powerful. The ink is derived from a potion distilled to its most potent form, and the magic is activated by the augmented person's blood when the potion is inked into their skin." She peered over her shoulder and glanced him over. "But you knew all of that already."

"Yep," he bluffed.

"You and your stupid tests."

"Where did that blood come from?"

"Don't worry, I only got Clean quality." She pulled a dark vial and pointed to the word "Clean" on the label. "He probably has a small army ready to donate the second he'll let them. In this ring of the city, they monitor donations pretty closely. You don't have to worry about Marked or Grime qualities until you reach the outer exterior."

He nodded as he quietly sifted through the deluge of information she had just given him. Apparently, blood quality was a closely regulated industry. As long as no one had died for the blood they needed, he'd let her take it.

"I heard they recently permitted Blue quality sales in the inner rings." Sophia let out a wistful sigh and looked out the window. "I'd love to toy with that. To see if wealthy blood does anything different to a potion."

Connor chuckled. "Maybe another day."

"Right." She pointed to the cabinet on the other side of the room, opposite the one that held the spellgust and blood. "That cupboard should have wine. Grab some, will you? It needs to be aged for at least ten years."

Eager to get this raid over with, he indulged her and strode across the room toward the other cabinet.

On her side of the store, the doors to the spellgust cabinet clicked shut. Mercifully, the green glow faded from the shop. The line of amber light from the streetlamps outside returned across the first few floorboards beneath the windows.

Thick rows of hand-carved grape vines surrounded the oak cabinet she had pointed out, and three sets of doors spanned the full width of the massive display. He opted for the center pair of doors and pried them open.

Inside, rows and rows of wine filled every available inch of space. Easily four hundred bottles sat before him with an array of beige and purple labels. They rested in a crisscrossing lattice of wooden planks, and he figured Murdoc would've started drooling if he'd been here.

Connor tugged one of the bottles out of its diamond-shaped tube and scanned the label.

Five years.

He returned it and tugged out another two rows above it.

Three years.

With an impatient groan, he hurried through the bottles, tugging and returning dozens of them as he went. Most had only been aged five years, and it took several minutes of scanning to finally find the right row.

"How many do you want, Sophia?"

Something rustled behind him as her boots tapped along the floor. "Seven."

He balked and stared at her over his shoulder. "Are you brewing a potion or trying to get Murdoc drunk?"

"Connor, we don't have time for this." She set a brilliant purple flower with blue pollen stems into the cauldron. "It'll be dawn soon."

"All right, fine." He shook his head and grabbed seven of the bottles. After a moment's hesitation, he also grabbed one of the bottles aged three years as a present for Murdoc. "Did you get everything else you needed?"

"Everything for the Hackamore, a few batches of Rectivane, and a few other fun experiments." She tapped her fingertips together with excitement as she peered into the cauldron.

"I said to only get what you need."

"Trust me. You'll be glad I made these."

He shook his head as his eyes stung with exhaustion. "How much is all of this going to cost?"

The necromancer paused, her fingertips still pressed together as her brows knit with confusion. "Are you unfamiliar with what the term 'steal' means?"

"I'm well aware." With his arms full, he leaned his shoulder into the cabinet doors and nudged them shut. "I am a merchant's son, after all."

"Why am I not surprised?" She rubbed her temple. "You and your damned conscience."

He shrugged.

"Connor, we need that money. We don't know what we'll encounter between here and the tomb. There's plenty else we need to spend it on, like—"

"Clothes?" He set the wine on the glass display beside him and tugged on the royal blue fabric draped over his torso.

She grimaced.

"Tell me the total cost. Don't make me sort through everything you have in that pot. You know I'll do it."

"Don't," she warned, not bothering to mask her irritation.

"Tell me the damn cost, Sophia."

She scratched at the back of her neck and muttered bewildered curses under her breath. "Twenty-three."

"Coin?"

"I'm afraid not."

He winced. "Silver?"

Her weight shifted onto one hip, and she crossed her arms as she let the silence make her point for her.

He scoffed. "Are you serious? Twenty-three gold?"

Without moving the rest of her body, she simply nodded.

"Fates above." He genuinely hadn't expected it to be nearly that expensive. "Did you shove the deed to a royal estate in there? Maybe a few jewel-encrusted statues?"

"We need everything in that cauldron," she said with a nod toward the pot. "I'm not putting any of it back to ease your damn conscience."

"I can't take you anywhere, can I?"

"You asked," she hissed under her breath. "And that's why we can't leave our money. We don't—"

"It's my money," he corrected. "And if that's the cost, then that's what I'll pay."

He shrugged off the pack on his shoulders and rifled through it to find the coin purse the potion master had given him. When he tugged on the string, the little pouch opened, and gold glittered from within.

It stung to think of parting with so much money, but he wouldn't stoop to theft.

As he counted out the gold pieces in his palm, an idea struck him like a lightning bolt to the chest. "Can they figure out what you were going to make based on what you stole?"

"Probably not." She lifted the cauldron into her arms, and she mumbled incoherent curses as her fingers slipped along the bulky pot. Her voice thinned with the strain of carrying something so awkwardly large, and she let out a groan of effort as her nails dug into the iron. "If the shopkeeper is really good, maybe, but I doubt it. Everything we took is used in an array of potions."

He scanned the tables again. "Let's grab some random ingredients too, just in case he calls in someone who can figure it out."

Sophia's eyebrows shot up her head. "That's really smart."

He yanked out an extra gold piece and poured the handful of coins onto the glass display. "Since your hands are full, tell me what to take."

Her eyes darted across the tables, and she bit her lip as she tried to choose. "Those peace lily flowers, those brown mushrooms, and that sprig of witch hazel flowers."

"What quality?"

"It doesn't matter," she admitted. "Those are just extra ingredients I can use in a large number of potions. Most brews don't require the same attention to detail as a Hackamore."

"Noted."

He grabbed a handful of the fresh white lilies out of a vase. Water dribbled off the tips of their stems and onto his boots as he reached for the long branch of yellow flowers he assumed were witch hazel. His fists full, he nodded toward the nearest basket of dried brown fungi shaped like clams. "Are these the mushrooms you're talking about?"

She nodded.

He raised one eyebrow as he stared her down. "These are reishi mushrooms."

"I'm well aware of that." She groaned and stumbled, fighting to keep her hold on the bulky cauldron in her arms.

Unbelievable. She really didn't remember.

"Reishi mushrooms," he continued impatiently. "As in, the reagent you said you wouldn't take as payment. I brought plenty because I was going to use them for barter."

"Oh, right." Undeterred, she pursed her lips and scanned the tables again. "Grab that sprig of dried white flowers, then."

He shook his head in irritation as the sorceress tested his patience. Indulging her, he grabbed a sprig of white flowers he'd often seen growing in the Ancient Woods. If he'd known yarrow was a reagent, he would've tried to sell some in the local towns as he'd drifted through.

He set the reagents in her cauldron and lifted the iron pot from her arms. "You carry the wine."

"Thank the Fates." She let out a heavy sigh and shook out her arms. "I wasn't going to admit how annoying that was to hold."

He chuckled.

"I saw a sack in the storeroom. We can use that to carry the wine." As she collected the bottles in her arms, the sky outside lightened with the coming dawn.

The last of their heavy darkness slipped away into the waking sun, leaving only the half-light for them to hide in. They didn't have long before the sun rose, and that meant almost no time at all to travel to an entirely different ring of the city.

They would have to move quickly.

Sophia led the way into the lavender-coated hallway. As he followed, Connor glanced at the dried petals on the ceiling and wondered how his father would've reacted to the mixed blessing of a break-in and a pile of money.

He would've probably danced a little jig at the sight of all that gold.

As he darted out into the last shreds of the night, Connor grinned at the thought of his father twirling with joy. Ideally, when the shopkeeper woke in an hour or so, he would feel the same.

CHAPTER FIFTY-THREE

CONNOR

With the massive iron cauldron in his hands, Connor led Sophia down a narrow third-floor hallway above a tavern in the outer exterior. Though he'd expected someone to spot them on the way through the ground floor pub, their only company had been a snoring bartender taking a nap behind the counter.

They'd made it with seconds to spare, really, and had nearly run out of alleys to hide in as more and more soldiers poured into the streets with the start of a new day.

As he neared the rooms they had rented, a dying flame in the lone sconce at the end of the hall cast distorted shadows across the corridor's wooden walls. A man shouted from the room next to Sophia's, his voice muffled by the closed door. Glass shattered on the other side of her neighbor's wall, and something heavy crashed to the ground.

The necromancer trailed behind him with the sack of wine slung over one shoulder. Together, they paused in the corridor to watch the wall as the quarrel rumbled through the room next door.

"What, no daring rescue?" She heaved the sack of wine over one shoulder, and the bottles clinked together as she reached for the knob to her room. The door handle glowed green beneath her touch, charmed by an enchantment she had used to secure their space in their absence.

"Too tired." Connor's eyes stung with exhaustion, and he shoved his shoulder against the door as she unlocked it. "Besides, it's not my business."

"That's never stopped you before."

He shot her a warning glare over his shoulder as he led the way into one of the two rooms they'd rented.

The wall thumped again as the brawl raged on, though he doubted the splintered boards of this seedy lodge could handle much more abuse. The nearby streets had enough makeshift kindling wedged into the nooks and crannies of the patchwork homes to start a bonfire. One overturned torch in the night, and this entire sector of Oakenglen's outer ring would go up in flames.

As he walked in, he groaned at the sparse room. One straw bed. One hole in the wall that served as the window, with a thin sheet draped over it in a futile effort to keep out the cold night.

He set the cauldron on the floor beside the mattress. "Is this honestly better than a tree? At least branches don't cost anything. Why pay for something like this?"

"Because I don't have to tie myself to the bed for fear of falling." She kicked the door shut behind her.

A breeze rolled through the window-hole, carrying with it the suffocating rot of boiling cabbage. The sting of manure followed on the wind, so thick in the air that it coated his tongue with a vile blend of fermenting carrots and dirt.

His nose wrinkled in disgust. "We're not staying here a day longer than necessary."

"Believe me, I don't want to be here, either." Sophia set the sack of wine on the floor, and the clink of glass tapping against glass filled the air like the chime of a bell.

As she set to work unpacking the bottles, the sheet over the window lifted in a second gust of putrid wind. A knee-high pillar of bricks stood by the window, previously hidden by the makeshift curtain. Firewood had been piled on top of the baked clay, the logs angled against each other and ready for a flame.

After she emptied the sack of wine bottles, Sophia set one foot on the bed and lifted her skirt. Her leg appeared from between the layers of crimson satin, along with a black sheath strapped to her calf.

Connor frowned as his gaze impulsively wandered up her bare thigh, toward the rest of her buried in the thick layers of satin. "What the hell are you—"

With a flick of her wrist, she yanked out a dagger from the hidden sheath and threw it at the curtain fluttering in the breeze. The blade dug into the wood and pinned the sheet against the wall, away from the fire pit.

"I can't exactly pull the curtain aside, now can I?" She adjusted her skirts and brushed off her corset as the grotesque breeze rolled through the open window-hole. "Problem solved."

He pointed to the bricks and firewood. "Where did you get all that?"

"I didn't steal it, if that's what you're implying."

They hadn't spent much time together, but he already knew her well enough to assume she had, in fact, stolen all of it. His mind hiccupped and buzzed with fatigue as he debated whether or not to reply. He ultimately sank into the lumpy mattress as he rubbed his tired eyes with the heels of his hands.

After a twelve-hour surveillance shift and a high-stakes heist, he was too spent to fight her on it.

"You need sleep." She reached into the cauldron and, one by one, pulled out the reagents they'd taken. Blooms. Sprigs of dried flowers. Baskets of mushrooms. Bottle after bottle of things he couldn't even name, from powders and nuts to shaved bark. The boxes and satchels covered almost all of the floor, each side by side in Sophia's militant little rows.

They'd taken more than he had realized. Now that he saw it all laid out on the floor, he understood the cost.

When she had emptied the cauldron, she grabbed the handles and let out a strained grunt as she hoisted the bulky thing on top of the pillar beneath the makeshift window. Its iron legs scraped across the brick, and she centered it over the firewood.

With the pot ready, she reached into the depths of her skirt. From seemingly nowhere, the Firestarter dagger appeared in her palm, its gems glistening in the morning light as the sun streamed through the open hole in the wall.

He barely stifled a yawn. "Where did that come from?"

"Hidden pockets in the skirts."

"Fun."

With a modest little shrug, she held the dagger's blade against the wood. Her fingers twitched, and an enchanted flame shot down the weapon from the hilt. The fire ignited beneath the cauldron, its flames licking the iron as the logs cracked and split from the sudden heat.

"The entire second exterior looks ready to go up in smoke." Connor nodded to the open window. "You're not going to set the neighborhood on fire, are you?"

"It's fine." She sheathed the Firestarter and tossed it on the bed. "I've done this a hundred times. In the outer ring of the city, no one cares about anything but their next meal. They'll ignore us as long as we don't cause trouble. With the bricks as our base, nothing will catch fire." She paused and tapped her finger on her lips. "Unless Murdoc knocks it over."

"I'll keep him out of here."

She snorted derisively. "Not that he'd get the chance to come in."

"You certainly talk about him a lot for someone who says she's not interested."

"Don't start with me, Wraithblade." Her eyes narrowed in warning, but a smile tugged at the corner of her lips.

At her mention of the wraith, he pointed again to the window. "We should keep quiet."

Sophia waved the thought away with a bored twirl of her hand. "We're in the upper stories, so no one can hear us. Besides, I'm pretty sure our neighbors are occupied with whatever started that brawl. Like I said, no one cares."

She knelt in a rare stretch of open space on the cluttered floor and set her satchel in front of her. As she opened the flap, Connor peered over her shoulder to find more impossibly small bottles lined in militant formation in the bag. As she reached into it, her hand once again shrank in size.

It couldn't have been a trick of the eye this time. Not here in broad daylight.

"What the hell?"

Sophia flinched and looked at him over her shoulder. Her eyes darted between him and the bag, and for a moment she didn't say anything.

"I—uh—damn it." She sighed in defeat. "It's an enchanted pack. It took a small fortune to create this, but my whole life is in here. Anything I put in here shrinks, which means I can fit more in."

"That's clever," he admitted.

She smiled, and the skin around her eyes creased with a flicker of genuine delight. "Thanks. I modified the recipe myself."

The necromancer pulled out a box of vials, each of them separated by a thin plank of intersecting wood. A familiar bottle of metallic liquid with a metal cork stood out from the others as she set it aside, and he leaned away on impulse. With a quick scan, he counted about twenty vials.

"Are those all potions you've brewed?"

She nodded.

He whistled. Impressive.

She reached again into the pack and pulled out a scale. The large leather-wrapped tray on one end teetered as she lifted it from the bag, and the counterbalance shifted along the metal base in response.

"Carrying that around seems like a waste of space." He lifted one of the bottles of dried petals they'd taken from the potion master. "This has the measurement on it already. Why lug that thing around?"

She set the scale on the floor. "Never trust someone else to measure your reagents. Don't trust someone else's scale, for that matter. That's how you ruin a potion."

She's good, the wraith king admitted. *Even better than I thought. She understands the nuance of potion making better than most.*

Sophia pushed herself to her feet and lifted her crimson skirts as she stepped over the cluster of flowers and baskets covering nearly every inch of the floor. As the fires crackled atop her makeshift fireplace, she grabbed one of the bottles of glowing green dust and popped off the cork. Wisps of light coiled off the lip of the glass, and little tendrils of magic snaked through the air as she shook the cork over the empty cauldron.

Connor gestured toward the expensive bottle of spellgust she was apparently throwing into an empty pot. "What are you doing?"

"I thought you were tired." With a frown, she peered into the cauldron and didn't bother looking his way. "Are you really going to watch the entire show?"

"Maybe. I believe you were explaining what this is." He gestured to the cauldron as a whole, waiting for her to focus.

She could huff and grumble all she wanted, but he would still get his answer.

The necromancer sighed. "You have to check the cauldron's heat before you add anything. When the spellgust smokes, it's ready. If the iron isn't hot enough, you can ruin the—"

"—entire potion," he finished for her. "I'm sensing a common theme with potion making."

"It's not for the impatient." She cast another sidelong glance at him and returned her attention to the pot.

Though his body ached for sleep, and though his eyes kept drooping to near-closed as he leaned the back of his head against the wall, he forced himself to stay awake and watch her work. He'd never seen a master make a potion before, and he didn't want to miss this.

"How can a potion make someone tell the truth?" he asked. "It just doesn't seem possible."

"The same way a drunk speaks more freely than a sober man. It lowers inhibitions." She hesitated and cast a shifty glare toward the window. "Among other things."

He frowned, instantly suspicious. "What other things, exactly?"

"You can't just let me have my fun, can you?"

He laughed and, instead of answering, pointed again to the bottle of spellgust in her hand. At the silent command for her to continue, she chuckled.

"This potion is expensive and difficult to make because it requires three extremely rare reagents." She pointed to a clump of green stalks with blue thorns. "Everglade bloom petals allow you to control water, but the stalk creates peace of mind and a sense of safety instead. When mixed with the rest of the potion, that makes your victim speak more candidly."

Connor resisted the impulse to laugh with surprise. He'd always thought a single reagent did just one thing, but apparently different parts of the plants had different reactions to spellgust.

Fascinating.

As the flames crackled beneath her cauldron, Sophia pointed to a second pile of brown stems by the door and the small handful of twisted roots lying beside the mound. "In case you don't recognize it, that's heart-shaped moonseed. Though the leaves are used in glamours, its stalks and roots weaken willpower and motivation when mixed with spellgust. That ensures your victim answers your questions, even if they don't want to."

He rubbed his jaw as he drank in the knowledge he'd managed to wring from her. One day, he'd have to find a book and study these reagents.

"See that flower?" Sophia pointed to a large purple bloom, and its long blue seedling stems twitched in the breeze. "That's a maypop. It's the rarest thing here, and I was worried he wouldn't have one. Its petals connect to the soul, and when combined with the rest of these ingredients, it gives you full access to your victim's mind." She gestured to the dozens of piles around her. "Death cap mushrooms, elderflower roots, maidenhair tree bark, lionsmane. I could go into detail about each one, but your eyes are already glossing over."

He chuckled and rubbed his temple. "That's from exhaustion, Sophia. I happen to find this enthralling."

"Hmm." She shook the spellgust cork over the cauldron again, releasing just a few grains of the magic powder into the pot. This time, a ribbon of smoke snaked into the air. "Good. I can finally start."

She snatched a bottle of wine from the floor and tugged another dagger out of the mysterious folds of her dress. As she dug the tip of the blade into the cork, Connor adjusted his weight and leaned his elbow against his knee. "How long will this take?"

"Eight hours to cook." With one final tug, the cork popped out of the wine bottle. "Fourteen in total. It'll be ready for our raid tonight."

"And what exactly is your plan to ensure he doesn't notify the Lightseers of what we're doing?"

The sizzle of wine splashing over hot iron filled the room, and she stared down at the stream without answering. The bottle emptied in seconds, and she set it on the floor.

"Sophia."

"Not everyone deserves the life they've been given," she said softly as she reached for a second bottle of wine.

He scoffed. "And who are you to decide that?"

Her ruby lips settled into a grim line. "I know better than most. I know who this man is, Connor. You don't."

"Then tell me who he is. Tell me why you hate him so much."

The tendons in her neck tightened as she swallowed hard. Her gaze never left the cauldron as she poured out the wine. Her eyes glossed over, and even after the bottle emptied, she held it over the pot.

"Sophia," he said again, more gently this time.

Her breath caught in her throat, and she blinked herself out of her daze. With a shaky sigh, she set down the empty bottle and reached for a third. Its cork popped in the heavy silence as she opened it.

Though she refused to speak, Connor waited. If he let the quiet linger, perhaps he could wrangle a confession out of her.

Before they went into that mansion, he had to know the truth. The *whole* truth.

"Richard Beaumont is a murderer." Her voice barely registered over the glug of wine pouring into the cauldron. "He's a double agent. A thief. A hitman. An assassin. He's whatever the Beaumonts need him to be. If there was ever a shred of dignity in that man's soul, it was burned out of him a long time ago."

Connor studied her as she reached for more wine. Her movements flowed without thought, as if she had gone to another place and muscle memory had taken over.

"What he did to me—" She squeezed her eyes shut as she steeled herself. "I don't even want to talk about it. Saying it out loud has always felt wrong. I don't want him to know what it did to me. How it broke me. I will tell you this, though. I'm not his only victim, Connor. I'm one of many. I've seen who he is. I've seen the real man behind the mask he wears when he talks to those in power. I've seen the twisted wart that is his soul."

"You waited to mention him," Connor pointed out. "You did that intentionally, didn't you? You knew we would have to come here to get to the tomb. Finding Richard was part of your plan, right down to the price you gave me. You knew we would have to go through Richard to get the bloody beauties. Am I right?"

The bottle emptied, and its last few drops fell into the cauldron before her. Without looking away from her work, she nodded.

She had played him.

His jaw tensed with his rising anger, and it took concentrated effort not to jump to his feet and tear into her for hiding this from him. When they'd struck their deal, she had sworn to tell him the truth.

One lie, one omission of truth, and you get nothing. You're done, and there's no second chances with me.

That was what he'd told her, and yet she had still tried to con him. She hadn't lied outright, but she had omitted the truth in a dangerous way. He'd always known he couldn't fully trust her, but now she had taken it too far.

He pinched the bridge of his nose and forced himself to clear his head. To think rationally about this.

Pain and vengeance blinded people, and even someone as powerful as her could've fallen prey to that trap. Richard had clearly done something horrible to her. She had been useful, thus far, and he wanted to give her a chance to salvage this.

Only the truth could save her.

"Why?" he demanded. "Why hide this from me?"

Sophia absently ran her hand over her mouth, and her eyes glossed over. "You were too smart for me to con you into helping me get revenge. I could tell as much pretty quickly. After I saw the wraith—once I knew what you were—I knew I couldn't leave you to take the fall for his murder, either. You would've hunted me down and killed me."

He didn't answer. She wasn't wrong.

She gestured to the room around them. "I had to play my cards right to get us here, and I had to do it in a way that wouldn't get any of us caught."

"I warned you." He shook his head and pushed himself to his feet. "I warned you not to play me. I warned you not to keep anything from me, Sophia."

"Connor, please." Jaw clenched, she simply looked at him. "Please, just listen."

He'd warned her back in the field that even one lie meant she would get nothing. He'd meant it, too. As she stared up at him with those wide eyes, though, his resolve wavered. The only other times she had ever said "please" were when she rolled her eyes or scoffed derisively.

Now, however, she watched him with such intensity that he sighed and gestured for her to continue. "You get one shot, Sophia. Use it well."

And if she didn't—if it was clear she only wanted to use him—he would disappear in the night.

His father had trusted the wrong man, and that had gotten his entire family killed. Connor refused to make the same mistake. He'd lived most of his adult life as a drifter wandering alone through the woods, and he could go back to it easy enough.

It didn't matter that he enjoyed relying on a team. It didn't matter that he rather liked having others around to help. Others who shared his goals and ambitions.

Trusting the wrong person wasn't going to be his downfall, too.

CHAPTER FIFTY-FOUR

CONNOR

Connor glared at the sorceress. He cracked a knuckle as he waited for her to finally tell him the truth.

Given her record thus far, he wasn't going to hold his breath.

The necromancer tucked a strand of silky black hair behind her ear and grabbed another bottle of wine. This time, after she popped the cork, she took a long drink before she tilted the open end over the cauldron and poured the remainder into the pot.

"Back in the forest, you and Murdoc both asked me why I left Nethervale. No matter what you've heard about that place, you don't know the half of how horrible it is. Half of the trainees who go to Nethervale die," she said, unknowingly echoing something the Wraith King had already explained. "Did you know that?"

As he stood by the door, Connor crossed his arms over his broad chest and nodded.

"Of course," she whispered. "It's so damn hard to tell what you know and what you don't, but I guess that's the point."

He didn't reply.

She sighed. "Do you know why half of the students don't make it through?"

Still tense and furious, he simply shook his head.

"We take four exams before we can graduate," she answered. "Each exam is to unearth intelligence on one of your classmates. Something dark. Something dirty. Something you can use against them. Sometimes, that information even gets them killed for treason."

Despite his boiling anger, his shoulders relaxed. If she was telling the truth—and he still wasn't convinced of that, yet—this place sounded appalling.

"That's not the reason half the students die," she admitted. "Our final exam comes in our tenth year. We had to kill a classmate in a closely monitored duel. If you found out who you're supposed to fight and killed them ahead of time, you were given a higher rank and additional enchanted weapons as a reward. If you killed the wrong person, you were sent to the dungeons to die of starvation."

His eyebrows shot up his head.

"Repulsive, I know." Sophia nodded. "I didn't know anything about Nethervale when my parents shipped me off. One day, a carriage appeared out front, and my mother said it was for me. They hadn't even let me know ahead of time. Not because they were afraid I would run, but because no one cared enough to remember. My brothers, my sister—everyone knew about it except for me. No one but my mother even woke up before the carriage left." She swallowed hard. "And she only saw me off because someone had to answer the door. Mother said this was my fault because no one wanted me. I wasn't pretty enough to marry off. She didn't know what else to do with me, and she said I wasn't welcome home until I graduated Nethervale—which she insisted I'd never do."

Connor rubbed his jaw in shock. "Sophia..."

That sounds like my mother, the Wraith King interjected. *What a bitter and horrible woman. She's lucky I turned out as well as I did.*

"Not now," Connor whispered to the ghoul.

"I don't want pity." Sophia absently opened another bottle and tipped it into the cauldron. "I just want you to understand."

He didn't reply. Though she might've been playing him, she didn't show any of her usual tells. No eye twitch. No shifty glance. Nothing.

Steam billowed from the cauldron. The rich aroma of grapes and apples masked the stale cabbage outside as she reached for another bottle.

"Richard and I entered around the same time, but his family name gave him a guaranteed path through the training. He couldn't die, you see. He was too important."

She grimaced with disgust and set the sixth empty bottle aside. The gurgle of splashing liquid echoed against the pot as she let the silence linger.

After a while, she rubbed her eyes and let out a weary sigh. "I had to start from the bottom. Even though he had a seat reserved for him in the Necromancer Chamber, I clawed my way to Nyx's side by myself. Every day was a matter of survival for me, but he treated Nethervale like a retreat. He only graced us with his presence when the Lightseer academy went on holiday."

She sneered and grabbed the final bottle of ten-year wine off the floor. The cork popped in the lingering lull, and she raised it over the bubbling vat of wine. Even as the bottle emptied, she held it over the steam and stared vacantly into the cauldron.

"Sophia," Connor said gently to snap her from her daze.

She flinched. "Right. Because of his family connections, he'd been chosen as a double agent to infiltrate the Lightseers. It made him better than the rest of us mere foot soldiers. He got off on his superiority. It fueled him. He used it as a weapon."

She set the bottle aside and reached her palm into the billowing steam above the cauldron. Her fingers wriggled, but Connor had no idea what she was doing. Testing the heat, perhaps, or just messing with his head.

Both seemed possible.

Sophia stared into the steam. "He got off on his power. He loved being important. Loved the way it made people tremble. Over time, he started using his position within the Necromancy Chamber to coerce the temple's women to spread their legs for him." A muscle in her jaw twitched as she scowled at the boiling pot before her. "And if we didn't do it willingly, he saw it as a contest. The hunt made it more fun, and those of us who resisted him became his favorite toys to play with. He found ways to force the most dangerous necromancers on the continent to do whatever he asked, and he laughed while we danced."

Connor rubbed his jaw as he listened. He wouldn't decide her fate until she was done, but she hadn't betrayed even one nervous tick. No shifting gaze. No tension. No warble in her voice. Absolutely nothing implied she was lying.

As awful as this was to hear, it seemed as though the necromancer was actually telling him the truth.

With a resigned sigh, Sophia placed one foot on the mattress. She peeled back her skirts to reveal her toned leg. As she pulled back her dress, the satin hooked briefly on the sheaths hidden on her calf and thigh.

He averted his gaze out of respect as more and more of her leg became visible. "Sophia, I don't—"

"I'm not seducing you, idiot," she snapped.

He let out an impatient sigh at her tone and waited as she pulled the skirt up to the top of her thigh. On her hip, a scar as wide and tall as her palm marred her otherwise smooth skin. A shield surrounded two letters, and the whole mess had been carved in crudely drawn lines that overlapped each other.

R.B.

Her voice dropped to the barest whisper as she stared at the scar. "He didn't have his brand on him that day, so he used his knife."

A jolt of fury shot clear through Connor's chest.

The hate burned in him, crackling like an inferno. His body tensed with revulsion. His hands went numb. Blindsided that a man would ever do this to a woman, to anyone—he could only stare at the mark as he silently fumed.

A warlord's tactic to mark your slaves, the Wraith King interjected. *It marks human property and reminds them of their place. I haven't seen one of those in centuries. I'd thought the world had forgotten.*

"Tell me you didn't do this to anyone," he demanded of the ghost. "Tell me you're not this revolting."

"What?" Sophia's brow knit with confusion.

"The wraith," he corrected.

I preferred total domination and control, the ghoul said with a bored hint in his tone. *If your prey needs a scar to remember you, you're not truly worthy of their fear. Relying on such primitive means was beneath me. However, I will confess that a large number of Saldia is most likely descended from my bloodline.*

Connor grimaced with disgust.

Don't be jealous, Magnuson. The ghost chuckled. *It's petty.*

"You don't know the kind of man he is," Sophia said as the cauldron boiled behind her. "I saw this mark on forty-seven other girls in Nethervale, even on new recruits who came in after he and I had finished our training. Whenever a recruit died, I checked their bodies in the morgue." She grimaced. "Nearly every woman who passed into the crypt had his mark. Some of the men, too, especially the ones he had killed."

Connor scowled and paced between the piles of reagents covering most of the floor. Too much anger coiled in his chest for him to stand still. He needed to move and burn off this rage, or he'd break something.

Or someone.

"Do you think he'll stop?" Sophia gestured out the window. "Do you think he saves his hate for Nethervale? Hell no. If anything, he's more tempered in a tower surrounded by magic users. I guarantee that every girl in that brothel has his mark, too. There are probably dozens of innocent people in this city with his putrid scar on their bodies. Maids. Soldiers. Mothers. Servants. Nobles. Warriors. No one is safe from him. Because of his name and his power over others, no one dares to do a damned thing about it. That hideous gremlin of a man walks free because he's a Beaumont!"

With a strangled scream, she grabbed one of the empty bottles off the floor and hurled it against the far wall. Even with her augmented strength, the thick glass bounced harmlessly off the wood and rolled across the floor, unbroken. The necromancer shoved the heels of her palms into her eyes and took a deep breath. For several minutes, no one spoke.

There was nothing to say.

When her shoulders finally relaxed and her breathing returned to normal, she set one hand on her hip. The necromancer stared into the steaming cauldron before her, silent once again.

Connor had gotten the confession he wanted, but he hadn't expected it to be anything like this.

"Please. I just—ugh." Sophia cursed under her breath and turned her back to him. "I can't believe I'm begging. I never thought I'd be in this position, begging for revenge that's mine, but if that's what I have to do, so be it. Just give me this, Connor. If we interrogate him and let him live, I'll never get another chance to get this close. He'll get more guards. He'll realize he should fear the enemies he's spent his life making, and he'll learn. He won't be cocky anymore. He'll truly be untouchable."

"Is Richard all you wanted?" He looked at her over the bridge of his nose. "Did you even want the bloody beauties?"

She nodded. "I need them for a potion."

"And what potion is that?"

Sophia scowled and returned her attention to the boiling cauldron. "I've spilled most of my heart to you already. Don't make me spill the rest."

He rubbed his temples. For all he knew, the flowers could've been the final reagent in a potion to kill him. As he studied her, though, he doubted it. He'd traveled with her for days, and the more time he spent around her, the less annoying she became.

Kind of like Murdoc.

His gut warned him there was more to the story. Eventually, he would have to wring it out of her. As for Richard Beaumont, she had relived enough of her pain for one day.

He let it go, and his shoulders relaxed. As the loathing for that man reduced to a simmer in his soul, the sharp sting that came with exhaustion burned against the back of his eyes. He rubbed them to quiet the ache and debated his options.

Technically, he had little in the way of proof for what she had claimed, but such was the way with crime families. No one but the crown dared go against them, and even then, it rarely happened. Rumors painted them as masked terrors in the night who could silence anyone who threatened their power—usually with a knife to their throat while they slept.

"Listen." Sophia pinched her eyes shut and steeled herself, as if she didn't want to go through with what she was about to say. "You're right. I broke the terms of our deal, and despite my own best judgment, I still tried to play you. You weren't supposed to figure it out, but that's my mistake. Let me offer you an amendment of sorts."

"I'm listening."

"This is my offer. A Hackamore is expensive, but we can brew another one. This once—and, truly, I mean this once, Connor—I will take a Hackamore and answer whatever you ask until it runs out. Any question. Anything. With what I know about Nethervale, reagents, and the politics of this world, that's something I'll never offer again. Just let me have this. Let me have Richard." She crossed her arms, her eyes wide as she waited for his answer. "Give me fifteen minutes alone with him to get my closure, and then let me kill him."

Connor scanned the reagents littered across the floor and ran his hand through his hair as he debated whether or not to let the necromancer before him kill a crime lord's nephew. To decide another man's fate seemed wrong, but if she was telling the truth, this man's fate had been sealed years ago.

He'd gotten away with rape, murder, and torture because no one had been brave enough to step forward to swing the axe at his neck. A man like that didn't stop. As the years passed, he would only get more dangerous. More brazen. More emboldened.

"I'll give you ten minutes." His eyes narrowed as they locked on her.

Sophia's breath quickened, and she blinked rapidly in disbelief. Though she didn't speak at first, she managed to nod while she collected her thoughts. "Thank you."

He stepped over a pile of mushrooms to reach the door. "I need sleep. Don't let anyone figure out what you're doing in here."

With that, he walked into the hall and shut the door behind him.

In the hallway, he paused with his hand on the knob. His head had cleared the moment he'd stepped into the corridor, and now he wondered if he should've offered more sympathy. Given all she had told him, she had suffered immensely, and she had carried her torment alone.

The necromancer had said she didn't want pity, but he figured her callous exterior served as her armor against the world.

If anyone had done to the Finn girls what Richard had done to Sophia, he wouldn't have been able to stifle his fury. He would've gone into a bloodlust and killed anyone involved. He would've made sure it hurt them twenty times more than it had hurt the girls.

With that in mind, he forgave her hatred.

As he reached across the hall and turned the knob to the room he and Murdoc shared, the handle glowed green beneath his touch. Sophia had enchanted both rooms, and yet again, she had proven herself immensely useful.

"Check the brothel tonight," he whispered to the wraith. "When we pass it on the way to Richard's mansion, I'll try to slow us down long enough for you to scan the rooms. See if any of the other women have the same mark."

You are wise to not trust her, the wraith said. *Though you are foolish to kill so sparingly. A simple murder will give you her undivided devotion and respect, and yet you hesitate? Who cares if he's innocent?*

"I care. I don't kill innocent men."

The dead warlord let out an irritated sigh. *Suit yourself, Magnuson.*

As he stepped into a room identical to Sophia's, the sheet over the window-hole fluttered in a breeze. A fresh wave of boiling cabbage rolled in, and the stench burned his nose. He groaned with disappointment as he locked the door behind him.

"Home sweet home." He tossed his pack on the floor and stretched across the straw mattress.

He would never admit it to Sophia, but even a straw mattress like this gave him better rest than the trees. As he drifted off to sleep, the itchy straw reminded him of the hay sticking through the sheets back in the Finns' house. He smiled, and his world went dark.

SOPHIA

As the door shut behind Connor, Sophia stared into the steam wafting from the cauldron. The gurgle and pop of boiling wine blended with the distant conversation on the street below. Oakenglen stirred and woke around her. Though the stink of manure still rolled through on the breeze, the boiling wine before her masked most of the disgusting odor.

Her augmented senses could barely stand the stench of the city, but she couldn't fathom what it must've been like for Connor. The Wraith King made him truly remarkable.

As much as she feared and respected that man, she envied his raw power.

More than that, she wanted it for herself. It tempted her, but she hadn't clawed her way through life only to give in to such a selfish urge.

Her throat still stung from holding back tears. She hoped to the Fates she hadn't let any loose while she had poured her soul out to the Wraithblade, of all people. As the bottle finally emptied, she dabbed her finger around her eye to ensure nothing had escaped.

Dry.

Good.

"You're a damn fool," she muttered to herself as she chucked the empty bottle onto the straw mattress. "Telling him so much. Being so honest."

Her throat burned again. She swallowed hard as she tried and failed to clear it.

You've always been my favorite, he used to say. *I love the way you squirm.*

Richard's breath on her neck. His hand on her waist. The agonizing bite of his blade in her thigh. The shame. The self-loathing that she had let him win—again.

The memories had been so close to the surface, but she would never let herself relive them. They would stay in the dark, and Fates willing, they would die there.

Even though the cauldron needed her attention, she squeezed her eyes shut and stuffed the memories back into the darkest depths of her withered heart.

Always lie. It was the only way to survive Nethervale, and the lesson had saved her life countless times.

With Connor, however, her motto had nearly ruined her.

He'd been about to break their deal. He'd caught her in a lie, and she had been forced to think fast. Even with Nyx, Sophia had woven webs of lies every day. The woman had never had her loyalty, even if everyone in Nethervale had thought otherwise.

The Wraithblade struck her as different. Strange. In recent days, she had begun to feel a flicker of something she hadn't felt since her parents had shipped her off to die.

Loyalty.

She cleared her throat loudly to kill the brief buzz of hope and scooped up a bottle of spellgust. She knelt before her scale and busied herself with pouring it onto the leather plate as she slid the counterbalance along its railing. The glimmering powder piled onto the scale, flawless and perfect.

Usually, she had to make do with whatever awful V4 quality garbage she could find out in the villages. She hadn't had the blessing of using flawless V1 Firebreath spellgust since her days at Nethervale.

A treat she would cherish—and why she had taken far more than they needed for a single Hackamore potion. Connor hadn't seemed to notice her greed, which suggested he didn't understand potions and spellgust as much as he wanted her to believe.

No matter.

With two hundred and fifty grams of flawless spellgust measured, she lifted the scale and poured it into the boiling wine. Steam rolled off the bubbles as the spellgust blended with the alcohol, its magic already casting a soft glow throughout the pot. In minutes, it would shine as green as the grass beyond the walls, and then she could begin adding her reagents.

She scanned the piles of flowers, mushrooms, and powders littered across the floor. It would take hours for her to store the leftover reagents in her enchanted bottles, but the effort wouldn't be wasted. With the Expanstic charm she had cast on her bag, she had all the clout and power of a potion shop on her back.

Still a bit shaken from her confession, she ran her fingers through her dark hair to comb out the tangles. When she had started this, she had only wanted two things: a bit of revenge and the bloody beauties for her potion.

It truly seemed as though Connor would give her both.

This man had stormed into her life and overturned everything she had created. The cottage she had built, gone. Her clientele, gone. After a visit from that Lightseer, Sophia would never be welcome in Bradford again.

Without question, she feared Connor and his wraith. During their duel, she had only had a chance to win because he hadn't been trying to kill her.

Despite the undercurrent of fear, she couldn't deny that she kind of liked the camaraderie. As annoying as Murdoc's advances were, she rather enjoyed having a team. After so many years alone, she had forgotten that relying on others was even possible.

As her mind wandered, she lifted the massive maypop flower into her hands. The purple bloom filled both palms, and its blue pollen stems shivered in the putrid breeze rolling through the window.

Years of planning had culminated in a chance encounter with the right man to help her execute her revenge, but that was how her life had always worked: research, prepare, and wait for the opportune moment.

Tonight, she would face Richard Beaumont for the first time in nearly two years. She would discover what he knew about the night he helped her escape Nethervale. Most importantly, she would learn who else he had told.

After that, she would slit his throat, and she would watch him die.

When she faced the man who had tried to break her, she would have the power of the Wraith King at her back—and two allies at her side.

"Give me this one thing," she begged the Fates. "For once, let me have something good."

CHAPTER FIFTY-FIVE

CONNOR

With his handkerchief over his nose to hide his face, Connor knelt on the roof of Richard Beaumont's house as the midnight moons gleamed overhead. The house's clay shingles dug into his knee, but he resisted the impulse to shift his weight and get comfortable. Considering the soldiers posted at the four corners of the property, he had to keep still.

His pack barely pulled against his shoulder, uncomfortably light after he'd emptied it to make room for the rope he would need to use in just a few moments. All of his belongings waited for him in the secret passage they had used to enter Oakenglen, since he'd needed to travel light on this mission.

The idea of everything he owned sitting in a heap in the most lawless part of the city set his nerves on fire, but the overflowing pack would've weighed him down. When they made their move, it had to be swift. A man like Richard Beaumont had enough money and training to wield deadly magic.

Connor wouldn't give the man the chance to fight.

As he crouched lower and listened to the moonlit night, he hooked his fingertips over the ridge of a roof tile for balance.

On the balcony below this patch of the roof, the orange glow of a candle flowed through the open doors to the master bedroom. A teacup clinked against a saucer, and the soft shuffle of a finger against paper followed.

Aside from Richard's wife reading in her bed, only the distant crackle of the fires in the streetlamps below hummed through the evening air. Much to his surprise, not even the wind rolled through the city tonight.

It was as if Oakenglen held its breath as it waited to see which man would prevail—the Viceroy or the Wraithblade.

To think he was finally here, with everything he needed to get answers about what he was and what the Lightseers wanted from him, seemed impossible. A peasant had found a way into a city that hunted him and even made it to the sectors of town forbidden to people like him.

You're a survivor, Connor, his father had always told him. *It's just what you do.*

His muscles ached from the hours he'd spent thus far on the roof, just waiting. Listening. Biding his time. He stretched out his hands to ease the tension in his body, but his bones hummed with anticipation. Impatient urges pushed him to hurry, to save the waiting for those with the luxury of time, but he suppressed the thought.

"Wraith," he whispered, careful to keep his voice low so that neither Richard's wife nor the soldiers would hear him. "What did you see in the brothel earlier?"

Nine of the girls had his mark, the ghoul confirmed. *The rest had their clothes on.*

Connor stifled a groan of disgust as he tried to understand what could drive a man to do such a thing. "Sophia was probably right, then. They must all have his mark."

Most likely.

In the bedroom below, a book snapped closed. The rustle of bedsheets across skin drowned out the gentle pop and fizzle of the candle's flame. Footsteps tapped along the floorboards as a shadow stretched onto the balcony, and in seconds, the shadow sharpened into an hourglass silhouette. The balcony doors swung shut, and the candlelight snuffed out moments later.

With the wife finally headed to bed, Connor shifted his weight onto his feet and kept low to avoid a guard spotting him. His fingertips brushed along the shingles for balance as he darted up the steep incline to the other side of the house, and he reached the peak of the roof in seconds.

The clay shingles gave him cover as he scanned the back gardens. Amidst the weeping willows and assorted flowers planted beside a small pond, one guard rested with his back to a tree. With one arm hooked around his drooping spear, his head leaned forward as he snored. The other soldier leaned against a tree on the opposite end of the gardens, with his head perched in the crook between two branches.

Asleep—or as close to it as they could get while standing up.

He climbed over the peak of the roof and inched his way to the edge, looking for the balcony they had monitored for the last four days.

The one that led to Richard's office.

True to Sophia's word, the man had a routine. Every night, he stayed in his study until roughly two hours after midnight. No breaks. No visitors. He simply sat at his desk, shuffling his way through papers with the doors open to the spring air. On alternating evenings, he would visit the brothel. On nights when he didn't, he walked into the bedroom he shared with his wife. Last night, muffled whimpers had escaped through the open balcony doors, followed by the hour-long smack of skin on skin.

Her torment—and that of Richard's other victims—would end tonight.

Somewhere in the house, Sophia and Murdoc scoured the place for servants, company, or anyone else who would've possibly heard a scuffle and come to help their master. He'd given the two of them enough time, and since no alarms had gone off, he could only assume it had gone to plan.

He peered over the edge of the roof. Orange light poured out of the office and illuminated the balcony eight feet down, but no shadows passed in front of the flame. The creak of a chair cut through the night, followed by a man muttering to himself as papers shuffled.

With the balcony directly below him, Connor scanned the gardens one last time. Neither of the guards in the backyard so much as shifted their weight.

It was time.

He eased himself to the edge of the roof and jumped. Silent as a ghost, he landed on the balls of his feet and crouched. With his fingertips pressed against the stone beneath him for balance, he scanned the office through the open balcony doors.

A plush leather chair sat in front of an empty fireplace on the right side of the room, and two windows framed the mantle. A man hunched over a desk against the left wall, his back to Connor. Stacks of papers covered every available inch of space on its surface, and the end of a jet-black quill trembled above his head as he scratched out a letter.

Richard's dark hair hung over his shoulders as he craned his head over the papers in front of him. With no satin ribbon to tie back his hair as he worked, the black strands hid the open balcony from his line of sight.

On the third floor of his mansion, the fool probably thought he was safe.

With his bag over one shoulder, Connor stepped into the office and drew one of the silver blades from the sheaths on his back. He gently eased the doors shut behind him and slipped the sword through the curved metal handles, locking them in place. The hilt squeaked softly as it rubbed against the metal latch, and his head snapped toward Richard at the sound.

Except for the quill in his right hand, the man didn't move.

Connor let out a quiet breath and braced himself. With whisper-silent footsteps, he approached the man from behind. The tip of the quill scratched in the silent office as the Viceroy mumbled obscenities under his breath.

Now or never.

With a violent and lightning-fast movement, Connor pressed his palm against the back of Richard's skull and smashed the Viceroy's forehead into the desk.

The man went limp. His arms knocked aside a pile of parchment and toppled the inkwell. Its black ink seeped across his freshly scrawled notes as his hair slumped onto the stacks of papers around him.

Out cold, but not for long.

As Connor grabbed the backrest of the man's chair, he briefly scanned the papers on the desk. The scribbled ledgers featured line after line of names he didn't recognize, followed by various offenses. Robbery. Loitering. Arson. Loitering again. Panhandling. More robbery. A fine followed, along with the date of the offense.

Busy work.

His brow knit with confusion at the idea of a Lightseer Viceroy busying himself with the sort of task usually relegated to poorly paid clerks. As he scanned the other piles of paper, he found the exact same information, written in three copies.

By hand.

Not busywork, then, but drudgery. Punishment, even. Apparently, the Lightseers liked this man even less than Sophia had thought.

He dragged the man's chair into the center of the room and cast a wary glance out the windows. Through the sheer curtains drawn across the glass, he could see clear into the night beyond. Moonlit silhouettes of the garden's towering trees blocked everything else from view. No neighbors' lights burned in the dark. No one rushed through the shadows to give aid.

To be safe, he still debated snuffing out the half-dozen sconces lighting the office. He and Sophia would've been able to see in the dark, even if Murdoc couldn't.

Perhaps that would've only garnered more suspicion, though. Because the soldiers outside guarded a man who kept the same schedule every night, they might've gotten suspicious if the lights went out too soon.

Richard moaned, and Connor opted to leave the lamps lit despite the risk. He released his hold on the chair, and the front legs hit the floor with a thump. Connor grimaced at the sound. The Viceroy's head lolled, blood still streaming from his nose, but he remained unconscious. Though the soldiers probably couldn't have heard that from outside, he had to be careful.

He yanked the rope out of his bag and got to work, tying off Richard's wrists and ankles. With the binding kept tight enough for color to drain from the skin, it would be harder for Richard to properly summon most of his augmentations.

Though he hadn't studied the man long enough to know all of the

Viceroy's magic, he'd learned quite a bit about augmentations from watching Quinn and Sophia fight. Every use of their powers required a specific movement, and this would at least slow the man down.

Probably.

The wraith materialized before him in a swirl of black smoke. The ghoul's haunting skull twisted on the base of his bony spine as he examined their captive. *Magnuson, you fool. What are you doing?*

Connor tightened the last knot around the Viceroy's wrist. "I feel like that's fairly obvious."

Your servants should be doing this, not you. For the Fates' sake, man. Even if you're not a king yet, you still represent me. Have some dignity.

He snorted. "My 'servants' are a little busy."

The muffled patter of feet against the hallway floorboards caught his attention—the shuffle of boots on wood brief and barely audible in the night. He stood, shoulders tense as he summoned a shadow blade into one palm. Black smoke rolled over his forearm as the sword appeared, and he approached the door with slow and steady steps. The blackfire crackled along the obsidian steel, and his hand wrapped around the knob as he prepared himself for what he might find.

He didn't want to have to kill anyone else tonight, especially not someone in the wrong place at the wrong time.

A floorboard creaked, just beyond the door. He waited, but the footsteps didn't retreat. Whoever it was, they lingered in the corridor beyond—which meant they would overhear anything that happened in the room.

Damn it.

To maintain the element of surprise, he threw open the door in a rush and raised his blade. He glared out into the hallway, ready to pin them to the wall if he had to. Maybe he could yank them into the room and blindfold them before they saw—

Outside the door, Sophia and Murdoc flinched in unison. They waited in the dark hallway with cloths over their noses and mouths to hide their features. Both of them froze in place and stared up at him with wide eyes.

He let out a breath of relief and dismissed the blade in his hand.

Murdoc cleared his throat and stepped into the room. "Fates above, mate. You're terrifying."

"Thank you," Connor said dryly. "Now hurry up."

Sophia adjusted the enchanted satchel on her shoulder as she entered, and her dark gaze landed instantly on Richard. He groaned with pain and furrowed his brows as he slowly came to, and her body stiffened at the mere sound of his voice. Her breath caught in her throat, and she absently tapped her fingernails against her thigh as she studied his bound body. The corner of her eye twitched as the door shut behind her.

"Remember." Connor leaned in, his mouth inches from her ear as he whispered his warning. "Mission first. Revenge last."

She nodded.

"Tell me what you found in the house," he ordered.

"No one is here but the wife, and I fed her a Dwelldaze after her light went out. It will make her sleep for about four hours, and there's mild memory loss in the moments leading up to the potion taking effect. She will remember someone forcing her to drink something, but she won't remember much about our faces."

"Will she sleep through shouting?"

"She would sleep through a house fire."

"Let's not set the house on fire, then." He rubbed the back of his head as Richard muttered slurred curses from his chair. "Looks like our man is waking up. Are you ready for this?"

Though her eyes never left Richard, Sophia rested the heel of her palm against her chin and tilted her head to the side. A sharp crack cut through the air, and she shook out her shoulders. "I've been ready for two years."

The wraith crossed his bony arms over his black cloak as he glided through the air and paused in front of Richard. His tattered robe billowed in the winds of the dead, and he stared down at their captive in silence. His hood cast shadows across his bony features, and Connor couldn't see the dead king's face.

It has been so long since I enjoyed a proper interrogation, the wraith confessed. *I suspect this will be quite fun, given the woman's clear experience in matters like this.*

"You should really learn their names," Connor chided under his breath.

The wraith shrugged.

Murdoc collapsed into the chair by the empty fireplace and draped his long legs over one of the armrests. His head dangled over the other, and he moaned happily as he stretched and sank into the well-worn leather. "Captain, will you buy me one of these? This is like a cloud."

We face a substantial threat, and he lounges like a fool, the wraith muttered. *Why you keep that idiot is beyond me, Magnuson.*

"Be nice."

No.

Richard lifted his head and blinked at the ground. His nose sat at an odd angle, but the blood streaming from it slowed to a trickle. As his long hair fell in his face, his eyes slipped in and out of focus.

Time to ensure the Viceroy understood the danger he was in.

Connor stood to the wraith's left with his hands at his waist and scowled at their captive. Apparently following his cue, Sophia stood to the ghoul's right with one hand hooked on the strap of her bag.

"What—" The Viceroy spit blood onto the wooden floor and winced. His hands tugged against his bindings, and he gaped at the rope around his wrists. "What the hell?"

"One shout for help, and I'll let him have you." Connor nodded to the ghoul beside him. "Even one use of your augmentations or any enchanted items you have on you, and you'll die. No matter how good you think you are, a wraith is faster. I guarantee it."

The shadowy ghoul tugged back his hood to reveal the long crack in his skull. With the dark holes that served as his eyes trained on Richard, he glided closer until his bony teeth were inches from Richard's face.

The Viceroy gasped, and he leaned his head as far back as he could. The ropes strained and creaked as he tried to put distance between them, but it didn't do any good. He stared into the wraith's skull as though the terrors of the afterlife waited in the darkness beyond those empty eye sockets.

Richard's gaze darted to Connor, and he gritted his teeth even as his hands trembled with fear. "You inbred peasants don't know who I am, do you?"

"We're well aware. In fact, we brought you a present." Connor nodded to Sophia.

The necromancer tugged a bottle of iridescent white liquid from the pack on her shoulder. As it gleamed with all the fire of a liquid jewel, she found a clean stack of papers and set her bag aside.

Richard's eyes went wide—even wider than when he'd seen the wraith—and he swallowed hard as he fought against the ropes binding him in place. "Don't, woman. Don't do it. That's a Duvolia, right? I'll pay you whatever you ask, give you anything—"

"It's not a Duvolia, idiot," Sophia snapped. "There are cheaper ways to kill you."

He let out a sigh of relief, and his shoulders briefly relaxed even as his gaze shifted to Connor. He opened his mouth to speak, but Sophia pinched his nose with her thumb and pointer finger, blocking off the airway. His mouth popped open, and he gasped for breath as he scowled at her.

As her thumb popped the cork out of the bottle, she shoved her palm against his eyes and forced his head back. He choked as his neck craned over the backrest.

Richard scoffed as his strained breath whistled through his pinched nose. "You'll never—"

She shoved the open bottle down his throat until half of it disappeared behind his teeth. He gagged and tried to tilt his head away, though her palm kept him mostly in place. He struggled against the bindings as the white liquid seeped out of the bottle and into his mouth, bit by bit.

When the last of the potion drained into his mouth, Sophia squared her shoulders. In a seamless motion, she tossed the bottle aside and grabbed his jaw. The glass shattered against the floor as she forced his mouth closed and held him in place.

His hands balled into fists as he sputtered and strained against the ropes. He puffed and gasped. White foam frothed over his lips as he fought to spit out the potion. With her hand firmly locking his jaw shut, his ragged breaths hissed through his teeth.

As Connor watched the spectacle, he pointed to Sophia. "Do you need help with—"

"No," she interjected, never taking her eyes off the man before her.

Richard tried one last time to yank his head away, and the chair skidded over the floor. Sophia hooked her foot around his leg and pinned him in place. Seconds later, she yanked his head farther over the backrest. He yelled, the cry muffled through the potion and her grip on him.

She has done this often, the wraith observed.

"No kidding," Connor muttered.

Richard's eyes pinched shut, and he finally swallowed.

She didn't release him.

If this went on much longer, he would pass out from the lack of air.

Connor cleared his throat. It seemed like the necromancer had begun to enjoy this a little too much, and she needed to focus on the mission at hand.

She didn't move. "He faked it."

Richard groaned with fury and fought against the bindings, even harder now than before. A bit of the rope around his leg gave, though it didn't unravel completely. He slammed his foot against the floor and let out a gargled scream.

Before Connor could even step forward to retie the binding, the Viceroy gulped hard. Sophia finally released him, and the man let out a string of curses profane enough to make a whore blush.

"You bastards." He spit a watery clump of the white potion onto the floor. "You diseased, sore-riddled cunts. I'll kill you for this, I swear to the Fates. For fuck's sake, that tastes like mold."

Sophia sneered down at him, her nose creased with wicked pleasure. "Only the best for a Beaumont."

"And who are you, then?" He gave her a quick once-over as his dark hair fell into his face. "Forgotten lover? Did I forget to pay you after I bent you over a chair? What is it? What do you want?"

Murdoc snorted derisively. "Well, isn't he charming?"

Richard spat again, though none of the white potion left him this time. "I'm not dead, so that wasn't a Duvolia after all. Not many potions look like that. It was a Hackamore, wasn't it? You cunts."

"You'll see." Sophia crossed her arms and turned her back on him.

"How long?" Connor asked.

"Two minutes."

Richard took a settling breath, and air whistled through his broken nose. The lines in his forehead faded, and he stretched his neck as he leaned back into the chair. "That's it, then. You've captured a Lightseer Viceroy, and now you want to ask me questions."

"That about sums it up," Murdoc admitted from the chair.

"Nothing to do about it now." With a shake of his head, Richard pointed to the bookshelves with a bound hand. "Since we have some time, why not open up some wine? In the cabinet on the bottom, I have a bottle from Wildefaire. Aged one-hundred-and-fifty years, no less, and from Queen Whitney's own stores. That sort of wine is meant for potions, but I let myself have the odd indulgence now and then. Pour me a glass before I spill my soul to you lot, huh?"

Murdoc jumped to his feet and clapped his hands together. "I'll take some of that."

"It's poisoned," Sophia warned.

The lines of fury instantly returned in Richard's brow as he scowled at her. His expression shifted as quickly as someone taking off a mask. "It seems like you know all of my tricks, don't you?"

"Most of them." She leaned against the desk and crossed her arms as she glared at the man, her figure barely visible around the wraith king's shadowy form.

"Hmm." The Viceroy's eyes narrowed with recognition as he studied her. "Your voice sounds familiar."

Her head tilted as she met his glare. "It should."

I am bored, the wraith complained. *Kill him already.*

"Have a bit of patience," Connor chided.

"Patience?" Richard's gaze darted toward Connor. He barked out a harsh laugh as his fingers drummed anxiously along the armrest.

The Viceroy opened his mouth, probably to spew more hateful bile, but his face contorted before he could speak. He tried several times to clear his throat. His face turned beet red as he grunted from the strain of fighting off whatever was happening inside of him.

Like a spark of fire in the night, a white glow ignited beneath his cheeks. His hands strained again against his bindings, and a crackling flame sparked to life in his palm.

"I warned you." Connor summoned one of his black blades. In the same breath, the wraith at his side drew his own sword as well. "I warned you not to—"

"It's the potion." Sophia raised one hand as she watched the spectacle. "It was an impulsive reaction. He doesn't know he's doing it."

Strange. The wraith studied her as he sheathed his blade. *Given her lust for this man's pain, I assumed she would jump at the chance to punish him.*

Connor frowned, his suspicious gaze also locked on her as he dismissed the blackfire sword in his palm.

Gleaming white light, brighter even than the moons outside, coiled down Richard's neck. He sputtered and tried to fight off the potion, but the light only grew stronger. As the glimmer seeped down his wrists and into his fingers, he groaned with discomfort. He jerked at the ropes, though each tug had far less fervor than before. The strained tendons in his neck slowly disappeared into his glowing skin as the Hackamore took him over.

"This had better work," Connor muttered.

"It will," Sophia promised.

With a long exhale, Richard Beaumont leaned back against his chair. Every muscle in his body relaxed, and his head lolled back and forth on his neck. The white glow under his skin rumbled and churned like thunderclouds.

The Viceroy eased into the chair. The ropes around his wrists and ankles went slack, and he surrendered to the potion in his blood. A smile tugged on the corners of his mouth as the high hit him.

A muscle twitched in Connor's jaw while he waited to see what would happen, and he crossed his arms as he forced himself to be still. Soon, he would either have the answers he needed, or he would lose everything he had worked for thus far.

His very survival hinged on what they learned tonight.

When Henry had fused with the wraith, he'd had his family's fortune to insulate and protect himself. He'd raised an army and conquered a kingdom, all in the name of the people and a higher calling.

In the Ancient Woods, Connor had nothing. No home. No path. No purpose. Now, he had a team. He had direction. He had drive. All things he'd lost when his family had been killed. Things he thought he'd never get back.

Perhaps, in the midst of all this chaos, he'd found a bit of himself again. Maybe that shriveled part of his soul had a bit of life left in it.

Either that, or the wraith had begun to corrupt him without his even realizing it. After all, he'd illegally stolen into the city. He currently stood in another man's home, about to interrogate a high-ranking official. In moments, he would hear secrets about Saldia most men wouldn't even dare to ask.

He squared his shoulders and focused on the task ahead.

One threat at a time, Connor, he thought. *One threat at a time.*

CHAPTER FIFTY-SIX
CONNOR

In Richard Beaumont's office, Connor braced himself for the interrogation that lay ahead.

Still bound to his own office chair, the Viceroy hummed a happy little tune, drugged by the potion in his blood. He absently tapped his fingernails against the armrests of his chair, apparently oblivious to the restraints. Beneath the man's skin, the white gleam of the Hackamore potion rumbled like storm clouds and cast an otherworldly glow against the collar of the man's dark gray tunic.

"This feels nice." Richard shrugged. "Like sitting on a cloud. Why do people always complain about this? I rather enjoy it. Perhaps I'll have to brew my own. After I slaughter the three of you, of course, and find a way to control that thing," he added with a relaxed nod to the ghoul.

The wraith bristled. *Make wise use of your time, Magnuson. If he makes any additional threats against me, I will sever his head from his spine.*

"You'll get your chance," Connor assured him.

Sophia sat on the desk behind her and gestured to the Viceroy. "All yours."

For the past few nights, Connor had sifted through the questions he wanted to ask. He had to use his time well, and he needed to take certain precautions to make this worth their effort.

First, he had to get a clear understanding of whether or not the potion worked by asking questions to which he already knew the answers, same as he'd done to test Sophia.

"Tell me your name," Connor ordered.

"Richard Beaumont."

"Are you a necromancer or a Lightseer?"

"I'm both, and I'm neither." He smirked with pride and blinked like a drunk after his tenth beer. "I do whatever my uncle needs me to do. I am whoever my uncle needs me to be. I went to the Lunestone Academy as a double agent for the necromancers, and I graduated Nethervale at the same time thanks to special accommodations my uncle, shall we say, *encouraged* Nyx to make. Shall I continue?"

Connor nodded.

"Very well. I hold seats on both Chambers. I tell Nethervale about many of Lunestone's secrets, though I keep the best ones for myself. I tell the Beaumonts about Nethervale's secrets, and I am loyal to no one but myself. I feed the Lightseers bits of my family's crimes, just enough to be useful without destroying my uncle's legacy. I play them all against each other, and I raid the treasuries any chance I can."

Murdoc sat up in the leather armchair and whistled under his breath. "That's a lot of honesty."

"It certainly is," Connor admitted, far more impressed than he'd expected he would be.

This would work. By some miracle, they had truly found a way to wring a Lightseer of his secrets.

Well, not by some miracle. By Sophia's experience with a cauldron. Despite her lies, she continued to prove herself useful.

Connor cast a sidelong glance at the woman who sat on the ink-free edge of Richard's desk. Her dark eyes narrowed as she watched the Viceroy pour out his soul. Her fingers curled around the lip of the desk, and she tensed like a beast about to attack its prey. Consumed as she was by her hatred for the Beaumont before them, she didn't even seem to notice him look her way.

"You chose the wrong man to interrogate." Richard closed his eyes and hummed happily to himself. "I'll carve out your hearts once I break free. Or maybe I'll do that to one of you and make the others eat it. I'll decide later. Just know that when I kill you, I'm going to make it hurt like nothing you've ever imagined. I'm going to make the pain last until you bore me. We'll go until your whimpers aren't fun to listen to anymore."

"Fates be damned," Murdoc muttered. "This man is ill."

"You won't break free." Sophia leaned forward, apparently unfazed by the threat.

Richard laughed, and his drugged head lolled as he shifted his attention to her. "I suppose we'll see, harlot."

"Hey!" Murdoc shouted. "Don't speak to her that way, you deranged piece of—"

"Enough." Connor raised one hand to get him to stop. Sophia had faced worse things in her life than petty insults from a crime lord's nephew. "Richard, who is the uncle you mentioned? Is he Gibor Beaumont, head of the Beaumont crime family?"

"He is." Richard drummed his fingertips against the armrests binding him in place. "And he's going to skin you alive for what you're doing right now. He's going to peel back the crusts of your soul, inch by inch, and I'll laugh while he does it."

A chill snaked through the room at the lackadaisical confession.

"Fates above." Murdoc pointed at the Beaumont as his glare shifted between Connor and Sophia. "These people are twisted. How can he say all this so calmly?"

"It's the potion," Sophia explained. "At least, some of it. He's a depraved bastard, but the potion corrodes his self-restraint. No matter what he says, he won't react until it starts to wear off."

"I truly hate you all." The Beaumont's voice remained calm, as though he were speaking to a lover. "It's been years since I faced a threat like you three. I forgot I could hate this much. And you," he added with a nod to Sophia. "You may have a scarf over your face, but I can tell you're attractive enough to not be a waste of my time. It's only fair to warn you, my dear, that I will have you one way or another. When I get out of this chair, I'm going to drive a knife through each of your arms and pin you to the wall. While you're wriggling, I'll lift those skirts and make use of you even after you've bled to death."

Murdoc growled and rolled off the couch. As he stood, the rush of steel over leather hummed through the room, and he lifted the blade of his sword to Richard's throat. "Over my dead body."

"Stand down," Connor ordered.

"But Captain, he—"

"I know, and he won't get the chance." He pointed to the hallway. "Keep watch. Check every room and window you can find and make sure no one's on their way. Notify me if someone approaches."

A watchman would help, but the bar had been set. The Hackamore clearly worked, and the questions he had for Richard involved truths he hadn't yet shared with the former Blackguard.

Murdoc's eyes narrowed as he sheathed his sword and begrudgingly strode toward the door. He stormed out and cast one hateful look at Richard over his shoulder as the door shut behind him.

The Viceroy laughed. "You don't need him to keep watch, and you know it. You managed to get into my house, so I can only assume you've monitored me for days, if not longer. You know they won't come to my rescue unless I call for them. Why did you send him off?"

"I ask the questions," Connor reminded him.

"I see." The man's head nodded back and forth on a drunken tilt. "You want to ask me things he doesn't know about, don't you? Does he know what you are?"

Connor crossed his arms. "And what am I, exactly?"

"The Wraithblade." With his wrists still bound to the armrests, Richard stretched his fingers wide in a dramatic flair. "You fused with an abomination, and you're damned for it."

The wraith bristled, and his bony hand wrapped around the hilt of his sword.

"Enough." Connor stepped between Richard and the ghost, and he shot a warning glare over his shoulder at the undead king. "Don't."

He tests my patience.

"And mine," he confessed.

Richard squinted at the ghoul. "You can talk to him. Fascinating. What other little secrets does the great and fearsome Wraithblade have for me to learn?"

He ignored the Viceroy's taunt. "Who knows about me? Who's after me, and why?"

Richard pursed his lips and looked off to the side, his eyes glossing over as he silently sifted through names. "The Lightseer Chamber, of course. Everyone on it. Otmund is particularly interested in you, though I still don't know why. He says he wants to bottle the ghoul, but I think his sniveling obedience is a ploy to get what he wants. I've always suspected he's more clever than we realize."

"Who else?"

"Zander and Teagan, obviously. No matter what the others on the Chamber may want with you, only those two men have any say over what happens. They want to bottle away the ghoul, but that seems like a horrid waste of power."

"Anyone else?"

Richard laughed. "The world, you stupid peasant. The whole world wants you. That Quinn girl is on the hunt, and when she finds you, you're dead." Richard grinned and leaned back in his chair. "Now there's a stunner. The things I would do to her if I could chain her to a bed—"

"Focus," Connor snapped. "Give me names."

A lock of dark hair fell in the Viceroy's face. "Victoria Starling knows something. That's Teagan's eldest daughter. She knows something more than the rest of us. As for Celine, she escaped the city on the night Henry died. I don't know if she knows anything, since she never sat on the Chamber."

"So, just about everyone." Sophia crossed her arms over her chest. "Like I said."

"Everyone." Richard pointed one finger at Connor as his head tilted limply to the side. "And we have plans, peasant. So many plans. We'll kill you, obviously, but there's so much more to the game. Those Lightseers preach their morality to anyone who will listen and shove it down the throats of those who don't, but they want what we all want." He leaned forward. "They want power."

"What are Zander's plans, exactly?" Connor pressed. "And Teagan?"

Though he didn't know much about Teagan, any Starling posed a real threat to him.

"Teagan wants you dead. He gave Quinn the sole duty to bring you in. As for Zander?" Richard nodded to the balcony. "He's out there, Wraithblade, waiting for you. There have been whispers through the castle, you know. Word that he disobeyed his father. Rumors that he's waiting for you in Slaybourne with a weapon that can kill even you." The man's gaze shifted to the phantom. "A weapon that can kill even that."

In unison, Connor and Sophia looked at each other.

Wait, she had told him. *Wait and listen.*

The next time the Lightseer went on a mission alone to an isolated area, they would attack. Few had any inclination of where Slaybourne even was, much less how to get there.

It didn't get more isolated than a warlord's ruin. Unfortunately, Sophia now knew a weapon existed that could kill a wraith.

Nothing to do about that now.

"Look at those somber expressions, so stiff and serious." Richard laughed so hard he snorted. He craned his head over the backrest as he enjoyed himself. "You—you're actually going to go, aren't you? What idiots! Are you too stupid to realize you're walking into a trap?"

After a settling breath to suppress the surge of annoyance he felt at Richard's constant stream of insults, Connor rubbed his jaw through the cloth across his face. "How many men did he take?"

The Beaumont raised one eyebrow. "None. He didn't want to scare you off because he knows he can take you by himself."

"This man sounds cocky."

The Viceroy slowly shook his head, and his long hair swung side to side with the motion. "You've never seen Zander fight, you poor fool. You don't stand a chance."

Sophia examined her nails, evidently impatient for her turn. "What else do you know about Zander's trap?"

Richard shrugged and shifted his weight in the chair. "That's everything."

"The rest of the Chamber, then," Connor pressed. "What do they want with me?"

"We want that wraith." Richard nodded to the ghoul. "We want those swords Henry used to summon on the battlefield. We want the world to tremble before us. And you," he added, his gaze darting to Connor. "You're in our way, and you've made this far more difficult than it ever needed to be. When Quinn drags you to Lunestone in chains, we're going to rip out your guts and strangle you with them. We're going to parade your corpse through the street on a diseased old horse. You'll be immortalized as the peasant who dared to kill a king. As your corpse rots in the streets, the people will cheer."

Connor stiffened. The shadowy magic of his blades coiled beneath his palms, aching to be freed. He forced himself to be still and glowered at the man who had dared threaten him so brazenly.

It seemed as though the fool didn't know he was going to die. He still thought he could wriggle out of this mess.

"Every kingdom has spies looking for you," Richard continued. "Our people are selling bread. Clothes. Beer. They're in the taverns and inns along the road. Our eyes are out there, waiting for you to stumble into view. Otmund gave us a sketch, and even with that cloth over your mouth, we recognize you."

Under his mask, Connor frowned. Now, it made perfect sense that the Starling woman had managed to find him—she had a sketch.

Damn it all.

"Yours is the most famous face we've never seen," Richard continued.

"It's those eyes. I can tell you're feral just by looking at you, and you can't ever hide that. Before long, your face will be on every wall in every kingdom on the continent, and the world will hunt you down. You'll have nowhere to go. Nowhere to hide. When you die, you'll beg for your life at my *feet*."

Fates be damned, the wraith said. *I almost admire the brutality. If he hadn't been foolhardy enough to threaten me, I'd be enjoying this. These Lightseers are far more brutal than I ever imagined.*

Connor hooked his thumb on his belt loop as he tried to ignore the ghoul. "None of you Lightseers will ever get the chance to see me in chains."

"Are you sure?" The Viceroy grinned. "That Quinn girl is out there, looking for you, and she's one of our best. Zander wants your heart on a spit. From what I can tell, Teagan is brewing some sort of scheme to use your death to get his family on the Oakenglen throne. Do you think the powerful people in this world care if you killed Henry or not? You're a pawn, you buffoon. You're nothing to them but a means to an end, and they'll laugh as you burn for their sins."

As the warning settled into his bones, Connor's gaze drifted to the closed balcony doors. He knew the Lightseers were after him, but he could never have anticipated just how deep this coup went.

Wrong place. Wrong time. Wrong enemies.

Richard laughed. "Your face! That somber glower! Are you afraid?"

He shook his head. After eight years in the blightwolves' forest, he didn't fear much anymore.

"You should be," the man snapped, his smile fading. "I would be."

"Why? What happened the night Henry died?"

The Viceroy shrugged. "He crossed the Lightseers, and they dealt with him. You're nothing but a scapegoat who stepped into the line of fire. The Starlings never trusted me, those clever bastards, so I inferred what I could after it happened." He pointed to the piles of paper on his desk. "To keep me busy and out of their way, they tasked me with this garbage record keeping. All in my own hand, four copies of each, to be finished every night. Why do you think I go to the brothels? I have to vent my hatred for those Lightseer cunts somehow."

Connor rubbed his temple in frustration. "Fine. What is the Deathdread?"

A little gasp escaped Sophia. In his periphery, she scowled at him. The necromancer must've finally realized she'd given that away to someone who had, in fact, not known a damn thing about it.

"The Deathdread is a collection of notes Aeron Zacharias left behind. We assume it has everything he ever wrote about the simmering souls." Richard gestured at the ghoul despite his still-bound hands. "The Lightseers were never able to open the book, but they believe it'll tell you everything about the souls and the powers that come with them. How to control them."

In Connor's head, the wraith growled with rage. *No mortal controls me, Magnuson, and neither do the dead. Remember that.*

He rubbed his jaw as the prickle of the wraith's glare burned across the back of his neck. He opted not to answer and instead focused his attention once again on the Viceroy as their minutes ticked by. "Where is the Deathdread hidden?"

"In Aeron's Tomb." Richard shrugged, as if that were obvious. "Deep in the Mountains of the Unwanted, where we keep the monsters too deadly to allow in the wild. The things in there…" He shuddered, and the white glow beneath his skin glowed brighter. "I went in once as part of my inauguration as a Viceroy, and that was enough for a lifetime. Zander forced me to stay there for twenty-four hours to prove my mettle and worth to join the Chamber, but I suspect he wanted me dead. A scorpion the size of a horse nearly ripped me in half. I'll never go back."

"How do we get in?"

Richard scoffed. "You want the Deathdread bad enough to face a scorpion with a stinger as large as your head? To face those glowing eyes in the dark? There are things in that mountain people thought were myths, Wraithblade. Only a fool would go in there."

"Tell me," he ordered.

"The entrance is in the depths of the Hazeltide castle. It's guarded at various points along the way by a squad of soldiers at each door. No one goes in and nothing comes out unless Hazeltide permits you through, but everyone knows that fat old king does anything Lunestone demands of him."

"And a map? How do we get one?"

"You can't. The only maps are in here." Richard leaned forward and strained against the binding on his wrist until he could tap his finger against his forehead. "And let's be honest, shall we? There's not much time left in this potion. Do you want to waste your last minutes to make me draw you a map I might not finish?"

With a frustrated growl, Connor paced back and forth across the office. "How can you lot not have a map to something so important?"

"It's a security measure to protect the world's deadliest treasure. You need a Starling or a Viceroy to enter, and I would rather spear myself through the neck with my own sword than set foot in that place again. No matter what you try to do to me, you can't keep me complacent forever. Potions wear off. Enchanted items break. The first chance I get, I'll slit your throats in your sleep and watch as you choke on your own blood."

"That answers my next question," Connor admitted.

"Once we're in, how do we get out?" Sophia asked. "Is the entrance through Hazeltide the only way?"

Richard's head rolled back and forth on his neck as he nodded. "One way in. One way out. That's the point."

Damn it all.

Connor rubbed his face as he debated what to do with this unfortunate turn of events. That meant no other chances to enter undetected. If they wanted into the mountains, the king would have to let them in.

This complicated things.

The white glow under Richard's skin dimmed ever so slightly, and the churning cloud of magic slowed. They didn't have much longer, but Connor had a few questions left to ask.

"Who has the Bloodbane daggers?"

Richard chuckled. "That's not a real thing. Is that a real thing? It sounds like something you made up."

He doesn't know, the wraith said. *How disappointing. I had so many inquiries about magic that advanced.*

"You and me both." Connor frowned. "Next question, then. Where is Otmund Soulblud?"

"Last I heard, that conniving asshole went back to Mossvale. Good riddance, too. I hate that man."

"You hate most people." Sophia tossed a pile of his papers onto the floor. They scattered across the rug, and their ink smeared from the fall.

"You sound so familiar." Richard squinted this time as he repeated himself. "Why do I know you? Take off that scarf so I can see your face."

She scoffed with disgust, and her attention shifted to Connor. "There's not much time left on the potion. Anything else to ask?"

"There is one thing," he admitted.

He crossed to the Viceroy and leaned his palm against the back of the chair. The seat tilted backward under his strength. The front legs lifted off the floor, and Richard watched him with the vacant expression of a man numbed by magic.

Connor had one final question. He'd saved it for the end because the mission came first, but he needed to know how this sick man's mind worked.

"Those women in the brothel," he said, his voice dangerously low. "Did you carve your initials into them?"

"I did." Richard hiccupped and grinned like a schoolboy showing off a prize fish he'd caught. "The brand was always easier to use. It made cleaner lines, and I liked the sizzle of hot metal on their skin. But the knife is a fun little challenge for when I'm bored."

Connor's hand coiled around the backrest, and the wood cracked under his powerful grip. He glared down at the grotesque human before him, his nose flaring with disgust as he resisted the urge to break the man's teeth. "You're revolting."

The Viceroy raised one eyebrow. "Tell me you wouldn't do the same."

"No sane man would." He released his hold on Richard's chair, and it thudded to the floor.

Richard shook his head, the loose strands of his dark hair swinging back and forth as he clicked his tongue in disappointment. "Every man thinks he's moral, Wraithblade. Every man can justify whatever he does. There's no good. No bad. No evil. There's just people, and we're all twisted inside. You were born poor in a world that discards its garbage. Even with those fresh new clothes, I can tell you have nothing. You *are* nothing. If you had money, I know the man you would be. You would be like me. Like Zander. You'd be hungry. You'd be fierce. You'd be brutal, same as us."

"Don't be so sure."

"Don't play coy. You're exactly like me." Richard snorted with disdain. "You're just too stupid to see the world for what it is. If life dangled its temptations and pleasures before you, ripe for the taking, pleasure would bore you. If women threw themselves at you because they wanted to marry rich, you would look for the sort of conquests that could make sex interesting again. That's why I brand those girls in the brothels. It's the only way I can get off anymore. It's taken years to perfect carving my initials with a knife, but I like the way they squirm." He hummed with pleasure as he leaned back into the chair. "I like the way they whimper as I pin them in place. Most of the time, I do it while I'm in them, just to listen to them cry."

Connor grimaced, and the urge to split open the man's temple flooded through him. He shook out one hand to distract himself and paced along the floor instead. "You're deranged."

"And you're not?" Richard laughed, his eyes creasing as he shook his head. "Look at where you are, peasant! Look at what you've done tonight. I can only assume you did this with next to nothing, but what if you had more? What if you had everything? Where would you stop? How far would you go to taste the high that comes with conquering something weaker? The difference between us is you have nothing, and I have more money in this house than you've seen in your miserable life. Money turns men rancid, Wraithblade, because it exposes what lies at the core of a man's soul—rot and disease. People like you deny what you are. I simply embrace it."

"Money didn't do this to you." Connor shook his head as he examined the miserable stain of a human before him. "Men aren't evil, and neither is money. From what I've seen, coin is like a Hackamore. All it does is show the world who you really are."

The Viceroy tilted his head in the silence that followed. The ropes around his hands creaked as they studied each other, and the Viceroy's eyes slipped briefly into focus. "That's fine, peasant. Tell yourself what you need to hear to sleep at night. The rest of us know the truth."

You are running out of time. The wraith stretched out his bony hands as he stared at the Beaumont tied to the chair. *I was promised blood, and that meager amount staining his nose is no longer enough to sate me.*

"He's all yours." Connor gestured to their captive as he fought to control the blazing revulsion he felt for this man.

Richard shifted his attention to Sophia, evidently unfazed by his own confessions.

The woman pushed off the desk, her shoulders stiff as her eyes darted to the door. "We're almost out of time, and you said I could have ten minutes alone."

He snared her with a cold glare, and she went eerily still. Though he ached to punch Richard in his miserable face, he instead pointed to the balcony. "My sword is locking the doors, so bring it out when you're done. The wraith will stay with you to ensure Richard doesn't escape."

She balked. "That thing can't—"

The ghoul's skeletal head spun on his spine, though the rest of him remained impossibly still. Only the tattered shreds of his cloak fluttered around him in the hush that followed.

The necromancer cleared her throat. "It—uh, *he*—is of course welcome to stay."

With a frustrated grunt, Connor ripped open the door and stormed into the empty hallway. He did his best not to slam it behind him as his blood pumped, searing and violent, through his veins.

"Control yourself," he growled under his breath. "Snap out of it. You're better than this."

He rested one hand on the opposite wall, his palm flat against a floral tapestry a servant must've hung to keep the hallway warm. Sophia's muffled voice slid under the door, and with a strained grimace, he pinched his eyes shut as he tried to listen. His ear twitched, and though he'd given her ten minutes alone with the man, he needed to know what they discussed.

If he didn't remain vigilant, Sophia's secrets might get him killed.

Murdoc's head popped out of a nearby room. Wordlessly, the ruffian lifted one eyebrow as he pointed at the closed door.

"She has unfinished business."

"Is it the kind I should be jealous of?"

Connor briefly smirked, but the Viceroy's confession about the people he had tortured weighed on him. The man had justified his crimes with lies about the human soul, and he'd felt nothing. No remorse. No guilt. He simply enjoyed watching people suffer.

Over the years, Connor's father had warned him that no man could decide another's fate. The judges and kings did, yes, but they carried the guilt with them to the grave. His father had believed they bore the sins for the people. Fate and destiny weren't for the rest of them to decide.

Tonight, however, Connor had given a verdict. He'd sentenced Richard Beaumont to death at the hand of one of his own victims, and he would sleep fine when the deed was done.

Sophia had been right. A man like that didn't deserve the life he'd been given. Tonight, the Fates had come to collect on justice that was long overdue.

Murdoc stepped back into the darkened room. As Sophia's voice drifted through the door, Connor tried to listen to her half of the interrogation. Though he could hear her clear as day, his eyes kept slipping out of focus.

The same words looped through his head, again and again.

Do you think the powerful people in this world care if you killed Henry or not? They'll laugh as you burn for their sins.

His jaw tensed as he glared at the floor, knowing full well what waited for him outside these walls.

Zander had set a trap, but Connor would meet the challenge. Though the Starling heir struck fear into Richard's heart, Zander had walked into the wraith's territory. That meant they would fight on land that belonged to the dead.

Land that belonged to Connor.

He had waited for an opportunity to strike at one of the two men who carried a weapon that could kill him, and that patience had paid off. Now, he would take back what was rightfully his.

Not even a Starling would stand in his way.

CHAPTER FIFTY-SEVEN
SOPHIA

In the hush after Connor had left, Sophia rested one hand on her hip and watched her prey. Drugged as he was and with nothing else to occupy him, Richard craned his head back over the chair and stared vacantly up at the ceiling. His long hair dangled behind him, a trademark of the family name.

Dark hair. Dark eyes. Pale skin. Strong build. The perfect Beaumont.

It took every ounce of her self-restraint to not drive a dagger into his neck.

The Wraith King glided along the floor, his cloak drifting around him as he floated behind their captive. The ghost leaned over the Lightseer Viceroy and stared into the man's soul. Despite the potion in his blood, Richard stilled as he stared up at the beast, and his breath quickened with fear.

With horror.

With knowing.

When the potion wore off, he would do everything in his power to break free. They didn't have long, and as much as she wanted to kill him, she had questions as well. Though she hadn't intended on having an audience, it seemed rather inevitable in retrospect. Connor's enhanced senses dwarfed even hers. He would've heard everything she said through the closed door, regardless.

Sophia would simply have to improvise. In the end, she and the Wraithblade wanted the same thing.

The Deathdread.

With a light tug on his bound hands, Richard lifted his head and sighed as his unkempt hair fell across his face. His eyes fogged over, and he studied her through the disheveled strands. "You don't want to know what I'll do to you when the potion wears off, my dear. You only have about twenty-five minutes."

"Ten," she corrected. "I couldn't find maypop fruits."

"Ah. I always forget that you common types have to go without things." As he stared at the floor, his brow furrowed with disdain. "What a miserable life you must lead."

Sophia curled one hand into a fist. To vent the pressure building in her body, she pressed her other palm against it and squeezed until the knuckles cracked. "Yes, I know how much you're used to taking what you want."

He nodded. "I am. Money, reagents, potions. Other people's bodies. Now, with your remaining minutes, is there anything you'd like to ask before I rip out your spine?"

She chuckled. "Same old Richard."

He frowned, the lines around his mouth creasing despite the heady buzz coiling through him. "You think you know me. I want to know why."

"Oh, there's no question." She crossed to him and rested her palms against his forearms as she studied his handsome face.

Chiseled jaw. High cheekbones. The sort of face women dreamed about at night if they didn't know about the monster lurking beneath the bravado and false charm.

As she leaned against his arms, Sophia dug her nails into his skin. He winced as she clawed through his sleeves with her enhanced strength. Despite the drugs in his blood, he twitched under her grip.

With him pinned beneath her, she rested her cheek against his and whispered into his ear. "I know everything about you, Richard. For years, I watched you slink between Nethervale and Lunestone. For years, I took side passages to avoid you, to no avail. You told me you liked the challenge of conquering a necromancer, but I wonder how many girls in Lunestone have your mark as well."

"Eight."

"Only eight?" She leaned away, lips pouting as she mocked him. "You must've gone soft."

"Stricter surveillance." He peered down into her cleavage as she leaned toward him. "Unlike Nyx, Teagan cares what happens to his students—provided he's not the one having his way with them."

She raised one eyebrow in surprise. How interesting. Perhaps she could use that if she ever ran into one of the Starlings again.

"You're from Nethervale, obviously." The Viceroy cast a hungry glance over her body and nipped playfully at her neck. She darted out of range before his vile mouth could touch her, but he just laughed. "You're quick. I like that. I don't recognize your voice enough to place you as one of the elite, so I can only assume you were one of the foot soldiers."

She scoffed and pushed off of him. To taunt him with what he would never have, she crossed her arms beneath her breasts to amplify the line of her cleavage. "Keep guessing."

The wraith's head tilted toward her, and that long crack in his skull drew her eye. His intense glare pierced her, and a chill snaked down her spine. She froze in place, the bubbling terror she always felt in the ghost's presence amplified now that they were essentially alone.

The Wraith King wanted death. Blood. Chaos. From what little she had been able to glean from Connor's mumbled one-sided conversation, the ghost probably wanted her to hurry up and kill the bastard already.

She cleared her throat and tugged on the ends of her hair to soothe her nerves. Everything she needed to discuss with Richard was a closely guarded secret, something she hadn't shared with anyone but him—and even then, only against her will. She had wanted to tie up that loose thread tonight, but the wraith complicated things.

No more playing with her food. She had to use her remaining minutes wisely.

With her thumb and pointer finger, Sophia flicked his broken nose. He winced, his brows twisting as he leaned as far back as he could, and his pain made her smile. "How many victims do you have, Richard? In total, across Saldia."

"Victims is a strong word. Maybe they like it."

Her nose wrinkled with disgust. "They don't."

"Agree to disagree." Richard shrugged and adjusted in his seat. "I always found counting to be irrelevant. It's a hobby, and keeping track became dull. I prefer to look at a woman and wonder if I've had her yet."

"I wish I could say I'm surprised." Unable to even look at him, she turned her back and scoffed.

"I must not have given you a scar. With eyes like those, I would remember you. From what I can see, at least, you look like a Beaumont should."

"That was the point." Her silky black locks slid across her neck as she looked at him over one shoulder. "The perfect disguise allows you to hide in plain sight."

Richard frowned, his brows pinched with confusion. "What do you mean?"

She ignored him. "Who was your favorite? Your favorite conquest. The one that sticks out the most."

His eyes snapped into focus, and his fingers stretched wide as he briefly came to. The potion swam through his body, its white glow a little dimmer now as the effects began to wear off.

She had to hurry.

The churning white glow beneath his skin strengthened again. His head lolled to one side as the potion overtook him once more, and he relaxed into the chair. "You wouldn't know her name."

"Try me."

"Leah," he answered. "My cousin."

She stiffened at the name she hadn't heard in years. Even though she had braced herself for it, she still hadn't been ready.

His eyes narrowed in recognition, and a smile stretched across his face. "It's you, isn't it? This is the new body you found?"

Sophia didn't answer. She didn't need to.

Her shoulders still tense, she glanced up at the wraith hovering behind her cousin. The empty sockets where his eyes should've been remained focused on her, and his bony fingers tapped against his frayed cloak.

Silent and ominous. The perfect weapon. The perfect spy.

Without a doubt, Connor had heard everything thus far from the other side of the door, and she would have to tread carefully from here. If they parted ways tonight, she wouldn't get the reagents or information that waited for her in the mountains. Whatever came of this, she had to ensure they made it to Aeron's Tomb.

From there, she would have what she needed, and Connor would no longer matter.

Her heart panged with guilt at the thought of leaving them, but she hadn't gotten this far in life by trusting others. She buried the hope for a better life into the withered creases of her soul and did her best to focus.

"I must say, I approve." Richard tilted his head as his eyes swept again over her body. "I never saw you from the front, but I suppose that was our deal. You got to keep your new face a secret, and I got one last ride."

She grimaced with disgust. "You've somehow become even more repulsive. I'm truly astonished."

He laughed. "I'm amazed your ritual worked, Leah. I figured the augmentation would've faded by now. I never thought you, of all people, could've surpassed the rest of us and done what we all aim to do." He sighed wistfully. "To defy death, the necromancer's ultimate dream. I figured you'd died within a few weeks."

Her hand impulsively flew to the augmentation on her sternum, and truth be told, he was right. She didn't have long, but he didn't need to know that.

"I never would have guessed you were the gifted one," he confessed. "You were the spare child the family never needed. The thing that lost its usefulness. No one expected you to have talent."

"It wasn't talent," she seethed.

Sophia grabbed his collar and, with her augmented strength, lifted him toward her face. The chair hovered off the floor as she held his full weight in her hands. His foggy eyes bored into hers, wide with surprise, but her hate had overtaken her common sense. The blood. The broken nose. It wasn't enough. The pain he'd felt in all of his life, in everything up to this moment—it just wasn't enough.

He needed to suffer.

Her voice lowered to a furious whisper. "It was work. It was sacrifice. It was the kind of pain and hardship Uncle protected you from because you were the golden son. Misery made me who I am today. Hatred and vengeance fueled me through the pits of that Fates-forsaken dungeon in Nethervale, and I clawed my way to the top of the tower. It wasn't talent, you sniveling twat. It was everything you've never known because you've always been the favorite."

As he stared into her eyes, he grinned.

It only made her hatred burn hotter.

"And now we come to those final moments." She dropped him, and the chair banged on the floor, the thud muffled by the rug. Wood splintered somewhere beneath him, but the legs held. His head snapped back. He groaned with pain, but she didn't care about his comfort.

Richard lifted his head and licked a bit of blood off his front teeth. "And what moments they were."

She ignored the taunt. "That night you followed me to Mother's home, you saw something you shouldn't have seen. Who did you tell?"

"Uncle. I had to lie, of course. I told him you bested me, since I couldn't tell him the truth. If he knew I'd let you go for something as petty as a fuck and a brand on your hip, he would've killed me. I knew I could get away with it, though. I always do. It was worth it to hear you whimper one last time."

He laughed while she growled with barely contained rage. Seething, she dug her fingernails into his neck. He gasped as she choked him, his stupid smile finally gone.

One of her fingernails drew blood. "Who else knows?"

Richard winced. "I only told Uncle, but who knows who he told? Besides, you shouldn't care. After what you did, you're dead to them."

"I was always dead to them." She released him and paced the floor. He coughed and wheezed, sputtering for air, but she ignored him. Her fingernail tapped lightly on her lip as she debated her next move.

"I wasn't going to let you go, Leah." He spat out blood onto the rug. "With you bent over that couch, your old body lying by the fireplace in front of us—I was biding my time. I wanted to make it last before I turned you over to the family."

"I know." Her nose creased with revulsion. "That's why I poisoned you."

"A clever move." With a flourish of his bound hand, he feigned tipping his hat to her.

"It should've killed you. When did you develop a tolerance to it?"

"It's a staple of all Lightseer training."

Of course.

Sophia ran a hand through her hair, ready to ask her final questions and end this. "Is there a Grimm on me?"

"Don't be an idiot, Leah. You killed a high-ranking member of the family. Of course there's a Grimm on your life. There has been since the day you left, but it's hard to collect on one when no one knows what you look like." He smirked. "Well, until now."

"What's the reward?"

"A favor from Gibor himself." Richard lifted one eyebrow. "Any request, any desire, instantly fulfilled. Have you ever seen a Grimm with such a generous prize? I certainly haven't."

Sophia bit her nail at the impressive bounty. Though Gibor had all but ignored her in her days as a Beaumont, at least she mattered to him now. In a sick way, it was rather flattering. "What are his terms?"

"They have to find you, prove who you are, and bring you in alive so Uncle can interrogate you himself." Richard shook his head and clicked his tongue in disappointment. "He's quite upset with you, Leah."

She suppressed a shudder at the idea. The screams she had heard coming from the bowels of his house still sometimes haunted her dreams.

"I wonder what Uncle would do if I handed you over to him?" Richard smiled and let out a dreamy sigh. "I wonder what I could ask for? The throne? A new title? What would—"

He groaned and coughed. His head fell limply to his chest as he heaved in breath after breath. His body tensed in the chair as he fought off the Hackamore, and the ropes around his wrists creaked with the strain of holding him in place.

No time left to play, apparently. Too bad.

With calm and measured steps, Sophia walked to her bag on the desk and opened the flap. Her fingers drummed against the air as she debated her next move, but something he'd said earlier gave her a wicked little idea.

With a twisted smile, she reached for another bottle of iridescent white liquid. As her hand entered the enchanted pack, an all-too-familiar pain splintered up her arm like a crack of lightning. Wincing, she gritted her teeth to ride it out. The modified Expanstic charm certainly had its drawbacks, but she and pain were old friends.

As she tugged out the bottle, she lifted it and gave it a little shake.

"Another Hackamore?" he asked, irritation bleeding into every word.

The white glow beneath his skin faded completely as the potion finally wore off, and his eyes snapped fully into focus. He tugged against his restraints. As his fingers flexed against the rope, he snuck a peek at the sword lodged through the balcony door handles—no doubt looking for an escape.

As powerful as he was, he wouldn't get one.

The wraith drew a jet-black sword from the depths of his cloak and set the tip of the blade against the back of Richard's neck. The man instantly froze and gaped as he stared dead ahead. His body leaned slowly forward to avoid the deadly sword, but the blade only shifted with him as he tried to escape it.

"All right." Richard's open palms flashed in surrender, and he took a shaky breath. "Everyone be calm. You and me, Leah, we can barter. Just like old times. You've asked me for help in the past, and all I ever wanted was a favor. Now, the roles are reversed."

Her boots passed silently over the rug as she stalked closer, ready to watch him die. Ready to cause him just as much pain as he had caused her for so many unjust years.

Without moving his head, his eyes darted to her. "There has to be something you need. Coin? A husband? Do you want the Grimm removed? I have sway over the family, Leah. I can make Uncle welcome you back. Just tell me what you want, and it's yours."

The edge of her mouth twisted into a sinister smile.

This, right here.

It was all she had truly wanted from the start.

She gestured to him with an open palm like an actor addressing an audience. "Look at the great and powerful Richard Beaumont. Begging for his life before the girl his family threw away." A happy little sigh escaped her while she drank in the scene. "It's beautiful."

A growl built in his throat. Behind him, the wraith's sword inched ever so slightly up his neck, and he flinched. "There has to be something you want, Leah. Just tell me."

"My name isn't Leah anymore."

"Fine, harlot," he snapped. "Tell me what you want! I've told you everything I know. There's no need for you to shove another truth potion down my throat."

"Oh, I know." She uncorked the bottle as she stood above him. "This isn't a Hackamore."

"But…" His gaze drifted to the vial. The pearly liquid inside shimmered with ribbons of pink and gold as it caught the candlelight. His brows knit in confusion at first, but a slow look of utter horror crept across his face as he figured it out. His jaw dropped. His eyes widened. His air left him, and in his panic, he struggled to breathe.

His terror tickled her soul almost as much as his begging.

Even with the wraith's sword against his neck, Richard struggled against his bindings as his fear overrode his common sense. His head snapped back as he tried to lean away from her. The sword squished as it dug into the base of his skull, and he let out a strangled yell of agony as his eyes rolled into the back of his head.

A muffled string of curses blended with his grunted efforts to break free. "Uncle is going to kill you for this! You're dead, Leah. You're dead!"

For a few moments, she let the words linger and simply enjoyed his fear. After so many years of suffering through his torment, this tasted sweeter than any honey.

As his ragged breath grew rougher, she smiled. "That makes two of us, then."

"Guards!" With wide and panicked eyes, he leaned toward the balcony. "G—"

The wraith grabbed his hair and yanked the man's head over the backrest. The otherworldly sword drifted to the ghoul's side as Richard gagged, his Adam's apple bobbing against his exposed throat.

With him pinned and helpless, Sophia debated grabbing her knife and taking her time as she sliced him open—just as he'd done to her. Though tempted, she ultimately shoved the open bottle into his mouth. Unlike the Hackamore, he only needed a few sips of this one. Death by Duvolia would cause him far more pain than any knife could manage.

So many ways to kill a man. Sometimes, it was hard for her to choose.

When enough of the potion drained into his mouth, she shoved his jaw flat against the roof of his mouth with her free hand. To her surprise, the wraith kept Richard's head pinned against the headrest.

An undead ghoul, helping.

She hadn't expected the Wraith King to assist. From the legends she had heard, the dead king preferred to do things himself.

As Richard squirmed in her hands, his hands and legs thrashed against the restraints. Her enhanced strength matched his, and the muscles in her augmented arms flexed with the effort. Her hand slipped along his mouth, and she grimaced with disgust as she fought to hold him in place.

Carefully, she set the half-filled bottle on the floor as far away from the chair as she could. Duvolia potions were expensive, after all, and a bitch to brew.

With her other hand now free, she pinched his nose and pressed her palm against his eyes, same as before. He would drink the potion, or he would suffocate.

His choice.

Flames sparked to life in his fingers, but she slammed her knee between his legs to silence his magic. He let out a strangled groan as her knee crushed his member, and he moaned in agony. In that moment, through the gasps and choking, he swallowed.

The deed done, Sophia released him and wiped her hands on her gown. With quick and fluttery breaths, she watched and waited. Her heart thudded against her chest.

Any second now.

"You conniving whore." He coughed and spit on the floor, but no amount of hacking or spewing would get the potion out of him now.

Behind Richard, the wraith raised his sword, poised to strike.

"Wait." She reached her hand to stop the ghost from cutting off his head just yet. "Wait. He's already dead."

To her surprise, the ghost hesitated.

Flames erupted across Richard's hands, and his cold eyes snared her. "Maybe, but think of what I can do to you in the precious moments I have left."

The fire of his Burnbane augmentation raged across his fingers as he glared at her. The ropes smoked, not yet broken. He tugged hard, and a few loose strands of the bindings fibers snapped. As he pulled against the burning ropes, his gaze never shifted away from her face. She had seen that expression time and time again, usually in the moments before he ran someone through with a sword.

It was a face she used to fear.

Richard gagged. He broke eye contact and dry heaved into his lap.

His face paled, and he mumbled obscenities. The fires dimmed as the last of the ropes burned away. He coughed, trying to clear his airway, and a puff of frost rolled from his mouth.

He gaped at the frozen breath in dismay. The last of the fire died with his raw terror.

"Your greatest fear." Sophia let out a wistful sigh. "I'd always wondered what a man like you could be afraid of, Richard. I've thought about it more than you can fathom. That look of terror on your face when you thought the Hackamore was a Duvolia—"

"You—I swear I'll—" He stuttered, and more frost puffed from his mouth with every word.

Her eyes went wide, and she feigned a breathless gasp as she mocked him. "Oh, my. Is it getting harder to breathe? Like there's a snow flurry in your chest? I hear it's painful, dear cousin. Freezing to death from the inside out—quite an awful way to go."

He huffed, and his shaking hands curled into fists as he struggled to look at her. With the ropes long gone, he leaned forward and wrapped his arms around his stomach. Splintering frost spread over his skin, inching up his neck and across his cheeks. "W-why?"

Sophia leaned forward, just out of reach. She met his gaze as he strained to look at her. With her palms resting on her knees, she smiled. "That look of terror in your eyes charmed me," she answered, quoting something he'd said to her the first time he'd pinned her to a wall. "I simply couldn't resist."

He huffed again, trying to speak, but puffs of icy breath coiled into the air. He shivered as the frost coated his fingers. His lips turned as blue as a summer sky. As he shivered in disbelief, a milky film covered his eyes. The irises faded until nothing remained but the snowy gaze of a blind man. The frost coating his body hardened. Bit by bit, the pinks and yellows in his skin faded until he became a stunning shade of blue, and only then did he stop shivering.

In the chair before her sat the ice sculpture that was once Richard Beaumont. It wore his clothes and a mask of hatred, immortalized in the frost.

Behind Richard, the wraith raised that massive black sword again. This time, he swung it clear through Richard's icy corpse. As the supernatural steel pierced the ice, Richard shattered, and the deadly blade sliced his chair clean in half.

Shards of Richard Beaumont slid across the floorboards. His frozen head bumped against the leather chair Murdoc had admired, and one of his hands drifted clear to the balcony doors. Sophia stared at the remnants of the man who had tormented her for so long, and she relished every thrumming pulse of this sweet, blissful vengeance.

With him went her secret.

She glanced toward the door, in the vague direction of the man who would eventually figure out what she truly was. Not just as a Beaumont, but as an undead abomination not unlike the wraith before her.

Everyone in her life had betrayed her eventually. Though that same stupid flicker of hope fluttered again in her chest, she snuffed it out. In the end, Connor would be no different than the rest of them, and she wouldn't let a foolish dream get her killed.

Not after everything she had endured to survive this long.

CHAPTER FIFTY-EIGHT

MURDOC

The putrid stench of rotting vegetables stung Murdoc's nose as he trudged through the ankle-high stream of fetid water. At the end of the tunnel they'd used to sneak into the city, the cool blue glow of moonlight promised clean air and a river that hadn't been stained brown.

His two teammates sloshed through the muck ahead of him, their fine clothes drenched with the sewer water as they escaped Oakenglen. With their silhouettes framed by the light ahead of them, neither so much as glanced his way.

They trusted him enough to turn their backs, which he honestly found rather odd. Either that, or whatever had happened during the interrogation had stunned them both into a furious silence.

Probably the latter.

Deadly quiet. Tense shoulders. Connor led the way, the fingers on his right hand stretching wide and curling into a fist, again and again. Neither he nor Sophia would look at each other.

Neither of them had said a word since they'd left Richard's house. The longer the strained lull lasted, the more this felt like the end.

No more makeshift family. No more band of misfits. Murdoc had seen this coming, and yet it still stung.

Whatever Richard had told them in that office, it had broken their little truce. With their peace fractured, he would inevitably witness the next battle in the mini-war that raged between them.

Though he had tried to listen through the door, he'd only caught a few muffled curses or the odd mention of Henry. None of it had made sense without a Hearhaven charm to enhance his ears, and he'd given up.

That was, until he'd peeked into the office after Sophia had left. Richard Beaumont had disappeared. Only a splintered ice sculpture with an uncanny likeness to their target had remained.

His future wife had killed the Beaumont, and he didn't feel a shred of remorse. Though he hadn't witnessed anything of note during his surveillance, he'd heard enough about the Beaumont crime family to assume this man had it coming.

As they finally neared the forest, the bubbling rush of the shallow river echoed through the tunnel. The moonlit glow of a woodland evening illuminated the first few feet of the tunnel.

As he ached for the open sky, a lifeless rat floated past Murdoc's foot. He grimaced and lifted his chin, opting not to look down at his feet anymore.

Connor took the first step into the forest's soft blue haze. The trees loomed over them as a fresh breeze rolled across Murdoc's face, and he sucked in a greedy breath of clean air. The muted greens and browns of the woods mingled with the moonlight, and the clear river water tumbled past with an almost otherworldly white glow.

This forest had tried to kill him time and time again, but bless the Fates, he was glad to be out of that wretched city. Better the blightwolves than a sheriff.

Their Captain didn't pause to enjoy the night, however. As the water deepened, Connor fought the current and reached for one of the willow branches dangling above the knee-deep river. He used it as a makeshift rope and hauled himself onto the high bank above.

"We need to regroup." Sophia finally broke the tense silence. "We need a way to find—"

"You're a Beaumont." Connor turned his back to them both as he stood on the bank above them.

Murdoc's heart skipped a beat. In his surprise, he tripped over a rock in the riverbed. Water splashed into the air. To keep from tumbling face-first into the river, he set his palm against the towering riverbank, its sandy walls even taller than him.

He must've misheard.

"Captain, could you speak up?" He dug his pinky nail into his ear to clear it. "I could've sworn you said—"

"She's a Beaumont." Connor set his hands on his hips and finally looked at her, his brows knit with fury.

Murdoc's lungs deflated. He could barely breathe. He smacked his chest with his hand to snap himself out of his daze and cleared his throat. "I heard you correctly, then."

Sophia stood between them, her crimson skirts floating around her knees as the river swept past. With her dark hair framed by the moon's soft glow, she looked like a nymph come to lure him into the woods. Immobile. Calm.

Ready.

With Connor to her right and Murdoc behind her, Sophia's only escape would've been to scramble up the steep bank to her left. As Murdoc scanned the forest above them, however, the wraith emerged from the shadows between the trees.

Her last exit, blocked.

Trapped.

Between the three of them, she had no choice but to stay rooted in place. She hadn't even flinched as Connor revealed her secret, but ribbons of shock still snaked through Murdoc's mind. He tried to understand how she could've been a Beaumont when they had just killed one.

Beaumonts didn't kill their own. That was more of a Redgrave family trait.

The incessant chirp of woodland crickets hummed around them as the canopy swayed in a gust. The forest carried on, oblivious to the trio unraveling beneath its leaves.

"Explain," Connor demanded.

At her side, her fingers tapped absently against her dress. With her satchel still draped over one shoulder, her dark eyes darted briefly toward Murdoc. They swept past him and back down the tunnel, as if she were considering a way out.

Murdoc set his hand on the hilt of his sword and stepped in front of the sewer. Her eyes snapped into focus as he stared her down. His other hand twitched as he fought the impulse to grab the length of enchanted chain hidden in his pocket.

"My secret was mine." Her head tilted backward as she looked up at Connor. "We got the information we needed, didn't we? Why are you—"

"—furious?" he finished for her. "Why wouldn't I be? You led us into the lion's den to kill your cousin, Sophia. Or should I call you Leah?"

"Don't ever say that name again," she warned, her voice dripping with contempt.

Leah.

Even her name was fake.

Murdoc flinched. A bolt of disbelief hit his head, strong enough to root his heels to the riverbed beneath him. "Richard was your cousin?!"

She cast an irritated glare his way.

Connor crossed his arms over his broad chest. "Who did you kill?"

"I've killed a lot of people." Sophia shrugged. "You're going to have to be more specific."

"To get the Grimm." He jumped off the bank and into the water, apparently tired of her games.

The splash hit her face. She let out an exasperated groan as she wiped off her cheek and shook her hands to dry them. He trudged through the current, closing the gap between them, and she took several wary steps away.

A Grimm.

Murdoc's breath left him in a rush, and he shook his head as he fought to process everything he was hearing. Though he tried to stay focused, to be the wingman Connor needed him to be, it was all too much.

No wonder he found her to be so attractive. He'd known she could kill him with a flick of her wrist, but now he realized her penchant for pain went blood-deep.

If he was going to fall for anyone, it only made sense it'd be a born and bred criminal.

"Why does Gibor want you dead, Sophia?" Connor continued. "Why is he willing to pay such a high price to make sure you're found?"

Sophia's jaw clenched as she looked up at the man towering over her. Step by step, he approached. Inch by inch, her retreat took her to the other side of the river. When she ran out of room to evade him, she set her palms against the cliff-like riverbank blocking her way out of the water. She had nowhere else to go but through him, and she had already experienced a battle with him once before.

Murdoc doubted she wanted to do it again.

"I killed my Mother," she confessed, swallowing hard. "Gibor's sister."

Connor set his hands on his waist and pinched his eyes shut in frustration. "Fates be damned, Sophia."

Fast as a blur, she darted past him. He didn't react. He barely even moved. With a lightning-fast motion that matched her speed, he grabbed her arm and threw her against the steep cliff of sand and dirt behind her. Her shoulder dented the wet soil. She nursed the arm he had grabbed and glowered up at him.

"Ow," she said dryly.

"You can't run from this," he warned.

"We can't stay here!" Sophia gestured back to the tunnel. "We don't have time for this! We killed a Viceroy, and we need to get as far from Oakenglen as we can before the soldiers realize what we've done. They'll come after us, Connor, and we won't be able to hide from them in the trees."

He rubbed his jaw, his intense glare still trained on her. "Oh, I'm aware. First, I need to decide whether or not to let you join me."

"What?" Her shoulders drooped as she stared up at him in disbelief. "I kept my end of the bargain, damn you! I got you the information you wanted. I got—"

"You got revenge," he interrupted, his voice sharp and commanding.

The forest went silent, and in the hush that followed, only the crickets chirped. The wind wandered through the canopy, slow and steady, unaffected by their anger.

"You're right. I did." She poked Connor in his muscled chest. "You promised me as much, and after what he did to me, it was earned."

Murdoc bristled at the thought of Richard laying a hand on her. His grip on the hilt of his sword tightened. Even though the man was dead, Murdoc's need to protect what was his—or would be some day, at least—blistered through him.

"What did he do to you?" Murdoc demanded, his voice dangerously low.

Connor and Sophia's heads both snapped toward him. Though Sophia held his gaze, their Captain's attention returned to her, and he subtly shook his head. "With all the time he spent in the brothel, Murdoc, I think you can guess at what he did."

Sophia's nose creased with hatred as she glared down at the water.

That *bastard*.

Murdoc wished he could've gone back and broken apart the remaining shards of Richard with his sword. His teeth ached as he clenched his jaw to restrain himself.

"I said you could kill the man who abused you, but this went beyond vengeance, didn't it?" Connor scowled as he leaned in. "He saw what he shouldn't have seen. He knew you're a reanimated corpse. He knew you'd found a new body to hide from your own family, and you wanted the truth to die with him. That makes me question what you'll do now that the wraith and I know your secret."

Murdoc gaped at the two of them as they glared at each other, talking so calmly about secrets and magic he thought were impossible. His mind splintered with disbelief, and for several moments, he just blinked at the two of them in awe.

"I need to interject for a minute." Murdoc lifted his pointer finger in the air to pause the conversation. "Every time I think I can't possibly process any more supernatural nonsense, one of you says something else that makes no damn sense."

"How is that possible?" Connor asked, ignoring Murdoc. He never even took his eyes off Sophia. "That's more advanced than anyone has ever been able to replicate. How did you figure it out?"

She crossed her arms with an indignant little huff. "I'm good at what I do."

"But not good enough to make it last," he countered. "Richard made a comment about it fading, and you went silent. It didn't work perfectly, did it? You did something wrong. Is that why you need the bloody beauties?"

"Damn you." The Beaumont squeezed her eyes shut and turned her back on him. "I was afraid you'd pick up on that. Why can't you be an idiot like Murdoc?"

She pointed at Murdoc, not even bothering to look at him while the insult hung in the air. He frowned. Usually, he let insults slide off his back, but not from her. Not one made so dismissively.

Fine. She was about to learn which of them had been the fool.

He fished out the Bluntmar chain and sloshed through the water toward her. Connor and Sophia both paused, watching him as he neared, but he waited to get close enough to act.

She was fast, and he had to be faster.

As he reached them, he grabbed the end of the chain and slung it at her wrist. She flinched, but the enchanted chain wrapped around her forearm before she could dart out of the way. With a practiced turn of his wrist, he yanked on the metal links and dragged her toward him. As she neared, he wove the chain around her wrists with skilful ease and rammed her against the tall bank behind them.

Connor didn't so much as blink. He simply crossed his arms and watched the scene, no doubt waiting to see where this would go. A man like him could intervene if the situation deteriorated, and Murdoc had been foolish enough to show his cards.

Perhaps he shouldn't have let her get under his skin, but he could feel the three of them fracturing.

The anger. The resentment. The unspoken lies about to bubble to the surface. If they weren't going to remain a team, he didn't need to care what they thought of him. He didn't need to be underestimated anymore.

Beneath the water, Sophia's foot hooked against his. He dug his heels into the riverbed and set one hand against her flat stomach. With a push, he trapped her against the bank. In the current, her foot slipped harmlessly over his as he retook the advantage.

Trapped against the sandy bank and temporarily stripped of her magic, Sophia gasped up at him in surprise. Her fingers flexed, no doubt trying to summon a spell, but the enchanted chains drowned her power. A loose strand of her silky black hair hung in her face, and he suppressed the impulse to tuck it behind her ear.

"How did you..." Eyes wide, she simply watched him as her hands strained against the chain locking them in place. "But *you*—"

Murdoc leaned in. With his nose hovering by hers, he looked her dead in the eye. "As a Blackguard, I fought the darkness most people don't have the balls to even imagine. I killed things most people don't know exist. I fought necromancers more powerful than you, and I did it as a scoundrel." He spat the word he'd always hated, but he used it to make his point. "I almost always win in situations like these because magic folk like you underestimate people like me. Time and time again, you lot think we're useless. That's what always gets you killed."

He rooted her in place even as her gaping shock faded. The worry lines in her brow disappeared. Her forehead relaxed. As she stiffened beneath his grip, her dark eyes searched his face, wandering across his features like she was seeing him for the first time. Those ruby red lips he'd wanted to bite for so long curled into a devious little smirk.

"You thought I was an idiot because I let you think that," he cautioned her. "If you're as smart as I think you are, I'm sure you've realized your mistake."

With that, he unwove the chains from around her wrists. Her chest heaved with hungry breaths as the Bluntmar enchantment fell from her arms. Those slender fingers massaged the red marks the metal had left behind, and she studied him carefully.

No longer caring if they saw, he grabbed his hidden flask and tossed the chains aside. They plunked into the water. Through the churning surface of the river, the tiny spellgust stones embedded in each link glimmered with lingering magic.

The whiskey burned his mouth, and he pressed his eyes shut as he waited for the booze to numb the fog of loss that followed him everywhere. He hated talking about the Blackguard brotherhood. He hated having the past slap him in the face with shame and self-loathing again and again.

All he wanted was his honorable death, and yet it refused to come for him.

Water sloshed behind him, but he couldn't bring himself to care about what they were doing. Sophia let out a breathy sigh, and it hit him like a summer breeze.

Fates above and below, how he wanted that woman. The fact that any conversation with her could've ended with a knife in his throat only made him want her more.

"We're going to discuss those chains in a moment, Murdoc." Connor's voice broke the fog, and Murdoc impulsively stiffened at the unspoken threat. "First, Sophia, you're going to tell me everything about that night. Start to finish. Leave absolutely nothing out."

The necromancer balked. "Connor, I can't just—"

"Now," he ordered. "Or we're done."

From somewhere behind Murdoc, his future wife groaned with irritation. The woodland crickets chirped in the silence that followed, but her sultry voice eventually broke the lull. "It took years to perfect my plan. You have to understand, the most difficult part of this wasn't the recipe itself. It was how I'd get away, when I had to escape both Nethervale and my family. They hated me, but I still knew too much for them to simply let me leave. If I'd just left, I wouldn't have lasted more than a season or two because they all knew my face. I had to find a new body to get my chance at a real life."

Something sloshed through the water, and Murdoc took another long sip of his flask before he tucked it away. He retrieved his chains from the river's depths. The cool water soaked his skin as he snatched the metal links from the riverbed.

Behind him, Sophia climbed onto the edge of the steep bank. While the ghoul floated between the trees behind her, her legs dangled over the river. Water dribbled off the ends of her soaked skirts as she looked up at the moons through a gap in the canopy.

Connor, however, hadn't moved. He remained rooted in place, his stance wide and his arms crossed over his chest as he listened.

She toyed with the ends of her hair. "It took three years to refine the process. The potion required so many rare ingredients and so much testing that I almost gave up on it several times."

"You tested it?" Connor asked.

"Of course." She shrugged. "On rats, mostly. You don't try a new potion on yourself, especially not one like this. It requires immense amounts of death and blood, plus a live sacrifice. Nethervale is still trying to understand why, but the moment of death amplifies many spells."

Their Captain nodded with understanding. "That's why you killed your mother."

Sophia pulled again on the ends of her hair, still looking up at the sky. "She made my life hell. When she sent me off to Nethervale, she sent me off to die. Why kill some random person from a town, when I can get a bit of revenge at the same time?"

The muscle by Connor's temple twitched. "That's twisted, Sophia."

"Maybe," she conceded without looking at him. "I need to do it again, and I need the bloody beauties to brew it."

"Do you need them all?"

"No. I asked for extra so that I had backups in case it failed again."

Their captain rubbed his eyes. "What else do you want from the Mountains of the Unwanted?"

Murdoc frowned. "The mountains of what, now?"

Connor's gaze darted toward him, and the man simply shook his head. *Not now,* the motion said.

Murdoc rubbed his neck and pulled out his flask again. These two would keep him drunk. He just knew it.

"I need the Deathdread, too," she confessed.

"The *what?*" Murdoc asked.

They both glared at him in a silent command to stop talking. He let out a strangled groan of frustration and took another shot of whiskey.

"You want to see if it has notes you can use?" Connor guessed.

She nodded. "I need to refine my recipe, but I've done everything I can think of. If anything can help me, it's—"

Her eyes darted to Murdoc, and her lips shut abruptly.

More secrets. More lies. He grumbled in frustration and paced through the water.

"I can't trust you." Connor turned his back on her and trudged through the current toward the other bank of the river. "You can't come."

"Don't you dare!" Clumps of sand plopped into the river as she slid off her perch. Her boots splashed into the water, and she stormed after him. "I told you everything you needed to know. The only parts I left out were for my own protection, and you know it!"

He turned just as she reached him, and they once more glared at each other with barely restrained venom.

Hands in fists. Scowls on their faces. Fury, raging beneath the surface. No trust left. The lull sat heavy in the air as they watched each other, inches from another duel.

Sophia had said her piece, but Connor had yet to respond. In moments like these, Murdoc usually assumed the wraith had interjected. Though he often wondered what the two of them talked about, he had a feeling he didn't really want to know.

Connor's eyes darted toward Murdoc, and the intense frown on his face deepened as his gaze narrowed. Murdoc stiffened, already hating where he figured this would go.

"You surprised me," the man admitted. "You notice a lot more than I gave you credit for."

Sophia took a step back, and her expression softened as she turned her attention on Murdoc as well.

He took a swig of whiskey and shrugged. "That's what Blackguards are trained to do. We—*they*—have to go unnoticed but see everything. They're an army, hidden in plain sight, with no loyalty to any crown. That's their way of life."

Connor nodded toward the metal links slung over Murdoc's shoulder. "Those chains are enchanted."

"They are."

"With what?"

"Bluntmar," Murdoc confessed.

"You're full of surprises." Though the rest of him didn't move, Connor's head tilted to the side. "You fight well. You're clearly skilled. Why exactly did the brotherhood force you to leave?"

Murdoc's throat closed at the question. He tried to swallow, but he choked instead. He took another drink from his flask to clear his windpipe. Though his body tingled with the booze in his blood, it wasn't strong enough to drown out the shame.

He needed more to numb the pain.

"Murdoc," Connor warned.

Gulp after gulp of whiskey burned Murdoc's tongue, and he only stopped when the prickle of phantom pins stabbed at his fingertips. A merciful lack of sensation flooded his body, clear down to his toes, like he was floating. Only then did he shove the cap back on his flask.

His mind buzzed, hot and heady. He coughed to clear his throat, but the burn remained.

"A mission went wrong," He rubbed the back of his head and let out a frustrated sigh. "A lot of good men died, and I took the blame."

Connor didn't respond. In the silence, the gurgle of the brook drowned out even the rush of the southern wind through the trees. By now, Murdoc had thrown back just enough whiskey to numb the pain. He could relive the past, now—but only some of it.

"I was in the Blackguards from a young age." He patted the disgraced mark on his chest. "Inked at fourteen, if you'd believe it. Never been prouder. Worked my way up to Second Lieutenant and was given a new unit. Our first two missions were easy. They went fine. But the third sent us to a town up the northern road called Norbury. We had to dispatch a sheriff who'd gotten greedy. Taxing people to starvation and only giving a portion to the crown. Raiding homes. People going missing in the night. The town was dying, and the king didn't care."

He rubbed his face as his men's haunting screams rang through his mind, but he shoved the memories down deep.

"My unit was young, a lot of sons and nephews of the higher ranks. All of us were eager to prove ourselves. We were the chosen, the next generation of Blackguards setting out to show that we were ready to take the helm."

The meaty thud of a head plopping lifelessly to the dirt echoed through his memory, and he shut his eyes to block it out.

Murdoc rubbed his face as he braced himself. "When we got to Norbury, the governor had a necromancer for a bodyguard. One of your lot." He pointed a finger at Sophia, who frowned. "An elite. He was a bitch to kill, but we managed. We did what we'd set out to do, and we hadn't even lost a single man. A few lost an eye or a hand, but that comes with the job."

A jolt of pain shot through his palm, and he grimaced as he curled his hand into a tight fist. A joint in his wrist popped from the strain, but he barely noticed. In the year since it had happened, he still couldn't bring himself to say it out loud. Even when telling his General what had happened, he'd left so much out.

"They ambushed you," Sophia said for him. "The elite."

He grimaced and set his hand over his face to quell the tide of self-loathing that churned beneath the drunken numbness.

"I can guess how this ends," Sophia said under her breath. "After a slight like that, Nyx would've sent a small army. Twenty? Maybe thirty other elite?"

"Forty," he whispered, his voice catching.

Her brow creased with surprise. "Curse the Fates, forty? She wanted you to learn a lesson."

He pinched his eyes shut. "They slaughtered us. One by one, I watched my men die. Burned to death. Cut in half from head to toe. Frozen with—" He cleared his throat, unable to finish as his gaze darted toward Sophia.

Unable to hold his eye, she shifted uncomfortably and instead studied the river as it bustled past them.

"They left me alive." Murdoc shrugged. "They sent me back as a warning to the others not to interfere. For weeks afterward, boxes with the fallen soldiers' heads kept appearing at their parents' homes."

Connor grimaced in disgust and walked away. Water splashed against his legs, and his head shook as he turned his back on them both.

"You want to know why they made me leave, Captain?" Murdoc scratched his beard. "The general blamed me, that's why. They all did. A leader should've known to call in reinforcements, they said. To shift focus. They said I could've saved lives if I'd been better prepared. If I'd called off the attack. If I'd abandoned the people who needed me and let the town die, their sons would still be alive."

He drank again from the flask, wondering how much whiskey could even be left. He hated this humiliation, this second chance at life he hadn't earned, and he wondered when death would take him already. It had certainly taken its sweet time.

Perhaps that was his ultimate punishment—to wait. To live with the self-hatred a little while longer.

A hand grabbed his shoulder, and he flinched as he looked wildly around. Connor stood beside him, silent as a ghost on his way over—but that shouldn't have surprised Murdoc, not at this point.

In the sober hush that followed, his new Captain simply watched him. His grip on Murdoc's shoulder tightened ever so slightly as he let the silence say what didn't need to be said. Connor's face relaxed, and Murdoc had seen that look once or twice before.

Forgiveness.

The tension in Connor's body had long since faded, and with that subtle gesture, all was pardoned. He took a deep breath and patted Murdoc's back before he walked downstream.

Murdoc stared after his captain. "Huh."

Apparently, he wouldn't lose his ragtag family today, after all.

"You're not the only one keeping secrets," Connor admitted over his shoulder.

Sophia sucked in a tiny breath of disbelief, and her head pivoted toward him.

"Let's get out of this water." The man climbed the riverbank. "Besides, Murdoc, you should sit down for this."

CHAPTER FIFTY-NINE
CONNOR

As Connor leaned his back against a trunk, the wet ends of his pants clung to his shins. A chill snaked through the cold spring night, but the longer he spent with the wraith, the hotter his body burned. Unaffected by the cold, he slipped his thumb through one of his belt loops and studied the two people he'd traveled through the Ancient Woods with thus far.

Sophia shivered as she sat on a fallen tree beside Murdoc. The dead oak's mangled roots stabbed at the air, clumps of dirt still stuck to them long after it had toppled. Whether by a storm or a blightwolf, something big had taken it down in its prime.

Beside Sophia, the former Blackguard stared at the ground, his face pale as the moon. His chest stilled, and his eyes widened with disbelief. A moment later, he sucked in a greedy breath.

In his shock, the man had forgotten to even breathe.

Connor had explained everything, and he'd left nothing out. Now, he simply had to wait and see how Murdoc would react.

After all, he was the darkness Murdoc had been trained from a young age to kill.

In the lingering hush, he braced himself for the inevitable chorus of steel against leather. A battle would inevitably follow, and he would try his best to merely injure Murdoc. Even if the man wanted an honorable death, he wouldn't get it from Connor.

This traveling band of theirs couldn't last. With Sophia's constant secrets and surprises, Connor didn't want to wake up one day to find a Beaumont in his camp or a necromancer's blade at his throat. Now that Murdoc knew the truth, he wouldn't want to stay.

Yet again, Connor would be on his own. Perhaps it was for the best. At least alone, he knew what to expect from the world—nothing.

Still frozen in place and unable to move, Murdoc's gaze finally drifted to Connor. "You're the Wraithblade."

"I am."

"That ghoul is the Wraith King."

"He is."

"King Henry is dead."

"Yes."

"There are two daggers out there that can kill you and the wraith."

"That's right."

Murdoc rubbed his beard, his eyes glossing over as he sifted through it all. He fumbled for the flask he'd set on the log beside him. When his hand merely scraped against the dead bark, he absently turned his head to find it lying just out of reach. He grabbed it and tossed his head back as he took a long swig.

He coughed and sputtered. As he leaned his elbows on his knees, the last of the whiskey poured onto the ground. If he noticed, he didn't react.

"Fuck," Murdoc said under his breath.

Connor nodded. "That's why I didn't tell you."

As the moments slipped by, he leaned his head against the bark behind him and waited for the unavoidable duel to start.

Above, the twin moons shone through a hole in the trees. A cloud crept in front of one of them and, backlit by the moons, the cloud's misty edges glowed silver. It reminded him of moonlight gleaming off the ocean waves, and a pang of nostalgia gutted him.

Life takes work, son, his father had told him one night as they'd rowed out into the sea. *Your mother doesn't like what I'm doing—what I've asked you to help me do—and that's why you heard her crying in the kitchen. That's why she slammed the door as we left. But that's life, son. You don't always get your way. You'll upset people, you'll hurt people, and you'll make mistakes. If you care about them, and if the relationship is worth saving, you find a way to work through the hurt.*

His father and mother had worked through the hurt of that night. She had forgiven him, agreed with him even, within weeks of their fight in the kitchen.

Despite her cold fury, despite the moments of terrifying silence as she refused to even speak to him, his father had persisted—because she mattered to him.

Connor rubbed his neck as he shifted his attention to Sophia and Murdoc. The two of them stared at the ground, shoulders slumped.

Defeated. Just like he'd been when he'd left Kirkwall.

"Everything in me says this is the honorable death I've been waiting for," Murdoc admitted as he stared off into the forest. "That it's my duty to run you through with my sword or die trying."

Connor stiffened.

Here it comes, the wraith warned. *As I expected it would. At least give me a little blood, will you? Even if you are too soft to kill him properly.*

As Connor did his best to ignore the stupid ghost, Murdoc shook his head in disbelief. "I should draw my sword, I suppose, but I've seen the man you are, Captain. Underneath all that power, you have a good heart. I respect that too much to try—and fail, might I add—to kill you."

The wraith groaned in annoyance, his bloodlust unfulfilled.

With a quiet sigh of relief, Connor relaxed into the tree behind him. Though admittedly grateful he wouldn't have to kill Murdoc tonight, he didn't know how to respond to a comment like that.

The former Blackguard rubbed his eyes and let out a frustrated groan. "You've got a world of pain coming for you, Captain. The Lightseers and Starlings want you, sure, and now we have the Beaumonts to contend with." He added with a gesture toward Sophia, who didn't even acknowledge him. "The Blackguards won't care if you're a good man. They'll come, but

I would fight my former brothers to defend you. Wherever this road takes us, I'm at your side. Debt or no."

A smile tugged at the corner of Connor's mouth, and he simply nodded in gratitude.

"But you're buying me more whiskey," Murdoc warned. "Loads more."

Connor chuckled. "Fair enough."

Murdoc stood and offered his hand. Connor took it, and they shook.

"And me?" Sophia asked.

Connor frowned and set his hands on his waist. She leaned subtly forward, and the line of her cleavage deepened.

"I understand why you did it," he admitted. "I hid who I was from Murdoc, same as you hid your Beaumont heritage from us both. You're powerful, Sophia, but I want you to listen closely to what I'm about to say."

The dark temptress waited, her lips pressed tightly together while the wind meandered through the leaves above them.

"I've seen the way you look at the wraith." Connor's eyes narrowed in warning. "I've seen that greed. That envy. I know you want him for yourself."

She didn't reply.

He stalked toward her, calm and steady, and her eyes followed him. She leaned back as he neared, and he only stopped when he stood right in front of her. The banished Beaumont craned her neck as she tried to meet his glare.

"You've been through hell and back." He shook his head, impressed that anyone could've survived what she had endured. "I don't blame you for your bitterness. But if I so much as catch a hint that you might try to kill me, I will gut you. I won't leave enough time for you to heal like I did for the Starling woman. Do you understand?"

Despite the death threat, Sophia didn't flinch. In the brewing wind above them, she kept his gaze and merely nodded.

"In that case, you can stay," he said.

Don't be a fool, the wraith chided.

Connor ignored the ghost. He had already tried the drifter's life, and now he finally had a team. While he still didn't know if he would eventually be forced to kill Sophia, she had proved immensely useful thus far.

You cannot keep them, the wraith insisted. *They are a distraction. They make you weak.*

"Stop talking," he warned the ghoul.

Magnuson, the specter snapped, still invisible in the night air. *Send them off this instant. They've both served you well, but you no longer need them.*

He grimaced, too tired to deal with the ghoul's arrogance. After the night they'd had, he needed sleep.

Magnuson, answer me!

Connor growled with annoyance. "The worst part of you being loud and irritating is that I'm the only one who can hear you!"

"What?" Murdoc asked.

Exactly.

The wraith materialized in a cloud of black smoke before him. Murdoc and Sophia flinched and leaned away in their surprise, but Connor met the old ghost's gaze. The gleaming. soulless skull hovered inches from his face.

You and I are linked, Magnuson. When Zacharias brought me back, he thought he'd tricked me into a life of servitude, and his pride cost him dearly. I knew that whatever poor soul I fused with would cave to my will eventually—even him. Even you.

The phantom drew his sword and lifted it to Connor's throat. The blade hovered a breath away from his skin, but he didn't care. In his periphery, Murdoc drew his sword with a familiar swish of leather and steel.

"You can't kill me," Connor reminded the ghost.

I can't, the wraith confirmed. *But I can kill them.*

"Don't you dare—"

The skull disappeared, and the thick black fog blocked Connor's view of the forest around him. He waved his hand through it to clear it away. As it dispersed, a ribbon of dread slithered through the trees, and the ghoulish figure finally reappeared.

The wraith now waited behind Murdoc, his blade lifted to the former

Blackguard's throat. Murdoc impulsively leaned his head back as the steel pressed against his neck. The ghoul's bony hand gripped the man's shoulder tightly, and Murdoc winced with pain.

Sophia stood, her eyes narrowed with anger. At her side, the fingers on both her hands spread wide as another chill rolled through the woods. A thick layer of frost coated her palm in a silent warning for the wraith to let Murdoc go.

Connor's knuckles cracked as he curled his hand into a fist. "Release him immediately."

The ghoul shook his head, though the hood over his skull cast a long shadow that hid the sockets where his eyes used to be. *Your team is your weakness. You care too much. I have tried and failed to control you, but now I see they are leverage that anyone—not just me—can use against you. You will send them away, or I will end them both.*

"Stop this before you do something you can't take back." His shoulders stiffened, and his biceps flexed as he prepared to test what sort of damage he could do to the ghoul. "Drop your sword. Now!"

The wraith laughed, the sound as harsh and grating as a creature's dying breath. *And why would I do that, Magnuson?*

"Because you're better than this."

Sophia snorted derisively.

At least she understands, the ghoul said with a nod toward the necromancer. *Yet again, Magnuson, you think too much of others.*

"I truly don't." Connor straightened his back as he stared the ghost down. "You have a bit of humanity left in you. I've seen bits of your human side that you thought were dead. I've watched you care about others, in your own demented way. You're not a heartless monster. Not anymore. You say my team is my weakness, but you're part of it—even if you are a royal asshat."

"Hey, Captain?" Murdoc's Adam's apple bobbed against the wraith's sword. "Maybe don't insult the brutal dictator's ghost, huh?"

"I hated you at first," Connor confessed, ignoring Murdoc as he focused on the wraith about to kill his friend. "I thought you were a nuisance to control and tame, but I was wrong. You've shown me I was wrong. All I want now is for you to work *with* me instead of making things so damned difficult all the time."

The wraith went still as he listened, though his grip tightened on Murdoc's shoulder. The man winced again, and his body tilted toward the bony hand as it threatened to break his bones.

"This, right here?" Connor gestured between the four of them. "This is the life you never got. This is a second chance at the good things you say you've forgotten about the world. The things you probably never even had to begin with. Let yourself have them now."

The Wraith King didn't answer. For several moments, nothing but the canopy shifted around them. The forest night sang with the chorus of insects in the darkness, and the rush of water over rocks gushed from the river nearby.

Inch by inch, the blade lowered from Murdoc's throat.

Magnuson, I'm impressed. You have done what none before you has managed.

He tensed, sensing a trap. "And what's that?"

The ghoul sheathed his sword, and Murdoc let out a low sigh of relief as he stumbled across the forest floor toward Sophia. He sat on the log and gulped in breath after breath. Beside him, the necromancer dismissed the ice from her hands.

You have earned my respect, the ghoul admitted.

Connor's eyebrows shot up his head, and he simply stood there for a moment in surprise.

You wanted to know all of the skills you acquired through your connection to me. It's partly why you sought the book, yes?

He nodded.

In that case, you already know.

His eyes narrowed in suspicion as he tried to figure out the wraith's riddle. As he sat with it, however, the truth dawned on him like the sun over a mountain.

You discovered most of them on your own, the phantom admitted with a lazy flick of a bony wrist. *The rest, you earned. Your one and only flaw is that you underestimate your power. You ripped apart an iron gate with your bare hands, and yet you cannot seem to fathom how to properly use that power in a fight. Even with an augmented warrior's might and magic, none should ever stand in your way. You are power incarnate, Magnuson. Though men fear me, you are the true wraith of the night. I will no longer allow you to live as less than your truest potential. When I am done with you, you will be as you always should have been—a man the world rightly fears, despite that infuriatingly noble heart of yours.*

Connor went still as he listened to the dead king's confession.

Power incarnate. The true wraith of the night. To think he had access to even more power than what he already possessed seemed impossible.

That book still has value, of course, the wraith continued. *Though there's nothing more the Deathdread can teach you about me, you should still find it when the time is right. The other simmering souls are out there, my brothers, and they will give you the strength to face what lies ahead.*

Connor frowned. Hunting for even more untested magic seemed unwise, to say the least.

The ghoul scoffed and dismissed Connor's silent scowl with a shake of his head. *You may have been born a peasant, Magnuson, but you have the soul of a king. If anyone can control the simmering souls' vast power, it's you. Fates willing, I will ensure that when Death eventually comes for you, you will go to Him as an emperor.*

A breeze trundled by, rustling the underbrush. Without another word, the ghoul dissolved into the southern wind as it passed.

"I really hate it when he does that," Murdoc admitted.

Connor brushed his thumb across the stubble on his jaw as he sat with the wraith's words. He stared at his hands and leaned into the magic in his blood, savoring the rush of power as it swam beneath the surface of his skin.

The swords.

The shield.

The enhanced senses.

The rapid healing.

The raw physical strength, unrivaled by any living man.

He'd already figured out the riddle that had baffled the kings and lords who had come before him. Though his eyes stung with exhaustion, he allowed himself a brief moment to relish his victory.

"He's not coming back, right?" Murdoc's voice broke the spell. "Because I do not want to do that again."

Snapped from his daze, Connor rubbed one eye with the heel of his palm. His bones ached for sleep, and he glanced back in the vague direction of Oakenglen. "Listen, both of you."

Still standing by the old log, Sophia crossed her arms beneath her breasts and waited for him to speak. Murdoc pushed himself to his feet, and in the soft blue glow of the forest, moonlight glinted off his sword as he finally sheathed it.

"If you're coming with me, there are no more secrets." He had to draw his line in the sand and set a boundary for them to cross at their peril. "No lies. No holding back. We have to trust each other," he added with a glare to Sophia. "We're a unit, and we work as one. Is that clear?"

Without even a pause, Murdoc saluted. Though the Beaumont beside him tossed her hair with an indignant huff, she eventually nodded.

Connor motioned for them to follow. "Good. Let's go."

"Where to?" Sophia grabbed her satchel and slung it over one shoulder. "I don't have to sleep in any more trees, do I?"

"We're heading south to regroup. After what I've been through tonight, all I want to do is get some damn sleep."

"So, trees?" she asked with a disappointed groan.

"Yes, Sophia." He laughed and stifled a yawn. "We're sleeping in the trees."

CHAPTER SIXTY

CONNOR

As the mid-morning sun broke through gaps in the leaves overhead, Connor lay in the grass with his pack serving as a lumpy pillow. His eyes stung with fatigue from the long night of hiking and climbing as they'd sought to put some distance between themselves and Oakenglen.

Though his tired eyes had ached for sleep, the shrill trumpets had rung off the city walls like howls in the night. Evidently, someone had found Richard's body far sooner than expected. The shouts of men through the darkness kept him and his team moving as soldiers had fanned out into the moonlit woods. Apparently, the people of Oakenglen didn't fear the blightwolves as much as they should have.

The morning breeze rolled over his bare chest as he lay in the shade. A campfire crackled nearby, the soothing pops fizzling as his eyes drifted shut. He'd picked this spot on the outskirts of Murkwell because they were far enough away from the road that no one would find them.

Every time he tried to surrender to sleep, a memory surfaced.

The wraith, extending one bony hand as he spoke of the power Connor had yet to understand.

Connor's eyes snapped open, but his vision blurred with exhaustion.

His father, ruffling his hair on a summer day at the coast.

He opened his eyes again, so tired he hadn't even noticed them close.

Sir Beck, wiping the back of his bloodstained hand along his sweaty brow.

Though Connor tried to open his eyes again, to fight the memories from surfacing, he couldn't. As he drifted off to sleep, he wondered what had become of his former mentor—and if the man had ever made it to his daughter's house in Briar Meadow, to live out his final days in peace like he'd wanted.

CONNOR

With a strained grunt, Connor swung his axe at the log he'd placed on the chopping block outside Beck Arbor's barn. The blade sliced the wood with a loud thunk, and the log split in one blow. The wood tumbled into the shade of a nearby willow, just out of reach.

He grinned with pride as the blocks of wood toppled onto the grass. It had taken ages to get strong enough to split a log in one go, but the new calluses on his hands made it easier to hold the axe.

In the hot summer's evening, a fanged horse nickered from the fenced field nearby. Flecks of caked mud dropped from its dappled coat as it stomped through the grass. A lock of its long gray mane caught on the foot-long fangs protruding from its bottom lip, and it whinnied in the fading day. Its nostrils flared as it lowered its head to sniff at the grass, probably hunting for another squirrel to eat.

Greedy thing. Connor placed the split log on the chopping block to cut it a final time for the fire. He'd already fed the horse three raw venison steaks today, but it never seemed able to eat its fill of anything.

Rusty hinges groaned in protest from somewhere in the barn, and Connor winced as the screech cut through the air. The horse spooked and galloped off, its hooves thundering over the grass as it ran to safety.

In the side of the barn, a brown door with faded red paint swung open. A wrinkled man with a slight hunch to his shoulders walked out of the shadows. He squinted up at the sun, as though he were accustomed to the darkness and unfamiliar with the bright orb in the sky.

Connor wiped the hem of his shirt across his face to mop away sweat as Beck Arbor limped toward him. The former soldier's wrinkled face contorted into a more severe version of its permanent scowl, and he muttered obscenities under his breath. The tendons in his neck tightened with each hobbling step, and Connor figured they were due for rain if his mentor's old war injury was acting up.

The story changed every time he asked about the limp. At this point, he assumed it had probably come as a consequence of a stupid mistake Beck didn't want to admit he'd made.

"Good evening, Sir Beck." Connor smirked as he feigned a bow and nodded to the dwindling pile of logs beside him. "Want to try your hand at chopping some wood for me? I could use a strong back like yours."

The old man wagged his finger in warning. "One of these days, I'm going to kick you out."

Connor laughed and set another log on the chopping block. He'd been making that threat for three seasons, now, and it was clear he wouldn't follow through.

Beck crossed his arms and turned his permanent scowl on the pile of logs. "Do you plan on finishing this year?"

"I'm almost done." He swung his axe and split the log in a seamless blow.

"Good. Your lesson starts now, then. I want to go to bed early."

Connor clicked his tongue in mock disappointment as he set another log on the block. "That wasn't the deal, Beck. A day's work for room, food, and two hours of lessons every night." He paused and pointed to the brightly lit sky. "Don't shortchange me my training just because you're a grumpy old man."

"Just wait until you're the grumpy old man," Beck warned as he sat on a nearby stump in the willow tree's shade. "You'll need your sleep, same as me."

Jokes aside, Connor needed to hurry. He didn't want to lose any of his training time to the old man's impatience, so he quickly grabbed another log to cut.

"Today, we're going to talk about retreat." Beck let out a miserable groan as he adjusted on his stump. He lifted his injured foot and rested it on his opposite knee. "When should a man stand his ground, and when should a man run? Do you know?"

"You run when you're going to lose, I suppose."

Beck laughed—one of the few he'd ever heard. Connor furrowed his brows in surprise, distracted by the sound even as he swung his axe. It sank into the grass by his feet, and he cursed under his breath at his own carelessness.

He'd almost taken off his own leg.

"I didn't know you could laugh, Beck."

"Bah." The old soldier dismissed the jibe with a wave of his wrinkled hand. "You don't wait to run until you lose. That's how cowards think, and you're no coward."

"What's the answer, then?"

"You run to gain the advantage. If you ever lose the upper hand, step aside until you can take it back."

"Huh." Connor yanked the axe from the grass and took aim at the log as he thought it over. The blade hit to the tune of splintering wood, and another log for the fire plopped onto the grass.

"Take the night I met you, for instance," Beck continued. "In that bar, you were hustling those fools at darts. With aim like yours, you could've robbed them blind while an audience jeered, but you showed mercy. You quit when you were ahead. You didn't get greedy. You knew when to retreat, whether you realized it or not. You needed to keep the advantage against men who were bigger and better armed than you. That's when I saw your potential. I saw more than a conman in a bar. I saw a young man with talent who merely lacked direction."

Connor leaned the head of his axe on the chopping block and rested his arm on the long wooden handle. He watched his mentor with furrowed brows, not sure what to even say.

"That's the only reason I offered this to you." Beck gestured to the farm around them. "Because I knew you could see the opportunity. I don't save people, you see. When I find someone with potential, I give them the chance to save themselves."

With a smirk, Connor grabbed the axe and waved it in the air. "I thought you just wanted free labor."

"Perhaps a bit of that, too." The former king's guardsman gestured to the remaining logs. "Speaking of, now, back to it."

With an exhausted groan from his long day in the field, Connor reached for one of the few remaining logs and set it on the chopping block. "What's the answer, then? It sounds like you think me stopping while I was ahead is tantamount to retreat."

"It is." Beck shrugged. "And it isn't. You kept the advantage. That's what matters. Sometimes, keeping the advantage means walking away. Other times, you have to run headfirst into the fray to keep it. Each battle is different, and what you choose to do depends on how you want to be perceived."

"What do you mean?"

"With anyone you face, you must ask yourself—do you want them to fear you, or do you want them to respect you?"

"Respect, obviously." Connor swung the axe again.

Beck clicked his tongue in disappointment. "You're better than that. Don't fall into the gullible trap of nobility and honor that gets so many foolish knights killed. Sometimes, you must make a man fear you. There will come a day when you have no other choice."

"That goes against everything my father ever taught me."

"He didn't serve on the king's guard," Beck pointed out. "He didn't learn this the hard way."

Connor's jaw tensed as the old man's words scratched at old wounds. Instead of replying, he turned his back on his mentor and reached for one of the final logs in the pile.

"Think about how you handled that game," Beck continued, oblivious to everything but his lecture. "You laughed with them and shrugged off your skill as luck. You quit when you were ahead. You let them think they were right, that you were nothing but a lucky kid. You showed them mercy instead of shaking them down. You won their respect, even if you did it in a roundabout way. It was an interesting choice, one I don't see made often, and it made me respect you as well."

Connor grinned and raised one eyebrow. "You respect me, do you?"

"Not if you don't finish your work and stop interrupting me."

He laughed and gestured for the old man to continue.

"The point is, sometimes respect is the best choice, and other times you must choose fear."

Unable to agree, his smile faded as he took aim at the next log on the chopping block.

"Fear makes cowards listen," Beck explained. "Sometimes, to survive, you must be brutal. You must be vicious. You must slit throats and draw a line in the soil that no sane mortal would cross. Sometimes, you truly must be feared to stay alive. There are wounded people in this world, Connor. They've been hurt and burned too often to believe good men still exist, and they must fear you at first. With time, you will earn their respect. It can evolve."

A bird twittered on the summer air and darted past them. It sailed over the horse in the field, who reared and snapped at the meadowlark's wings. The bird darted out of the way with seconds to spare, and the horse thundered off after it as it escaped unscathed.

Beck scratched his wrinkled chin. "Of course, there are some you will never sway. Crooked men most of all need to fear you because they can't respect anything or anyone but themselves. Their greed is rooted too deeply in their hearts. They don't know anything else."

"It's probably best to just avoid men like that," Connor lifted the last log onto the chopping block.

The retired soldier let out a sarcastic snort. "You can't avoid corrupt men. Eventually, you will face at least one. It's inevitable. There are too many."

"Hmm." He tossed the last of the cut logs aside. "It sounds like your default is to inspire fear."

"Not at all," his mentor corrected. "Respect is the best weapon for a leader to carry. It's earned through that nobility and honor you like to live by, so it suits you, but respect is also a way of life. It's the way you carry yourself and what you do with every breath. A king always leads the charge into battle. Wherever you settle down in life, you must rule your own little kingdom the same way—from the front."

"But how can I know?" With his chores finally done, Connor sat on the empty chopping block and placed his axe in the grass at his feet. "When I meet someone, how do I know whether to show mercy or be brutal?"

"That is the question, isn't it?" Beck adjusted his injured foot again as it began to slip off his knee. "Every leader is faced with that choice—to be feared by your people, or respected? To inspire dread or devotion? Only you can know, and when the time comes, it won't be a difficult choice to make. All you need to do is watch. Listen. Wait. If there's greed or fear in a person's heart, it will roll around them like a fog. You can't miss it, and when you inevitably see it, you must decide for yourself what to do. Can you tempt them toward the light and make them respect you, or are they too far gone?"

As the summer sun baked the grassy field around them, a bead of sweat dripped down Connor's neck. "I'm not a leader, Beck. I'm just an orphan lost in the woods."

The old man scoffed and shook his head, like Connor was missing the bigger picture. "Take it from an old soldier. True leaders—the ones history remembers—they don't choose to lead. Most of them don't even want to. They simply reach the point in their lives where they have no choice but to step up to the challenges given to them by the Fates. I've watched it happen time and time again, but I've also seen what happens when a weak man is given an enchanted sword. When I meet a man, it's always obvious to me where he falls on that spectrum. I already know where you fit into the world, Connor. Do you?"

As he sat on the chopping block, his axe laying on the grass beside him, Connor simply stared at the ground and thought it over.

"Stack the firewood." Apparently uninterested in getting an answer, the old man nodded toward the barn. "Meet me in there with your swords, and we'll resume. Don't keep me waiting."

"Yes, sir," Connor said absently.

The retired soldier groaned with pain as he pushed himself onto his feet, and he limped back toward the barn. Connor watched him walk away, and despite the urgency, he didn't move.

Beck's entire lesson struck him as odd.

Mercy and brutality. Respect and fear. Leading from the front and ruling his patch of dirt like a king. None of it applied to the common folk, and he had no patch of the world to his name. Back in Kirkwall, the king's guard had burned his family home to the ground, and he had nothing left to go back to.

It didn't make sense, and he frowned with frustration at the wasted time. It simply wasn't a lesson an aimless vagrant like him would ever get the chance to use.

CHAPTER SIXTY-ONE

QUINN

As Quinn wandered through the mid-morning crowds in Oakenglen's second interior, she kept her head down. The oversized hood on her blue cloak covered her fiery hair, and she kept her chin lowered even as she scanned the throng.

Ladies in emerald-green and rich golden dresses giggled as they passed by, barely even looking at her. Now and then, she snuck a glance at their hair, at the hundreds of intricately woven braids that must've taken hours to do. The young women fanned their painted faces, whispering nonstop, sometimes even talking over each other. One wore a hat shaped like a swan, woven from reeds.

With a small shake of her head, Quinn plowed onward. It didn't matter that she had been raised in the halls of palace after palace. The way these nobles strove to both fit in at court and draw attention to themselves had never made sense to her.

Raiding the coffers had been a tad more difficult than usual, as both her father and Zander had appeared around almost every turn. She hadn't even been able to get all of the enchanted items she wanted. Thus, why she had risked walking through Oakenglen in broad daylight.

Much to her frustration, their interference had forced her to leave Lunestone empty handed. Instead of getting what she needed from the vaults, she now had to waste several days to do a bit of shopping.

After what she had overheard, even looking at either of them made her skin crawl. They had kept her under close watch while she had been home, and she needed to be extra careful while in the cities. Zander and her father each had spies across Saldia. To buy herself time, they had to truly believe she had chased some fake lead down the western road.

With only fourteen days left before her father tried to break her spirit, time was something she couldn't waste.

The chatter of hundreds of people bubbled through the square as she risked a glance at the vendors nearby to ensure no one paid her any mind. Customers in vibrant reds and blues darted in and out of the shops. A honey-sweet breeze carried a hint of roses and fresh toast through the air.

The Spell Market always hummed with life at this time of day. If she'd had more time, she would've waited until closing to meet with her contact. In the last hour of daylight, the streets emptied as people shifted to the dining district. Walking through a crowd always set her nerves on fire, but it had to be done.

Saldia's new Wraithblade lurked somewhere in the shadows. Whatever it cost, she would find him.

In the corner of the wide square, soldiers clad in golden armor scanned the throng of people. They squinted through the gaps in their helmets, and each rested his hand on the hilt of his sword.

Hunting.

Quinn averted her gaze and slowed her gait to match the pace of four women who passed between her and the soldiers. Two wore gowns made of rich blue silk and lace, the fabric only a shade or two away from her own cloak. Another of the girls carried a parasol that blocked the soldiers from Quinn's view, effectively hiding her in plain sight.

Even though they likely weren't hunting for her, she wouldn't risk it. If anyone could've recognized her in this crowd, it would've been the men in the king's guard. They'd accompanied the Starlings on enough missions through the years to easily spot her.

A glamour would've been the best way to travel unnoticed through a mob of shoppers and women with stupid hats. Unfortunately, she needed her contact to recognize her, and a glamour was out of the question.

Though she had left Lunestone several days ago, doubling back and hiding Blaze in the woods had wasted precious time. The trip through the abandoned tunnels beneath the city had taken hours, and coordinating in secret with her contacts had cost even more time.

Hopefully, Blaze didn't do anything stupid in her absence. Given that he'd nearly lost an eye to one of the giant owls in the woods, she wasn't going to hold her breath.

He was an idiot sometimes, but he was her adorable idiot.

The bubbling crash of a fountain cut through the murmuring crowd as the road opened onto another square. In the center of the wide brick courtyard, a statue of King Henry towered over his people, with roses and frothing water at his feet. With his sword raised and his crown immortalized on his head, he stared off into the distance with all the determination of a warlord calculating his next move.

Soon, a new king would stand in Henry's place on that fountain. She scowled, knowing how fervently her father wanted to weasel a Starling onto the throne—and how desperately Zander wanted his own face on that statue.

"Stay focused," she quietly chided herself.

As she took a side road downhill, the crowds thinned, and she could breathe a little easier with fewer people around. Though most augmentors' shops could be found on the upper hill of the Spell Market, the best of them had been banished to the fringes of proper society for the crime of being a woman in a man's field.

Tove Warren—arguably the continent's greatest augmentor, and too damned modest to ever admit it.

The late morning sun warmed the cobblestone beneath Quinn's boots as she finally reached Tove's door. Overgrown hydrangea leaned into the path, and the soft purple blooms shivered in a light breeze.

The shop windows on either side of the entrance featured framed art to showcase her drawing style and entice window shoppers to enter.

A rose woven around a dagger, its thorns lying in a pile beneath the blade.

A dragon, its tail curved around a tower as it roared into the air.

A crown hung haphazardly on the hilt of a sword, as though the king didn't care for it after all and had left both behind.

Sketch after sketch sat in militant rows across the window displays that protruded over the flowers, each drawing done in her signature blend of imperfection and elegance. Rough lines. Graceful curves. The flawless blend of mystery and precision that had first lured Quinn inside years ago on a whim.

Before darting into the shop, she paused at the entrance to listen. Two women spoke, their voices muffled by the door. A floorboard creaked mere feet away from her, suggesting another client waited for Tove's attention.

Company.

How disappointing. She simply didn't have the luxury to wait.

Quinn scanned the street as a father ushered three young boys up the hill, but she had a better chance of going unnoticed in Tove's shop than she did out in the market. With a resigned sigh, she let herself in.

"…and I told him to buy his own tobacco, then, if he's so damn picky about it," a stranger said.

"Uh huh," a familiar voice replied.

Tove, hard at work.

A bell chimed above Quinn, soft and delicate, and she kept her gaze to the ground as she entered. With her hood still over her head, she immediately stepped into the comfortable retail area on the right side of the store and turned her back to the voices.

A tall mirror mounted to the wall nearby bounced the light across the room and brightened the space. While the woman droned on about tobacco and shopping, Quinn used the mirror to scan the building behind her.

Nothing had changed in the last few weeks. In the half of the store where she stood, rows of shelves nailed to the wall held a colorful array of potions in bottles of every shape and size. A thick blue curtain draped against the back wall hid a hallway to the rest of the house, and the left half of the store was reserved for the act of augmenting itself.

Tove's golden augmenting throne sat on a raised platform against the wall, framed by floor-to-ceiling bookshelves painted as white as snow. Books covered every inch of available space, each of them a reference guide to one reagent or another.

A blonde sat on the throne's black satin cushions, and the skirts of her flowing blue gown cascaded over the platform beneath her like a waterfall frozen in time. Her right hand blurred through the air as she punctuated each word with a gesture.

Beside her, a woman with dark hair sat on a simple stool and held the blonde's forearm with a firm grip. A long table sat at an angle behind the brunette, its surface covered in stacks of white towels and half-filled jars of emerald green ink.

"…but he never listens." The woman rolled her eyes.

"Yeah," Tove answered from the stool, her eyes focused on the woman's skin while she worked.

The artist's thick brown hair flowed over one shoulder, and her brows knitted together as she focused. A green augmentation of a rose coiled like a vine up her neck and to the base of her jaw, glistening with the magic in its ink.

That one was new. Quinn wanted to get a closer look, but she resisted the urge to wander over and inspect it. Tove always saved the best sketches for herself—and, she claimed, for Quinn.

"And he had the gall to ignore me." The blonde scoffed.

"Huh," Tove muttered, still consumed in her work as something hummed in her hands.

It took everything in Quinn not to laugh. Anyone who hired Tove should've known better than to talk during the augmentation. An army could've laid siege to the kingdom, and she wouldn't have noticed until her client tried to stand up.

A floorboard creaked again, and Quinn pretended to look at the shelves of potions around her as she scanned the rest of the shop through the mirror. A little girl sat in a small lounge chair beneath the other window on the left side of the room. No more than twelve, her slippered feet tapped at the floor while she waited. Her lips bleached from the effort of pressing them together, most likely because she had been told to keep quiet. With her hands in her lap, she stared at the floor and fidgeted in her seat. The floorboard creaked again under her slipper, and she cast a wary glance toward Quinn.

Quinn turned her head enough to hide her face, just in case the girl happened to look in the mirror.

"And then I said, 'you fool, who do you think you're speaking to?' He wouldn't even answer. Can you believe it?" The woman huffed and shifted in her seat.

As the blonde moved, Tove flinched. With the lightning-fast reflex of a practiced augmentor, she lifted a small device previously hidden from view by her shoulder. It looked like dozens of tiny quills fused together with gold, and it hummed with a life of its own. Green ink glowed at its tip, and a drop splattered onto the woman's forearm.

"Please remain still." Tove grabbed a fresh towel from behind her and wiped away the ink from the woman's skin. "I know it can be uncomfortable, but we're almost done."

"Does it hurt, Mama?" the little girl asked, apparently unable to keep silent any longer.

The woman glared at the child. The girl sucked in a frightened little breath of air, like she had been caught stealing cookies.

Quinn frowned.

Undeterred, Tove glanced up at the little girl and smiled. "It depends on where you get the augmentation, dear. On the forearm here, it barely hurts at all." Tove gestured to the woman's half-finished design of a flower. "But up here, you're going to really feel it." She moved the needle toward the inside of the woman's elbow and winked.

"Amazing," the girl whispered.

"It is," the woman said dryly. "And I would like it to be finished today, please."

The skin around Tove's eyes creased as she strained to hold her smile, and she simply nodded.

Quinn scanned the shelves of potions along the wall to occupy herself while Tove finished—and to keep from blowing her cover to teach this woman some manners. A small placard sat in front of each cluster of bottles, the paper covered in Tove's elegant handwriting.

Rectivane Charm—heal your loved ones with the power of the best potion masters in Oakenglen. They don't have to know you bought it. One gold.

Rootrock Charm—no plant will ever die on you again! Control the earth with all the power of the seasons. Two gold.

Rushmar Hex—it's a delight when your husband surprises you with flowers. Don't let him surprise you with a child, too. See me for the price, my Hexes Permit, and my approval of sale papers.

The little girl tapped her toes against the floor. Still perched on her bench, she leaned toward the augmentation, even though she was a good ten feet away. "What are you drawing?"

"Maize, honestly," the woman snapped.

"It's all right," Tove tucked a loose strand of hair behind her ear and resumed her work. "Your mother asked for a poppy, so I designed one especially for her. It's your father's family symbol. Did you know that?"

"I did!" The girl smiled broadly. "It represents loyalty to the crown."

If you say so, Quinn thought as she stifled a groan. The nonsense these nobles went through to weasel their way into the court never ceased to baffle her.

The little girl tugged gently on the ends of her hair. "Can you draw anything you want in an augmentation? Or do you have to use the same drawing every time?"

"What a good question!" Tove grinned and wiped the towel across the woman's forearm as she finished with the leaf.

Quinn smirked. The augmentor wouldn't talk to adults while she worked, but she never seemed able to resist a child's charm and curiosity. It was a wonder she hadn't married and had a few of her own already, but she still had plenty of time to find a man who wouldn't force her to close her shop.

If anyone ever tried to shut this place down, Quinn would see to it they changed their mind—by force, if necessary.

"Look here." Tove pointed to the nearly finished drawing of a poppy bloom with a single leaf beside it. "What you draw doesn't affect the potion we use in the ink, so you can draw anything you desire. Isn't that neat?"

"It is," the girl confessed, breathless. She leaned forward again, still trying and failing to get a better look. "Mama, can I get an augmentation?"

"When you're sixteen, Maize, and not a moment before." The blonde shifted her frigid glare to Tove. "Are you done?"

Quinn frowned. Only fools rushed a master.

Tove's cheek twitched with annoyance. Quinn had seen that look plenty of times before. The augmentor had barely managed to suppress a frown at her client's interruption.

"If you're happy with what you see, then yes."

"It's fine." The woman didn't even glance at the augmentation.

Maize leaned against the edge of the seat. "May I stand? What potion did you get in the ink, Mama?"

"Yes, yes, on your feet." The woman stood, and Tove barely pulled the ink pen out of the way before the woman's arm ran into it. "I got a Hygenmix charm, which is all you will be allowed to get."

Unbothered by her mother's curt tone, the girl's eyes widened in awe. "What does that do?"

Tove set the ink pen on her small desk. "It makes you smell nice. You can customize any perfume you like, and you'll smell that way for two whole years."

"I like roses!"

Tove smiled broadly at the little girl as she wiped down the throne's armrest. "Then I'll make you one with the best rose petals I can find. Would you like me to tell you about all the reagents I used today? I would be happy to teach you anytime."

"Yes, please!" The girl clapped her hands together. "If I get a hyg—a heg—whatever Mama got, does that mean I won't have to take anymore baths?"

"Maize, that's enough." The woman snapped her fingers impatiently. "Come. We're leaving."

The girl's smile fell in an instant. "But I have more questions."

"That's why we're leaving." The woman glared over her shoulder at Tove. "I'm disgusted, Miss Warren. You come from a good family, and you could have done so well for yourself. It's bad enough that you chose this life. Don't drag your clients' daughters into it, too."

Tove bristled. Quinn set her hand on *Aurora's* hilt out of impulse, but she forced herself to relax and let out a slow breath.

If she hadn't needed to maintain her cover, she would've had quite a few choice words to share with this woman.

Maize rubbed her thumb against her fingernail as she nervously glanced between the two women. "What do you mean, Mama?"

The blonde ignored her daughter. "If you didn't have such a unique art style, Miss Warren, I never would have come in here. I wanted to give you a chance, but that was clearly a mistake I won't make again. Don't fill my child's head with nonsense. Unlike you, she has a chance at a real future."

With that, the woman grabbed her daughter's wrist and stormed out into the street. The bell chimed as the door swung shut behind them, and its delicate note pierced the stunned silence that followed.

Tove let out a shaky breath. Tears glistened in the corners of her eyes, and she arched her back as she stared out the window after her client.

Quinn tugged off the hood of her cloak. "Don't let that horrible woman get to you."

The augmentor flinched with surprise. The moment her gaze landed on Quinn, however, she smiled and wrapped her in a tight hug. "What a pleasure!"

Never one for embraces, Quinn indulged her anyway with a few awkward taps on her back.

"Are you here to pick up—"

"Yes," Quinn answered with a tense glance toward the unlocked door. "I also have some questions about an active manhunt."

"Ah, I see." Tove's smile fell. "When the order came through, I thought—I hoped—you were joking. You've surprised me with odd requests before, but this is beyond anything I've ever done."

"Did you have trouble?"

Tove shook her head. "It worked perfectly. I just pity whomever you use this on."

Quinn's heart skipped a beat with anticipation. "Let's see it."

Her failsafe. Her way out of whatever the Wraithblade threw at her. The man had threatened to kill her should they ever meet again, but this would ensure she survived his wrath.

Tove was right. Whatever fool ended up on the other end of her failsafe would meet a quick—and painful—death.

CHAPTER SIXTY-TWO
QUINN

As Quinn stood with Tove in the woman's shop, she glanced again at the open windows and unlocked doors.

"Right," the augmentor said. "To business."

Tove flitted to the entry and peered out the front windows before sliding the bolt to lock out the public. With a practiced flourish, she drew the curtains over the windows. The room darkened, lit only by the glow of sunlight around the shades.

"Thank you for the order, Quinn. It was the most interesting thing I've done all year." Tove smiled and hurried over toward her stool. She knelt in front of it and reached one hand under the seat. Something clicked, and a hidden compartment in the red cushion popped open.

A small blue box rested inside, barely larger than the woman's palm. The augmentor scooped it into her hands. As she returned, she opened it to reveal the necklace Quinn had been waiting days to see.

On a small black cushion, a golden necklace glittered in the rooms low light. Its blue stone, easily larger than an eyeball, cast rainbows against the wall as it caught a sunbeam. Metal spires radiated from the stone like the rays of the sun. A thick piece of gold jutted from the bottom, like the blade of a sword.

"Just as you ordered." Tove stood a little taller, barely able to restrain her proud grin.

Quinn let out a sigh of relief. "I knew you'd come through."

The augmentor bit her lip as her gaze drifted down to the necklace.

"This is dangerous. Even for you."

"That's the point." She lifted the necklace into her palm. The second it touched her skin, it hummed with power. The enchanted pendant buzzed with all the barely restrained energy of a captured lightning bolt.

"I've never seen a Voltaic recipe like the one you sent over," Tove confessed. "I hope you don't mind me adjusting my notes based on what I learned from it."

"Not at all. I considered that part of the payment. Did you receive the gold, as well?"

"Bless the Fates, yes. You paid me too much."

"Nonsense. Consider it a rush fee." Quinn examined the camouflaged spellgust stone in the center of the pendant. "You charmed it perfectly. It genuinely looks like a sapphire. There's not even a hint of green."

"There will be, once you use it," Tove warned. "Quinn, are you sure about this? The Voltaic hex is highly volatile on its own, but an enchanted item with that much power? I mean, for the Fates' sake, woman. That stone is bigger than the one in *Aurora*."

As she put it on, Quinn didn't answer. The necklace dangled next to the Starling crest. Its chain sat tight around her throat, too short to slip over her head—an intentional choice to ensure no one tried to steal it. The pendant itself hung from a second chain attached to the first with a small sapphire, and the golden enchantment disappeared into her cleavage.

Hidden. Perfect.

The necklace buzzed against her chest. "And the lock? You got the Locklose hex to work?"

Tove nodded. "You know, Quinn, when you insisted I keep a vial of your blood on hand, I thought you were insane. But I get it, now. It's for moments like these, when you need me to make you something that only you can use. No one can take that off but you."

"Exactly. And the Strongman enchantment worked?"

"Perfectly. No one can break that chain, and the spellgust stones for those enchantments were small enough to hide in the links by the clasp.

But this…" The augmentor gestured to the necklace. "What are you up to? What in the Fates' name are you after?"

"Not what," Quinn admitted. "Who."

"Ah, right. Your manhunt."

"Exactly, but—"

"—you can't tell me about it, I know," Tove finished for her. "You never can, but I'm worried for you. Here, come talk to me while I clean up."

While the augmentor wiped her hands on a towel, Quinn sat in the golden chair, just as she had done a dozen times before to get her own augmentations. Much to her father's disappointment, she had foregone any of Lunestone's official augmentors in favor of the art she got in this chair. To this day, she still got letters from the other augmentors, begging her to return to the chairs the Starling family had sat in for generations.

She ignored them all. In her opinion, none of them could compete.

Tove lifted the small device she had used to augment the woman's poppy. One by one, she tugged out the quill-like tubes and set them in an empty jar on the table.

"That's new." Quinn pointed to the ink pen.

The augmentor smirked with pride. "My own design. I enchanted it to use dozens of tiny needles, instead of the large single needle those fools on the upper hill use."

"I thought your designs looked great before. Why the change?"

The augmentor laughed. "An artist can't get complacent. When you need yours retouched, they won't just look good. They'll look incredible."

Quinn shrugged. "No complaints so far. They haven't lost their potency."

With an exasperated sigh, Tove set one hand on her hip. "You Starlings are something else. Everyone else needs retouching every two years or so. It's been, what, three years for yours?"

"Roughly."

Tove clicked her tongue in disappointment. "I'm so jealous. I'd love to figure out why your family is different from the rest of us."

Quinn chuckled. "You can't dissect me. Sorry to disappoint."

"That's not what I meant." The augmentor smacked Quinn with a clean towel as she tucked the pile of dirty ones under one arm. "I just want a challenge. I want something *hard*. These hygiene augmentations are all I ever see, and the business I do get only comes in because of, well…"

"Because of what?"

"Because they want a chance to see you in person." Tove sighed as she knelt and tossed the pile of towels into a basket hidden underneath the throne. "Almost everyone asks when you're coming in next."

Quinn sighed and rubbed the back of her neck. "No one from Lunestone came?"

"Not even one." The augmentor ran a hand through her thick brown hair as she frowned. "Thanks for trying, but no warriors come to me. None but you." She hesitated and watched Quinn for a few moments in silence. "What's this manhunt you talked about? Does this have to do with your brother's mission?"

That caught her attention.

"What mission?" She curled her fingers around the edge of the armrest as she studied the augmentor intently. "What did you hear? I need to know everything."

Tove's eyebrows shot up her head, and for a moment, she gaped at Quinn in silence. With the clean towel still in her hands, she clutched the cloth tighter.

Quinn scanned the artist's face, genuinely confused by her reaction. "What's wrong?

"You're scary when you get like—well, like this." The artist gestured at Quinn's face. "Whatever's happening right now must make grown men piss themselves."

To put the augmentor at ease, she did her best to relax her shoulders and sit back in the chair. The tendons in her neck tightened, however, and it took everything in her to not jump to her feet and pace while she listened.

"That's not any better," Tove admitted with a curt laugh. "But thank you for trying, I suppose. I've heard rumors from Lunestone that Zander is headed into the Decay. Something about setting a trap for someone powerful, and something about a special weapon. It doesn't make any sense, though. Why would he head out that way? There's nothing but dead trees and cracked dirt for miles."

The Decay.

Of *course*.

Quinn rested her jaw on one fist and closed her eyes as she pieced it all together. The Wraith King's ruins must've waited at the heart of the only dead part of their world. Her brother must've charged into the void, armed with information he'd probably scrounged from the vaults she had never been allowed to access.

If Zander killed the Wraithblade, the truth she craved would die with him.

Quinn let out an irritated sigh as she rubbed her eyes with one hand and sank into the chair. She had heard the warning in his tone back when he and Teagan had discussed the Wraithblade. Even then, that hint of disobedience had hung in the air as he spoke.

She could've sworn she had more time. For him to act so soon, something must've happened.

"This is bad." She pinched the bridge of her nose and let out a frustrated sigh.

"I thought you knew," Tove said quietly.

"I should have." Quinn leaned back in the throne and stifled an irritated groan. "I'm discovering there's a lot I don't—no, never mind. Let's focus. Is there anything else I should know about this mission of his?"

The artist shook her head. "That's everything I've heard. Aside from that, the other important news from Lunestone is the death of a Viceroy. Richard Beaumont died in the night. Not to be unkind, but good riddance. I never liked him." She shuddered.

"Neither did I, but this is the first I've heard of it. Foul play, or natural causes?"

"He was turned to ice and broken into hundreds of pieces." Tove raised one eyebrow. "I wouldn't call that natural causes, but your line of work is more dangerous than mine."

Quinn whistled, impressed. "Duvolias are rare."

"That they are."

"Any suspects?"

"Not a single one. Folks are saying the Fates came for him in the night. Justice served, based on what a few of the women in the brothel districts are telling me."

With a frown, Quinn sat up straighter. "Do I want to know?"

"You don't." Tove's gaze drifted to the floor. "Besides, it doesn't matter. He's dead. Justice served, like I said."

"A Beaumont dying mysteriously in the night suggests foul play. That was probably a Grimm or some other contract on his life."

"That's what we all think. No one but his uncle is going to miss him."

"Provided his uncle isn't the one who killed him."

"True."

"What else, Tove?" Quinn wove her fingers together as she waited for more news. "You know everyone and everything that goes on in Oakenglen. Have you heard any other news? Anything out of the ordinary?"

"Oakenglen always has gossip, Quinn. You need to be more specific."

That wouldn't be a problem. After quite a bit of thought over these last few days, Quinn had narrowed her request down to two warning signs Tove could monitor.

For starters, anything the Lightseers tried to hush or make disappear could've easily been connected to her father's attempt to steal the Oakenglen throne. She needed to know his movements as he pulled the city's strings.

Second, she needed Tove to listen for any signs of the Shade or general necromancy. While charm and hex classes of magic were permitted, curses were forbidden inside Oakenglen's walls. Though it was a bit of a shot in the dark, any powerful necromancy in the city might've been a clue that could lead her to the sorceress—and therefore, to the Shade.

However, the less Tove knew, the less danger she faced. For the augmentor's own safety, Quinn had to remain as cryptic as possible.

She tapped her finger against her lips as she carefully chose her words. "There are two things I need you to find out. First, I need to know if anything happens in the city that Lunestone tries to silence. Murders, thefts, disappearances. Things like that."

"Murders?" The augmentor shook her head. "Quinn, the Lightseers would never cover up a murder, right? That's the whole point of… of…"

Tove trailed off as Quinn held her gaze, trying to say what needed to be said without uttering the treasonous words aloud.

They do, she wanted to say. *And they will.*

"Oh, my." The artist sat on her stool and leaned her elbows on her knees as she tried to process what was being asked of her. "If that's the first thing, what the hell is the second thing you need me to do?"

"I need to know about a man. Some call him the Shade."

"Huh." Tove rubbed her hands together as her eyes glossed over. "Well, now. Isn't that funny timing."

"You've heard of him?"

Tove's eyes snapped back into focus, and she smirked. "Quinn, look who you're talking to. I'm the most insufferable gossip in this entire city. Of course I've heard about him."

Quinn chuckled and rubbed her eyes. "Inform me then, oh great and wise Tove Warren, Master Augmentor of the—"

"Yes, yes, I know you're hilarious." The woman waved away Quinn's dripping sarcasm. "The Shade is a myth from the Ancient Woods, but a lot of people have been talking about him the last few days. You're saying he's real? I thought he was just a folk legend."

Quinn stiffened, but she didn't dare hope too hard for a solid lead. "What are they saying?"

"Mostly just ridiculous nonsense that's obviously made up. He controls the southern wind, he fights for the common man, all of the mythical nonsense you usually hear with legends. But the other night, Gerald—a friend of mine who runs a potion shop in the first exterior—was robbed.

Whoever stole from him must have been a necromancer because they used a Brackenbane curse to melt his alarm, and they had enough strength to somehow break his enhanced locking system."

"How? What potion did they use?"

"They didn't." Tove raised one eyebrow. "They broke it by hand."

"By hand?" She scoffed. "That's impossible."

"Is it impossible for this Shade fellow of yours?"

Quinn frowned and rubbed her jaw as she stared at the ground. "Maybe. To be honest, I'm not sure, yet. Anything else?"

"The bandits left money on the counter."

The baffling statement froze Quinn in place. She squinted at Tove, certain she had misheard. "They did what?"

"You heard correctly. The thief paid. Apparently, the pile of gold was enough to cover what they took and then some. Gerald joked that he'd like more people to rob him if they overpaid like that. Honest thieves, suspicious strength, and forbidden potions only the necromancers use—it's all rather suspicious, don't you think?"

It was, but Quinn didn't admit it out loud. "Anything else?"

"Oh, I could talk your ear off for days," the augmentor promised with a flick of her wrist. "I'm sparing you about fifty other stories right now, Quinn, because I know you value your time. Most of it is truly garbage. You can't sneeze in a tavern lately without someone bringing up the Shade, so who knows? Maybe it's a dead lead, but I've never heard of anyone from Nethervale paying for what they steal."

Quinn rubbed her cheek as her eyes glossed over. If he'd saved those lovers in the woods between Bradford and Murkwell, the Wraithblade had clearly been heading north. He could very well have been in Oakenglen, but the risks of being in the Capital outweighed any benefits that came to mind. It seemed far too risky for a smart man to do, but even Zander's contacts had heard whispers of him coming to town.

If the Wraithblade had infiltrated the city, something desperate and dangerous had driven him here. No matter what he wanted, this wouldn't end well for anyone involved.

Tove set her disassembled ink pen in an empty basket. "Why are you hunting this man?"

"That's a very complicated answer," she admitted.

"It's all right. You don't have to tell me. I know King Henry isn't a fan of vigilantes, so my best guess is he probably sent you after this Shade fellow to set him straight."

Quinn hesitated at the offhand comment as Tove set her stool against the wall. At ease and relaxed in her shop, the augmentor clearly hadn't understood the gravity of what she had just said.

Tove didn't know that the king was dead—and if Tove didn't know, the country didn't, either.

Her father had mentioned Zander wasn't needed in Oakenglen anymore, and now she wondered if the two of them had pulled strings to ensure the power void in the Capital would only grow. His choice involved immense risk. The longer Henry's death remained a secret, the worse the riots would be when the truth finally leaked to the people.

For her own safety, Tove needed to leave.

"I need you to listen closely." Quinn cleared her throat and simmered over the best way to word what she wanted to say.

The augmentor froze in place, watching with bated breath in the silence that followed.

"You need to have resources in place in case the situation in the Capital deteriorates. You need a way to escape to a safe place without being noticed."

"Situation?" Tove's brows knit together, and she took a wary step backward. "What situation? What are you talking about?"

"Be ready. You'll know it when you hear about it, and you need to be able to leave in a heartbeat. Do you understand?"

"Quinn, what do you mean by—"

"Tove," she interrupted. "Tides are shifting around us. Oakenglen isn't safe. Hell, Saldia itself may not be safe, and you can't breathe a word of that to anyone. Is that clear? Not a soul. I'm only telling you because you're the closest thing to a friend that I have, and I don't want you to get hurt. I don't—" She groaned with frustration as she tried to explain the danger without saying it outright. "I don't want you to get caught in the crossfire, all right? This is real. If you stay here, you could die."

At first, Tove didn't answer. Any sane woman would have trembled with terror or clutched her hand to her chest in breathless disbelief.

Not Tove. The augmentor grinned.

As the broad smile stretched across her face, she poked one slender finger into Quinn's shoulder. "You just admitted I'm your friend. It took years, but you finally said it out loud."

That broke the spell of unspoken dread, and Quinn laughed. "What I said was—"

"Oh, you can't take it back now." Tove pursed her lips and shook her head with playful scorn. "Too late. I'm your friend. It's official."

Quinn laughed harder. "You're insane."

"Maybe a little, but I have to be in this profession." Tove gestured to the shop around them and leaned against the wall. "You've got a heart in there, Quinn. It's nice to see. Despite all that money and magic, you're just the right kind of squishy."

"Look, will you—"

"I will," Tove promised. "I'll prepare, and when I hear something about the Lightseers or this Shade fellow, I'll leave it on a scroll under the throne." She nodded to the chair. "I don't know how you get in to retrieve those, and I won't lie—it always unnerves me to see them suddenly disappear."

Quinn shrugged, not one to give away her secrets.

"You stay safe out there." Tove's smile fell with the warning. "I know you live in a different world than the rest of us, but you can still get hurt, too."

The comment crawled under her skin and took root in her bones. Zander had complicated everything with his plot to trap the Wraithblade, and now she had to hunt through the Decay to find him before he killed her chance to get the truth.

And as for the would-be assassin, so many unknowns remained. She had already tasted an approaching death after just one encounter with this man, and she couldn't lie to herself—she had no idea if their second encounter would get her the truth she wanted.

But she had to at least try.

CHAPTER SIXTY-THREE
CONNOR

With a jolt, Connor sat upright.

His hand smacked impulsively against his bare chest, his fingers tensed and ready to summon one of the shadow blades. His nail brushed across the black mark on his sternum, and the wraith's scar glowed briefly green at his touch.

Instead of a Beaumont attacking him in his sleep, however, a leaf fell into his face from the tree overhead.

With a muffled string of curses, he brushed it off and scanned the forest around him to get his bearings. Dappled patches of amber sunlight flitted across the grass as the canopy shifted and swayed in the wind. From somewhere out of sight, the crackle of a fire mingled with the birdsong and the vibrating buzz of cicadas.

The lingering image of Beck Arbor limping toward the barn flashed again in his mind. As quick as it had come, the vision faded like a fog burned away by the sun.

Just a dream. Just a memory.

His eyes stung, and he rubbed them to clear away the lingering grogginess of rough sleep. With a dazed groan, he leaned his elbows on his knees and shifted his weight as he tried to get comfortable. A stick lying on the uneven dirt jabbed into his thigh, and he grimaced.

You're finally awake. Though the wraith's voice echoed in his mind, the specter didn't appear. No cloud of smoke. No skeletal face beneath a hood. Just another spring day, fresh and vibrant.

A blue bird darted past, twittering as it banked into the breeze and soared into the leaves above, unaware of the ghoul in its woodland.

"Yeah," he muttered as he yanked the stick out from under his thigh and chucked it into a nearby bush. "I'm up."

The phantom snorted derisively. *You slept like a cursed princess, and you snore.*

Connor chuckled, opting to ignore the dead king's jibe until he'd at least eaten something.

Another gale ripped through the trees, and their branches creaked under the southern wind's might. Though the thick oak leaves obscured the sun, the amber tint to the light suggested dusk would hit them soon. They needed to regroup and plan their next move.

Zander waited for him in the Decay, and the man had something Connor wanted.

A log on the campfire behind his tree shifted in the pile, and the pop of roasting bark mingled with the snap of the flames. He peered around the trunk to find Sophia sitting in front of the flickering light with her back to him. She once again wore the dark dress from the field where they had met. Even as he shifted and woke, she didn't move.

Lost in thought, perhaps—or simply waiting. For what, he couldn't tell, but the lingering tension from last night hit him square in the chest.

He and Murdoc had made their peace, but she still walked the line between friend and foe.

Strewn across the various branches of a tree on the other side of the campfire, their clothes swayed in the wind. Before setting up camp, they'd cleaned what they could in a nearby river and set them out to dry. With a glance down at the vile blue pants he still wore, their hems stained brown with the muck of the sewer tunnel, he pushed himself to his feet.

Time to burn these atrocious things and finally wear something familiar.

He walked around the campfire, conscious of Sophia's gaze on his shirtless back as he grabbed his cloak and squeezed the fabric to test it.

Dry, thank the Fates.

"A man with scars like those has stories to tell," Sophia said.

As he tested the fabric of his tunic—also dry—he peered over his shoulder to find her watching him. She held a long stick, one end of it stabbed into the flames and forgotten.

"I'm sure you have a fair number of scars, too—on both bodies."

Her lips pressed together in a thin line, and she looked back at the fire without responding.

He scanned the small clearing. "Where's Murdoc?"

"We need food. The town markets are cheaper than the city, so I sent him to forage and buy whatever he couldn't find on the forest floor. Murkwell's quite a hike from here, so he'll be a while."

"Are you sure that's a good idea?" Connor tugged his shirt off the branch. "The last time he foraged, he tried to feed you slime rats."

"Oh." Her brow creased with a frown as she realized her mistake.

As the conversation died, Connor tugged on his shirt. A shrill bark cut through the air, high-pitched and distant. He'd heard it plenty of times before in the Ancient Woods, but he'd never been able to find its source.

Sophia pinched her eyes together in defeat. "You and I need to talk."

"About what?"

"The Grimm. Any sane man would fulfill it."

Uninterested in yanking off his pants in front of her, he opted to finish changing after she said her piece. He leaned against the tree and crossed his arms. "I guess I'm insane, then."

"Don't play coy." Her features contorted into a surreal blend of anger and hope. "Come, now. It must be tempting. Anything you ask, given to you instantly by one of the most powerful men in Saldia. He has connections that could get you whatever you wanted, whenever—"

"I don't need anything he can give me."

Her dark hair slid over her shoulders as she shook her head. She frowned and sat upright with a skeptical huff. For a moment, she simply watched him, like she wanted to believe him but couldn't bring herself to do it.

Skepticism. Doubt. Distrust.

As he watched her struggle with the emotions, it all finally made sense.

"You must feel trapped." He scratched the back of his head as he tried to think of this from her perspective. "Without the bloody beauties, you die. You want the Deathdread because you think it'll help you perfect your recipe. You won't ever admit it out loud, but you need someone else to survive. You need *me*."

Sophia frowned and glared into the fire, but she didn't protest.

He shrugged as he pieced it together. "And yet, you've survived this long by not trusting anyone. By covering your tracks. You needed Richard, and the deal you struck with him—" Connor's nose creased with loathing for that vile worm. "Sophia, I'm not that kind of man. As long as you don't betray us, you're safe. I will only send your family after you if you try to kill me." He paused, thinking it over. "Or Murdoc."

Her stick went limp in her hand, and she became deathly still. She watched him with a guarded expression, one he couldn't even read. Whatever she was thinking, he couldn't decipher it from her face.

He grabbed his clean pants off the branch and tossed them over his shoulder, assuming the conversation was done.

As he turned his back on her, however, she cleared her throat. "Wait."

"I want to change, Sophia, and I would rather do it without an audience."

"I need to know about that scar." She stoked the fire with her stick. "That scar on your back—it's not magical. If you were just a merchant's son, how did you get a scar like that?"

A fair question, given all her doubts.

His body tensed at the mention of the long red line from his left shoulder and down to his right hip. Wide as a hand, it had burned for a solid year after the incident. He'd seen it in a mirror, once, after he'd gotten a bit of help to heal it, and the scar burned against his skin like a brand. Any time he'd bedded a woman or had a fling with a farmer's daughter, they had all gasped at it in horror and asked questions he didn't want to answer. Over the years, he'd been so careful to keep his shirt on, but last night he had dropped his guard.

He sighed and rested one hand against a nearby tree as he looked at her over his shoulder. He'd never told his story to anyone, not even to the witch who had healed him.

After last night, however, they were all coming clean. He might as well tell one person what had happened.

"Back in Kirkwall, I came from a respectable family." Connor braced himself. "My sister and I didn't have the finest tutors in Kirkwall, but we still had a bright future ahead of us. I was only fourteen when Henry took the island. After that, the city changed."

As the memories of the augmented soldiers on unicorns trotted through his mind, he rubbed his jaw. After Henry's men had executed the royal family, fear had taken root in the island's very soil. Curfews had kept people trapped in their own homes. Soldiers had dragged men from their homes despite having no evidence of a crime.

"Henry started taxing everything that came into the port," he continued. "Prices soared, and the local economy all but collapsed. He didn't need the money. He just wanted to keep us dependent on the rotted food he shipped to us. To keep his prices low and give back to the widows who had lost their husbands in the war, my father started smuggling."

"Oh," Sophia's brows lifted. "I wasn't expecting that from you, of all people."

He smirked. "That's why it was perfect. No one expected it of my father, either. A law-abiding man. Always courteous to the soldiers, even though he hated them. Told them jokes. Made them laugh. Gave them free food and spices to send home to their wives. And under their noses, he stole from the king."

"That explains a lot about you, actually." Sophia stabbed the fire.

"He was a good man." Connor grinned and crossed his arms, his clean pair of pants still draped over one shoulder even though he badly wanted to change. "We were nervous at first, but we hired a warlock to help us.

Someone adept with potions. I'll never forget his name."

Bryan Clark.

A feckless stain on humanity.

Connor glared off into the forest as he tried to suppress the surge of hatred that rose each time he thought about that man. "Bryan gave us Prowlport potions each time he came, and he enchanted our wagon into utter silence. It worked for two years, and we let down our guard. We would row out in the dead of night to the ships beyond the harbor, buy our wares, and carry them into town."

"But enchantments wear off," she said, guessing at where things had gone wrong.

He nodded. "One night when I was seventeen, the wagon seemed louder. Bryan assured me it was the way of magic—that you get used to it."

Sophia scoffed.

"Exactly." Connor grimaced, his nose creasing with disgust. "Bryan had lied. I watched him re-enchant the wagon that night, but he must've done something wrong. Bought bad spellgust or had the wrong reagents. The guards heard the wagon and chased us down. We abandoned everything we'd bought. Two full seasons of supplies that had cost a small fortune, and we were forced to leave it all in the street."

He sighed and rubbed his eyes as the sting of it all resurfaced. Even eight years later, he still wished he could've gone back to that night, knowing what he knew now.

All he could do was relive it.

"We ran for our lives along a cliff toward the forest. We figured if we got into the woods, there was a chance we could escape without them identifying us. The guards were fast, so Bryan—" Connor braced himself for the words he'd never said aloud. "Bryan shoved my father into the soldiers to slow them down."

Sophia let out a breathy sigh. Though she didn't say anything, her brows tilted upward with remorse.

Connor cleared his throat. "I went back for him, of course. I wasn't going to let the guards have him. As I tried to save my father, I guess I got in Bryan's way. He shoved me over the cliff, and the last thing I remember about that night is the crunch my bones made when I landed on the rocks."

The salty sting of the sea rolled through his mouth at the memory, burning his nose and lungs with all the fire of a brush with death. The crackle of the campfire popped and fizzled in the forest around him as he lost himself in thoughts he hadn't allowed to the surface in years.

Sophia, to her credit, didn't speak. She let him sit with it in silence.

"I woke up on a hidden shore, but I don't remember how I got there." He stared off into the trees. "The soldiers probably left me for dead. Hell, at one point, I was convinced I really had died. But I climbed my way back to the top of the cliff, broken and battered, barely able to move. When I finally made it home, I found it in ashes."

Sophia stiffened, like she couldn't believe there was more.

As he'd staggered toward the torched remnants of his childhood home, in so much pain he could hardly walk, he'd felt the same way.

He shut his eyes and listened to the wind through the trees. "In the ruins, I found my mother and sister. They were nothing but burnt corpses, huddled together by the back door. The soldiers had barricaded it to ensure they couldn't escape. The town square was littered with a dozen men's heads on spikes, including my father's." His voice caught, but he cleared his throat. "They'd found other smugglers that night. His friends. Captains of the ships at sea. Other good men in the city, just trying to make a living, but not Bryan. That bastard got away."

She cursed under her breath.

The gentle crash of the wind through the leaves filled the silence that followed. Cicadas buzzed with their incessant song, but the forest's energy had otherwise shifted as dusk settled into its branches. The birdsong had faded, replaced by the deafening croak of frogs.

Sophia rubbed her eyes. "I shouldn't have asked."

"It's fine," Connor lied. "Besides, I'm not the only one of us who knows pain."

Her hand wrapped around her chin, and as she looked up at him, she merely nodded.

Without another word, he headed into the woods to clear his head and change out of the vile pants he'd worn last night. He wove through the trees until the roar of the fire faded, and even when it did, he continued his hike.

He'd left his bag behind, as well as the irreplaceable silver swords his former mentor had designed. He had nothing but the shirt on his back and the fresh pair of trousers in his hand, and yet he trusted they wouldn't disappear in his absence.

How strange, to trust again.

A gust tore through the trees, and a blinding flash of sunlight broke through a gap in the canopy ahead. He squinted at it, keen for a distraction. As he neared, the blinding light became a vista.

He paused at the edge of an overlook, watching as the leaves below rippled like waves in the wind. On the western horizon, the sun settled into the distant peaks of the mountains and cast an orange glow on everything it touched.

A man needs a purpose, son, his father had told him as they'd rowed out to the sea on that final night. *What will your purpose be?*

As a merchant's son, he'd figured his purpose was to take over the shop and build the family fortune. Maybe get into the Kirkwall royal family's good graces and rise in the ranks of society.

As an orphaned young man, he'd thought for a while that his purpose was to run Bryan Clark through with a sword.

As a drifter, he'd thought of himself as a survivor, and time had soothed some of his hatred. He wasn't really living, but he wasn't dead, either. It was something. Some days, the only thing that had kept him going was the idea that to give up and die meant his family had suffered for nothing. His rage and grief had driven him onward, but it hadn't given him anything more than the will to take another breath.

Now, he had a chance to build something better.

However unintentionally, his life as a vagrant had prepared him to be the Wraithblade. It had honed his resilience, resourcefulness, and adaptability. He had his swords and his wit, and he could overcome whatever tried to crush him.

Instead of taking life one threat at a time, he would look into the future.

A cloud of black smoke rumbled through the trees beside him, and he waited patiently as the Wraith King materialized from the void. The dead man's skeletal face pivoted toward the forest below, and he clasped his bony hands behind his back.

The trees rustled in the silent song of this timeless wood, and for a moment, the two of them simply listened to the ancient melody.

A brief calm before the inevitable storm of chaos.

Connor crossed his arms as he stared out over the forest below. "Power incarnate, huh?"

Your advanced training will not be gentle, the ghoul warned. *Nor will I be kind. You will adapt or die. Is that clear?*

His jaw tensed as he considered what lay ahead for him, but he eventually nodded.

Good. The wraith lifted his chin to the sky. *Now, to address the more immediate threat. Zander waits in Slaybourne. He stands between you and the stronghold that is rightfully yours.*

"And Otmund wants me dead. Both of them probably had a hand in sending the Starling woman after us."

Most likely. Tell me your plan.

Connor chose to indulge the specter, despite the old ghost's demanding tone. "I'll hunt them both down."

He would face them like the man his father had always known he could be.

And? the ghoul prompted.

Connor listened to the enchanted southern wind for a moment as he thought through his options. "Henry said I was a dead man walking, and maybe that's true. One thing's for certain—I won't make it easy for the people who want to kill me. I think it's high time I carve a place for myself in Saldia. I've drifted long enough. I've always been a fighter, but at least now I have something to fight for."

Hmm. The ghost's curious hum echoed through Connor's mind, as though the dead king were studying a rather fascinating puzzle. *What is it you fight for, then?*

"For myself," he answered without hesitation. "For the Finns. For Murdoc and Sophia. All I ever wanted was a way out, and I'll fight for anyone else who wants the same. I think you were right, wraith. It's time we go home."

A wise choice. You will not be disappointed. A twinge of excitement snaked through the wraith's voice. *Slaybourne is the perfect fortress, and it can be further fortified both with the magic in its mountains and with external aid. Perhaps it's time we hunt down the dragons and invite them back to Saldia. I suspect they would enjoy Slaybourne, and we could easily indulge their lust for chaos.*

Connor smirked. "If you're right—if they do still exist—I think the continent has enough death without adding dragons back to the mix."

The ghoul sighed. *Suit yourself. Be warned, Magnuson. A dire threat stands between you and our fortress. It was Zander who took my fingers, and he is an adept warrior. Even when you reach your fullest potential, he will be a threat.*

Connor rubbed his jaw as he sat with the warning.

The moment we arrive in Slaybourne, your training will begin. You no longer have the luxury of remaining unaware of your true power.

"If Zander is this much of a threat, you could just tell me now."

A soldier does not become a general the moment he lifts his first sword, Magnuson, the ghost chided. *It will take time. You have begun to understand and use your true strength, but you don't yet have true command of it. Though I would like to begin your training on our journey to the Decay, reaching Slaybourne takes precedence. We will never get another opportunity to face Zander alone. Provided you do nothing stupid, you and I are strong enough to take him together.*

"Good to know," Connor said dryly.

The dead king absently scratched at the exposed bone of his jaw. *Reaching Slaybourne is an arduous journey from here by foot, so you must buy horses to save time. Take the towns two per day. Sleep in the inns to ensure your horses aren't eaten in the night. Sell the mounts in the last town before the Decay, as they will likely die in the endless nothing that surrounds the citadel. This will allow us to arrive within ten days.*

"That's a decent plan as long as my wanted poster isn't hung in every town. When Murdoc returns, I'll see what he noticed."

Bah. The ghost waved his hand to dismiss the concern. *Knowing you, you'll either massacre anyone foolish enough to attack, or you'll adopt them like you did those two.* He gestured back in the vague direction of Sophia's fire.

Connor grinned.

You will need to be at your best for the fight, the ghoul cautioned. *That means another day of rest before you face Zander. Between now and the Decay, you must finally allow yourself to eat your fill. Are you prepared?*

"I am."

You've faced a Bloodbane dagger before. You know what to expect.

"And I've faced a Starling before," he added.

The Quinn girl was never prepared to face you, the ghost corrected. *Judging by the look of shock on her face when she saw me, she couldn't have known what I am. What you are. Zander does.*

"That's why I won't be walking into this alone."

Right. A hint of disdain dripped from the word as he looked over his shoulder toward the campsite. *Bringing Murdoc as a sacrificial lamb to distract Zander is most wise.*

Connor chuckled. The wraith could pretend not to care, but he'd noticed the subtle shift in the ghoul's tone—and the hint of respect underneath the haphazard threat. Hell, he'd even remembered Murdoc's name this time.

If the ghoul had lost his humanity in life, it seemed as though he'd reclaimed a bit of it in death.

CHAPTER SIXTY-FOUR
QUINN

In the five days since Quinn had left Oakenglen, the passage of time had blurred into an endless streak of green leaves.

Only nine days remained before her father became suspicious.

Blaze banked toward the east as the sun set behind them, another day lost to her flight over the Ancient Woods. Dusk rolled through the forest below as shadows pooled between the trunks. Her vougel's white and gold feathers trembled as air rushed by.

As the roar of the southern wind rolled across her face, she had ample time to plan her next move.

No matter how she looked at what lay ahead, she would never be able to reach the Wraithblade first. Zander had laid his trap in a location only a handful knew. Despite wasting several days to speak with every one of her contacts in Oakenglen, she hadn't been able to figure out specifically where he'd gone. While he sat in one place, the Wraithblade seemed incapable of staying in one town for more than a few hours.

He and Zander would have their duel before she found either of them, so she had to adapt her plan accordingly. A fight between two masters wouldn't go unnoticed, and the lightning from her brother's Voltaic hex always betrayed his location.

Few had mastered the chaos of a storm—not even her.

Her new pendant rested against her chest, buzzing with life, and she brushed her fingertips against it. Magic and power hummed through her hand, and she relished its raw energy.

Volt. An appropriate name, if nothing else.

The enchanted pendant gave her more control over the Voltaic hex, though she ached to master her augmentation. She had always felt as though something blocked her when she reached for the lightning magic inked into her skin, as though something held her back, but the anarchy of a storm obeyed few.

She simply needed to practice more and rely on her Burnbane augmentation in the meantime.

Though finding her brother had proven to be a difficult task, the true challenge lay in keeping her secret from him. She couldn't let him know she had overheard their father's plan for her, and that meant he had to believe she was still loyal to Teagan and the Lightseer Chamber.

If she interrupted his battle with the Wraithblade, she would have to fight on Zander's side. Quinn shuddered with disgust at the thought, but it had to be done.

A hazy beige streak simmered along the eastern horizon, and she squinted at the expanse in an effort to make out details. Devoid of all color, the stretch ate away at everything she could see. The line of muted browns cut through the otherwise endless ocean of green.

As they barreled closer, the stretch of desolate nothingness only grew larger. The edge of the Ancient Woods approached, and the first withered tree beyond it came into focus. One by one, the dead carcasses of once-great oaks stretched into the distance.

The Decay.

An endless expanse of cracked soil stretched before her. Though no one had survived the expeditions to map it out in its entirety, scholars believed it stretched to the ends of the continent.

In the distance, the smooth horizon betrayed nothing. No hint of mountains. No water. No life.

Her vougel growled into the wind, and Quinn steeled herself for what lay ahead. Few who went into the Decay ever returned. As for those who did make it out, the wasteland changed them. Even if they stumbled back to civilization, a piece of themselves died in the void beyond the southern forest.

The people feared this land for a reason.

As Blaze flew over the line of death, the southern wind roared louder. They had crossed into the Wraith King's land, into the stretch of the Ancient Woods that still oozed with his timeless magic.

Into the world he had, long ago, killed and claimed for himself.

ZANDER

As he sat on a fallen log in the Decay, Zander stared into his campfire. A gust rolled past him in the dark night, tousling his hair, and he frowned as he flattened it again.

The trees around him swayed. Their thin trunks bent in the wind, all of it less than a few decades old. Sprouts of grass poked from the cracked dirt at his feet, but he had yet to find anything out here to hunt.

To his surprise, he'd had to travel the few hundred yards to the edge of the new growth to find wood dry enough for a fire.

At the tail end of his flight, when he'd finally reached Death's Door and the sheer cliffs into which it had been built, this clump of new growth had huddled by the gate like an oasis in a desert.

The only life in a hellscape.

He peered over his shoulder at the massive black gates of Death's Door. The stone gleamed in the sparse moonlight, as sleek and smooth as a polished gem. They towered over him, as tall as the cliffs on either side—the only portal into the dark mountains and the hidden city beyond.

In this tiny patch of forest surrounded by days of rot, only the wind rustling the young leaves broke the heavy silence.

If life had begun to return, perhaps Slaybourne's magic had begun to fade.

A white and gold heap lay at the base of the mountain, and he grumbled in annoyance at the jagged spear-like rock through his vougel's neck. The stone lance twisted around itself like a gnarled old branch made of mountain rock, its tip smeared with blobs of his mount's blood.

Enough of the citadel's magic remained to keep him from entering, at least. In his hours spent so far at the gate, nothing had flown over the mountains, and nothing had come out.

True to Otmund's word.

The helm he'd ripped from his dead mount's forehead lay at his feet, and he lifted the golden circlet to examine it in the firelight. On the inside of the large ring, two spikes protruded from the metal. They glistened, ready to spear their next victim. He flipped it over, and the oval spellgust gem that powered the spikes glimmered in the night.

Too large for a man's head.

With a grunt of effort, he snapped the front stretch of the helm from the rest, until he had only the important elements—the spikes and the stone—both embedded in the same broken stretch of gold. It would be easier to shove into the Wraithblade's forehead this way, and it served him better than the potions he'd brought.

Otmund believed Zander was stupid enough to trust the man with his life, and that suggested the Lord of Mossvale was getting sloppy. Either that, or he'd made an error out of fear. It was time to figure out what the man truly wanted in all of this, and unfortunately, Zander had nothing else with which to fill his time while he waited.

Even with one of the fastest vougels in the fleet, it had taken him six days to reach Death's Door. From the air, the long-lost mountains had dominated the horizon for the last two days of his journey, and the gates themselves had nearly blended into the endless line of black mountains.

With no mount to make a quick escape if the need arose, he risked a long wait in the Decay.

No matter. When he left with the Wraithblade as his mindless servant, maneuvering the wasteland would hardly pose a threat.

Now, he had only to rest and prepare himself for his first battle with the peasant—and his second with the wraith.

SOPHIA

At yet another tavern in a long string of exhausted nights, Sophia collapsed into the straw mattress and closed her eyes. She had never come to Charborough before, but she didn't even have the energy to explore anything in the town except for the tavern and the inn. After her shopping trip in Oakenglen, she already had what she needed to face Zander Starling.

A ball caught in her throat at the thought of Zander, and she coughed as panic flooded her chest. The Starling woman had nearly killed them all, and Sophia didn't look forward to facing off with the woman's brother.

Her legs ached from their ride through the last two towns on the southeast road, and the rest of her throbbed from passing through eight others in half the time it should've taken. Normally, she would've taken a Rectivane to soothe the soreness, but they had to reserve their stores.

Footsteps thudded in the hall, approaching fast, and she groaned in annoyance. All she had wanted was a bit of peace before Murdoc's unbroken stream of chatter stabbed her in the ears again.

The door creaked, and the aroma of roasted meat rolled through seconds before Connor shoved his way in. Another man walked past the open door without even looking their way as Connor balanced four plates on his arms. The platters overflowed with turkey legs, piles of chicken, charred carrots, and a heap of steaming potatoes. A long loaf of bread hung from his mouth as he kicked the door shut behind him, and the wall trembled from the force.

When no one walked in after him, she sat upright. "Where's Murdoc?"

Connor set the platters of food on the other corner of the straw mattress and took a bite out of the bread. "There you go, asking about him again. Are you worried your future husband has run off with another woman?"

She rolled her eyes and aimed her pointer finger at him. With a twitch of her fingertip, she shot a thin blast of ice at the bread.

A puff of smoke rolled across the plates as Connor summoned a great metal shield onto his left forearm. Ribbons of light snaked through the black metal, and her ice splattered uselessly across its surface. The Crackmane magic dissipated into harmless steam.

He dismissed the shield with a smirk and took another bite of bread. "Ass."

She shrugged. "Yeah, I am. I was wondering when you would use that in front of us."

"You knew I had it?"

"Of course. I know everything."

In the silence that followed, Connor frowned and raised one skeptical eyebrow as he chewed.

"You're no fun." She crossed her arms. "Fine, yes. I stayed up that night and pretended to sleep while you played with it."

"I should've known. To answer your previous question, Murdoc is off selling the horses."

"I guess we won't need them anymore. Besides, those beasts probably hate us for what we just put them through."

"Most likely. Mine wouldn't even look at me when I handed off the reins."

Sophia reached for a roasted potato on one of the plates. In her periphery, Connor summoned one of his shadow swords. Quick as a flash of lightning, he smacked the flat of his blade against the back of her hand.

"Ow!" She shook out her fingers as ribbons of pain splintered up her arm. "What in Saldia was that for?"

"This is my food." He popped the last bite of bread into his mouth.

"What—" She frowned in confusion as he rubbed his hands together to rid them of lingering crumbs. "How could you have possibly eaten that entire loaf already?"

"I'm not holding back anymore." He grabbed a turkey leg off one of the platters and shrugged. "I need to have energy for the fight ahead of us. You said you studied the wraith before, so this shouldn't surprise you."

"I only heard rumors." Sophia studied the feast before her and pointed to the pile of chicken. "Are you truly going to eat all of this by yourself?"

He nodded and ate half of the turkey leg in a single bite.

Her nose creased with revulsion. "That's simultaneously disgusting and impressive."

Connor laughed, not pausing again to speak as he picked the turkey bone clean.

As her stomach grumbled, she leaned back against the wall and adjusted her seat on the scratchy mattress. "We'll reach the Decay tomorrow night. Are you ready?"

"There's no running from this, Sophia." When nothing remained of the turkey but bones, he grabbed a potato and bit into it. Steam rolled over his face from the uneaten half of the tuber, and it only made her hungrier. "Zander has one of the daggers, and against the four of us, not even he can win."

"You're sure about that?"

For the first time since he'd entered the room, Connor stopped eating. His gaze briefly searched her face before he looked her dead in the eye. "Are you not?"

"You don't understand." Sophia rubbed her jaw and stared at the floor while she spoke. "Even in Nethervale, the elite are terrified of the Starlings. They're boogeymen to us. We were lucky when we took on the Starling woman because the wraith surprised her, but Zander has a decade more of experience. He's even better than she is. He's been molded in his father's image." She shuddered. "That family is barely human, Connor. They're practically gods."

He popped the final bite of his potato into his mouth and crossed his arms, watching her as he chewed. His brows knit together, and she couldn't for the life of her read the expression on his face.

"You don't have to come," he said quietly. "You can stay here. We'll come for you once Slaybourne is secured, but I'm getting that dagger from him even if it kills me."

Sophia groaned. "That's what I'm worried will happen, you oaf. Back in the camp outside Murkwell—what you guessed about me—ugh." She cleared her throat, hating what she was about to say. "You were right. I need you and that Blackguard idiot. If you lot die, so will I."

Connor grinned, his eyes creasing with mirth as he shook his head. "Be careful, Sophia. It almost sounds like you're getting soft."

She groaned and snatched a potato off his plate. Before he could protest—and with the help of her Spelsor hex—she managed to dart out the door before he could grab her. Even as she left, she couldn't suppress the small smirk tugging at her mouth.

"Ass," she muttered as she bit into the delightfully warm potato.

CHAPTER SIXTY-FIVE
CONNOR

Connor knelt on a patch of grass in the Decay, tired of the waiting. Tired of the endless days of walking. More than ready for the fight he'd been preparing for these last two weeks.

Six days of marching through a wasteland.

Six days of camping under the stars.

Six days of eating whatever stores they had to keep up his strength. The wraith had assured him that game and water awaited in the citadel, but watching their reserves deplete to nothing had left him on edge.

His body hummed with anticipation. His fingers twitched, eager to summon the shadow blades.

On his back, the familiar weight of his silver swords pressed against his spine. He debated taking them off, but he'd fought with them for years. Even if he didn't use them against Zander, he wanted to go into this fight with as much steel on him as possible.

Given what little he knew of the Lightseers, Connor had to assume Zander wanted to kill both him and the Wraith King. Now, he had the chance to face the Starling warrior alone. If he allowed there to be a next time, Zander had the resources and influence to bring an army.

Tonight, it was kill or be killed.

The smoldering char of campfire smoke billowed past. The orange glow of distant flames illuminated a field at the base of a cliff. Above him, the Black Keep Mountains towered into the sky, each sheer face of rock far too steep for even him to climb and too high for even the wraith to peer over.

A smattering of stars shimmered in the dark night, and a soft blue glow from the twin moons swept through the young forest around them. Oak trees bent in the southern wind, barely a few decades old, and patches of pale green grass clumped across the once-cracked dirt.

The specter grumbled, hidden from view as they stalked their prey. *There is too much life in these woods. The enchantments I left must be fading.*

"Or we could not kill everything around the citadel," Connor muttered under his breath, careful to remain quiet.

Not everything. I kill only what's outside. Approaching invaders must understand that a siege on your stronghold will end with them as dead as the forest around them.

"Fair point. Now, go see if he truly came alone."

The wraith chuckled. *How comfortable you are to make commands of a king.*

"Yep."

Behind him, Sophia and Murdoc knelt against the grass. Sophia's head tilted, her eyes glossing over as she listened to something, but Murdoc simply glared at the campfire.

Ready.

Waiting.

The dagger is here, the wraith said, interrupting Connor's thoughts.

His world tilted, and his stomach churned as the ground disappeared. He bit back a rush of nausea as the trees around him blurred into nothing but streaks of blue and black.

After a few disorienting moments, his vision finally cleared. He stood on the outskirts of a meadow as he watched the world through the wraith's eyes.

A man with a squared jaw sat on a toppled log, his hair rife with the reds and golds of a flame. With his elbows on his knees, he stared into the campfire. The orange glow flickered across his features. His rich green tunic contrasted the fiery strands of his hair, and the golden threads along the hems suggested immense wealth. Strapped to his side, a massive sword waited in its sheath.

Zander Starling. It had to be.

Beside the man, a Bloodbane dagger sat upright in the log. Its enchanted green blade glimmered as magic churned through the steel. Runes covered the edges, their etched lines glistening with ribbons of gold.

The man by the fire lifted his chin and looked right at him, as though he could see through the wraith and into Connor's soul. Zander stood, his shoulders squared as he tugged the dagger from the log and stowed it in the empty sheath on his belt beside his sword.

I will check the woods for reinforcements, the wraith said.

Connor's head spun, and he set his palms flat against the dirt as the wraith's vision faded. He groaned with irritation as he tried to get his bearings, and he rubbed his temple to root himself back in the moment.

Fates above, he hated it when the ghost did that.

A shrill and distant cry floated on the wind, too far away to name. His ear twitched, and he frowned as he glared off toward the west.

Impossible.

Nothing lived out here. In their six days in the Decay, they'd seen no life at all. No deer. No rabbits. Not even a slime rat had ventured out into the deadlands. Though it had been a nice change of pace to camp beneath the stars instead of in a tree, the oppressive silence had weighed on his shoulders, broken only by the howl of the wind.

After nearly a week in the overbearing hush of a wasteland, his mind must've played a trick on him.

Murdoc pointed toward the orange glow. "Can you see anything?"

Connor nodded. "Zander's here, and he wants to kill us. Even though he's a Starling, you have my blessing to return the favor."

"With pleasure." Sophia cracked her knuckles as she studied the distant campsite. Despite her bravado, her fingers trembled ever so slightly, betraying the depths of her fear.

And yet, she stayed.

Murdoc tugged the enchanted Bluntmar chain out of his pocket. "Technically, he just wants to kill you, Captain."

Connor frowned and studied the former Blackguard in silence.

The ruffian cleared his throat and awkwardly rubbed his neck with his free hand. "Right. Murder and mayhem, per usual. Scarves up."

"Not this time." Connor summoned one of his shadow blades, and the blackfire roared across the dark steel. "I'm the Wraithblade, and the world already knows it. You heard Richard. No use hiding anymore."

"Suit yourself, Captain." Murdoc draped his chain over one shoulder and tugged a loose cloth from his pocket. "Sophia?"

She shook her head. "There's no point."

"At least one of us needs a bit of anonymity," the former Blackguard argued as he tied his scarf over his mouth and nose. "I guess I'll be stuck doing the shopping from now on."

The necromancer beside him smirked, and her dark eyes briefly darted toward him.

"Everyone remembers the plan?" Connor asked.

Sophia stretched out her arms. "Surround him, get the blade, and kill him. I have a few potions ready at the top of my bag in case my augmentations aren't enough."

"And don't die," Murdoc added. "That part is important."

"Right." Connor stretched his neck to limber up for the battle. "You have your chain, Sophia has her potions, and the wraith has his homicidal insanity."

"Exactly," the necromancer muttered. "What could go wrong?"

His mount is rotting in the forest, the ghoul interjected. *Speared by one of my enchantments. At least some of my magic still works.*

"Hmm." Connor rubbed the stubble on his jaw as he glared at the great gates above him. "Can we lead Zander into Slaybourne? Maybe activate some of the traps?"

I doubt he would be so foolish as to follow.

"Fair point."

That said, no one else is here. It seems he truly came alone.

Connor stood, ready to end this. "Then he's a damned fool."

QUINN

As the twelfth day of her hunt through the Decay came to a close, Quinn rested her back against a shriveled old tree with Blaze's massive head in her lap. He purred as she stroked his silky soft ears, and his claws slipped in and out of his paws as he enjoyed their nightly routine.

Only three days left.

From what she had gathered, Zander had left Lunestone several days before she had left Oakenglen. He'd probably reached Death's Door a week ago, and she had no idea of how much time remained before he and the Wraithblade faced each other—if they hadn't already.

Dusk sank into the endless expanse of dead trees and cracked soil that stretched for eternity in every direction around her. With no cover but the tree at her back, she kept watch across the endless expanse of nothing as she debated her plan.

Ordinarily, her fire would've been a beacon to the deadly things in the night, but nothing lived out here. As her hunt approached its two-week mark, she hadn't seen so much as a lizard crawling through the dusty soil.

Just… nothing. In every direction. Miles and miles of *nothing*.

The Decay had proven to be an endless stretch of emptiness, no doubt intended to disorient anyone who dared hike through it. The Wraith King had probably created the wasteland to kill anyone who didn't come in prepared—and to slaughter the hope of anyone who did.

Within a few days, she would need to rethink her plan. Wandering aimlessly through this expanse risked her missing her window of opportunity, and the Decay was so much larger than any map had suggested. Without landmarks or life, the desolate stretch of dead things skewed her sense of direction and warped her sense of time.

As she lost herself in thought, a piercing howl cut through the empty night.

Familiar and unsettling, it chilled her to the core. It echoed through the wasteland, eerily similar to the howling she had heard in her travels through the Ancient Woods.

In unison, she and Blaze sat upright. His ears perked forward, and she craned her head while they waited for it to happen again. The evening winds whistled through the dead branches, but nothing else broke its incessant roar.

Out here, only the southern wind had ever wandered by. For a cry like that to make it all the way to her, something had to be—

Another howl cut through the air again, interrupting her thoughts, just as shrill and somber as before. This time, she and Blaze looked at each other.

Time to move.

She jumped to her feet and grabbed his saddle off the dusty ground. Though his tail twitched with anticipation, he kept low as she threw the leather seat on his back. The satchels hooked to the saddle shook with the force, but with everything at stake, urgency mattered more than a few broken bottles.

They needed to move.

Blaze stood, allowing her to tighten the straps with a few practiced tugs from their years of traveling together. His claws sank into the cracked dirt, and he glared up at the starlit night while she strapped *Aurora* to her waist and climbed into the saddle.

In mere moments, they were in the sky.

The cool night air rolled past Quinn's face as they soared, and she scanned the endless stretch of dead trunks and fallen logs in search of whatever had made the noise. For it to have been that shrill, that loud—and for them to both have heard it—this couldn't have been a hallucination.

At first, the hazy horizon only darkened, as empty and void as everything else. The trees waited below, same as they had for nearly two empty weeks. Barren. Void of life.

An endless stretch of rotting wood, same as always—until she spotted a cloud of dust billowing into the distant sky like a brown fog.

Her chest panged with dread, and a bead of sweat rolled down her neck despite the cold night. Though she never would've admitted it aloud, her body tensed with panic. With horror.

With fear.

She refused to believe the blightwolves were out here. They'd always kept to the Ancient Woods, and this stretch of the forest had been dead for centuries. Assumptions aside, she must've made a mistake. This had to be something she had stumbled upon that would make sense the moment she reached the cloud of dust.

Blaze banked toward it, and his magnificent wings rocked as the powerful southern wind fought them. Even with his exceptional speed, it took quite a while to reach the distant cloud. As they approached, they circled it from behind. Her vougel gave the storm a wide berth, and beneath her seat on his back, he held his breath.

At the front of the murky cloud of dust, a silver wolf bolted through the dead forest with ease. It towered over the crumbling trunks around it, far larger than the biggest horse she had ever seen.

A blightwolf.

Its fur glinted like metal in the last shreds of sunlight as it led the charge across the Decay. As it shot through the night, silhouettes in the dust cloud chased after it. While Quinn circled, she squinted and tried to make out what pursued the creature.

At least fifty more blightwolves charged after the wolf at the front of the pack. Her lips parted with horror as she realized they weren't chasing it, but following.

Their alpha.

She cursed under her breath, but the obscenities faded into the roar of the wind.

In the Frost Forest north of Lunestone, Quinn had killed three carnivorous unicorns with her bare hands to rescue a lost child in the woods. To earn *Aurora*, she had gone into the Mountains of the Unwanted and sliced open twelve of the carriage-sized scorpions crawling its walls. Once, during an ambush on the eastern road, she had taken on ten of the Nethervale elite and lived to give the report to her father.

But she had never seen anything like this.

She gaped at the stampede of blightwolves, their ragged breaths louder even than the wind. Her vougel growled, his shoulders tensing beneath her, and she could practically taste his fear.

One of the blightwolves at the rear of the pack craned its head toward her and Blaze. It howled into the night, warning the rest of them. Its unnerving cry sliced through the air, and within seconds, the others joined. The collective howl of fifty blightwolves rumbled through the Decay like thunder, shaking her to her bones.

An omen of death, the southern locals had always said.

One leapt into the air, its jaws snapping as it tried to bite Blaze's leg, but it fell back to the dusty earth before it even came close. The vougel growled and climbed higher anyway, his wings slapping against the turbulent air as the southern wind tried to take them down.

With nothing to hunt out in the Decay, the creatures must've been heading toward the only living thing for miles.

Zander.

"Follow them, Blaze," she ordered.

The wolves tore across the dead expanse, and her vougel struggled to keep up with their incredible pace. When Death's Door finally came into view, she and Blaze would have to race ahead to steal precious minutes from the blightwolves.

Provided, of course, Zander didn't kill her quarry first.

CHAPTER SIXTY-SIX
CONNOR

Blackfire engulfed Connor's enchanted blades, licking the air as he held them at his side. He strode through the young forest outside of Death's Door, weaving through the trees to the crackling chorus of the bewitched flames. Their roar mingled with the snap of the distant campfire obscured by the oaks between him and the meadow.

Zander waited for him at the gate into Slaybourne, and he'd come to meet the man's challenge.

The campfire's flickering amber light rolled over his boots as he neared the clearing. Through gaps between the trees, he caught sight of a silhouette by the fire. He impulsively tightened his grip on the hilts of his weapons.

He stepped past the last tree and paused at the edge of the field. The backlit silhouette crossed its arms, already watching him. Already waiting.

As ready for this battle as he was.

The figure took several steps forward. Despite the low light, Zander's features came into sharp focus as Connor's eyes adjusted. The campfire's orange glow flickered across half the man's face, and the vibrant reds and golds of his trademark Starling hair melted together. At his side, green light buzzed along the edges of the Bloodbane dagger's sheath.

The bait for his little trap. Bait Connor had gladly taken.

Zander gave a mockingly halfhearted bow. "You must be the famous Wraithblade. I'm honored."

"I can't believe you actually came alone," Connor admitted with a shake of his head. "And you actually brought the dagger with you."

"Of course. I couldn't have you scampering off when you realized it wasn't here, now could I?"

"Leave," he warned, unfazed by the taunt. "You're outnumbered."

"That's never stopped me before." With his free hand, Zander patted the green dagger in the sheath at his waist. "Speaking of, where is that abomination of yours?"

"That's not your concern, and that's not what I meant."

To Connor's left, Sophia stepped into the light from the depths of the forest. She set her hands on her waist and lifted her chin, silently daring the Starling to attack. From the woods opposite her, Murdoc stepped into the meadow with his chain over one shoulder and his sword already drawn. The former Blackguard sank into his stance, both hands clasped around the weapon in his hands as the steel glistened in the firelight.

"Followers, already?" Zander mimed tipping a hat to Connor. "I'm impressed. Here I thought you were a useless peasant."

Do not underestimate this man, the Wraith King warned, still invisible as he glided through the young forest around them. *To kill him, we must overwhelm him. Tonight, Magnuson, we must fight as one.*

Without a word, Connor nodded his agreement.

"Very well." Zander let out a bored sigh and drew the Firesword at his waist. Flames erupted along the golden weapon as he scanned the three of them. "For your crime of treason, I sentence you to death. Per my duty to the people, I will deliver your sentence myself, and you will die on *Valor's* blade."

Valor.

With a twinge of envy, Connor wondered if he should've named his blackfire blades as well.

In a blur of pale skin and green cloth, Zander reached into a pouch on his waist. His arm swept across the field as he unleashed a wide spray of steel darts, each no larger than a fingernail. Light glinted off the dark gray steel as the arrowheads carved through the air toward Connor and his team.

The fight for Slaybourne and the Bloodbane dagger had begun.

As four darts careened toward her, Sophia rolled out of the way, and the arrowheads pummeled the tree behind her. Murdoc twirled, and his body contorted as he avoided the spray of metal. He cursed under his breath and hopped aside at the last second as a final dart sailed by.

Connor, however, merely summoned his shield and stalked toward Zander, unfazed by the threat. Though the blackfire sword in his left hand dissolved into a cloud of smoke to make room for the shield, the large circle of metal hummed with magic and life in the night. The darts tinged against its blistering hot surface and fell harmlessly to the grass.

"You're full of surprises," Zander admitted.

From behind the fallen log, a wave of black smoke rolled across the campfire. In a rush of darkness and shadow, the Wraith King's skeletal face emerged from the haze. His jet-black sword lifted above Zander as the man focused his full attention on Connor.

The wraith swung his undead blade, ready to cleave the Starling's head from his shoulders.

With barely a second to spare, Zander spun on his heel and raised *Valor*. Their blades hit, and the clang of crashing steel echoed through the quiet night.

"Now!" Connor charged, mere moments away from attacking one of the most powerful men in Saldia.

Sophia threw her enchanted daggers. With his sword still locked against the wraith's, Zander twisted his body to avoid them. They sailed past, slicing his tunic on their way by, and they sank into the dirt.

Together, Connor and Murdoc raced into the fray as the wraith grabbed the Starling warrior's collar. The bony hand clutched his tunic, but Zander drew the Bloodbane dagger and sliced at the ghoul's forearms. With an enraged growl, the Wraith King dissolved in a rush of black fog as he narrowly avoided a severed arm.

Freed from the phantom, Zander sheathed the dagger once again. Connor reached him and swung at the man's neck. In the same breath, Murdoc threw the Bluntmar chains at Zander's leg.

Odds were at least one of them would take the man down.

The Starling warrior jumped onto the log, as calm and relaxed as if he were sipping coffee on a winter morning. Murdoc's chain thudded uselessly against the grass, and Zander leaned backward as Connor's blackfire blade almost sliced open his gut. The dark flames singed the fibers on the soldier's tunic but left him otherwise unscathed.

Close, but not close enough.

Another surge of black fog billowed around Zander as the wraith appeared again behind him. Before Connor could even swing his sword a second time, the ghoul's undead blade sliced through the mist.

It landed against Zander's weapon with a resounding bang. The Firesword's blood-red flames billowed into the air, fueled by the blow.

Unnatural speed. Unparalleled reflexes. Zander seemed to know what would happen seconds in advance, every time.

Two could play that game.

Connor shoved his shield into the Starling's gut. The man fell backward through the cloud of ethereal smoke and landed hard on the grass. As Connor cocked his arm to break the man's nose, Zander grabbed his shoulders and used their momentum to throw Connor over his head.

With a string of muffled curses, Connor hit the ground rolling. His sword dissolved into a puff of smoke as he dug his fingers into the dirt to slow himself. His hand kicked up a cloud of dust and left behind a long gouge in the grass.

Zander kicked off the ground and drew the Bloodbane dagger as he jumped again onto the log. He sliced at the lingering fog of black smoke. The wraith's white skull dissolved again into the wind as he narrowly avoided a blow from the only thing that could kill him.

Murdoc darted into the light and grabbed his chain off the ground by the fire. Zander leapt off the log and swung *Valor* at the former Blackguard's head, but Murdoc dove across the grass as the blade cut through the air where his face had been moments before.

When Connor finally stopped sliding across the dirt, Sophia ran along the edge of the meadow until Zander stood between her and her daggers. She flexed her palms, and the enchanted blades flew through the air as they returned to her.

Black fog billowed over Zander as the wraith reappeared, and the Firesword clashed against the ghoul's blade. Sophia's daggers whistled through the air, and the Starling warrior's head snapped toward them as they raced at his skull. He backflipped through the air, effortlessly clearing her blades as he simultaneously avoided another blow from the wraith.

Zander landed on the grass nearby, not even winded. With a grin, he studied Connor's face. "Having fun?"

"Absolutely." Connor stood. With his shield still in one hand, he summoned one of the blackfire blades into his empty palm, ready for more.

In a blur, Zander pushed off the ground and raced toward him. Dirt sprayed through the air from under the man's heel, and he swung his golden sword. The blade clanged against Connor's shield. With a twist of his shoulders, Connor angled the shield to redirect the blade into the dirt.

It worked.

As his sword sank into the ground, Zander teetered briefly off balance.

The perfect chance to strike.

Connor stabbed his sword at the man's chest. The Starling warrior grunted with effort and shifted his weight. With a twist of his hand, he blocked the blow at the last second. The enchanted steel shoved the blackfire blade aside. Flames erupted along both swords, each fueling the other as they hit.

He has somehow gotten even better, the wraith observed. *Even faster. Even more deadly.*

"Great," Connor muttered.

Over by the log, the ghoul disappeared in a swirl of churning black mist, only to reappear once again behind Zander. In the same breath, Connor attacked.

The Starling warrior raised his Firesword to block Connor's blade and, with his other hand, drew the green dagger at his waist. With Connor's blade trapped against the enchanted Starling weapon, Zander sliced at the ghoul's wrist.

The Wraith King darted backward, managing to keep his hand with only a moment to spare. A furious growl rumbled through Connor's head.

Zander smirked, his attention shifting to the ghoul. "You're not so terrifying when you face a real weapon, now are you?"

"I wouldn't taunt the undead warlord." Murdoc charged from the edge of the field, his sword flashing in the firelight. "But you Starlings can do what you want."

The former Blackguard swung, and Connor stepped back to avoid the blow as they fought in such close quarters. Zander ducked, and the Blackguard's weapon sailed overhead. Before Murdoc could recover, Zander landed a sharp kick in the man's stomach. The ruffian doubled over, gasping for air.

Connor swung at the back of Zander's exposed neck, but the soldier dropped to his hands and knees. In a blur, he swiped Connor's legs out from underneath him. Connor fell hard onto his back, and the air left his lungs in a rush. Though he managed to hold tight to his sword, the shield dissolved in a burst of black fog.

Murdoc wheezed nearby, still struggling to catch his breath. Zander crouched on the ground, and Connor recovered enough to stab his blade at the man's face. The Lightseer stumbled backward, out of range. The blackfire crackled as Connor's sword drove into the dirt. The grass around it caught, consumed by the enchanted flame.

Barely a second later, Sophia's enchanted daggers sank into the ground by Connor's submerged sword.

"He's so damn fast!" The necromancer spread her fingers wide as she scanned the battlefield. The blades beside Connor trembled in the ground at her silent command. They levitated and returned to her with the whistle of metal through the air.

Zander rolled onto his back and used his momentum to kick off the earth. With a polished flourish, he landed on his feet and settled into a light stance as the flames on his sword billowed across the steel. In his other fist, the blinding green glow of the Bloodbane dagger blurred through the air as he rolled out his shoulders.

Connor stood and summoned his shield as he and his teammates regrouped.

The wraith emerged from the shadows at his side, and the undead warlord's grip tightened on the hilt of his sword. *I can't get close enough to take the dagger from him. This infuriating maggot just won't die!*

"Stay calm," he chided. "Don't let him rile you."

"As fun as this has been, I have other things to do." Zander sheathed the Bloodbane dagger and reached again into the pouch at his waist.

Sophia's eyes widened. "Take cover!"

Before anyone could even move, Zander hurled another spray of darts.

A thick cloud of shadow rolled over them as the wraith disappeared, only to reappear behind the Starling warrior. The clash of their steel rang through the air as Connor raised his shield against the darts. Sophia dropped to the ground, but Murdoc tripped over a root as he tried to contort his body yet again.

The man fell right into the line of fire.

Connor grabbed the former Blackguard's collar and dragged him behind the shield. Several darts clattered off the sizzling metal, and one sped through the air where Murdoc had stood moments before.

"Much obliged, Captain." The ruffian gave him a mock salute. "That's two life debts, now."

"Focus!"

"Yep." The former Blackguard fished the enchanted Bluntmar chain out of his pocket. "Shutting my mouth."

Flames roared across *Valor's* blade in the pitch-black night. The fire burned brighter as the wraith loomed over Zander, their swords locked. The specter's hood had fallen off at some point during their duel, and his skeletal face leaned toward the Starling warrior.

Connor and Murdoc raced again into the fray. At the same moment,

Sophia charged as well. Ice splintered up her arms, and Connor skidded to an abrupt stop. He grabbed Murdoc's collar and yanked the man out of harm's way as the necromancer summoned a pearly blue orb into her palm.

He and the former Blackguard hit the dirt with only seconds to spare. With a stifled grunt of effort, Sophia hurled a blast of frost at the Starling warrior's face.

Zander cursed under his breath and dove across the grass as the wraith's sword cut through the empty air above his head. The blast of ice passed harmlessly through the ghoul and splintered across a tree. The oak groaned and cracked as it toppled.

As the redhead skidded to a stop, his eyes narrowed. His gaze shifted to her, and he grinned. "You shouldn't have shown me that."

With the Firesword in his right hand, Zander stretched his empty palm toward her. A stream of fire billowed from his fingers, as hot and furious as the fabled breath of a dragon. It roared through the field, dwarfing the campfire as it consumed everything in its path.

"Sophia!" Murdoc jumped to his feet and raced toward her.

A brilliant blue glow dwarfed the fire's orange light as the necromancer summoned a tidal wave of ice. It streamed from her fingers, and she let out a strangled groan as she leaned into the magic. Her glowing azure frost railed against the searing fire, just as massive as the torrent of flame.

The two spells hit each other with the hiss of boiling water, and a thick wave of steam rolled across the field like an evening fog. The sizzling haze drowned out the trees and coiled over the grass, obscuring the world from view.

Sophia faded into the cloud, and the fog churned as Murdoc darted into it. As Zander's fire raged on, Connor bolted toward him to end this before the flames dwarfed Sophia completely. Her ice crackled against his assault, its light weakening as the Starling warrior's fire burned hotter.

The steam thickened as their battle raged on. Everything faded into the white fog, until only Zander's face glowed orange in the mist. Connor reached the man just as the wraith's skeletal features emerged from the haze on the soldier's other side.

As both Connor and the wraith swung at Zander's head, the churning steam obscured the man completely.

The deafening clash of steel hitting steel rang through the mist. Instantly, the roar of fire faded, and its bright glow through the fog disappeared. Overhead, a blood-red light hummed through the cloud to the distant crackle of burning wood.

As Connor stood alone in the haze, he craned his ear to listen. The hissing sizzle of his blackfire blade filled the night. As the mist cleared, he found his sword locked with the wraith's.

Zander was gone.

The ghoul muttered a stream of curses and disappeared in a rush of black smoke. Somewhere in the mist, Sophia screamed. Murdoc shouted something unintelligible, but the pop of smoldering bark quickly dwarfed the distant sound of his voice.

"Your people are dying, Wraithblade," Zander taunted from the depths of the fog. "Do you care?"

Connor stifled a furious yell and swung at the sound, but he sliced through empty air.

Zander's Firesword appeared suddenly to his left, and Connor barely lifted his shield in time. The blade sang against the metal, and vibrations from the attack rang clear to his bones. It drove his heels into the dirt, and his teeth rattled from the blow.

Strong. Fast. Brutal.

Zander Starling was the perfect warrior, but Connor had vowed to get this Bloodbane dagger no matter the cost. In the hands of someone so deadly, it posed a threat unlike anything he'd ever known in his life.

The man disappeared again into the fog, and Connor cursed under his breath. He'd told Sophia he would get the dagger even if it killed him—and, curse the Fates, he'd meant it.

CHAPTER SIXTY-SEVEN
CONNOR

In the thick steam obscuring the meadow around him, Connor listened. Black mist mingled with the suffocating white steam. Seconds later, another clang of steel echoed through the fog. The screech of swords hitting each other rang through the night as the fight between Zander and the Wraith King continued somewhere in the thick haze.

Beyond the battle, the roar of a torched forest raged on. A red glow permeated the mist, brightening as smoke coiled into the air.

The man had set the forest on fire.

Sophia had screamed into the night. Murdoc had disappeared. Not even the wraith could land a blow. A single man had the power to decimate his team, but Connor would stand between them and the Firesword if that was what it took to protect them.

He'd just learned to trust again. He refused to lose it so soon.

Despite the fury scorching through his blood, he briefly shut his eyes and forced himself to take a settling breath. With his shield in one hand and one of his enchanted swords in the other, he waited—just as Sophia had suggested all those weeks ago.

Wait.

Listen.

The moment to strike would reveal itself.

In the mist, a single footstep thudded against the grass—too heavy to be Sophia, and too quiet to be Murdoc.

Connor's eyes snapped open, and he swung.

His blade railed against a pillar of steel. The violent blow cleared a small circle of the fog around him.

Zander stood mere feet away. *Valor* hovered mere inches from his face as it blocked the blackfire blade. The Starling warrior's nose creased with hatred as he met Connor's eye.

"You're good," the Starling admitted. "But I'm better."

With his free hand, Zander grabbed a dart out of the pouch on his belt. Before he could throw it, Connor dropped his blackfire sword and grabbed the man's wrist. With a violent twist, he wrenched Zander's arm. The man grimaced, and his fingers popped open. The dart fell, and the fog churned as the arrowhead disappeared at their feet.

Undaunted, Zander shoved his shoulder into Connor's chest and swept out his leg. They both went down, and the flames erupting along the Starling's enchanted sword blurred through the dispersing fog.

The back of Connor's head smacked hard against the dirt. Overhead, *Valor* barreled toward him. He cursed under his breath and barely rolled out of the way before it impaled the grass where his head had been.

Zander got onto one knee for balance and swung again. Connor pressed himself flat against the ground as the fiery sword barreled above his face. The heat singed his eyebrows, and the firelight glinted across the shield on his left arm.

In the split second after Zander's sword passed, Connor used his shield as a weapon. The metal sizzled with its otherworldly heat, and the Starling warrior barely leaned back in time. He lifted his jaw to avoid the shield, and he narrowly avoided having his throat crushed from its blunt edge.

There you are, the wraith's voice echoed in Connor's mind. *You can't hide forever.*

The ghoul appeared behind Zander and drove his blade right at Zander's heart. The Starling rolled into the thinning mist, and the ghoul's blade pierced the grass.

The wraith's growl built again in Connor's head as the dead man dissolved into black smoke. Damn it all—the phantom's anger was getting the best of him.

Connor darted into the mist after Zander, watching for the orange glow of the Firesword even as the mist hummed with the crackle of a wildfire tearing through the young forest around him. Red light simmered through the air as the hellfire raged.

From the red and orange mist, a blast of fire sailed toward his face. Running on instinct, he lifted his shield to block it. Something massive cracked against his shield, and vibrations shot clear through to his toes.

Zander's eyes appeared in the fog, though most of his face remained shrouded in the mist. Connor didn't hesitate. With every ounce of his strength, he drove his sword at the Lightseer's gut.

The Starling warrior pushed off the shield, using Connor's own protection to build his momentum as he jumped backward.

But not even Zander Starling was fast enough to avoid the blow.

The tip of his magical blade pierced the man's stomach. Zander stifled an agonized yell with a string of curses. His eyes met Connor's as he stumbled backward, and the warrior disappeared once again into the mist.

"Sophia!" Connor shouted, refusing to believe Zander had killed someone as resilient as her. "Do something about the damn fog!"

"I'm trying!" she shouted back.

Despite his conviction that she hadn't died, he let out a breath of relief at the sound of her voice.

"She can't do anything with those burned hands." Zander's disembodied voice floated through the mist, and Connor frowned as he scanned the thick cloud. "How quickly do her Rectivanes work, Wraithblade? Faster than mine?"

The Firesword barreled toward him again, and he raised his sword to block it.

But he wasn't fast enough. He missed, and Zander's blade barreled toward his skull.

No, he thought. *This can't be how I die.*

Before *Valor* could slice open his head, a surge of black smoke rolled over his shoulders. The wraith's jet-black sword emerged from the shadows and blocked the sharp steel. The clang of metal sang through the fog.

The Wraith King had saved Connor's life.

Connor gaped in shock at the crossed blades, time briefly suspended as he processed the undead warlord's selfless act.

Before either he or Zander could move, the ghoul barreled toward Zander and grabbed the man's shoulders. He drove the Lightseer backward, and the two of them disappeared into the swirling mist.

A gust of air ripped through the clearing, so powerful and strong that Connor dropped to one knee to keep from toppling over. The mist swirled and churned, thick enough to fight the gale. Bit by bit, it slowly dispersed. The crackle of the burning forest became a deafening roar, and a large stretch of the torched meadow appeared once again.

Sophia stood with her back to the great gate in the mountains. Her blackened palms flattened against the air, aimed toward him as the gale continued. Murdoc crouched on the ground beside her, that trademark satchel of hers in his arms as he returned a vial to its depths.

Tears burned in Sophia's eyes as she controlled the gust. She gritted her teeth as branches sailed overhead. The wildfire in the canopy bellowed and roared as it ate every living thing around them. Its flames shivered in the gale.

Though dark smoke still coiled into the air from the burning forest, the last of the steam dispersed. The necromancer collapsed to her knees, and her arms shook as she struggled to sit upright. Murdoc tugged another vial out of her satchel and held it to her mouth.

She must've used one of her potions to summon the wind, but Connor didn't know how long the power would last.

"Nicely done!" Connor shouted.

She nodded weakly in thanks, but they couldn't celebrate yet. He scanned the meadow for his target. He and his team needed to finish this before Zander regained the upper hand.

At the far end of the meadow, black smoke churned around the Starling warrior as the wraith popped in and out of existence. The Firesword's enchanted flames blurred through the thickening smoke as the soldier parried every blow, always a breath ahead of the wraith.

Connor pushed off the ground and raced toward the Lightseer. Shield in one hand. Blackfire blade in the other. Silent as a ghost, he lifted his sword as he reached Zander, ready to end this.

Ready for this brutal man to die.

As he raised his sword to cut off Zander's head, the Starling warrior glared at him over his shoulder. Their eyes met, and Connor steeled himself as he prepared to deal the final blow against one of the most powerful men in Saldia.

White sparks danced across Zander's neck. He set his left palm on Connor's shield, and his skin sizzled against the metal.

Move! the wraith shouted in his head.

He didn't. There simply wasn't enough time.

Lightning shot from Zander's fingers. It rippled into the shield and blistered through the metal.

Pain tore through Connor. His joints popped. His arms stung, as though the attack ripped the muscles from his bone. He barely stifled an agonized yell as the lightning roasted him through the shield. The metal took most of the blow, filtering the blistering magic that would've probably killed him otherwise. His sword dissolved into a puff of smoke as his mind fractured from the agony.

The glimmering ribbons of light in the shield fizzed and sparked as the metal threatened to shatter under the attack. Jolts of pain rooted him to the ground.

Immobile.

Trapped.

As he pushed through the unyielding wave of pain, he forced himself to open his eyes. In his periphery, just beyond the edge of the shield, the Wraith King hovered in a shadowy haze. His bony fingers stretched wide as lightning scorched through the black smoke around him like a thundercloud. His toothy jaw sat open in a silent scream as the magic paralyzed them both.

Whatever power Zander wielded, it transcended even what the Lightseers had given the Starling woman who'd come after them once already.

Over the crackle of burning trees, the whistle of metal through the air sang through the night.

Murdoc's Bluntmar chain barreled toward them. Barely visible over the edge of Connor's shield, Zander gritted his teeth as he fought to control his lightning. His head snapped toward the sound, and he let out a muffled curse. At the last possible moment, he stumbled backward to avoid the chain.

The lightning paused. For a brief and blissful moment, Connor could breathe.

It didn't last.

Instantly, Zander summoned the blinding magic once again. The bolt hit Connor's shield, and the torment continued. The jolts of pain squeezed his heart with its jarring static. He yelled as he forced himself to push through it.

To fight.

He refused to let this man win. He leaned into the shield, grimacing with agony as he blocked out as much of the pain as he could. Despite the splinters of chaos numbing every muscle in his body, he managed to take a single step toward his enemy.

Only one step, but he'd managed to move. A victory.

"Impossible," Zander growled through gritted teeth.

Two daggers glinted in the light of the wildfire as they whistled through the air toward Zander. They blurred through the gathering smoke. Connor shut his eyes as he forced himself to take a second step, and Zander shouted a string of obscenities into the night.

The thud of a body on the grass interrupted the stream of lightning, and Connor collapsed to his knees. He sucked in a greedy breath as he tried to stand, but he merely stumbled again to the grass. His arms went limp as the assault finally ended, but he didn't have time to rest.

Only a few yards away, Zander pushed to his feet and glared into the smoke. "I've had enough of this!"

"What's the matter?" Connor coughed as his tortured body screamed in protest to every movement. "Aren't you having fun?"

Zander didn't reply. As Connor struggled to stand, the Starling soldier unleashed a spray of tiny arrowheads into the night. Dozens of darts sailed blindly into the smoke, in every direction.

With an intuitive twitch of his arm, Connor raised his shield. Four of the darts bounced off the metal, though the shield creaked in protest from the strain of everything it had endured tonight. Three more sailed harmlessly through the Wraith King as the dead warlord vanished into a cloud of black fog.

Six more darts hissed through the air as Sophia and Murdoc emerged from the gathering wildfire smoke. One sailed right at Murdoc's face.

He didn't have time to evade it. His eyes merely widened with shock.

Connor forced himself to his feet and stumbled forward, but even he knew he'd never make it in time.

He still had to try.

As the dart reached Murdoc, Sophia shoved him out of the way. They fell together, and instead of impaling either of their skulls, the arrowhead merely grazed her neck. It drew a thick line of blood, from her jawline to her ear.

Connor let out a sigh of relief. As his body fought to recover from the lightning, he dropped to his hands and knees.

His teammates collapsed into a heap of tangled arms and fabric. As they slid to a stop, Sophia winced and held the wound.

"I knew you loved me." Murdoc planted a kiss on her cheek.

"Make sure she's all right!" Connor ordered as he returned to the fight. For all he knew, Zander had laced the darts with something deadly. If so, he trusted Murdoc to get Sophia a potion in time to heal.

The clang of steel echoed through the night. The wildfire raged around them, its hellish red glow their only source of light. Black smoke swirled around Zander as the wraith swung again and again, disappearing and reappearing with each blow. His Firesword blocked every attack seconds before it could hit.

Connor joined the fray and dismissed his shield in favor of his second blackfire blade. He swung the first, and Zander ducked. He swung the second immediately after, and the Starling warrior blocked it with his blade *Valor*. The flames crackled and roared as the two enchanted weapons met.

The wraith appeared behind the soldier and swung. The Starling man dove out of the way, and the wraith's blade sliced through Connor instead.

His heart skipped a beat in shock, but the undead warrior's blade passed harmlessly through his throat. Though the ghoul had said he couldn't kill the Wraithblade, it hadn't been something Connor had ever wanted to test.

Not yet dead, he let out a breath of relief and squared his shoulders. No time to rest.

Zander rolled to his feet, only a few yards away, and Connor charged. In the same moment, the wraith reappeared between them. The swish of steel against leather cut through the crackling wildfire, and a green glow rolled through the thickening smoke.

The Bloodbane dagger.

The glow disappeared. As Connor reached them, green light sliced through the wraith's dark cloak.

An unholy scream echoed in his mind. His chest ached, as if someone had sliced it open. Searing agony ripped through him as the wraith took a devastating blow.

His world blurred, and he dropped to one knee as he fought off the agonizing pain. He tried to stand, but his legs gave out. He fell. Something hard smacked against his shoulder, and his head snapped back against the grass.

Orange and brown blurs smeared across his vision as he strove to clear his head, but the pain only worsened. The scream in his mind echoed until it became a roar that drowned out everything. His thoughts. His sense of time. His plan.

There was only the scream.

He grimaced and shook his head, trying to clear the noise from his mind. It didn't work. His world only tilted more violently.

A silhouette appeared above him as the blurry forest swirled. The weight of the blackfire swords in his hands faded. Through the haze of his unyielding pain, he yelled with fury and fire. He wouldn't let it end this way.

Not here. Not this close to victory.

The yell dwarfed the scream in his head. For a second, his mind cleared, and he touched just enough of his rage to summon the shield.

If tonight ended with a sword through his chest, he'd take the Starling warrior to hell with him.

"It's been years since I had a worthy opponent." Zander's voice pierced the chaos as the silhouette paused overhead. "You've been an enjoyable challenge. I suppose I should thank you for that, peasant, but I want that wraith, and you're in my way."

Connor sucked in a pained breath through his teeth and glared up at the blurry figure above him. "Come and get him."

The billowing Firesword came into focus as the soldier raised it above Connor's head. He tried to stand—to take the blow like a man and deal one back—but the searing ache in his chest rooted him to the ground.

Get up.

His father's voice echoed again in his head.

No matter what life throws at you, son, I want you to always get back up.

Ripples of pain shattered his legs, but he forced himself to his feet. He wobbled, and his chest throbbed. He couldn't see the wraith, but it didn't matter.

These final moments were between him and Zander.

As the Starling warrior's face finally came into focus, Connor stifled an agonized groan and squared his shoulders. His fingers twitched at his side, and he summoned a blackfire blade into his empty palm.

Zander sneered at him. "You just don't know when to lay down and die."

A deafening roar cut through the air, followed by the flutter of wings above the smoke. Zander glanced toward the sky behind Connor and scowled.

The distraction was all Connor had needed. Just a few more seconds to catch his breath and clear his head.

He rammed his shield into Zander's chest. The man stumbled backward, and Connor pivoted his hips to redirect their momentum. With all his remaining strength, he lifted the shield and slammed it against the man's nose. Blood splattered into the air. The Starling warrior's head snapped back, and he collapsed to the grass.

"Zander Starling!" a woman's voice boomed across the fray. "You damned fool!"

A winged tiger with golden stripes dove through the smoke, and a familiar young warrior with fiery red hair sat on the vougel's back.

Quinn Starling.

Fighting one Starling was bad enough, but the Fates must've truly hated him if they'd sent two.

Connor cursed under his breath. "This can't get any worse."

The wraith snorted derisively as he appeared at his side in a puff of black smoke. *To quote that Blackguard buffoon, don't tempt the Fates.*

As Zander writhed on the ground, the wraith drove his blade at the man's head. The soldier rolled out of the way with seconds to spare and jumped to his feet. With his enchanted blade in one hand, he rested his other hand on the hilt of the sheathed Bloodbane dagger.

The winged tiger landed between them, and sweat coated the beast's neck. It panted, still trying to catch its breath, and its tail hung low to the ground.

Quinn dismounted, and her gaze darted between the two of them. "A pack of blightwolves are on their way. We have ten minutes at most before they reach this field."

Excellent, the wraith said as he glided to Connor's side. *Reinforcements.*

"I wouldn't count on it. They barely left me alive last time."

Hmm. The ghoul's voice dripped with doubt as he tapped his bony finger against his exposed jawbone.

Quinn glared at her brother as smoke billowed into the air around them. "You're interfering with an official matter. Regardless of your feelings about it, this is my mission. Not yours!"

"I outrank you, baby sister." The man spat blood on the grass as he raised *Valor*. "Fall in line and obey your superior. This fight was never yours to begin with."

She arched her back in the silence that followed, and her fingers twitched as she stared him down. Still facing her brother, she drew her own sword as well. Fire engulfed the blade, and his furious glare shifted toward her.

Demanding that she choose a side.

Without a word, she turned her gaze on Connor and settled into her stance. The dazzling blade in her hand blurred through the air, now raised toward him.

"I warned you." He struggled to breathe, though the stinging in his chest mercifully began to fade. "I warned you that you'd die the next time we fought."

"You did." She twirled her blade, and the fire carved orange streaks through the smoky haze. "I guess it's time to see what kind of man you are."

CHAPTER SIXTY-EIGHT
CONNOR

The blightwolves were coming, and now Zander had backup. This duel to conquer Slaybourne and the Bloodbane dagger hadn't exactly gone to plan.

With the Wraith King at his side, Connor lifted his shield and prepared for the battle to continue. His mind buzzed with half-baked ideas as he debated how he could possibly retake the advantage.

He had to come up with a new plan, and he needed to do it quickly.

Standing just a few feet in front of her brother, Quinn watched him with the same intense glare she had worn in the field by that withered old tree. Determined. Focused. Unshakeable. Flames raged along her sword as she held it aloft. In the silence that followed, only the crackle of flames from the burning forest around them filled the air.

Zander joined her, his golden Firesword blazing even more brightly than hers. "Give up, Wraithblade. Tell your abomination to stand down and come die like a man."

I despise this cretin, the wraith said.

"You and me both," Connor's grip tightened on the blackfire blade in his right hand. The straps securing the shield around his left arm creaked under his grasp, and he prepared for war.

In his periphery, Sophia and Murdoc staggered along the edge of the thickening smoke. She coughed and teetered. Blood still seeped from the wound in her neck. Her eyes rolled into the back of her head, and she collapsed. Murdoc grabbed her, and together they fell to the ground.

"Sophia!" The Blackguard patted her face. "Sophia, what's wrong?"

She clawed at the scratch on her neck, and her fingers slipped on the stream of blood. Her lips parted, but before she could speak, her hand went limp. Her head rolled back, and her dark hair spilled across Murdoc's lap.

"What did you do to her?" Connor's glare darted back to Zander. "What was on that dart?"

"Oh, this?" Zander pulled an arrowhead out of the pouch at his waist and pinched the small sliver of metal between his fingers. He studied it, twisting it this way and that as the glow of the wildfire glinted across the tiny weapon.

His gaze shifted abruptly to Connor. With a blurred twist of his hand, he threw it. Unfazed, Connor lifted his shield. The dart tinged off the metal and fell harmlessly to the grass.

A twinge of lingering pain shot through his chest where the wraith had been stabbed, but he gritted his teeth and rode it out. The surge of agony had mostly faded, healing much faster than the stab wound he'd gotten from Otmund.

"Sophia—" Murdoc patted her face as she lay in his arms, but she didn't answer.

In Connor's periphery, a vine coiled around Sophia's arm. The ground quaked, and dozens of roots shot from the dirt. Clumps of soil and dust soared into the air as hundreds more swarmed her body.

"What the—" Murdoc held her close. A vine slithered over her neck, but he ripped it off of her. With each second, dozens more circled them.

The former Blackguard reached for his sword on the ground, just out of range. As he shifted, she rolled onto the grass, and the hundreds of roots coiled tightly around her. In seconds, they consumed her in a sphere of earth-covered roots.

With a string of curses, Murdoc hacked at the vines. The sword sliced out a chunk of the roots, but more grew over the cut. "Captain, what the hell is this?"

Connor's grip tightened on his shield as he glanced again at the former

Blackguard. "Stand down. That looks like her magic."

Murdoc growled with frustration and stepped away as the ball of roots hardened around her unconscious body.

As Quinn's winged tiger stood behind its master, it growled and spread its wings. Its tail twitched back and forth as its gaze narrowed on Murdoc, and its nose wrinkled. The beast snarled, ready to pounce.

If it tried, Connor would slit its throat.

"Blaze, no," Quinn chided, without even looking toward her mount. "Keep watch for the wolves."

It moaned in disappointment, and its ears flattened against its head.

"Now." Her glare shifted toward the vougel.

The creature grumbled and launched into the air. As the wind from its wings rolled over Connor's face, the tiger cast one last forlorn look over its shoulder. Moments later, it disappeared into the smoky haze above the meadow.

"Wraith, go to the alpha," Connor said under his breath, his mouth hidden by the raised shield as he glared over the top at the two Starlings. "Slow them down and buy us more time to get the dagger. Once they come, we might lose what little advantage we have."

The wraith growled with frustration, but he disappeared in a rush of black smoke.

"I hope you're ready, baby sister," Zander jeered.

Cold and collected, she merely nodded. "Ready to show you how it's done."

In unison, the two Starlings raised their left hands, and a torrent of fire billowed from their empty palms. The blaze raged through the meadow, narrowly missing Sophia's nest of safety. With Connor's shield as the only available cover, he bolted toward Murdoc. The phantom injury in his chest protested with every step, but he forced himself onward.

Pain wouldn't be his undoing.

He grabbed the man's shirt and dragged him behind the shield. They knelt as the fire scorched the meadow around them. Through the metal, the oppressive heat singed off the hair on Connor's forearm, and he let out a strangled yell as he pushed through the searing burns.

"Be ready," he warned over the roar of the fire.

A bead of sweat rolled down Murdoc's temple, but he readjusted the cloth over his masked face and simply nodded.

The stream of fire ended, and they bolted to their feet in unison. Quinn and Zander charged, and the clang of all four swords crashing against each other echoed through the Decay.

Murdoc threw a left jab at Quinn's jaw, but she ducked to avoid it. With an effortless flourish, she dropped to the ground and swept the Blackguard's legs out from under him. He hit the ground with a thud but used his new angle to kick out her knee. His boot landed with a heavy thud, and she winced.

Mere feet away from their duel, Connor circled Zander. The Starling warrior watched him, shoulders tense, and sparks danced down the Lightseer's arm.

More lightning.

Not again. Connor wouldn't allow it.

He slammed the shield into Zander's chest. The man groaned, the wind knocked out of him, and the sparks sputtered out.

They fell to the ground, cursing each other as they rolled. Connor drove his blackfire blade at Zander's neck, but the Firesword parried the blow before it could land. With a twist of his hand, Connor cracked the hilt of his sword against Zander's already broken nose. More blood snaked over the Starling's mouth.

"You vile maggot!" Zander's fist erupted with flame, and he broke his knuckles across Connor's jaw.

Pain splintered through Connor's head. The blow sent him rolling, and he couldn't tell the sky from the ground. Red and white flashes of light blinded him. Smoke strangled his lungs. He coughed, and the rusty tang of blood pooled on his tongue.

The world came slowly into focus as he tried to push himself to his feet. Barely ten yards away, Murdoc swung at Quinn's face. She leaned back and easily avoided the blow, but the former Blackguard spun and swung the sword again. It grazed her shoulder, drawing blood, and she let out a string of muffled curses as she dropped the sword in her hand.

Instantly, her arm went limp. She glared at him and grabbed her Firesword with her left hand as her right hung uselessly at her side. "That's enchanted, isn't it?"

Murdoc grinned. "Want another taste?"

The world blurred again, and Connor winced as his head thundered. He squinted and scanned the meadow around him, unwilling to let his guard down no matter what the Starlings did to him.

Roughly five yards away, Zander stalked toward him. The Bloodbane dagger glowed in its sheath at his waist.

Connor had to buy them time until the wraith returned. As he glanced again at the injured Quinn, an insane idea popped into his head.

The Fates might've hated him, but damn it all, he still hoped this would work.

He jumped to his feet. As he released his weapons, both his sword and the shield dissolved in a rush of black fog.

Instead of racing toward Zander, however, he bolted toward Quinn.

Her head snapped toward him, and she swung her sword at his neck with her left hand. Despite the perfect aim, he leaned backward and slid the last few feet toward her. With his momentum, he kicked out her legs. She collapsed to the ground beside him, and he wrapped his left arm around her neck.

With his new captive pinned to his chest, he jumped to his feet and dragged her with him. She barely weighed anything, even as she clawed at his forearm. Her nails drew blood, but he blocked out the pain and summoned a blackfire sword. The blade pressed against her side, and its dark fire singed her clothes.

Quinn had become his shield against her own brother.

Zander paused, *Valor* still in his hand even as his sister's great Firesword lay on the ground between them. The warrior's shoulders relaxed, and he laughed.

Despite the dire situation, Connor raised one eyebrow in surprise.

The Starling warrior gestured at his sister with the golden Firesword in his hand. "Honestly, Wraithblade, I'm disappointed. Do you think I care if she dies?"

"You bastard!" Quinn fought against Connor's grip, even more furious than before. A fresh ripple of agony shot through the phantom injury in his chest as he barely kept her contained.

Zander's smile faded. He scowled at her, the rest of the burning field forgotten in their moment of shared hatred. "Which of us is the bastard, Quinn?"

Still pinned to Connor's chest, she seethed and let out a string of curses obscene enough to make even a sailor blush with shame.

"Well," Murdoc muttered quietly from somewhere behind them. "I certainly wasn't expecting that."

Connor's bicep flexed as he fought to keep her contained, and the lingering pain in his chest flared again. He grimaced and tightened his hold around her neck as his blackfire sword pressed harder against her side.

"Stop moving," he snapped, trying to figure out how he could salvage this.

She stilled, but her nails only dug deeper into his forearm as she glared at her brother.

In a blur of pale skin and dark metal, Zander threw more darts—this time at Quinn.

Out of reflex, Connor summoned his shield to protect them both. The arrowheads clinked against the metal, and Quinn stilled with surprise.

"I guess he truly doesn't care if you die," Connor muttered to her.

She said something, but the words slurred together as his world tilted. The air around him thickened, and his vision blurred.

No.

Not now.

The sky swirled into the ash-covered grass, and his stomach churned as the wraith once again took over his sight. In mere moments, the smoky haze of the burning meadow became the cool blue glow of the twin moons as they illuminated a vast stretch of the Decay.

Glowing eyes stared into his very soul.

The silver blightwolf that had nearly killed him once already stood before him. It growled as the hazy silhouettes of four dozen other wolves fidgeted in the shadows behind it. The pack towered over the withered trees around them, and several yipped in the cold night.

"You will move." The alpha's harsh whisper slithered through his ear. "We claim the Starling man. He has killed two of my pack. Hunted our brothers and sisters. He dies tonight."

Without you here to speak for me, I cannot hold them off for long, the wraith warned. *I hate to admit it, but you were right. They are ravenous. Furious. They will eat you all.*

Something landed hard in Connor's gut. He groaned and fell. His palms hit the dirt, and his shield dispersed in a cloud of black fog. His lungs ached from the thickening smoke and from whatever had just hit him in the stomach.

Quinn rolled away. In a flawless motion, she grabbed her enchanted blade off the ground with her left hand and jumped to her feet. Though her right arm still hung limply at her side, her Firesword erupted in flames. A smoky haze swept through the forest behind her, thicker than ever before.

"Murdoc!" Connor shouted above the growing roar of the wildfire. "Get to high ground!"

"But the high ground is on fire!" the former Blackguard shouted back.

He tried to answer, but smoke caught in his lungs. He coughed, trying to clear his head.

Out of the corner of his eye, Zander charged.

Fueled by instinct and intuition, Connor summoned a blackfire blade into his hand. The swords met with a resounding clang. Zander glared down at him as the man pressed his weight into their crossed blades.

"Just surrender, damn you," he seethed.

Quinn grunted with effort from somewhere out of view. Familiar black smoke billowed across the field, blocking what little Connor could see of the charred meadow.

Kill him, the wraith demanded. *The Blackguard and I will keep the other Starling at bay.*

With one of his blackfire blades locked against Zander's Firesword, Connor summoned the other into his empty palm and dragged it across the Starling's forearm. The man cursed and stumbled backward as blood poured from the wound.

Both of them struggled to breathe, their chests heaving as the smoke thickened around them. While Connor pushed himself to his feet, Zander reached into his pocket and pulled out a shattered helm similar to the one Quinn's tiger wore. The spellgust stone in it glimmered in the light of the bonfire. The Lightseer ripped off a carrot stuck to the other side of the spellgust gem, revealing two spikes in the metal.

Whatever the man wanted to do with something like that, it wouldn't end well.

With his Firesword in one hand and the broken helm in the other, Zander circled. Connor summoned his shield, and he gripped the blackfire blade in his right hand even tighter. He eyed the Bloodbane dagger in its sheath at Zander's waist.

All he had to do was grab it. If he got close enough, he'd also be able to stab Zander with it, and this would be over.

But how? he wondered.

Zander had his darts, but Connor couldn't throw his shield or blackfire blades. The moment they left his hands, they disappeared. He had daggers hidden in sheaths across his body, but Zander moved too quickly. Before he could even reach one, Zander would attack.

He rolled out his shoulders, trying to think of a plan as they circled each other. The crossed sheaths strapped to his back resisted the movement, and the familiar weight of his silver swords gave him an idea.

Since he'd gotten the blackfire blades, he'd barely had a use for them. In fact, Zander hadn't so much as glanced at them thus far.

It was worth a try.

As quickly as he could manage, he dismissed the blackfire blade in his right hand and grabbed one of the silver swords from his back. Just like the darts he used to throw in the taverns when he hustled drunk idiots, he threw it with perfect aim.

It sailed toward Zander's face, but he already knew the man would duck out of the way.

Zander leaned aside, and his gaze followed the silver blade as it sliced through the air inches from his face.

It was all the distraction Connor had needed.

He charged the Starling warrior and rammed his shield against Zander's chest. The soldier swung his sword, but it was too late.

Connor's empty hand wrapped around the dagger's hilt, and he wrenched it from its sheath. In a fluid movement, he drove the cursed blade into Zander's side.

The Starling screamed with agony. Sparks raced across his arms, and the tendons in his neck tightened. He grabbed Connor's shoulders, and the sparks brightened.

They tumbled to the ground, and Connor rolled out of the man's grip. As the Lightseer struggled to stand, Connor drove the dagger into Zander's shoulder as well.

Zander let out another agonized scream. His nose flared as he fought through the pain, and he slammed his boot against Connor's jaw.

Connor's head snapped back from the blow, and he rolled across the dirt. Flashes of red mingled with the mind-numbing pain splintering through his head. Though the shield disappeared from his hand, he managed to keep his hold on the dagger.

He skidded to a stop. The phantom injury in his chest flared again. He gritted his teeth and pressed his sweaty forehead against the dirt.

"Get up," he growled to himself.

Teetering, barely able to move, Connor pushed himself onto one knee and leaned his elbow against his thigh for balance. His fingers tightened around the glowing Bloodbane dagger in his right hand.

After everything he'd endured to get it, not even the fires of hell could've taken it from him now.

Barely ten feet away, Zander pressed his palms against the wounds. Though he'd somehow managed to stand, his shoulders slumped, and he grimaced with pain. He glared at Connor with all the hatred and fury of the Fates themselves. He tried to speak, but he merely sputtered slurred nonsense.

Connor nodded. "It hurts, doesn't it?"

"You filthy peasant." Zander groaned and swayed, barely able to stand upright.

"You came here to kill me. Don't expect me to show you any mercy."

He had the Bloodbane dagger, but this wasn't over. He had to kill Zander before the blightwolves arrived, or he risked the man escaping.

Facing Zander had been hard enough. He didn't want to face a Lightseer army, too.

He summoned a blackfire blade in his empty hand and staggered to his feet. Zander grabbed his Firesword with bloodstained fingers.

Grit and glory, to the bitter end—a motto they both seemed to share.

Connor swung at Zander's head, but the Starling blocked the blow. Even though the Lightseer held *Valor* aloft, its enchanted flames flickered and died.

Before either of them could lift their weapons to strike again, growls permeated the forest. Dozens of snarls rumbled through the night. Connor looked at Sophia's ball of roots in the center of the field, hoping it would be enough to protect her.

"Murdoc!" he shouted.

"I'm safe! Get the hell out of there!"

The thunder of a stampede reverberated through the smog.

In unison, he and Zander looked at the sheet of gray smoke that hid the approaching danger. The Starling man staggered backward and sheathed his Firesword. He stumbled, barely able to stand, and he kept Connor's eye as he walked into the line of fire.

Right into the path of the wolves.

Baffled, Connor studied the fool's face. "What the hell are you doing?"

"You'll see." Though blood poured from his broken nose, Zander smirked.

No.

Even if a blightwolf sank its teeth into this man's neck and dragged him off, Connor refused to let Zander leave the meadow alive.

He dismissed the blackfire blade in his palm and grabbed a short knife from a sheath on his belt. As Zander stood taller, one hand pressed against the worst of his injuries, Connor threw it right at the man's heart.

A silver blur tore through the meadow, nothing but a metallic streak of teeth and fur. It grabbed Zander's injured shoulder. The man let out a garbled yell of agony, and they were gone.

Connor's knife passed through the air where Zander had stood moments before, and it sank into the dirt.

He'd failed, and now he was going to die.

Dozens of silhouettes raced by, backlit by the wildfire engulfing the young forest outside Death's Door. Snarls and yips pierced the night as the stampede continued. Connor braced himself, knowing one would sink its teeth into him.

Any second now.

He gripped the Bloodbane dagger tightly, ready for the battle to continue.

A raucous howl mingled with the growls and barks as the blightwolves charged through the torched field. One by one, the others joined in the piercing cry.

The thunderous scream rocked Connor to the core.

He braced himself. Any minute now.

Slowly, the rumble faded. The howl became a distant moan. As the seconds passed, their chilling screams withered into the air, dwarfed by the crackle of the burning forest and the ringing in Connor's ears.

Shoulders still squared, he scanned the blazing field around him. Aside from Sophia wrapped tightly in her ball of roots, he stood alone in the scorched meadow. Smoke billowed through the air from the torched canopy, casting a murky haze across the Decay.

A massive silhouette appeared in the smoke. A dark head emerged from the smog, its glowing eyes a sharp contrast to its black fur. The blightwolf snarled, its snout creasing as it approached.

Connor dug his heels into the ash-covered dirt and took a settling breath, prepared for the worst.

"We will spare the rest of you," the wolf growled, its voice a deeper pitch than the alpha's. "Unless you contest our claim."

His fingernails dug into the hilt of the dagger, ready to strike the moment the creature dared to bare its teeth. "Your claim to what?"

"We claim the Starling man."

You can't have him, Connor wanted to say. *That bastard is mine.*

Zander had chosen the blightwolves over him, and that meant the Lightseer had a plan. Connor had seen it in the warrior's eyes. Unafraid. Unfaltering. If he didn't end this tonight, Zander would be back, and he'd return with a vengeance.

When should a man stand his ground? Beck Arbor had asked all those years ago. *Do you know?*

Connor gritted his teeth and let out a frustrated sigh. "He's all yours."

"A wise choice," the wolf growled.

It howled into the air, and the ground trembled under the shattering wail. In the distance, dozens of cries answered. The blightwolf darted off into the smoke, and just like that, it was gone.

As the wildfire crackled around him, his ears rang in the silence.

Connor studied the Bloodbane dagger in his hand. Enchanted with magic powerful enough to kill the undead, it glowed brilliantly green in his palm. Yes, he'd gotten what they'd come for, but he hadn't truly won.

Someone had crafted this blade for Zander, and that person could probably make another.

He'd witnessed enough of the blightwolves' fury in the forest to assume the man was dead, but fighting Zander had been like fighting a demigod. As much as he wanted to believe the wolves could finish him off, Connor knew better than to assume he had one less enemy.

After all, the Ancient Woods had a strange way of killing a man's hope.

CHAPTER SIXTY-NINE
CONNOR

Smoke billowed from the wildfire burning away the only life in the Decay. It coiled into the sky, and its murky haze thickened in the charred meadow. It scorched Connor's lungs, and he coughed to clear his airway.

His grip instinctively tightened around the Bloodbane dagger in his palm as it glowed with all the power and light of a Rift. How strange to think something so small had caused him and the wraith so much agony.

"Captain!" Murdoc shouted over the roar of the fire. "Connor, where the hell are you?"

"Stay there!" he ordered.

They still had one more Starling to kill.

Since he didn't have a sheath for the Bloodbane dagger, he needed to be careful. He couldn't risk Quinn taking it from him now that he'd finally stolen it, but he wasn't going to shove it in a loose pocket and risk stabbing himself.

He coughed again as he stumbled through the smoke toward Murdoc's voice. In the blinding haze, only thirty yards were visible at a time. He swatted at the cloudy air, and the smoke churned with each bat of his hand.

Familiar black fog rolled through the gray haze, and he angled toward it. Moments later, the wraith's form appeared in the smoke. With his back turned, the ghoul's sword rested against Quinn's neck. She glared up at him, her back pinned to one of the only trees not currently on fire.

As calm and collected as ever, the Starling warrior held her Firesword to the side. Flames rolled along the blade, still primed and ready to strike. Her eyes darted toward him as he approached.

Movement in the branches above Quinn caught his eye, and Murdoc peered through a break in the tree's leaves. "Captain! Thank the Fates."

The former Blackguard jumped to the ground, and a plume of ash wafted into the air from under his feet. He coughed and swatted at the cloud to clear it.

"Get Sophia out of there," Connor ordered with a nod behind him. "We need to heal her and figure out what poisoned her. While you're over there, see if you can find my silver sword, too."

"On it." Murdoc saluted and darted off into the smoke. It stirred and swallowed him as the thud of his footsteps faded.

With that handled, Connor shifted his focus to Quinn. He studied her stance as he tried to guess her next move. The last time he'd thought he had her trapped and ready to surrender, she had merely used the moment to catch her breath.

He stood beside the wraith and crossed his arms, unsure of what to do with her. "I warned you that I'd kill you the next time we fought."

"You did." Her gaze didn't waver. She didn't even flinch.

Interesting.

He gestured to the Firesword in her hand. "Did you name yours, too?"

"*Aurora.*"

"Hmm."

Orange light glinted off the polished hilt as she held it, and her hazel eyes narrowed with suspicion. Her back arched, but she otherwise remained motionless.

A wise move.

"Let me guess." He studied her features. "You're here to kill me, too?"

She shook her head, but the wraith's blade dug deeper into her neck as she moved. Though it didn't break the skin, her gaze darted to the ghoul, and she froze in place. "My mission was always to arrest you. I had strict orders to bring you in alive."

"Had?" He tilted his head skeptically. "Past tense?"

Her eyes shifted back to him, but she didn't reply.

To kill her or not? Such a difficult choice. With his free hand, the ghoul scratched absently at the long crack on his exposed skull.

Connor only killed if the situation called for it. Besides, they needed a Starling or a member of the Lightseer Chamber to get into Aeron's Tomb. Unless she posed a threat to him or his team, it made the most sense to keep her alive.

Whether she lived or died depended on what she did next.

His grip on the dagger tightened. "The last time I thought I had you cornered, you wriggled out of it. What are you going to do now?"

For a moment, no one spoke. They stood there as the wildfire raged on, and she watched him with an expression he couldn't read.

With an irritated sigh, she stabbed her Firesword into the dirt at her feet and lifted her palms into the air. "I surrender, Wraithblade."

Cool. Calm. Collected. Unfazed by the phantom's sword at her throat.

A roar cut through the smoke, and Connor glared over his shoulder into the haze. Murdoc shouted obscenities, and the swish of steel through the air mingled with a vicious snarl. Connor summoned his blackfire blade into one palm, ready to defend his team.

"Blaze!" Quinn shouted into the smoke. "Stand down!"

The roar ended abruptly, and an irritated snarl followed.

"Hey!" Quinn shouted, frowning. "I mean it!"

The snarl faded into a grumble, and a silhouette prowled toward them through the haze. Connor raised his blade, but as the tiger appeared, it lowered its head and slunk over to Quinn. It sat with an angry thump and pinned its ears to its head as it glared at the wraith.

"Thank you!" Murdoc shouted from the haze. The dull thud of a sword slicing into wood echoed through the night.

With the threat neutralized, Connor dismissed the blackfire blade. "Tell me what's in those darts that hit Sophia."

"They're experimental." Quinn kept her hands in the air as she answered. "Zander wasn't permitted to use them because they're not cleared for battle yet, so I can't say for certain if he tinkered with them. If he didn't change the formula, they should be nothing more than a fast-acting Dwelldaze draught. She'll wake up in a few hours with a headache, but she'll be fine."

"For your sake, you'd better be right."

Quinn lifted her chin in defiance, but she didn't reply.

Another silhouette approached them from the haze, and Murdoc appeared from the fog with Sophia draped over his arms. The smoke around them thickened, and the Blackguard coughed violently into his shoulder, away from her face.

Without taking his eye off Quinn, Connor turned his empty palm upward and took a step toward Murdoc. "Do you have your Bluntmar chain?"

"Yes, Captain." The Blackguard knelt and set the unconscious Sophia on the ashy ground. Soot smudged against her cheek as he tugged the chain from his pocket and set it in Connor's open palm.

Connor wrapped the chain around Quinn's wrists. The second the metal touched her skin, the color rushed from her face. Her shoulders slouched as the chain cut off access to her magic. An almost inaudible moan escaped her, and her fingers twitched as Connor wrapped the chain tighter.

"We'll get you some proper cuffs or a collar as soon as Sophia wakes up," he promised with a final tug on the chains. "Wraith, take us to the gate."

With pleasure.

He grabbed her shoulder, and the wraith lowered its blade as Connor pushed her ahead of him. She let him guide her through the haze, and her vougel followed close behind. The wraith darted ahead of them, and Murdoc lifted Sophia once more into his arms.

They trudged through the smog and passed the fallen log where Zander had waited for them. With each step closer to the mountains, the air cleared a little more.

A gust swept across the torched meadow, ushering away the smoke. The towering black stone of Death's Door loomed above them, as tall as the cliffs on either side. In the dark sky above, Saldia's twin moons cast their light across the Decay.

The wraith set his bony palm against the dark gem-like stone. With his touch, ribbons of green light snaked through the rock. Locks and gears appeared in the light, brief and fleeting, as the wraith's magic worked its way up the length of the door.

There are traps along the way, the Wraith King warned. *We must tread carefully. If you would like to push the Starling woman or her blasted tiger into one, simply let me know.*

Connor shook his head. "Let's minimize the death."

Something massive unlatched within the gate, and the click boomed like thunder through the Decay. The dual gates of Death's Door creaked open to reveal a channel through the mountains. Though moonlight seeped into the narrow passage, it couldn't pierce the black void.

On the ground by the door, a skeleton lay on the rocky terrain, half-emerged in the shadow and frozen in its moment of death. Its arm reached for the door, its bony fingers inches from freedom.

Home, the wraith said, a wistful hint to his voice.

"Yeah," Connor said as he led the way into the darkness. "We're home."

CHAPTER SEVENTY
ZANDER

Pain cascaded through Zander's body. The Bloodbane dagger's poison pumped through his blood. His skull ached. His heart struggled to beat. Every breath clawed against his throat. Blood pooled in his mouth. The stab wounds in his side and shoulder seared. He jostled, playing dead as the blightwolf bit down harder. Its teeth pierced the bone in his shoulder, and he barely stifled an agonized yell.

The stench of rotting meat rolled over his face with each of the blightwolf's huffing breaths. He gagged. His legs dragged along the dirt as the wildfire receded into the distance. Behind the silver wolf, dozens more silhouettes stampeded through the darkness. Their paws thundered over the cracked ground.

This was a desperate plan, but it had to work. If it didn't, he'd be a dead man.

The silver blightwolf darted past the withered trees in the heart of the Decay. His back struck a rotted log, and the wood splintered from the force. A jolt of pain shot down his spine, adding to his agony. A fresh wave of anguish blistered through his two Bloodbane injuries, and he let out a string of curses.

Enough of this nonsense. They were far enough away from the Wraithblade that he didn't have to feign death anymore.

With his injured shoulder in the silver wolf's mouth, he summoned fire into his other hand and grimaced with effort as he struck the beast's face. He smacked his palm against its metallic fur and dug his fingers into its eye.

It yelped and crashed into the cracked dirt. Zander tumbled across the ground, kicking up dirt as he rolled. The wolf collapsed into a rotting tree, and splinters soared into the air. The blightwolves growled. A cloud of dust rolled across his feet as the other wolves slowed and circled in the low light of the moons.

The silver wolf—the one he'd always assumed to be their alpha—snarled and shook its head. The flame burning away at its fur blurred through the night, creating orange streaks in the darkness as the creature tried to put out the fire.

The others yipped and snarled as they closed in. One charged, and Zander channeled a blast of lightning through his good hand. The splinter of light arched wildly through the air, and a crack of thunder deafened the valley around him. Feral and untamed, his magic flared with all the unbridled chaos of a storm. His head throbbed, foggy from the incessant ripples of pain, and that would throw off his aim until he healed.

He didn't care. For his plan to work, he only needed one of the wolves alive.

His lightning crashed into the blightwolf. Its eyes glowed white, and the charred stench of cooked meat coiled through the air. As the blast of light faded, the beast collapsed in a heap. Smoke spiraled off its corpse.

The alpha snarled, the flame on its face finally out. It bared its teeth and lowered its head, stalking closer. The other blightwolves circled, giving their leader space to make the kill.

A foolish move.

From his pocket, Zander pulled out the broken helm he'd meant to use on the Wraithblade.

Perhaps this would work out for the better.

The silver beast charged, and Zander summoned a gust of air with his battered and torn right hand. His body screamed in protest, and he gritted his teeth to numb himself to the pain. As blood dripped down his arm, he groaned with the sheer effort it took to channel the southern wind.

For whatever reason, it always fought him—but in the end, he always won.

His gust nailed the silver blightwolf hard in the side with the force of a hurricane. The beast fell, and the ground shook. The alpha slid across the dirt, and Zander ran toward it. Though he limped from his injuries, slower than he usually would've been, he pushed through the pain.

A Starling never quit.

As he neared, the blightwolf's claws ripped at the air. He ducked backward, narrowly avoiding a claw to the eye, and the Bloodbane injuries rattled his bones. His muscles ached, as if unseen hands were ripping apart the open wounds, and he stifled a pained yell as he tried to focus on his task.

Still laying on its side, the blightwolf snapped at him. Though he ordinarily would've ducked out of the way, his body protested every movement. He needed to end this fight quickly, or he risked making a stupid mistake that would cost him his life.

He summoned a wave of fire in his good hand and grabbed its snout. Fire raged again across its face, and it yelped in agony as smoke spiraled into the air. It rolled onto its back and slipped out of his grip as it snapped blindly at the sky.

As its teeth gnashed at anything that came close, Zander inched around the blightwolf until he had a clear sightline to its forehead. His body stung. His world tilted. His legs threatened to give out on him, but he refused to let the peasant win.

With a furious grimace, Zander channeled every ounce of his augmented strength into his hand. He slammed the shattered helm into the beast's forehead. The spikes drove into the blightwolf's skull, and the beast howled with pain.

He needed the barbs to remain in its head until the enchantment took effect. If the beast shook it off before then, Zander would die in the Decay.

One of the beast's claws nailed him hard in the chest. It kicked the air out of him, and he flew backward. His ruined shoulder hit the dirt, and his world flashed white as the pain shattered him. He arched his back as the anguish swallowed him whole. He couldn't see. His world blurred. The agony ripped him apart from inside as the Bloodbane wounds burned with all the fury and fires of the afterlife.

On your feet, his father had always said. *Be a man. Face the pain and laugh at it.*

Zander huffed, sucking in breath after strangled breath as he forced himself to his feet. He staggered blindly through the wasteland until the ground evened out again.

The shrill ringing in his ears faded, and his vision slowly returned. The blightwolves circled him, snarling as their gazes swept from him to the silver wolf and back.

Trying to figure out what to do. Trying to figure out whether to strike or obey the alpha and wait.

The silver wolf shook its head, snarling as it clawed at the helm embedded in its skull. It bucked and rolled, fighting the enchantments already swirling through its blood.

The panicked yips around Zander became a howl. When the alpha didn't return the cry, four of the blightwolves charged at once.

Damn it.

His injured arm hung limply at his side, but he managed to channel another blast of frantic lightning at them. The magic snaked through him, and his arm shook from the sheer effort it took to contain the anarchy of a storm.

Three of the blightwolves skidded to a stop. Their paws kicked up dust as a branch of the wild lightning crashed against the cracked dirt in front of them.

The fourth, however, effortlessly darted around it. With its ears pinned to its head, it bared its teeth and pounced.

Zander unleashed a torrent of fire at it. The flames billowed from the air in front of his fingertips, but the blightwolf sailed through the blaze. The wolf's snarling face emerged through the billowing plume as the ends of its fur glowed orange.

So full of hate, it couldn't even feel itself burn.

Its teeth sank into Zander's good shoulder. His mind snapped, threatening to shut off from the sheer pain he'd endured tonight.

The wolf tossed him across the field. Hot blood poured down his arm, and he landed with a dull thud on the dirt. He skidded across the cracked ground, kicking up a cloud of dust with each lifeless tumble.

The blightwolves yipped in victory, their voices echoing over the wasteland.

When he finally slid to a stop, it took every ounce of his strength to simply breathe. His lungs threatened to quit as he bled onto the dry dirt. Every inch of his body begged him to give up and just die.

He refused.

Though the world blurred around him, he leaned his weight onto his forearms and glared over at the silver blightwolf.

It growled and clawed at its forehead, still fighting the helm. It nipped blindly at the air, fierce and furious as it slowly lost its mind.

Not much longer left.

Zander spit out the blood pooling in his mouth and staggered to his feet. Pain cracked through him, eerily similar to all the times his father had unleashed hell on him in their training.

He pushed through. A Starling always persevered.

Inches from death and no longer caring what he took with him to the grave, he preemptively channeled lightning into the ground around him to keep the beasts at bay. Crashes of thunder split the air. Flashes of light froze each moment in time as the blightwolves circled.

His magic struck everything around him as he channeled his pain and rage into his attacks. Trees splintered. Wolves whimpered. He didn't aim because he didn't care what he hit.

As long as he lived, any collateral damage would suffice.

Lightning splintered through the air, merciless and violent. The light blinded him and froze the world around him in a haze of white.

Eventually, his legs gave out. He fell to one knee, exhausted. The last flashes of lightning splintered through the air like sparks off a campfire, but they faded into nothing.

In the aftermath, flames roared across several logs around him. A dozen smoking corpses lay on the caked earth. Coils of rot and smoke spiraled into the night, and he coughed to clear his battered lungs.

The blightwolves waited in the darkness beyond the meager firelight. They snarled, ears pinned to their skulls, heads low.

This time, however, they wisely kept their distance. It seemed they finally understood the strength of their opponent.

In the distance, beyond the carnage and smoking carcasses, the silver blightwolf staggered across the cracked dirt. Though it still shook its head and pawed at the helm, its half-hearted movements slowed with every step.

Finally, it stilled. With the golden helm still embedded in its skull, it lifted its massive head toward him. The green spellgust stone glowed brightly in the dark night, and the beast watched him with cloud-white eyes.

"Come," Zander ordered the magnificent beast.

The silver blightwolf stalked over to him and lowered its head to his. It stared down at him, each of its milky white eyes as big as his fist.

"Kneel," he commanded.

The blightwolf knelt before him, and Zander pushed himself to his feet. Though his body quaked with agony, he grabbed the silver fur with his bloodstained hands and hauled himself onto the beast's back.

The blightwolves around him snarled, but he didn't care. He owned them, now.

Zander reached into his pocket and pulled out his emergency Rectivane potion. The cracked vial leaked onto his hand, and he cursed under his breath. He popped off the cork, but the glass at the top half of the bottle shattered as its final support faded. The potent potion dripped over his fingers, and he lifted the broken vial to drink what little of the potion remained. Glass slid into his mouth, and he pushed it against his cheek to keep from swallowing it.

When he'd downed as much of the potion as he could, he spit out the glass and a bit of blood. The potion worked its magic through his body, and he groaned with relief as it got to work on the Bloodbane injuries. Hot ripples of magic snaked through him, and he craned his head back as he let out a shaky breath.

He'd wanted to do this from the moment the Bloodbane dagger had stabbed him, but his life had been on the line every second since. This was the first moment he had to finally breathe, and he relished it.

Without the entire vial, he would have scars. At least he wouldn't die, and at least he didn't have any serious wounds on his face. The only visible scars worth having were the ones he'd earned in a victory.

He looked down at the blightwolf beneath him—his new pet. Tonight hadn't been a triumph, but it hadn't been a total loss, either.

"Command your wolves to follow me," he ordered.

"I cannot," the blightwolf replied.

Zander flinched with surprise as the beast spoke, and he suppressed the impulse to draw the Firesword still mercifully strapped to his waist. As his heart rate settled, he glanced across the blightwolves gathered in the shadows beyond the burning logs. "Why not?"

"Our only law is that of respect." The blightwolf's raspy voice came out as a harsh growl. "Even if they respect me, they have no respect for you. As long as you control me, they will ignore everything I say."

Zander cursed under his breath, his plan ruined.

At least he had one of them.

"Fine. Can you swim?"

The great wolf nodded.

"Good. Take me to the northern edge of the Ancient Woods. I will guide you to Lunestone from there."

The silver blightwolf darted off into the night, and Zander kept low to the great beast's back as it barreled through the Decay. Wind snapped against his face, stinging his eyes with the creature's unparalleled speed.

The rumble of paws along the dirt chased after them, and he cast a wary glance over his battered shoulder as the stampede followed.

An interesting turn of events, but it changed very little.

Despite the Rectivane, Zander still needed to heal. As his new pet darted across the Decay, he silently fumed at his loss. Not only had the Wraithblade taken Slaybourne, but he'd stolen the Bloodbane dagger as well.

When he faced the Lightseer Chamber, he wouldn't be able to lie. Given his failures against such a significant opponent, he would be forced to drink a Hackamore before he gave his report.

If Zander was lucky, the Wraithblade had already killed Quinn. His father would be furious, of course, when he learned she had been left behind. Not even a blightwolf would ease the Lightseer Master General's rage at losing his beloved miracle child.

It didn't matter. In the end, this defeat only proved Zander had been right all along. His father should never have sent Quinn on this mission. From the start, Zander should've been dispatched to end the peasant before it could've ever gotten this out of control.

As he rode through the Decay on the blightwolf's back, he lost his last shred of respect for his father. Teagan's fury didn't scare him anymore. Nothing did.

A man needed a purpose, and Zander had his. In his lifetime, he would destroy every simmering soul in existence, once and for all—starting with the Wraithblade.

THE SOUTH WIND

As dawn broke across the northern border of the Ancient Woods, a towering silhouette darted into the open fields beyond the South Wind's domain.

Forty other blightwolves skidded to a stop at the woodland's edge as their alpha raced into the unknown. A lonesome howl rang through the air, long and mournful, but the silhouette ignored them.

Like so many others who visited the cursed forest, their leader had lost his way—and abandoned them to die.

CHAPTER SEVENTY-ONE
QUINN

In the whispers of daylight that tend to come in the seconds before a dawn, Quinn sat on a fallen column in the ruins outside of Slaybourne. Taken captive, just as she had intended.

A new Bluntmar collar pressed against her throat a little too tightly to be comfortable, but she resisted the urge to scratch at it. The necromancer must've done something dark to it, because this one didn't just block her magic.

The collar seemed to drain it.

It took more effort to sit upright than it should have. Her body ached from the fight, but at least she had regained full function in her arm. She flexed her fingers, still uncertain of what enchantment could've been on that ruffian's sword. Every muscle screamed in protest any time she moved, even when she simply adjusted in her seat. Her eyelids drooped. Sleep threatened to take her at any moment. Even breathing took effort.

These sensations reminded her too much of her brush with death by the withered tree outside of Bradford, but she had expected to be collared. She had come prepared, even if the slow drain of her magic had come as a surprise.

The Volt rested between her breasts, beside her Starling crest—hidden from sight and ready. No matter what the necromancer tried to do to Quinn's magic, and no matter what weapons or potions they took from her, they couldn't take that.

Isolated in a clearing with no view beyond a thick forest, Quinn waited.

The Wraithblade's necromancer kept watch from the shadows, probably eager for any excuse to kill her.

Blaze lay on the ground nearby, his ears pinned to his head. He wouldn't even look at her. His tail twitched as he growled, pouting in their defeat. He knew they could've won, and that she had given in.

"Don't be a sore loser," she chided.

His ear twitched at the sound of her voice, but he simply grumbled in reply.

The canopy swayed overhead, and the thick shadows between the trees blocked out everything. Normally, she would've listened to the silence and heard what no one else could hear, but the Bluntmar collar had blocked every single one of her augmentations.

This necromancer of his had talent.

With a sigh, she closed her eyes and listened to the woodland around her. Birds chirped. Insects hummed. Something rustled the nearby underbrush, and the Wraithblade had apparently gone in search of water he knew to be here.

Slaybourne was a haven. It didn't at all resemble the legends of a desolate wasteland, rotting away in a forgotten valley.

Yet again, the world had lied to her.

Which of us is the bastard, Quinn?

Unbidden and unwelcome, Zander's voice rattled in her brain. She sucked in a sharp breath through her teeth, but it didn't quell the surge of hatred that came with hearing his voice. Either he'd been messing with her and trying to throw her off her game, or he had finally revealed why he'd always hated her with such fervor.

Despite her fire-red hair, he'd chosen to believe she was somehow illegitimate.

To vent her anger, she snatched a rock off the ground and squeezed. Without her Strongman augmentation, though, the dark stone resisted her grip. Its jagged edges dug into her palm, scratching against the scars from the knife she had broken in her rage—intentional reminders of her father's betrayal, just in case she ever lost her way.

If the blightwolves had killed Zander, she wouldn't mourn his death. As she toyed with the Starling crest on the second chain around her neck, however, she knew better than to hope too hard.

Starlings weren't that easy to kill—not Zander, and certainly not her.

CONNOR

In the coming dawn, a flood of golden light broke across the inky stone of the Black Keep Mountains. The new day poured its sunshine over the crags and cliffs, glinting off the smooth rock as it sipped at the last few stars lingering in the sky. Clouds obscured the peaks, their fluff stained with the pink and orange of a spring morning.

Nestled in a verdant valley and surrounded on all sides by the steep cliffs, a city lay in ruin—much as Connor had suspected it would.

Slaybourne. He'd finally reached it.

As he stood alone on a rocky overlook at the farthest end of the valley from Death's Door, he surveyed the land below. Endless mountains circled the stretch of fields and forests on all sides, while boulders and blocks of what were once walls littered the patchy woodland.

In the distance, a towering citadel loomed over the vale like a grim specter of crumbling black stone. By some miracle, the primary fortress had remained relatively intact all these centuries later, though most of the other structures had rotted away. In the rubble, the patchwork foundations of a metropolis remained, ready to be rebuilt.

Behind him, the soft trickle of lake water lapping against the shoreline mingled with a gentle breeze through the leaves of a solitary old maple. It grew alone on the shore, the only tree for a hundred yards. He set his hand against the ancient bark and stared out across the water as a school of fish splashed along the surface of the lake.

Plenty of game to hunt. Ample water. A fortress, locked away behind a gate only he could open. A rediscovered haven, once lost to the world—

and his new fortress.

Birdsong mingled with the mellow wind through the maple tree, and a streak of yellow blurred through the air over the water. A sparrow landed on the branch above him, unbothered by his presence. It chirped and sang into the morning light as its head hummed with the brilliant glow of the sun. The vibrant colors of its body faded from yellow to green, and its long tail ended with a bead of light at the tip of each feather. Its head tilted to the side as it studied him, and moments later, it darted off into the valley to continue with its day.

Somehow, this place had changed its creatures. No bird he'd ever seen in his life glowed like that—as if with the power of spellgust itself.

He knelt at the lakeshore and slipped his hand beneath the crystal-clear water. Brilliant blue and white stones rested on the lakebed, and the muted reflection of the clouds above rolled along the surface. The edges of his fingers distorted beneath the ripples as the icy water rolled over his palm, and he gathered a bit of it to drink.

It flowed through him like a potion, bright and refreshing.

He rested his elbows on his thighs as he squatted by the magnificent lake. No wonder this city could've survived a siege—it had everything. Its own water supply. Its own ecosystem. Thus far, they had discovered several horned rabbits and a herd of fanged deer with stripes and tails unlike anything he'd ever seen. Instead of running, one of the bucks had wandered over to him and sniffed his shirt.

Unafraid. No natural predators. A new breed, completely isolated in a valley the world had forgotten.

He ran the back of his hand over his brow to wipe away the sweat from his hour-long hike. The sky brightened, and the sunshine glinted off a pile of fist-sized stones deeper in the lake. Flecks of gold shimmered in the otherwise black rock, their surfaces as smooth and polished as a gem.

Perfect.

Connor rolled up his sleeve and chose three of the polished rocks. Droplets of water rolled off his arm as he set the three stones side by side on the shore and arranged them so that they faced the sun.

His family had never left Kirkwall, but they would've liked it here.

All those years ago, he'd thought his purpose and drive had died with them. A dead warlord, a dishonored scoundrel, a banished crime lord's niece, and a grieving family isolated in a cursed forest had, by some miracle, rekindled it.

A puff of black fog blipped to life in the center of the lake, and dark smoke rolled across the pristine surface as the cloud grew. Connor waited for the inevitable specter to appear from the darkness.

Sure enough, a familiar cloaked ghoul strode from the smoke. With his hands clasped behind his back, the dead king stared out over the valley.

You will need to attract subjects to restart the farms. Much of what I built is overrun and rotted, so you will need carpenters to rebuild.

"If only we knew one of those." Connor smirked, still watching the natural spring as sunbeams glinted off the rippling water.

The Finns were going to love it here.

The wraith ignored him. *There are hundreds of miles of catacombs to excavate. I stored most of my fortune and enchantments below ground. I confess to be most disappointed that more of the citadel did not survive. If the builders were still alive today, I would execute them as punishment.*

Connor laughed and pushed himself to his feet as he stood beside the ghoul. Evidently, the dead didn't know how to rest.

The wraith gestured to the Black Keep peaks around them. *There is more gold and spellgust in these mountains than a man can spend in his life. It will take time to recover, but it is ours to rebuild.*

Connor stared out over the valley, and his smile fell. Somewhere by the citadel, Sophia guarded their new captive while Murdoc collected whatever food he could find. True to Quinn's word, the necromancer had woken with a terrible headache, but at least she had survived.

"That Starling woman will either be a blessing or a curse. Maybe both."

She surrendered with intention, the wraith agreed. *Given what we witnessed in the field outside of Bradford, she still had plenty of fight left in her before she gave up her sword.*

"I know." Connor rubbed his jaw, irritated with himself that he hadn't figured out her plan yet. "In the meantime, she's cuffed and blocked by the Bluntmar, which we know worked on her before."

Will you kill her?

"If she gives me a reason to."

The old ghost groaned with frustration. *There is still so much work to do to make you into the fearsome warlord you can become. We must begin your advanced training at once.*

Connor chuckled and rubbed his tired eyes, not even bothering to reply. Instead, he drank in Slaybourne, the paradise he'd never expected to find beyond Death's Door. If he looked beyond the skeletons littered across the valley from whatever had happened the night the Wraith King died, this place had everything he needed.

His own little kingdom of ruin.

His father—and Sir Beck—would've been proud.

CHAPTER SEVENTY-TWO
OTMUND

Vile things croaked in the darkness as Otmund tapped his heels against his horse. Torchlight cast a dim orange glow across the rippling swamp water on either side of him, and a brown tint obscured the murky depths. He didn't want to know what creatures made the incessant chorus of growls and moans that always rolled through this swamp. Instead, he focused on the submerged wooden path before him.

His horse trudged through the water, its hooves splashing with each step as they followed the raised trail through the depths of the marsh. The helm around his mount's forehead glinted in the low light, and the beast's eyes fogged over from the Bridletame enchantment.

Towering trees bent over them and blocked out the night sky, while moss dangled from nearly every branch. Every breath of the bog's air clawed at his throat as the thick humidity practically strangled him.

Behind Otmund, the lone guard he had brought along lifted their single torch. The oppressive darkness swallowed most of the amber light. The soldier shifted uncomfortably in his saddle, and the man's horse snorted nervously. A twig cracked from somewhere in the muck, and the guard cursed under his breath as his head snapped toward the noise.

The weight of eyes on Otmund's neck sent a shudder down his spine. He kept his gaze focused on the wide bog ahead of him as they neared their destination. As long as he stayed on the path and out of the swamp itself, he would be fine.

Dark things lurked in the depths. Things Otmund never wanted to meet.

The path rounded a bend in the damp forest. In the center of the swamp, a massive tree loomed before them, its branches long dead. He craned his neck at the night sky visible through the break in the bog's canopy above the towering tree, but he couldn't see the moons from here.

They never seemed to shine on Nethervale.

The narrow path ended at a gnarled old root spiraling from the tree. Three long gouges in the bark betrayed the rotted wood underneath, as black as the sky.

"My lord." The soldier pulled his horse beside Otmund's. "Whatever are we doing out here? What is it you need to find, sir?"

Otmund frowned at the commoner's audacity to speak so candidly, but they were still used to his father's rule. His father had always told him to honor the warriors protecting their home, but they were bound by their own foolish sense of duty and had to do it anyway. It had never mattered to Otmund if they were content or not, and he'd never even bothered to learn this man's name.

He ignored the soldier and pulled on the horse's reins. As they stopped before the tree, a deadly silent hush rolled through the forest. The croak of the bog frogs faded, and the howling screams of everything else died in the same breath. Moss dripped from the branches above like wax from a candle, as still and immobile as a dead man's chest.

Nothing in the marsh dared to move as the bog studied the intruders. There were protocols to follow, and Otmund didn't have much time before the vile things he so loathed grew impatient.

"I come bearing gifts," he shouted into the canopy.

The soldier stuttered with fear. "My lord? What—"

The deep water rippled, and Otmund faced the tree. Such was the rule—never watch.

He could only listen.

The water sloshed. The guard's horse nickered and snorted, its hooves splashing through the shallows as its rider tried in vain to shush it. A screech ripped through the swamp, the creature's roar hollow and deep, and the water frothed

"My lord!" the soldier shouted. "We must leave! Now!"

In Otmund's periphery, the horse backed up out of his line of sight. As it retreated, a talon as long as a flagpole shot from the bayou's depths. Though Otmund's horse remained immobile, stupefied into silence by its enchanted helm, the soldier's horse let out a panicked scream.

The guard yelled obscenities, but his voice ended abruptly with the meaty squish of bone impaling flesh. The torch plunged into the water. Its flames dissolving with a hiss, and the bog's shadows swallowed the meager orange light. Hooves splashed through the swamp as the guard's horse bolted, and the leather straps on its saddle flapped against an empty seat.

The soldier gasped for air as he tried to form words, but a heavy splash silenced them. Waves rolled over his mount's already drenched hooves as the spellbound beast stood there, patiently awaiting its next command.

With an impatient sigh, Otmund waited in the darkness.

A thunderous crack sliced through the air, and a jagged line of light cut down the middle of the dead trunk before him. Nethervale's secret doors opened on their hidden hinges, appeased by the sacrifice he'd brought for the monsters lurking beneath its roots.

Their pets, he assumed.

The door opened to a dark void. A cobblestone tunnel angled down into the depths of the swamp, but he didn't move. In the silence that followed, a few of the frogs croaked again. Seconds later, the growls and screech of the swamp returned, as though nothing dastardly had happened at all.

Along the tunnel's pitch-black walls, a sconce flared to life. Its orange and yellow flames licked at the air, casting a bright glow across the stone floor. Moments later, another sconce farther down the hall erupted with fire—his guide through the labyrinth of corridors.

He tapped his heels against his horse's side, and they rode into the fortress together.

The tunnel angled downward, steep enough that the beast had to take slow and cautious steps along the slick stone. The wet clomp of its hooves against the floor echoed through the empty hall, and Otmund craned his ear to listen for approaching necromancers.

Few could've detected one, of course, but he listened nonetheless.

A fog of dread clung to him, weighing on him with the gravity of what he was about to do. Quinn's deadline had come and gone, yet the girl hadn't returned. No notice. No word. In all her years as a Lightseer, she had never once missed her deadline. Zander, despite his power and experience, had yet to return from his mission into the Decay.

And yet, tales of the legendary Shade continued.

It seemed, by some cruel twist of fate, that the peasant had somehow bested two of the greatest warriors on the continent. His puppets had failed him. One by one, their strings broke, and his sway over Saldia lessened. Now, he needed insurance in the likely event the Wraithblade came for him next.

The trail of sconces ended in a door flanked on both sides by torches. Simple iron plates framed the wooden planks, and two nondescript iron rings served as the handles. Nethervale had never been one for creature comforts. He steeled himself for what lay ahead.

He dismounted and left his steed in the hall. With a settling breath, he straightened his shoulders and threw open the doors.

A chandelier hung in the center of the room, its candles flickering as he entered. Shadows obscured the walls, giving the room a sense of eternity, like a void about to swallow him whole. Beneath the light, a blonde wearing dark riding pants and a green blouse leaned over a massive map of the land he wanted to conquer.

A map he had always wanted to steal.

All of Saldia, from Wildefaire to Oakenglen and beyond, hummed with life in miniature. Water flowed down the Lucent River from Lunestone to the sea as wind rippled through the tiny trees. Oakenglen sat on its hill by the lake, and the mountains of their continent stretched to the edges of the table.

The woman rested the heels of her palms against the edge of the map and lifted her chin as he slammed the doors behind him. Her green eyes narrowed as a lock of her hair fell into her face, obscuring the scar across her eye.

Nyx Osana—the most terrifying woman in Saldia, and the only one immune to his charm.

"You have some nerve." Her deep voice came out like a growl.

From the shadows behind her, a man with white hair and ice-blue eyes stepped into the light. The hilt of a sword protruded from his back, and he reached for it as his glare landed on Otmund.

"Reaver." Otmund greeted Nyx's second in command with a curt nod.

Reaver Solomon didn't answer. He never did.

"Pleasantries aside," Otmund said, turning to Nyx. "I need an army, and I need it now."

At first, she merely stood there with her palms on the edge of the map, watching him with a scowl. Immobile. Statuesque. A grim reaper with blonde hair.

When she finally adjusted, it took everything in Otmund not to flinch with fear. She stood and raised one arm, showing him her palm. The small enchanted blade of a Nethervale elite soldier popped into her fingers as if from thin air—a silent warning to leave or die.

But he couldn't. Not without his army.

He braced himself for a world of pain. "You won't kill me."

Her brow creased as her frown deepened. "Are you certain? You've become less and less useful as the years go on. I'm frankly surprised I haven't killed you yet."

"Then let me be useful." He took slow and deliberate steps around the table as he swallowed his terror and stalked toward her. "I know what you want, and you know what I want. Give me my army and help me take Oakenglen. When you do, I will give you funding. Privacy. Dominion over Nethervale and everything in the north east. You will be left alone. I will force the Lightseer crusades to end, and I will grant you access to Troll Island—if not full control."

She stiffened at the mention of the fabled island just off Dewcrest's shore. Any who ventured onto the isle without proper approval became compost for the rarest reagents in Saldia.

Many necromancers' corpses rotted on that island, their augmented bodies reduced to food for greedy plants.

As quickly as her brief interest had come, it faded back into her familiar scowl. Nyx summoned her other blade, and the black daggers glinted in her palms as she took aim at his heart. "And if I see you for the sniveling liar you are?"

Of course.

Of course she had to make this difficult. Of course she had forced him to threaten her. A proud woman like Nyx Osana bowed to no one, and any compromise ended with a dagger in her business partner's back.

Luckily, he'd come prepared.

"If you refuse, I will decimate Nethervale." His jaw tensed as he threatened the only woman he feared. "Even now, there's a letter waiting to be placed on Teagan Starling's desk. If I don't return tonight to cancel the delivery, he will receive quite the shock in the morning."

Her green eyes narrowed, and her breath escaped in a furious whisper. "What have you done, Soulblud?"

"I've forged evidence." He held her gaze as he made the most brazen threat of his life. "According to the very convincing documents in that envelope, you colluded with the new Wraithblade most heavily. You assassinated our king and—"

"You vile grub!"

Though he hadn't yet reached her, the woman launched over the map faster than Otmund's eye could even track. Something hit him hard in the chest, and the floor disappeared from under him. The room became nothing but black and orange blurs.

Before he understood where he'd even gone, his back hit the wall with a painful crack. The blow knocked the air from his lungs, and he gasped as pain splintered down his spine.

When his vision cleared, her glowering green eyes blocked the rest of the room from view. Her blond hair hung in her face, the frayed ends mere blurs when this close. Her hand coiled around his neck, and something cold pressed against his throat. He squinted up at her and choked as her grip cut off his air.

By some miracle, he managed to wheeze enough breath through his strangled windpipe to finish his threat. "You'd be a fool to kill me now. If anything happens to me, that letter will reach him in mere hours, and that war you've always feared will begin."

"I've never feared that war."

A lie.

"I've spent years crafting this, Nyx," he wheezed. "Years, biding my time. You will never weasel out of it. It will come."

She glared at him, nose flared and brow creased with furious hatred as she gripped his neck tighter. A feral growl built in her throat, like something he'd only heard in the forest at night, and a prick of pain stung his neck. Something hot rolled down his shirt.

Blood.

This damn fool was going to kill him.

"That's low," She tightened her hold on his neck, and pain splintered down his spine. "Even for you."

"Those who behave are rewarded," he said through gritted teeth, with the last of his air. "Those who don't, die."

They held each other's glares, but at this point, he had to see this through. Blistering pain shot up his neck and through his jaw, clear to his teeth. Her hand shook as she barely restrained herself from killing him. Down here, she could have. Even as the Master Strategist of the Lightseers, Otmund's death wouldn't matter to Teagan.

The letter, however, would spark a crusade unlike any Saldia had ever seen. Conquering the Wraithblade would inspire all sorts of alliances.

Aside from the letter, there wasn't much he could use to sway or threaten her, and that limited his longevity. Once he had the Wraith King, he wouldn't have to worry about her anymore—or the handful of people with greater power than even she possessed.

Perhaps he would kill her, when that time came, just to be rid of a nuisance.

With a groan of disgust, Nyx released him. His throat stung, and he doubled over from the pain. He grabbed his neck and coughed. Air burned in his lungs. Nausea scratched at his cheeks as his stomach threatened to purge the roasted lamb he'd had for dinner.

His fingers slipped over the ribbon of blood flowing from the small stab wound in his neck, but he would recover. Since he hadn't collapsed on the floor, she must not have poisoned the tips of her enchanted blades tonight. How lucky.

He'd won—for now.

"Your best," he demanded through his sputtering coughs. "Only your best. I want two hundred necromancers to take residence in Mossvale by tomorrow evening."

The deadly woman snorted with impatience. "I'll give you forty, you toad. Then—"

"This isn't a negotiation. It's a demand from your new master."

Behind her thick blonde hair, those green eyes narrowed yet again. The room went deadly silent. In any other situation, her blade would've been through his skull by now.

And yet, as the pain in his throat subsided, his world didn't end. He still breathed. He still stood on his feet. He watched his new pet, enjoying the hold he finally had around *her* throat.

"Two hundred, then." Though her gaze never changed, the blades in her palms disappeared with the soft swish of metal over leather.

For the moment, he owned Nyx Osana, but he was no fool. His hold over a woman like this wouldn't last.

With the new Wraithblade on the loose, Otmund had to make every moment count.

EPILOGUE
CELINE

In the heart of Wildefaire, a morning breeze ambled up a mountainside dotted with bright pink blooms. Loose petals tumbled past on the air, dancing with the northern birds as they woke to the spring. In the distance, the white towers of the Wildefaire castle rose above the forests as its golden spires pierced the low-hanging clouds.

From her perch on the silver throne her cousin Whitney had commissioned for her exile, Celine simply enjoyed the view.

A plush blue cushion provided relief from the otherwise solid silver chair. Placed on a patch of grass at the edge of the overlook, her intricately carved throne had no place in the wilderness.

She didn't care.

With her legs curled underneath her in a deliciously unladylike manner, Celine lifted a cup of tea to her nose and breathed in the sweet aroma of jasmine. Steam rolled off the surface, and her eyes fluttered shut as she allowed herself to savor the day.

And yet—she still couldn't smile.

Celine had assumed coming to Whitney's kingdom would've inspired a hint of joy in her life again, but she had been wrong. Try as she might, she hadn't felt happiness since the night she had agreed to Otmund's terms.

The night Henry died, her soul had died with him. Only spite remained in the void he left behind.

As she let out a soft sigh, her snow-white hair caught in the breeze and nearly fell into her cup. She tucked the loose lock behind one ear, grateful to be more Stormglass than Starling. She'd had a white head from the day she was born, and that had been a source of pride for her family. At least she had a bit of regal blood in her, and not just the hotheaded rage of those fire-breathing Starlings.

Footsteps thudded up the brick path through the trees, and she suppressed an irritated groan. However kind it had been for Whitney to provide servants, they never seemed to understand the concept of leaving their mistress alone.

As the man's haggard breathing drew closer, she sipped her tea. The sweet bite of the jasmine blended beautifully with the green leaves from South Haven. As the last of the kingdoms to fall, South Haven had nearly been burned to ash as punishment for their bloody eight-year rebellion against Henry. Celine, however, had insisted he keep them alive and instill heavy taxing structures instead.

Their land had the best tea, and she refused to live without it.

The raspy breath of a man unacquainted with running up steep mountain trails grated against her augmented hearing, and she grimaced with annoyance at his obscene ruckus. As her nose wrinkled with impatience, she took another sip of her tea.

His presence sullied the otherwise idyllic experience of her mountain throne. If he didn't leave soon, perhaps she would simply kill him to be rid of the noise.

With her back pressed against her ornate throne and uninterested in her company, Celine Montgomery sipped her imported tea.

Boots slid against the paved path, and the man muttered under his breath as he tripped across the grass where the bricks ended. Cloth rustled, and the wet slick of skin over sweat plopped through the otherwise delightful day.

A muscle in her jaw twitched. Too bad she hadn't brought her daggers with her today.

"Your Majesty," he wheezed from behind her. "I bid you a fond morning and good tidings. I pray you're well?"

With an irritated sigh, she ignored him. On a branch to her left, a sparrow sang to her before it flitted off toward the Moonbright Mountains that separated Wildefaire from the sea.

The servant cleared his throat. "I—uh, that is—I beg your pardon for my intrusion. If you would be so kind, I ask for only a moment of your time."

Celine lifted her tea to her lips and took another heavenly sip. The soothing heat from the piping hot brew seeped through the porcelain, and its divine aroma coiled in her senses.

"That is—uh—" The man chuckled and lost his trail of thought, apparently unsettled by her lack of conversation.

Perhaps he would take the hint, then, and leave before she speared him through the eye with her teacup.

"I shall skip the formalities, Your Grace, if that is what you prefer."

In answer, she watched a pair of bluebirds chase each other through the pink blossoms.

"I see, yes," he stuttered. "To the point, then. Queen Whitney received a note from Lunestone, one they claim to have sent out across the continent. The Lightseers wish for you to speak with them."

As the brew swirled through her mouth, she sat with the beautiful flavor. It warmed her chest with every drink, and she closed her eyes to savor the experience.

And yet, she still couldn't smile.

"They're desperate, Your Majesty," the servant continued. "They say only you can help them. They're pleading, begging even, for your military experience. They claim Saldia will fall without you."

She grimaced. Those irritating conmen. Otmund wouldn't have written something so garish, so it must've been Zander or Teagan who'd penned the note. Those two prideful fools should've known better than to think common flattery would've worked on her.

As she lifted the teacup to her lips again, she debated how she would kill this man for wasting her time. A bolt of lightning through the eye, perhaps, or a spear of metal into the heart.

The world and its trivial conflicts hadn't mattered to her in years.

"I am also supposed to tell you the wraith has been spotted again." His voice trembled with fear. "The letter said, 'the ghoul has a new master,' though I'm afraid I don't understand what that means. The Lightseer Viceroys seek your assistance at once."

Her cup went still as it pressed against her lips. With her favorite tea barely a breath away from her mouth, she shut her eyes. The calming rush of the northern wind sang through the cherry blossoms, teasing her with the barest hint of summer warmth.

Teagan, that fool. He'd gotten cocky. He'd sworn an oath to act quickly, bottle the abomination, and then immediately burn all record of its existence, but he'd failed.

Celine had warned him not to disappoint her, and yet, he hadn't taken the threat to heart. In the end, they all inevitably disappointed her. Perhaps she had been the fool to expect anything more.

That settled it. The old man's family had ruled this land for too long. The phoenix bloodline had met its match with Aeron's abominations. Despite plenty of opportunities to be the stewards Saldia needed, they had proven themselves unworthy.

When she was done, not even they would rise from the ashes.

"Y-your Grace?" the servant behind her stuttered. "Is there anything you would like for me to repeat?"

His voice snapped her from the spell of hatred, and though she didn't move, she listened once again to the forest around her. A bird chirped in the sunshine, though she couldn't spot it from here.

This servant had annoyed her, certainly, but he'd delivered important news. Killing him wouldn't vent her fury, and she opted instead to save her ire for the Starlings.

"Do you have a family?" After so many weeks of silence, her voice had a chillingly alien tone, even to her.

He swallowed hard, the gulp painfully audible even as his boots shuffled backward across the brick in a slow retreat. "I do, Your Majesty. A wife and a young daughter."

"And you love them?"

"Y-yes, of course."

"Hmm."

Celine allowed herself one final sip of tea. As it swam through her senses, she sighed with the wind. From somewhere deep in the mountain forest, an animal yipped as blossoms floated toward the grass from the branches.

"Leave Saldia, then," she warned.

"Beg your pardon? Did you say—"

"Yes," she interrupted.

"But your Majesty," he said under his breath. "We love this land. What have I done to deserve banishment? Please, Your Grace, allow me to redeem myself."

"You misunderstand."

The former queen wrapped her fingers around the porcelain cup and squeezed. It shattered. Steaming tea drenched her beautiful gown, but she didn't flinch. The blistering liquid burned her skin through the dress, but the pain only sharpened her focus on the horizon.

"You aren't banished," she explained. "You've been warned. When I'm done with the new Wraithblade, this world will be on fire. The wraith will get the hellish war he's always wanted." Her eyes fluttered shut as the wind soothed the burns along her legs. "But this time, it will come for *him*."

Thank you! PLEASE READ

To the amazing soul reading this right now, all I can say is thank you. Sincerely, and from the bottom of my heart. You took a chance on this book, and I hope you feel that investing your valuable time into this story was well worth it.

Getting this book to you involved a year and a half of drafting, writing, rewriting again, rewriting *a third time*, lots of debate, analysis, tweaks, and intense editing. Now, the first installment of *Wraithblade* is finally on the shelves. It's surreal, and I'm over the moon!

On that subject, a few notes:

First: Please, please, please consider rating and reviewing *Wraithblade* on Amazon, as well as any of your other favorite book sites. Many people don't know it, but there are thousands of books published every day, most of those in the USA alone. Over the course of a year, a quarter of a million authors will vie for a small place in the massive world of print and publishing. We fight to get even the tiniest traction, fight to climb upward one inch at a time towards the bright light of bestsellers, publishing contracts, and busy book signings.

Thing is, I need all the help I can get, and that's where wonderful readers like you come in!

Second: If you want to join my publisher's growing community, be sure to jump into the conversation at:
- the Wraithmarked Creative's private readers' group on Facebook, where we geek out about magic and nerdy things.
- the Wraithmarked Patreon, where you can get early art, early access chapters, and whole books months in advance, at patreon.com/wraithmarked.

Third: If you're curious about what this book means to me, you can read my author's note over on my website.

Regardless of whether or not you choose to review, reach out, or support me elsewhere, thank you again for taking the time to read *Wraithblade*. I'll see you in the sequel!

Your biggest fan,
Boyce

Printed in Great Britain
by Amazon